The Miracle Game

BY THE SAME AUTHOR

Fiction

The Cowards
Miss Silver's Past
The Bass Saxophone
The Swell Season
The Engineer of Human Souls
Dvorak in Love
The Mournful Demeanour of Lieutenant Boruvka
Sins for Father Knox
The End of Lieutenant Boruvka
The Return of Lieutenant Boruvka

Non-fiction

Jiří Menzel and the History of the *Closely Watched Trains*
All the Bright Young Men and Women
Talkin' Moscow Blues

The Miracle Game

■

JOSEF SKVORECKY

Translated by Paul Wilson

Alfred A. Knopf *New York* 1991

THIS IS A BORZOI BOOK
PUBLISHED BY ALFRED A. KNOPF, INC.

 Published in the United States by Alfred A. Knopf, Inc., New York. Distributed by Random House, Inc., New York. Published in Canada by Lester & Orpen Dennys, Toronto and in Great Britain by Faber & Faber, London. Originally published as *Mirákl* by Sixty-Eight Publishers, Toronto, Canada

Library of Congress Cataloging-in-Publication Data
Škvorecký, Josef.
[Mirákl. English]
The miracle game / Josef Skvorecký: translated by Paul Wilson. —
1st American ed.
p. cm.
Translation of: Mirákl.
ISBN 0-394-57220-3
I. Title.
PG5038.S527M513 1991
891.8′635 — dc20 90-53116 CIP

Diagrams by Jonathan Gladstone, j. b. geographics

Manufactured in the United States of America

FIRST AMERICAN EDITION

Author's Acknowledgements

My thanks to Sam Solecki for his help in preparing this English-language edition, and for much other assistance; also to Eileen Thalenberg for checking my rusty German, and to Gleb Zekulin for doing the same with my almost non-existent Russian. My special thanks to Bobbie Bristol and Louise Dennys, who stood by me through all the years of moody book markets, and to Gena Gorrell, for — among other things — detecting my crimes against logic and consistency.

J.S.
Toronto, April 1990

Translator's Acknowledgements

This translation was completed in the aura of another miracle — one anticipated by the events of the novel — the "gentle revolution" in Czechoslovakia in November and December 1989. Such events create their own pressure, and in the final stages of the work I was, and am, enormously grateful to Gena Gorrell for taking some of that pressure off me. My thanks as well to Louise Dennys and Bobbie Bristol, and, as always, to my wife, Helena, for holding the fort during my many absences. I would also like to acknowledge my gratitude to the Canada Council for its generous support.

My one regret is that my father, Cecil Wilson, did not live to read this book. To the end of his life, he took a lively interest in my work and, through it, in all things related to Czechoslovakia. It was he who brought Josef Skvorecky and me together in the mid-seventies, and it is to his memory that I dedicate this translation.

P. W.
Toronto, April 1990

"'You're a danger. That's why we kill you. I have nothing against you, you understand, as a man.'"

Graham Greene, *The Power and the Glory*

". . . it's so easy to kill real people in the name of some damned ideology or other; once the killer can abstract them in his own mind into being symbols, then he needn't feel guilty for killing them since they're no longer real human beings."

James Jones, in a *Paris Review* interview with Nelson W. Aldrich, Jr.

"Take free will away from man and there is nothing to save."

Saint Bernard of Clairvaux

To Honzlova:
So little for so much

1

■

The Virgin Mary under Mare's Head Hill

I.

I lifted Saint Joseph by his brightly coloured head. There was a crudely fashioned peg protruding from the bottom of the statue, and in the pedestal — which was much newer, and covered to excess with the conventional ornamentation of a later time — was a hole, partially stuffed with worn-out packing so the peg in the statue would fit it snugly. The statue itself had a new coat of paint applied by Mr. Rericha's hand — a mark of the political revival of 1968 — and so far it had managed to withstand the subsequent reversal of fortune as an earlier version of enlightenment once again established its sway.

Saint Joseph — eighteen inches of ancient wood, his termite holes plugged with plaster — lay in my hand. His cheeks were bright pink, his robes grass-green, and under a raffish head of raven-black hair his eyes bloomed like forget-me-nots. As I looked at him, I found I couldn't remember what he'd looked like years ago, before the Communist Party (in one of its periods of temporary derangement) let him be tricked out in these fancy togs. Or had he looked like a tree-frog even then? God knows. At the time I hadn't paid much attention to such details. How could I know the Lord would choose him, of all His servants, to show a handful of Hronov grannies the mystery of His ways?

Mr. Rericha had painted his version of the miracle directly onto the glass of the oval window to the left of the altar, and a garish light came through it and fell on the gaudy statue. The proportions of his painting were influenced by Gothic art; the style and coloration by Panex, the toy factory in Hronov where he worked. The picture showed an enormous, radiant Saint Joseph (in a grass-green gown, of course) looming precariously over the believers, who in his presence shrank to the size of hummingbirds. Their twisted faces and their tiny hands held up in supplication were presumably meant to suggest religious ecstasy; unfortunately, given the composition, their pose looked more like the natural reaction of people upon whose heads the Colossus of Rhodes was about to topple. Mr. Rericha made his living by painting rubber ducks and other toys, and not even his great faith in God could make a Rembrandt of him.

On another window, to the right of the altar, shone Mr. Rericha's depiction of the parish priest who had once been the spiritual custodian of the little church. Him I could remember well enough: his clean-shaven, deeply lined Sunday face, his grey brush-cut hair, his brown eyes faded by the sun. In the hands of the pious doll-maker the face of this earthy priest had become a pink moon with bright blue eyes, and although the priest was still a living memory in the district, the painter had adorned him with an Old Testament beard. Perhaps, sensing the inadequacy of his own art, he was trying to add to the priest's stature by providing him with some patriarchal features, but he only succeeded in making the Father look like a particularly cheerful hippie. Such unintentional up-to-dateness was not diminished in the least by the fiery declaration written in would-be medieval lettering against a background of hellish black: O GLORIOUS MARTYR, PRAY FOR US!

I turned my back to the altar and looked around at the remaining windows, but time had run out on Mr. Rericha. Through the open door I could look far out into the countryside and see the succulent meadows and dark forest that separated Pisecnice from Hronov and the world. Hronov and its main street — which over the past thirty years had been named after Eduard Benes, Frederick the Great, Stalin, Lenin, Professor Nejedly, Thomas Garrigue Masaryk, and finally, once more, Lenin — were lost in the early evening mist like a small heap of stones in a poisonous green basin of meadows and fields. On the western horizon the Ruler of the Universe, playing at being a baroque engraver, had produced a masterly fantasia of cloud and light. An array of sunbeams as precise as though drawn with a ruler connected a steely cloud to the mystical pond where, twenty-one years before, a rather questionable young water nymph had gone skinny-dipping.

Suddenly the doll-maker's work no longer seemed inadequate. It belonged in this fairy-tale, along with the fragment of countryside visible through the doorway, and the pond gleaming like the tranquil eye of a fish hypnotized by the Creator's ethereal finger. It was not, as it were, of this world. I frowned and lifted Saint Joseph up to put him back on his pedestal, but with his glossy coat of fresh paint he slipped from my hands and fell to the floor. Tenderly I knelt down to the miracle-worker who had survived, in the solitude of this chapel under Mare's Head Hill, for more than two hundred years, and I saw that his end had finally come. The impact had split him lengthwise, opening him up like a book.

When I looked into the statue I felt the touch of God's hand once more, and I knew that, against His own interests, He was giving me a sign. The phallic protrusion on the bottom of the statue was not an integral part of the saint, but was in fact a plug glued into a cavity bored in the base of the statue.

I worked the peg out, breaking part of it off as I did so. There were traces of white glue around its upper circumference. If the statue hadn't been so old, I would have sworn the glue was ordinary office paste.

But the statue was from the eighteenth century. I drove the peg back in, fumbled around in my pocket for a piece of string, and firmly bound Saint Joseph's legs back together. Then I carefully replaced him, inserting the peg into the packing around the hole in the pedestal. I had to laugh, even though I didn't feel much like it. The memory this phallic game provoked in me was too vivid, too absurd.

2.

The history of my part in the miracle also began with a phallus — not a symbolic one, but my own, afflicted with a bad case of gonorrhea that I could only have got from a Russian teacher called Irena Znenahlikova. Three days before a compulsory mid-term course I was attending in Hradiste ended in a gala farewell party, she'd arrived fresh from Bulgaria, where she'd gone as a volunteer to help build a large pig farm. A brigade of black Brazilians had worked on the job with her. They were men whose profession was youth and progress, and they were travelling around the world as payrolled warriors for peace. So my gonococci had circumnavigated the globe — which may help to explain their special resilience, because they turned out to be all but indestructible.

The gonococci first announced their presence on the train to Hronov. A furious itching drove me to the washroom, where, with a sinking heart, I discovered a discharge and a rapidly spreading inflammation of the foreskin. I lifted my gaze from this little surprise and looked out the window of the moving bathroom at the green countryside. The train was crawling through it like a snake, towards the ruby apple of the setting sun, and my mood sank to zero. That evening I administered first aid with cold water, but when I got up the next morning my instrument of sensual delight had grown to almost twice its usual size, and my foreskin resembled an over-inflated inner tube oozing grey drops—exactly as described in the clinical textbooks. By now the itching was unbearable. But after fashioning a primitive jockstrap from pieces of gauze, I left to take up my new position as teacher in a vocational school dedicated to training young girls as social workers and nurses.

Disquieting thoughts tormented me. Could I afford to begin my stay in this small, lilac-bowered town with a visit to the venereological ward of the local hospital on my very first day? I was certain the nurses would be graduates of the school, and although discretion was theoretically guaranteed in the ward, nurses were only women, after all. Was it realistic to hope they would keep quiet about a new teacher who came all the way to Hronov seeking a cure for the clap?

The more I thought about it, the more I felt my courage ebbing away. How could I bring myself to expose this ghastly, misshapen organ to the eyes of recent graduates? And when I met my first class—an extraordinarily buxom gaggle of young females—I was hit by a wave of black despair. It was early spring and the girls in third form were sitting there, alert and expectant, all of them wearing tight-fitting cotton T-shirts. I supposed they had just come from a gym class; it was not until much later that Vixi admitted that the T-shirts had been deliberate, and that the sight of row upon row of virginal tits had been intended to embarrass me, excite my passion, or in some other way put my manhood to the test. But lust was the furthest thing from my mind. While I muttered some dry and indigestible remarks about Stalin's contribution to the science of language, as the syllabus required, my mind wrestled with the larger question of whether the discharge, also described in the textbooks, would eventually soak through my trousers and betray me.

When my uninspired lecture had gone on for about half an hour and I was still sitting behind the master's desk like a stump, one of the girls suddenly put her hand up. She had a remarkably pert little nose, wide green oval (and all too knowing) eyes, and a set of freshly licked full lips gleaming beneath them. When I nodded at her, she stood up and asked if she could go powder her nose. A titter went through the classroom and at first I didn't know what to think. But one more look at that sly, foxy face told me that here was another test of my endurance. My only previous experience teaching girls had been with ten-year-olds at the municipal school in Police; that had been before I attended the fateful political schooling in Hradiste, where my command of Marxist jargon made such an impression on the all-powerful principal of the Hronov Health and Social Workers' School that I found myself transferred, in mid-term, to his paradise for young maidens. "If you must 'powder your nose'," I said, with all the icy deliberation I could muster, "then you may go," and Vixi (the nickname occurred to me in a rush of feeling that was something like love at first sight) swaggered out of the room in her tight navy-blue skirt and the translucent white T-shirt, beneath which I could see the outline of an amply filled brassiere, swinging her hips like a seasoned streetwalker. A buzz went through the classroom. I tried to draw the girls' attention back to Marshal Stalin's thoughts on slang, but it was no use. The tittering continued, then came to a sudden stop as the door squeaked open and the chestnut-haired Vixi swung back into the room. There was something different about her, but it took me a moment to see what it was. Underneath the T-shirt, instead of the ample brassiere, there were two magnificent hemispheres, and through the tightly stretched fabric I could see two round, dark patches glowing at me like eyes. In the absolute silence that descended upon the room, Vixi walked slowly past my desk with the hemispheres bobbing up and down in a way that cannot be described in words. I too was silent.

The spell was broken by a rapidly spreading sensation of discomfort in my trouser leg, and then by a sudden wall of white pain. As I writhed in agony behind the instructor's desk, a new wave of whispering spread through the classroom like a spring breeze. My efforts to save the situation by coming back to Marshal Stalin's linguistic ruminations ended in utter failure, and I could feel the steam rising from the back of my sweat-soaked shirt.

When I finally made it to the staff room, hunched over and hiding my wet fly behind my copy of *Stalin on Language*, there was a fellow standing there, elegantly dressed (in those times of sweaters and cords), talking with Ivana Hrozna, the vice-principal. He even wore a moustache and a brightly coloured tie, but in spite of that Ivana Hrozna's smile was more glowingly optimistic than it had been that morning.

"Come in, Comrade Smiricky!" she said eagerly. "You don't know each other yet, do you? This is Comrade Dr. Gellen. He's a physician and teaches hygienics here." The fellow looked at me with narrow eyes that had the striking colour of ripe blueberries. With an instinct that cements such brotherhoods everywhere, I at once saw in him an experienced and probably very successful pussy pirate, and realized that I was saved.

"You've done yourself proud," he told me in his office, when I showed him my grotesquely swollen organ. "What school did you say you taught at before, Mr. Smiricky?"

The formality with which he addressed me created a sense of trust and intimacy between us that the less formal "comrade", which was compulsory usage in the school, would have made impossible.

"The municipal school. In Police."

"My God! You mean to say our young pioneer girls are so — immoral, shall we say?" He grasped my swollen member brusquely but professionally in his fingers.

"This comes from the mid-term political school, Dr. Gellen."

With a roguish look in his eyes, the doctor quietly sized me up, then gave my penis a squeeze. Out came a few drops. "Well, well, what's this we have here? You realize, I hope, that venereal disease has been officially eliminated in this country?"

I explained that my bacilli in no way contradicted the government's claim because they were a Brazilian import. He perked up his ears at that and asked for the name and address of the carrier, Znenahlikova. In a spirit of sheer revenge, I gave them to him.

"As a member of the Youth Union, possibly even a member of the Party, she ought to know that it's her responsibility, once infected, to seek an immediate cure," he said, looking at me intently with his blueberry eyes. "But in case she's neglected to do so, I'll report her to the proper authorities myself. That, in turn, is my responsibility." He paused and then added, significantly, "As a doctor." He still had a professional grip on my diseased organ. "You," he said slowly, "have already fulfilled your responsibility. As a pedagogue and — "

" — and a politically aware non-Party member," I said, to fill in the blank left by his pause. Dr. Gellen gave my wretched member one last squeeze, as though he were shaking my hand, and told me to button up. Then he went to the sink and washed his hands.

"This will have to go under the microscope," he said. "There's always a chance it's just some exotic form of balanitis. But I wouldn't put any money on it."

"Are you going to examine it yourself, doctor?"

He grinned slyly under his elegant moustache. "No, the lab nurse will deal with that. But have no fear, Mr. Smiricky. Our nurses don't gossip." My skepticism must have shown, because he added at once, "You'll see for yourself when you meet them. And if it turns out to be what we're afraid it is — as I'm sure it will — I'll enter it in the records as an inflammation of the urethra. All right?"

He smiled at me like the owner of a private practice. "You know, it really is bad luck," he went on. "I'm truly sorry for you. You land a job at a pussy joint like ours just when you're in no state to enjoy it. If I were you, I'd probably go out and get drunk. Now that sounds like a good idea. Would you mind if I joined you?"

At the hospital he introduced me to a nurse with the improbable name of Udelina and I understood at once why he'd been so sure of her discretion. She was an imposing bride of Christ, somewhat advanced in years, who went about her job in a businesslike way and spoke with a dry, objective pragmatism that reminded me of Western journalism, except that it was underpinned by a deeper certainty.

"Smiricky . . . ," she said reflectively. "You wouldn't by any chance have an uncle who's a parish priest in Budejovice, would you?" And she gestured energetically for me to take out the object under investigation.

Her mention of the good priest made me feel even more embarrassed. For as long as I could remember, my uncle had visited us regularly. He always brought me a gift of some kind, usually a box of chocolates, and he always made the sign of the cross on my forehead when he was leaving. He deserved better than this.

"Yes. That is — he's not there any more."

"Is that a fact?" Sister Udelina heated a piece of thin steel wire with a tiny eye in one end over a bunsen burner and deftly inserted it into my urinary tract. I accepted the discomfort as part of my punishment. "Did they move him to another parish? He should have been a dean long ago, that's what we always said. He was such an exemplary, well-read man — and kind, full of real Christian humility." She gave the wire a twist. It burned like the devil and I gasped in pain.

"They collared him," I blurted. "I mean, they arrested him."

The nurse pulled the wire out and held it up to the light. "Did they now?" she said, as though I'd just told her that my uncle was heading up a devotional retreat in Svata Hora. "What sort of charges did they dream up?"

I buttoned my fly and the nurse skilfully spread the fluid on the wire over a small glass slide.

"He read something — a pastoral letter from Archbishop Beran, I think — from the pulpit."

"They go after that kind of thing like ferrets. I hear the archbishop's in jail too," she said, almost blithely, inserting the glass slide under the microscope. "A saint. A real saint! He spent six years in a concentration camp under the Germans. We knew him from before the war; he'd come and serve us Holy Communion when we were still at Vinohrady Hospital in Prague. Anyway, here he is in prison again. Some people say it's only house arrest, but if it is, prison can't be far behind," she added, again with what seemed almost like satisfaction. "Aha! Here we are! Come and have a look." She stood aside and let me look through the microscope. "Gonococci always come in pairs. They look like two little seeds side by side, like twins. See them?"

I saw them all right, these offspring of my not entirely Marxist interests at the political school. "Damn the little buggers!" I said with feeling.

"There's no point cursing them," said Sister Udelina as she pushed me away from the microscope. "They can't help it. But sinning doesn't pay."

"I guess not. Some kinds of sinning don't, anyway."

"No kind of sinning pays," she replied, looking through the microscope again and making notes on a form. "No, it never pays. Sometimes, at the beginning, it may seem as if the Lord has forgotten the sinner, left him out of His reckoning. But that's an illusion. The mills of God grind slowly, but. . . ." She stood up from the microscope and brandished the form, looking me straight in the eye. "You have gonorrhea, Mr. Smiricky. There's no mistaking it. Now, will you take this back to the doctor yourself or — "

"No, no, please, I'll do it myself!" I said quickly, and I avoided her eyes by staring at her gigantic coif. It was bathed in a gloom of milky light from the high windows. Over the black habit of her order she was wearing a wide white apron; a black rosary swung from her ample waist and her pale blue eyes stared at me from a plump face that might have belonged to a country housewife. On the whole, Sister Udelina seemed in very good spirits.

I couldn't just take my shameful verdict and walk out. I felt I had to smooth things over, to justify myself somehow before my arrested uncle. So I hesitated before leaving, and asked, "Did they — were you transferred here from Prague?"

Unlike the elegant Dr. Gellen, the nun felt no need to sound me out before speaking her mind.

"Yes indeed," she replied, again in that odd tone bordering on enthusiasm. "They've banned most of us from any activity. The teaching and the contemplative sisters have already been sent to Broumov — they set up a special convent there, they call it a concentration cloister. So far the hospital sisters have only had to leave Prague and work in the countryside, but the word is that we'll soon have to leave the hospitals altogether, and work in hospices for the congenitally disabled and the incurably ill."

I didn't know what to say — such things didn't come up in general (or prudent) conversation — so I fell into an inane question: "Is that because these places are short-staffed?"

"Well, you know how it is. Those who are badly disabled from birth are the most wretched people in the world. Most of them can't even move on their own, let alone walk. They need looking after twenty-four hours a day. Usually their parents don't want them, or can't have them at home, and lay nurses — well, it's too much to expect of them. So these poor dear cripples have no one in the world but the good Lord."

Some radical had recently demanded, in *Rude Pravo*, that even congenital cripples be freed from the shackles of superstition — in short, that the hospices too be secularized — but Sister Udelina obviously didn't read *Rude Pravo*.

"You said — a concentration cloister?" I'd never heard the term before. Clearly I wasn't keeping up with the latest achievements in the class struggle. "What exactly is — ?"

I hesitated, somewhat embarrassed. The best way to keep such things secret is to encourage a general indifference to anything that doesn't affect most people's everyday life. Like many others, I gave little thought to the problems of the clergy, the holy bishop, or incurable cripples.

"There are two of them," said Udelina matter-of-factly, "one for men and one for women. Both in Broumov. They bring together — or 'concentrate' — people under vows, no matter what order they belong to, and they all have to work in some factory or other. Originally they assigned all the nuns to a small weaving mill in Olivetin. They had old equipment, all self-acting twiners, if that means anything to you, and it took a lot of running around. But not long ago they split them up and sent them to several different factories in Broumov, because they were — "

Suddenly she stopped and stood up. I felt my senses sharpen. Even this woman who lived beyond the range of political fear had stumbled onto a topic she couldn't bring herself to talk about. Or perhaps it wasn't political fear that made her hesitate. Had the nuns started having it off with the foreman? Surely not — official ideology would have welcomed anything like that . . . of course! Scattering the nuns around several factories would provide more opportunities for concupiscence to flourish.

"To work!" cried Udelina. "I've talked far too much already. Just look at the gallons of urine I have to deal with today!" In a wooden holder stood a neat row of test-tubes filled with liquid covering a colourful range of yellows. But I couldn't resist probing a little further. Adopting a tone of officially admissible jocularity, I asked, "What was the trouble, weren't the sisters fulfilling their quota?"

Udelina looked at the shameful form I held in my hand, then at me. She sized me up the way Dr. Gellen had and said, "On the contrary! We're very hard-working. Sloth is one of the seven deadly sins, after all. But someone pointed out that the sisters were fulfilling their quota better than any of the other factories in Broumov — by about a hundred and fifty per cent — *and* on the oldest machines. It made for a lot of bad blood among the workers."

She took a test-tube of urine and squeezed some drops into it, creating a cloudy solution that looked like anise liqueur with water. I smiled at her, stuck my verdict into my pocket, and went back to Dr. Gellen, who entered it in his books as inflammation of the urinary tract brought about by a chill.

It soon became clear that the Hronov Health and Social Workers' School was a real house of shame. Theoretically it was a co-educational institution, and I heard that the previous fall there had in fact been one boy in the first form. But after withstanding the combined onslaught of 260 girls for a month, he had dropped out. With him out of the way, the girls now turned their energies in two main directions: towards the local school for stone-cutters and sculptors, and towards the military academy. There was also a vocational school for saddle- and bridle-makers in town, but they ignored that; the trainees were mostly country yokels, and our girls — whose favourite subject (and, before the Communist takeover, main subject) was cooking — thought of themselves as intellectuals.

My arrival had promised to liven things up, but I turned out to be no fun at all. Perhaps as part of God's punishment and purpose — or so I thought at the time; later I would deliberately avoid such theological speculations, but *quia turpe, quia indignum* — the clap gave way to an actual case of inflammation of the urethra, and the balanitis remained long after the gonococci had been exterminated. So for some time one function of my organ was painfully difficult, and the other practically impossible. My only resort was continence, and the hope that the girls would write me off as a lost cause and leave me alone.

My restraint, however, had roughly the same effect on them as a glimpse of ankle had on my grandfathers. The experiment with the brassiere was merely the beginning; it was followed by a series of other attempts, both individual and collective, to unbalance me. A fashion for incredibly daring, low-cut necklines swept the school (or at least my classes). Once, someone accidentally jammed the lock on the girls' changing room during gym, and all the girls showed up in my social studies class wearing gym shorts. And on my way home to my rented room on the edge of town I would, with suspicious regularity, run into one of my students all by herself — a different one each day. It was exemplary teamwork and, as I learned later from Vixi, it developed into a kind of contest, one the girls would make bets on. Each time it happened, the student would look at me with wide-eyed intensity and something would slip out of her hand: a book, a briefcase, a handkerchief. But these ploys were so exaggerated that I finally came to believe the girls saw me not as an object of sexual desire, but as a butt for their pubescent female humour.

I also received a lot of passionate letters, and someone, obviously a soul fraught with genuine longing, sent me ration tickets for milk, the kind distributed to mothers breastfeeding their babies. I was too embarrassed to use them in Hronov, so they went to waste. Despite all these efforts, I remained cool, distant as an iceberg. But the girls didn't give up. My aloofness merely drove them to greater, more ingenious strategies.

A new stage in the game was initiated by none other than the girl with the pert nose and the wide, foxy eyes.

"Vlasta," I said to her one day when I was substituting in political economy for Ivana Hrozna, who was at a meeting, "go to the board and write down the formula for calculating declining profits in advanced capitalism."

Vixi, wearing a brassiere this time but in a skirt that wouldn't have had far to go to match the much later mini (to achieve the effect she had rolled the waistband over and over on itself), looked at me sullenly.

"Comrade Smiricky, sir, I would prefer you not call me by my first name."

"I beg your pardon?"

"I don't want to be called by my first name."

The class mumbled in assent. "Yes! Don't use our first names!" came a muffled shout from some carefully concealed protester at the back of the classroom.

Vixi, at the blackboard now, continued, "We're not children any more and we don't like it when you call us by our first names."

I measured her with what I hoped was a shamelessly bold look. No, she was certainly not a child.

"Very well, Miss Koziskova. As you wish. Now, tell us all about these declining profits," I said, with heavy professorial irony.

She couldn't answer the question, and I happily gave her a zero. Ten minutes later, in the staff room, I said to the sixty-year-old superannuated Czech teacher, "What do you make of this, Annie? The third form won't let me call them by their first names."

The incident grew into a problem that took a special staff meeting to sort out. The third form's demand was a flagrant violation of the norms of the time, and for Ivana Hrozna, who had meanwhile been appointed principal (the former principal, Comrade Prochazka, had been appointed regional inspector), modes of address were not just a question of etiquette and grammar, but of world view and making the new people's democracy truly more populist in spirit.

"It's the last thing I expected, comrades," she said, her maternal breast swelling with indignation. "Here we are, trying to eliminate the old, bourgeois forms of address. There was to be no more 'sir' or 'miss' to the teachers and no more 'Miss Koziskova'. And now the comrades in third form come to us with this deeply reactionary demand. I won't deny that I feel very hurt, but I don't know what to do about it." Her homely face was the picture of regret.

"If I were you, Ivana, I'd send around a memo," said Evzenie Vikusova, who had once taught cooking and now taught the theory of nutrition. Not long ago Vikusova had come within a hair's breadth of ruin because of her father's overpriced sausages; he had owned a wholesale smoked meat business, and his sausages were still part of living memory. To complicate matters, she had a complete set of gold dentures, which made it impossible to hide her family's former affluence. In the Soviet Union, where they knew nothing of her doubtful class origins, her best-selling cookbook *Secrets from the Czech Kitchen* had recently been published, and that, together with the fact that she had joined the Party after President Gottwald issued a general appeal for new members, saved her from the liquidation that some Hronov radicals were demanding for her. "Just write a memo, Ivanka," she said, "and lay down the law: the girls have to address their teachers formally — I mean informally — and no two ways about it."

Ivana shook her head. "That would be a mistake, Comrade Vikusova. I don't think it's appropriate to introduce the kind of radical measures in a school that you'd use in everyday life. The struggle between the old and the new has to be different here. It has to take our girls' youth into account. We Communists must try to understand and persuade, not punish or hand out ultimatums the way bourgeois teachers would. Though I admit this whole business really pains me — "

"I'd tell them to do what they're told and that would be the end of it!" insisted the nutritional theorist. "But if you think it would help, maybe we should call a meeting of the Youth Union and — "

"You may be right," Ivana nodded, uncertainly at first, but then her enthusiasm for the idea grew rapidly. "And then I'll talk to them — or no, it would be better if one of *them* were to do it, say Pecakova from 4B. She could tell them how informality serves a completely different function today — "

I was trying to find the right moment to slip in a word about the use of informality in my particular case, but Zdena Prochazkova, the former principal's wife, beat me to it.

"Look here, Ivana," she said, "don't you think we'd better find out why the girls want the comrade here to address them formally in the first place? That would be entirely in accord with good pedagogical principles, and I think Marx would have approved too. First you uncover the real causes, then you look for a solution."

Ivana's face betrayed a mixture of respect and chagrin — she realized she'd been caught in a fundamental sin against the dialectics of education.

"You're absolutely right, Comrade Prochazkova. First we have to analyse the matter. And I think — I'm afraid — that among our girls there are still many comrades who grew up in bourgeois surroundings, as well as some who are daughters of larger farmers. And after all, it's only been a year since the victory of the People. Perhaps that's just too short a time to get them used to the notion of comradely informality. It may require some special tutoring — "

"I'm not so sure about that, Ivana," said Zdena Prochazkova, glancing at me. She was sitting there in the staff room in her sweatsuit. She was at least forty years old, her body overtrained, her face ruddy and windburned from too many canoe trips, her hands callused from using the horizontal bar, or perhaps from field hockey. "Maybe it's more complicated, or much simpler, than whether our girls come from farms or are tradesmen's daughters. The comrade here is young — about twenty-five, is that right?"

I nodded.

"And our girls are fifteen to nineteen. They feel uncomfortable when young men like the comrade here call them by their first names. Now, if the comrade were fifty or sixty, it wouldn't bother them at all, but — "

"You know, Zdena, that never occurred to me!" exclaimed Ivana. "But I suppose you're right — though I wouldn't underestimate the influence of those bourgeois — "

A debate ensued that dragged on and on, until it finally ended with an unprecedented solution: given the fact that opposite sexes were involved, and given the closeness in our ages, I was officially allowed to address the pupils in the two highest years formally, by their surnames.

Later, when I was walking through the fragrant spring air with Zdena Prochazkova towards the lilac-bowered streets on the edge of town where we both lived, she said as we neared her house, "Look here, Danny, I hope you don't mind if I call you by your first name."

"Why would I mind?"

"Well, I'm old enough to be your mother."

"You'd have to have had me when you were ten."

"Seventeen, boy, when I was seventeen." She sighed. "Well, good night."

She reached into her large handbag, fished around under a skipping rope and a bathing cap, pulled out a set of keys, and unlocked the garden gate. Though her husband was now in Prague, preoccupied with the problems of regional school inspection, she was still living in his family's house. I waited until she had locked the gate, and as she was running up the stairs to her door I waved goodbye.

"You know what I call you?" she called back at me in the slowly gathering darkness.

"No, what?"

"Mowgli."

"Why?"

"Because you're a human boy-child," she said mysteriously, "among the comrades."

I didn't know what she meant, but I laughed and walked off towards where the road disappeared into the dusk among thick purple bushes. I accepted her nickname without questioning it and then forgot about it. Maybe she thought she had some special insight into me. So many things in life remain a mystery to us and — as Sister Udelina might have said — we carelessly toss away most of the opportunities we have to do good.

Dr. Gellen was fascinated by the tenacity of my inflammation. One evening when he was on night duty he invited me to the hospital, and as soon as his office door clicked shut behind us he followed up on the suggestion he'd made after our first conversation. From an old penicillin box he pulled a rare commodity: a bottle of genuine Scotch whisky. Then, from a refrigerator where he kept perishable drugs, he removed a large metal bowl full of ice. He broke the ice into pieces on the tabletop and assembled two scotches on the rocks.

"Your health!" he said, raising his glass. "Frankly, as far as your penis is concerned, I'm afraid this cure will be as effective as any." He took a swig of his drink. "Of course, there's always a more radical solution." Seeing that his remark had alarmed me, he added reassuringly, "I don't mean amputation — just circumcision."

I took a drink and the good whisky calmed my nerves. Dr. Gellen topped up my glass at once.

"To the health of our Party!"

"*Our* Party?"

"You're a progressive non-Party member just like me, aren't you?"

"I'm certainly non-Party."

"And you're progressive too. Non-progressive non-Party members aren't allowed to hold responsible positions like yours." He grinned.

For a brief fraction of a second I wondered if the doctor might hold a secret position in addition to his official one. But he seemed too intelligent for that.

He was silent for a while, sipping the yellowish liquid and swirling it so that the melting iceberg tinkled against the glass. Sitting in his white lab coat against the background of the refrigerator and stroking his moustache with his index finger, he looked a little like a devil. Then he shook himself out of whatever private visions he was having, drained his glass of whisky, and said, "Have you ever noticed the interesting semantic qualities of the negative prefix — " At that point someone knocked on the door. Gellen shouted with disgust, "Come in!"

One of the Franciscan nuns rushed into the office and said the doctor was needed in emergency to deal with an ugly injury.

The injury awaiting us in the emergency department was not ugly at all. On the contrary. A young woman was sitting on a revolving stool and staring at the doctor in alarm over the edge of a white handkerchief she held pressed to her nose. Beside her stood a husky young man in corduroy pants who was staring at us in even greater alarm.

"Well, what happened?" asked Dr. Gellen severely.

"Doctor, I — " the young man began, " — we were — we just got married on Saturday — and I — I guess I'm just extra-clumsy or something because we were splitting wood together and I — I cut Liduska's nose off!"

"Oh, my, my," said Gellen with undisguised delight. "Let's have a look at you."

Very carefully, the young woman lowered the handkerchief. The sight that greeted us was bloody, but far from tragic. The husband had obviously sharpened his instrument well, because he had sliced off only the fleshy tip of the girl's nose. The tip now hung by a thread of skin and swung gently back and forth against a backdrop of full lips that were curved downward in a tearful pout.

"Doctor," said the young man in a whisper, probably because of my presence, "I'll make it worth your while. Only please do your best for Liduska, so she won't be disfigured. I can get you all the poultry you want — and never mind ration coupons."

Dr. Gellen and the young woman disappeared into his office, and I sat in the corridor with the poultry supplier while he worried out loud about his wife and whether she was suffering any pain. By asking me a few clumsy questions he very adroitly determined that I wasn't in the Party, and then asked if I'd mind going in and telling the doctor that another goose would be neither here nor there if the doctor would just give his wife an injection to ease the pain. I declined politely, and assured him that his wife was in the best of hands.

At last the wife appeared in the doorway. Her eyes, no longer full of alarm, peered out over an expertly fashioned gauze bandage that covered most of her face. The new husband sprang to his feet and tried to press a banknote into the doctor's hand, but Gellen told him not to bother, that he didn't need money. "I understand," said the young man, in a half-whispered, conspiratorial tone, and then he tenderly led his wife down the long corridor to the exit. A horse-drawn buggy was waiting for them in front of the hospital.

As they walked away, I noticed that the wife had extraordinarily pretty legs. I looked into Dr. Gellen's blueberry eyes.

"You know how it is, Mr. Smiricky," he said. "In a progressive hospital, a doctor has a stable of young pussy right under his own roof. But what do I have here? The Order of St. Francis! So a man takes what he can get from the emergency patients."

"Aren't the students at the school enough?"

"Our girls are too interested in getting married," the doctor replied. "You'll see what I mean when your little problem clears up."

Oddly enough, Vixi was never one of those who lay in wait to snare me with a dropped handkerchief as I walked home. What I didn't realize was that this was only because she was studying me closely and gathering information about me, about my habits and my interests. Once I told a first-form class about my otherwise secret past as a sax player. Another time, on the occasion of some official state anniversary, I substituted for the singing teacher (who had conveniently fallen ill) and played the national anthem and the Internationale on the piano. Then one afternoon shortly after four o'clock, when the corridor was filled with the delicious smells of a lesson in nutritional theory that had barely finished in the school kitchen, Vixi knocked on the door of my office and stepped in.

Her chestnut hair was pulled back and tied with a blue ribbon, she was wearing one of her tight-fitting T-shirts of a nondescript yellow, her navy-blue skirt was hitched up above her knees, and she had filthy tennis shoes on stockingless feet. She had a roll of sheet music in her hand and her foxy eyes wore an exaggerated look of tempered respect. Standing there in a cone of light from the window, she turned my office into a sanctuary consecrated to spring and its longings.

"Sir," she began, "may I ask you a favour?"

"Go ahead."

She moved closer to me, out of the light.

"Sit down," I offered.

She did so, poking a rather grubby pair of knees in my direction.

"Sir, you're an expert in jazz — "

"Now wait a minute, expert's a — "

"You told the first year you played saxophone in a jazz orchestra right up until the end of the war."

I allowed as how I'd done something of the sort. "So what?"

"I'm taking piano," said Vixi, still very properly, "but all I ever get to play is études and sonatinas, you know? And now I've come across some jazz music and I don't know quite what to do with it. So I was wondering if you'd be kind enough to play it for me?"

Those foxy eyes looked at me with such patently counterfeit respect that if it hadn't been for my troubles, I might have reached for her instead of her sheet music.

"Let's have a look."

She handed me the music. It was for three ancient hits, and for a moment I forgot all about her blatant ulterior motives. I've always had a weakness for the twenties, with their honest obscenity and gaiety — perhaps because ever since I attained the age of reason, as it's sometimes called, I've lived under the shadow of various terrors. Vixi's songs came from an age before the nightmare began.

"Where did you get these?" I sat down at the piano that stood in my office (I was sharing a room with the sickly music teacher) and started playing. As the syncopated melody bounced along I said dreamily, "A Charleston . . . you know, the Charleston's been out of fashion for a good twenty years!"

"No kidding?" I heard her say behind me in a voice of exaggerated awe. She sounded closer than good manners might have dictated. I tinkled away, turning the song into a boogie. Syncopation never failed to arouse in me the fleeting sensation of absolute happiness. Then I realized that the girl was as silent as a fish. This struck me as odd and I glanced around, but all I encountered was the egregious politeness of those improbably innocent eyes.

I opened the second piece of music. A tango. I played it too, but with less enthusiasm. Vixi was still as quiet as a mouse. I glanced around again and this time I could see a questioning look in her eyes. The third piece was a waltz. As I played I puzzled over what the question meant, and it made me uneasy. I stopped in the middle of the song and spun around on the stool to face my student.

"This one isn't jazz at all."

"I know," said Vixi.

"Do you still want me to play it for you?"

She took in a deep breath. Her pointed breasts, charms of far more ancient allure than the Charleston, heaved under her T-shirt and drew nearer.

"Not if you don't want to — "

It was a simple statement, but it held out many meanings. A swelling in my trouser-leg reminded me of my former sin and I quickly spun the stool around to face the piano again. Once more I felt her silence, with its unspoken question, hovering behind me.

In my embarrassment, I began to examine the well-fingered covers of her sheet music. The tango showed a girl, her hair in a roaring twenties bob, stretching her arm towards a man with slicked-back hair. On the Charleston a man in a checkered shirt much like the one I was wearing appeared to be getting ready to remove his trousers while a girl, likewise with bobbed hair and wearing a gossamer negligée, reached out to him with open arms from a rather soiled-looking bed. "I LOVE YOU ONLY, a tango" and "DON'T BE LATE, MY HEART CAN'T WAIT!, a Charleston" said the titles in bold banner lettering. Vixi's audacious message was starting to come through.

The waltz was called "COME TO THE CHAPEL THIS EVENING!" and the cover displayed a small ecclesiastical structure about to be desecrated by a pair of very un-Catholic lovers. Such a chapel stood on a little knoll behind my rooming-house. To get to it you had to walk through a lilac bower which was just now in bloom, and the place was so obviously made for lovers' trysts that it cast suspicion on the intentions of the merchant who had built it in the eighteenth century as a gesture of gratitude, so the town chronicles said, for his safe return from distant voyages. I glanced at the lyrics to the Charleston. "Take off your shoes now, don't be late," the ancient flapper from proletarian Zizkov was urging the man with his pants halfway down, "Don't make me, make me, make me wait!"

There could be no doubt about it. God damn Irena Znenahlikova! I snapped the music shut and turned to face Vixi.

"Take these away," I said, again playing the role of the high-school teacher to the hilt. I looked at my watch. "There's still time," I said. "The showers are open till five. That helps — at least, it does with boys."

Vixi lifted her pert nose with an offended air. This time the expression was authentic. She practically snatched the music out of my hands and said, as though poison were dripping from her lips, "Very well, *sir*!"

The door slammed shut with a loud bang behind the yellow T-shirt, behind the blue ribbon carefully tied in a lovely bow, behind the lovely tennis shoes.

May you roast in hell, Znenahlikova! My own pedagogical virtue, so entirely a product of necessity, made me sick. In fact, the whole notion of pedagogy in relation to the seventeen-year-old Vixi was a bit of a joke.

But there's no rest for the wicked. In the silver moonlight outside my window, flowery purple clusters nodded in the breeze, transforming my bed-sitter into a perfume shop. In the kitchen, a tiny cell of the Moravian

Brethren were holding their regular Thursday worship service. They had no house of prayer of their own, but they did have two pastors, both sons of my landlady, the widow Ledvinova. One of them, a casual labourer in the steel plant, played the lute, and the other, who worked in a local cotton mill, was torturing a violin. The widow herself played a harmonium which had last been tuned sometime before the First World War, and a Mr. Hribek, a secret believer, added some timid continuo on a bass viol. Three women of uncertain age raised their voices to address the Creator:

From the depths of the ages, O God, our Father,
You speak to us of never-ending love. . . .

I couldn't stand it any longer. I jumped out of bed, angrily smashing on the floor the little jar of orange ointment that represented my last hope, then crawled through the open window. As I raced up the hill through the sweet-smelling lilacs like a killer running from the law, I could see the white chapel up there glowing in the Hronov night, inviting me to a different kind of never-ending love. I ran faster and faster, and because I was badly out of shape I arrived at the small plateau in front of the chapel gasping for air, as though I were suffering from a terminal attack of asthma.

Vixi was sitting there on a bench, looking at me intently through the darkness. The night made her eyes seem black. When she spoke, there wasn't a trace of respect in her voice. "If you'd come sooner, you wouldn't have had to wreck yourself like that," she said simply.

I came up beside her and slumped onto the bench, puffing and panting.

"You should take up sports, *sir.*"

It was a while before I could respond. Then I said, "Aren't you being a little insolent?"

"No. I just know what this is all about."

She laughed. Her breasts cast two round, tantalizing shadows. The moon, looking as if it were fresh from the silversmith's workshop, hung over the iniquitous town, an invitation to anything but chaste meditation. Vixi's eyes flashed. The light transformed her carefully brushed hair into sparkling silk and my nostrils, dulled by an onslaught of lilac, were invaded by the healthy smell of young skin. I touched her naked arm. It was like warm velvet slightly cooled by the evening. I gave her a long Hollywood kiss on the mouth.

"Be gentle with me," she said, because that was what girls said in those days, and she slipped her arms around my neck in a proprietary fashion. At that moment, the Lord reminded me that I had a long way to go before my punishment was over.

Biting my lip against the searing pain, I freed myself from Vixi's moist embrace and tried to stand up. I couldn't, so I crouched down in the grass instead. It smelled almost as sweet as the lilacs.

"Hmm?" said Vixi. It sounded like a question.

I couldn't speak; my entire anatomy was urging me to yell out in pain and I was afraid to open my mouth. The God of my honest uncle was giving me a taste of what it was like in hell. Vixi stood up.

"If you're worried someone's going to see us, let's go down there into the trees. Come on!"

She took my hand. I pulled it out of her grip.

"Hey, don't start playing professor all over again!"

I looked around me, seeking some escape from this trap. Rising before me was the virginal chapel, its small white tower glowing against a background of stars like a mystical bride. It whispered to me, maliciously and perhaps as part of an absurd plan, a pious lie.

"Look, Vlasticka," I said, trying in spite of my pain to speak in the worldly-wise tone I had used as a tenor sax in the Embassy Bar, "you've got it all wrong, understand?"

"You mean you're not a professor?"

"No, that's not what I mean. But I've got reasons for acting this way, maybe reasons too big for your brain to handle."

"That's an insult! Just because you gave me a goose-egg in economics doesn't mean I'm stupid. What reasons — and reasons for what?"

I got up and walked down towards the grove of lilac trees. She ran after me, dragging her white tennis shoes through the succulent grass. In the deceptive light those shoes were the same colour as the chapel, as the moon bathed them in a loving light.

"You're chicken!" she said.

"You've got me wrong."

"You are. You're chicken. You're afraid of Ivana, afraid she'll throw you out on your ear."

"Completely wrong."

We walked through a screen of dark purple blossoms. Vixi ran ahead of me, then turned and stood in my path, blocking my way. The shadows under her breasts deepened, the silken head sparkled in the moonlight. Her full, soft, seventeen-year-old lips pouted in defiance.

It was inhuman. The tips of her breasts gently touched my shirt — again she wasn't wearing a brassiere — and her stiff nipples poked into my skin like two arrows shot from the traditional bow. We could hear the wheezing worshippers in my boarding house, and I held out my hands in helpless supplication while they sang:

Oh Lord, our God and our refuge,
Lead us through mystery to see thy eternal truth. . . .

I took Vixi's velvet cheeks in both hands and hungrily kissed her lips. They smelled of sex. Then the Lord gave me a hard kick in my *centrum peccationis* and my vision went dark with the pain. I turned and, hunched like our ancient ancestors, hobbled back to the little house that stood between two enormous lilac bushes. The wheezing harmonium was artlessly imitating the voice of the Middle Ages.

Vixi came skipping after me in something that resembled a dance step. She was astonished at my behaviour. I stopped just outside my open window and tried to stand up straight. Vixi gazed into the darkness of my room, and suddenly thought she understood.

"In there?"

"No," I said. "It's probably too much for you to comprehend, Vixi, but it's out of the question."

"Coward!" she hissed. *"Coward!"* And she danced around me like a sneering naiad.

"You're right. I am afraid. But not of Ivana."

"Have you got a girl in Prague?"

"I'm afraid of God."

"Who?"

"He's already punished me severely for the same sin. And I don't feel like testing His patience again."

"You're joking!"

"No. I'm — if you have any idea what this means — a devout Catholic. And I'm trying to live the way a Catholic should."

She stopped her dance and stood in front of me, astonished, looking at me as though I were some fairy-tale apparition.

"Gosh!"

She was still standing there as I climbed in my window and looked back out. The nymph of Hronov, this seventeen-year-old embodiment of pure sex. The moon, swollen by the tensions of the night, set a crown of silk on her head and placed its own dark umbra below her breasts. She looked at me in amazement, and as she raised her head her little nose caught the moonlight and turned white. Then she said, in the voice of that persistent classful of girls who, without the slightest interest in the scientific method, had tried every experiment they could think of to get to the bottom of my erotic inclinations:

"Gosh, sir, if that doesn't take the cake!"

In the end Dr. Gellen's radical measure worked, and Vixi's persistence bore fruit. Then, with my back to that other bride who also glowed whitely into the countryside, I saw another Vixi: white as chalk and terrified, because like so many women she had a tendency not only to sin, but also to be superstitious. Desperately she dragged me away and we staggered headlong down a path through the woods, away from the Chapel of the Virgin Mary under Mare's Head and down towards the poisonous green meadows surrounding Hronov, heedless of my hangover, which turned our flight into hallucination. For the murmuring of peaceful Sunday-morning prayers had lulled me into a half-dream, and to be awakened by a sudden, wailing pandemonium that suggested the torments of hell (I had no idea what was happening, although the voices were shrieking, "A miracle! A miracle!") and then to see Vixi suddenly fall to her knees in an attitude of prayer — none of this did much to support my faith in the solidity and substantiality of the real world.

We fled before the fading clamour and the rocky cliffs hung over us at crazy angles while an absurd wind, perhaps related in some way to the *miraculum,* roared through the birches. With the chapel out of sight behind us, we rounded a sharp turn in the path and ran straight into Dr. Gellen. He looked a little like a devil, with enormous black circles under his eyes and his face the colour of the woods around him. He was jogging along in a track suit and breathing in the fashion recommended by fitness experts.

He stopped. "You're in rather a hurry. Don't tell me you saw it too?"

"Meaning what?" I shot back at him.

Gellen stared lasciviously at Vixi, who was trembling like a rabbit. He reached into the back pocket of his sweat pants, pulled out an absurdly inappropriate pocket flask, and handed it to my girl.

"The same thing that terrified our young friend here," he said, watching as Vixi, who had refused to touch a drop the night before, took a healthy swallow of the invigorating beverage.

"Golly!" she said with a sigh. "Were you there too, Doctor Gellen?"

He shook his head. "Unfortunately not. I only woke up half an hour ago, after a night of heavy indulgence in iniquitous immoderation," he said, allowing a well-practised leer to flit across his face, "and I'm trying to atone for it by taking a run. But some hiker with a rucksack came pounding down the trail ahead of you just now, and told me there had been a miracle in the chapel up there."

"There was!" Vixi took a deep breath and shuddered again. "At least, it sure looked like it."

"You seem a little shaken," said Gellen.

"Who wouldn't be? One of those carved wooden saints — "

I squeezed her hand so hard she hissed with pain.

"Ow! But the hiker saw it too!"

"Did *you* see it?" Gellen asked me.

I shook my head. "Signs like that only appear to heathens," I said, looking at my girl. "Never to backsliders."

Vixi grabbed my hand. "Sir! If something did happen, then it's all because of me!"

The expression on her face was an unusual one for her — absolute sincerity, with none of her usual foxiness. The result was mildly comical. Dr. Gellen laughed, but not at Vixi. He asked me: "Say, what faith are you backsliding from?"

Angrily, I looked into his devilish eyes. In the shadows of the wind-tossed birches and the towering cliffs, they were almost black.

"I have to get going," I said. "I have a district conference to attend this afternoon. So long."

We parted. The greenish Gellen set off at a leisurely trot towards the chapel, and Vixi and I quickly put the miracle behind us — for almost twenty years.

2

■

The Dead Priest

I.

He was still the same elegant, youthful man with the same anachronistic moustache he'd worn when he'd first laid eyes on my wretched implement of love in his office, beneath portraits of the generalissimo and the president, and a spark of understanding had jumped the gap between us. He was twenty years older now but still in splendid condition, thanks to regular games of tennis — a habit acquired back when his father owned a gynecological sanatorium. By his age — he was approaching fifty — most of his more proletarian colleagues had started looking like beer barrels, having never cultivated the iron habit of dividing their time between work, recreation, and sleep, no matter what. This regime was yet another inheritance he had brought with him from capitalism into socialism, along with his luxury cottage under Horse's Saddle. He was a full professor of gynecology at Charles University, one of those indestructible people who had learned a trade in time and, along with it, acquired the art of saying nothing, of observing the world and its crooked ways from the ivory tower of a specialization no social system could do without. He had carefully avoided signing any of the manifestos reflecting the vicissitudes of the times, and only in the narrow circle of his closest friends did he ever let on that he was already living in the next century, when the mythic battles of ideology would appear as ridiculous as an earlier era's debates about the sex of angels. Now, in the early days of the Year of Our Lord 1970, he was sitting in a chalet not far from an army base that had been commandeered by a tank division of the Soviet Army of Occupation. The chalet had been built during the Depression by the famous and expensive architect Gocar, and it was supplied with a recreational bookshelf full of detective fiction and English translations of Solzhenitsyn, Djilas, and other, lesser lights of disillusionment.

He was sitting by the fireplace, a bottle of Vat 69 beside him, and with gentle cynicism was reminiscing about his Aunt Laura. I had learned of her death in that morning's *Rude Pravo,* where an anonymous hack had characterized this once beautiful woman as "a comrade who, during the difficult trials of the 1950s and then of 1968, remained faithful to the tenets of Marxism-Leninism, unlike so many others."

"Cancer runs in the family, I'm sorry to say," Gellen said reflectively, without the slightest trace of emotion. "She was a magnificent girl! My only venture into incest. But when she lost her sense of judgement, she lost it in spades. That's always the way it was in upper-class families. In the old days daughters used to rebel by having affairs with the chauffeur; when we were young they were climbing into bed with the local Party organization. But Laura didn't deserve all those knock-out punches. It was just a little too much for one essentially tender young girl."

He raised a glass of whisky as though offering a toast to her memory.

"She was only a year older than me," he said dreamily, looking into his glass. "My aunt. A magnificent creature. She was always a bit morbid about our relationship, probably because of the kinship factor. Once she swallowed a tube of Veronal on an empty stomach, but she hadn't a clue about medicine, poor thing, and she underdosed. After they pumped out her stomach, they made me go and visit her in the sanatorium. Because I was family. The theory was that I could help her slowly get over it." Gellen grinned as only he knew how. "She got over it with my help, all right, but only in the sense that she stopped fantasizing about getting papal dispensation from the taboos of kinship, and instead became adept at a very ancient art. Before her conversion to a more modern world-view, she used to be of your faith, did you know that?"

"You know the story of my faith," I retorted.

"Me? I can't say that I do."

"Never mind," I said. "My sin was blasphemy, never incest."

"You don't know what you've missed, my friend. Laura was an exceptionally quick study."

The deceased's aristocratic face, unproletarianized even by her long love affair with the Party (and, concretely, with several of its members), came to my mind, ravaged by the approach of death but still as fresh as — but then, it hadn't been that long ago. The flames in Gellen's fireplace flickered through her image in my mind. The fireplace was overlaid with Gothic tiles, and the naively executed reliefs on them depicted the agonizing demises of virgins tortured to death for Christ. Beside the fireplace hung a crucifix — not as an expression of the owner's faith, but as a gesture towards one of the current fashions in interior design. It had obviously been stolen from an abandoned chapel in the countryside, but instead of flogging it to an American tourist the thief had sold it to Gellen, who happened to have a stash of hard-currency vouchers. A haggard Christ with a bird-cage chest hung on the cross in his original worm-eaten form, unretouched by any devout doll-maker and therefore not to the most sophisticated taste of the time. A halo had been chiselled into the wood around his head. I looked away, into the flames. The sight of that suffering face, rendered in the expressionistic folk-style of the baroque era, was unpleasant. It reminded me of things I didn't believe in any more.

"Anyway," he went on, "after she converted to her more modern world-view, the Party gradually destroyed our relationship, the way it does everything nice. And when she fell for that idiot Fischer, she moved on to a phase of saccharine Stalinism. No more free love, but a noble relationship between a man and a woman who would be faithful to each other, build socialism together, and give birth to a new generation to carry on the task after them. The wonder is that, when the Party came up with all those other medieval discoveries to replace old, bourgeois prejudices, it didn't come up with some hygienic version of the chastity belt too."

He puffed on his pipe, veiling us both in an aromatic cloud.

"So there it was — suddenly she didn't want to come across for me any more. She threw herself body and soul into marital fidelity. She saved everything for her hairy Jew, Fischer." He blew out some smoke and another cloud rose to meet the fine wood panelling in the ceiling. Some of it formed a second halo around the head of Christ — translucent, pastel-coloured, transient. That was a nice funeral oration, I thought. He's remembering the best of Laura, the things that will remain — if anything does — in the fleeting memory of the world.

"Anyway, all things come to an end, and when we split up I didn't try to poison myself or anything like that," said my friend. "I didn't even get drunk. The only hard part was finding another woman half as quick to learn the arts of love."

A red log crashed to the hot bricks of the fireplace and sighed. A small swarm of sparks swirled up the chimney. When I had first heard of Laura, I reflected, Fischer had already been in his grave a long time. What I had learned, I had got from the mouth of another one of her admirers.

2.

In the courtyard in front of the ministry building a group of young idiots were swirling around in a circle-dance, honouring the anniversary of some allied nation. It was like a bad joke since, that same morning, news had come through that a Russian freighter was steaming straight for the American battleships that were blockading Cuba, and all the signs pointed to war — an atomic one this time. For several days now the streets had been swarming with pot-bellied reservists in uniform; my landlady had carried her entire supply of canned food into the basement, where she intended to sit out the radiation, and the Prague art galleries had moved their most valuable holdings to a depository somewhere in the country. In other words, the diagnostic picture was almost unmistakable, yet here were a group of obsolete lunatics in blue Youth Union shirts, yelping and prancing under a many-coloured oriental flag as though it were all business as usual. As I walked past them, I noticed that the youth of the people executing this *dance macabre* was rather threadbare. But they were professionals and therefore could be counted on to deliver the prescribed dose of *joie de vivre*, whatever the international situation.

I had gone to the ministry on business that was clearly going to be delayed by this sudden turn in world events. It was a job passed on to me by a friend of mine called Slavek Machal — assistant to the minister, and part-time dramaturge with the Illusion Theatre, a company of international repute that toured abroad and paid in hard-currency vouchers. The idea was that I would concoct a musical comedy for them, and I had the unfinished synopsis for it in my pocket.

When I opened the door of Slavek's office, he was just pointing out the window to a hillside across the Vltava River, to the empty spot where the gigantic Stalin monument had stood until its destruction the year before. Now all that was left of it was the base, which looked like the dark side of a Mayan pyramid, with wide granite steps on either side leading to an empty platform at the top. Slavek looked around as I came into the room, his arm dropped, and I noticed a man sitting in an armchair opposite his desk. From the dark colour in Slavek's face, I could tell they were not exchanging pleasantries.

"Comrade Barta," said Slavek, introducing me, and then raised his arm again to point towards the enormous granite platform. He said nothing, but merely stood there with his arm outstretched, like a public prosecutor pointing at the accused. Then Comrade Barta spoke.

"It's a demagogic bogy-man, nothing more," he said. His voice was utterly calm and expressionless and I felt alarmed because Slavek's outstretched hand led me to misunderstand his remark. But his drift became clear at once. Slavek brought his arm around in a half-circle to point directly at Comrade Barta's bright red, fashionably knit tie, which sat beneath the folds of his impassive chin like a handsome direction marker, and said rather loudly:

"You're talking like a Chinaman, Tonda! Surely you know how little it would take to turn all of Bohemia into a wasteland! I maintain that the missiles they put in Cuba are a terrible risk, and it's cynical of us to pretend they aren't. If there's war, we're the ones who'll buy the farm, not them. They've got space, they're not living like sardines in a can the way we are. And they know it damn well. I'm sorry, Tonda, but I *do* care if someone wants to use this small nation as cannon-fodder!"

Barta remained unruffled. "I repeat," he said calmly, "it's all demagoguery. And you know as well as I do that we're going to evacuate the children. Fifteen hundred of them are in Bulgaria already, far from where we assume the bombs will fall."

"How many more do you think we'll manage to evacuate, eh? Twenty thousand? Fifty?"

"It will be a bloody war, no question about it. But the Party has done its homework. According to studies, twenty thousand children are enough to regenerate a nation of ten million within a few generations."

I'd been accustomed to reading about the horrors of nuclear war only in the Western newspapers and magazines an acquaintance of mine, a waiter in the Alcron Hotel, sometimes stole and passed on to me. To hear this kind of talk straight from the lips of an important Party official gave me a feeling of unreality. But I was hearing it with my own ears.

"So far, the Party has always demonstrated that it knows what it's doing," Barta went on, ignoring the obvious rebuke of the bald granite pyramid across the river although his fish-eyes were looking straight at it. "Great goals demand great sacrifices, sometimes at the extreme limits of what society can bear."

"But *whose* sacrifice? Certainly not theirs!" Slavek shouted angrily, pointing dramatically across the river again. "That's the only shelter!" he shouted. "The only atom-bomb shelter in the whole goddamned city of Prague! You know that! And who'll be using it? Children?"

"The Party leadership, of course," said Barta, without blinking.

I looked at Slavek. He seemed to be on the point of apoplexy, struggling for air. "Of course!" he managed to say finally. "The best and the brightest. Led by the president himself!"

"It's not a question of what you or I or any other individual thinks of these men. The Party must be able to give leadership even in a crisis and, as you say, there's only one shelter." Barta was wearing sparkling garnet cufflinks. "As far as the president is concerned, well, that's where you and

I differ. In my opinion, it's only thanks to Comrade Novotny that things haven't gone as far downhill in this country as they have in other places I could mention."

A formation of jet fighters streaked ominously across the sky above the empty dais. For a moment I stopped listening to this conversation and remembered how hard it had been to destroy that statue of Marshal Stalin. The first detonation had failed to do the job, and they had had to blast away at the colossus bit by bit, until gradually the familiar figure was transformed into the ghastly outlines of one of Giacometti's monstrosities. Day after day the editors of the writers' weekly paper took pictures frame by frame, on movie film, from a window in the editorial offices. The documentary film that resulted was never shown in cinemas, of course, but I attended a private screening and saw the enormous statue shed its recognizable form, twist, succumb to what looked like a fatal convulsion, and suddenly collapse into a heap of stones. It was like watching, in reverse, one of those botanical time-lapse films in which a lily of the valley sticks its head out of the ground, zooms up to full size, and rolls out blossoms. And it had given me the same sense of unreality that I was feeling now.

"Anyway, all nations will integrate with each other in the future," I heard Barta say in the tones of a political indoctrinator. "The nation, as you know, is a historically derived form of social cohabitation, and as such it will one day become historically obsolete. Humanity will amalgamate to form a single unity."

All at once, without really wanting to, I found myself blurting, "And how will people talk when that happens?"

Barta turned his fishlike eyes on me. "I take it you mean, what language will they speak?"

I nodded and the impassive man laughed, but only with the lower half of his face. "That's hard to say."

"Russian?" said Slavek angrily.

"Perhaps," said Barta. "It is, after all, the language of the first socialist revolution."

Slavek exploded again. "Language is an attribute of nationality, Tonda, not of historical events. And if you think everyone's going to speak Russian — "

"I didn't express myself precisely enough," Barta interrupted. "Perhaps individual nations will maintain their own languages. But Russian will be the lingua franca. Something like medieval Latin used to be, perhaps."

"Latin was a neutral language — practically a dead language — in the Middle Ages! Has it never occurred to you that one nation might not want to learn the living language of another?"

The look Barta gave Slavek suggested he had just dropped him from the ranks of those who deserved to survive. I wondered if Barta had a pass that would get him into that bomb shelter across the river. Probably not. But for the first time a question surfaced in my mind — one I would ask myself many times after that, without ever finding an answer. Could this creature, Barta, be a human being? And if he was, then what was I? Or was he perhaps that hypothetical *Übermensch* — risen like a phoenix out of the fire of socialist humanism, which in becoming international had gone beyond the limited horizons of my bourgeois sensibility?

I tried to shake off what amounted to a pathological tendency to dramatize things. The poker-face in front of me was not that of an *Übermensch*, merely of a relatively important member of a confraternity whose actions were always correct, if occasionally erroneous. But that wasn't his fault. He was not the author of those ideas, merely the agent. His honour lay not in sensitivity but in fidelity — fidelity to the absolute truth, which — as the founder of the confraternity so cleverly defined it — is the sum total of all relative truths that succeed each other in the process of historical development and that retrospectively appear, in the light of the confraternity's activities, to have been mistakes.

"National friction and chauvinism will not exist under Communism," I heard Barta declare. "When I said Russian was the language of revolution, I meant that the Russian nation — I mean the Russian people," he corrected himself, "have made undeniable contributions to history, such as being the first in history to carry out a socialist revolution. In the moral sense, Russian undeniably has the right to become the language of Communism."

By now even Barta was beginning to lose his cool, detached manner. Both men started interrupting each other and their shouts, echoing in the uncertainty of a tense historical moment, sounded like the voices of madmen arguing in some other wilderness than the one where a voice had once cried.

"All kinds of nations took part in the revolution! They only spoke Russian because they lived in the czarist empire! Even the revolutionary leaders weren't Russian: Stalin was a Georgian, there were a bunch of Jews, maybe even Lenin himself — "

"It's irrelevant how these non-Russian nations came to speak Russian. They fought in the revolution and adopted Russian as their own language. In the ideological, not the linguistic sense — "

"But the old revolutionaries were counting on some kind of artificial language to carry the day — something that would be the logical equivalent of Latin," Slavek insisted. "Besides, you can learn a language like that in a month; it doesn't have any grammatical peculiarities, or any idioms — "

"Which is precisely the trouble with artificial languages. They're dead before they're born. They haven't a chance of catching on. People need an international language that has some skin and bones to it, something that isn't just a cosmopolitan abstraction — "

The image of a nation far from Russia appeared to me out of the mists of this delusion — the Xhosa tribe, perhaps — as in some utopian future they suppressed their own clicks and labials and wrestled with the human skin and bones of the three genders and seven cases of Russian grammar. But at that moment the unreal argument was interrupted by a brisk knock on the door, and the language of revolution was suddenly forgotten as a stunningly beautiful blonde stepped into Slavek's office.

At the time I didn't know she was Barta's wife, so my first impression of her was unspoiled. She was a charming woman in a light spring dress, white shoes, and nylons. The buckle on her low-slung belt was shaped like a heart and hung directly over her pudenda. Earrings that looked like daisies sparkled in her ears. At the time, she was thirty-eight years old.

"Excuse me," she said, and "Hi, Slavek!" and then, to Barta, "Can I talk to you for a moment?"

Slavek shot out of his chair. "Welcome!" he said. The blonde granted him a smile and then turned her back to us. Our view of her as she walked out was obscured by the broad back of her impassive husband, who got up and followed her out of the room.

"A very interesting person," I said. "Who is she?"

"Her name's Laura," said Slavek.

Slavek was — in his own words "once", by my observation "still" — madly in love with Laura, and he spoke of her husband with an anger rooted in differences that went far deeper than ideology. As we walked up the winding streets of Mala Strana towards Prague Castle, he admitted to me that once, long ago, he had been very much like Barta. Like him, he had come from proletarian origins and, under the tutelage of Party instructors, had cultivated the proper class hatred. Then he had turned its sharp edges against a certain Wideman family, because he'd fallen in love with their daughter, Laura.

He first met her when she was going through what Gellen had once described to me as her Youth Union, avant-garde phase of misalliance with her Party cell. From what Slavek told me, I concluded that he'd only figured in her life as one of many tools she'd used to punish her parents for bringing her into the world in a luxury apartment instead of a slum tenement. Shortly before he met her, she'd taken the cure in the sanatorium and changed from a good little Catholic girl into the bedmate of her nephew, the progressive non-Party scientist Gellen. Her relationship with the Communist Party helped her shed a number of other inhibitions as well, but not all of them, for she never put out for Slavek. So he vented his frustration on her mother.

"I tell you, man, I hated that woman," he confided to me as we trudged up the winding street. "Whenever Laura and I were sitting in her room and her mother knocked — she always knocked — and then stuck her head round the door and said, 'Wouldn't you like a nice cup of tea with us, Mr. Machal?' I always felt like saying something really obscene to her — and sometimes I did. At four o'clock in the afternoon what you did was drink tea, end of discussion. And there were Laura and I, in her room, talking a blue streak about whatever we were interested in, and she comes in with her 'Wouldn't you like a nice — '"

"What were you interested in, anyway?"

"Politics," he said. "The Marshall Plan, I kid you not. The tax on millionaires. Can you believe it? You saw Laura — she's still a looker, right? Well, you have no idea what she looked like then."

"I think I might have," I said. "In that department my imagination's pretty good."

"Then crank it to the limit, man, crank it to the bloody limit," Slavek said. "But this is even harder to imagine: I'm sitting there next to this beautiful woman, shooting my mouth off about Klement Gottwald's statement on the nationalization of the Batas' goddamned shoe factories."

"That's nothing. I was in a situation like that once — of course, I was a lot younger at the time — and what I talked about was dinosaurs."

"Was she interested?"

"Of course not. Neither was I — not at that moment."

"See what I mean? And we actually *enjoyed* it!"

I'd been spared the joy of such peculiar passions. I had never succumbed to the charms of Klement Gottwald, or of any more significant statesmen, either.

"What else did you do?" I asked. "Didn't you ever let your hands wander — "

"Of course I did," said Slavek, "but she'd always crack me across the knuckles. Sometimes we'd even kiss, on that beige couch of hers — but every time we got down to it her goddamned mother would come in with her 'Wouldn't you like a nice cup of tea?' routine. She'd even enunciate the 'of' clearly, for God's sake."

"Obviously there was some fancy mother-and-daughter teamwork going on," I said. "In some of the better families that kind of thing was a highly developed art."

"You're wrong there. Laura hated her mother."

"Then maybe it was a deliberate ploy on her part. She knew the family always had tea on the stroke of four, so she'd get you excited according to a very precise schedule. Did you masturbate while you were still there, or wait till you got home?"

Slavek was not a complete romantic, so he wasn't shocked at my question.

"As a matter of fact, sometimes I did it right there in her bathroom." He looked into the sun and squinted. "But no, she didn't do it deliberately. We were just comrades. She already had a boyfriend, some doctor or other. I was young and fairly good-looking and she was young and Jesus, Danny, she was beautiful. But usually, instead of wanking off in her toilet, I'd take it out on her mother."

"You mean the mother came across for you?"

"Still got a dirty mind, eh, Danny?" laughed Slavek. "You know what I mean. I'd give her a hard time all during tea."

As we reached the top of the hill a strange procession of three bulky armoured vehicles rattled past the castle gates, reminding me of the Cuban crisis. In the midst of it, according to Slavek, Laura was getting ready to divorce her husband — as though the future still had some meaning.

"Why do you think she's divorcing him now?" I asked.

"Why?" Slavek said. "How should I know? She doesn't let me in on her private thoughts. And Barta, well, he's just a government swine, never tells me anything. I tell you, man, that fellow gives me a bad conscience," he said unexpectedly.

"You mean you carried on with her behind his back? Marriage was so disappointing that she finally came across, right?" Slavek said nothing. "Come on, you can tell me. I'm notorious for my discretion."

"You're an asshole, Danny. No, I hate to say it but there's never been anything like that between us. Anyway, that's not what I meant about a bad conscience. But did you notice how he always has an answer for everything?"

"It's impossible not to notice."

"He's always going on about the law of large numbers. You know, I believed in that too, once. Or — " He stopped. "Of course, I still believe that in politics the law of large numbers applies."

"I'm not so sure about that."

"What I mean is," he began, slipping dangerously into areas of discussion that were really Barta's territory, "pitting the politics of individual happiness against so-called collectivist politics really is demagogy, know what I mean? Because if collectivist politics are done properly, really and truly properly — " A quarter of a century in the Party had certainly left its mark on him.

"Politics have never yet been 'done' really and truly properly anywhere in the world," I interrupted. "Let's talk about women instead."

Slavek nodded and gave me a good-natured poke in the shoulder. "Good idea!" he said. "I'll tell you what, Danny. Let's talk about those two women who sat there with me drinking good bourgeois English tea, may God strike me down."

"Was the mother good-looking too?"

"I suppose she was. She had a fabulous figure. She played a lot of tennis and she swam — that was one of the things I didn't like about her. Once we were lying out on the deck at a private bathing club down by the Vltava — the Widemans rented a cabin every summer and I used to really rub it in, never let her forget it. Now I rent one there myself. But I do it for the kids — she only did it because it was the swank thing to do. Jesus, what an ideologist I was in those days." Slavek sighed. "Anyway, it was the hottest days of summer, a fantastic time to be down by the river. Laura was as brown as a nigger and her mother was lying on one of those inflatable mattresses — a rare thing in those days — all bronzed and shiny, and she'd whine, 'Oh, my head! My poor head! Why don't you and Laura go for a swim, Mr. Machal?' and then a bit later she'd say, 'Oh, my back. Laura darling, could you possibly pass me the thermos bottle' — there was tea in it, of course — 'and my pills?' And it went on like that all afternoon, Mama whining and Laura fussing over her, bringing her pills and pillows. I mean, I hardly knew her, she'd never kowtowed to her mother's whims that way before, not that I knew of, and her mother was whimpering and whining and talking like your stereotypical spoiled bourgeois parasite. So finally I couldn't stand it any more and I let her have it with my heaviest dose of left-wing sarcasm: 'Madam,' I said — this was 1947 and the expression was still in serious use — 'you know what would cure those aches and pains of yours in a hurry? An honest day's work!'"

"So the mother was mortally offended and from that time on you had to neck with Laura in Stromovka Park."

"The hell we did!" said Slavek.

"She wasn't insulted?"

Slavek spat over the railing onto the tile rooftops of the ancient houses below us. "She died."

"What?"

"She died. Not right away, about a month later. She had cancer."

"Jesus."

"She already knew she was dying that afternoon at the pool," said Slavek, turning his blue eyes on me. "It's irrational. It doesn't mean the stereotype is wrong. But I tell you, man, it's been haunting me ever since. From then on, I was never able to be as good a comrade as that son-of-a-bitch Barta."

"You should thank her from the bottom of your heart for that, shouldn't you?"

"I don't know. My basic beliefs are a lot like his. Yet I quarrel with him all the time. It's irrational."

"Relax," I said. "Even Comrade Barta doesn't tackle everything rationally. He just has a different make-up than you do. His kind can make a real mess of the most rational system in the world."

"That's easy enough to say, my friend," Slavek sighed, "but what if my kind can never turn a real mess into a rational system?"

"Then we're in deep shit."

I wanted to add something else, but I swallowed it. I didn't belong to his Party; it wasn't up to me to teach him how to solve the Party's problems. And it wouldn't have made any difference anyway. I didn't know how to solve them any more than anyone else did.

"Poor Mama," I said. "How did Laura take it?"

Slavek shrugged his shoulders. "At the funeral she cried her eyes out like any proper daughter. But I don't think it really affected her. By February of '48 she was working for the Ministry of the Interior; then she went over to Counter-Espionage, dumped her doctor boyfriend, and married Fischer. And then — well, you know the rest."

3.

It was almost dark. The flames cast a shadow of the termite-infested Christ's wooden halo onto the ceiling; it looked like a quivering black moon. The wind that was howling through the rocks outside hadn't changed a bit in twenty years, and even with Soviet tanks squatting in the darkness not far away, the Vat 69 in my veins transformed the world into a safe, though still adventuresome, place.

"What was the name of your girlfriend, anyway?" asked Gellen innocently. "The one with the cute nose? She had a kind of worldly-wise look in her eyes."

"You mean," I said slowly, "the one who was with me the night you plied me with whisky, the night before the miracle?"

"My goodness, the miracle! I'd almost forgotten that. As I recall, she was quite terrified — poor thing."

"She was a good kid. She thought religion was a joke, but when she saw that wooden statue start to — "

"She was a cute little number, if I remember rightly," Gellen interrupted me. "Not my type, unfortunately. Or maybe it was just as well. At least she never got in the way of our friendship."

He sat there opposite me, under the crucifix that might have been carved from a weatherbeaten fencepost. He was wearing a pair of fashionable striped slacks, and with his long legs resting on a leopard-skin hassock he looked like a professional gigolo. You're lying, my friend, I said to myself. It doesn't really bother me — but you're lying, and I know it.

4.

I was standing outside the record shop in Wenceslas Square when I heard the anachronistic greeting. Inside they were playing an imitation Melanesian love song rendered by the Kucera Family Singers. You could hear it all the way out on the sidewalk.

"May the saints be praised, if it isn't Mr. Smiricky. Sir!"

I turned around and there at the pedestrian railing at the edge of the sidewalk — a place where the zoot-suit crowd usually hung out — was Vixi. She was smiling at me over a battered, fifty-second-hand baby carriage.

"Vixi!" I cried. I was genuinely happy to see her. My mistress at the time, Margitka, had just changed her mind again about divorcing her husband — something I hadn't asked her to do in the first place — and the decision had ushered in a brief period of marital fidelity. "How great to see you!" I shouted, and my voice was immediately drowned out by a piercing wail from under the cheap plastic hood of the baby carriage. "Don't tell me this little angel is yours?" I said, looking at the red-faced infant under the hood.

"There's nothing wrong with it if you're married, is there?" said Vixi, putting on a familiar, unbelievably virtuous expression. "Do you know, I can still recite the catechism — how can I forget it when everything my hubby does reminds me of it?" Those foxy eyes, void of any morality, were inviting; they took me back to that time of lilacs six years before. Vixi examined me with a friendly, cheerful audacity, the way she had always done. "Anyway," she said, "I've always had this incredible luck with Catholics, and it can't just be coincidence. I mean, when you think about it, here I am, a poor little orphan girl, and one Catholic picks my cherry and another saddles me with a brat — "

The baby stopped squalling and the colour of its face returned to normal. It looked like the wife of a senior alderman. It was terribly overfed, and had angelic blonde hair and eyes so blue they were almost black.

"But the other one married you, too. Or was that a third Catholic?"

"I beg your pardon!" said Vixi. "Of course he married me. I didn't even have to ask. *And* it was a church wedding!"

"So you were finally christened after all?"

"I had to be, otherwise he might not have married me. When it comes to religion, my husband's as much of a pious old maid as you are. Sir."

The green eyes mocked me.

"Or maybe you aren't any more, but you certainly were back then."

"I got over it," I said. The baby stared at me with its wide, dark eyes, as though it had seen a ghost. "Who did you manage to collar, anyway?" I asked. Looking at Vixi's sweet face, with that silken halo of hair tied with the traditional blue ribbon, I found myself slipping into her old schoolgirl idiom.

"You don't know him, sir. Somebody called Novotny."

It was the most common name in the phone book. "Vixi! Surely you have more imagination that that!"

"When did you ever pick anyone because of their name?" she shot back. She was, after all, Vixi the *parvenue.* If I'd told her of the main charm of my mistress of the moment — a girl with the gloriously aristocratic name of Margitka Kolowratova — she wouldn't have understood. There was no room in her for the resonance of old myths. If I had known Laura at the time, and had told Vixi that every woman called Laura evoked "a face in the misty night" and was immediately halfway to winning me over, she'd have said, "Baloney, sir! What if she's hunchbacked?" She understood everything with a down-to-earth realism. But even she could display some modest aspiration.

"I know, it's a stupid-sounding name: Vlasta Novotna. But my husband's in the same line you are, in a way. Except that they won't publish what he writes. He doesn't write the sort of lightweight stuff you do."

"Wait a minute!" Without knowing why, I looked at the baby, who was now staring at me intently with eyes the colour of blueberry pie. "You married *Vojtech* Novotny?"

"You know him?" she asked uncertainly.

Of course I know him, Vixi. How could I not know that almost saintly prophet of orthodoxy, who surpasses — in his capacity to cleave to the Catholic faith, if not in his art — all the stars of the diminishing ranks of the literary underground?

Despite the rash of sudden raids and arrests by the Secret Police, the underground still had its own king, the poet Vincenc Hollar. Hollar had once written postwar hymns to the Red Army, our Liberator (he was awarded a state prize), and then, influenced by the show-trial justice of the Party, had taken to writing sonnets on the Czech saints (his state prize had enabled him to survive the change in subject). When his best friend, the poet Jan Kopula, was arrested, he withdrew into his private life and deliberately turned himself into a notorious hermit. He stopped going out of doors, but because he enjoyed company — especially that of young ladies — many people, women in particular, undertook pilgrimages to the small Renaissance house where he lived, provocatively stuck on the hillside just below Prague Castle. More than one young ballet dancer came away with a handwritten poem by the Master, complete with dedication — usually a sonnet of mingled erotic and Catholic imagery wrapped in magic Czech, on the unfailingly entertaining theme of feminine beauty.

Vojtech Novotny was one of the most persistent, if not the most welcome, pilgrims to Hollar's sanctuary. I had met him there. He looked like an earthy farmer from the flatlands of Moravia, with pious blue eyes in a round face, and he suffered for his faith in that although he had a solid education in the humanities (they had thrown him out of university in the wake of the Communist takeover, before he could complete his doctorate) he worked as a corpse-washer in the General Hospital. Everywhere he went, his faith went with him; like Peter, he was a rock of faith and a steadfast pillar of orthodoxy. He would always cross himself whenever he passed a wayside chapel (once, in a streetcar, I watched him ostentatiously cross himself whenever we passed a Catholic church; the Protestant ones he ignored), and it was over the question of orthodoxy that his adorational friendship with Vincenc Hollar finally broke up.

Like so many poets, Hollar not only loved ballet dancers, but also had a passion for crime fiction, and he loved Graham Greene. He enjoyed bringing Greene up in conversation and it was soon clear to me that Novotny, who would usually add long, eager commentaries of his own to the Master's statements, was unusually silent whenever the famous convert's name was mentioned. Once, however, Novotny broke his mysterious silence, and this led to an event that became a legend in the annals of the Catholic literary underground. The Master was just waxing ecstatic about *A Gun for Sale*, and as far as I could understand from his rambling eulogy, he was identifying the dancer with Mary Magdalene and the hired killer with the thief who was crucified on Christ's right hand. At this point Novotny scowled and, in the sepulchral voice of a scholastic interpreter, announced, "If I may make an observation, Master — I think that

Greene sometimes goes a bit too far. There are even times when I have doubts about the man's salvation."

A sudden silence descended upon the Master's study. The Master was a man of great (literary) passions and I knew that anyone who messed with his saints was lost. Novotny must have known it too, but he couldn't help himself. Now, having uttered the unretractable judgement, he cowered back in his seat, and we cowered with him, while the Master, his eyes burning and wide with disbelief at what his ears had just heard, pulled himself up in his cubist chair, got to his feet, walked over to a surrealist picture called *Suffering on the Cross*, in which a painted lamb was nailed to a cross with real nails, dramatically covered his eyes as though he were shooting off a brief prayer to heaven, then spun around and like a prophet of doom stabbed his finger towards the washer of corpses, who was now cringing between two ballet dancers. "Mr. Novotny," he thundered in a voice that made us all tremble, "I would rather go with Graham Greene to the place where there shall be weeping and wailing and gnashing of teeth, than spend a single second of eternity in the Kingdom of Heaven with you!"

Novotny slunk away from the little house in disgrace that night, and both ballet dancers carried word of the Master's retort to other underground gatherings. Indeed, Novotny owed his relative notoriety more to this famous expulsion from paradise than to his own boring litanies. It was a sign of how out of touch Vixi was with the literary world that she first heard the story from me, in the Julis Café, where I took her (along with the baby in its buggy) for coffee and cake.

"There's still no call for you to make fun of him," she said. The story had mildly offended her. "He takes it seriously. You always just lied through your teeth."

"Me? Vixi, how can you say — "

"This Greene," she interrupted, "Vojta really hates him, and he read me something about him a while ago in a magazine. Some reporters asked him about his religion, and he told them religion was like an incurable disease. That's just the way you are, you know? Except your disease was curable."

From the look in her eye, I understood that by some careful prying Vixi had managed to uncover the secret of my faith, despite being so poorly informed about her own husband. Later I discovered that he didn't interest her a great deal. But in the Julis Café I exploded. "Who told you that, Vixi?"

"Guess!" she said, and those little teeth which, at the time of my venereal agony, could have driven me into rage, sank into a Sachertorte. But very soon the light went on in my lighthouse, as she might have put it.

There was only one other person in the whole world who had known about my indisposition. He was not a writer, and therefore not prone to gossip. If this person had told her, they must have known each other very well.

I looked at her while she put her waistline in jeopardy with the torte, which came slathered in whipped cream. It was a nice waistline, and Vixi was still slim and shapely. She wasn't one of those women who appeal to some men and not to others. In any case, I knew this non-writer very well; he liked all types.

Suddenly I remembered an almost forgotten telephone conversation — how long ago had it been? With the help of my fingers I made some quick calculations, and soon I had the answer.

"Vixi," I said, "what was it you wanted of me last summer?"

Immediately, she withdrew inside the armour-plating of an unlikely insolence. "Do we have to talk about it? You must have known what it was about. Anyway, you basically told me to get lost, so I don't want to discuss it."

She turned her attention from the unfinished Sachertorte and pulled the child out of the carriage beside her. It was strapped into its bedding with old-fashioned Czech swaddling bands. Vixi took a spoonful of whipped cream and stuffed it into the baby's mouth. The baby opened its eyes wide in astonishment, the way it had when it first looked at me, and swallowed the unfamiliar delicacy with loud slurping and smacking noises. I suspected that whipped cream was a rare commodity in the corpse-washer's household.

"What kind of mother are you, for God's sake?" I said. "Stuffing him with whipped cream like that! How old is he, anyway?"

"In the first place, it's a she," Vixi said, looking proudly into the creature's face — which so far displayed no signs of belonging to either sex — "and in the second place she's two months old, so she can eat anything."

"I'm not so sure about that. If Evzenie Vikusova could see you — "

"At least, it never seems to bother her," Vixi added uncertainly. "Anyway, what do you care what kind of mother I am? I don't like you!"

I was now remembering with more clarity that sunny Saturday morning the previous July when suddenly — after five years filled partly with military service, and partly with new girlfriends and forgetting — the call of Vixi's voice came out of the past. "Hi, prof!" Over the telephone her voice sounded quiet and caressing but as wily as ever, the kind of wiliness that must have been common among the houris of Babylon. "How'd you like to come over? I've borrowed a friend's flat and I'll be here through Sunday. All by myself. So why not come over, prof? You know, I'd really like to. . . ." This Circe from Hronov needed say no more; her voice was moist and undressed, like the July morning. But as luck and the devil would have it, that was the very day Margitka's husband was supposed to go away on business — his first trip since she'd turned the biggest eyes in all of Greater Prague on me in the Mysak sweet-shop and begun to fall for my eloquence. So I had to turn down this tempting call from the depths of my lilac-bowered past. Margitka's call came, and I got into a cab and drove to the *fin-de-siècle* villa in the Hanspaulka quarter where the hitherto faithful aristocratic wife was waiting for me, perfumed and nervous.

Now I made another quick calculation and everything figured. I looked into the hungry infant's wide eyes, and that figured too.

"Vixi, you bitch!" I said. "You wily little fox! Whenever you play hide-and-seek with me, you lose."

She pulled an exaggerated look of incomprehension from her repertoire. "I don't know what you're talking about," she said, unconvincingly.

"Come off it, Vixi!" I said. And I took her bare arm, which was as warm and velvety as I remembered it, and pointed with my other hand to the baby. "The daddy of this little thing is Doctor Gellen, isn't he?"

"You know what you are?" said Vixi reproachfully. "You're a disgusting, mean-minded . . . *schoolmarm*, that's what you are."

"Well, is he or isn't he?"

"Okay, he is."

"And you wanted to do the Mendelssohn March with me, right?"

"Well, yes, I did. But" — and her green eyes were filled with real reproach — "you weren't exactly against getting married back in Hronov. So you come off it, too."

It was my turn to feel ashamed, because she was right: I hadn't been against getting married. The heady mixture of lilac trees and my own intensely randy youth, the ancient magic of her seventeen-year-old breasts, her eyes, the blue ribbon in her silken hair, all of that had made me go on with the Catholic farce I'd begun until at last my intentions became entirely serious. I encouraged her to go to Father Doufal to learn the catechism — Vixi was an unbaptized heathen — because if she was in the Church she would be eligible for a Christian wedding, and in addition it would support my explanation of my chastity — at least until the Brazilian clap allowed me to abandon it.

I burned like paper, as Vixi might have said. I caught fire in the lilac night with a pure flame, and it wasn't extinguished until the army high command had the inscrutable idea of calling up university graduates for military service far earlier than usual, in midsummer. That directive from on high put out the flame and confirmed the truth of the old saw: Vixi was out of sight, and her place was taken by a certain Ludmila Neumannova-Hertlova, and then by a sad officer's wife called Jana. That same summer Vixi went to Zeleny Hradec to wash floors in the local hospital, and from there, thanks (or so I'd thought until that afternoon in the Julis Café) to some clever scheming on her part, she got work washing floors in the Mother of Cities, until she finally landed a job as a nursing assistant in Prague General Hospital. By that time my good friend Dr. Gellen was an assistant professor of gynecology there, and it was about that same time that I sat down one afternoon in an empty chair at a table for two in the Mysak sweet-shop, having asked the prim ex-aristocrat Margitka Kolowratova, "Is this seat taken, miss?"

But back when Gellen's dextrous scalpel brought an end to my abstinence, I was still burning with a clear, unsullied flame. In a cottage belonging to Professor Hepner from the School of Sculpture, which I'd borrowed on the pretext of meeting a fictitious fiancée from Prague, Vixi, though still a catechumen, finally succeeded in storming the barricades of my Catholic principles.

In the process, a mildly embarrassing thing happened.

It was five in the afternoon when we first came together, softly and tenderly, suffused in the brown light seeping through the wooden shutters so that against the green of Hepner's sheets Vixi's skin appeared to be radiating burnt umber. Thanks to my long abstinence I exploded inside her after only a few seconds, but I had accumulated such a rich supply of fluids that I was granite-hard again in less than half an hour, and this time we lingered an uncommonly long time in a paradise of bliss. At last Vixi got up and walked over to an alcove, where she splashed herself with water; then she came back in a polka-dot bikini and opened the window and the door, letting in the blinding late-afternoon sunlight. I was still lying on the bed, luxuriating in my nakedness, when I heard someone speak outside. I rolled off the bed onto the floor and crept under the window to the chair where my underwear was — because the voice belonged to Dr. Gellen, and he was beginning to flirt through the window with Vixi.

Gellen quickly guessed that the bikini'd Vixi was not alone in the cottage, and he soon found out who was with her. When she went to put on some more clothing he became uncharacteristically matter-of-fact, professional interest taking precedence over erotic curiosity. He listened to my report and made the pleasing observation that removing the *praeputium* often made the *instrumentum amoris* less sensitive, and thus had a beneficial effect on the patient's staying power during the act of love. The success of his operation on me put him in such good spirits that he invited us both for supper at his cottage, which stood a little way down the hill, nestled between two large formations of rock called Mare's Head and Horse's Saddle.

The party got off to a bad start. There was a portable grill in front of the cottage, and beside it stood a well-groomed brunette from Prague who could only talk in banalities. Her presence made us feel like newlyweds on an official visit, and I was overwhelmed by the unpleasant sensation of having been annexed. Fortunately, Gellen had a small but highly varied collection of liquor arranged on his mantel, and with his doctor's perceptiveness he immediately felt the stiffness in the atmosphere. The evening passed in anything but sobriety. I drank quickly to drown the feeling that I'd just been yoked, but the liquor only made it worse. Meanwhile the cooking instinct had been aroused in both women, and they fussed around the charcoal grill, perspiring and exclaiming with delight over the meat. At last, their eyes begging for praise, they presented us with burnt steak topped with mustard and garnished with little flowers carved out of radishes. It looked like the outcome of a home economics assignment.

At that time I was unusually sensitive to the perverse details of the world: I noticed how Vixi tore off enormous chunks of steak with her teeth (meat of that quality was something practically unknown to her), and how Gellen was constantly pouring drinks for himself and me. As the feast progressed, my unpleasant sensation that I was being roped into marriage grew into a panic of nightmare proportions. Finally Vixi and the Prague concubine helped me stumble back to Hepner's cottage, where I spent the rest of the night unconscious. At nine in the morning, Vixi energetically shook me awake — into a clanging hangover.

"You're right, Vixi," I said, handing her a handkerchief so she could wipe off the whipped cream that was now smeared all over the child's face. "I wasn't against getting married. But be thankful it didn't work out. As a husband I'd have been a disaster."

"If you think things are so great with Vojtech, then you're way wrong. I don't know if it would have been any bigger a mess with you."

"Of course it would. First of all, because I know only too well where those blueberry eyes came from — unlike your husband. By the way, why didn't Gellen help you out? Things like that shouldn't happen to a gynecologist."

"It happened because I thought I was being smart," Vixi said. "And all the time it was the other way round."

"The other way around?"

"I knew what he'd want to do," she explained. "So I waited until it was too late, because I reckoned — "

She stopped and looked at me. I understood what she'd been about to say, and smiled at her.

"I'm dying to know one thing, though. How did he get off scot-free when abortion was out of the question?"

"Well, he gave me a choice," she said, lowering her eyes. "It was either child support or Vojtech. Gellen got him that job in the hospital. He knew what a pushover Vojtech was, and how all I had to do was snap my fingers and Vojtech would come running." Her big, beautiful mouth formed an expression of exaggerated indignation. "Isn't he a rat, sir?" But there wasn't a trace of hatred or moral judgement in her voice; she was merely stating a fact. "Isn't he the biggest rat under the sun?"

"But he's also Mr. Generosity. Try to be fair, Vixi. He did offer you child support, no strings attached."

"Because he knew I'd do anything in the world to avoid a scandal. Grandad would've whipped me if I'd ever showed up with an illegitimate brat," she said, with old-fashioned propriety. "And you were a real disappointment, you know that? It wasn't till you turned me down that I saddled myself with my Catholic."

"You mean to say you'd have had the cold-blooded gall to saddle me with this?" I said, pointing to the well-fed bundle in the swaddling clothes.

"I've always been fond of you, sir," Vixi protested. "I still am. It wouldn't have been cold-blooded at all. And maybe I'd even have told you the truth."

"When?"

"Not before I had you collared, of course," said Vixi.

Her expression told me she saw nothing wrong in all this. And in a while I realized that she was right: there *was* nothing wrong in it. Among her many other virtues, Vixi often spoke the truth.

"Well, that's something. But you didn't tell your husband."

"I wasn't in love with him, was I?" she said, wiping away a disgusting mixture of saliva and whipped cream that was dripping down the baby's triple chin onto the floral-pattern bib. "And why should I spoil it for him? He's crazy about Anezka. He wants to have at least two more kids," she added, with a very ancient resignation. "Wouldn't you love her, even if she wasn't yours? Just look how pretty she is!" As she raised the bundle for me to look at, a ray of light struck the child's eyes; she closed them and turned into a miniature fat lady again.

"You're prettier," I said. The same ray of sunlight also caught the silken crown of hair with the blue ribbon in it. As she held the child up and admired her with her crafty eyes, the curves of her body above and below described irresistible question marks, and her slender legs, covered with fine, soft hair, were bronze and gold in the sun. She wasn't wearing tennis sneakers any more, but fashionable high-heeled shoes with metal buckles.

And that's how chapter two in my rather pleasant affair with Vixi began.

5.

Apparently the poet had no idea he was infertile. Certainly it never occurred to him that I was the father of his second child, a son, though by the time he was eleven Vojtech junior was looking noticeably like me. Nor did he ever suspect that Anezka, who had long since ceased looking like an alderman's wife, had not inherited her ripening beauty from her mother alone. He was not even alerted by his wife's uncanny frugality, although she was somehow managing to dress her children like a pop-star's offspring, on a corpse-washer's pay. (To my surprise, both Gellen and I turned out to be, if not good fathers, at least good providers.) Instead of taking an interest in his wife's daily activities, he concentrated on building an extraordinary mountain of manuscripts in the depths of his desk.

He respected me, rather ingenuously, as an insignificant (I wrote operettas) but politically uncompromised man of letters—particularly after I began placing his less ostentatiously Catholic poems about nature as fillers in illustrated weekly magazines, where I had some friendly connections. Thus, with my help, his passion to write was kept at the boiling point, and Vixi was easily able to mask her infidelity (I had the impression that, as time went on, the field she played occasionally included other interested parties) by listening to him reading his religious verse. Over time, Vojtech established a position for himself somewhere between those poets who were allowed to publish small volumes of verse and those who were forbidden to appear even in the illustrated women's weeklies. Then, in 1968, one of his lifelong dreams came true: the Catholic publishing house Velehrad, revitalized in line with the new freedoms of the Prague Spring, scheduled the release of an anthology of his work, to be called *The Wayside Cross.* In the chaos after the tanks arrived, they even managed to get it out. In the course of that hot spring and the hellish summer that followed, as poetry readings moved out of private salons to become popular public events, he even managed to gather a small circle of followers.

But one thing I had to credit him with: he was not egocentric. Despite the fact that Hollar had banished him from paradise, Vojtech Novotny never held it against him. He even put his growing reputation to altruistic use in the struggle to rehabilitate, posthumously, the Master's good friend Kopula, who'd been sentenced to twenty-five years of forced labour in 1949 on charges of high treason and espionage. It later came to light that Kopula's high treason had consisted of saying something insulting about Jan Hus—who was a hero to the Communists because the Church had burned him at the stake in the fifteenth century—and circulating poorly reproduced photographs of the archbishop, who had just been placed under house arrest. The charge of espionage was a mere judicial error. When Kopula died in 1959, a month after his release from prison (he was suffering from an incurable illness and the authorities preferred that he die at home), an underground legend began to circulate about a brilliant poem he'd written in prison and smuggled out into reliable hands, with the help of a guard who'd been converted by the poet's piety.

In the early sixties, when I first heard the legend, it was said that Kopula's poem was based on his unshakable belief in a "miracle" the Secret Police had exposed, more or less credibly, as a naive hoax. This supposed miracle had happened in the summer of 1949, about the time the poet was arrested. Kopula was notorious for his obsession with miracles; in an earlier work he had celebrated the miracle in Fatima, where the Virgin Mary was said to have temporarily stopped the earth's rotation. For reasons that were entirely personal, I was more interested in the far more modest Czech miracle. But for years the poem was only a rumour, and I finally forgot all about it.

6.

Forgot it, that is, until the *annus mirabilis* was upon us and the legend surfaced as literary artefact. Vojtech's hands trembled with emotion as he took the rare and precious hand-written copy of Kopula's poem out of its velvet folder and, in his most sepulchral voice, began to read how the poet, who was already behind bars at the time of the miracle, imagined it to have been.

It was the first time he had read the work. Later, "Litany to Joseph's Wife" made it as far as the Prague "Hyde Park", where Novotny recited it to a crowd of ten thousand young men and women so wrapped up in their enormous and fantastical dreams that they were open to anything. But that first evening, he read it at what amounted to a private seance for a narrow circle of friends.

The devotions were held at the Novotnys' apartment, which consisted of a kitchen, a tiny bathroom, and a sitting room that doubled as a bedroom for the parents and the two children. The room was lit with candles, and a large dish of small, round poppyseed cakes sat on a table, a culinary homage, perhaps, to the poet's Moravian roots. Under an enormous Candlemas candle with a cross of black wax on it sat Juzl, Vojtech's *intimus* — an expert on ecclesiastical art and an editor with the Catholic daily *Lidova Demokracie.* The son of a famous Catholic novelist, also deceased, sat on the threadbare couch with a rosary peering out of his pocket. On one side of him sat Vojtech's epigone, Sadovec, and on the other side the only person who didn't really belong there. She was not in Vojtech's circle at all; she was a colleague of Vixi's from the gynecological clinic where Vixi had gone to work when the children were old enough. I had a strong suspicion that she was also Vixi's confidante in matters having nothing to do with Catholicism. She had dropped in unannounced, but when she saw the candles and the food she ignored the poet's pointed remarks about the lateness of the hour. Vojtech finally gave up and decided to let her stay for the privilege of the First Reading. He no doubt reasoned that, since the other Novotny — the dangerous president — had abdicated by then, there was no longer any risk.

In the end — and here again an incomprehensible Providence seemed to be at work — it was the uninvited guest who set the mad merry-go-round of Juzl's crime story spinning.

Vojtech gave a passionate reading of the work. Against all my expectations, it radiated a darkly poetic beauty, thus refuting the idealistic belief that truth alone gives greatness to literature.

All during the reading the unknown acquaintance noisily sampled the poppyseed cakes, and as soon as the poet had finished, she broke the sacred silence. She had a voice that grated with its innocent ignorance, like a film ingenue's. "So what's this miracle all about?"

The woman's question hung in the silence like a blasphemy.

Vixi made a face at me behind her husband's back. Her part in the miracle, as well as the fact that I had once taught her social studies in the lilac-bowered town, had remained a secret between us. I saw Vixi's husband stiffen as a wave of righteous ire seemed to rise in him, and I was expecting a replay of the scene in that little Renaissance house beneath Prague Castle so long ago — only this time the fiery sword would be wielded by the one who had himself been driven out of paradise. But at the last moment, Juzl intervened.

"We're talking, of course, about the miracle that took place in the Chapel of the Virgin Mary under Mare's Head, in the spring of 1949," he said drily. "During a sermon delivered by Father Josef Doufal, an early baroque folk statue of Saint Joseph moved in a way that could only be explained as a *suspensio legis naturae* — a way that defied all natural law.

Eyewitnesses claimed that the statue appeared to be giving a sign to the faithful."

"Is this true?" asked the friend. With an apologetic grin at Vixi, she helped herself to another cake.

The novelist's son now joined the conversation. "You mean to say you've never heard of it?" he asked tartly.

The ingenue shook her head, not realizing that in the corpse-washer's household such ignorance amounted to complicity, *post factum*, in the regime's version of the event.

"Where in the world were you?" asked the novelist's son. "The newspapers were full of it at the time! Of course, they went to great lengths to prove that it was no miracle at all," he added sarcastically, more to the others than to her. "In those days they could prove whatever they wanted."

The woman quickly realized that frankness was out of place here and she began to backtrack. "I mean . . . well, now that you mention it, I may have actually heard. . . ."

I felt sorry for her and wanted to divert the conversation to the poem we'd just heard. But Vojtech had brought his anger under control, and when he spoke it was with the voice of Christian charity. "We mustn't be too surprised that some people weren't aware of it. Don't forget, the whole affair was quickly hushed up, despite the fact that they'd sounded the trumpets so loudly at first. It was all very suspicious. The priest was never brought to trial, and that was the end of it."

"Why wasn't he?" asked the ingenue.

The assembled company exchanged sad, knowing glances.

"Because to the best of our knowledge, miss," said Vojtech, "they tortured him to death before they could put him on trial. We don't have any concrete proof. But the priest wasn't the only one who vanished without a trace at that time. He had no next of kin, and people like that were easy to liquidate because who was there to take an interest in their fate?" He looked around with a bitter expression, then went on, "I don't think there can be any doubt about it. Like Jan Kopula, Father Doufal died a martyr's death."

The faithful nodded their heads, and the wick on the Candlemas candle above Juzl sputtered in the silence. Then the woman spoke again, but now she no longer sounded like the voice of blasphemy.

"What did you say the priest's name was?"

"Father Josef Doufal," said Vojtech.

She thought for a moment, the cake suspended halfway to her mouth, while little wrinkles appeared at the base of her fleshy nose. I suddenly had an odd feeling, as if the group was sensing, collectively, that what she was about to say would have a bearing on the case — and as if, once again, I was being touched by something predetermined. Of course, that could be said of any coincidence. If coincidences exist.

"Listen, I don't know if I should say this or not," said the unknown acquaintance, "but I guess it's all right to talk about it now. I mean, the papers are writing about all sorts of rotten stuff that went on, even the business about Jan Masaryk dying like that — " She still hesitated. The inhibitions of twenty years in a people's democracy were too powerful. Embarrassed, she looked at Vixi's husband.

With a kindly severity he said, "What were you going to say, miss?"

"It was something strange that happened. . . . I've never told anyone about it, because Dr. Dvorak told me to keep my mouth shut, but — " She stopped, that habitual fear struggling inside her. But the Prague Spring was building up a full head of steam now; the first madmen were revealing the truth about the various ignoble acts that together had constituted the noble class struggle; people were starting to feel the intoxication of non-dialectical freedom. The cake-eater too plucked up her courage. "Still, it was practically twenty years ago," she said, "and even Nazi collaborators aren't punished any more — " She hesitated again.

The poet wanted to say something, but Juzl beat him to it. "Of course. There's nothing to be afraid of, miss. Anything you say will be in strictest confidence, even though nowadays we all have a responsibility to — otherwise, how will we ensure that such things never happen again?"

He fixed her with an eager stare, and the woman began to spill the beans.

"I really don't remember anything about that miracle. But when you said his name — the thing is, I remember Dr. Dvorak made a silly joke — "

"Joke?"

"I remember him saying to one of the nurses in reception, 'So his name is Do-fall? Well, that was some fall he took. I don't give him much hope.' That was when he was washing his hands after the operation. Doctors can get pretty cynical sometimes, as you probably know. But this Doufal was a lieutenant of some kind — that's what the policeman who brought him in said."

The faithful exchanged meaningful glances.

"He was the first patient who ever ex'd out on me," she went on. "I'd just started working at the Military Hospital, that's how I remember the date."

"And what was the date?"

"The summer of 1949."

"What did he die of?"

"Well, the operation was for a perforated ulcer, at least that's what Dr. Dvorak put down on the death certificate. But what it really was, I couldn't say. He was a real mess, though, I can tell you that."

Once again the faithful exchanged glances, and I looked over at Vixi, who was staring at her friend with an expression that was not in her usual repertoire.

"What do you mean, 'a real mess'?" Juzl probed gently.

"The cop said it was a car crash. Said they'd flipped their car. But I'd seen a few accident victims by that time. And the cop who brought him in didn't have a wrinkle or a tear in his uniform, let alone an injury — nothing — but he talked about 'our car'. The patient had a broken leg — fine, that fits. But then he had these strange bruises all over his body, and that doesn't make sense — at least, not that many. And the main thing was — " and again, as though astonished at herself for having said so much already, she stopped and looked around the room. "I don't know. Should I say it?"

Juzl leaned over until he was close to her. His eyes were ablaze in the light of the Candlemas candle. I realized that I had seen just such a flame in the eyes of some Party members, back in the days before the flame had petered out. "Miss," he said, "perhaps God has chosen you to testify to things that others can no longer testify to!"

Under the weight of such a trust, the woman nervously swallowed the rest of her cake and blurted, "Two things — " Her voice faltered. "On his right hand, the patient's fingernails were — missing," and she stopped, although this time what stopped her seemed to be the ugliness of her own memories. I glanced at Vixi; her eyes were closed and her jaw was clenched tight. Juzl had turned noticeably pale.

"It must have been a strange car crash, is all I can say," said the woman. The room was silent. No one said a word.

"What was the second thing?" asked Juzl after a pause.

"When they were taking him out of the operating room, I noticed his hair. It was thick and grey and it was cut short, but right here on his crown," and she reached up and touched her bun, "there was this small bald spot, like priests have done to them. I mean, it seemed strange, but they said he was a lieutenant and who was I to — "

She stopped. And then the assembly was given a sign, for suddenly, without warning, the Candlemas candle sputtered and went out. Vojtech looked up in alarm and stared at the candle. He reached for it weakly, took it out of the candle-holder, and raised it towards the ceiling. He stood there for a moment, then quickly knelt. The novelist's diminutive son slipped off the couch; as he thumped his knees loudly on the hardwood floor, his rosary tumbled out of his pocket. Juzl slowly sank to the floor, and Vojtech's epigone followed suit. Only the two women remained sitting on the couch. I stood up.

In his most funereal voice, Vojtech Novotny began to pray: "Our Father, who art in heaven. . . . "

7.

I opened my eyes into a bright Sunday morning and squinted at Vixi in her polka-dot bikini. Nature, awakening through the wonder of dewdrops and the buzzing of rested insects into another fleeting day, always reminded me of death — the prodigal flowers that would soon fade, the desiccation of butterfly wings. I was not a nature lover. Vixi, annoyingly chipper and fussing over the small alcohol burner, took a water-can and jogged off to the pump.

Then, quite unexpectedly, the sounds of a church organ came drifting in on the perfumed air, bringing with them an atmosphere of sin and bad conscience. All that was lacking was the aroma of incense to drive out the acrid smell of overheated oil from Vixi's frying pan. But the distant voices of pious old ladies made up for it. I could hear them chanting in an inimitable heterophony:

> Mary, gracious Mother,
> Mother of our Lord. . . .

Their voices quavered through the moist smells of morning, wailing in a malicious negation of my morning depression — these voices keening on the edge of the grave yet as fresh as the ridiculous caterpillar, all hungry for life, that was inching along the lintel over my head. Vixi stuck her head through the window. "Sir! They're celebrating mass in the chapel down the hill!"

"So what?"

"So shake a leg!" Vixi pulled the green blanket off me. "We've got a golden opportunity to be forgiven for the sin we committed last night."

"Vixi, will you get off my back?"

"You've got the sin of intemperance to worry about, too." The catechism was still fresh in her memory, but she was invoking it for her own facetious ends. "And if you don't get up you'll be guilty of sloth as well, and that's another one of the seven deadly sins."

I got up. A hot needle of pain shot through my head, and I blasphemed while those pious old women in the distance sang:

. . . cattle and horses, donkeys and sheep,
Oh Holy Virgin, oh Mother so sweet. . . .

When we entered the wooden chapel, the priest was already in the pulpit. On the gospel side of the altar, wreaths of wildflowers were heaped around the base of a statue of Mary, and the Blessed Virgin was up to her waist in fresh geraniums. Someone had remembered the Guardian of Our Lord on the other side of the altar, because a wreath of daisies had been set at his feet.

We squeezed into a place in the last row of pews, beside a Sunday hiker in plus-fours with a rucksack on the floor between his knees. The sermon was well under way by now, but he was still kneeling over his pack with his head in his hands, and he peppered us with nasty glances for interrupting his meditations. Perhaps he'd been drawn to the chapel because he thought he could attend mass without the risk of being seen by the town informer. A feeble old lady at the other end of the pew blinked a single malicious eye at me as we tried to slide in past her; her other eye was glassy and motionless, perhaps blind. Vixi immediately knelt down beside the hiker. Her breasts bobbed up and down and her thighs, covered by nothing more than a thin skirt, pressed against the kneeling man, who shrank indignantly away from her into the far corner of the pew. Over his head was a painting in which some wide-buttocked Roman legionaries in late baroque armour were nailing a wan and pale Christ to the cross.

The instant I sat down, I became desperately drowsy. The wooden rafters, steeped in the incense of times gone by, smelled sweet. The priest was reciting his sermon in a droning voice. I dropped off before I even knew what his homily was all about. Sweet, dreamless sleep engulfed me. I came to my senses when Vixi whispered in my ear, "Don't fall asleep, now!" I caught the malevolent eye of the old crone beside me and forced myself to listen to the sermon.

It was essentially a story — nothing at all like the homilies of Father Urbanec, the Franciscan I'd once gone to hear preach with the family of Papa Nedochodil so I could be near his pretty daughter Julia. Father Urbanec was fond of examining scholastic questions like the relationship between body and soul in the light of Aristotelian teachings on form and content as modified by Saint Thomas Aquinas. As I sat there listening to the preacher in the chapel under Mare's Head talking to this assembly of old women in their Sunday best and bald-headed old men in shiny, ill-fitting suits, I wondered if he had ever heard of such matters.

He was tall and ungainly, with grey hair cropped short in a kind of brushcut, and his square face was lined with deep wrinkles that made him look like an old-fashioned Czech farmer. He was so tall that when he leaned over the edge of the pulpit to emphasize a point, I was afraid he would topple out. As he rested one wide hand on the railing, I could see his ring finger with the last joint missing — an unusual injury for a priest — while his other hand, its index finger extended, gave stress and rhythm to the story that was the subject of his sermon. Both the story and the priest seemed to be aspects of a single, simple-minded, anachronistic world.

The story he told was about a girl who was born blind but never doubted God's goodness, despite her disability. Each day she would come to the foot of a rock that had been called Mare's Head for as long as anyone could remember. At that point a spring of water emerged from the rock, and the girl would kneel and pray to the Mother of Christians to intercede with God on her behalf and grant her sight. The priest's enormous hands kept beat to the rhythm of the story as it headed for its inevitable and obvious conclusion: "One morning, the maiden felt raindrops on her cheeks," whispered the priest, in a voice that was accustomed to calling cows. "It was odd, you might even say strange, for God's sun was shining, a cricket was chirping in the grass, and then suddenly — there were raindrops from heaven!"

At that point I fell asleep again. Several confused dreams followed in rapid succession; in the worst of them, it was Ivana Hrozna, not Gellen, who was staring into the cottage at me while Vixi shamelessly paraded her bare ass around the room. "Comrade Smiricky," Ivana was saying in a wounded voice, "I never expected this of you! You've no idea how this pains me — " when something like a sudden blow from an invisible hand rescued me. I opened my eyes to find a sea of waving arms in front of me. The priest seemed strangely diminished; I could scarcely see him over the edge of the pulpit, and it slowly dawned on me that he wasn't standing any more, but kneeling, staring in wide-eyed alarm towards the altar and crossing himself while the old women, all on their knees too, were shrieking like banshees, their hands outstretched beseechingly to the statue of Saint Joseph on the right side of the altar, while amid the screeching the man in the pulpit was saying, in a voice of thunder, "Our Father. . . ."

At that moment the hiker beside us jumped to his feet, knocked over the trembling Vixi, squeezed roughly past me, and almost pushed the one-eyed old woman off the edge of the pew. The hobnails in his shoes clacked across the floorboards, a shadow blackened the door for an instant, and a draught carried a small cloud of incense and wrapped it around the priest's head. Vixi's teeth were chattering.

"What's going on?" I hissed in shock, still half asleep.

"Do you think it's because of us?" Vixi wailed in a thin little voice.

"*What's* because of us, for God's sake?" I shot back. My voice was almost drowned out by the chorus of brittle voices gripped by the passion of piety: "Thy kingdom come, Thy will be done . . . ," the old women were shrilling over top of one another, and one of them was even waving her rosary in the air, while the priest's rural voice stood out over them all: " . . . and forgive us our debts. . . ."

"What in *hell* is going on, for Christ's sake?"

Vixi clapped a damp hand over my mouth. "Jesus, Mary, and Joseph, this is no time to take the Lord's name in vain!" She began to beat her chest as if she'd taken leave of her senses, and then she added her voice — slightly out of kilter, perhaps because she didn't know the words very well — to the babbling voiceband of the faithful:

"And lead us not into temptation. . . ."

3

■

The Monastery

I.

Juzl had invited me to come around because of a casual remark I'd made that night at the Novotnys', about knowing Father Urbanec. I should have watched my tongue, of course, and not mentioned it at all—I'd only known the priest superficially, a long time before, and I'd all but forgotten about it—but Father Urbanec's letter, which the editor read to me, reminded me of a discussion on the essence of miracles that the erudite Franciscan had once unexpectedly put a stop to, in Papa Nedochodil's dining room.

It had happened at one of the monthly meals that Madame Nedochodilova held in the priest's honour. They were sumptuous affairs, more like banquets, and they always ended with a general blessing from Father Urbanec. I especially looked forward to these blessings because we all had to kneel to receive them; I always knelt slightly behind Julia so that I had a good view of the back of her charming legs while above us, in the fading aroma of roast turkey, the priest made the sign of an enormous cross with his hand. He was immensely fat and once, when I was alone with Julia, I took the liberty of poking mild fun at his gargantuan appetite. Julia put me in my place. "If the Venerable Father is fat," she said primly, "it's a sign that he's leading an abstemious life." I expressed surprise that she could speak of abstemiousness barely half an hour after the priest had demolished two turkey drumsticks, eight large dumplings, and a variety of hors d'oeuvres and desserts. "In their love for God, priests deny themselves other worldly pleasures," Julia explained, and, stupefied by her fragrant virginal presence (her perfume smelled of myrrh), I didn't realize that she was referring to the very pleasures she had been denying me for some time. "So they occasionally deserve a substitute," she said. "And that's what Mama gives him."

Mama Nedochodilova rewarded the priest's privations in the most opulent possible way, for her husband was an important layman in the Church and the manager of a chain of Catholic agricultural co-operatives. Thus, in the period of general shortages after the war, Father Urbanec feasted on home-made sheep's-milk cheese that came in little wooden buckets, a gift of the grateful monks of Slovakia, washed it down with mead from another monastery in southern Moravia, and stuffed himself with every delicacy the co-operatives could supply. And while he was eating, he and his host discussed different questions of exegesis.

At one of these banquets, Julia's brother Jiri, an overly pious student of molecular chemistry, talked about a theory of miracles that seemed quite modern. He explained the parting of the Red Sea using higher mathematics instead of the traditional and unconvincing argument of unusual tidal action, and what he said struck me as passably convincing. The theory was based on something he called "acausality in the microcosm" — the notion that the laws of cause and effect did not always apply. There were causes and impulses in the microcosm, he claimed, that were not followed by any discernible effect, and effects that had no apparent cause. It was as though God had squeezed through the interstices of infinitesimal possibility, applied the non-law that He'd prepared for cases like this, and thus been able to multiply the loaves and fishes and give the blind man back his sight.

I was completely ignorant in matters of chemistry and so added my own silent admiration to that of the two women, who, in the best Catholic tradition, took no part in the men's conversation and merely refilled their plates with food. Only Papa Nedochodil (who on principle understood absolutely everything) and his son participated. Father Urbanec, whose enormous presence dominated the end of the table, sat with a goblet of golden liquid in his hand and was as silent as I was, for the same reason, I thought. Still, he seemed rather sullen to me. After examining the matter from all sides, both father and son sat back looking pleased with themselves for having scientifically explained phenomena that defied science and yet formed the cornerstone of their faith.

But then the priest shook his head and said, "No, no, Jiri! No, your arguments are made in the proper spirit of piety but they are wrong and therefore not to be commended at all." Jiri looked as if someone had slapped his face; Papa's hand, holding a tiny pigeon drumstick, hung motionless in the air; Mama looked disapprovingly at her son; and under the table, Julia squeezed my hand excitedly — she'd been holding it all evening, mainly to prevent me from slipping it under her skirt. "Who else, my dear Jiri," Father Urbanec continued, in a kindly tone now, "gave the universe, nature, and all of creation its laws, if not the Lord? Even the law you mention, which I have to admit I've not heard of, is part of the divine dispensation. Don't you think it would be denying God's omnipotence if the phenomena that elude those natural laws — which is why we call them miracles in the first place — could be explained as something that merely takes advantage of a hitherto undiscovered aspect of those laws?" And he gave the young man a warm but penetrating look.

Jiri stammered something that sounded contrite, Papa brought the pigeon leg to his mouth, stripped it majestically, and nodded, and the women enthusiastically refilled our glasses with mead. "That's the way it is," said the priest humbly. "Explaining the miracles of Our Lord Jesus Christ as 'natural', as not going against the laws of nature, is a vain and foolish exercise, and therefore pointless and, yes, even harmful. Indirectly, it deprives God of His most essential attribute. For the One who determined that everything be as it is can also, when He so desires, make everything other than it is."

For me, these suppers came to an end in the autumn of 1948, when I finally deflowered Julia and was immediately afterwards unfaithful to her with her best friend — which helped Julia overcome her guilt at committing a sin. For Father Urbanec those beautiful times ended a year later, when they arrested him and sentenced him to twenty years of forced labour. As in the case of Jan Kopula, the charge was high treason and espionage for the Vatican. He was sent to work in the uranium mines, where a faithful civilian miner took a picture of him in the underground shafts. Some former Catholic Boy Scouts reproduced the snapshot and old ladies kept copies of it in their prayerbooks. In the end the Secret Police discovered the Boy Scouts' darkroom (they were sentenced to fifteen years for circulating anti-state material and spying for the Vatican), but the portrait of the suffering priest, oft-kissed and faded because of poor reproduction techniques, survived in breviaries throughout the country.

Julia had one, of course, even many years later when I ran into her in Charles Square in Prague. She was now an office worker with a state enterprise called Heat-Tech, and she had five children. She had long since forgiven me, though losing her virginity must have given her many sleepless nights, especially before her wedding. Her husband was a graduate of the Conservatory of Music and in 1948 had accepted the position of organist and choirmaster with the Jesuits. Consequently, at the time of his marriage and for seventeen years afterwards he worked as a refrigerator repairman. As we sat talking on a park bench in Charles Square, Julia let me see her copy of the devotional picture: it showed a gaunt Father Urbanec in a prison shirt leaning against a pick-axe. The shaft was sticking so far through the metal head that it took no theological imagination to see it as the Cross of Peter — an image that Vojtech Novotny later wrote a poem about. The priest's right hand was raised in the familiar sign of blessing and he was looking straight into the bold lens of the camera.

Juzl read me the letter from Father Urbanec over the phone: "My dear Mr. Juzl," it said, "I firmly believe that the affair surrounding the Hronov case was an attempt to deny the glory of God, which our Heavenly Father revealed to us with such moving simplicity in the chapel of the Virgin Mary under Mare's Head. The Hronov miracle was a real miracle, genuine and undeniable. That is why the police made every effort from the outset to explain it to the public as a fraud engineered by the late Father Josef Doufal himself. I laud your efforts, sir, to cleanse his bright memory and establish the guilt of those who, in all probability, stained their hands with his blood. But I urge you, do not accept *a priori* as true their claim that a mechanism had already been installed in the chapel *before* the inexplicable events took place. Otherwise, despite being guided by the most Christian of ambitions to clear the martyred priest's reputation, you run the risk of unwittingly helping to extinguish the Light that once shone from that simple altar. I beg of you, Mr. Juzl, please visit me first before you take any further steps in this matter."

"They took the Reverend Doufal behind the altar and made me stay back under the choir," said Father Urbanec. "There, they showed him a device that they alleged he had put in so that he could make the statue move without leaving the pulpit. Then they brought him back in front of the altar and, gentlemen, a remarkable change had come over him. By the grace of God, I've seen a similar transformation in many people. When I used to instruct converts to the faith in the catechism, I would wait for it to happen, that strange, inimitable expression that appears in the face. I was never in any hurry to perform the rites of holy baptism until I saw that expression. It was a clear sign to me that the spirit of divine grace had entered the catechumen."

Until recently this gaunt, etherealized priest had been mining uranium for Soviet bombs; long years ago he had dined on roast pigeon at the table of good Papa Nedochodil (who had died in police custody after trying to take his own life); now he sat in a *fin-de-siècle* armchair, in the white light of a cold spring day, while outside the window two black-gowned nuns from his improbable order chased piglets around the yard.

"When Father Doufal came back in front of the altar, gentlemen, he had precisely that light in his eyes, as though he had just looked into the face of Truth itself."

We were silent. Outside, the piglets squealed. Then Juzl asked respectfully, "How do you explain it, Reverend?"

The priest spread his arms apart. "I can only tell you what I think. He alone knew the truth — he and Almighty God. I heard him say to the police, 'All right then. Do whatever you want, and I will do what you ask.'" By that I understood he meant making the film, and, may God forgive me, I thought they'd broken him. I'm ashamed to admit it today. They brought out the vestments, Father Doufal put them on, they took him to the pulpit and very roughly — but I don't want to talk about that — they forced him to mount the pulpit. Then they ordered me to walk up to the altar. They had floodlights and a movie camera all ready and there were two men in uniform and several in civilian clothes, and one of these said to me, 'When I say "now", I want you to point slowly at that statue over there,' and he indicated the Blessed Virgin. And because I had not, like Father Doufal, been given a sign from God — I was not worthy — I refused. I prayed silently for the strength to prevail, because I was determined not to participate in their work of blasphemy, even if they killed me." Father Urbanec smiled and nodded his head. "Of course, you know whom they did kill. Father Doufal was in the pulpit with a man standing to his left, and they were measuring the distance between him and the camera with a kind of measuring rod, and just then Father Doufal called something out to me and, believe it or not, gentlemen, he sounded almost happy! And again, I'm ashamed to admit it but I failed to understand. I had forgotten those wonderful old legends about the early Christians entering the arena of death with a joyful song on their lips because their faith was strong and they knew they would soon be seeing their Saviour face to face."

"I know," said Juzl. "In fact, he — "

"Like the early Christian martyrs," the priest interrupted. "Happily, sir, almost joyously, he called out to me: *'Erat miraculum, fratre!'* — 'It was a miracle, brother!' I assume he said it in Latin because he didn't want the police to understand him. But the one who was standing beside him, the one with the measuring rod, hit him in the mouth so hard that blood spurted from his lips and fell on the railing of the pulpit."

He stopped and bowed his head, and his lips began to move silently. He was obviously praying to the saint of his bloody tale. Beyond the window we could hear the ancient farm sounds, the wheezing of the geese, the squealing of a captured piglet, the voice of a nun calling chickens. Father Urbanec raised his head. "I was incapacitated by fear," he said. "I was afraid I wouldn't be able to stand what I knew was coming. I did not understand Joseph's sign. To overcome my fear, my horror, I began to shout, 'I won't help you. I will not become an instrument of your blasphemy!' Then they began to beat me."

He looked out the window. The once plump face, long emaciated by the hunger of the work camp, was now slowly filling out again, and under his habit the outlines of another dignified paunch were beginning to appear. Julia would certainly have felt a pious admiration. His nuns were taking care of him as her late mother once had; he was clearly still living an abstemious life, alone though he was among so many women.

2.

"You really missed something, my friend. There hasn't been a better program on television since they snatched it back from the hands of the counter-revolution," said Gellen, pouring another two fingers of Vat 69 into his glass. He was lit on one side by the flames in the fireplace and on the other by the pale light of the stars that spangled the night over Mare's Head and the Horse's Saddle. "Not only could you hear all the delightful things Pinkava was saying about dear Sasha Dubcek, you could also *see* him — that is, you could see what were supposedly his hands on the steering wheel of his Mercedes. The story was that, by the miraculous power of the Party, they'd not only bugged his car but installed a hidden camera as well."

"Do you think they'll bring Pinkava to trial?" I asked.

"I hope so. It's getting to be a bore. The most refined counter-revolution in the history of the working-class movement, and they haven't hanged anyone yet."

I looked out the window. There was a big, beautiful star directly over Mare's Head — the very one that had been there the night a freshly washed Vixi and I walked across the meadow to this same cottage for a party.

"But wasn't it a little obvious? A tape-recorder maybe, but to say they'd hidden a camera in Pinkava's private car. . . ."

"Not at all. Ever since old Nikita came out with his book of revelations, they've stopped even pretending subtlety. They know no one's going to believe it, but they also know everybody will pretend to." He glanced back at me from the fireplace. "In fifty years, they've come as far as you Catholics have in two thousand."

The joke of my Catholic orthodoxy in the lilac-bowered town of

Hronov was still fresh in his memory. Sitting there with the fireplace behind him, he had a devilish aspect. Or maybe he looks more like God, I thought. God is a cynic too, after all; in these times, can wisdom be anything but cynical?

"But," my friend went on, "they made good and sure the Mercedes logo on the hood was visible. They claimed Pinkava was driving, but all you could see was that pair of hands on the steering wheel. You can't identify anyone from that, not unless they have a finger missing or something. But everybody knew Pinkava's voice, his Moravian accent. He gave too many speeches in 1968. So they managed to bug his car — or more likely his apartment — and then they just added footage of somebody's hands and created a new reality."

A fire-resistant knot exploded in the hearth. We were silent for a while. The whole Pinkava affair was embarrassingly like those elephantine frameups in the fifties.

"Theoretically, people ought to get hopping mad," Gellen went on. "They're broadcasting an unconstitutionally bugged conversation, after all — "

"Oh, people will get upset, all right," I interrupted him, "but not because of that. And the police aren't going through this charade to make people pretend to believe, but to make them lose their faith altogether."

"Faith? Where, except maybe in a madhouse, is there any faith left to be lost?" Gellen's surprise as he said this sounded almost sincere.

"Not the kind of faith you mean," I said. "Not faith as revealed by Party resolutions and public prosecutors. But until not long ago, people still had illusions about men of the people like Pinkava. Now they've lost them. If a man like Pinkava says things like that about his old boss — and not at a trial, after proper brainwashing, but of his free will — then who can you believe? The relatively obscure dirty trick of illegal bugging won't do any further harm to the image of the Party, but it'll hurt the image of Dubcekists like Pinkava. No indeed," I said, reaching for my glass, "they're not as unsubtle as they seem."

Gellen stood up and, as though the flames in the fireplace weren't enough, he lit a fat, decorative candle on the table. It was almost like the Candlemas candle that had mysteriously gone out when the woman who was so fond of poppyseed cakes had made her revelation about Father Doufal. Flames can symbolize everything, I thought. Both heaven and hell.

"You may be right," Gellen said. "It's a remarkable method, come to think of it. Hearing Pinkava say such nasty things about Sasha the Simple — why, he even got me upset. It must have been an atavistic response — I was almost offended. It made me quite ashamed."

"Because he called our unforgettable Sasha a kindly idiot?"

"Of course not! Because I found that I can still be upset by the truth."

3.

It wasn't until I walked right up to the pulpit that I noticed it: on the upper side of the railing Mr. Rericha had painted a row of ruby-red drops, outlining each one with a tiny corona of gold paint. The church had been entirely given over to the memory of the martyred priest, and it was obvious that the doll-maker had been carefully following Juzl's series of articles in the newspaper. Near the last Gothic drop of blood there was a round hole filled with white plaster and surrounded by a jagged border of black paint, from which the silhouettes of pitch-black demons emerged. It was through this hole that a thin steel cable had been passed and then, over a series of small pulleys, carried back behind the altar to the miraculous statue. Juzl had taken his technical description from an old official report that, at the time, was reprinted in all the newspapers.

"The statue was made to move by pulling on a handle located inside the pulpit and out of sight of those present," the report said. "Given the relative darkness in the church, the advanced age of the majority of those present, and the hysterical atmosphere created by the priest's inflammatory rhetoric, there was very little risk that the steel wire would be noticed." It was upon this uncomplicated device that Father Urbanec had based his hypothesis about what had led the martyred priest to utter his final exclamation in Latin.

4.

"Father Josef originally accused them of installing the mechanism in the church themselves, so they could use him to bring dishonour on the Church," he said quietly in the white light of that melancholy day. "And they tried to get me to confess to having ordered him to install those things, and to having acted on orders from His Eminence the nuncio of the Holy Father. But when they led him behind the altar and he first saw the device, he was filled at once with the certainty that it had been a miracle after all. *Erat miraculum.*" The priest touched the cross he was wearing around his neck and bowed his head. Then he went on: "How, you may ask. How could he be so sure? And I would reply to you: perhaps it was a direct revelation. The grace of God, which needs no proof. Then again, perhaps he saw something behind the altar that proved the installation was fraudulent, something they'd overlooked. Something that didn't fit."

The old Franciscan's eyes blazed the way they used to when Julia, who was almost but not quite a sinner, knelt beneath his lightning-bolt stare and practically put her arm out of joint crossing herself. Then the priest picked up the thread of the idea that had once, a long time ago, put Julia's brother to shame.

"But perhaps it's blasphemous to try, like the hero of some detective novel, to get to the bottom of what Father Josef saw. Isn't it enough to know that it filled him with a faith so great that he was willing to die a martyr's death? Should our faith be smaller than his? Ought we to seek reasons for what, to him and through him to us, was revealed?"

There was a knock on the door. It was the Mother Superior with coffee. She was at least seventy-five years old now, but I remembered her from the time when she was an occasional guest at Papa Nedochodil's well-stocked table. She always sat beside her apoplectic husband, who had once, from the profits of his farm in Sedlcany, bought an enormous clock for the steeple of the Church of the Most Holy Heart. Thus reconciled with God, he died before the state could give him the compulsory opportunity to become a miner. His large farm devolved to the working people, who let it go to seed and expressed no interest whatsoever in the old manorial house in the woods, a good five kilometres from the barns and the village. The widow was allowed to go on living in it, but without servants the manor quickly became a haunted castle. Then the husband of one of the widow's friends died, and because the pension he left behind was not enough to support his wife (he'd been a general in the pre-war, capitalist army), she was glad to accept her friend's invitation to live in the haunted house. Soon afterwards a third friend was widowed and joined the growing commune. Twenty years after the owner's death, the population of the manor house in the woods had grown to include about fifteen elderly widows who pooled their minuscule old-age pensions and spent all their leisure time in prayer. Finally one of them came up with the idea of founding a religious order. Naturally they did not seek the approval of the Office for Ecclesiastical Affairs — monastic orders had been outlawed long ago, and in any case the widows acknowledged only the imprisoned archbishop as their spiritual leader, and time had endowed them with a sharp nose for politics. The very first thing they did (they were women, after all) was to design and sew themselves a set of habits. Next, they inscribed the rules of the order in an account book, took vows, and began to live through prayer and work. They set up a hen house, and started breeding angora rabbits, and a Catholic conspirator in the local council entered them into the district records as a people's co-operative.

There was just one thing that bothered the widows: mass was celebrated in the Sedlcany church only once a month. The nearest priest had seven parishes to tend to and he couldn't do it more often. Rather diffidently, they asked him if he might celebrate a private mass with them on some week-night in the manor-house chapel. But the priest refused on the grounds that he was already over-extended. In truth, he was afraid of being indicted for espionage for the Vatican, although so far news of the unregistered order had never spread beyond the borders of the village — most of the villagers were still religious.

But a solution was finally found, one that the widows attributed — perhaps correctly — to a special act of divine grace. Naturally they were among the admirers of Father Urbanec, the underground martyr, and his familiar photograph had hung in the cloister all during his imprisonment. The women had even had it enlarged and mounted in a baroque frame they'd taken from a picture of a shepherd and his sheep. Long before, some of them had regularly attended his services and heard him preach his fascinating sermons, and they were among the first to hear rumours of his release after seventeen years in prison. Because the conditions of that release included a ban on holding any position in the Church, the newly liberated prelate accepted an offer they made him. Instead of working for the Prague Sewage Department, he was officially engaged as an accountant for the people's co-operative in Sedlcany, and he became the spiritual head of the pseudo-monastery. The Sedlcany Party organization (consisting of two comrades who were living together out of wedlock) kept sending stubborn denunciations to the district Party office, but by the mid-sixties the general atmosphere no longer favoured faithful Leninists. So this odd female cloister with its own Father Superior existed secretly for two years, until the Prague Spring tied the informers' tongues and the widows, full of confidence, asked the Church authorities to appoint their spiritual guide as parish priest in Sedlcany.

"If, however, we are prepared to seek trivial explanations where the late lamented Father Doufal left us the blood-stained proof of his own faith," said the abbot, who by now had been utterly drawn into the scholasticism of his own thought processes, "why do we not try to read the signs that already exist, and are, to my mind, conclusive?"

"Signs?" said the astonished Juzl eagerly.

"Yes, signs," said the priest. The widow, who had asked and been granted permission to remain with us, crossed herself. "Two things are remarkable here, although naturally *they* failed to notice them. First of all, there is the apparently illogical nature of the miracle." I expected him to talk about why the Almighty, who had the power to raise Prague Castle (along with the First Secretary) into the air and in a divine rage hurl it into the Macocha abyss, had instead chosen to express himself in the manner of an itinerant puppeteer. But Father Urbanec had something else in mind.

"Are you aware of the event that led Princess Landsfeldova to build the chapel under Mare's Head in 1723?" asked the priest. "As a matter of fact, that was the theme of Father Doufal's sermon on the day of the miracle. I know this because there was a reference to it in the papers at the time. On that very spot, the Mother of God appeared to a girl who had been blind from birth. Rain fell from a clear blue sky onto the girl's uplifted face, her eyes were opened, and she saw. It was one of the many times the Holy Virgin has favoured our land with a miracle. Princess Landsfeldova, who was herself christened Mary, was so moved by the miracle that she prevailed upon her son-in-law, the Duke of Korutany, to donate a memorial statue of the Blessed Virgin that had stood in the chapel of the family château for as long as anyone could remember, and to place it in the newly built church. The chronicles say the transfer was accompanied by great church festivities. The chapel was consecrated by the Archbishop of Prague himself and the statue was carried by twelve priests, all the way from the Landsfelds' château in Turyne, on a pearl-encrusted litter."

He stopped. Some litter, I thought, if twelve portly prelates could fit underneath it — especially since the statue was so small it could have been taken there in a doll's carriage. But perhaps the discrepancy made the priests feel the kind of humility that all authorities should submit to now and again.

The priest interrupted my disrespectful ruminations.

"Now, pay attention! A Mary chapel, built in honour of a visitation by the Holy Virgin. In it, an ancient statue of the Mother of God that is an object of adoration." He paused, his blazing eyes fixed on us. "*But it was the statue of Saint Joseph that moved!*"

We were speechless. Juzl's jaw dropped.

"And why do you suppose that was?" asked the priest quietly.

We had no answer, nor was the priest expecting one. He sat up straight in his chair, clasped his hands over his stomach, and began to toy with his cross.

"For many, such a circumstance may be meaningless," he said. "But for me — and for both of you as well, I believe — " he added, including me in his company of believers (he didn't know I'd deflowered Julia, since by that time she'd had another confessor), "it must speak a comprehensible tongue. Father Doufal's Christian name, after all, was Josef. In other words, he was named after the holy spouse of the Virgin Mary, the Guardian of Our Lord Jesus Christ."

He bowed his head; so did the widow, and Juzl quickly followed suit. Finally I bowed my head too, so as not to spoil their delight, which was enormous.

"Therefore I ask," Father Urbanec went on, "what if God intended, through this apparently illogical miracle, not only to indicate to believers that he is always immanent in this world, but also to suggest to those fortunate enough to take part in that holy communion that he had chosen their spiritual pastor, Josef, to receive the greatest honour a Christian can hope to attain — to die for the faith?"

Again he paused to give us time to absorb the overwhelming theological implications of this. Juzl turned as pale as a wax candle and shuddered. It had begun to rain outside, and his face, full of an incredible faith, was outlined against the background of the sharp, cold light coming through the window. I felt as though I'd been transported to some unreal country, far from Prague, far from the Year of our Lord 1968, and set down in a novel by Georges Bernanos. But then I remembered that time was out of joint, that the Communist Party of Czechoslovakia had just gone to confession. I began to doubt my own doubts. Perhaps, I thought for an instant in the cold, mystical light of that cold spring day, perhaps this is exactly what the truth is. *Quia absurdum . . . quia imbecille. . . .*

"And the second thing," said the priest. "You said that, according to the nurse, Father Josef died the tenth day after the miracle, on the twenty-first of June. Do you know which saint that day is consecrated to?"

Naturally none of us did, not even the widow.

"Saint Aloysius," said the priest quietly. "The beautiful old Czech name that was given to Father Josef's mother at her christening."

His burning eyes looked at us, and the cross sparkled on his incipient belly. There was a tomblike silence in the room. Outside the window a beautiful rainbow appeared, like an embarrassing symbol — like an illustration in an old-fashioned biblical history for Catholic schools.

Juzl, the unlikely detective, sat beside me on the black seat of my Felicie sports coupé and stared at the moving countryside. Its contours and other features made me feel that we had touched another time, a time outside of time, or had perhaps passed through a secret entrance to regions inhabited by the simple baroque Ruler of the world, and thus escaped the graceless Year of Our Lady 1968 in which, just beyond the fairy-tale horizon, invisible armies were rattling and clanking through a set of highly suspicious military manoeuvres.

We were passing through lovely countryside, with gently rolling hills carpeted in green grass and dark forests. A pair of storks were circling lazily overhead and on the horizon, on a lone, geologically inexplicable outcropping of rock, stood a castle with medieval spires. The sun was burning away the afternoon clouds and spreading the russet tones of evening over the land, while the long shadows of poplar trees confined the road, gently but implacably, to the narrow dimensions of bygone centuries. I was gripped by a powerfully retrograde emotion — a longing to sink into this forgotten countryside for ever, for my convertible to become a carriage, for a damsel in a wimple and veil to beckon from the highest parapet of the castle. But the feeling was short-lived. I knew that the castle had been built on old Gothic foundations by a *nouveau-riche* postman who'd been raised to the aristocracy for his faithful service to the post office, and I knew that, glorious as it looked, the only thing about it that worked was a brewery built just outside its walls, and that the balconies led directly into the payroll and accounts department. I rebelled against this sweet moment of weakness. Juzl, who was still deep in some mystical meditation, suddenly irritated me.

"I hope you plan to go on writing those articles," I said. "Father Urbanec may be satisfied, but the rest of us live in a heathen world, where you need solid proof." I stepped on the gas to escape the hypnotic power of the postmaster's castle. "Anyway, you know an *advocatus diaboli* is an essential part of any miracle."

"I won't play that role," said Juzl. "I believe the miracle really took place."

"But the Church always engages one. And it's as well to be on the safe side. Think of Saint Christopher," and I pointed to a plastic image of the patron saint of motorists that Suzi Kajetanova, my platonic love, had bought me a year before in Italy. "They say he and a lot of others won't make it through the authentication process. You have a chance to put Father Doufal in one of the available slots."

My lack of respect obviously bothered Juzl, so I quickly continued:

"And Father Urbanec may prefer faith without proof, but it's interesting that Father Doufal himself doubted the miracle, and didn't begin to believe in it fully until they showed him what they said was material proof of a hoax."

From the corner of my eye, I observed the rapid demystification of the pious journalist. Thoughtfully, he said, "That business about Saint Joseph is interesting."

"Of course it is. I mean, they must have known it was the Virgin Mary who traditionally performed the miracles in that chapel. So why did they wire up Saint Joseph?"

"For all we know," Juzl replied, "the Lord may have visited their minds with confusion."

The two storks came to rest like a pair of lovers on a nest built at the very peak of a slender tower. That's not an entirely stupid explanation, I thought. God confused them. But, as Marx (or maybe it was Engels, or both of them) once wrote, the problem was to extract the rational nut from the mystical shell.

"Maybe," I said, still goading him, "maybe as far as they're concerned it's all just superstition anyway. One statue's the same as another. So they just took a blind stab, and instead of hooking up the Virgin Mary, they got the Guardian of Our Lord."

I could see that Juzl didn't like my offhand manner. As though he hadn't heard me, he said, "But there's still one thing I can't explain."

"What's that?"

"Why did Father Doufal let them make that movie of him?"

The question hung unanswered in the air. I stared at the road unwinding between the yellow fields of rye striping the light green countryside. The earth was cupped like a large hand and the countryside lay within it, like a romantic landscape painting, festooned by evening clouds. Sunbeams slanted down through the air, connecting the greyish clouds with the green hill ahead of us and, on it, a white village touched with gentle fire. I had seen Father Doufal in a countryside like this, one that had also lain before us like a cupped hand, and it had been evening then, too.

5·

He was sitting on a bench made of boards as grey and cracked as both statues had been before the doll-maker had repainted them. He was wearing a shiny black suit and vest and black lace-up boots, and his rural, sunbaked face emerged incongruously from a yellowed clerical collar. He sat there and I thought he'd never get up, as in a calm voice, untouched by the big city and its poisonous fumes, he told me about the habits of waterfowl and how, as a boy, he'd made a wonderful collection of birds' eggs. Every now and then he would interrupt his story, which entranced me for reasons he could not imagine, and listen to the scrawking and cackling of birds in the reeds of the edge of the pond. He was able to identify each species immediately. The horizon sliced the red monstrance of the sun in half, and from the far shore, where the pond was covered with a green carpet of algae, the evening assembly of frogs declared its presence, and the priest slowly began to find it odd that creatures on our side of the pond who should have gone to sleep when the frogs came out were still in full voice.

That day I'd come back after lunch to find that someone had slipped a note under my office door. "IS IT REALLY TRUE?" the note said—nothing more. But I understood the meaning, and despite the neat block letters I knew who had written it. After four o'clock, as I was walking through the lilac bower up to my sublet room, I saw a girl in a white T-shirt sitting in the lavender shadows. She had a red ribbon in her neatly brushed hair and from a distançe she watched me trudging heavily up the steep slope.

I wanted to turn into the house and pretend I hadn't seen her, but the picture was too attractive: the vision of seventeen-year-old Vixi, radiant through a purple filter of lilac blossoms, worked on me like the Apple. My legs carried me past the window where the widow Ledvinova was reading from Chelcicky, and took me directly to the Serpent's helpmate in dirty tennis shoes.

"Really, sir?" she said by way of welcome. "Is it really true you're such a die-hard Catholic?"

I looked around cautiously. My colleague Evzenie Vikusova lived a short way from the widow Ledvinova's house and I could see her inside, just walking by an open window. Fortunately she was short-sighted.

"Look," I said, "let's get out of here. People can see us."

Obediently, Vixi jumped up and skipped along beside me, deeper and deeper into the lilac bower. Soon it became a pine wood, thick and full of ferns, and I led her along meandering pathways lined with moss where you could smell the mushrooms and the resin on warm pine-tree trunks.

"I don't believe you," she said into the murmuring treetops. "How come you kissed me, then?"

"Because you're pretty, and sometimes a guy can't resist temptation. Even if he's Catholic."

"That means you're a bad Catholic."

"I'm trying to be good."

"Hmm," she said, and then she was silent. Maybe she was thinking. The trees sighed and the woods hummed with a provocative sexual energy brought to life by the warm spring air. A large dragonfly darted out of a dark shadow in front of us and stopped in midair right in front of Vixi's nose, where it hovered, a green reservoir of insane energy. Vixi stared at it like a hypnotized rabbit and then, suddenly but very deliberately, shrieked and flung herself around my neck.

"Yieee! It's going to bite me!"

Everything happened just as she knew it would. Through my shirt I felt her breasts squashing against my chest, and her hot thighs pressed against mine. My wretched, battle-scarred organ struggled to be let out.

It took me all my strength to disengage myself.

"Vixi! Don't play those games with me! You're not a city girl; I can't believe you're afraid of an insect."

She was unexpectedly insulted. "You think I'm stupid because I'm from the sticks?"

"Stupid, no; primitive, yes. What a cornball ploy! You should be ashamed of yourself."

She was ashamed, and walked on, silent and subdued, beside me, kicking the caps off mushrooms with her tennis shoes. I suspected she was thinking up a better ploy, but I had no idea what a quick learner she was.

Then she asked, "Do you seriously believe it's bad?"

"What?"

"You know. *That.*"

"*That* is one of the most wonderful things in the world. That's why the Church, in its wisdom, requires us to use it with discretion. So it won't become commonplace."

"Are you using it with discretion?"

"What do you think?"

"Nothing. Only you sure don't look the type."

At her age, sometimes the whole of existence is just one big provocation.

"In the first place, I have a certain position here, and so do you."

"Sure. You're afraid of Ivana."

"Naturally, I wouldn't exactly be thrilled to get locked up because of you."

"You can't get locked up because of me any more. I'm past seventeen."

"To get the sack, then."

"You wouldn't get the sack if you married me."

I looked at her severely. I was twenty-five years old and not yet a confirmed bachelor, and the treacherous wiles of her seventeen years might yet bring me to ruin.

"But I wouldn't marry you, Vixi."

"Well, in that case they probably *would* throw you out of the school. Maybe they'd even lock you up, because I'm an orphan."

"That's exactly what I'm talking about."

That seemed to me a perfectly logical end to this strange conversation. But I underestimated the power of her female logic, which was heading inevitably towards its own ends.

"But that's not a religious reason," she said. "What I want to know is, do you really think it's a sin?"

"Yes, I do," I said firmly, though not firmly enough, because I was trying to keep the lie out of my voice.

"And you never sin?"

"Of course I sin. But this particular sin has already had dire consequences for me." I said this with a suggestion of tragedy in my voice, so she wouldn't get the wrong idea, while angry memories of the infectious Miss Znenahlikova flashed through my mind. But my tone misled her completely.

"I'll bet you have to pay somebody child support."

Astonished, I shook my head.

"No? Then I'll bet you had some serious complications, right? Like you got someone pregnant and she had to get rid of it — "

She belonged to a generation that had been protected, to a certain extent, by the generous state-wide Action VD program, which had been so successful in eliminating the gonococcus that it now had to be imported. But I had an idea. "You see, Vixi," I said, "you simply don't understand. You're neither Catholic nor Protestant, are you?"

"No. I don't belong to any church."

"You can't imagine any other kind of punishment. You don't realize that there are other ways for a man to suffer."

Vixi's green eyes flashed with a light that came, not from theology, but from glossy magazine romanticism. "I know!" she said. "You're suffering from unrequited love!"

I had to laugh. I'd last known that condition of the soul in puberty. At the time it had been extremely intense, but when I'd grown up, I'd grown up completely. Since that time, I'd directed all love towards myself. I shook my head, laughing, but it was obvious that Vixi didn't believe me.

We walked out of the woods, out of the darkness, into the dazzling light of a spring afternoon. Before us lay a countryside apparently untouched by civilization. Insects performed mating rituals in the hot air, and close by the edge of the woods, set in a periwinkle meadow, the Creator had placed a pond with a still, quiet surface. On the shore of the pond someone had built a wooden shack the size and shape of a village outhouse. Outside it stood a backless bench made of grey, weatherworn boards supported by four unpeeled logs. The pond might once have been a private swimming hole belonging to one of the later princesses of Landsfeld, or perhaps some farmer's wife came here to refresh herself; the tiny cabin with its wooden bench was the only visible object fashioned by human hands. Otherwise there was only an undulating green and yellow plain that rose gently to a low, craggy mountain with grey sandstone outcroppings. A narrow path wound through the fields in graceful arcs towards these rocks, vanishing now and then behind the green hill strewn with white snowdrops.

Vixi sat down on the grass beside the pond and let the gathering of silken hair tied with a red ribbon fall across her bosom.

"Come here," she said. "It's as clear as day now. You're in love with someone and you want to stay faithful to her."

Again I shook my head. "No, Vixi. I'm suffering from something you've probably never known. A bad conscience."

"A bad conscience I know only too well."

"Except I didn't do anything, just that particular sin. And I doubt you'd bother your little head much over that one."

"You didn't get her pregnant?"

"No."

Her green eyes looked straight into mine. She had my number. "I don't believe you, sir!"

My unworldly pangs of guilt had failed to convince her. She was silent for a while, then came up with a new ploy.

"Gosh, it's hot," she said.

She lay back in the grass, pulled her white T-shirt up to her breasts, and rolled the hem of her skirt high above her knees. Her stomach was beautifully concave, and she had a deep-set navel. She closed her eyes. The sun burned down.

"It's all bull, bull, bull. You're afraid of Ivana and you're just trying to make yourself seem interesting."

Suddenly I realized how nice it was to be with Vixi, and how my theological bunkum merely increased the terrible longing I had to reach under her shirt and do what would be appropriate under the circumstances. I gritted my teeth and, gathering all my strength, forced my mind back to theology.

"You don't understand at all," I said. "The girl's a Catholic too. And God also punished her with a bad conscience." Then physical desire turned my theology in a direction that was far more interesting. "It's far worse for her because she was a virgin." My reminder reminded me of the charms of Julia Nedochodilova, and then her best girlfriend, but I said nothing to Vixi about that.

Vixi interpreted this in her own way. "Sure, sure. It's obvious. You're madly in love and she doesn't want you any more."

"You hopeless heathen!" I said, lying down on my stomach in the warm grass beside Vixi. "My sin is all the greater because I *didn't* love her."

"Then why did you do it?"

"You're asking me? You don't love me either, and just last night you were dying to do it."

"Maybe I do love you."

"That's bull," I said, using her word.

"No it's not. I said 'maybe'."

I said nothing. I looked at Vixi through narrowed eyes — at her navel, her closed eyes, that pert little nose. Her mound of Venus rose invitingly under her thin skirt. An emerald light, inflamed by the sun, shone suddenly from under her eyelids. She in turn was looking at me through half-closed eyes.

"Sir — " she said, as though the discussion was over. She lifted a bare arm and ran her fingers lightly through my hair. I didn't react. She turned over on her side and took my earlobe in her pouting lips. Then she began to nibble it with her teeth. I felt a searing pain — and not in my earlobe. I shook my head and met her taunting eyes.

"Boo!" said Vixi.

"You're a nitwit."

"Gobble-gobble!"

"The Communists have really led you astray."

"Boo-hoo-hoo!" she said. "I was led astray by someone from the Moravian Brethren."

"That's not what I'm talking about. You think everything to do with religion is stupid."

"No, what's stupid is the idea that a roll in the hay has anything to do with religion."

"You're ignorant and blinkered. You can't see things from someone else's point of view."

"Yes I can," she bantered. "You'd be surprised." She sat up. On her back, between the waist of her skirt and her rolled-up T-shirt, her spine stood out under her warm silken skin like a string of large pearls. It made me think of the backbone of some graceful dinosaur under the slick clay of a prehistoric river.

"I've already seen things from your point of view. But I don't believe it. I mean, I don't believe it's a sin."

"Don't, then!" I shot back. "One of these days the Lord will show you."

"Why hasn't He shown me already?"

"Maybe He's giving you a chance to reform."

"If He doesn't give me a sign, I won't believe it."

"Maybe He'll give you a sign sooner than you think."

Vixi turned towards me. "Really?"

I shrugged my shoulders. She stood up and stretched, deliberately taking her time about it.

"It's hot," she said again. "Spring's hardly begun and it feels like summer already." She gave me a sidelong glance and announced, "Let's go swimming!"

"I don't have my bathing suit with me."

"Neither do I. But who needs a bathing suit?"

"Look, Vixi," I admonished her. I was beginning to understand the principle of hell.

"Then I'll go in by myself, if you won't go."

"Come on, Vixi!"

"And don't you look, either," she added. "Since you're such a high and mighty Catholic, you'd better look away so you won't get caught sinning."

And she skipped off to the shack.

I buried my forehead in the grass. A wise man would have left then and there, but I lay on my belly in the bright grass while the imp of a perverse longing pinned me to the ground in a full nelson. Reason told me to go, but my will refused, although I was suffering like a dumb animal. I heard a button click against the shack's wooden wall. The sun, already sinking towards the west, was still warm, and the desperate enemy of chastity was straining against my trouser leg like a creature independent of me, a creature being denied something that was rightfully his and struggling to claim his due.

Suddenly I heard the padding of bare feet in the grass, and Vixi's voice crying, "Yii — ii — ii — iii!"

As I heard and felt her running naked towards the pond, the devil gave me a push and twisted my neck around with a crude wrench. I looked at her in classical fashion, peering through the fingers I was using to cover my eyes. She was standing by the edge of the pond, sticking her foot cautiously in the water. "Brrr! It's freezing!"

Slowly she advanced into the pond. The stones on the bottom must have dug into the soles of her feet, because she held her arms out for balance. The red ribbon was still in her hair; it was the only thing she was wearing that she hadn't been born with. She was as willowy as a branch, with a firm, white, beautifully rounded bottom. The water slowly welcomed her, rising along her slender thighs, kissing her white bottom, reaching around her hips to moisten the growth surrounding her soft sanctuary.

Then something terrible happened. As I watched the red ribbon fluttering against her magnificent naked back, and the two dimples just above the crease that separated those wonderful white hemispheres, my straining, wilful organ could bear it no longer. A splash of delight overwhelmed the pain and a spurt of hot fluid shot down my leg.

"Brrr!" shrieked Vixi. "It's freee — eeezing!"

She fell forward with a splash into the water and cried out maliciously, "You can look now!"

I sat up, pulled my knees to my chin, and took a handkerchief from my pocket.

"The water's awfully cold!" she announced again. "But it's great! Come on in!"

"Lay off, will you?"

I looked down and saw that my semen was seeping through my cotton trousers. Vixi dived under the water and I quickly ran my handkerchief into my fly. When she surfaced a short distance from a patch of reeds, I turned onto my side with my back to her and wiped my thighs and the inside of my pants.

"Some birds have built a nest here!" she informed me. I finished cleaning up the mess and sat up straight again. Vixi was up to her waist in the water, imperfectly shrouded by the reeds, and with an interest about as convincing as her other exaggerated hypocrisies she peered into the green shadows where a family of ducks was quacking frantically.

"Don't you want to come and have a look?"

"Come out and get dressed!"

"Do you think this is a sin too?"

"Of course. Enticing to fornication is a major sin in itself."

"My, you Catholic boys have a tough life, don't you?" she said, and walked slowly out from behind the screen of reeds. And so I first saw her naked breasts. They were firm and round and proportionate to her size, and they glowed whitely in the shadow of her body. She was standing with her back to the evening sun and drops of water sparkled as they dripped into the pond.

"Get dressed!" I groaned. "Don't play games with God!"

"Ha-ha!" she retorted. "I don't want to play with Him anyway. I want to play with you."

And she began to walk out of the water, emerging with slow and sophisticated motions — like an experienced stripper — until the precise moment when the waterline coincided with the top of the bushy overgrowth on her mons Veneris.

"Boo!" she said, and stopped. "I'm a devil woman and I'm coming for your soul, *sir*!"

She raised her arms luxuriously over her head, her fingers like Gothic talons, and began to move forward again. Her white breasts bobbed resiliently and her dark triangle rose out of the water.

At that moment a tall, gangly man in a black suit walked out of the woods into the full light of the setting sun, wiping his face with a red handkerchief. Both Vixi and I saw him at once. Vixi showed marvellous presence of mind, slipping under the water like a snake and disappearing into the reeds without a single splash. The only thing that betrayed her presence was an excited twitting of waterfowl, but for the time being the man didn't notice it.

He approached along the path and, when he was a short way off, called out a friendly greeting. "God be with you!"

"Good evening," I said, and suddenly noticed that he was wearing a clerical collar. "God be with you, Father!" I corrected myself, with ill-suppressed delight; I'd just realized what a wonderful opportunity this was for revenge.

The priest stopped and looked at me. "Just a moment," he said slowly. "Aren't you — of course! You're the new teacher at the Social Workers' School."

"I am," I nodded, and then added somewhat more loudly, so Vixi could hear me in the reeds, "Won't you sit down, Father? It's so lovely here, and such a beautiful evening!"

The priest walked over to the wooden bench, wiped his face with his handkerchief again, and sat down. "Smiricky," he said thoughtfully, as Sister Udelina had done not long ago. "You aren't by any chance related to Father Smiricky from Budejovice?" Clearly my uncle was almost as popular among clerical people as the imprisoned archbishop.

There was a splash in the bullrushes, but the priest looked at me with tranquil expectation in his pale eyes. Thanks to my uncle, the ice was quickly broken between me and the man whom Providence and the Secret Police had destined to die a martyr's death.

And so — while Vixi huddled in the cooling water among the reeds, pestered by insects and threatened by aggressive mother ducks — the Venerable Father Doufal recounted several of his immensely boring but, at that moment, welcome tales of his encounters with my uncle. The sun sank until it touched the horizon and the priest began to flap his red handkerchief about to drive away the growing numbers of mosquitoes. I lit a cigarette to help keep them off. A cloud of them circled above us and then, with a gentle hum, swarmed off towards the patch of reeds in the water. As he watched them go, the priest started a long, drawn-out story about some mosquitoes that had once tormented his native village of Stepanovice in Central Moravia because of an enormous swamp that lay on the east side of it, and how the farmers — and for him everyone who worked on the land was a farmer: the local kulak with thirty hectares and his own father with six — joined their efforts and on the advice of the local priest drained the swamp and thus, with God's help, rid the village of mosquitoes. . . .

A strange birdcall came from the reeds, a spluttering squawk resembling a sneeze. The priest pricked up his ears, shook his head, and said, "I wonder what that was. A coot, perhaps? No, it sounded more like a female blue heron. But — " and he began talking about his egg collection. At that moment the angular hill on the horizon took its first bite out of the red sun and started to swallow it. By the time the sun was gone, I had learned everything there was to know about the collection that the priest, as a country boy, had preserved in oakum. I'd never realized there were so many varieties of fauna around a single dumb Moravian village. When he finally got around to describing how he felt when the teacher of the local one-room school decided to display his collection in the school office, where the regional inspector himself praised it, the moist spring stars were already beginning to twinkle in the sky; the warmth was quickly fleeing the countryside and I was beginning to feel chilly. But I gritted my teeth and hung on.

Being a farmer, the priest didn't feel the cool of the spring evening, and he began naming the constellations with great enthusiasm as they came out. "The Big Dipper!" he said, with wonder in his voice, as if he were seeing that too-familiar sight for the first time. "If you follow the line of the last two stars in the Dipper, you come to the Little Dipper, and then a little farther over, right there, is Cassiopeia, then Draco. . . . Isn't it magnificent, God's heaven?" And he stared up at it, and the black buttons on his vest glimmered like majolica in the starlight, and his large hands rested quietly on his black trouser legs, and broken farmer's fingernails shone at the ends of his thick fingers. "On a night like this you can almost touch the glory of God," he said, and though I wasn't sitting here for the glory of God, it touched me in a strange way as well. I almost forgot about Vixi — who by this time must have been half dead from the cold — as I too stared at far-off worlds like jewels that an incomprehensible God had scattered prodigally across His elegant heaven. Suddenly I began to shiver. "My goodness gracious," said the priest, "here I am, carrying on like this, and you're only wearing a shirt. You must be cold!"

"A little," I admitted. The priest jumped to his feet. "Well, let's be off then, let's be off!" He pulled a bulbous pocket watch from his vest. "Goodness! Eight-thirty!" Then he noticed that I was looking at the watch with interest and he added, "My great-grandfather was given this by Prince Lobkowicz. It has to be wound with a key," and he gave me a demonstration of that miracle of old-fashioned technology. Then, at last, we set off down the path whitewashed by starlight.

When we reached the first pines on the edge of the wood I excused myself for a moment and disappeared into the ferns. The fresh night magically flooded the countryside with light and I saw a water nymph rise white against the dark waters of the pond and flit to the wooden shack.

Satisfied, I smiled, then ran back to join the waiting priest.

Next day, Vixi sat through the third-form social studies lesson with a red nose and watery eyes. She was wearing a woolly blue sweater over her yellow T-shirt. She kept interrupting the lesson with her sneezes, and I was malicious enough to scold her several times. She glared at me with tear-filled eyes and, on my orders, blew her nose loudly into a tiny, damp handkerchief.

After four o'clock there was a knock on the door of my office.

"Come in!"

Vixi entered the room and stood there. I looked at her silently, but then I couldn't help laughing.

"You're awful!" she said.

"God was punishing you. You asked for it."

"And don't blaspheme!" she shot back. "I know you don't believe it, but I do, now!"

"Wonderful!"

"And you don't even know *how* He punished me." She sneezed.

"Did you get the flu?"

"Worse than that!" she wailed. "While you were passing the time of day with the priest, I was bitten by a blood-sucker *this big*!" And with her hands she indicated a creature as long as a large eel.

"Where?" I asked.

"On my bum," said Vixi, then gave an enormous sneeze.

She spent the next three days in bed, and when she came back to school she expressed a desire to join the Catholic Church.

6.

Juzl and I were driving through a darkening countryside towards the city. The first suburbs were glittering like nests of glass eggs on both sides of the river.

"I've decided to continue the series," Juzl decided suddenly. "I'm going to accept their game. I'll use *them* as *advocati diaboli.* "

Before I went to bed that night, I reread the first article of what would become Juzl's series — the one that had prompted the letter from Father Urbanec.

"I think, therefore, that we are fully justified in posing several questions," Juzl had written in conclusion, and then he had posed the questions with rhetorical pathos:

Is the "Lieutenant" Doufal who died on June 21, 1949, as a result of an "automobile accident" — in which he inexplicably lost all the fingernails on his right hand — one and the same with Father Josef Doufal, arrested and charged with fraud on June 12, 1949, and missing since that time? And if so, what confessions did his interrogators force him to make through such inhuman torture? As far as the second question is concerned, I think we are justified not only in asking it, but also in suggesting an answer: they forced him to admit to installing a mechanism which they had put in the chapel themselves!

4

A Detective Story

I.

Several days after our trip to the monastery in Sedlcany, Juzl and I were sitting in the Slavia Café in Prague and he showed me another letter. This one was not from Father Urbanec.

> Dear Sir,
>
> You are right it was them who framed Father Doufal, he was innocent, that morning I put flowers around Saint Joseph and the Blessid Virgin and there wasn't nothing like that there or I would of seen it and they arrestid me and I got five years in prison. It was a Miracle, Father Doufal didn't set it up. It was those communist swine and I wonder how the Lord can bear the sight of them, respectfully,
>
> Albina Knizakova, Na Brezince 13, Prague XVI
>
> I'm old now and living with my daughter and soninlaw, they are both very good to me.

"A marvellous document!" I said. "It's the concrete proof you've been looking for — unless they installed the device so cleverly that they can say the old woman didn't see it."

"They can't say that!" cried Juzl, jubilant. "At the time, they published an official report with photos, and they even included a sketch. Now they're going to pay for being so sure of themselves. Look at this!"

Juzl took a file folder out of his briefcase and set it on our table; it was marked "FATHER JOSEF DOUFAL" in calligraphic lettering. He took some photocopies of a diagram out of it.

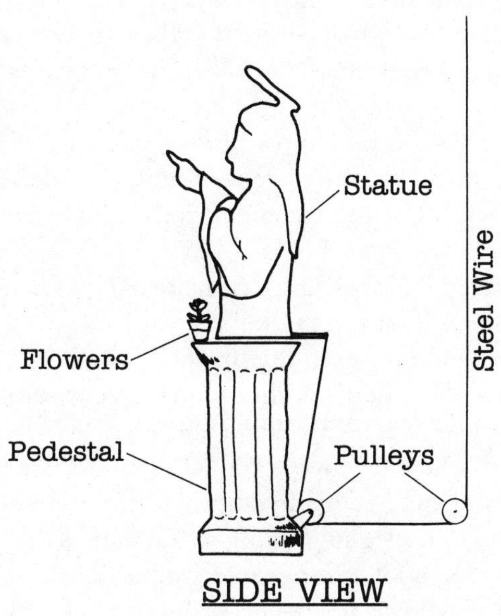

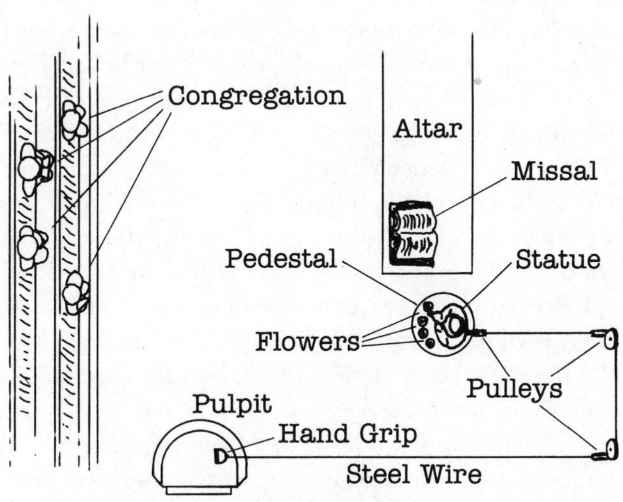

I looked at the diagram of the simple mechanism. There was a certain sophistication about it — not technical but psychological sophistication. They knew the priest was from a small farm. Their man in Hronov had undoubtedly told them that Father Doufal's hobby was woodcarving. So they must have guessed that he would have a certain manual skill, and the mechanical imagination to think up a device that might have come from the age of Leonardo da Vinci. But like all criminals, they'd forgotten something. Back in those days, when so many goods were in short supply or simply unavailable, thin steel cable was a rarity. In any case, a country priest would hardly have used cable: binder twine and wooden pulleys would have been more natural in his hands, with their calluses and broken nails.

"She'd have had to be almost blind not to see all that rigging," I said, putting my finger on the system of pulleys. "Besides . . . it strikes me that this looks just like the sketches criminal investigators make at the scene of a *murder.* "

As I'd expected, this uncanny coincidence made an impression on Juzl's theologically influenced thinking.

"Would you mind if I used that insight?" he said.

"Be my guest. But don't bother naming your source," I said. "By the way, how old was Mrs. Knizakova at the time?"

"Fifty-seven. She's seventy-seven today, but she's still a chipper old gal," said Juzl, warming to his hypothesis. "So it's impossible that she was too doddering to notice something as obvious as this. When I went to visit her, she told me a lot of other interesting things, too. For instance, those flowers in the flowerpots — according to the official report, they covered the mechanism so the believers couldn't see it from the pews. But Mrs. Knizakova brought those flowers in that morning, just before mass. She said there were flowerpots there from an earlier service and the flowers in them were dry, so the first thing she did was set them aside behind the altar, here," and he pointed to the sketch. "In other words, she'd have seen the mechanism when she moved the flowerpots. But even if she'd been completely blind, she'd have tripped over this wire *here.* According to the official description, it was about ten centimetres off the floor and led to a pulley in the wall behind the altar."

I followed his finger as it moved across the diagram and I could see that he was right. It was pretty damning evidence.

"There's another detail, too," Juzl laughed, and for the first time since he'd begun investigating the miracle he sounded almost lighthearted. "A family of swallows had built a nest in the corner above Saint Joseph, and Mrs. Knizakova discovered that the floor behind the altar was covered with their droppings. She took a broom, a rag, and a bucket — she kept them in the small sacristy behind the altar — and swept up the mess and then scrubbed the floor. See what I'm getting at? That was right where the wire was supposed to be!"

I looked at him with new respect. He was a pale, rather slick-looking young man of not entirely unblemished reputation. He had once spent a year in a seminary but had then left and studied art history at university.

"Mr. Juzl," I said, "I take my hat off to you. I think that with this evidence, the only way you can explain the events in Hronov is the way Father Urbanec did."

Juzl nodded. It was a triumphant nod.

"It contradicts science," I went on, "so it can't be the way it happened, but — "

"It's an enormous responsibility," he said, looking at the documents which testified so persuasively to the miracle, and then he stuck them back in the file. "I would never have imagined that I would be chosen to — I'm certainly not worthy — "

"One reformed sinner . . . ," I said quietly.

The café lights shone in his slicked-back hair. He was looking past me, at something I could never see. Perhaps, I smiled to myself, I was the unworthy one; all I could see was the waiter walking past us with a glass of vermouth for an elderly, worried-looking gentleman who was sitting at the next table reading *The Times* of London mounted in a bamboo newspaper holder. Not long ago they'd allowed the café to carry it. The page he was reading displayed a sober headline: TOP KREMLINOLOGIST SAYS CZECHS GO TOO FAR.

Juzl's meditations, however, ranged forward over centuries. "It's no longer just a matter of a couple of articles in a newspaper," he said. "This may well be a case for sanctification. Naturally it needs more witnesses, though. And who knows how many are still alive?"

He had no idea that one witness was sitting at the table with him — but I had no desire to take part in a trial, even if it was only in the Holy See. I was afraid the Kremlinologist quoted in *The Times* was right. In one corner of the café, out of sight from the big windows, a group of radical writers led by the world-famous playwright Hejl was having a meeting. Recently — if the Kremlinologist's prophecy was correct — Hejl had been behaving as though he wanted to follow in the footsteps of the priest and become a martyr to the ideals of the *annus mirabilis*. I was certain he would. Ultimately, everything in the world turns out for the worst.

Although for the moment I had no other way of explaining the phenomenon in the Chapel of the Virgin Mary under Mare's Head, I couldn't put much faith in Father Urbanec's theory. Still, *Credo, quia*. . . .

Unlike the world-famous playwright, Father Doufal had never acted as though he was deliberately trying to win a martyr's crown.

2.

"Why the hell did you want to learn the catechism in the first place, if you still have doubts about everything?" I shouted at Vixi. "Certain things belong to the mystery of faith and no one will ever explain them to you. Either you believe them or you don't!"

We were sitting in the clover on the edge of a field, hidden by hazel bushes from the eyes of passers-by. Below us Hronov was humming with the throes of socialist construction, and above us was a high, bright spring sky. Vixi had got over her flu and now she was suffering from doubt.

"But how can you believe Jonah was swallowed by a whale when a whale has a mouthful of balloon?"

"Baleen," I corrected her. I was irritated. "And anyway, the Bible doesn't say it was a whale, just a large fish. It might have been a giant shark."

"A shark would have chewed him into little pieces. Sharks don't swallow their prey whole."

"Anyway, stories like that don't belong to the mysteries of the faith."

"Why are they in the Bible, then?"

I sighed. "Look. The Bible was written at a time when there was no such thing as natural science. Mankind— "

"I know. That's what the priest says too. People were still ignorant then and God had to hand it all to them on a platter—I mean, explain it to them by example. And you know what I asked him? I asked him why God didn't make people clever right away, so they could understand the way things are right from the start."

In my heart I pitied the priest. Teaching Vixi something as full of contradictions as the Catholic catechism was not an enviable job.

"And he said it was like when a child is born and the parents try to explain the difference between good and bad, and they tell it fairy-tales. Sure, I said, but people don't know how to make babies who are anything but stupid. But God should be able to, shouldn't He?"

"And he didn't clip you one?"

"Him? He wouldn't lay a hand on anyone, not even the bratty little altarboys. He's awfully kind. He gives me a piece of cake almost every time I go."

"Cake? I didn't know he had a housekeeper."

"He doesn't, he makes it himself. And I'll bet he does it just for me.

Nobody else is taking catechism, because everyone else is afraid."

"I hope you're being careful, like you promised."

"Don't worry. I always climb over his back fence. No one can see me from there. But he makes fantastic cake. Better than Vikusova."

"And you pay him back by asking impertinent questions."

"I do not. I like him. But I can't help it. Everything seems only half worked out. Like for instance that stuff about God being all-powerful and all-knowing and all-loving. It doesn't fit," she said, raising a problem that has tortured adherents of the religion since the beginning. "If He's all-knowing, He knows we're going to sin — and then He punishes us for it even though He could easily arrange it so we wouldn't sin in the first place, since He's all-powerful and all-loving. The way it is now, He comes out looking pretty mean." Then she thought of something else. "Hey, you know, it's like — did you know Joska Sala?"

I did. He was the fat, roughneck son of the biggest hotel-keeper in Hronov, and I suspected he had designs on Vixi. But he was no longer a rival. Not long ago he'd been arrested and convicted of taking part in some ill-defined anti-state activity and sentenced to fifteen or twenty years in prison.

"Well, listen to this," said Vixi. "Kamila Doruzkova's going out with an undercover cop, and he was bragging to her that they knew about Joska for a long time. But all Joska ever did was meet a bunch of his buddies and drink in the back room of the hotel and shoot their mouths off. But then one of his buddies joined the cops, and the cops let them go until they'd all said enough to get them in deep trouble, and then they collared the lot of them." She looked at me as though she'd made a profound philosophical discovery. "And that's exactly the way it is with God. Instead of helping us, He waits till we get ourselves mucked in and then acts as if it was all our own fault. And then bingo! Off to hell with us!"

I was horrified. "Do you actually say things like that to Father Doufal? He must be delighted."

"Well, I didn't put it exactly that way. But how do you explain it? All that stuff about God being all-powerful and all-knowing and all-loving — how do you fit that together?"

"Me?" When I was still in high school the Venerable Father Meloun gave us a rather sophisticated explanation, but he never really made it clear, and I was never all that interested anyway. "How did Father Doufal explain it?"

Vixi was sitting in the clover with her arms around her bare knees. She'd taken off her tennis shoes; her toenails were painted different colours, the even ones red and the odd ones silver. The girls at the school got up to some strange things. She stuck a clover blossom in her mouth; it made her look like a well-groomed rabbit. She was thinking.

"Well — as a matter of fact, he didn't really explain it. He said God loved us so much that He wanted us to be as much like Him as possible, just like parents want their children to be like them, he said. So He gave us free will and He gave us love, the two most important qualities, for God and for people. Father Doufal said if we didn't have free will we wouldn't be like God and we wouldn't be worth saving. And if there was no love, then we couldn't be saved from our sins anyway. It's because we love God that we have the free will to choose good, because we know He likes that."

"There! That's not such a bad explanation."

"No, it's not. The only thing is, what's *good*? Is *that* good?"

"What?"

"*THAT,*" said Vixi. "You know — diddling."

"Naturally," I said confidently. "But only under certain circumstances."

"I know. It's supposed to be an image of the act of creation, and that's why God made it so much fun, see? I mean, that's how babies are made. Like, they're created. But I told him, 'Father Doufal, it's still fun even if you do it with a safe.'"

"My God, Vixi, did you actually tell him that? What did he say?"

"He turned red," she said. "He did, he was red right to the roots of his hair. He said true pleasure only comes in marriage. When you're married it's real love, otherwise it's only lust." She laughed, but it wasn't a mocking laugh. "He's really a funny old priest. He has a red and white striped eiderdown."

"Jesus, how do you know that?"

"Well, I mean, he's got a bed. I saw it through an open door. He stacks the bedding up really high, like my grandfather did. By the way, let's go visit my grandfather someday, okay?"

I nodded. A fat bumblebee landed by mistake on the clover blossom Vixi was just about to put in her mouth. She stroked its furry abdomen gently with her index finger. The fingernail was painted purple. The bee grumbled.

"I still don't know why you're taking catechism. It's a big risk — if anyone saw you — "

"I'm taking it so I can know true pleasure," she said, looking at me out of the corner of her eye. I said nothing. I was hot, and itchy in those places where the weight of sin was still being lifted from me by chlortetracycline.

"Do you see what I'm getting at, sir?"

I stopped listening to her. God knows why, but I imagined the priest sleeping peacefully under his candy-striped eiderdown. And although I fancied myself a thoroughly cynical man, I hoped Vixi's catechism was not interfering too deeply with his sleep of the just.

3.

Hejl, the world-famous playwright, had clearly turned the Café Slavia into the secretariat of his future opposition party, because I saw him in his corner again, surrounded by young coeds instead of writers. The café was becoming a regular haunt for Juzl and me too. He invited me there two days after he published an article about the testimony of the woman who had changed the flowers. In this instalment he came right out and stated that the moving statue of Saint Joseph in the Chapel of the Virgin Mary under Mare's Head had been a genuine miracle. This was a time when even the social democrats were beginning to come out of their closets, but Juzl's hypothesis was a daring one all the same, and it drew at least one response — a rather mysterious anonymous letter. We examined it by the window while beside us the elderly gentleman, who was becoming something of a fixture here too, anxiously studied *The Times*.

> Your conjecture is a nice one, and very brave. I'd be a happy man if I could believe it, if only because certain people would be highly upset if it were true. Unfortunately, however, I must disappoint you. Saint Joseph was moved not by the power of God the Father, nor the Son, nor the Holy Ghost, and certainly not by the Virgin of Virgins, but by the power of the Secret Police — even though the means they employed were somewhat more sophisticated than the ones they ultimately served up for public consumption. The whole operation was codenamed MIRAKL — a Russianism, but what else would you expect from them? I'm sure you understand *unde inspiratio* — a term for what unfortunately did not take place beneath Mare's Head Hill. The scheme was worked out by two leading Marxist-Leninists, both of them government ministers at the time: Kopecky, from Information, and Cepicka, of National Defence. They entrusted the execution of their scheme to three officers of the Secret Police: then-Lieutenant Albert Sulc, Corporal Josef Pecen, and Lieutenant Koernerova. First, these three carried out the necessary research in their files on all the priests and in the calendars of local church festivals, so they could choose the most suitable place and time for the operation.

After consultations with expert advisers in psychology and Church history, they settled on Father Doufal and the Mary chapel near Hronov. Pecen and Koernerova came to Hronov sometime in the middle of May, registered as man and wife in the Rock City Hotel, and secretly made photographs and sketches of the chapel. Using these, a radio engineer for the Secret Police called Neuhofer designed a special device that Pecen, who was a trained electrotechnologist, then constructed in the workshops. They installed the device in the statue on the evening of June 10, 1949, a day before the "miracle" took place. It worked with remote-controlled electromagnets and looked approximately like this:

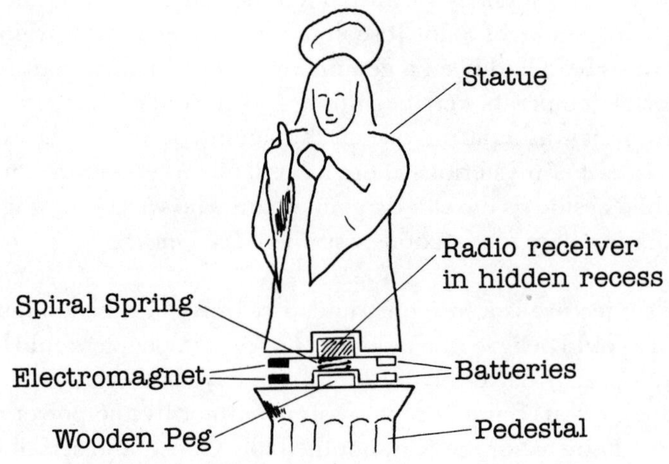

When the circuit was closed and the electromagnets were activated, the statue leaned to the right, that is, towards the hand raised in blessing. This lifted the statue a little on one side, but not enough that its base would be higher than the raised edge of the pedestal. Because the pedestal was almost two metres high, the base of the statue was far above the eye level of people sitting in the pews and there was no danger of the woman who replaced the flowers on top of the pedestal noticing anything. The transmitter was hidden in a rucksack belonging to Corporal Pecen, who attended the mass disguised as a hiker.

I repeat again, my dear sir, that I regret very much having to destroy your hypothesis, which is a courageous one, even today. But that is the simple truth about the "miracle" in the Chapel of the Virgin Mary under Mare's Head Hill. I'm sure you hold with the newly repopularized slogan "The Truth Will Triumph", and you will therefore understand that it was this not entirely truthful principle, and this alone, which led me to write you this letter, which, for reasons you will no doubt appreciate, I will not sign.

Yours in friendship,

A Destroyer of Myths, All Myths

PS: You are right about one thing: all that clumsy apparatus with pulleys and wires was actually installed in the chapel *after* the "miracle", by a group of Secret Police investigators, when they occupied the chapel and closed it to the public. After all, to turn a village priest who was not outstandingly intelligent into a Marconi would have been more than implausible.

"I'm very sorry," I said, almost sincerely, for there was disappointment in Juzl's face. "The man seems to know a lot about it. That is, if he's not making it all up. But you could probably check on some of his details." I was dismayed by Juzl's dejection and wanted to cheer him up. "Even if it turns out that Father Doufal wasn't a miracle worker, he *was* a martyr, and now you can prove he wasn't a fraud."

Juzl nodded sadly. "Some of the names mentioned in the letter weren't pseudonyms, that much is certain. Sulc existed and he's now somewhere in the diplomatic service. So far I haven't been able to trace Koernerova. But this fellow Pecen, there's something rather odd about him. Someone by that name was working for the Ministry of the Interior at the time, but shortly afterwards he died and I haven't been able to find out how."

"In a people's democracy, deaths of indeterminable cause almost always have the same cause, don't they?"

Juzl nodded again. "And they also admitted that the so-called lieutenant who died after an ulcer operation really was Father Doufal." He raised his bluish eyes and looked at me. "You know, I never knew Father Doufal personally but I can imagine what he was like. God often chooses his saints from people like him. I remember them from the seminary: simple village boys, their mothers would send them parcels filled with muffins, and they had a terrible time with Latin and Hebrew — but they had something in them, I don't know, something holy, something I didn't have. It's from people like them that God chooses His best servants — and sometimes He even rewards them with — "

He stopped, and his blue eyes wandered somewhere in the general direction of the triglyphs on the façade of the National Theatre. The man reading *The Times* wiped his brow with a paper napkin and angrily turned the page. Muffins from home — that's a nice detail, my friend, I thought. But why in God's name does your God, who produced such a scientifically complex universe and wants us to be like Him, demand a low IQ as a condition for salvation?

"But *why* people like that? Don't you find it a little strange?" I said.

The blue eyes turned back from the sky above the National Theatre and looked straight at me. At the beginning of this spring of madness, Juzl had published an extraordinarily erudite study of Czech literature from the baroque period; this former would-be priest was not one of God's simple people. For me, he was as much a mystery as Julia Nedochodilova's brother. Jiri Nedochodil had become a chemist and eventually made a name for himself by discovering a fibre twenty times stronger than nylon. But once when I was showing a visitor around the Holy Mountain, I met Jiri and his new bride — she was the niece of one of the imprisoned bishops — and they were offering a wax doll and a prayer for fertility.

"I know what you're thinking," said Juzl. "But I — you know, sometimes — and it happens more and more these days — sometimes I wonder whether our entire modern era might not be described — metaphorically, you understand — as a counter-offensive of the fallen angels. They were pretty arrogant, after all. Maybe God's trying to tell us that we're on the wrong track. That we're depending too heavily on reason. You know what Saint Paul wrote?"

"You mean the one who liked drinking and whoring?"

"You're not taking this seriously. I'm thinking of his first letter to the Corinthians."

I suddenly realized what he was talking about. That letter had been a favourite of Lida Neumannova-Hertlova, who almost got me sent to prison once. She loved to quote from it, from the book of Ecclesiastes, and of course from Solomon's song of praise to the ancient Jewish houris.

"'If I speak in the tongue of men and of angels, but have not love, I am nothing,'" I recited, the way Lida used to do; when she said "love", of course, she was thinking about what Vixi called "diddling". Juzl nodded and picked up the quotation: "'And if I have prophetic powers, and understand all mysteries, and all knowledge, and if I have all faith, so as to remove mountains, and have not love, I am nothing.'"

We were both silent. From the corner of the café came the loud voice of the world-famous playwright holding forth while at least seven young women gazed at him intently.

"By the way," I said, "if you don't mind my asking, why did you leave the seminary in the first place? Listening to you now, I'd say you wouldn't have made a half-bad priest." Juzl looked as though he wanted to object, so I continued quickly, "Those theology students with muffins from their mothers — maybe they are potential saints, maybe the old women in their congregations will wear out their heels following them. But I'll bet they won't bring many new people into the Church. You might have been able to. I read your anthology of baroque writing; do you know, you actually managed to rehabilitate the Jesuits?"

Juzl waved his hand dismissively. "No, no," he said. "I wouldn't have made a good priest, I didn't have the vocation. I only thought I did." That was his way of saying, euphemistically, that he couldn't get along without women. When he was still a student of art history he'd followed Saint Paul's advice, but his wife had left him shortly after their marriage. She could soon be heard in the Prague bars, claiming that she had nothing against fulfilling her marital duties or even having children, but that she drew the line at turning herself into a sexual assembly-line for the mass production of progeny. Since Juzl would not contemplate divorce, a chain of iniquity followed, as the wife shacked up with another failed priest and Juzl periodically succumbed to sensitive young students.

"But God must have loved you," I said. "Given your uncompromising character, you might have ended up just like poor Father Doufal. They beat him to death for nothing, in fact. I mean, if there had really been a miracle, then at least — "

He looked at me imploringly.

"You mean you still think . . . ," I said, taken aback. "After this?" And I tapped the anonymous letter.

"I don't know," said Juzl, and in his voice I could hear a great distaste for the facts that had just been revealed. Perhaps it was a proper distaste, for there is a convention, and it may be a healthy one, which dictates that facts revealed anonymously should be discounted. "Sulc is off on an embassy posting somewhere, I don't know anything about Koernerova, Pecen is dead. How are we to know whether this," and now he tapped the document, "isn't just another hoax?"

"Who would want to — "

"Remember what Father Urbanec said in Sedlcany."

He explained what he meant in his next article, his third such epistle to believers. At my request he left me out of his vivid description of the trip to the cloister, but the inspiration he'd received from the priest from the uranium mines breathed from every line. He concluded:

I too originally believed that the Secret Police had installed the pulley mechanism in the chapel sometime before that special mass, that during Father Doufal's sermon some agent had operated it, and that after Father Doufal was arrested it had simply been "discovered" and rearranged so that the wire led to the pulpit. But a witness to the investigation of the Venerable Father Doufal at the scene of the "crime", Father Urbanec, and the letter of Mrs. Knizakova, which practically eliminates the possibility that the mechanism as officially described was installed *before* the mass, have convinced me that the phenomenon near Hronov was in fact a miracle. Why? Let us look at certain facts. First: the final words of Father Doufal, "*Erat miraculum!*" are scarcely explicable unless the late priest saw some evidence behind the altar of which we are not yet aware. Secondly: the testimony of Mrs. Knizakova provides us with clear proof that the device was installed *post factum.* And now, for this very reason, an anonymous "Destroyer of Myths" appears on the scene and reveals the alleged existence of another device. This device, however, is so complex that I can't help wondering whether it too was not invented *ex post,* i.e., after my last article, in order to invalidate Mrs. Knizakova's testimony. Of course, it is almost impossible today to authenticate the anonymous correspondent's information — even though I am doing everything in my power to do so. But let me be permitted again to ask at least two questions. The anonymous correspondent displays extremely detailed knowledge of the top-secret "Operation MIRAKL". Who would have access to such information but a member of the Secret Police? And why is he coming forth with this information now, when the question at issue is not whether Father Doufal was a victim of police murderers or not — since that was admitted by a representative of the Ministry of the Interior — but whether the phenomenon in the Chapel of the Virgin Mary under Mare's Head Hill can be explained by natural means or not?

5

■

Hyde Park

I.

The big log in the fireplace looked like the shrivelled corpse of a martyr burned at the stake.

"This is good stuff," said Gellen, and he read from an article in *Tribuna*:

> The havoc wrought by the counter-revolution reached a peak in the spring and summer of 1968. Increasingly, honest Communists became the target of slanderous attacks and took their own lives, unable to bear the sight of everything they held dear and had struggled long years to achieve being daily spat upon, reviled, and trampled in the mud. Psychological white terror soon became the terror of blood.

He put the newspaper down on the coffee table beside the black candle. Thick black tears of wax were running down its shaft.

"Very juicy writing indeed," said my friend. "It must make quite an impression on comrades in the West. They only see what goes on here through the window of their own left-wing press, which is like seeing a landscape from an express train. That marvellous apocalyptic imagery, with 'terror of blood' at the end to parallel the idea of white terror, when you're expecting red terror instead. But that would hardly do, here. Notice also the clever use of the vague plural 'honest Communists' in conjunction with another vague plural, 'took their own lives'. Semantically it's a first-class piece of work. It conjures up the idea of mass suicide."

He leaned towards the black candle, ignited a used match in the flame, and then lit the fresh tobacco in the bowl of his pipe. "As a matter of fact, I happen to know a little about those mass suicides; the Department of Forensic Medicine is attached to our clinic. Do you know how many took their own lives, according to my information, because everything holy was being trampled in the mud?"

I didn't, but I did know who had written the philippic he'd just read to me. It was Vohnout, a sometime poet, editor-in-chief, and political essayist, and in general terms a party hack who'd developed his own personal method of scientific generalization based on analysis and subsequent synthesis of the fixed ideas put in circulation by the Party leadership.

"Three," said my friend, holding up three fingers for emphasis. "There were a few other mysterious deaths the boys would have liked to pass off as suicide, but because they were dicey — Masaryk's suicide is an open-and-shut case by comparison — they were finally just brushed under the rug. The three 'suicides' they did claim weren't exactly kosher either, but the boys could get away with presenting them as such. Number one was an army general. He apparently got mixed up in that sick little putsch the general staff wanted to pull off to 'give voice to the will of the people'." Gellen didn't have to tell me who he had in mind; people already knew of the abortive putsch through the grapevine. The generals appeared to have mistaken Czechoslovakia for Bolivia. Their plan was to bring a tank division to the Party Secretariat building and intervene in the discussions of Dubcek's Central Committee. But there was a Judas among them, and the tanks which had set off at someone's orders were halted on someone else's, and the will of the people, as always, got short shrift.

"That one's the most believable," said Gellen, "although there's some disagreement about where he shot himself, and whether it was in the temple or in the mouth. In any case, they reported it as suicide. May mother earth rest lightly upon him!"

We raised our glasses and drank a toast to the memory of the general who either had weak nerves or knew too much.

"Number two was a judge," my friend went on. "As a matter of fact, he was supposed to be another belated victim of Youth Unionitis, something like Laura. He used a clothes-line and a bottle of red wine rather than a gun, and he wasn't entirely efficient about it. According to a set of photographs the boys gave our pathologist, his legs were bent out of shape even as he hung from the tree, from which we deduced that *rigor mortis* had set in before he hanged himself, and that he'd conveyed himself to the suicide site in the trunk of a car. When our pathologist pointed this out, the comrades from the Ministry of the Interior took the photographs back for retouching." Gellen released an aromatic ring of pale blue smoke from his mouth. "This dear departed started out as a craftsman, just like Him," and he pointed to the cracked torso that resembled a bird-cage. "But Jesus didn't start poking His nose into public life until He was thirty. This one was only nineteen when the Party ordered him to train as a judge, and by the time he was twenty-two he'd handed down an undetermined number of death sentences — that was his contribution to revolutionary justice. Then it was discovered they'd all been judicial errors. To be more precise, it had been known all along in Party circles that they were errors, but it was assumed that the Party, in its inscrutable wisdom, required human sacrifices. Then the Party, in its inscrutable wisdom, found it had to start condemning such things in order to silence the clamorous enemies of humanity, especially in the West. And then evil tongues began to whisper things about the honest Communist-carpenter. Meantime he'd been appointed to the Supreme Court, and when they passed him too close, people stopped talking altogether."

2.

"Suppose I tried to poison myself because I was madly in love with you, prof."

"That'll be the day," I said. I could see right through her; she was trying to twist the holy catechism to serve her own ends.

"This is just an example. And suppose you came across me just as I was about to do it and you knew the only way to stop me was to do what I wanted."

"If there was no other way, I suppose I'd marry you."

"You're kidding — you're not that big a Christian. I know you better than that."

"Well then, I'd give you a good spanking."

"No, you'd know it wouldn't help. So you'd do it with me, then. And the priest says that in a case like that it wouldn't be a sin."

"Now, don't you kid *me.* I can't believe you talk to him about things like that."

"Not exactly," she admitted. "But he said it was okay to kill in self-defence or to save somebody else's life. The ends justify the means, those were his exact words. He said that was Saint Ignatius's idea."

"*In extremis.*"

"In what?"

"It's okay if there's no other possible way."

"That's just what I was saying. So what if there was no other way to stop me killing myself except, you know, doing it?"

"Vixi," I sighed, "you're not the type to commit suicide, and besides, Saint Ignatius definitely did not have *that* in mind."

Vixi lifted one of her legs and pointed her sandalled foot towards the setting sun. Her short skirt slipped high above her knee and she wiggled her two-tone toenails.

"You're such a cold fish," she said. "I know it's a sin as well as you do. But I love you. And I'm willing to spend the rest of eternity in hell."

My eyes were riveted on her silky brown thighs; the only thing holding me back was the impossibility of it all.

"Now that's what I call love," I said. "Provided you believe in hell. But if you don't, it's just a sinful trick to get your own way."

3.

Gellen poured the rest of the bottle into the large glasses. A second toast was in the air.

"This judge," he grinned, "was no Rubashov, to wait until the Party, in its inscrutable wisdom, discredited him before the whole nation for a sacred principle. He began to raise a clamour himself, so that the Party — again in its inscrutable wisdom — arranged for a *Sonderbehandlung,* special treatment. But that may only be malicious gossip put out by the enemies of humanity. No doubt it was these same enemies who, in their legendary sophistication, caused that pathologically inexplicable distortion of his legs. Whatever the case, may the earth rest lightly on him as well."

Again we touched glasses and drank the excellent whisky. The martyr in the fireplace was slowly disintegrating, and I was reminded of the film of the destruction of Stalin's memorial statue. It occurred to me that if you ran the film backwards, you would see the statue rising out of the rubble. The creator of that statue had hanged himself too. But that had been long ago, long before the age of white terror.

4.

People had begun calling it "Hyde Park" but, unlike the antiquated London apostles of temperance and the Second Coming, the Prague apostles were ahead of their time. They held forth from the base of an idealized statue of a tall, slim Jan Hus (in real life he was fat and thus, according to Julia Nedochodilova's theory, a virtuous priest). Hus was burned to death at the beginning of the fifteenth century for preaching against the outrages committed by the ruling party of his day. Now Prague's Old Town Square had become one large rally of the faithful, and the overwhelming symptoms of green youth held sway: blindness to what was good in the social system cobbled together by their fathers and mothers, and absolute clarity about everything false in it. The sun was shining but the square was partly overshadowed by the twin spires of the Tyn Church. From the gallery of those spires Master Kampanus, a Protestant theologian of the time, had once looked down while the Czech noblemen who had fought to prevent the Hapsburg armies from giving "fraternal assistance" were beheaded for high treason. The square was as bright as a rag carpet, filled with long-haired young men in motley shirts and unbelievably beautiful young women in colourful miniskirts. Some had guitars with them, and in the intervals between speeches, songs were sung — as expressionistic as the statue of the martyred reformer, and full of high-pitched rock and roll descant:

> It was written there
> On a looking-glass,
> A curious message:
> WAR IS AN ASS!

I saw a man leaning against a column in front of the Tyn Church who was not noticeably filled with enthusiasm by the song. I was hardly surprised. He was the husband — the former husband, rather — of Laura Fischerova-Widemanova, and the man who, during the Cuban missile crisis six years before, had instructed Slavek Machal and me about the wise measures taken by the Central Committee to ensure its own survival in the event of nuclear war, and about the children stockpiled in Bulgaria to ensure the future of the nation — though while the proportions of the group, one boy for each girl, conformed to Christian morality, they were certainly not scientifically sound. Now he was observing "Hyde Park" in a summer suit of imported seersucker, and he was armed with a Leica.

> I stood and stared
> At the same looking-glass,
> And the same strange slogan:
> WAR IS AN ASS!

sang the hippie leader at the base of the statue. Beside him was a young man who looked like Christ, except for a flashy Aztec headband.

But the hippies were only a small, exotic island in that enormous sea of people, who must have numbered over ten thousand. The majority were tidy long-haired university students and comely coeds, and for perhaps the first time in their lives they were collectively animated by politics instead of rock and roll. This generation had come into the world at a time when the class enemy had already fled the country — or, having been caught in the attempt, was mining uranium for the Soviet "peace bomb". From their pre-school days on they had been conditioned by socialism and yet, with the unerring instinct of their light-hearted age, they simply eliminated from their socialism everything they didn't like, especially the Communist Party. Now, silent and attentive, they listened to the Jewish messiah, who was shouting into a bullhorn.

"When we raise the question of free speech, they tell us we don't need an opposition party. They tell us public opinion can be expressed through the mass organizations, they tell us mass organizations already work as an opposition. But this notion is based on the faith — and faith is all it is — that the government will *voluntarily* take suitable actions in response to public criticism. Democracy is not based on faith, it is based on *guarantees*. And if the most important condition of democracy is an open, public debate between different points of view, then the foundation of democracy is something else: a public and legal contest for power. If, instead of legalizing the contest for power, the government merely allows the debate between conflicting points of view, this opens the door to all kinds of undemocratic forms of politics. And it is just as big an illusion to believe that those who hold a monopoly on power can ever be a guarantee of democracy. I'm referring, of course, to the only political party that actually exists — the Communist Party of Czechoslovakia!"

Applause started up in different spots around the square and quickly spread until the whole crowd was clapping and cheering wildly. Unlike the automatic and obligatory applause that for so many years and at so many meetings had always followed any mention of the Communist Party, this applause was not for the Party but for what the young man had said. I glanced at the man with the Leica. He was not pleased, but the shadow of a sardonic smile had appeared on his face. The youth with the Christ-like beard took a swig from a bottle of cola handed to him by a fellow clutching a flag in his other hand, and then put the bullhorn to his mouth again:

"Yes, democratizing the Party, if that's all these reforms amount to, is one big illusion — if it's not something worse. One of the bitter experiences of all revolutions is that if the group that seizes absolute power does not move quickly to establish some external means of control over that power, then sooner or later the group loses all self-control as well, and begins to degenerate. Every pressure for self-control inside the ruling group, every drive to improve the quality of the leadership, inevitably dies if it is not sustained by pressure from outside. Instead of permanently regenerating itself, the leading group's development is arrested, it becomes fossilized and more and more alienated from reality. When the situation finally becomes unbearable and untenable, the first random shock can lead to a general explosion — and then we have bloody palace revolutions, back-room conspiracies, murderous political trials and suicides."

This was too much for the man with the Leica. He turned away and, as if repulsed by the new roar of approval from the crowd, quickly retreated through the mob of people under the arcade seeking shelter from the sun.

I saw him duck into a Gothic taproom a short distance away and I followed him inside. The place reeked of the usual mixture of smoke and nicotine, and the usual buxom waitresses were rushing about bearing trays loaded with half-litre mugs of beer. There was another kind of "Hyde Park" going on here. Unlike the huge assembly outside, this crowd was limited by the dimensions of the beer hall, and in place of the idealistic rationalism of the young man with the bullhorn, there were other mental processes at work. Barta headed for the sole unoccupied table, which stood by the wall. It could seat only two people, and so the convivially minded beer drinkers had avoided it. I noticed that Hertl, the head stagehand at the National Theatre, was holding forth at one of the big tables. He was an Old Testament opponent of Bolshevism, and the father of the dangerous Lida, who had given me more than one sleepless night — and not just because of her sex appeal. When I tried to slip by him unnoticed, his beery eyes registered my presence and he raised his glass.

"Danny, my boy! Long live Thomas Garrigue Masaryk! Cheers!"

"Cheers!" I said, ignoring the provocative invocation of the founding father of the republic, and slipped quietly into the chair opposite Barta.

Barta looked at me with his fishlike eyes. "It's probably more obvious to me than to a lot of others that some of our policies have got to change. But if we go about it so demagogically," and he nodded his head towards the window looking out on the square, where the bullhorn was still roaring, "there's a real danger we'll toss the baby out with the bathwater."

"You're right," I said. "It produces something like mass hypnosis; that's already happened here once, and it did more harm than good."

A hint of suspicion, which I'd managed to disarm earlier by pretending to share his misgivings, reappeared in his fishlike eyes. The head stagehand, drunk as much from the unexpected feeling of immunity that now prevailed as from the Pilsners he'd consumed, shouted for what was probably the fifth time, at the top of his lungs, "I say send all the Commie swine to the gallows!" A nerve began to twitch in the corner of Barta's eye, and I hurried to allay his suspicions. All I wanted was to learn more about what he thought, because his opinions interested me.

"Take President Novotny, for instance," I proposed. "Of course, he made all kinds of mistakes. But I didn't like the way he was swept out by psychological pressure."

A non-Communist speaking well of Novotny must have seemed to Barta as improbable as sheep grazing among a pack of wolves. Again he vetted me with his eyes. But he saw what he supposed was the real basis for my fears, and concluded that I was one of the far-sighted ones who were trying to get on the good side of people like him, just in case.

"Yes, Novotny did make mistakes, we must have no illusions about that," he said sternly. "But we have to give him credit for one thing: he always defended — I'm not saying he was always very clever at it — but he always defended some of the essential principles. And you can't just abandon those principles and expect to get away with it. If he'd been able to hang on, if Dubcek hadn't pushed him out, things might not have gone this far." And again he nodded towards the window.

As his fishlike eyes tried to see into my soul, something occurred to me — a small detail. Barta had not admitted that the former president had made mistakes until the young man with the bullhorn had begun pointing them out.

About an hour earlier, at the Writers' Union Club, I'd seen the old prose writer Marie Burdychova stretched on the rack of psychological terror. There, in the meeting room of the club, people were also settling their accounts with the past, except that the most popular drink was wine rather than beer, and the account-settlers were armed not with atavistic memories of our founding fathers but with hard documentary evidence.

Marie Burdychova was not originally on the program; she crawled onto the rack by herself. Once she had been a decent enough writer, but twin misfortunes befell her. First, Party literary scholars chose to lavish bombastic solicitudes upon her until she lost all sense of herself; then, as honorary chairwoman of many Youth Union congresses she managed to arouse in young people an invincible aversion to reading her books. By 1968 she could no longer bear her terrible isolation, and she complained to Jan Vohnout, who at the time was still editor-in-chief of the publishing house run by the Writers' Union. Vohnout described his conversation with this laureate of three state prizes (each awarded under a different regime, while the theme of her writing remained unchanged: the sanctity of manual labour) in a reproachfully sentimental essay aimed at young writers: "Here she is, a lonely old writer," he wrote, "longing for the company of young talent! But it would seem that young writers have no idea where she is, although she lives in the very heart of the capital city." One of those talented young authors, a pugnacious poet called Vostrak, published a polemical response in a monthly which, at the time, was already in the hands of the group around Hejl, the world-famous playwright. In his reply, Vostrak inconsiderately mentioned a fact that the widow, in the pain of her isolation, had forgotten: "In 1952," he wrote, "when the Communist Party was preparing for the judicial murder of eleven of its leading functionaries — including the First Secretary, Rudolf Slansky — Marie Burdychova published an article in which she personally demanded the 'highest punishment' for the entire 'centre of conspiracy'." Vostrak put all those Marxist-Leninist phrases in quotation marks, and continued: "Marie Burdychova should therefore not be surprised if young people avoid her today. All our young authors — at least, I know of no exceptions — fully support the demand made by the Club of Non-Party Writers for the abolition of the death penalty, which has already happened in a number of capitalist countries. Marie Burdychova is a writer and therefore represents a profession whose practitioners in the past have almost without exception been spokesmen for humanism and frequently — and I mention only the case of Emile Zola — have actively defended victims of arbitrary justice. It is difficult, therefore, for young writers to understand how Marie Burdychova could have publicly demanded someone's death. Her horrifyingly sadistic article will always stand between her and young writers. And it will be a difficult barrier to remove."

The Party authoress was crushed by such frankness. In the past this kind of treatment had been reserved for people outside the Party and other victims of the class struggle, and to apply the same rhetoric to a state prize winner was something akin to blasphemy. So, supporting herself on two crutches, she hobbled into the meeting, where a whole list of tantalizing executions (though not hers) were on the agenda, and stuck her own neck into the noose. Now she stood sobbing on the podium, with no visible response from the audience — which consisted of several trembling writers waiting to be pilloried themselves; the leading Party literary lights who had changed course in time or had been overcome by bad conscience, and were therefore proof against sentimentality; and a flock of Vostrak's peers who came armed with the kind of pitiless anti-sentimentalism the leading Party lights had been applying for years to the victims of Party campaigns, so that they now felt coldly aloof when some of those leading Party lights happened to fall victim to their own machinations. In addition, there were many victims of Party campaigns present who were boiling with not only moral outrage but a sense (generally justified) of personal grievance.

Faced with such a gathering, Burdychova tried vainly to explain how it was that she who had written so sensitively about the lives of young girls in barren mountain villages could have longed to see eleven men hanged by the neck until dead, especially when some of them had been personal friends of hers. She finished speaking and dabbed her eyes with a damp handkerchief. One of the long-haired men by the wall stood up to speak; it was Brebera, a concrete poet, and, predictably, he asked an unfeeling question: "All right, but could you please explain how you could write such immoral crap in the first place?"

"Comrades!" pleaded the prose writer — and, noticing the frowns that appeared, corrected herself rather unhappily: "Friends! I'll tell you quite frankly how it happened. Perhaps I'll have to say something I shouldn't, but to tell the truth, comrades," and because she was edging towards hysteria she no longer bothered to correct herself, "I just don't care any more. I'm at the end of my tether and I'm going to tell you exactly how it was."

This promising beginning was not followed by any sensational revelations, however. It merely came out that at the time when the Party was preparing for one of its series of judicial murders (as Vostrak called them), Burdychova had just returned from two years as the Czechoslovak attaché in Moscow. Soon after that, she published a book about her time there — which, as it turned out, was also her last book. The work was a standard account presenting the Soviet Union as a heaven on earth, the kind of thing that more cunning authors turned out by plagiarizing existing books, and that gullible Western enthusiasts wrote after being given the standard Potemkin tour of factories and collective farms. Burdychova, as it turned out, belonged to the latter group, for she said, "I came back still enchanted by the Soviet Union, somehow. After all, comrades, it was a country we had looked to all our lives with love! And I was scarcely in the door when the Comrade Minister Kopecky came to me, and you know, comrades, I'd always liked him, he was such a cheerful man, and he said, 'Marie, the Party needs you to do something. We've just discovered a terrible thing and we're all extremely upset about it. Marie, Rudla Slansky was a spy!' Comrades, you can believe me or not, but I felt as though I'd been struck by lightning!"

She put her handkerchief to her eyes again, and as she wiped them a pinkish trickle of water ran down her chin. The handkerchief was a cheap one and the colour in it bled.

In the first row, close to the platform, sat the hard-of-hearing translator Josef Stipek, a one-time anarchist and a long-term member of the Party; in some confusion he held up his transistorized hearing-aid first to Burdychova, then to the loudspeaker. He had once confided in me, before the Prague Spring but after the old political show trials had begun to smell to high heaven, about a meeting he'd had with the jovial Minister of Propaganda, Kopecky. At the time the minister looked pale and shaken, and when Stipek joked that it must have been a good party the night before, Kopecky replied, "Like hell it was a party, Joe. Everything's all right now; Comrade Stalin's decided that that kike Rudla is the one to go down the chute. But I'm telling you, Joe, Klem Gottwald and I were *that far* from being dumped ourselves!"

It was highly improbable that Stipek had made this story up. He was a windbag, but he was also a translator; he had no narrative fantasy of his own.

Meanwhile the authoress was continuing her tale. "'Marie,' said Comrade Kopecky, 'the long and short of it is, we need you to write an article. People respect you, they like your books, and you've got to help the Party out in this difficult crisis!' And so, comrades, I wrote the article!" Burdychova's voice broke and she moaned into her now streaky handkerchief. "Comrades, I couldn't sleep! Rudla Slansky! Everything in me said, don't believe it! But Comrade Kopecky said it was true, and after all, comrades, he was a member of the Central Committee! Comrades, how could I not believe him?"

She looked around desperately, but her faith in authority failed to move the steely hearts of the literary avant-garde. The concrete poet Brebera stood up again and said, "That's not the point. It's entirely possible that you did believe it. But how could you, as a woman and a writer, demand someone's *execution*?"

"I didn't demand it!" Burdychova was almost shouting now. Then she backtracked. "That is — not in the first version. But then — " and before everyone's eyes she began to shrink — "Comrade Kopecky brought the article back to me and said, 'Look, Marie, I know this is hard for you. You were fond of Rudla and so was I. But it's not wise to write — as you did here, for example — "The heart does not want to believe that someone who has done *so much good* for the Party and for working people" and so on. The thing is, it's turning out that Rudla Slansky was a spy *right from the start,* that he was *already* a spy when he joined the Party. Naturally this throws an entirely different light on his activities. So I hope you won't mind rewriting this. The Party has to mete out exemplary punishment to the entire band, and it needs comrades like you, whom the people down below love and respect, to give it their full support. Do you understand what I'm saying?'"

According to Burdychova, she proceeded to display the energy and industry of the young Hemingway in the subsequent revisions of her article. In the course of seven visits from various friendly and highly placed comrades, she rewrote the piece twenty-two times. They finally accepted it because it had to go to press, although an editor rewrote it once more, while it was being typeset. So now Burdychova could claim that the bloodthirsty result was only partially her doing.

I've never been an artist and so, unlike the young poets present, I found the old woman's story almost moving. She was sitting on a chair in front of the microphone, on the edge of hysteria; a hairclasp had come undone and a strand of grey hair dangled over a wild eye. Although one of her crutches had fallen to the ground, she managed to stand up suddenly and shout:

"And from that time on, comrades, from that time on I have not been able to write a single line! Not a single line! I was completely broken. And then I learned that it was all a lie, comrades. A lie! Even though Comrade Gottwald himself claimed it was true! And they had to take me to the sanatorium. Not a line, comrades — for sixteen years! I can't write any more!"

She reached for her crutches but couldn't find them, and two secretaries from the translators' section took pity on her, caught her under the arms, and led her from the hall. Prochazka, the vice-chairman of the Writers' Union, came up to the microphone and said that Comrade, or rather Mr., Kocour had asked to speak next. Burdychova and her tragic fate were quickly forgotten. In the twenty years since 1948, we had all got used to tragic fates.

"Yes, the case of Dr. Divis may be more complicated," said Barta. "It seems he did employ methods that can scarcely be approved. Of course," he said meditatively, picking up his untouched glass of beer, "we mustn't forget that this was at a time when foreign agents were actually murdering Communists."

He was obviously referring to the isolated but oft-cited case of the two sons of an anti-Fascist fighter executed by the Nazis; the sons escaped abroad, went over to the Yanks, and then, outfitted with the latest sophisticated technology, came home to carry on their father's crusade for democracy, cowboy style.

"It was class warfare, after all. And Lenin once wrote that terror can't just be threatened; it has to be actually carried out or its effects will rapidly diminish. With Communists being shot at, the Party had to resort to methods that were sometimes excessively harsh."

I looked at Barta as I would at an odd but not uncommon freak of nature. Which came first, the chicken or the egg? But the double standard he was still using, even now, obviously didn't bother him. He even sounded a little more human. He took a sip of his stale beer and explained, "All I'm trying to say is that in the case of Dr. Divis we can't rule out the psychology of the time. And his age — he was a young man in the fifties, and clearly somewhat blinded by enthusiasm. And no one," he said with great emphasis, "has *any* right to present him to the public as a common criminal. You know yourself that these things were not quite so simple." He looked into my eyes. "It was the way they wrote about Divis that finally drove him to suicide. You must have read that statement his wife made?"

Of course I had. The woman's tone had been reminiscent of Marie Burdychova's lament. The wife (his third) had described how journalists from the newly liberated press had badgered her husband to say publicly whether it was true that once, as a prison doctor, he had refused an injection to a prisoner suffering from a gall-bladder attack until the man confessed to high treason — or maybe it was espionage. The man finally confessed and was given his injection, but the inflammation in his gall-bladder had progressed so far that he had to have it removed. They didn't hang him, however, until he'd completely recovered.

Instead of giving a statement to the press, Dr. Divis hanged himself in his bathroom.

So Lenin had apparently been right: a practical application of theoretical terror could induce so much fear, at least in weaker people, that they were afraid to go on existing. When I'd gone to the Writers' Union Club that afternoon, sitting right by the door had been a victim of the fear which had been aroused twenty years earlier but still persisted — the gifted non-Party novelist Nabal. The prevailing terror had driven him to such heights of virtuosity that although his novels depicted contemporary reality with detailed exactitude, the Party had vanished without a trace: he couldn't say anything good about it, and didn't have the courage to say anything bad. When I came into the foyer, he was at a table by the corner, perspiring over a sheet of paper. The moment he saw me, he jumped up and came rushing over.

"Did you get one of these too?" He stuck the sheet of paper under my nose. It was an application to join the Club of Non-Party Writers. The world-famous playwright had recently formed the club, probably as a core for his future opposition party.

"Yes," I said.

"Do you think we should join?"

I shrugged my shoulders. I put on the mask of the saxophone player at the Embassy Bar, and it hid the turmoil in my stomach. "Hard to say. It all depends on how things turn out."

"But what do *you* think?"

Again I shrugged my shoulders and lied. I knew how it would turn out. I'd had a traumatic revelation, during the war, of the lengths to which Communists would go, and it had equipped me with an absolute lack of faith in any permanent victory over Communism. But to the terrified Nabal I said, "I'm on pretty uncertain ground over this one. Usually I have a good nose for these things, but now I really don't know. I'm sorry, my friend, but I just don't know."

And I walked off towards the hall. The novelist stood there with an agonized expression on his face, and looking back over my shoulder I saw him sit down at the little round table again and take out his pen. He unscrewed the top, brought it close to the paper, and held it uncertainly in the air. Then he set it down beside the form and put his head in his hands.

As I was going through the door into the hall, Pinkava, a member of the Central Committee of the Party, bumped into me. What he told me did nothing to improve the condition of my stomach.

"Danny, hi!" he said jubilantly. "Listen, I was at Ludva's place yesterday and he told me you're going to join the executive committee of his society."

My legs began to tremble. "I haven't made up my mind yet," I said evasively.

Once upon a time Ludva had been famous, but then he'd got locked up for a long stretch and people had forgotten about him. Now he was just an ambitious pop-song writer, and he'd had some hits that I'd written the lyrics for. He was upset when someone beat him to forming the Club of Committed Non-Communists, but then he got an idea. Drawing ideologically on the United Nations' Universal Declaration of Human Rights, he founded a society in support of the document.

"I haven't decided," I repeated. "Do you think it's worth doing?"

"Ludva reckons that later on it might be turned into an opposition party."

I couldn't believe my ears. A second opposition party! I must have looked at Pinkava in some astonishment. He'd been a favourite of Novotny, the former president, and had toadied to him for many years, gaining a number of posts and rubbing shoulders with the powerful. I wasn't at all sure what he was up to now.

"Isn't that a bit foolish?" I said. "An opposition party?"

"Why?" said this member of the Central Committee of the Communist Party. "It seems to me like an interesting idea, basing it ideologically on the United Nations— "

Again—and this time with utter certainty—I knew that after twenty years we were plunging headlong into another disaster.

5.

Gellen constructed a new funeral pyre on the crumbling corpse of the burned martyr. I was standing by the window; the moon had just come out and the pastoral valley shimmered with a million dewdrops. In that valley Hronov stood darkly against the sky, like a town in a medieval painting.

"And then the third one, Dr. Divis," said Gellen behind me. "His contribution to the revolution was to pull out good teeth and leave the bad ones in till they became abscessed. For some inexplicable reason he chose the noose instead of taking an overdose of sedatives, as you might expect a doctor to do. Perhaps someone helped him make up his mind, too."

I turned around. He was sitting in his leopard-skin chair again.

"Look, don't you think—just to be completely fair about this—that someone may have *ordered* him to pull out those good teeth and leave the bad?"

My friend grinned. "They were given general directives, of course. But the teeth were his own personal contribution to the art. In the end, though, the method was never actually approved, and the Party had him transferred out of Pankrac prison sometime around '55. Then he worked as the district stomatologist in Prague 8." He thought for a moment, swirling the amber drink in his round glass. "Sometimes the Party reminds me of Maria Theresa," he said finally.

I looked at him in astonishment. "But she was loved by her subjects."

"How can you know that? Were you there? Did you put your finger into their gaping wounds?"

I admitted that I hadn't.

"But that's not what I meant," said Gellen. "There are all kinds of parallels, however—some of them less obvious. For example: before Maria Theresa, torture in the Austro-Hungarian Empire was carried out on a 'do-the-best-you-can' basis, and of course there were excesses. So the empress banned private innovations and had a law of torture drawn up. This included a list of permissible means of torture, as well as the appropriate instruments, and a detailed and binding set of instructions on how they were to be used. That, my friend, was progress. No more kicking prisoners in the nuts or sliding red-hot needles under their fingernails.

From that time on, throughout the realm, they were only allowed to stretch prisoners on the rack, break them on the wheel, and draw and quarter them. And that last measure could only be taken after the prisoner had been executed with the sword or the rope."

Again he swirled the liquid in his glass, then took a drink — he drank quite a lot, but in that he was no different from most other people. He went on in a somewhat dreamy tone of voice. "Once, I performed an appendectomy on a secret policeman. They brought him in at the last minute. He was petrified of having an operation, and if I'd got him on the table an hour later it would have been too late. The nurses told him this afterwards and he couldn't thank me enough — for saving his precious life for him, and for the revolution, of course. So we became buddies, so to speak, and believe it or not, this undercover cop loved complaining about the system just like everyone else."

He paused, as if expecting me to question this unlikely story. But like him, I belonged to a generation that knew only too well that absolutely everything was possible — even the impossible.

"What he complained about most was the bureaucracy. He came to me once, more upset than usual, and said, 'Dr. Gellen! It's terrible. The boss used to be able to approve all torture, but now we've got to go all the way up to the Minister of the Interior for permission. Do you know how long it takes for those goddamn pen-pushers to give us the okay? By the time they get back to us, all the excitement's gone!"

"You must be kidding," I said to Gellen, *pro forma*.

"I thought I was hearing things too. But don't forget, that was twenty years ago — during the fifties. Why are you surprised to hear about it now?"

"I'm not surprised they tortured people, just that they had instructions — "

"Mind you, they had no instructions as to what methods to use. In that sense they were far behind Maria Theresa. But — " Gellen stopped, then said, "Listen, when you were in the West you must have had some contacts with the Communists there, just for appearances' sake. They have that reprehensible skepticism regarding the crimes of our Party. But you have lived here all these years. . . ."

"You're right," I said. "Just because I was lucky, I tend not to believe those who weren't."

Gellen laughed and refilled our glasses. "That cop," he added, "was so pissed off that in the end he quit his job and became district secretary of the Union of Czech-Soviet Friendship in Pelhrimov."

"I guess he got rapped over the knuckles for his improvements."

"Not at all. He wasn't a sadist like Dr. Divis, he was just a faithful employee of the security services. He tortured only in approved cases. Once," said Gellen, laughing as though the memory were a pleasant one, "I went to operate on someone in Troubel, where he'd just been transferred; there was a brand-new prison there. He invited me in for a game of badminton and I accepted. When we were walking down a long corridor to the officers' gymnasium, I noticed that along one side there was a line of doorways with no doors in them, and that each one led to a small bathroom with a bathtub." Gellen dipped his lips in the whisky and then stroked his moustache. "'Well,' I said, 'I see the prisoners' hygienic needs are well looked after. But why didn't you install showers instead? It's more economical and it's healthier too.' My friend just waved his hands and said, 'Come on, Dr. Gellen, these are torture chambers. We had the architect include them in the plans, since they were building the whole place from scratch anyway. The bathtubs are for holding people under water. "Swallowing angels" — you know the expression? It's kind of a technical term. The method's very effective. Right — but almost before they finish putting in the tiles we get a stop-torture order! Only in exceptional cases, and even then you need about a hundred and fifty signatures to make it legal. Who wants that? So now all the tubs are good for is keeping Christmas carp alive for the whole garrison!' At the time he thought it was a pretty good joke, but the decommissioning of those rationally planned torture chambers was what finally finished him off. A month later he was district secretary of the Friendship Union."

6.

In the farthest corner of the hall I sat down at the table occupied by non-Party writers, where the energetic author of socio-critical novels Sarka Pechlatova was arguing with the science-fiction writer Paternoster. They had broken off their debate while Burdychova was speaking, and now they were at it again. At the second-farthest table, occupied by a group of men and women who were rightly suspected of harbouring sympathy for Novotny and his deposed regime of personal power, a deathly silence reigned. The surrealist and perennial avant-gardist Kocour was just making his way to the microphone, armed with a dangerous-looking file sprouting bits of yellowing newspaper clippings. At the table where the faithful Marxist-Leninists were sitting, Kocour's long-time acquaintance and sometime friend Vohnout watched darkly, his face a burning red. Sarka Pechlatova could be heard assailing Paternoster in a stage whisper that carried across the hall: "Why not, you old fool? Now's the time to smash them in the face! Knock them cold, you lily-livered pansy!"

To which the cautious delegate to so many international congresses on utopian literature asked her, under his breath, to get a grip on herself because her adrenalin level was getting dangerously high.

Kocour peered at the audience over the top of his glasses to check the level of attention. The room was tense. Someone opened the door and squeezed in among those who were standing, and through the opening I caught a glimpse of Nabal, still vainly awaiting the advent of courage. Again he withdrew his pen from the paper, and anxiously asked a question of Bozena Pokorna, the six-foot-tall translator of Russian classics. Approaching him from the left was the world-famous playwright, on his way back from the bathroom.

The door closed again and the loudspeakers crackled as Kocour sorted through his papers.

"Ladies and gentlemen," he said, and then got right to the point. "Five months have gone by since January, since the process of renewal began, but Comrade Jan Vohnout is still a member of our union. In fact, he's sitting here with us today. And because instructions to purge all social organizations of unworthy individuals have come down from the highest places, allow me to take a closer look at this comrade."

I looked at Vohnout. He appeared to have turned a shade darker. "Comrade Vohnout," Kocour went on, speaking too loudly into the microphone so that his amplified voice thundered and shook the hall, "is a member of the Party, and of all the principles of Marxism-Leninism the one most in evidence in his past activity is the law of evolution as a struggle of contradictions. Comrade Vohnout entered our literary life, or perhaps it's better to say our public life, in 1936 with this text."

Kocour paused to leaf very slowly through his file of yellowed bits of paper. He deliberately drew out the manoeuvre, and the audience, expecting great revelations, silently inhaled the smoke of many cigarettes. Finally Kocour extracted a clipping that had turned almost orange with age, carefully glued to a piece of cardboard. He adjusted his spectacles and began to read in a tone of high pathos:

> The basis of our nation, its very flesh and blood, has always been and will always be the peasant. The Czech farmer, tilling the family soil by the sweat of his brow, has no sympathy for the intrigues of the Benes-Masaryk clique entrenched in the lofty heights of the Castle, or for the treacherous plots of the agents of Moscow operating under the cloak of the Communist Party. At key moments in our national destiny, the Czech peasant has always supported politicians like the chairman of the Agrarian Conservative Party, Josef Beran, who unyieldingly. . . .

The audience was rapt, and many forgot to smoke while Chesterfields smouldered forgotten in hands and ashtrays. The young writers, in their long hair and beards, may not have been sure precisely what the point was — the Agrarian Party, supported by large landholders, had vanished long before they came into the world — but the unflattering references to the Communist Party and also to Masaryk and Benes left them in no doubt that the text was highly inappropriate today from all points of view. An angry muttering came from their ranks and spread to the tables occupied by the middle generation. Only the table of Marxist-Leninists remained unruffled. Kocour finished reciting Vohnout's ancient appeal on behalf of Josef Beran and then said:

"In the final years of the bourgeois republic, then, Comrade Vohnout supported a movement based, in the terminology of the time, on blood and soil. After the Munich *Diktat*, however, he underwent a transformation."

He took another yellowed document from his file. This time it was a text that appealed, not to the agrarian roots of the nation, but to the holy traditions of the national saint, Wenceslas.

> At fateful moments in our nation's history, Saint Wenceslas has always held his hand out in blessing over this land and shown it the only true path: the path of light that leads to Christ, to Humility, to Peace, and to Mutual Understanding.

Kocour peered at the audience over his glasses and said, "The mutual understanding that Comrade Vohnout had in mind actually took place several months later. In March of 1939, to be precise, in the office of the Chancellor of the Reich. Shortly afterwards, Czechoslovakia was occupied by the Germans."

In talking off the cuff, Kocour lost his place in the prepared text, and he spent some time trying to find it again. I looked around and saw that the indignant group of radicals had settled down somewhat. There was scattered laughter at the piously religious pronouncement, but the large group that had been grumbling by the window was now as quiet as the Marxist-Leninists. Vixi's husband was sitting among them — so he too had made it into the Writers' Union. Someone opened the door again and I could see Nabal still sweating blood in the foyer. He was sitting at his little table, his tie loose, distractedly trying to follow an argument that had broken out between Bozena Pokorna and the world-famous playwright.

"In 1942," a voice thundered from the loudspeakers, for Kocour had found his place, "at the height of the Nazi occupation, Comrade Vohnout offered *this* to the Pavel Publishing House, where I was working as an editor." Kocour held high in his hand, for everyone to see, a sheaf of bound pages. They too were yellowed, but they were not newspaper clippings, but a manuscript.

"This is a book of selected short stories translated into Czech from the Imperial German original by Comrade Vohnout. He chose the author himself and translated the work on spec, without a contract, purely because — he said — he was fond of this writer's work. The author whose work Comrade Vohnout chose to translate — and this, remember, was the same year Heydrich was assassinated — also happened to be the chairman of the *Reichskammer der Kultur*, or the Imperial Chamber of Art. And this same author was awarded numerous literary prizes by the National Socialist Workers' Party of Germany. His name was — Hanns Johst."

The bomb exploded. Kocour had got himself a sensational scoop. To translate the work of a man whose most lasting contribution to the arts was the dictum about going for one's gun whenever the word "culture" was mentioned. . . . Vohnout — who had obviously never dreamed that anyone would go to the trouble of digging an unpublished manuscript out of the forgotten archives of a defunct private publishing house — grew another shade darker, while an excited murmuring spread from the young bearded writers to the older generation. Again, the Catholics joined them; only the faithful Leninists were maintaining their silence now.

"Pavel," said Kocour, raising his voice above the rising storm in the room, "the *bourgeois* publisher Pavel, tried to explain to *Comrade* Vohnout why he was reluctant to publish his translation. But *Comrade* Vohnout refused to listen to the *bourgeois* publisher Pavel's arguments and stressed the national and socialist character of Johst's work. Finally he threatened to complain to the *Reich* authorities. So the bourgeois publisher Pavel relented and accepted the work for publication, but he kept delaying the typesetting on various pretexts until finally Vohnout lost interest and asked for his manuscript back so that he could 'rework' it — by now it was the fall of 1944 and the tide was turning. But before the work could be sent to him the Gestapo arrested the *bourgeois* publisher Pavel, because it appeared that he had published, under the pen name Jan Jeremiah, a collection of poems called *Elegies* that had in fact been written by the Jewish poet Jiri Pick. After six months in custody, the bourgeois publisher Pavel died in the concentration camp at Buchenwald. Comrade Vohnout," and by now Kocour had dropped his mask of objectivity and was speaking with open sarcasm and hatred, "did not dare come right out and ask for the manuscript back for 'revisions' from *Treuhänder* Seep Dürenheld, whom the Gestapo had appointed to run Pavel's publishing house. In the end, however, the manuscript wasn't published anyway, because with the war on there was a shortage of paper."

I looked around at the man who had survived all these ups and downs with his skin intact. He appeared to be on the brink of a heart attack. The Marxist-Leninists were still sitting proudly and loyally by his side, but someone in the audience whistled provocatively. I wondered if I was witnessing the last moments of another victim of white terror.

"After our liberation by the Red Army in 1945," the thundering voice went on, "some non-Communist writers moved that Comrade Vohnout be expelled from the newly created Syndicate of Czech Writers, which he had been among the first to join. The motion was not passed. Comrade Vohnout had also been one of the first to join the Communist Party after the liberation, and the Communist members of the syndicate unanimously supported his membership."

The whoops and bellows that followed this revelation sounded like a crowd at a rock concert. Someone who knew what he was doing threw an empty wine bottle at a portrait of the late Party poet laureate S. K. Neumann, and above the roaring of the assembly came the penetrating soprano voice of Sarka Pechlatova shouting, "Pfui!" Up to that point the story had merely seemed bizarre; now it had become a farce. But Kocour's facts were unassailable. He circulated Vohnout's yellowing translation of Hanns Johst's fiction and his manifesto in support of the Agrarian minister. Filled with the afflatus of dialectic, I imagined to myself how Comrade Barta would explain this example of inscrutable wisdom. For a moment the hubbub in the assembly hall faded and I could almost hear his subdued, expressionless voice going on like a talking fish: "We know Vohnout isn't a real Communist at all, but objectively we can absolutely rely on him because we have him in our grip. Subjective motivations don't interest us." I frowned, and mentally answered this phantom voice as though I were Dr. Gellen: "Certainly Comrade Vohnout was not one of those who led the Party to power; that was accomplished through the aggressive idealism of young radicals. But the Party, in its inscrutable wisdom, knows only too well that if aggressive idealism is allowed to carry over into the period of power, it could well lead the Party to a position of powerlessness once more. There is no danger of this from Comrade Vohnout."

Kocour's voice interrupted my imaginary dialogue and again the excited crowd fell silent. "But Comrade Vohnout," he roared, "had occasion to pay the Party back for its help and support, and he did so when the Party needed it most. In 1952 he published in the main Party organ, *Rude Pravo*, an article entitled 'We Demand a Just Punishment, The Highest Punishment!'"

A new, somewhat less yellowed clipping was now produced from the damning file, and Kocour read from it with relish. It was a somewhat impersonal (but at the time, adherence to stylistic models was mandatory) and only slightly more bloodthirsty variation on the heavily edited statement published by Marie Burdychova:

> This disgusting band of traitors, this filthy effluent from imperialist sewers, this phlegm from the lungs of the Party and the people, cannot properly be punished at all as they deserve. The death sentence is too good for them when we consider what a vast number of the most heinous crimes they committed, this rats' nest of international Zionism and cosmopolitanism. . . .

Hana Bojanova, an author of socialist-realist nature novels, had tears streaming down her cheeks. She pulled out her handkerchief and ran from the room, crushed. Even the stronghold of Marxist-Leninists is beginning to crumble, I thought. Once again, the open door afforded me a view of Nabal. So far, his situation remained unchanged.

"'These inhuman creatures'," Kocour quoted in a ceremonious voice, "'stopped at nothing in their inveterate hatred for socialism. Had it not been for the alertness and vigilance of Comrade Gottwald, and of comrades Kopecky, Bacilek, Zapotocky . . . ,'" and then followed a long list of other dignitaries who had not drawn the short straws, starting with the president's son-in-law and proceeding according to Party hierarchy. I looked at the hirsute faces of the experimental authors; they seemed to have been transformed into a fresco by Giotto, a crowd of people gazing with innocent eyes on the presence of a repulsive miracle. They listened in astonishment to this text, as though it were the distant cry of an awakened Godzilla, and in my mind I heard the voice of a lovely woman speaking from the depths of an unclean time — the voice of Gertrude Mendelova, who had the experience of two hells behind her and was still very much alive.

7.

"She carried on like a lunatic, Danny," I could hear Gerta say. "Screaming that she didn't even want to see Fischer, that she wouldn't talk to a traitor, that she'd as soon strangle him with her own hands as look at him. It was so awful that even the guard said, 'Comrade, maybe if you just said a kind word or two to your husband. I mean, they're hanging them tomorrow, comrade — Slansky and all the rest of them.' But that drove her into a frenzy, and she ranted on about how such a rotten, vile excuse for a man didn't deserve a kind word, that all she would say was how disgusting he was. And when they finally brought him in, she lit into him, Danny, she was shrieking at him, saying she was going to give their son another name so he wouldn't have to be ashamed of being conceived by a monster like him — it was awful, Danny, awfuller than you can imagine. We heard everything and so did all the condemned men. We were sitting in a row of little cubicles with a grille between us — and you can imagine how it affected the guys. In the end, Fischerova had a fit of hysterics and the guards had to drag her away by force, and the first thing Robert said to me after was that we should give our son Robert another name too, and that I'd be better off forgetting about him. He said the minister, Kopecky, had promised him nothing would happen to me, so I should forget him and start a new life. But Danny, I could never have done that!"

She was telling me all this in the Julis Café, where several years before I had dragged from Vixi her trifling but human secret. At the table next to us a textbook secret agent was rocking back on the hind legs of his chair, with his enormous ear leaning in our direction, and Gerta said, "Look at him, the weasel! Well, let him listen." And she told me a story that was also straight out of the textbooks, but nevertheless true. It was the story of how she and Robert had first met on the sorting ramp at Auschwitz, in front of Dr. Mengele, who would imperiously point his thumb to the steel of heaven or the slag-heap of earth. There, a textbook spark jumped between them, and because Dr. Mengele jerked his thumb towards heaven twice in a row, the spark smouldered in dangerous, out-of-the-way corners between the barracks, under the stars that winked at them intermittently through the black smoke from the Auschwitz chimneys. Gerta was pregnant when she returned from the concentration camp, and instead of having a big wedding in a synagogue the two joined the Party together, because of all the stars that had glowed above that village in Poland, the most realistic had been an unreal one, a red star with five points.

Gerta had been a pampered daughter of a well-to-do family, just as Laura Fischerova had been, but the war had made her an orphan. She had inherited a lingerie factory, but when she submitted her Party application to the secretariat she brought along a set of transfer papers drawn up by a lawyer turning the factory over to the Party. Her clever husband stood out in a Party ravaged by the Gestapo and diluted by the post-war tide of Vohnouts. From the generations of Jewish pedlars stretching from the crowded *stetlach* of Central Europe right back to the mythological times of the first Czech princes, he had inherited a talent for wheeling and dealing, which he put at the service of the revolution. Three months after the February Victory in 1948, he was sent to England on a trial run to negotiate a trade agreement between the new Communist state and the oldest capitalist empire in the world.

"Robert carried it off so brilliantly," Gerta said, "that Gottwald invited us to a private dinner at the castle. Just the two of us! Do you understand what that meant, Danny? Just Robert and Klem and Marta and I. Gottwald got drunk during the meal, but he was hammered all the time anyway, and by that time — and after the trials, especially — he practically never sobered up until they finally did him in, too," Gerta said, and the undercover cop's ear quivered, perhaps with pleasure. "That evening all he wanted to do was drink to Robert and his trade agreement with the English. Finally he fell on him, put his arms around his neck, dribbled wine down the front of his new suit, and said, 'Mendel, you old Jewish rascal, you suckered the Anglos so royally you deserve the Order of Lenin! Unfortunately I can't give it to you for a swindle like that, but don't worry, Bertie, I'll never forget you for it. I'm for ever in your debt!'" said Gerta. Four years later they hanged Robert, partly because, according to the prosecutor, the trade agreement he'd negotiated had damaged the economic interests of the People's Democratic Republic of Czechoslovakia. But Gottwald may well not have forgotten him. He drank himself to death six months later.

"Mind you, Gottwald wasn't the only one whose promise got reneged on back then," Gerta added. The cop, his ear already hypertrophically enlarged by frequent use, kept leaning farther and farther back in his chair. "For instance, you remember that rat Kopecky? And how he promised Robert nothing would happen to me? Well, you should have seen what happened! They were at our door before they'd taken Robert down from the scaffold. They came for his assets, they said; then they proceeded to walk off with everything except my lingerie — the only thing that obviously hadn't been Robert's — and some silk handkerchiefs that Aryan friends of ours had kept for my parents during the war, that were monogrammed with my maiden name. They threw Bobby and me out of our flat so fast I didn't even have time to close my suitcase properly. And then I collapsed so they took me off to Bulovka Hospital, but when the head physician made his evening rounds and discovered who I was, I was tossed out of there too, with a temperature of a hundred and three. If it hadn't been for Evzenia Mahlerova — she let Bobby and me stay in her tiny bachelor flat — it would have been the end of me at last."

8.

"Not very many years later, in 1959," Kocour thundered, "Comrade

Vohnout, who by that time was editor-in-chief of *Literarni Listy,* published in that journal the following literary essay." Kocour's supply of yellowed documents seemed inexhaustible. "'Pasternak,'" he declaimed, reading from the text, "'never revealed his inner self better than in the libellous, counter-revolutionary pamphlet *Doctor Zhivago.* This mystico-religious mishmash attempts to conceal the real meaning of the revolutionary changes in Russian society by describing them as just another bloody episode in the millennial tradition of Russian despotism. Small wonder that the gentlemen in Stockholm awarded Pasternak the Nobel Prize for his anti-Soviet pamphlet. In the eyes of the Soviet readership, however,'" and Kocour raised his eyes from the text to interpolate a comment. "Here, of course, the text is somewhat illogical, since to this day the novel *Doctor Zhivago* has not been published in the Soviet Union. Perhaps Comrade Vohnout was referring to readers of *samizdat.* But to continue: 'In the eyes of the Soviet readership, however, that prize, which Pasternak did not refuse, will be an unerasable symbol of shame!'

"Another three years went by," Kocour roared on, "and Comrade Vohnout, who by then was editor-in-chief of the monthly literary review *Ohen*, published several new pieces from his translation workshop. This time, however, it wasn't German he was translating from but Russian." From his sinister file Kocour pulled out a well-preserved copy of the magazine *Ohen.* "They were 'The Poems of Dr. Zhivago', from the novel *Doctor Zhivago* by Boris Pasternak," he said.

This new example of reality-turned-farce altered the mood in the hall. The concrete poet Brebera began to chuckle, and that started Vojtech Novotny laughing as well. Another empty bottle flew from the ranks of the bearded young writers, this time towards a portrait of Alois Jirasek, the ultra-reactionary Czech Walter Scott, who had been accepted into the Red Valhalla and made compulsory reading in schools because his lovely daughter was the mistress of the Communist Minister of Culture. The younger writers, educated exclusively in post-revolutionary schools, obviously considered Jirasek a Communist too.

I got up and left to go to the bathroom. In the foyer Nabal was still undecided, his pen drawn and ready but as yet unused. Over Nabal's shoulder, the world-class playwright was urging Bozena Pokorna to sign up with his Club of Non-Communist Writers.

"Organization is everything. We can't just go on opposing professional politicians like them with nothing but ideas!"

I stood there listening. Pinkava stopped beside me; he was just coming back from the place I was headed for, and was doing up his fly.

Pokorna studied the handsome, slightly plump young playwright with a distrust born of experience. She'd started studying Russian during the Nazi occupation out of a love for things Slavic. After the war she taught Russian in high school, but when the Communists took over she lost her job for being apolitical. During the next few years she worked in an iron foundry and in the evenings and on weekends she produced a stunning translation of Lermontov's *A Hero of Our Time*. Stipek published it under his own name, although he didn't even know the language. The whole thing was kept quiet. Stipek was given a Writers' Union prize for the translation, but he admitted the truth as soon as things began to thaw, thus making it possible for Bozena to change jobs once more. (He kept the prize money, though.) So at last Bozena could devote herself to her beloved work, and now she was gazing at the radical young playwright with radical mistrust.

"Everyone who's concerned about democracy simply *must* join," said Hejl. Unfortunately the terms he used were the ones she most mistrusted, because they'd been in common use ever since the fall of Nazism. Nabal's eyes darted anxiously from the playwright to Pokorna. There was now a large crowd gathered around the table, listening to the argument. A pot-bellied sweater worn by Central Committee member Pinkava stood out.

As I expected, Pinkava couldn't bear to listen passively for very long. "Mr. Hejl is right, Miss Pokorna," he interjected. "This is no time to be standing around on the sidelines."

Pokorna shook her head energetically and the playwright added quickly, "Today the only possible answer is yes or no. There's nothing in between."

A chair scraped against the floor; Nabal was trying to make a getaway. But Pinkava put a hand on his shoulder and he sank back into his seat again. Pokorna pushed her glasses up onto the bridge of her nose and saw the novelist's frightened expression, and the healthy skepticism within her triumphed.

"I'm sorry, but I will not sign it," she said, enunciating her words like a Czech teacher. "I'd rather not become entangled in politics."

With this historical if momentarily unpopular pronouncement, she turned and forced a passage through the crowd towards the exit.

9.

"Believe it or not, Danny," said Gerta, "I still get the shakes when I think about it; I guess my nerves are shot. Yesterday I got summoned to Party headquarters. Ten years later, Danny! I mean, I almost fainted. What could they want of me now? So I popped some downers and off I went. Well, they were awfully kind to me and took me in to see some spiffy-looking comrade in an office crammed with armchairs, and this comrade informed me that the Party had gone back over the trial of Slansky and Co. and had discovered that, in all points of the indictment, Robert was innocent, that he'd been wrongly sentenced and wrongly executed and they were going to rehabilitate him. And the spiffy comrade told me they knew nothing could take Robert's place but as a sign of good will, and to help me out financially, the Party was willing to offer me financial compensation, as much as I wanted. Within reason, he added quickly, in case I asked for a million. I was livid. I remembered Robert in that tiny cubicle on the other side of the grille the day before they hanged him, and I thought I was going to have an attack of hysterics right there and then, just like Fischerova. The filthy bastard! Within reason! For Robert? And like a fool I'd given them a whole factory worth at least ten million! But never mind. The downers must have saved me — I just told him to keep his money, but there was one thing he could do. When Robert was sentenced to death the verdict was printed on page one of all the newspapers, so now I wanted them to print the news of his rehabilitation in all the newspapers, again on page one. And now hang on to yourself, Danny; can you guess what Mr. Nice Guy said?"

"That you could demand as much compensation as you wanted, and never mind the 'within reason'?"

"Guess again," said Gerta. "He said, 'Comrade, you have to understand that the Party can't do that. Given the international situation and the situation at home, it might hurt the Party, and not even your husband would want that.' I was so outraged I wanted to slap his face and tell him that, thanks to the Party, my husband was dead so there was no way this jerk with his ass stuck in his armchair could know what he'd want. But before I could throw that at him, he leaned out of his armchair and, you won't believe this, he actually *whispered*," and for emphasis Gerta leaned towards me over the marble table and whispered too, while the undercover cop tilted backwards as far as he dared, "'In any case, comrade,'" Gerta whispered, "'it wouldn't make any sense to publish it, because word will get around anyway. In a month everyone will know he's been rehabilitated, even without publicity!'"

The undercover cop brought Gerta's tale to an end: the chair suddenly toppled over backwards and he clattered to the floor, striking the back of his head on the edge of a marble table on the way down. While the waiters hovered around trying to revive him, we quickly paid and left, in case he expired and they tried to pin the blame on us.

10.

Kocour left the podium and his place was taken by an apoplectic, profusely perspiring Vohnout. I wondered where he found the courage to mount the platform at all.

"Comrades," he wheezed. "This is a terrible shock. To have someone take my — my mistakes, which I admit I made, take them out of context and — and — attribute completely different intentions to them. It's demagogy. But I'm too upset now to respond coherently. All I can say in my own defence is that as far as Slansky is concerned, and you can believe me or not, I truly believed he was guilty, and in the case of Pasternak I hadn't read the novel and I took my information from Soviet sources, which I also believed — "

He never had a chance to explain the case of Hanns Johst, because the members of the young and skeptical generation were so disgusted by this monumental faith that they began stamping their feet on the floor, drowning out the loudspeakers. Vohnout turned around, looking for an escape route; his shirt-tail was hanging out behind. He bumped into a canvas screen at the back of the platform and stumbled out through a back door.

After the meeting I was sitting across the street in the Cloisters Wine Room with the science-fiction author Paternoster, Sarka Pechlatova, and two television producers. The producers looked tired and worn down. They'd brought along a cheaply reproduced leaflet which had been published, illegally but with impunity, by a group of "Old Communists" in Liben, a factory district of Prague. The author of the leaflet was someone called Herodas. The name seemed too embarrassingly symbolic and I asked the prettier of the two producers, a charming young woman in a miniskirt, "Don't you think this *nomen omen* is just a tasteless *nom de plume*? And isn't the whole leaflet a fraud, to discredit the conservatives?"

"Oh no!" said the prettier of the producers, Jana Hloubava. "That's his real name. He's an old idiot. He had a sinecure in the Ministry of Domestic Trade for fifteen years, and now they've put him out to pasture."

The leaflet was an apology for President Novotny, recently deposed. It consisted of a list of his merits, among the greatest of which was this: "It is to his credit that the Communist Party of Czechoslovakia never carried out a *full* rehabilitation of the criminals sentenced during the so-called trials." Then it went on about the present activities of those criminals who had survived the mass execution of justice and had merely been sent to prison for "deservedly" long sentences. In a style strongly reminiscent of the Aryan movement a few decades before, the pamphlet added to each name an additional surname. "Sik, a.k.a. Schonberg," it read, "hasn't a good word to say for the socialist method of economic planning, yet praises to the skies 'market relations', faithfully seconded by Hajek, a.k.a. Haisenberger, and Kladiva, a.k.a. Hammerstein. Even the writer Pinkava, a.k.a. Pfinkelstein, has added his two cents' worth."

"I had no idea Comrade Pinkava was of Jewish origin," I said. "I thought he was a Moravian farmer."

"He is," said Jana Hloubava. She took the leaflet from me with nicotine-stained fingers. I'd seen her somewhere before, but I couldn't remember where. She looked nervous; she'd stacked up a neat pyramid of half-smoked butts in the ashtray in front of her. "Pinkava's no Jew. But try telling that to Herodas. He believes in *The Protocols of the Elders of Zion*, too."

"Why don't you stick him in front of a TV camera?" Paternoster asked. "Let him air his views?"

"We invited him to do just that," said the producer. "Several times, in fact. But he doesn't want to. He says he's just a simple man and on television they'd turn a pack of rabid intellectuals loose on him and make him look ridiculous." Jana Hloubava crossed her legs, displaying her other equally charming thigh, and stubbed out three-quarters of an American cigarette. "You get nowhere with people like him."

"It's not worth it either," said Sarka Pechlatova. "The only thing they understand is a punch in the teeth. I'd lock them up. This kind of thing," and she pointed to the anti-Semitic pamphlet, "is probably illegal, if not anti-state. Look at Karel over there," and she turned her head to look at the prose-writer Zalud, who was sitting not far away, hunched over a glass of Veltlin wine, as quiet as a mouse. He had just managed to get a novel set in the uranium mines published and now it looked as if he was beginning to regret it. "They chucked him in the slammer for a negative review of *The Fall of Berlin* he wrote for a Czech socialist flyer shortly after February '48. So if nothing else, this thing here" — she again pointed to the pamphlet — "can easily be qualified as incitement to racial hatred."

"You're pure adrenalin today, my dear," said Paternoster.

"Adrenalin, my ass!" Sarka retorted. "You're just scared shitless!"

Paternoster shrugged his shoulders. Nabal entered the restaurant with a new copy of *Literarni Listy* under his arm, and his necktie askew. He looked like a convict on the run. Sarka waved at him. The gifted novelist slumped into a chair and ordered a slivovice.

"So, did you sign?" I asked.

"Sign what?" Sarka wanted to know.

Nabal nodded.

"Well, what, for Christ's sake?" Sarka pressed.

"My own death warrant," said Nabal. "How much can they give me for it? Not more than two years, I hope."

"What in hell's name did you sign?" roared Sarka.

"An application to join the Club of Non-Party Writers," said Nabal. Bobbing out of his chair, he added, "Maybe there's still time to take my name off!"

Sarka grabbed his arm. "Have you gone off your rocker? Every decent person has got to sign it! You signed it, didn't you, Honza?"

The science-fiction author turned his eyes to the ceiling in resignation. "I don't really give a good goddamn. I used to be a doctor. When worst comes to worst, I'll go back to treating the girls in the clap department."

"But what about me?" wailed Nabal. "I was a teacher. They'll never hire me back. Just look at this!" He spread the newspaper on the table and pointed to an article headlined "The Truth about the Case in Louny", which described some ordinary judicial murder. "The author of that will get about five years. And for this," and he put his finger on an exposé of police wire-tapping, "two, maybe three years. In a collective cell, in Pankrac. This," and the finger slid to a headline that read, "Has the CP Let Us Down?", "ten years, minimum. And for this one, 'The Need for an Opposition'," he said, reading aloud the headline of an article by the world-famous playwright, "taking his other activities into account, he's obviously going down for life. That is, if they don't just hang him."

"Jesus, you really paint a black picture, don't you?" grumbled Sarka. "Look, everything's fine! The Russians wouldn't dare. They'd be in deep shit with the rest of the world if they did."

"It's us who'll be in deep shit," said the gifted novelist. "Just local, home-grown shit, but — " and suddenly he got to his feet. Evading Sarka's bright nails, he shouted, "I'm going to take my name off that list!" he ran out of the wine room.

The producer in the miniskirt laughed uneasily.

Where in hell had I seen her before?

Once more we stood under the baroque arcade on the edge of the square, several sheets to the wind. At least, I was; not Barta. The sun was slipping behind the Old Town Hall, but the youthful crowd in the square seemed to be swelling, reinforced by young factory apprentices who had punched out for the day. Maybe it was the alcohol, which was making me horny as usual, or maybe it was another of those overblown, embarrassing symbols of history, like the Virgin Mary under Mare's Head Hill shining white at the beginning and the end of it all, but to me the reform movement seemed to be swarming with pretty young girls, in numbers vastly disproportionate to their actual percentage in the population. I looked over those delectable fruits of my generation's love-making and remembered another movement, twenty years before, that had swarmed with overweight girls in blue shirts. Both my impressions were no doubt superficial, the one tilted by alcohol and the other by an antipathy that had only increased over twenty years. But these graceful young women reminded me of something else, too: a quotation from an author who had once got Vojtech Novotny expelled from paradise, and whom I, despite his unbelievable faith, worshipped as fervently as Vojtech did his saint. "I daresay you are wondering how Maria and me could make a beautiful girl like that one. That's an illusion people have about beauty. Beauty doesn't come from beauty. All that beauty can produce is prettiness. . . . Beauty diminishes all the time, it's the law of diminishing returns, and only when you get back to zero, to the real ugly base of things, there's a chance to start again free and independent." Like all quotations from my saint, this one meant many things. More than he knew himself.

I cast an inebriated glance over the motley square — flags of long, silken hair, the latest in hippie fashions, the incredibly serious faces, and those young breasts, their charms ignored now in favour of political rumination. The Jewish boy was still talking through the bullhorn and the crowd of ten thousand was listening attentively. They were inhaling the eternal belief (which later in life would be eternally frustrated) that right and wrong would always be as crystal clear as they were now.

"The Party that came into being to create the most strictly rational of societies," preached the bearded messiah, "creates only irrationality and chaos. It promises scientific leadership, and cripples science. It promises the most just of social orders, and puts into prison thousands and tens of thousands of people — in some countries millions — the minute they express the slightest doubt about the justice of that order. It promises equality to all, and creates a specially chosen social class to lead us out of the bondage of history. It promises a higher form of democracy, and eliminates even the limited democratic guarantees and institutions of the system it replaced. It promises the greatest freedom, and destroys the most basic freedoms we have. It declares that the deepest motivation for work is political correctness, and builds enormous camps for forced labour. It declares itself the embodiment of progress, yet it has become a special-interest group in which the remnants of an intellectual elite, careerists of all stripes, and gangsters stand side by side."

The young man spoke with passion, his words underscored by the flapping of the Czechoslovak flags the plump guitarist was holding high above him. He seemed to be speaking from personal experience of some kind — but it was probably just moral euphoria, exacerbated by youth.

"This party remains silent about acts that no progressive person can overlook in silence. Remember its silence over the fate of Communists in Egypt, its silence over Indonesia, its silence over the genocide in the Middle East, over the real causes of the civil war in Nigeria, over the anti-Semitic campaign in Poland. If this party does not break its silence, if this party does not expel from its ranks all those yes-men, those bloodstained judges and prosecutors, those careerists and incompetent managers — in short, all those so-called faithful Communists," said the young man, and the evening breeze carried applause from several points in the crowd across the square but the voice from the bullhorn was stronger, "then it will, of its own accord, have destroyed any chance it might have had to gather the progressive and creative people of this country into its ranks, to attract young people, to form a genuine left-wing movement capable of carrying out the revolutionary aims of socialist democracy. And these forces will have to gather beyond the range of the party's influence!"

The boy put down the bullhorn and the square erupted in thunderous approval. The shadow of a stone gargoyle fell across Barta's face and he smiled at me. I grinned back, partly as insurance against the time prophesied by the gifted Nabal back in the wine room. But the young man's speech had been tantalizing, and I was tempted to introduce a little disorder into Barta's eternally predictable world.

"You have to hand it to him," I said. "The boy's got quite a tongue. And there's some sense to what he says. It's not just all hot passions."

"What he says is only quasi-rational, based on half-truths," said Barta. "It's that old tried-and-true formula: talk about things as though the Party had never done anything good."

I had it on the tip of my tongue to point out that for twenty years things had been talked about as though the Party had never done anything bad, and that even when it finally (God knows why) began to wash its filthy underwear in public, the only permissible response was jubilation over the washing; anyone who pointed out how very soiled the underwear was, or suggested that sometimes the only solution was a complete change of underwear, was muzzled. But Barta beat me to it.

"Besides," he said, "if you could see through this fellow's purely rational argument, you might find there were some rather ordinary personal and irrational motivations behind it. I'll be seeing you."

He shook hands with me and walked away down the arcade, lashed by stripes of light and shadow as he walked. I didn't understand his final comment.

At this point another young man stepped up to the microphone and said, "Thank you, Vladimir Fischer. And now Blanka Valentinova, from the Department of Natural Sciences, will speak."

A girl in a white dress with a red ribbon in her neatly brushed hair stood as bright as a butterfly against the blackening statue of the medieval martyr. She was an agonizing reminder of my lost past, and of all the embarrassing symbols around — the church, the statues, the square — she was the most embarrassing; two hundred years earlier, some fatuous Delacroix would have painted her in a Frygian cap with her bosom bared, leading the students — where? To the barricades? Against what? Tanks? Tanks which would become the embodiment of what? Progress?

Suddenly I felt miserable. The young Christ jumped down from the base of the statue into the empty fountain. What was his name? Vladimir Fischer . . . the bits of the puzzle fell together in my mind. That was why Barta had taken his picture with that undercover Leica of his — not for the Ministry of the Interior's archives, but for his own interest. "If you could see through this fellow's purely rational argument. . . ." Vladimir Fischer. And Barta was right. Sooner or later, our parents have to die. Whether they die in bed or as a consequence of some specialized form of suffocation, die they must. It is irrational to let oneself be influenced, as Laura's son was, by the *causa mortis*.

I looked again at the white girl against the black statue — and I remembered where I had first seen the television producer. A three-hundred-pound general had rolled off the airplane — stripes down his trousers, medals on his chest, a surly face, everything you'd expect — and, fixed in the eye of a hand-held camera, had marched briskly across the tarmac. Suddenly a girl in a miniskirt hopped into the left-hand side of the picture, clutching a tape-recorder over her shoulder and a microphone in her hand. The general accelerated his pace; the girl had to break into a trot; the general sped up again until he was almost running. Even so, the girl managed to ask him a question in the adroit Russian of her generation: "*Tovarishch* General, is it true that as political commander of the Soviet Army you said that the Army of the Soviet Union is prepared . . . ," and here the general fixed her with a very evil eye and, despite his three hundred pounds, almost broke into a trot himself. But the girl managed to get the rest of her breathless question out: " . . . is prepared to carry out, as you said, its international responsibilities, if it is asked for help by some group of faithful Communists in Czechoslovakia?" They were running now, the general's medals clanking as the girl stuck to him like a guilty conscience. And she managed to add: "In other words, is it true that in such a case the Soviet Army would carry out an invasion of Czechoslovakia?"

By now they were running flat out, but now that the reporter had translated his facile euphemism into ordinary words, the general was enraged. He stopped abruptly, the girl bumped into him with all the force of her insignificant inertia, and he glared down at her from his enormous height and measured her tiny skirt with sullen, dangerous eyes. Then, in a voice accustomed to bold declarations of anything whatever, he said into the microphone she had deftly manoeuvred towards his mouth:

"*Eto glupost.*"

Having said that, he set off once more on his sinister walk across the tarmac, while the hand-held camera followed him for a few moments more. Right after his historic statement — "It's balderdash" — the girl fell out of the camera's range of vision and the liberated general marched towards the airport building and his unknown mission.

That was where I had first seen Jana Hloubava, the young woman who had piled up in an ashtray in the Cloisters Wine Room enough tobacco to poison a weaker soul.

6

■

A Farce in Spring

I.

Vixi was full of surprises. It was never clear to me why she really began to go to catechism classes. Whenever I tried to pry the reason out of her, she would say it was so she could marry me.

And each time I'd reply, "But Vixi, I'm not going to marry you."

"Maybe you will," she'd say. "What do you know?"

I didn't know anything. We started having regular rendezvous at five every afternoon. In the interests of secrecy, we met not in the lilac bower behind my boarding house but in a small clearing in the forest where there was a statue of Krakonos, the legendary mountain giant, made by some graduate of the stonemason school in Hronov. Then we would stroll through the sweet-smelling woods like the shy, platonic lovers in the classic Czech novel *A Fairytale in May.* Vixi soon forgot the flu she'd caught as divine punishment, and each day—five times a week—she tried to seduce me. Each time, in agony, I resisted. She must have noticed how difficult it was for me to remain chaste, because her efforts became more sophisticated. One afternoon she showed up with a borrowed camera because she wanted, she said, to take a few snapshots as souvenirs in case I decided not to marry her after all. We wandered through the woods while Vixi took my picture in the company of assorted mythological beings. Krakonos was not alone; everywhere, from behind the bushes, peered out chubby Venuses (the school had employed the same model for thirty years), Achilles, and various discoboli and Doryphori, so that Vixi soon had a complete collection of figures from Greek mythology. Then we arrived at a clearing warmed by the sun where a sandstone satyr was giving a silent concert in the tall grass.

"Now you take one of me, prof!"

I waved my hand dismissively.

"Sir!" she said, with artful disappointment in her voice. "Don't you want me on your bedside table?"

"You know what would happen. First thing you know, Vikusova would see it through the window."

"Well, how about one for your wallet?"

"All right, stand over there."

Vixi looked at the statue, then at me, and an improper thought seemed to take shape beneath that blue ribbon. "But I want to be taken just as I am."

"What do you mean, just as you are?"

"Without my clothes on. In the nude."

"So long, then."

She was obsessed with the desire to copulate, and so was I. But I still couldn't permit myself the pleasure, and the strain was starting to impair my reason.

"Wait a minute, sir," she said, grabbing my arm as I tried to walk on. "Wouldn't it look good beside the statue?"

With a great effort of will, I forced myself to be reasonable. "If you're so anxious to have your picture taken in the nude, do it with the girls in the dormitory," I said resolutely. "Look — just pose there the way you are, and then I'll carry you in my wallet."

"Don't you want me in your wallet without my clothes on?"

"I'd leave it lying around somewhere and — and anyway, I don't want to arouse feelings of lust in myself, because that's a sin. And you, as a catechumen — "

"As a what?"

"A catechumen. Someone preparing for the sacrament of holy baptism."

"It's a nice word."

"Yes, it is. And what you're suggesting is hardly appropriate."

She donned an expression of exaggerated innocence. "It doesn't arouse feelings of lust in me, sir. Really, it doesn't. I only think it would go well with that statue."

"You're lying, and that's another sin. Besides, I'll have you know that it *does* arouse lust in me. So we share that sin between us."

"But I don't want that, really!" By this time her feigned innocence must have seemed improbable even to her, because she suddenly dropped the mask and appeared thoughtful. "Then you know what I'll do? You go on ahead, and I'll take my own picture. With the automatic timer."

I suppose that when it came right down to it I must have wanted that picture, but I persuaded myself that this would be the best way out of her trap, and walked away down a shady path. Naturally — and she knew this would happen, of course — I couldn't resist creeping back through the woods to the edge of the clearing and hiding in the ferns. The chance to see again what I had seen in the pond not long before knocked my will-power flat on its back.

Vixi had shed her clothes and was lying on her stomach on the other side of a large rock. She put the camera on the rock and then looked through it to get the sandstone satyr in her viewfinder. When she'd framed the shot, she pressed the shutter and ran to the statue. The mottled light flowed over her skin like a moving kaleidoscope and, in this second round, my will was given a knock-out blow. As Vixi leaned against the statue and assumed a lascivious pose, my hand went involuntarily to the centre of my suffering; relief seemed like a grotesque categorical imperative. But I was suddenly struck by a strange shame, a feeling that I was meanly avoiding my just punishment. It was a theological terror. Quickly I drew away my hand, which had been poised to commit the most intimate of sins, and I pounded my own head with it instead, and then fled through the woods to the edge of the forest where the medieval countryside began. There I found a bench made of birchwood and sat down on it, thinking about the ancient iniquities. Although they had gone out of fashion, there was something to them still. A warm breeze set invisible waves moving through the air and the greyish-white sandstone formation on the horizon quivered slightly, the way a backdrop might during an opera. Down below, where the woods bordered the sandstone towers, I caught sight of a white dot — some kind of building painted with lime.

Vixi finally found me and sat down on the bench close to me. Her clothing was very thin.

"I know what you were doing."

I was horrified and felt myself blush, because I thought my punishment for desiring Znenahlikova was about to continue with another demeaning revelation. I feigned ignorance.

"What? I don't know what you're talking about."

But the Lord saved me from embarrassment. With clever hypocrisy, Vixi replied, "You were praying for the strength to resist temptation."

Another time she sat silent and thoughtful, with her chin on her knees, chewing a four-leaf clover for luck.

"What's got into you?" I asked.

"I'm just thinking what a Judas you are."

"Me? How do you figure that?"

"He denied Christ too."

"That was Peter," I said. "Judas betrayed Christ."

She cocked her head with her ear on her knee and looked at me. "All right, so far you're only Peter. But watch out you don't turn into Judas one day."

"What are you talking about, for crying out loud?"

"Why are you always talking like a Communist when you're a Catholic?"

"Me? Talking like a Communist?"

"Sure. Remember what you told us in social studies today?"

I had told them something about how violent revolution was the only way to deal with capitalism.

"Now, wait just a minute," I said. "That's on the curriculum."

"So? Can't you leave it out?"

"Look," I said, "the priest has already told you how they gave Jesus that trick question with the coin, and he answered them and said, 'Render unto Caesar the things that are Caesar's, and unto — '"

"'God the things that are God's'," she said, looking into the distance. She was silent for a while, then said, "But you said it like you believed it."

"I do."

"And you call yourself a Catholic?"

"Jesus never had a theory about whether you could reform capitalism or not. And just because I believe in the need for revolution doesn't mean I'm happy about it. In fact, it's more the other way around. But don't forget, Jesus also said, 'It is easier for a camel to go through the eye of a needle — '"

"But they're such bastards!"

"Who?"

"The Communists, of course!"

I was surprised to find a poor orphan girl with such sharp class prejudices.

"Do you have any idea the nasty things they're doing to my grandad because he won't join their co-op? No, you don't. Look, prof! Let's go visit my grandad this weekend, okay?"

Again I promised to visit her fairy-tale grandfather — who seemed to be the only person she loved without reservation. Then I tried to teach her something about the principles of the class struggle, quite objectively and without taking a stand myself one way or another.

"You don't know what you're talking about, sir! Almost all the rich people who weren't totally dumb joined the Communist Party. Just look at Hronov. Look at Mr. Grimm — don't tell me he's a proletarian!"

She was referring to one of the many blatant exceptions: a local wholesaler who outdid his retail colleagues in his instinct for politics as well as business. He had not waited until 1948 to join the Party, as they had; he had joined right after the war. Now he was security adviser for the municipal Party organization. I tried to explain some of the peculiarities of the class struggle to her, and in doing so I paraphrased the Communist Manifesto, where it says that even some members of the exploiting classes may understand the necessity for —

"Of course they understand!" she interjected. "These types always understand which side their bread is buttered on. But isn't it rotten when they do things without really believing in them?"

I tried again, this time to explain the dialectic principle that subjective motivations are unimportant and that it's objective behaviour that counts. I thought it might be a little too learned for her; she was only seventeen, after all. But she understood.

"You mean why you do something doesn't matter, it's only doing it that counts, is that it? Because it helps the Communists?"

"Something like that."

"But that's exactly what's so rotten about it, supporting something you don't believe in!"

"It's subjectively rotten!"

"Objectively!"

So she hadn't really understood very much. I tried, for the fourth time, to explain the philosophical difference between subjectivity and objectivity. But her logical powers were too feminine.

"In my opinion, they're totally objective bastards — Mr. Grimm, our former principal Prochazka, all of them!"

I gave up on logic and resorted to primitive sociology. "You can't really believe that, Vixi. Not all of them are bastards. There are some decent Communists around who mean well."

"Sir! We're not in school now! And Marie Pecakova's not here either, so you don't have to play Commie."

"All right, what about Marie Pecakova?" I said. She was the much-feared Youth Union activist from 4B, the only one of her kind in the school.

"She only does it because she's got no tits," said Vixi baldly, "and she's got a nose like a cucumber and legs like a horse and on top of it all her feet are flat. And she weighs two hundred pounds. So what's she got left, since she's not religious?"

"And what about Ivana? Ivana's a good woman, isn't she?"

"She's madly in love with Joe."

"Joe who?"

"Stalin, who else?" said Vixi. "Grandad knows her. Before the war she was madly in love with T. G. Masaryk. She's got something seriously wrong with her head."

Vixi's horizons were hopelessly limited by Hronov.

Or was it that Hronov was hopelessly overpopulated by comrades who didn't fit any textbook view of things? I thought of Comrade Prochazka, the jovial, massive husband of the likeable gym teacher, who had chosen me as his apostle at summer school and had given me a job in his paradise for teenage girls.

"Prochazka? Sir, you're being a jerk!"

"Why not? He's always been just an ordinary schoolteacher, not a millionaire like Mr. Grimm."

"But he's a sadist."

"What does that mean? Does he beat Zdena?"

"I never thought of that!" Vixi's thinking suddenly changed direction and she burned with renewed interest. "Do you really think he beats her?"

"Now don't start getting crazy notions, for crying out loud. I never said anything of the sort. On the contrary: I think Prochazka's a decent man who believes in what he's doing."

"He's as cruel as they come," Vixi said. "He sent his own son Karel to a miners' school even though he was the top student in his class. Karel wanted to be a doctor. I knew him and we — anyway, his dad forced him to go to this miners' school just to make himself look good to the Party."

I ignored Vixi's unfinished sentence. "Is that a fact?" I asked.

"You can ask his missus," she said. "They almost got divorced over it."

I gave up any attempt to transform the mulishly conservative Vixi into a progressive young woman, and moved to the personal field. "So as far as you're concerned I'm one of the bad guys too, for teaching you Marxist social science."

"I suppose you are. You don't have to do it."

"And you still want to marry me?"

"Yes."

"Why?"

"Because I love you," she said.

For a moment I couldn't think of anything to say. Then I asked, "So what should I do? Become a bricklayer?"

"No, but you don't have to say that stuff as though you believe it. As Jesus said, 'Render unto Caesar — '"

"But that's exactly what I'm doing! I'm sending you to catechism and for government money I'm teaching you about revolution!"

"But that's not how Jesus meant it. He meant you have to do it in a way that gives the wolf his due and lets the goat go free."

In the silence that followed, I wondered whether she'd learned this interesting interpretation from Father Doufal. I concluded that it was the result of her own meditations.

Next day, during a social studies class, there was a knock on the door of the third form's home room and Zdena poked her head into the room.

"Comrade, could I have a word with you?"

Outside the classroom, she handed me a business envelope. I didn't even have to look inside. It was badly torn, and through the hole I could see a photograph of Vixi, from the waist up. She had no clothes on.

"The mailman just delivered this," said Zdena. "Fortunately I was alone in the staff room. I hope you don't think I've been snooping through your private correspondence, but you can see for yourself. . . ."

The mailman always left the mail in a box by the staff-room door. Every staff member had to sift through the pile to find his own mail. I didn't suspect Zdena of prying — on the contrary. But as I struggled to recover from my shock, I swore to myself that I'd tear Vixi apart.

"Well — I mean, this is — I can't understand — that is — "

Zdena looked at me like a sphinx. When she saw how embarrassed I was, she said, "Try to be a little more careful, Mowgli. I know you like the girls. But don't forget they're very young. And young girls — "

"Zdena! I swear to God I — "

"And also, Mowgli," she interrupted, "you mustn't forget that Hronov is a village. And not all the women on the staff are your friends. There may be one or two gossips, and one or two comrades as well. So long."

She walked away. I stuck the photograph in my pocket and stomped angrily back into the classroom. Vixi was sitting innocently in the row by the window, her chin in her hand, sending amorous glances my way. She always took advantage of social studies classes because she knew she was safe.

At ten after five, still in a rage, I stormed into the woods and burst into our clearing. There, a new surprise was waiting for me. Vixi was sitting on the base of the Krakonos statue with a paper chessboard spread out on the grass in front of her, pretending to be absorbed in trying to solve a chess problem. I sat down roughly on the sandstone and, like a domestic tyrant, swept the figures from the well-worn squares.

"Oh, sir!" she said defensively. "Now I have to start all over again."

"Why the hell did you send it?"

Her immediate reaction was to put on that implausible mask of innocence. "Send what?"

"You know damn well what. And you sent it to the school! You're out of your mind!"

"I wanted you to have a nice surprise!"

"Good Lord!"

"I thought it would be a bigger surprise if I mailed it."

"Then why didn't you send it to my place, at least?"

"I forgot your landlady's name. And your street number."

"You goddamned stupid goose!"

This hurt her. "Why are you getting so upset, sir?" she asked.

I flung the torn and as yet unopened letter down in front of her. "Do you see what could have happened?"

She laid a curious finger on her own nude portrait, conspicuous through the tear in the envelope. "Did you tear it like that?"

"That's just the point, damn it — I didn't."

"Jeepers creepers!"

"Jeepers creepers!" I mocked. "It's a good thing it was Prochazkova who noticed it. If anyone else had seen this, I'd really be up the creek. And so would you."

"Prochazkova saw this?"

"That's right. Fortunately, she's not a tattletale."

She looked at me and said nothing. My anger was gradually draining away. To make up, I said, "Vixi, you get the craziest ideas."

"Well, so what if I do?"

"They could have you thrown out of school."

"But they wouldn't."

"What makes you so sure?"

"Because you'd marry me and then it would all be okay!"

"Me marry you? You're a nut-case, Vixi."

"You'd have to marry me," said Vixi, "because otherwise they'd lock you up. You told me that once yourself."

Though she couldn't get a grip on the logic of generalizations, she was logical enough when it came to sex. Was this all part of a plan? I looked at her pretty, foxy face and experienced one of those rare moments in life when no proof is necessary. There was no plan here: she was just a seventeen-year-old girl, full of sex, a dash of romanticism, a lot of mischief, and a brain that, despite its limited horizons, was very clever indeed. But she was guided by a highly individual moral code.

I looked at the chessmen lying helplessly in the grass.

"What were you doing?"

"Oh, I was just trying to solve some problems."

"I didn't know you played chess. You're a dunce when it comes to math."

"This isn't math," she said. "I do this pretty well."

"So let's have a game."

"I'd rather not, sir."

"Why not?"

"Let's kiss instead," she said, and when she saw me hesitate she added quickly, "Catholics can kiss if they're engaged, Father Doufal said so."

All sense of reserve abandoned me. I couldn't play chess anyway; I only knew how the pieces moved. And the day before, Dr. Gellen had decided on a more radical surgical procedure to deal with my ailment. In the green light of the woods, woven through with the golden light of the sun in the west, her lips were literally the colour of strawberries.

"But only as long as lust doesn't set in," I pointed out. "I'm sure Father Doufal told you that too."

"He didn't mention it," she said, and with the ardent desire of youth she slipped her arms amorously around my neck. Kissing was definitely more fun than chess — even when lust set in like an earthquake.

Hronov's five-hundredth anniversary was finally upon us. The Communist Party and the Municipal National Committee had prepared what they described as a rich program for the weekend, to be climaxed by a soccer match between Viktoria Hronov and its traditional rival, Slavia Lesni Paka. The latter had recently decided, with one voice (the voice belonged to the chairman of the team's Party organization), to rename itself Dynamo Lesni Paka, after Dynamo Moscow. On the occasion of the gala match, the Hronov team was also to be given a more progressive name: Spartak Hronov, after Spartak Moscow. Originally the team was to be officially renamed by the Minister of Water Resources, but he fell ill at the last moment and his place was taken by the Minister of Health, Father Josef Plojhar. Thus the Church was unexpectedly represented at the celebrations — though only by an excommunicated priest. Otherwise, all references to it had been completely eliminated from the town's history.

According to Comrade Grimm, who spoke to a mass gathering of people in the town square that Sunday morning, Hronov, unlike the vast majority of other medieval towns, had been established not by royal decree but as an embryonic people's democracy. It had been founded near the sandstone rock formations in the fifteenth century by a group of politically persecuted craftsmen so they would have somewhere to hide if necessary, and this was in fact necessary several times not long after the town was built. The historical portion of Comrade Grimm's speech had been written by a professor at the Academy of Sculpture, and was more or less based on fact. It merely passed over in silence the fact that the founding fathers of Hronov had all been faithful members of the Catholic Church who had fled from the revolutionary Hussite town of Zeleny Hradec because they were afraid of being burned at the stake. They were craftsmen indeed, but they were led by a Franciscan priest, Father Prokop, who was later immolated by the Utraquists on orders from the Hussite commander Zbynek of Lapte, who had joined the revolution because he coveted the property of his devout Catholic cousin Zikmund.

The Venerable Father Doufal, the only direct and legitimate heir of the town's founding father, was not invited to the celebrations. Of his own accord, however, he preached a Sunday sermon commemorating the martyrdom of Father Prokop, thus coming in conflict with the municipality's secular authorities. The sermon was recorded stenographically by Mr. Mazl, the cross-eyed shorthand teacher to whom Comrade Grimm had entrusted the job of monitoring Church activity. Two days after Mazl turned his report over to the security chief, Comrade Grimm summoned the priest to his office and threatened to arrest him under the Defence of the Republic law if he repeated his offence.

The second highlight of the anniversary, though far less popular than the football match, was a gala evening in the Municipal Theatre on the theme "Lenin and Hronov". Considering the liberties already taken with Hronov's ancient history, the subject was not as absurd as it sounds. Not long before, an old citizen of Hronov — the owner of two run-down tenement houses and a saddlemaker's shop — had died. After the Communist takeover in February 1948 he'd managed to save his skin by suddenly remembering that, sometime before the First World War, he had given shelter, for a single night, to a Russian escapee whose name — he also recalled — was Ulyanov. The saddlemaker had been a rabid Slovanophile at the time and could prove this by press clippings. He had no proof of his historical act of hospitality, but that didn't prevent the Party chroniclers, who were desperate for things to write about, from jumping on his story. They gave him Party pamphlets and textbooks to read, and the more he learned from them, the more details about the visit he was able to remember. Eventually he could describe the famous refugee so exactly that there could be no doubt about his identity. According to an article written for the local paper by the historian from the Academy of Sculpture, the escapee had even addressed a few Leninist-sounding phrases to the master saddlemaker, one of which was quoted by *Rude Pravo*. "In but a short time," Vladimir Ilich was reported to have told him, "I will be with you once more. Not in the flesh, perhaps, but in the spirit, which will live on in my work."

It was shortly after the article appeared that the heroic saddlemaker died. Several years later, a teacher in a one-room school in Poklasni Lhota would discover, while reading *The History of the Communist Party (Bolshevik)*, that at the time Lenin was supposed to have made his historical pronouncement in Hronov he was at a congress of the Second International in London. So the legend would be quietly allowed to die. But at the time of the anniversary in Hronov the saddlemaker's fabrication still had the status of historical fact, and because Ivana had taken a shine to me she appointed me to deliver the ceremonial speech. I was considered something of a scholar in Hronov, and since I was not a member of the Party, my presence on the podium and my speech would stress the unity of Communists and other working people.

The gala evening was to be preceded by a simultaneous chess tournament with the national champion and international Grand Master Bukavec, who was practically a native of Hronov (he had been born a short distance away, in Poklasni Lhota). Because we had gone to high school together (we'd also visited a few brothels together in senior high school, but I didn't tell Ivana that) I was given another assignment: keeping the Grand Master company.

He arrived from Prague in a chauffeured limousine, and when we sat down together in his hotel room he looked weary and careworn.

"I've got to have a talk with you in private before it starts, man," he said.

"What's up?"

"You teach at the Social Workers' School or whatever it's called, right? Do you know someone called Vlasta Koziskova?"

I had a dark foreboding that I was about to learn of another of Vixi's escapades. Bukavec was a great womanizer but he'd recently got married, in Moscow, to the daughter of an important Soviet poet. Could he be worried about some earlier adventure with Vixi?

"Yes, as a matter of fact. She's in third form. Why?"

"What's she like?"

"Do you mean, is she good-looking?"

"No, I mean, does she do well in school? Is her father a teacher or an engineer or something?"

"I don't know," I said evasively, "and she doesn't either. Word of mouth has it he passed through town with a circus. Koziskova's illegitimate, if you follow me. And her mother died when she was born."

"Jesus!" said Bukavec. "But they say that can sometimes happen."

"What can sometimes happen?"

"Kids who grow up in difficult circumstances can sometimes cultivate exceptional talents."

"Koziskova's hardly what you'd call exceptionally talented," I said. "She's a completely average student. For instance, I just found out she doesn't have a clue how to handle fractions."

"Aha!" said Bukavec. "Then it could be like those cases you hear about with idiots, you know what I mean? You can't teach them to read or write but they can work out equations with two unknowns in their heads."

"You're missing the point, Jarda. Koziskova can read and write — it's figures she can't handle. And she's certainly no *idiot savant.* "

Bukavec sighed. "That was only an example. Forget it. Take a look at this!"

He pulled a silver cigarette case out of his pocket, but when he opened it up it wasn't a cigarette case; it was a miniature chessboard — a magnificent piece of hand-crafted work with squares made of ivory and ebony. Pushed into tiny holes in the middle of each square were tiny filigreed chessmen done in gold and silver, on minute pegs.

"That's a cute little thing," I said. "Where did you pick it up?"

"Sergei gave it to me. Petrofim, you know who I mean? It was a wedding present. He's my wife's cousin. As a matter of fact, he introduced us."

"Petrofim, the Soviet Grand Master?"

"Right," said Bukavec laconically. "Man, I tell you, I take this thing with me everywhere I go and I stare at it every spare moment I get, and it's driving me nuts. Here, take a look. White to move."

"It's all a mystery to me."

"Okay, look. We're five moves into this match. White's put his queen's knight on — " Bukavec began inundating me with names and numbers that made everything more obscure than ever. "I'm in a serious bind," he said, ending the lecture. "I moved my pawn to king's knight four, but. . . ."

"Why don't you concede, if you're in such a mess?"

He looked at me almost desperately. "I can't do that!"

"Who are you playing with, anyway?"

"With Koziskova, that's who!"

I almost fell off my chair. "With Vixi?"

"No. With Koziskova. She wrote me a letter — it was sometime last fall, a pity I threw it out. Said she was president of a chess club at the school in Hronov — "

"As far as I know there's no chess club at the school. I mean, it's a girls' school. . . ."

"You find madmen and fools among women too," said the Grand Master with resignation. "So she made it up."

"She makes up a lot of things."

"She probably wanted to impress me or something. Anyway, she wrote and asked me if I'd play a game of chess with her by mail. So I said to myself, why not give the girl a thrill? You know how I've always enjoyed giving the girls a thrill. I thought I'd wrap it up in a few moves, but here we are at the sixth move and *I'm* in trouble."

I could see from the unhappy furrows on his forehead that he was telling the truth.

"Look," he said, "this isn't doing my self-confidence any good. I mean, if word were to get out that I couldn't beat some little chick from Hronov — "

"I see your point," I said. "But don't worry. She's a hair away from failing in social studies. I'll find a way to fix her gambit."

"No. No, I wouldn't want that — "

"Or — wait a minute. Are you sure she's doing this by herself? Maybe somebody from the sculpting school is helping her out. Now that I think of it, one of the teachers there — Professor Hepner — is supposed to be a good chess player. I'll have a talk with him."

"No, please, I wouldn't want that either. That would be just as embarrassing — a nobody called Hepner — it's almost the same as losing to Koziskova. Worse, because if you're beaten by a woman you can at least pretend you let her win out of chivalry. . . . Do you suppose she talks about it? I mean with her friends?"

I shook my head. Here was another suspicious circumstance, though. I could hardly believe Vixi wouldn't have bragged to me about her match with the Grand Master.

"I'm certain she's never talked about it. If she had, I'd know. But maybe she doesn't know what she's doing. Maybe she has no idea she's got you on the run."

"Hang on! She hasn't got me there yet! I'll probably run my bishop up to — " and on his miniature chess set he showed me his probable strategy and what Vixi would likely do to counter him. I interrupted him.

"How about if I arrange a face-to-face match with her, to cut short the agony? Tomorrow afternoon at my place, no spectators?"

"Well — come to think of it, that's not a bad idea." The suggestion obviously appealed to him, and he became more and more excited. "In any case, I definitely have to meet her in person. She's bound to play in the simultaneous match this afternoon. We could set it up then, couldn't we?"

Ivana was sitting in the staff room with an important guest. The district school inspector, Comrade Prochazka, had come to honour his home town's anniversary celebrations with his presence, bringing with him the famous Youth Union poet, Jan Vrchcolab. As I came in the door Vrchcolab was babbling enthusiastically about the saddlemaker's fascinating historical revelation, which was news to him because he'd been in Prague, preoccupied with other things. He had just successfully opened a verse play dramatizing his wife's infidelity. Both in the play and in real life, the Party organization had sent the wayward woman on a forced labour brigade. In the play her waywardness was curbed and cured by collective living; in real life her degradation was consummated by a man called Gartner, of bourgeois origin, who was trying to get into university by demonstrating excessive zeal as a volunteer in the labour brigade.

Vrchcolab was suddenly seized by inspiration and asked Ivana if she could find him a quiet room where he could write a poem for the evening's celebration. Ivana, glowing with delight, shut him in her office, and I took the opportunity to ask her if she had a list of those who'd applied to play in the simultaneous chess tournament against the Grand Master that afternoon.

Comrade Prochazka laughed. "I have it, comrade," he said. "Who do you want to know about? I know the list by heart."

"Comrade Prochazka is a former chess champion," said Ivana.

Here, I thought, was my chance to punish Vixi a little. Instead of simply saying that the Grand Master was interested in the list, I revealed that he was playing a chess-by-mail match with one of our students, that the student was doing exceptionally well, and that the Grand Master was wondering whether she'd be on the Hronov team.

Ivana was thrilled, in her maternal way. "Really! Which one of our girls is it, comrade?"

"Koziskova, from third form."

"Her name is definitely not on the list," said Prochazka.

"Vlasta Koziskova!" cried Ivana. "But she's such a modest girl! She's an orphan, did you know that, comrade? Raised by her grandfather, a small farmer from up in the mountains. I'm sure she was too shy to register."

"She had no reason to be," I replied. "Jarda Bukavec says she's exceptionally talented."

"Does he really?" Ivana was aglow with her usual altruistic delight. "Oh, I must get Vlasta to change her mind! Comrades, we must persuade her to take part! Girls are so retiring," she said, and she took my ironic smile as agreement. "So often they have real talent and ability, but they're just too timid to put them to good use. Imagine! A match with

Comrade Bukavec! We must set this right at once!"

And she reached for the telephone.

Fifteen minutes later Vixi was standing before Ivana with an improbably submissive look on her face. Ivana was bubbling over.

"Vlasta, my dear! Why didn't you let us know you were so good at chess?"

"Please, Comrade Hrozna, I really don't know," said Vixi, and her eyes, now full of dark suspicion, shifted to me. Ivana noticed the look and interpreted it wrongly, as usual.

"Comrade Smiricky here tells us you're playing a game with Comrade Bukavec, the Grand Master!"

The eyes now cursed me silently. "But that's nothing, really. Chess by mail isn't like the real thing."

"Modesty is all very well," Ivana said with a smile. "But Vlasta, our society gives everyone the chance to realize his or her potential. Representing our school will be a real honour. And since Comrade Bukavec specifically asked for you to play. . . ."

That afternoon Vixi occupied the place of honour right next to Prochazka, the Hronov chess champion. She was the only woman among a field of fifty-seven. They were all sitting at tables set in a horseshoe around the auditorium of the Municipal Theatre, wearing their Sunday-best clothes. Jarda Bukavec sat in the centre, politely listening to a speech by the president of the Revolutionary Trades Union chess club, a progressive pastor in the Church of Czechoslovakia called Pandera. Vixi was dressed up too, not in any of her favourite T-shirts but in her one lace blouse — transparent, according to the fashion in those days — with a brand-new brassiere, also trimmed with lace, underneath. She looked like a decoration on one of those kitschy wedding cakes, and she was trembling visibly.

When she'd met Bukavec before the match, Vixi had blushed and stammered and hadn't been able to utter more than a few inarticulate sounds — which tended to support Bukavec's theory about *idiots savants*. Finally, she turned away in shame and ran back to her safe haven beside Comrade Prochazka.

Ivana and I were standing right behind the district inspector, so we could follow the match at first hand. As the progressive pastor finished his speech with the conventional set of "long live" cheers, Bukavec stepped up to the local champion, made his opening move, and then, accompanied by the pastor, strode quickly around the fifty-seven chessboards, making a lightning-quick move at each one. When he came back to Prochazka, he stood at his board for about a second, moved a piece, and then went on to confront Vixi. Whatever it was she had done, he now stood in front of her board for a good five minutes. Several times he looked from the chessmen to the hot and perspiring girl with a strange mixture of suspicion and astonishment on his face. Finally, with an uncertain hand, he edged one of his knights forward, and then continued his journey around the horseshoe. Ivana pressed my hand, nodded proudly, and pointed to her wristwatch. I looked at Vixi's pearl buttons and the red ribbon, the only aspect of her usual uniform she had left intact, and I had the odd feeling I was witnessing an anomaly. It was like the time the otherwise completely conventional Julia Nedochodilova demonstrated to me that she could write with both hands at the same time, in opposite directions. She told me the nuns in the Catholic girls' high school had taught her how.

Meanwhile Bukavec had gone quickly around the horseshoe, making perfunctory moves on each board. He stood in front of Prochazka's board for about four seconds, taking sidelong glances in Vixi's direction, and made his move, which drew a worshipful sigh from the district inspector. Then he turned to Vixi. She sat like a mouse while he stared at her in amazement once more.

"Comrade!" It was the progressive priest whispering loudly to Vixi behind the Grand Master's back. "In simultaneous play you have to have your next move ready by the time the Master comes back to you!" Vixi trembled and did something with a bishop, and then Bukavec spent a full ten minutes over the problem her move had created. Three times, Ivana pointed significantly at the watch around her chubby wrist. Prochazka, who had figured out his next move, studied Vixi's board out of the corner of his eye.

Finally Bukavec brought up his queen's bishop, and then he practically flew around the horseshoe, stopping at no one for more than a few brief moments and devoting only a demeaning wave of his queen to Prochazka, while the progressive pastor breathed a respectful "Check" behind him. Then he stood before Vixi once more. My girl moved something with a quick, nervous motion. The Grand Master frowned, and instead of picking up a piece, he pressed his chin with two fingers.

By now the chess fans in the audience had noticed Bukavec's long pauses in front of the girl in the lacy nylon blouse. A silent crowd gathered behind us, pushing us against the armrest of Vixi's chair. Glancing around at the faces staring at the sixty-four small squares, I saw the same skeptical astonishment that I'd seen on Jarda Bukavec's face. The Grand Master was standing motionless, his chin in his hand, while the spectators looked back and forth from his face to the chessboard with increasing frequency. After five minutes had gone by, Ivana pointed triumphantly at her watch again, and I began to suspect that Vixi was about to become the darling of the historical anniversary.

She soon distinguished herself, all right, but not the way I'd expected. After a pause so long that Ivana stopped looking at her watch and merely gazed proudly around at the tense faces of the aficionados, Bukavec let go of his chin, extended two nicotine-stained fingers towards the white knight, hesitated, then grasped it firmly by the head, made his move, and skewered Vixi to her chair with a piercing look. A murmur of appreciation went through the onlookers and behind the Grand Master the pastor, his voice cracking as he said it, uttered a single word: "Mate."

It was indeed a mate, and in four moves. Vixi, her face as red as a poppy, jumped up and pushed her way through the crowd. Ivana and I looked at each other and without saying a word we followed our vanquished young student out of the auditorium.

"There, there now, my girl!" Ivana had heroically overcome her disappointment and was pressing the sobbing Vixi to her maternal breast. "You're still young and Comrade Bukavec is an international Grand Master."

"But I'm soooo embarrassed, comrade!" wailed my secret girlfriend. "I didn't want to play. I told you!"

I found the sight of Vixi crying astonishing. The only familiar thing about her was that she was as full of surprises as ever.

"You're right, Vlasta, we shouldn't have forced you to play when you didn't want to," said Ivana consolingly, moved by Vixi's tears. "It was our mistake. And you were nervous, but everyone will understand that. Imagine, playing against a Grand Master!"

Callously, I intervened. "But Koziskova, how were you able to do so well in your chess-by-mail match?"

"That's an entirely different matter, comrade," Ivana reprimanded me, wiping Vixi's damp face with her handkerchief. "When you play by mail you're not nervous; you've got time to think each move through, no one's rushing you. . . ."

"Exactly!" said Vixi, shooting a hateful glance at me over the handkerchief in Ivana's hand. Fortunately the expression on her face was so exaggerated that I merely grinned, then left the remarkable girl to Ivana's motherly good graces.

For the evening program, a mixed Youth Union choir of students from the Sculpture Academy and the Health and Social Workers' School sang a Russian song, Maria Pecakova recited Mayakovsky's poem "Lenin", and I gave my talk on "Lenin and Hronov". No one recognized that I'd copied my remarks straight out of the town guidebook, altering them slightly by translating all the petrified Party clichés into non-partisan Czech. With tears in her eyes, Ivana crushed one of my metacarpal bones and promised that when Comrade Stalin's birthday came round she'd give me the chance to speak again. Somehow, she said, I had a way of putting things differently.

The high point of the evening was Vrchcolab's performance. He came on stage wearing a blue Youth Union shirt sparkling with various achievement awards — the usual Fucik and Tyrs badges, but beside them the coveted medal from the World Youth Congress. In a husky voice, he said that he had originally intended to recite one of his older poems about Lenin (by now he had enough for a whole collection, which he published soon afterward). "But your ancient town," he said, "which once sheltered the great Father of the Revolution, inspired me to write a new poem. I wrote it this afternoon, in the office of the principal of your Social School." He paused and then, in a voice that was a good imitation of the more histrionic Soviet school of grand recitation, he read some rhyming piece of twaddle that had the great sage of the Soviet revolution standing in the window of his temporary abode, inhaling the lilac-scented air of Hronov, and, as the legendary Princess Libuse had once done for Prague, predicting a glorious future for this town founded long before by a Catholic monk. The landlord saddlemaker who had invented all this in the first place made a cameo appearance in the clever guise of "a simple man".

Vrchcolab was young, with chestnut-brown hair, and he was given an enormous round of applause. His performance entirely overshadowed the greatest intellectual feat of the evening, a speech by Pastor Pandera, who had been chosen as a representative of Hussitism. The progressive clergyman, dressed for the occasion in the black uniform of his church, with a red chalice sewn to the chest, went one better than Comrade Grimm, who would speak on the same subject the following day in the town square. Pandera succeeded in squaring the circle, for without actually saying so, he managed to create the impression that Hronov had been founded without the approval of the king as a result of the direct influence of the Hussite movement — which, in a perverse way, was true. He was applauded, and after the choir sang a medley of the Internationale, the Soviet national anthem, the Czech and Slovak national anthems, and the Song of Labour, the crowd dispersed and went home.

After the gala, Prochazka gave a banquet for the Grand Master and the poet. Prochazka was in an excellent mood, for he had managed to salvage his reputation during the simultaneous match. By a Herculean effort he had extricated himself from an early attack on his king, and five hours later he was one of the remaining three — the rest had all been mated by Bukavec, who was in fine fettle — to accept the draw that was offered mainly because the attendants, with an ostentatious rattling, had begun setting up chairs for the evening event.

The banquet reminded me of those contemporary posters depicting the joys of life under socialism. The table was laden with mountains of pork, cabbage, and dumplings. Stupefied by the quantities of grease in the food, we sat around afterwards drinking beer, and Ivana said, "You know, comrade, when you took so long over every move I thought our Vlasta must be playing well, and yet — "

"I was a little taken aback, to tell the truth. Her moves — I don't know how many of you here play chess — " and Bukavec looked around the table, where the only other guest besides Prochazka and his wife, Vrchcolab, Ivana, and myself was a Comrade Ponykl, a Party worker entrusted with carrying out the collectivization of agriculture. He briskly shook his wrinkled head and Bukavec went on: "Those moves of hers were so unbelievably . . . bad. I mean, you can find a description of the opening I used in every textbook for beginners — "

"But you sure took your time figuring your moves, comrade," said Ponykl. "How come?"

Before Bukavec could reply, Ivana spoke up. "I know, comrade. You were surprised that her moves were so bad when Vlasta was doing so well in her chess-by-mail match with you, isn't that it?"

"Yes, it genuinely surprised me," said Bukavec uncertainly. "She was obviously nervous — "

"Stage-fright is a terrible thing," said Ivana. "But I've already talked to Vlasta. We're going to establish a chess circle in our school, and what would you say, comrade, if I asked you to be our patron?"

"Gladly," said Bukavec, but without enthusiasm. He quickly changed the subject and began talking about the popularity of chess in the Soviet Union. When he came to the clearly legendary claim, de rigueur in all such conversations, that Comrade Stalin himself was fond of playing chess, Ivana sighed happily and asked, "But who does he play against?" Her question caught Bukavec off guard, but with great presence of mind he said that Stalin probably played with Comrade Beria or Mikoyan, and then he changed the subject again to describe a simultaneous match he had played in the Urals against eighty Party secretaries from the local *gubernia*.

The vision of a purely Party competition appealed to Ponykl. Already well into his beer, he leaned across the table and said, "How's about doing something like that in our district, comrade? I'd get all the collective farm bosses together, they'd learn chess in a hurry, I guarantee you, and then you could play a big match with us, maybe on Nationalization Day. It would be great propaganda for collective farming. I mean, look, you guys in Prague should get off your butts and give us country guys a hand, instead of just flogging the dog in Dobris!" He was confusing chess players with writers, who had been given their own feudal retreat. Suddenly, he swore: "Christ, this damn thing's cutting into my gut!" He reached under his jacket, unfastened something, and tossed an enormous pistol in a leather holster onto the table. The beer glasses rattled with the impact.

The instrument of class struggle aroused silent respect among those present.

"Well, what're you gawking at?" said the armed man with a grimace. "This ain't the city, that's for sure. Out here the enemy's still powerful."

Jarda Bukavec, who was timid by nature — I remember how, in gym class, he used to be terrified of straddling the pommel horse — asked meekly, "Comrade, have the kulaks ever — well, used a weapon or something against you?"

"Well, not exactly," said Ponykl. "But the other day, over in Zalesni Lhota, old Hejda and his sons ambushed me and tried to beat the shit out of me with a bullwhip. But I yanks out old faithful here" — and he seized the gun and pulled it out of the holster, while Ivana quivered with romantic delight and Prochazka laughed, somewhat over-heartily — "and you should of seen 'em dusting away through the clover. No, they ain't got no hardware like this. They're all shit scared. And any guns they did have — mostly shotguns — they handed over during the Protectorate anyway."

"In South Moravia," said Vrchcolab, joining the discussion, "the head of a collective farm was murdered. But I gather they've apprehended the culprits. So far they've not confessed, but — "

"Now they have!" cried Ivana. "You can't have had time to read today's *Rude Pravo*, comrade, you must have left Prague too early in the morning. But they've all confessed. The whole business was organized in the West!"

"What the hell else do you expect?" asked Ponykl, as he lovingly slipped his gun back into its holster. "Capitalist bastards! But we'll soon have them all by the short hairs! As Lenin so rightly put it — and comrade," he said, turning to me, "you forgot to mention this in your speech today, which was pretty good otherwise — the only thing the bourgeoisie understands, Lenin said, is terror. But if it's going to be terror, then it should be proper terror, and not just goddamned pussy-footing around. You can't go making threats and not backing them up. You got to hit them with all you got."

Ponykl's folksy paraphrase of Lenin's notorious article on the implementation of terror made everyone feel like a participant in the grand processes of history. "Does this mean you've uncovered some actual agents, or something like that?" Bukavec asked.

Ponykl glanced conspicuously at Prochazka and Prochazka laughed. "As a matter of fact," he said, "I believe the comrades from the Interior are on the trail of something at this very moment. Comrade Grimm. . . . Anyway, the trail is leading us to Maselna Lhota. But let's change the subject, shall we?"

Bukavec then began a hurried description of how, right in the central office of the Revolutionary Trades Union, where he was (formally) employed as convener for Union-sponsored chess clubs, they had uncovered a conspiracy involving former Boy Scout leaders. It turned out that although scouting had been officially banned, two leaders still went on secret hikes with members of their old troops and taught them woodlore. Bukavec told the story in a breathless, incredulous tone. "In this case, the trail leads all the way to the Vatican," he said. "Not long ago they arrested some Franciscan monk, Urbanec or whatever his name is. He was running something called *Studium Catolicum*, which was supposed to be a school for adults who'd converted to Catholicism. In fact, it was a centre for espionage."

Ivana shook her head in horror. I felt a sudden chill, for scarcely a year had passed since I'd last fought with Julia Nedochodilova's hand under the table as she tried to prevent me from playing with her garters, while, with a pretence of piety, I'd listened to this agent of the Vatican expatiating on the joys of the eucharistic way of life.

That night, as I walked Bukavec back to his hotel, I asked him, "Is it true what you said about that guy Urbanec?"

"It sure is, man. I've never followed these things very closely—you know how it is, chess takes up a lot of your time. But I'd never have believed there were so many foreign agents around. They must have a fantastic network! It's a wonder we ever managed to come out on top in '48."

"It seems incredible to me too," I said cautiously. I had no way of knowing how far Bukavec, a Party member since 1945, had been Sovietized by his Russian wife.

"You know how it is; we both have other things to think about. I've got my chess, you've got— "

"My students." I said it for him, and though he had once been a great womanizer, he didn't catch the irony in my tone.

"Of course, you're a pedagogue now," he said, and I concluded that the Sovietization was already in an advanced stage. He promptly confirmed this.

"We don't really have any idea how these things work. We're naive, and they're incredibly sophisticated. Take that Boy Scout leader. He worked in my department, and because of him I was interrogated by some comrades from the security forces. They asked me if I'd seen anything suspicious about him, and like a fool I told them I hadn't. So they said, 'Has he ever praised any Western literature on chess? Or Western chess players?' Then, by God, I remembered something. It wasn't chess literature, mind you, but I knew he was reading an American novel, something called *For Whom the Alarm Goes Off* or something like that, and he was always talking about it. So I told the security guy and he wrote it down and checked it out at the university and sure enough, it turns out to be some Trotskyist novel about the Spanish Civil War. Anyway, their security guy coaxed some more answers out of me and I ended up being one of the main witnesses at the trial."

He looked at me as though he couldn't believe it himself.

"What evidence did you give?"

"Just about how he was always praising this book, *For Whom the Chimes Ring* or whatever it was, and some other stuff too, stuff I've forgotten now. Like once the guy said that Churchill was a reactionary but that he also played a major role in defeating Fascism. That really went against him. Afterward, the prosecutor told me privately that my testimony helped reveal the guy's true political profile, so he couldn't deny the charges. In the end he confessed that he was actually being run by a Jesuit priest and that he was feeding him information."

"What sort of information?"

"I don't know, man," said Bukavec. "It was top secret, so they didn't talk a lot about it."

"That's wonderful," I said, and my thoughts went back to that time not long before, when I'd obviously been surrounded by traitors without knowing it.

We were just walking past the girls' dormitory. All the lights were out, according to regulations, which meant the girls were sitting on their beds in the dark, talking about sex and comparing their vital statistics the way they'd read American girls did, in a magazine smuggled into Hronov by Kamila Doruzkova's cousin, who was a waiter in the Hotel Ambassador in Prague. And no doubt a secret agent as well.

"By the way," I said, "I've arranged it with Koziskova. You can finish your chess game — the mail game — at my place, instead of watching the football game."

"Can we?" he said uncertainly. "But I have to leave by four at the latest. I have another simultaneous match in Zeleny Hradec."

"Three hours will be enough. You finished her off in twenty minutes today, and the only reason it took that long was that when you saw her stupid moves you couldn't believe your eyes."

"All right. Thanks."

We were standing by the hotel entrance and Bukavec's face shone, somewhat absently, into the empty square. Our night-time conversation about improbable spies, and the beautiful thrill of Vixi's mysterious chess abilities, remained so firmly fixed in my memory that years later I could still see his face in my mind's eye, radiating only that highly particular intelligence that is the hallmark of the narrow specialist.

2.

Bukavec was the most silent of all those present in the Renaissance salon of the Hrzansky Palace, or on the terrace that hung suspended in space between Mala Strana below and the midsummer moon above. He moved like a disembodied being from group to group, very like a moon himself, his round face pale and exhausted from lack of sleep. Something was eating away at him — perhaps a knotty chess problem, worse than the one that Vixi had once confronted him with.

Standing in the doorway to the terrace, a folksy politician was telling a group gathered around him about a funny experience he'd had that day. He'd received an anonymous letter that said, "You will hang right next to First Secretary Dubcek, you hoor!" The politician was treating the incident as a joke and was telling everyone, at tiresome length, what a great honour it would be to be hanged next to the leader of the realm. Everybody thought this was hilarious. The only blemish upon the joviality was an awareness that there were only a limited number of solutions to the political dilemmas of the First Secretary (and most of those present), and that hanging was far from being the most improbable.

I escaped from this gaudy gathering into the salon. The prime minister, his face red (probably from drink), was conversing with a group of writers and ministers about his meeting that morning with the commander of the Soviet troops that had been on manoeuvres outside Prague for a suspiciously long time. "So I pounded my fist on the table," said the prime minister, fortified with the Hungarian wine known as Bull's Blood, "and I said to him, I said, 'Comrade General, I expect your side to keep to the terms of the agreement and have your troops off our territory in three days!' And I did an about-turn and marched out of the room. And by this afternoon, I got a report that the first units were moving towards the border."

He looked around triumphantly and took a sip of his wine. He and the other energetic men in the Party and state leadership had been in the eye of the world press for some time now, and I suddenly felt as though I were watching a Shakespearean drama performed by the Hronov Puppet Theatre. Perhaps all historical dramas look like that close up. Vrchcolab — who, unlike Bukavec, was one of the most convivial participants in this wine and cheese soirée — said stoutly, "That's the way to handle them! The Soviets have to understand once and for all that we mean what we say, literally. We expect equality, independence, non-interference in our internal affairs. In short, we're taking our own road to socialism!"

From the shadow of a gilded but unlit candelabrum, Bukavec, his face pale and confused, stared at Vrchcolab with unbelieving eyes. Vrchcolab had long ago abandoned poetry and taken up writing plays, which he churned out for his current mistresses, most of whom came from the theatre world. He had also abandoned the chaste blue Youth Union shirt and all the other paraphernalia of his green youth, and was now striking a raffish pose on the terrace in a suit recently purchased in Carnaby Street. His newest play was an existential piece in the style of the Theatre of the Absurd. Beside him Bukavec, who had evolved neither sartorially nor professionally — he was still a Grand Master — looked like a poor country cousin.

The Minister of Justice, one of the two token non-Communists in the government, stepped up to me and said, "How are you doing, Mr. Smiricky?"

He spoke with neither aggression nor irony, and a rapport was immediately established between us. The minister was used to peaceful collaboration in unexciting times; now, as a member of a revolutionized government, he was obviously not feeling quite himself. He had experienced — and, unlike many other politicians, had survived — one Communist revolution already, and as a result he adhered to the notion of moderate progress within the bounds of the law.

"Still writing, Mr. Smiricky, still writing?" he asked affably.

"I'm trying to, sir."

"I read that book of yours. Those detective stories. I quite enjoyed them."

"Thank you," I said. It was the first piece of fiction I'd published. The rest of my work — my non-detective fiction — was still hidden in my drawer, except for a satirical novel I'd written about the army. Dasa Blumenfeldova, the aggressive literary talent scout, had sussed out its existence, and Foglar, who'd become editor-in-chief of the Writers'

Union publishing house after Vohnout's humiliation, had managed to pry the manuscript out of me. I wasn't very happy about their interest. So far I'd managed to make an honest living writing operettas, which I called musicals, but as cultural life became more liberal I'd taken a chance and started writing crime fiction. But I still had grave doubts about my first venture into serious literature.

"Somehow," said the minister, and I could sense a kind of nostalgia in his tone, "your stories remind me of Karel Capek's mystery tales."

This was exaggerated praise, but his expressionless eyes were gazing unflinchingly into mine and he was nodding his head. Perhaps he was trying to tell me that he was a genuine Masarykian democrat, and that as a cabinet minister he was merely a puppet, not a Communist ogre. For years he had represented a non-existent political party, whose salaried members were trotted out on special occasions to inspire astonishment in uninformed Western delegations. Surely the man deserved more for his fidelity than to be drawn by his masters into yet another of their potentially bloody adventures.

I felt sorry for him, but we had nothing to say to each other. We stood there for a while, smiling, and then the minister nodded again.

"So keep on writing, Mr. Smiricky, keep on writing. We'll all look forward to the results."

And he walked away, taking with him whatever unexpressed worries he may have had.

From a table beneath a crystal chandelier came the sound of laughter. An important strategist of the revival process, Pinkava, was letting some young poets in on his political plans. "When I become a member of parliament," I heard him say in his heavy Moravian accent, "I will do my utmost to have this country withdraw from the Warsaw Pact and declare its neutrality."

I felt ill and hurried back out onto the terrace.

There, surrounded by a cluster of admirers, the First Secretary was sitting on a low wall while the world-famous playwright spoke to him with great urgency. Bukavec was among the listeners and he was gazing at Dubcek the way Ivana Hrozna had once gazed at the portrait of Marshal Stalin.

"You can take it from me, Mr. Secretary," Hejl was saying, "practically everyone in the country is for socialism."

The First Secretary was obviously not yet used to being called "Mr." Perhaps it gave him a bad conscience. He was wearing a smart summer suit with a silver pattern in it, no doubt recommended by his advisers. Behind him the wooded slope of Petrin Hill was murmuring in the evening breeze, and above the treetops a floodlit American flag fluttered over a small gazebo in the American embassy garden. Another of the embarrassing symbols of that summer. Above the First Secretary's head, with its nose tailor-made for caricaturists, schools of moist stars swam through the warm night air.

"Do you think so?" he said.

"Certainly!" said the playwright. "Take me, for example. My father was a millionaire, so you might say I'd stand to gain personally from a return to capitalism. But upon my soul, nothing of the sort has ever occurred to me. Property doesn't interest me. I make theatre — and theatre, potentially at least, is better off under socialism."

"Do you think so?" repeated Dubcek, and his eyes strayed to the heathen peace symbol dangling around the playwright's neck, a souvenir of his recent visit to the United States. In an interview in the *New York Times* Hejl had condemned the Warren Commission report on Kennedy's assassination and criticized President Johnson. He had also interviewed prominent anti-Communist Czech émigrés, and was now editing the tapes for publication in the leading Prague literary weekly. "Do you really think socialism has all this support?"

"You have my word of honour!"

"Perhaps it is so because you are talented. You find full satisfaction in your work." The First Secretary, whose first language was Slovak, was not entirely at home in Czech. "But not everyone can. Perhaps you and I, we mean it well. But it is a question whether everyone means it well. Even those who have no artistic talent."

"An absolute majority means it well," said the playwright decisively. "Socialism is the *epitheton constans* of the modern era."

"Do you think so?" asked the First Secretary again, in a careworn voice, while a fresh breeze rippled his silvery suit.

Bukavec saw me and grasped me by the hand.

"Danny!" He led me aside and said, in a whisper, "Is there any hope?"

"Any hope of what?"

"That they'll let him alone? That they won't try to strangle him?"

"You mean him?" I said, nodding towards the First Secretary.

"He's such a decent man. Much too decent for the job!"

"I hope he's only pretending to be decent."

"Not him!" sighed the Grand Master, looking unhappily at the small man with the large nose. Beyond him Prague, a tourist's dream, sparkled in the night. Bukavec's moonlike face was white against that kaleidoscopic background. All at once he turned to me and with a strange intensity, almost imploringly, he said, "Danny— "

"What?"

"Forgive me!"

"Forgive you for what?" I had no idea what he was talking about.

"Can't you remember?" he whispered, leaning close to me. "Recently it's all been coming back to me. Sometimes I think I'm going crazy. If—if only there were something I could do—to atone."

Everyone's gone crazy, I thought, and Bukavec here is a case for the funny farm.

"What the hell are you talking about?"

"I—I've hurt so many people," he babbled, and I realized that he was talking more to himself than to me. "I was young and stupid, but that doesn't excuse me. I was a swine. Don't you remember?"

Tears were flowing from his eyes. A minor detail swam into focus in my mind, a detail from the twilight of trifling memories.

"You don't mean the time you attacked me because of *A Game with Emilka*?"

His eyes widened, as if in fear. *A Game with Emilka* had been one of my light-weight musical farces, and I had put the words "Chess is a stupid game, and what's more, it's feudal," in the mouth of the female lead. It was a run-of-the-mill comeback; the heroine was merely taking a dig at her timid suitor, who'd offered to play a game with her, because she'd taken a fancy to him and was annoyed that he hadn't the courage to propose one of the more amusing games people play. The Grand Master had gone to school with me and had followed my artistic career, and he was understandably upset by the line. In an angry, venomous review in *Sports Weekly*, he fired his mightiest salvo: chess, he said, had been Vladimir Ilich Lenin's favourite game! To help me defend myself an anonymous but friendly reader from the Institute of Marxism-Leninism sent me a lengthy quotation from Engels, who was more interested in young women than in chess, and wrote far more disrespectfully of the game than I had. But Bukavec was an old friend, and I didn't have the heart to reply. Chess was his life and he had a right to feel insulted. Moreover, his article generated wonderful publicity. *A Game with Emilka* became the hit of the season and made a star out of an unknown singer called Suzi Kajetanova, so that my stock went up in her eyes—or so I thought at the time.

"You see what I mean?" said Bukavec. "I'd forgotten all about it. I was thinking about what I did to Koziskova— "

"Koziskova? Don't let that both you. She was happily married long ago. She has two kids, each by a different father and neither by her husband."

But Bukavec's distraught conscience had brought to mind yet another sin. "And then there was my testimony, man! Hisek-Kirsch," he said, naming a former colleague of his who had died in custody after falling head-first against a wall. "Danny! I testified against him! I said that at a tournament in Casablanca he had personal contact with Freddy Cohen. They told me Cohen was a CIA agent, and I believed them. What an idiot I was! Idiot? Murderer is more like it. It should have been as plain as day. Freddy Cohen was such a snotty-nosed little teenager — I mean, his idea of fun was riding the bumper cars in an amusement park. How the hell could anyone that childish have been working for the CIA? Danny, I was criminally stupid. *Criminally* stupid!"

He began pounding his clenched fists against his forehead so hard I was afraid he'd end up like Hisek-Kirsch.

"Hey, calm down," I said. "Did you actually fabricate any evidence against Hisek?"

"God forbid, no! I never made up anything!"

"They asked the questions, right? And you answered truthfully, to the best of your knowledge. Hisek drank Coke with Freddy Cohen in Casablanca, that's a fact. So what's the problem?"

But Bukavec went on drumming his fists against his brush-cut, moaning in moral agony. I lost interest. I saw madness everywhere I looked, and I was longing to meet someone sane. Vrchcolab trotted by me, hot on the heels of the prettiest young writer in Central Europe, Eliska Obdrzalkova.

"Look," I said, drawing the tormented man's attention to the chase. "Vrchcolab takes it differently. There's no repentance there. He believed everything, just as you did, and that's all the absolution he needs."

"He's different," sobbed the Grand Master.

The First Secretary got up and walked into the palace, followed by a train of admirers. The Grand Master forgot about me at once and joined the crowd.

I didn't feel like staying any longer. The night was tepid and reminded me, painfully, of the pleasurable side of life. I turned around. A short distance away, the Minister of Foreign Affairs was sitting on the low wall, now in close conversation with Sarka Pechlatova, while Paternoster, the science-fiction author, sombrely listened in. At least I could expect some low-level normality from Paternoster. I sat down beside him.

"Various social organizations will come into being," the minister was saying, in the tone of voice one uses to tell fairy-tales to children. In the distance beyond him, at a spot where, legend has it, Saint John of Nepomuk was thrown from the Charles Bridge, the black Vltava River reflected the moon. "And these organizations will represent the interests of various strata of the population. This way, pressure will be created in all directions and the Party will co-ordinate these pressures and point them in a single, common direction. Imagine it like a river," he went on, reaching for a parable with which to convey the Party's vision. "The river has different currents, whirlpools, and rapids, but the flow is determined by the riverbed, which meanders through the countryside and inevitably leads the river to the sea. That river, with all its internal currents and swirls and rapids — these are the pressures and conflicts between the social organizations. The riverbed is the Party. Now, what do you think of that arrangement, speaking as non-Party people?"

"Sounds nice," said Sarka.

"I'm glad," said the minister. "Because you know how it is: in exchange for giving up a portion of its power, the Party expects that our more politically-minded citizens will understand what we're trying to do and give us their support. We believe the class society has been essentially overcome. The former exploiters have been integrated into the masses, which means the class struggle *de facto* is over. That's why the Party no longer wants to rule, but merely to lead."

Then the minister was called away to the telephone. Berlin was on the line.

"Isn't it fascinating?" said Sarka, turning to me, aglow with enthusiasm. "'Not to rule, but to lead.'"

"But where?" I wondered, out loud.

"Up shit creek," said the author of utopias.

Sarka lost her temper. "Listen, you big jerk, I've had enough of your disgusting pessimism. Do me a favour and don't spoil this beautiful evening for me." She stood up and energetically walked to the other end of the terrace to barge in on Vrchcolab, who was eagerly instructing Eliska Obdrzalkova in something or other. Her dress, recently brought back from Paris, had a back so low-cut that you could see those seductive little dimples just above her buttocks.

That left Paternoster and me alone on the historic wall. Beneath us the medieval city was still sparkling with the beauties of the night, and a warm wind was pushing rococo clouds gently across the face of the moon. One of the swell seasons in our brief lives was running out. I felt a terrible rage welling up inside me. Paternoster obviously felt a similar emotion. "The *comrades* have already ruined our lives once," he said bitterly, as though he were filled with the allegedly vanished class hatred. "Now that we're starting to get things back together, they're going to tear it all apart again."

We were silent.

"When do you think they'll come?" I asked.

"I don't know. But they won't leave it too late, you can depend on that."

We were silent again.

"Most people are walking around in some kind of trance," I went on after a while. "They don't believe the Russians will come. But why wouldn't they? Things have always turned out badly so far."

"And they always will," said the author of utopian novels.

Vrchcolab and Eliska walked quickly past us, escaping from Sarka Pechlatova, who was now buttonholing Jan Nabal at the far end of the terrace. Nabal had been trying to make himself inconspicuous behind a fig tree since the beginning of the party, hoping to avoid compromising conversations. I looked around at the naked dimples of possibly the most beautiful writer in Europe, and felt a stab of pain in my heart.

"Another sorcerer's apprentice," snorted Paternoster. His eyes were following the same dimples mine were, but he meant Vrchcolab. "First they spend all their energy conjuring up spirits, and now — " He waved his hand and cursed.

"They were young and stupid then," I said.

"And we were old and wise?" he asked, turning his anger on me.

"Well, I suppose we weren't," I admitted.

Could the difference be explained by class origin? According to official statistics — published at last, after so many years, but for the information of sociologists only (who immediately spread it all over Prague) — almost two-thirds of Party members were, as they so discreetly put it, of "non-working-class origin". Before the war, Vrchcolab's father had been director of a joint stock company that owned steel mills in Poland and a car factory in Prague. After the victory of the people he had become director of the car factory, which was then nationalized. Dark, ungovernable forces live through us, and ideas serve only as guides. Who said that? Someone called Herbert Spencer. It was certainly not a Marxist sentiment.

I turned back to face the ancient city, and with a painful sense of helplessness I surrendered to the beauties of the night. There were spotlights in the distance over the Old Town Square and I could hear the sounds of mass chanting, and incomprehensible words booming from a megaphone. Otherwise it was a quiet summer night in a land where the class war had become nothing more than an embarrassing memory.

3.

Ivana Hrozna had been worrying for some time about how to reconcile two apparently disparate demands: the list of girls allowed to try their matriculation exams had to conform to the regulations drawn up, in the spirit of alertness and vigilance, by the Ministry of Education, but at the same time she had an intrinsic need to follow the dictates of her heart.

The ministry instructions from Prague were quite specific:

> There must be careful review of all cases of students whose marks indicate probable success in the matriculation examinations, but whose class origin and family background do not fully guarantee that they will use the knowledge gained in the building of socialism. Only in those cases where it is positively determined that, on the one hand, the student himself sincerely expresses a positive attitude towards our people's democratic system (e.g. by being a member of the Czechoslovak Union of Youth, taking part in voluntary work brigades, gathering scrap paper, etc.) and, on the other hand, the parents, despite their class origins, have understood the historical role of the Communist Party of Czechoslovakia and have joined in the building of socialism, can exception be made and such a student be allowed to sit for the final examinations.

The struggle in Ivana's soul was in turn shaped by two not entirely compatible theories: the classical doctrine, as she understood it from her crash courses in politics, of how one's class origins predetermine one's opinions and behaviour; and the legendary teachings of Makarenko, the great reformer of Soviet hooligans, who from the same classical Marxist sources derived the doctrine that every person was capable of re-education. To this dialectic Ivana added her own personal interpretation of Lysenko's notorious discovery that characteristics acquired during an individual's life are hereditary. Consequently, at the prematriculation meeting she expressed the opinion that not only were all our girls essentially re-educated, but they would pass their new convictions on genetically to their children.

The staff of the Social School might have been willing to accept Ivana's unique, scientific synthesis without digging into the matter further, had it not been for Milada Maresova, who taught Russian. Among her other strange abilities, this young woman could recall at will all the most unpleasant passages from the classics of Marxism; in this she differed fundamentally from Ivana, whose memory worked in precisely the opposite way. Frequently, and with great spirit, Milada would bestow her blessing on the liquidation of the class enemy, the democratic nature of dictatorship, and the justice of capital punishment in as many cases as possible. She also ridiculed the intelligence of all those thinkers who came before Marx, those around him, and those who came after him but did not follow in his footsteps. So Milada immediately countered Ivana's synthesis of Makarenko and Lysenko with a quotation from Marx's *The Eighteenth Brumaire of Louis Bonaparte*, and vigorously demanded the exclusion of at least fifty per cent of the senior class from the final exams.

Ivana — with the simplicity of a person who doesn't realize that using reality as an argument against the classics is heresy — said meditatively, "It's true Marx writes that the petty bourgeoisie can't go in their minds beyond the limits they get to in life. Comrade Maresova is absolutely right there. But Marx was obviously thinking of older people, and in any case," and she turned her guileless eyes straight at Milada, "isn't the act of joining the Party in itself a way of going beyond those limits? The doctrines of our Party are alien to the petty bourgeoisie, yet members of the petty bourgeoisie often overcome their background and join. Take someone like Comrade Grimm, for instance."

In the light of these contradictory hypotheses, the existence of the District Security Officer presented a considerable problem. It was hardly possible, under the circumstances, to declare him a "radish" — red on the outside, white on the inside — whose enlightenment owed more to the post-war law punishing collaboration with the Nazis than to the Great October Revolution. So Milada fell back on contemporary theories about typicality and declared that the former wholesaler was an atypical exception that merely proved the rule.

"In that case, comrade," retorted Ivana, taking her at her word, "isn't it possible that our students are atypical as well? Comrade Grimm is in his fifties and our girls are still teenagers. Young branches are the most easily bent. Just remember what upright people Makarenko made out of those twisted young juvenile delinquents! For example, during the campaign to collect non-ferrous scrap metal, which by the way is also mentioned in the ministry circular," and she waved the ominous document in the air, "our graduating class did marvellously. Let's not forget that because of them our school won the Red Banner as the best in the region."

Ivana pointed a stubby finger at the red flag with the golden tassel hanging on the wall between the portraits of Stalin and Gottwald. This argument silenced Milada for the moment, and the staff accepted Ivana's thesis that the graduating class consisted of six comrades of proper origin, and nineteen atypical exceptions.

Ivana, of course, had no idea how we'd really won the banner for collecting old metal, and I wasn't about to tell her. The roots of that success went back to the time when an elderly fellow teacher was given time off to go to a spa and left me with a list of pledges. I put it away somewhere and, because I had other problems, forgot about the whole thing. Then a message came from the regional board for all teachers in charge of metal collection to send in their results, and I was in the soup. I couldn't very well tell them we hadn't collected anything, so I decided to send the regional inspector a fictional tally slightly higher than our pledge. The only problem was that I couldn't find the mislaid pledge sheet. It was no use asking anyone else about it: the students had long since forgotten what they'd pledged and, besides that, I would have been admitting to my dereliction of duty. So I said nothing, and began to conduct a theoretical collection in which the school, again theoretically, gathered 297 kilos of copper, 303 kilos of zinc, 221.5 kilos of bronze, and 83 kilos of light metals. Almost half of this weight I ascribed to the graduating class. Why, I don't know; perhaps some inner voice was leading me.

I was a little worried that the regional inspector would ask to see receipts from the depositories where the metal had (theoretically) been sent for recycling, but in the end what I'd assumed would happen did: the referees didn't care about the metal at all, they only cared about the numbers, which they passed on to the regional school board. But my other assumptions turned out to be wrong: the figures I'd submitted were nothing like the actual pledges made by the students. The regional headquarters were very good at filing, and one day the chairman of the scrap metal evaluation commission himself appeared at our school bearing an enormous case. He took it to the staff room, where he pulled out a banner with tassels so golden they would have delighted a Russian general. It turned out that our students had collected 287% more copper than they'd pledged, 203% more zinc, 186% more bronze, and a credible 22% more light metal. The chairman gave a speech in the gym, the girls maintained an exemplary silence, Ivana recommended me for a raise in pay, and at a small reception afterwards in the principal's office the chairman of the evaluation committee got drunk on Soviet champagne.

Unfortunately the champagne went to Milada's head as well. In her eyes I was a hero basking in the glory of the red flag, and so, fervent Youth Union supporter as she was, she made a pass at me. Fortunately her resemblance to a woman was only approximate, and my poor, beleaguered organ didn't suffer. It was not politically wise to spurn such advances outright, however, so when she grabbed my hand under the table I let her hold it until the moment we toasted Comrade Stalin's health with vodka.

Milada was a member of the Party District Committee and the daughter of the head gynecologist at the Hronov hospital. Before the war the hospital had been a private sanatorium where the owner (her father) performed abortions for ladies from Prague high society. (During the war these were mainly the wives of high-ranking officers at the front who had become pregnant at a time inconsistent with their husbands' furloughs.) After the war, with great foresight, he had donated the sanatorium to the state. He had already joined the Party — just before the end of the war, in late April 1945 — and he quickly became an important functionary. The dangers of rejecting Milada were so frightening that if the state of my organism had permitted, I might very well have gone against my principles and plunged to my own destruction. For Milada was not a whore, at least not sexually. She dreamed publicly of a proper socialist marriage and spoke out loud, and frequently, about having children.

The day after the reception, however, she had a hangover and was determined to do something, in true Youth Union spirit, to erase any bad impressions her unseemly behaviour might have left. Over lunch, she invited me to go to a Soviet movie called *The Knight of the Golden Star* that Saturday. I refused on the excuse that I had to go to Zeleny Hradec to visit a relative, and then spent the whole weekend alone in my room at the widow Ledvinova's, with the blinds down (Vixi had gone to her grandfather's). I could not escape a concert of the Czech Nonet on the following Wednesday, but fortunately Ivana sat beside us, and because she lived in the same street as Milada I managed to say good night to her by her gate and then walk Ivana the rest of the way home.

Then the Red Army Ensemble came to Hronov. This would be a rather benign occasion, I thought, because attendance was compulsory for the whole school. They gave Milada the job of buying the tickets, however, with the result that on the evening of the performance the whole staff and student body sat in the orchestra, while Milada and I found ourselves upstairs, ensconced in a private box for two.

The constant swirl of somersaulting officers put me in a terrible mood that became worse with every somersault. It reached its nadir in the finale to the first half, when the troupe, in unbelievably shiny riding boots, paraded onto the stage and, before the astonished matrons of Hronov, produced out of nowhere an enormous portrait of Stalin in what looked like a gold frame. I could hear Ivana's explosive clapping rise from the orchestra, and I excused myself to Milada and spent the whole intermission in the washroom.

When I returned, the lights in the house had gone down and female army officers in folk costumes were spinning around like tops, their skirts flaring to reveal rather pretty female thighs. This helped me forget my plight.

But not for long. After the performance, Ivana got lost in the crowd and there was nothing I could do but take Milada to the café. To make matters worse, there was no one there we could join; there were only a few chess players sitting beneath wreaths of smoke, reconstructing games from Bukavec's recent tournament. Milada energetically manoeuvred me into an intimate booth, a relic of the more immoral times of the First Republic. As soon as we sat down, she opened her small eyes wide at me and sighed, "Wasn't that magnificent, Comrade Smiricky?"

"It certainly was."

I asked the waiter for two cups of black coffee, but Milada playfully protested.

"I'm in the mood for some wine!" she said. "An experience like that is almost worth celebrating, don't you agree, Comrade Smiricky?"

"We have Mavrud," said the waiter.

"So bring us some Mavrud," I said, resigned to my fate.

"That's Bulgarian wine, isn't it, Comrade Smiricky?" she said, blinking at me in what was obviously an attempt to be coquettish. "Comrade, I hope you won't take offence — we teach in the same school, after all — if I call you by your first name; you can do the same to me."

"Go right ahead," I grumbled.

"Milada," she said, offering me her hand.

"Danny." She took my hand in hers and pressed it firmly.

"You know, that's the only thing I don't like about you."

"What?"

"You call yourself Danny. It sounds so English, and you're a Czech. I'm going to call you something else."

"Anything you say. What do you want to call me?"

"Well — something Czech-sounding."

"My name is Daniel."

"That's kind of — it's too official."

"I agree."

"So what could we call you that's more colloquial — so long as it's not Danny?"

We thought about it for a while. It turned out that my name could only be de-Anglicized at a level of intimacy which Milada was not yet ready to adopt.

"How would it be if I called you Danik?"

"It sounds too much like Pepik. I hate that name."

"All right, what about — " and she paused, gathering her courage, "Danielek?"

"That's more a child's name. Can you imagine what would happen if the students found out? It would make my life impossible."

"Do you really think so?"

"I know so. I can just hear it: 'Danielek gave me a goose egg in social studies!' Why don't you call me Danas? Or Danak?"

"That seems too — "

"Too what?"

"Crude — vulgar — "

I could feel anger boiling up within me. "What about Danieles?" I suggested maliciously. That very day an article attacking Zionism had come out in *Rude Pravo*, and I expected to get a rise out of her. I was right.

"Pfui! Your name is so nice and that's so ugly!"

"It's a Jewish name. I guess that's why it's so hard to find Czech diminutives for it. Daniel was one of the prophets of Israel; they threw him into a lion's den or something."

"I think I'll stick with Daniel. Daniel," she repeated, as though trying it out. "It's not so bad after all. Daniel . . . Daniel . . . ," and she began to say it as though she were caressing me. It was awful. A drop of sweat began to roll down my back — and then, God knows why, I remembered the thighs of those Russian women officers in folk costumes and I got a marvellous idea.

"My Maria calls me Danicek."

The silence that followed was broken by the croaking voice of one of the old chess players in the smoke-filled room: "Mate!"

Milada twitched. "*Who* — calls you that?"

"My — let's call her my fiancée. Naturally we're not so bourgeois that we're actually engaged, not officially anyway — but we're going to be married next fall," I said, secure in the knowledge that by next fall I'd be away from Hronov and safely in the army.

Milada slowly turned pale. A dramatic struggle was going on inside her, woman versus loyal Party member. But the woman hadn't surrendered yet.

"Where does your fiancée work?"

"She's a dancer in the State Dance Troupe," I said, and then I went on to assure the fictitious fiancée a proper class pedigree. "She's an orphan. The Germans executed her parents. The Nazis. Her father was a foreman in the CKD foundries and he was mixed up in some sabotage and — well, you can imagine the rest. At the time, a lot of people got rounded up."

This watertight fairy-tale dashed Milada's hopes. She surrendered her progressive young man who had been roped in by this woman of impeccable pedigree, this daughter of a resistance hero of elite working-class origins.

"That's horrible!" she said. "The poor thing! The more you learn, the more you realize what a terrible thing Fascism is!"

Following this letdown, Milada revealed some human imperfection after all, and downed her glass of Mavrud as though it were vodka. I filled it up again, and kept on filling it until she'd emptied the bottle. Then I ordered another. Milada abandoned the theme of the fiancée and revealed her secret plan — which she would have no doubt abandoned, had I abandoned the daughter of the executed resistance hero. She had submitted a request to teach at one of the Czech schools abroad. In addition to Moscow and several other cities in the peoples' democracies, she was looking at Vienna, Paris, Chicago, and Rio de Janeiro. The Ministry of Education had decided to open experimental schools in these cities for the children of Czechoslovak diplomats, which would also be open — in special afternoon courses — to descendants of emigrants. The vetting of teachers for these schools would be exceptionally strict, said Milada, but she wasn't worried. She had top references from Hronov and from her university, and her father had recently been decorated with the order of "Builder of Socialism", since he'd been the first in the country to introduce the Soviet method of painless childbirth.

When I left her at her door that night, she was still babbling about it. "Daniel, I'm going to carry the struggle right inside the capitalist lair; I'll take our children right out of their arms, those stupid, disgusting capitalists." The alcohol had made her vulgar, and the romantic moon made her permanent wave glimmer. "I'll make contact with the comrades in the Communist Party of America, and with the comrade Negroes — oh my God!" she said suddenly. "I feel si — "

She vomited all over the sidewalk in front of her house, then fled inside. The next day she didn't come to school, sending a note saying she had "women's troubles" — an unheard-of event, for although she suffered from almost pathological pain each month, she was always heroic in her suffering, following the example of the model Soviet female worker — but to be sure everyone knew, she kept a tube of feminine painkillers beside her Russian composition notebooks.

After her romantic disappointment, Milada threw herself with renewed energy into the struggle to keep most of the graduating students from taking their matriculation exams. But Ivana always managed to fend her off, and on the eve of the final and decisive staff meeting she was still assured of full support. In the time-tested tradition of citizens in dictatorships everywhere, the staff members supported the source of power nearest them, so that in case of trouble they could always absolve themselves from responsibility by blaming it.

But on the day of the meeting — almost as if by arrangement — a bomb fell. Milada walked confidently into the staff room, a grim expression on her face and a copy of *Sudlice,* the weekly of the district committee of the Communist Party, in her hand.

Of course, everyone had read the article already. Ivana, who was normally the first to arrive at any meeting, was still in her office, where she was consoling a weeping Bozena Stoklasova. The article in *Sudlice* had the striking headline KULAK CONSPIRACY REVEALED, and it said, briefly but forcefully:

> Thanks to the alertness and vigilance of members of the National Security Forces, and the co-operation of our citizens, a dangerous conspiracy of local kulaks was uncovered in the community of Maselna Lhota in our district. These traitors [whom these class enemies had betrayed by conspiring against an enemy class, the article did not explain] formed an illegal, anti-state group the purpose of which was economic sabotage and the murder of functionaries in the United Agricultural Co-op movement and in the Communist Party of Czechoslovakia. A former farmhand, J.N., was also arrested for his part in these evil intrigues. The arrest was made by Com. Ponykl, an officer of the District National Committee in charge of economic questions, just as the villain was trying to poison pigfeed with mercury in the nearby village of Tresnova Lhota. Among the arrested are Martin Stoklasa, kulak (28 hectares), Josef Zima, kulak (26 hectares), Josef Benisko, kulak (24 hectares), and others.

The first of the diversionists, who were listed according to the size of their holdings, was the father of Bozena Stoklasova from the fourth form, a delicate, pretty girl who had worked with superhuman dedication over the past half-year to qualify for matriculation.

We sat around the conference table in tragic silence until at last the doors of the principal's office opened and a red-eyed Bozena hurried out. Probably in the desperate hope that it would help, she had worn her Youth Union shirt. Now — shorn of hope — she ran past the conference table and out into the hall. All the staff followed her with sympathetic eyes, except for one who gave her a dark look of correct hatred.

Then Ivana Hrozna emerged from her office. A button was torn off her white blouse, and there was a large wet stain on her ample bosom where the kulak's daughter had probably pressed her face. Part of her blouse was hanging out of her navy-blue skirt, and across her face, which looked very much like a caricature of Winston Churchill, bobbed a strand of greasy hair.

She sat down in a chair at the head of the table and, with her clumsy but calculated diplomacy, began the meeting.

"This is a terrible, tragic blow, comrades. Poor Bozenka is completely shattered by what her father has done. I've asked the girls in her year to keep an eye on her in case she tries to do something to herself."

The silence continued.

"Such a disgusting fellow!" Ivana continued, trying to fill her incorrigibly good-natured voice with hatred. "He has such a dear, talented daughter and he has no idea how his revolting behaviour could ruin her life! He deserves the strictest punishment! And we, comrades, must give even greater care to Bozenka now — "

"I agree," Milada interrupted her sharply. "She's a grown-up girl now and she must be given an opportunity to prove that she has a positive relationship to our efforts to build socialism, unlike her father. Of course we can't let her sit for her matriculation exams. But we can put in a good word for her, and perhaps they'll allow her to volunteer for some youth construction project, or for a steelworks, and then in two or three years — "

"Yes, comrade, I entirely agree with you," Ivana said, moving on to her second tactical plan. "We must give her an opportunity." Then she opened the floodgates of eloquence and told us the stunning news: the school doctor, Comrade Dr. Gellen, had informed her that Bozena suffered from Ménière's disease and could under no circumstances work at a machine or do heavy physical labour. And she had a cousin who, unlike her criminal father, had been declared Model Tractor Driver at the Agricultural Machine Depot in Rozemberk in South Bohemia. Despite her class background, Bozena had worked very well all year in the Czechoslovak Union of Youth, where she'd been in charge of membership fees; moreover, during the scrap metal drive she had collected an above-average amount. Ivana looked at me and I confirmed her statement, adding that the metal Stoklasova had collected weighed more than she did. Zdena laughed intelligently at my remark, inspiring the others to laugh too. This dispelled some of the gloom, and Ivana pressed her advantage. "And Comrade Stoklasova," she said, her voice rising, "wishes to make a commitment to volunteer as a social worker at the New Klement Gottwald Steelworks in Ostrava as soon as she finishes her matriculation."

But Milada was not to be moved. She stuck to her main point: a kulak accused of planning (if not actually carrying out) the murder of Party functionaries. When Ivana gave up trying to persuade her and proposed to hold a vote on the matter — an outmoded democratic procedure, but one that would have achieved her goal — Milada interrupted her in a cold voice:

"Comrade principal, I don't like to say this, but if you, comrades, vote to allow Stoklasova to take her finals, I will have to report the matter to the regional Party headquarters! The point is not what kind of person Stoklasova is, or how she studies. The point is that she was raised by a criminal, an enemy of our system. Where is your guarantee that she's not merely putting the best face on it? That, as a social worker, she won't have a negative impact — or worse — at an important place like the New Klement Gottwald Steelworks?"

A chill fell over the room. The more timid old women on the staff were frightened at the mention of the district Party headquarters. Ivana was also caught off guard.

"Yes, but — Comrade Maresova — " she stammered, "naturally — I value your approach — but consider the facts. She's a sick girl — and she's young — and green boughs are more easily — "

"They've been bending her for eighteen years," the good Party member said drily. "How do you expect to correct that in a single year, comrade? All I know is, she's had a reactionary upbringing, and she's a girl who obeys her father — "

At this point Ivana interrupted with an inspired appeal based on the latest Marxist method.

"But even so, Milada, I've already talked to her about it — and so far she hasn't made up her mind — you know you can't rush into these things, when the girl is going through such a difficult time — but she promised me she'd think about it. To make a long story short, I suggested she put an announcement in the paper saying that — well, that she renounces and condemns her father — and at the same time she could publish her pledge too, so I think — and what do you say to this, comrades? — that in that case we could all give her a full vote of confidence, couldn't we?"

She looked around the room at the staff members, her eyes full of entreaty and innocent guile. Her gaze came to rest on Milada.

"Pedagogically speaking, it's the perfect solution!" Zdenka Prochazkova said firmly.

"Isn't it? I think so too," said Evzenie Vikusova, although why they shouldn't let a student who had never failed take her final exams was a mystery beyond the range of her logical abilities. I grumbled my assent loudly, and one by one the old ladies became bold enough to agree.

"Did she actually promise?" asked Milada uncertainly. She couldn't immediately assess the ideological implications of such a solution.

"I gave her three days to think it over. For the time being, we'll leave her case open. Do you agree, comrades?"

We all mumbled our assent. Milada said nothing.

But Bozena Stoklasova displayed an unexpected stubbornness and refused to renounce her villainous father. We had to substitute for Ivana all next morning because she was in her office trying to persuade the unhappy student to change her mind. Occasionally she enlisted the help of Evzenie Vikusova and Anca Slavici, the senior member of the staff who taught history, but neither the home economics teacher's pragmatism nor Anca Slavici's historically informed relativism made any impression on the girl with her Catholic upbringing. Just before lunch Zdenka Prochazkova had a try, but oddly enough she gave up immediately. Ivana, sufficiently desperate now to exploit my erotic influence, called me in that afternoon.

Bozena, on the edge of hysteria, forgot about the recent edict that teachers were to be addressed as "comrade".

"Mr. Smiricky! I can't do this to my father! It would break his heart. My father's such a good man; he's never beaten me, he's worked all his life, and anyway he's completely innocent!" she wailed.

"Hush! Bozenka! Don't say that!" Ivana hissed.

I tried an old but proven tactic. "Look here, if I were your father I'd want you to do it. After all, your father loves you and I'm sure he only wants what's good for you."

She turned her majolica eyes back to me; her face was pale. She obviously couldn't imagine me in her father's place, and she burst into tears again. Her bony shoulders shook so violently that it looked like epilepsy.

Ivana and I gave up.

Or rather, I gave up. Ivana simply changed her tactics. That evening I ran into her at the post office sending a telegram. She took the night express to Prague and after lunch the next day — I was sitting in the staff room alone — there was a polite knock on the door and in stepped a ruddy, windburned man, robustly built, in a black, double-breasted Sunday suit off the rack, with a lace handkerchief in his pocket and, under it, an absurd Soviet-style medal.

"Stoklasa, Jan," he said, introducing himself in the old-fashioned way, and then he handed me a crumpled piece of paper. "I got this telegram so I took the express train right away, in case Bozenka tried anything, since my uncle got mixed up in that stupid — " He stopped, wondering if he hadn't chosen his words poorly.

I read the telegram. COME AT ONCE STOP YOUR COUSIN'S LIFE IN DANGER STOP FATHER ARRESTED STOP I HROZNA PRINCIPAL SOCIAL WORKERS' SCHOOL.

I read the rather Delphic message and offered the medal-wearer a seat. I was just telling him that the principal wasn't there when the door flew open and Ivana, just off the same afternoon express, rushed into the staff room. She grasped the man's right hand with both of hers and squeezed so hard I could hear the bones crack. Then she took him into her office and locked the door.

When I saw him that evening, still wearing his medal and clumsily trying to explain something to Milada Maresova among the lilac bushes, I was compelled to revise my opinion of Ivana's simple-mindedness. Later, as I was walking past the municipal café, I saw Ivana through the window in conversation with Comrade Ponykl, his pistol bulging ominously under his summer jacket. In the staff room the next day, when everyone but Milada was present, Ivana casually let it be known that she'd been to Prague on business yesterday and, among other things, had learned the sad news that Comrade Maresova would be leaving us in the fall. After a joyous pause, Ivana added that the regional inspector, Comrade Prochazka, had informed her that the appointment of Comrade Maresova to one of the new Czech schools abroad was virtually a certainty. The incorrigible gossip Vikusova (and this was part of Ivana's secret plan too) immediately told Milada the fresh news, giving what she had heard a new though essentially truthful twist, which was that Ivana had been to Prague to intervene on Milada's behalf. That afternoon Milada accompanied the ruddy medal-wearer to the station (no one knew where he'd spent the night, but he looked as though he hadn't slept much) and the Stoklasova affair was dropped. Ivana had proved herself a strategist worthy of her great model, the generalissimo.

But even the most perfectly laid plans are sometimes disrupted by unforeseen events. Another terrible blow was to fall upon the unfortunate Stoklasova.

Two days after a mollified Milada had stopped talking about her, Ivana summoned me into her office just as I was about to have lunch. She was unusually cool, but I could tell she was upset. When I entered the room I saw Stoklasova sitting with her face buried in her arms on the desk, her thin shoulders heaving, a picture of misery and suffering. A tight-lipped Milada was standing over her, and when she saw me she gave me a look of such imperious disdain that my heart plunged into my trousers.

"Comrade — comrade — " Ivana began awkwardly, radiating pure despair. "Look here — what — what can you tell us about this? How — how can you — explain this?"

I felt a sudden chill. My first thought was that someone had told her about Vixi and me. As if to confirm my fear, Ivana reached across her desk and handed me a photograph. "And Comrade Smiricky," Milada said acidly, "is already engaged to the daughter of a comrade executed by the Nazis."

With some trepidation I looked at the picture. To my relief, it was only a portrait of me taken by a local photographer for inclusion in the traditional graduating-class tableau. Across it, in the red ink we used to correct students' papers, someone had written:

To Bozena — thanks for the gift of your virginity — Danny.

The handwriting bore a vague resemblance to mine — at least in the sense that it came from a fountain pen with a wide nib.

"Comrade Milada — found this — " Ivana was almost gasping for breath — "in Comrade Stoklasova's — Russian composition notebook."

I turned to the unfortunate girl. First her father had been arrested for conspiracy to commit murder and now she stood accused of immorality. But I was beginning to see what was going on. I thought of that house of shame, the girls' dormitory, where the porter had asked for a bonus because night after night he had to patrol the back of the building to scare off the young sculptors and stonemasons trying to clamber up the ivy.

"Just give me a moment, comrades," I said. I reached for the telephone and asked the operator for Municipal Services, photography division. Bozena's sobbing grew louder while both teachers stared uncomprehendingly at me. The photographer answered the phone in the still respectful tones of the private businessman he had once been.

"Kominek, photographer. May I help you?"

Loud enough for everyone in the office to hear, I said, "Professor Smiricky here. Sir, I ordered some extra copies of my portrait. You may recall it was for the graduation-class tableau for the Social School."

The photographer's response satisfied me, and I repeated it out loud: "Aha. You say Miss Doruzkova picked them up for me? Yes, she's from my class. And that was a week ago? I see. She must have forgotten to give them to me. Thank you very much, Mr. Kominek."

And I hung up.

Under Ivana's supervision, Milada and I carried out a merciless inspection of the graduating class's schoolbags, purses, books, and scribblers. In half an hour we were back in the staff room, minus Stoklasova this time, with a collection of my portraits on the conference table in front of us — all of them bearing dedications that went far beyond the norms of ordinary pornography. The erotic spirit of the Social School had broken through its political shell with such vigour that, by comparison, the reference to Bozena's loss of virginity was practically a model of innocence.

We turned up eleven pictures in all, and Milada, who'd never got even with me for being engaged to someone else, now demanded that all the guilty parties not only be excluded from the final exams, but be expelled from school as well.

In a situation that, for the moment, seemed otherwise unresolvable, Ivana suddenly put her hand to her heart and passed out.

But the Lord can sometimes show mercy in His cruelty, and He now appeared to choose me as His agent in extending a helping finger to the unhappy principal.

While Dr. Gellen was administering first aid to Ivana and I was gathering the confiscated photographs from the table, an interesting detail struck my eye: five of the eleven pictures bore dedications written by the proletarian members of the graduating class. My political schooling, which so far had brought me nothing but the clap, suddenly came in handy, and I applied the key of class justice to the crime. By my calculations there were only six girls of bona fide proletarian origin in the class; if we went along with Milada's proposal, only one of them would get to sit for her finals. In light of the Ministry of Education's directive, that would be a serious political error.

When a revivified Ivana followed Dr. Gellen out of her office, I put on a look of grave concern and informed her of my discovery. She seemed surprisingly fresh after her seizure, and immediately summoned Milada and took her back into her sanctuary for a private conversation. Two hours later Milada emerged, glowering but clearly defeated, and Ivana, just to make sure, walked her right to the door of the staff room and into the hall. A great weight seemed to have fallen from her overburdened heart. Using the class approach, she had clearly been able to stave off the impending catastrophe.

And then our girls — Youth Union members all, with their residual Girl Guide morality — went and spoiled everything.

At half past three I was called to the telephone. It was the photographer, Mr. Kominek, with an apology. Those extra rush copies of my portrait that Miss Doruzkova had ordered after lunch today wouldn't be ready until half past five, he said, because his printing machine had broken down. The significance of this new move by Doruzkova was not immediately clear to me, but school was over for the day and I decided to put off any investigation of the matter until the next day.

By that time, however, an investigation was no longer necessary. First thing in the morning, a delegation from the fourth-year class — consisting of all the girls from whom we had not confiscated any photographs — showed up at the principal's office, led by Kamila Doruzkova.

They presented a dismayed Ivana with fourteen more photographs, each with a dedication (the ink was scarcely dry) that maintained the high standard of immorality set by the original inscriptions. They didn't want only some of their class to suffer, Kamila declared, because all of them were equally guilty.

At that moment Milada Maresova stuck her head into the principal's office and immediately grasped what was going on. The delegation piously filed out of the office, leaving behind a crushed principal who, in other circumstances, would have been pleased by such a show of class solidarity. Unfortunately, the solidarity again laid bare the class aspect of the affair. In the meeting that was quickly called to discuss the matter, Milada, as though it were criminally soft-hearted even to suggest such a thing, declared that she would no longer insist on expelling the girls and that she wanted to change her original proposal. Now, she said, all the girls should receive an official reprimand from the school, and only students of working-class origin should be allowed to take the finals.

"It's a harsh measure, comrades, I'm aware of that," she said, "but Bolsheviks have always been able to display harshness when necessary."

I thought the fate of the unfortunate class was sealed at last, but I didn't know Ivana. Fortifying herself with strong black coffee, she mobilized what was left of her powers for one final effort: that evening she called a meeting of the graduating class's Youth Union in her office. None of the other teachers was invited.

Around eleven that night, when I was walking past the school on my way back from a date with Vixi, the window of the principal's office was still open and glowing into the humid, pre-summer darkness. Inside I could see the backs of several girls. The office was packed, and the familiar voice of Comrade Ponykl drifted into the quiet, empty street. "I'm telling you, girl," he was saying, "it'll get you a good report card, it'll get all of you good report cards, comrades, and speaking for myself—" Then his voice was lost in the rustle of chestnut leaves. I didn't know what plot was being hatched by the homely Ivana and the sinister Ponykl, but I tipped my hat to Bolshevik tenacity.

A day later, the Hronov newspaper *Sudlice* carried, in a decorative frame, the following announcement:

> I hereby declare that I publicly renounce my father, the kulak Martin Stoklasa from Maselna Lhota. His despicable act has excluded him for ever from the ranks of our honest working people. I no longer consider myself his daughter, and I would ask all comrades not to consider me as such. At the same time,

I pledge that after completing the matriculation examinations, I will volunteer my services as a social worker among the comrades of gypsy origin at the HUKO construction site in Kosice, in Slovakia.

B. Stoklasova

Underneath it, in a different frame, was another manifesto:

We, the students of the fourth year in the Hronov Social School, declare that we are deeply shocked by the revelations regarding the conspiratorial reactionary gang in our district, all the more so because one of the reprehensible criminals is the father of a member of our collective. We fully stand behind her declaration above and we would like to add our own pledge to hers: after the matriculation examinations, we will voluntarily join a work brigade for one year at the Youth Construction site in Ostrava-Kuncice, in Moravia. Long live our working class, which vigilantly reveals and deservedly punishes all enemies of our people's democratic homelands. Long live the Union of Czechoslovak Youth!

For the Union members in the Fourth Form
of Hronov Social School,
Doruzkova K.

And that was the end of the affair. For health reasons, Bozena Stoklasova never did go to work on the gypsy construction site in Slovakia, and in one way or another the others wormed out of their pledges too. But the pledges had never been more than means perfectly justified by the ends they served. On the day the declarations were published, Ivana — to make a hundred and ten percent sure — undertook a new pilgrimage to Comrade Prochazka's office in Prague. She brought back with her a letter of appointment from the Minister of Education declaring that Comrade Milada Maresova, presently teaching at the Hronov Social School, was to be the new principal of the Czech school in Cicero, Illinois.

And that was how Ivana Hrozna led all her immoral little lambs into the promised land of matriculation.

4.

When I got home from the reception in the Hrzansky Palace in Prague, I found a copy of the Hronov *Sudlice* from the previous week in my mail. It had been sent to me anonymously by someone who obviously remembered my ancient tenure in the lilac-bowered town, and one article was marked in red.

> A QUESTION FOR THE PUBLIC
>
> On June 6, 1968, the district court in Hronov conducted a judicial inquiry into the case of the so-called "anti-state kulak group", involving Martin Stoklasa and company. It was determined, and confirmed by testimony, that the "group" was actually set up by an agent of the secret police, Jan Nohejl from Maselna Lhota, acting on orders from the state security forces in Prague. This action was intended to entrap credulous farmers. The court found that because the whole affair was a provocation, the charges brought against the accused were unfounded, all the more so since no actual sabotage took place and — according to testimony by J. Nohejl — no assassinations were planned at all. The court therefore reversed the charges on all counts against the men, and returned full civic rights to all those who spent many years in concentration camps: Martin Stoklasa (14 years), Josef Zima (12 years), Josef Benisek (12 years), Alois Safranek (10 years), and Antonin Sykora (8 years). In the case of M. Stoklasa and J. Zima, the rehabilitation is unfortunately posthumous. Charges were laid against the *agent provocateur*, J. Nohejl.
>
> But for citizens of Hronov, this is not the end of the "kulak group" affair. Most citizens of Hronov still have vivid memories of how the principal of the Hronov Health and Social Workers' School, Ivana Hrozna, using a combination of terror and threats, compelled B. Stoklasova, the daughter of Martin Stoklasa, to write a shameful denunciation which was published in this newspaper nineteen years ago. The girl was so upset by the experience that after graduating from the school she was hospitalized for more than half a year in the neurological department of the Hronov District Hospital. The same Ivana Hrozna is still principal of the Social School in our town. We ask: *quousque tandem . . . ?*

Thus does the world settle its scores, I said to myself. And thus the world turns and yet remains the same. I looked at the numerals in brackets, which indicated a different measure than the ones printed — my God! was it nineteen years before? — though they too were mentioned in descending order of magnitude. I wondered where Milada Maresova was now. She had married an officer in the Soviet Army stationed in Poland and had vanished from my horizon. I looked at my bookshelf and the row of librettos, my musicals, from which these and other stories were circumspectly missing. Among those musicals was the comedy once attacked by the Grand Master. His story, too, was missing from my works.

5.

On Sunday afternoon Bukavec and I went in his limousine to pick up Vixi at the girls' dormitory. She was already waiting for us at the bottom of the wooden staircase — dressed, for this private match, in the same lace blouse, perfumed, her lips a bright red. She'd even put mascara on her eyes (later she told me it was shoe polish). Her deathly pallor (she was still nervous) and the lace frill around her neck made her look somewhat like an inmate of the eighteenth-century girls' residence founded by the Princess Lansfeldova.

The regular Sunday worship service was going on in the widow Ledvinova's kitchen; the Moravian Brethren did not acknowledge the municipal jubilee because orthodox Protestantism had played no role in the founding of the town. So the lute, the harmonium, the bass fiddle, the violin, and human voices created a backwash of sound for the chess match. The song they were singing — thanks to frequent pauses, embarrassing rhymes, and incompatible syllabic quantities — sounded more like an anti-religious parody:

Mystery surrounds us
Blind men in the glooooom
But the light of Jeeeeesus
Shines forth in that roooooom.

It was half past one when Vixi and Bukavec sat down opposite each other at the cherrywood table where the widow served me breakfast. The Grand Master's chauffeur announced that he was going to take a nap in the lilac bushes, but I thought it would be brief; I figured the match would be over in about ten minutes. Then we could all go to a restaurant in the rock formations outside Hronov where the last surviving local swing band had found refuge from the wrath of the municipal Party committee.

The Grand Master pulled his tiny silver chess set out of his pocket; the figures were arranged the way they had stood after the final move in the chess-by-mail match. My student gave this jewel of Soviet chess technology a respectful look, and then looked at the Grand Master.

"It's your move, Miss Koziskova," said Bukavec.

Vixi brought her pretty little nose close to the chessboard, stretched out a finger with its nail fastidiously painted pink, gently touched the golden rook, then took it carefully from its little hole, moved it several squares forward, and pushed it back into the board. The Grand Master swallowed, gave a silly titter, nodded, and asked for a cup of coffee. I went into the kitchen to interrupt the singing for a moment. When I came back with the coffee pot, the Grand Master was sitting with his head in both hands and Vixi was squatted down opposite him, as pale as the ghost of the dead princess.

About an hour later Bukavec sent me for another pot of coffee. Vixi jumped up and offered to go and get it herself. I sat down in her place and looked at the little figures, which told me nothing. The strained face of Jarda Bukavec told me more.

"Looks like you're in a tight squeeze," I said.

The Grand Master gave a twitch and then, with great difficulty, pulled out of his trancelike state.

"This girl is a goddamn genius," he said. "I had everything worked out. I'd move my knight to — " and he began talking mumbo-jumbo. "But when she shifted her rook there — well, at first it seemed totally irrational, but the more I sit here, man, the more I realize she's just opened up an incredible opportunity for her bishop, who could go to — " and he went on talking his secret language, concluding with a rhetorical question: "So where do I go from here?"

"Why don't you just mate her and get it over with, instead of trying to figure out some complicated response?"

Bukavec angrily reached for his cup of coffee and tilted it into his mouth before realizing it was empty. Irritated, he said, "There's a simple answer to that, stupid. It can't be done."

"To be more precise, *you* can't do it."

"All right. To tell you the truth, I am, as you pointed out, in a very tight spot."

I told him what time it was and he was horrified. "What I can't figure out," I said, "is how you mated her so easily yesterday."

"Some players are like that. They just need time to think. Sometimes they need several days for a single move."

I looked at my watch again. "I think you must be one of them."

"Don't talk like a jerk!" He put his head in his hands and sighed. "This kid's a genius."

At that point Vixi came back with the coffee pot. The Grand Master began drinking his at once but, coffee or no coffee, nothing changed on the chessboard that day. Not long afterwards, the chauffeur pounded on the door and said that if they didn't hit the road right away the Grand Master would blow his simultaneous match in Zeleny Hradec. So the Grand Master, dulled by an overdose of caffeine, obediently hit the road — leaving me alone in the bedroom with Vixi.

"Mysteree surrounds us," sang the unflagging choristers in the kitchen, while I studied my neatly groomed girl in amazement.

"For crying out loud, Vixi, what kind of racket are you running here?"

"I beg your pardon!" she said, and a healthy colour quickly returned to her cheeks.

"Someone's helping you out, right?"

"Who? I mean, he's creamed Botvinik, and they say he once played Alyechin to a draw."

She was right. "So how do you explain it? Where does this talent come from?"

She shrugged her shoulders, stood up, and then unexpectedly came over and sat down in my lap. "I don't know, sir. That's just how it is. Comes all by itself. I'm sitting there staring at the board and suddenly something in my noodle goes *ping*!"

I thought of Julia, who could copy an article from *Holy Mary's Weekly Messenger* with both hands at once, in mirror writing. There is mystery in young girls. Not being entirely rational creatures, perhaps they can communicate with the dark forces of that other world — which of course doesn't exist.

"Maybe you're just an idiot," I said.

"What's that supposed to mean?"

"I mean you're a brilliant idiot. Haven't you ever heard of morons who can solve irrational equations?"

"You think I'm a moron?"

"No, I don't. But you're obviously, in a very narrow sense, a genius."

"That sounds a little better, sir."

"If you're not lying, that is," I said. "Sometimes I have the feeling you're a little too smart for your own good. Just be careful you don't end up having to pay for it someday!"

7

■

The Muddled Young Men on the Flying Trapeze

I.

The Prague Spring rushed madly on. The working class, traditionally conservative, kept a weather eye on their cottages and their motorcycles; intellectuals wrote manifestos and badgered their friends over the telephone for signatures. I myself signed one — I could not very well avoid signing it without discrediting myself in the cultural community — and it was this manifesto that the Party, struggling to reassert its authority, chose to damn publicly. It withdrew its damnation later the same day, but from then on I was more cautious; I stopped answering the telephone and left my apartment only for the most essential groceries. Others, more cautious than I, left Prague altogether. Paternoster retreated to a cottage in Pikovice, and the talented novelist Nabal went all the way to the Bulgarian seaside, where he passed himself off as a West German in case the local Leninists tried to lynch him as a counter-revolutionary.

I too was beginning to give serious thought to foreign travel when, as if in answer to a prayer, an invitation arrived from Vienna. The Austrian Arts and Letters Society was holding a summer conference on the French *roman nouveau*, and because my last operetta was called *Eva, Have You Read Robbe-Grillet?*, they had been misled into putting me on their mailing list. I sent them a telegram saying I was on my way, and packed my suitcase.

Meanwhile the telephone kept ringing, but I didn't answer it. Just as I was getting ready to slip out of my flat the back way, though, the mailman brought me a special delivery letter, mailed in Prague:

Dear Dr. Smiricky,

I couldn't reach you by phone, hence this letter. Dr. Zinner of the Austrian Arts and Letters Society called to tell me, among other things, that they'd invited you to a literary conference in Vienna, and that you'd agreed to come. I can't get away myself, so I'd like to ask you a favour. Sulc, one of the three people mixed up in the Father Doufal affair, is now working at our embassy in Vienna. If you have the chance, do you think you could see him and try to get him to talk a little? It would help me, and our whole cause, immensely.

Yours,
Vaclav Juzl

I crumpled the letter and tossed it into the waste basket. There was too much writing on the wall already, and the nineteen years since the miracle had taught me — unlike others — a lot. But man proposes and, as they say — no doubt correctly — God disposes.

From the very beginning of the conference on the *roman nouveau*, I found myself suffering from a sense of alienation I'd always thought was just another one of Karl Marx's overblown inventions. The sessions took place in the gilded hall of a Viennese Biedermeier palace, and the keynote address was given by the author who had dreamed the whole thing up. He was a slim, Gallic, cunning-looking man with a thin moustache, and he presented his views to the sluggish morning audience in a brisk, polished salon French. "I do not describe," he said, "I construct. That was long Flaubert's ambition: to begin from nothing and construct something that could stand on its own, relying on nothing outside the work. All contemporary novels have this ambition."

The founder of the movement was world-famous, and despite the early hour the hall was packed. Official delegates were seated in comfortable chairs on a raised dais and each of us was provided with a souvenir pen and a thick notepad. Beside me, already busy scribbling on his notepad, was the West German literary critic Steiner, while on my other side the Soviet delegate, Arashidov, was fighting off sleep. He had arrived late the previous night and before retiring had spent some time ironing out his jet-lag in the bar downstairs. I knew him from Prague. He had gone (three times) to see my operetta *The Naked Truth*, in which the well-endowed Suzi Kajetanova played one scene in the nude, though behind a backlit scrim, so that she looked like a figure in a Chinese shadow play. Arashidov loved it, and was especially pleased when, after his third visit, I invited him backstage. There was nothing like this, he told me, in all of Moscow.

The man with the moustache was inveighing against realism and the audience was rapt. The only other sound was a faint pop, like a fly stumbling over a caraway seed: Steiner, still writing furiously, had broken his pencil, but he replaced it at once from a supply he kept in a crocodile-skin pencil case beside him. The sound, slight as it was, aroused Arashidov just as the speaker began to talk about the need to renounce the use of details that in traditional prose, he said, "create the sensation that what one reads is actually the truth, since today such details are no longer of interest to the novelist." I saw Arashidov sit up and take notice at this, and I knew why: Arashidov's latest book had been violently attacked by Soviet critics (although they were not advocates of the New Novel) for showing an excessive interest in details that looked too much like the truth.

Since what the French author was saying had little application to my own operettas, I fended off boredom by applying his literary principles to the work of my friend from the East. It was not hard to do. Arashidov too did not describe; he constructed. For many long years, he had written novels that referred to nothing whatever outside themselves, and they stood so perfectly on their own that he had been awarded the Stalin Prize (although now, of course, it was always referred to in reviews as the Lenin Prize).

I looked over at the man who, in this bizarre fashion, had become a double laureate. He was now fully aroused and was nodding enthusiastic assent to each of the Frenchman's literary aphorisms. The silence in the hall continued. Steiner's pencil squeaked and he kept tearing page after page from his notepad. Behind me a bank of floodlights was turned on and I saw a man in a leather jacket readying a hand-held camera for action.

The speaker on the podium remained cool; he was used to the attentions of the mass media. Smoothing his moustache with an index finger that wore an antique gold ring, he kept up his delectable extempore, referring only occasionally to a set of notes on miniature index cards. Arashidov, perhaps thinking that the camera was taking him in as well, donned a frown of appropriate dissent, but went on listening anyway. The speaker's voice was like music full of muted overtones, and my feeling of alienation intensified. The speaker represented a form of experience different from my own, less traumatic and therefore more subtle. Erratic and thoroughly unpleasant memories of the Prague merry-go-round were aroused in my mind — the merry-go-round of the last nineteen years, which had turned some distance from its starting-point, yet always threatened to come back around to it. Although I lived in a land that had once been attracted to the traditions of the speaker's country, fate had now drawn me closer to Arashidov.

The divergence was manifest in the application of the Frenchman's discoveries. Both of them had written their most recent works on the theme of war. The Frenchman had done so with the help of his strange but brand-new method, and his aim, as he described it from the podium, had been to describe the matter in such a way as "to undermine our belief in it all, yet ultimately to confirm to us that everything is true." Arashidov had applied his usual technique, based on an imitation of Hemingway mixed with Saltykov-Shchedrin, for the purpose of undermining the official belief that Soviet soldiers captured by Germans in the Second World War were traitors to the nation and the working class, yet he had had not the slightest intention of confirming that the official belief was true.

By now, newspaper photographers were bouncing their dazzling flashes off the famous novelist's sculpted hair, while his beautiful, nasal French echoed off the gilded frescos of idealized Greek myths on the rococo ceiling. A bluish column of aromatic smoke rose above the bald heads of Western European literary scholars and the bronze coiffeurs of women writers from Manhattan. Then his speech was over, and the novelist bowed modestly and stuck his tiny sheaf of notes into his vest pocket. The camera-man pushed his way through the circle of photographers and knelt down at the front while the author, to deafening applause and the winking of many flash units, graciously descended from the podium.

Steiner began writing an endless and clearly polemical sentence on his notepad, and Arashidov bent close to my ear. His eyes reminded me of the eyes of the Grand Master Bukavec; I could see in them the immense distances of a land shrouded in mist.

"Daniel Josefovich — you know what I don't understand?"

"Nothing, right?"

Arashidov shook his head gravely, got to his feet, and picked up from the table a thick manuscript in a school binder. As he was the representative of the most important country (militarily speaking), protocol dictated that Arashidov speak next.

"What I don't understand is why Monsieur Alain was so strongly opposed to socialist realism when he was in Leningrad last year," he said, blinking the liverish whites of his eyes at me.

Steiner looked around in astonishment, but Arashidov had suddenly stopped resembling the Grand Master. There was definitely a rapport between us, a rapport that, from the standpoint of dialectical materialism, was impermissible.

Once Arashidov was behind the microphone, however, his resemblance to the Grand Master became noticeable once more, and as he got into his presentation I slowly began to understand why. He spoke, or rather read, from a manuscript in Russian, two or three sentences at a time, which the interpreter then contorted into a muddled German. After the suave Frenchman, Arashidov seemed awkward and a bit idiotic. "I am—I can't help it—a socialist realist," he said by way of introduction, and then, via a moronic simultaneous translation, he clumsily developed a theory radically different from the one he'd hinted at to me a short while before. Unlike most of those present, however, I had already heard many attempts to define this mysterious method, and so to me—unlike most of the others—Arashidov's definition did not seem at all naive. On the contrary: in the context of his time and country, I could appreciate his subtle and sophisticated innovations.

"The basic principle of socialist realism," he declared, placing his hand on his heart, "is a belief that can be expressed in the words of that most enlightened of Roman emperors, Marcus Aurelius: *Homo sum. Humani nihil a me alienum puto!*"

Steiner's head jerked up and he looked severely over his glasses at the speaker, then made a furious inscription on his pad. Whatever it was, he was so upset that the note was illegible and resisted all my attempts to decipher it over his shoulder. Meanwhile, having laid the foundation with his quotation from classical literature, Arashidov managed by some logical sleight of hand to include as precursors of socialist realism not only the obvious figures, such as Gogol and the author of *What Is to Be Done?,* but all the writers he liked as well: Dickens and Lautréamont, Thackeray and Kafka, Büchner and Hemingway, Voltaire and Dostoevsky, Milton (he was thinking, as he later told me, not of *Paradise Lost* but of the *Areopagitica*) and Allen Ginsberg. The mix he offered was so outlandish that when the erudite Steiner stood up to speak after Arashidov, he didn't even bother to rebut it with sarcasm, and merely corrected Arashidov's attribution of the Latin quotation. Then he went on to deliver an hour-long lecture, during which all the New York writers, one by one, left the hall. In his talk, he assembled an enormous pile of convincing proofs that everything the Frenchman had said had already been said by others before him, mostly in classical antiquity. Arashidov was not insulted by Steiner's swipe at his scholarship; he accepted the criticism and made his first and only note. A simple poet like Terence was, after all, politically more suitable than even the most enlightened emperor.

During the break I sought out Arashidov in the corridor. He was standing alone in a corner, with a silent man at his side. With my long years of experience in the lands east of Vienna, I had no difficulty guessing the man's function. Fortunately, since the conference was in Austria, they had provided Arashidov (whose only foreign language was English) with a German-speaking shadow. By denying any knowledge of either German or Russian, I could talk to Arashidov in English.

Arashidov was excited. "Is here Mike Morris? They tell me yes! You know him?"

"Yes, I do," I said. "He has a very pretty wife with him."

But it was the author who interested Arashidov, not the woman. Morris was a self-made Englishman from a working-class background. The earthy naturalism of his works was somewhat redeemed — at least in the eyes of Soviet literary criticism — by his anti-capitalist tendencies, and so Arashidov had been able to translate (and linguistically edit) Morris's shortest novel into Russian.

With Arashidov's KGB shadow on our tail, we went looking for Mike Morris. The crowd milling about in the corridor was colourfully cosmopolitan, and the cop was constantly distracted. His attention was first taken by a stocky Canadian novelist in a kilt; next, we almost lost him as he stared in shock at a black American authoress who, though wearing trousers, also had on a transparent blouse with no brassiere underneath. We found the Englishman and his pretty wife standing at the bar between two women writers from New York. The encounter was an emotional one. Arashidov flung open his arms, tipped his head towards one shoulder, charged the petrified Brit, and embraced him, planting a loud kiss on either cheek. Morris turned a deep shade of red. Then, while Arashidov was busy embracing and kissing Morris's wife, the undercover cop embraced and kissed the Englishman, then repeated the ritual with his wife. It was only when I offered him no more than a handshake, and kissed his wife's hand (she was so pretty she made a Pole out of me), that Morris became himself again.

We sat down at the bar and Arashidov ordered a drink he called "oo-iski". The barman was baffled by the Russian's pronunciation, but Morris was obviously an experienced drinker and understood at once. The barman poured them each a double scotch and Arashidov, a vodka-drinker, tossed his glass back in one quick motion, without blinking. Then he fished an ice-cube out of the glass with his fingers, put it in his mouth, and began to chew it, smiling fondly at Morris.

"*Nu vot — eto on!* It *is* you! Morris!" he said in Russian.

"Right!" said the Brit. "Let's have another one." We had another one, Arashidov began to speak fluent Russified English, and the cop had nothing to do but be bored. The black writer in the transparent blouse was sitting somewhere behind us, hidden in the crowd.

After several more whiskies (the polite Morris didn't have the heart to point out that one drank whisky differently from vodka) Arashidov began to take a keener interest in the pretty wife, but his advances were interrupted when Dr. Zinner came into the bar to announce that the next session of the conference was about to begin. The black writer in the see-through blouse stood up and, as the KGB agent gawked helplessly at her fantastic nipples, Arashidov took advantage of his distraction to ask, in a whisper, if Morris and his wife would care to spend the evening with him. Perhaps he was worried that his shadow was only pretending not to understand English, as I was pretending not to understand Russian. The English couple, who were made slightly ill at ease by Arashidov's conspiratorial tone, accepted the invitation, and we all went back into the hall.

I walked back with both Russians, behind the black writer in the yellow blouse. Steiner was trying to engage her in conversation, but she shook him off by disappearing into the ladies' room. The KGB agent mumbled something and blundered into the men's room right beside it; perhaps he thought he could sneak a peek at her through a ventilation duct. Again Arashidov took advantage of the moment, and said to me, in Russian this time, "Daniel Josefovich, I need a whore for this evening."

I looked at him in astonishment. "A whore? I had the impression you were sweet on Madame Morris."

"You don't understand," he said, with a sidelong glance at the door to the men's room, and then, instead of continuing into the hall, he cleverly pulled me back into the bar. There, over a vodka, Arashidov told me his plan. Looking straight at me with his sad eyes, he said he wanted to have a heart-to-heart talk with Morris. There were many things he wanted to ask him about. And—I would certainly understand—this would not be possible with Anton Pavlovich along. (By this he meant the shadow, whose given names were a parental joke; his surname was Chekhov.) Of course I understood. Anton Pavlovich didn't know, whispered Arashidov, that we'd arranged to spend the evening with the Morrises, so if Arashidov could convince him that he wanted to go with a whore in order to write an article about the degradation of women in capitalist society for *Ogonyok*, Anton Pavlovich might just let him do it. Of course, he wouldn't believe that that was Arashidov's real reason for wanting a whore, but Anton Pavlovich had one weakness — his only truly human weakness, Arashidov said with unexpected sarcasm — he was terribly fond of women. Anton Pavlovich didn't drink or smoke, but he made up for it by copulating. He might let Arashidov alone if he thought he wanted to sleep with a whore. Then we'd pay her, let her go, Arashidov would concoct something about Viennese whores for *Ogonyok*, and we'd go to join the Morrises. "A whore, Daniel Josefovich," said Arashidov hopefully, "he just might close his eyes to a whore." But she would have to be pretty. An ugly woman would only put him off.

I promised to keep my eyes open for a whore and deliver her that evening to the Kaiserhof Hotel. A scowling Anton Pavlovich appeared in the door of the bar; he had obviously been searching for us. His jacket was covered with plaster dust, and I speculated that maybe he'd actually tried to poke a peephole in the washroom wall. Arashidov waved excitedly, with a glowing smile on his face, and, so that there would be no doubt about his joy, called out in a booming voice:

"*Anton Pavlovich, idite syuda! Zdyes vodka!*"

The frowning Chekhov joined us and ordered a Coca-Cola.

As it turned out, I had no trouble at all fulfilling my promise to find a whore. At lunch I was handed an invitation to a five o'clock cocktail party at the Czechoslovak embassy, and when I arrived there — having gone partly out of curiosity, partly to avoid being considered disrespectful — I was welcomed by my old platonic love (I wasn't her type) Suzi Kajetanova. She was standing with the ambassador by the bar, wearing a dazzling dress, and the moment she saw me she rushed over and gave me an ecstatic and no doubt sincere kiss. I was the only one who, years before, had believed she had any talent as an actress. She was a phenomenal jazz and rock singer but had the reputation of being a piece of wood on stage, but I virtually forced the world-famous film director Jiri Vencl to give her a part in a film version of my musical comedy *Crime in a Night-Club*. I had written the part especially for her, hoping she would reward me in the traditional way. And I was vindicated: not only was she stunningly photogenic, she wasn't bad as an actress either. But the only compensation I ever got was seeing her act in the nude from the wings, behind that scrim — which could only deepen my platonic love.

But otherwise she was a spunky kid, and when I took her aside and explained Arashidov's problem she was immediately game to help out. She had her own reasons, I knew, for agreeing. Suzi had a number of private scores to settle with undercover cops. Several years before, when the Party was trying to stifle a wave of rock and roll sweeping the country, it had circulated a rumour — on direct orders from the head of the Cultural Bureau of the Central Committee, Comrade Kral — that Suzi had urinated on a delegation of workers from a balcony in the Pupp Hotel in Karlsbad. But the plan backfired: the rumour added to her popularity, if anything, and urinating from balconies became a popular sport among young people. So the Party resorted to more open tactics and arrested the Queen of Rock, as she was known, charging her with smuggling twenty-seven West German marks into the country in contravention of the currency regulations. She was given a suspended sentence of six months for damaging the state economy. I attended the trial, and my heart went out to her. The Party had put together a clique of faithful concierges and during the trial these rent-a-mob Leninists shouted out slogans read from pieces of paper hidden under the benches. One of them bellowed three times, "It's whores like you we work our butts off for!" (The last time, she misread her cue and shouted it just as the state prosecutor, a woman, was standing up to enter her final argument.) When a tearful Suzi finally left the courtroom, these sour-faced harpies formed a gauntlet of shame and hurled abuse at her quite *ad libitum.* But a crowd of Suzi's admirers, who hadn't been allowed into the courtroom, were waiting for her on the sidewalk. They got mixed up in a discussion with the Marxist women, with the result that some time later another trial took place and six Fascistoid hooligans were sentenced to a total of fifteen years. One of them jumped bail and defected to Canada.

So Suzi promised to go to the Kaiserhof Hotel with me that evening, appropriately dressed as a Viennese hooker, but only, she said, "if the Russian won't turn around and want to take the whole thing seriously." Not long before, she had married again (for the fourth time), and one of her most realistic roles was that of the faithful wife. I assured her that if anything happened I would personally clean the Russian's clock. My only worry was that, in her role as a hooker, she might crank her extraordinary sex appeal up so high that Anton Pavlovich himself started lusting after her. But before I could warn her, she was approached by the founder of the *roman nouveau*, who had seen her singing the evening before (and making hard currency for Czechoslovakia) in the Schwarzweissklub. I had no desire to exchange opinions on the Prague political reforms with a foreigner right there in the Czechoslovak embassy, so I retreated into a *fin-de-siècle* corner where I had seen several empty armchairs behind a fig tree.

There I found the literary critic Brousek drinking cocktails with red cherries in them with someone who was obviously a comrade. Brousek looked uneasy and was obviously relieved at my arrival. He introduced me hastily, then vanished, as though it were the changing of the guard. The comrade turned out to be the Second Secretary, and his name was Schultz. By the time I realized that this was the "Sulc" Juzl had mentioned in his letter, it was too late to back out.

Sulc too was transparently an undercover cop. He had greying hair and wore a well-fitting double-breasted suit from which, somewhat absurdly, the face of a small-time fairground boxer emerged. He even had a scar, and looking at that scar, and the flattened nose, I lost all desire to help Juzl out. But Sulc raised the matter himself.

"Comrade, I understand you do a little bit of writing for the papers from time to time," he said, in a tone of voice from years long past — a tone I was no longer used to hearing. He obviously remembered that I occasionally wrote pop song reviews. "You wouldn't know someone called Juzl, would you? An editor or something like that?"

"A little," I replied non-committally.

"I only ask because he wrote me a letter. They're publishing this series of articles about the so-called Pisecnice miracle, if you recall that business."

"I think I may have read something about it, yes," I said, sipping the cocktail Brousek had left behind, scarcely touched, with even its red cherry intact. "I have to admit I only skimmed them. I had the impression Juzl really believes in miracles."

"Somebody should try to persuade him otherwise," said Sulc. He slurped at his cocktail, then tried to fish the cherry out with his tongue.

Suddenly the devil of temptation sat on my shoulders and whispered in my ear, and what it suggested was too sweet to resist. So I said, "You mean he shouldn't believe in miracles?"

"No, let him believe in all the miracles he wants," said Sulc. "We have guaranteed religious freedom. I mean the provocations. Someone — " and he looked at me with a look that was also out of the past, and I realized that the Czechoslovak security organs never sleep, not even during a Prague Spring, " — *someone* should try and persuade him to change his tune." He stressed the indefinite pronoun in a way that made it sound very definite indeed.

"You may be right," I said. And since the security forces already knew about my contacts with the pious editor, I began cautiously to play my little game. "Of course, if that anonymous informant was right when he said there was some kind of remote-control device in the base of the statue — "

"Anonymous letters belong in the waste-paper basket," he snapped.

"Of course. I was only raising the possibility — "

"He's trying to slander the security forces, right?" said Sulc. "Somewhere he dug up the information that I was assigned to that case — " He looked at me. "It's getting so you almost need guts to admit you worked with the police back then, isn't it?"

"Unfortunately that's true. But it's obvious to me, Mr. Sulc, that not *everyone* who was sent to prison back then was — "

"Exactly what I'm trying to say," he interrupted me, and then he exploded. "That whole business about remote control is a load of crap! Listen, comrade! Why should we go to the trouble of making a complicated device just for some goddamned Bible-puncher? All there ever was at that church was those wires and pulleys, just like they wrote in the papers. What that old biddy who put the flowers up there says is ridiculous. Think anyone can remember exactly what happened twenty years ago? Especially an old bag like her!"

"I admit she's not a very reliable witness," I agreed. "And as far as that goes, I don't believe in miracles either."

Sulc angrily took another drink of his cocktail and it seemed to calm him down a bit.

"Besides — this guy Doufal finally confessed. First it was like, who me? I just work here, kind of thing. But when we took him behind the altar and showed him the set-up — and he had no time to dismantle it because our boys moved in fast — he came clean."

Another attempt to lick the cherry out of his glass failed. Beyond the fig tree I could hear Suzi's contralto laughter pealing over a resonant, seductive, nasal bass, and I wondered if her fourth stretch of marital fidelity might be drawing to a close. I also noticed, as Sulc spoke, that the vocabulary of those long-dead years was asserting itself over his smooth, diplomatic demeanour more and more. I forced myself to go from the present tense of Suzi's voice, back to the perfect past.

"The priest died or something, didn't he?" I said.

"Look, comrade," said Sulc unpleasantly. "He got a slap or two, there's no point denying it. It was a tough time, and they weren't treating us with kid gloves either. Besides, the comrades had no way of knowing he was in such bad health. His ulcer ruptured."

I decided not to mention the priest's peculiar manicure. Sulc was getting angrier all the time.

"He confessed! I know — the smartass commentators say now that confession isn't the same as proof. But if you ask me, the proof is that he agreed to act in that movie we made about him."

"You mean he played himself?"

"Of course he did! I was there when they made it. He was as docile as a lamb, very co-operative." Sulc gave up trying to snare the cherry with his tongue, extracted it with his fingers, then tossed it into his mouth. "In the movie you can see they didn't treat him as badly as Juzl claims. There weren't any bruises or anything like that. He got a couple of slaps, but otherwise it's all crap. I recall they even took a few closeups. You could see his hand pulling the handle with the wire that led to that statue — "

He stopped suddenly; the cherry stone had lodged in his throat and he gagged and tried to cough it up, turning as red as the cherry.

I was completely confused now. It had been so long, nineteen years. But after all, I'd known Father Doufal, and I'd seen the movie, in the Lido Cinema in Hradec Kralove, and I knew they'd used someone else to play him. It hadn't seemed odd at the time; it made sense that they wouldn't use the criminal himself. However, the actor in the pulpit might better have been cast as Savonarola. He'd worn black-rimmed glasses and had looked like a hollow-faced fanatic. But at the time I thought this was a deliberate artistic choice.

"Yes, I remember the film a little. There were no signs of beating or anything like that. He was sort of tall and skinny, wasn't he, with glasses — "

"I can't remember," Sulc interrupted, between fits of coughing. "It was twenty years ago."

"Nineteen."

"Nineteen, what's the difference? And anyway, I only saw the Bible-puncher for a couple of hours all told."

He fell silent. He'd stopped coughing and his colour was slowly coming back. Nineteen, Comrade Sulc, I said to myself. Not twenty. That may be an important difference. Nineteen years and you might still hang for it. Twenty, and even murder comes under the statute of limitations. Not that I believe in the gallows. But I do believe this was murder.

"I don't even know if they ever used that footage," Sulc added. "It seems to me they had to redo some of the shots. The negative got exposed to the light — something like that. I can't remember. I never even got to see it. I was shifted to another case."

This is all rather strange, Comrade Sulc, I said, again only to myself. Suzi emerged from behind the fig tree. The father of the *roman nouveau* was trying to keep her to himself, and when he saw us he put on a sour, distant expression, but Sulc seemed willing enough to leave and did so. I didn't. Feeling somewhat piqued, perhaps at Suzi but certainly at the father of the *roman nouveau* — and to remind Suzi that she had a husband in Prague and me in Vienna — I kept them company behind the fig tree until the cocktail party was over.

2.

The Venerable Father Doufal lived alone in the large baroque vicarage on the square. When at long last he had sorted everything out, he invited Vixi and me, as prospective fiancés, for coffee. We entered his place from the back, through a hole in the fence and across an overgrown garden, so no one would see us.

A wooden staircase with two landings led to the second floor. On the first landing stood a statue of the Virgin Mary, painted with a fresh coat of sky blue, and on the second was Saint John of Nepomuk, his halo of stars glittering in the late May sunshine like pure gold. Father Doufal met us at the door and took us into a large room that smelled of old furniture, candle wax, wooden floors, and incense. Between two windows, a large ivory-hued Christ was fixed to the wall with his arms stretched out, and the rococo shelf opposite was full of black-bound books with Latin words in faded gold shining on the spines. A painting of the crucifixion hung in the corner; at that angle the light reflected off it, and all that was visible against the dark background was the white body. Underneath it was a carved wooden prayer-stool with two worn spots in the red cushioning. Clearly the priest used it a lot. Above it was a red glass container with a flame burning inside, which cast a reflection in the shiny surface of the oil painting — a mystical ruby right where the heart would have been in the snow-white body.

In a corner by the door, a light brown escritoire caught my attention. It had a large, strange-looking object on it, something of gold and silver and silk. "That's an old reliquary from the seventeenth century," said Father Doufal. "It contains a fragment of Saint Anastasia's shin-bone and two fingernails of Saint Beatrice of Worms. Here, look!" As he pointed to some unenticing, dirty white fragments that lay in tiny caskets of gold and glass, his own broken fingernail caught the light just as the surface of the painting did. "I'm repairing this in my spare time," he said. "The silver's worn away and some of the parts have come loose. It's three hundred years old, after all. And much of the fabric has disintegrated, so I'm sewing in some new material."

He stroked the faded silk with his broken fingernail. On the wooden construction, visible through the holes in the material, the goldsmith had fixed silver cherubim with golden wings. Tiny rivets, some of which had fallen out, held winged heads with Bohemian garnets for mouths in place among the clouds of pink and pale blue silk, a heavenly host all reaching towards the eye of God set in a golden triangle. From this eye strips of gold emanated like rays from the sun; some were bent, others broken, and still others had been repaired — the priest had straightened and soldered them. On the escritoire, beside the reliquary, the tools of his craft were laid out: a tiny screwdriver, a little hammer, tweezers, cotton batten, pieces of silk, a needle, and two spools of pink and pale blue thread.

"You're an artist, Father," I said.

"Oh now, Mr. Smiricky," he said modestly. "I just tinker around for fun when I have a little time. I've always loved old things like this. They're pretty, aren't they?"

Meanwhile he had picked up one unattached seraph and put it in his wide, almost circular palm. His fingers were short and stout and I noticed that the last section of his ring finger was missing. The skin of his hand was hard and callused beneath the beautiful, freshly polished angel silently blowing its trumpet.

"I'm a country man," said the priest. "In winter there isn't much outdoor work to do, so I put my hand to various things inside. I always did enjoy sewing — usually fancy harnesses, but I also made shirts and Sunday-best trousers. Where I come from, people still used to wear their local folk-costumes to church. And I did other things too, wood-carving for example." Then he stopped, as though he felt he was talking about himself too much. "But I don't know if any of this interests you — "

I assured him it did. "I love old statues," I said.

"This one's not old," said the priest, and he opened a small door in the escritoire. "It's not finished yet," he apologized, pulling out a piece of wood. The smell of pine seemed to fill the room. There was still bark around the base of the piece, but from it emerged the long, slender, and still rough outline of a human body, widening into a chest that suggested a limited knowledge of human anatomy, shoulders, a raised arm that was too long, and a carefully carved head. The wood was fresh and bright, but the head was identical to the faces of those puppet-like saints that used to hang in mountain farmhouses and that I would later sometimes see in the apartments of my more pretentious friends.

The priest stood beside me in his black shiny suit, smiling awkwardly as he held the medieval messenger in his hand. "I'm not much of an artist, as you can see," he said. "But when I get it polished and painted, it will be Saint John the Baptist. I want to give it to the nursing sisters in the hospital. They like my little carvings, at least they say they do. But I certainly can't do one that good," and he pointed to a plaster statue of the Virgin Mary which had probably been bought in Charita, the Catholic supply store. She looked like Deanna Durbin.

The evening light outside the window was deepening into yellow and wine. The sun cast a reddish glow across the tablecloth, over the deep yellow slices of cake, and the porcelain plates and coffee cups with their pink roses and green leaves.

"Father Doufal baked this himself, didn't you, Father?" said Vixi, and the priest almost blushed.

"My mother taught me how. When I was a boy I always wanted to be a cook. You know what kids are like. I got the idea from fairy-tales. I imagined myself going out into the world and across nine magic mountains to seek my fortune." He laughed. "I didn't know much about the world. We lived a pretty isolated life." And he stopped and regarded the cake. It looked like a Van Gogh sunflower. "Of course, my mother only baked a cake like this once a year, when the priest had his name-day. Did you know, Miss Koziskova," he said, turning to Vixi, "that we Catholics have always celebrated name-days rather than birthdays? Do you know why?"

"Because," said Vixi, but she didn't know the answer.

"Because at the sacrament of holy baptism, when the child is given a Christian name after one of the saints, it's as though he were being born, really, for the first time. We say we are born in spirit, in Christ. And that's why when you take the sacrament of holy baptism, Miss Koziskova, you must remember the date well. It will be an important date in your life." He looked from Vixi to the cake and then said, "So now, come to the table. I hope you like the cake."

The wine-coloured light falling on the silver reliquary took me into the world of the Czech country novelists of the previous century. I took a bite of the cake and, like the angel in the priest's hand, I was suddenly small again, at my pious grandmother's place, surrounded by the same wood and cake-icing, and I walked with my hand in hers, beside her long, black, rustling skirt, into the eleventh-century stone cathedral in Kolin, where everything was long, narrow, attenuated, high, and it was full of old women like my grandmother, and the priest was singing the litany to Saint Prokopius in a magnificent voice: ". . . You who slapped the face of one who blasphemed against you . . . ," and there was the wailing of old women. I sat in my grandmother's kitchen, stuffing myself with a cake just like this one, and the wine-coloured light darkened and Vixi, in a lace blouse, was as bright as a baroque cloud. "Poor Venerable Father Venhoda," Father Doufal said. "He suffered greatly."

"Was he sick?" asked Vixi.

"No, no," said the priest. "Well, as a matter of fact he was, but not until afterwards. He died a beautiful death — Archbishop Beran himself administered the last rites. But he had a dreadful time during the war."

"Did they lock him up?" asked Vixi.

"They did," said the priest. "He tried to help a family in Destne. They had a young daughter and he tried — but let me get this straight now," and he raised his round hand and, with the aid of his index finger, explained. "The family was of the Jewish faith, the only one in Destne. They knew they'd be sent to prison, but someone told them of a way to save their daughter, at least. The trouble was that it was almost too late. Christians weren't allowed to marry anyone of the Jewish persuasion any more. But anyone Jewish who already *was* married to a Christian could stay behind and didn't have to go to prison." He talked quietly, using an old-fashioned word for the death factories and confusing race with religion. Dark wine-red light flowed over the wrinkles of his face, as though he were walking past a stained-glass window depicting a bloody martyrdom, though it was only the setting sun. I filled myself with yellow cake despite my attempts to be moderate. The delight of sugar, eggs, and butter was too much for me.

"And so the parents — Mr. Stein had a grocery store in Destne — arranged a marriage with another family, Christians, in Olesnice. Mr. Soukup was a farmer, a very good and decent man, and his son was a decent, religious boy too. The Venerable Father Venhoda married the young people secretly. Then he entered their names earlier in the marriage registry, by erasing another marriage, so it looked as if they'd been married before the new regulation was made."

He noticed that I'd finished my coffee, and poured another cup for me and Vixi from a pot with a golden bee perched on a pink rose. I reached for another piece of cake.

"I'm glad you like it," he said. I realized that I was the only one eating and felt embarrassed.

"And what happened then?" I asked quickly. "Did someone turn them in?"

"No, no." The priest shook his head. "Thank God, there was no one like that in Destne, nor in Olesnice either. Our people had all kinds of weaknesses but no one was that mean. But you know what the Germans were like, they had records for everything, and when they sent around the summonses to prison, they sent one for Hanicka too. That was the daughter. Mr. Stein tried to point out that it was a mistake because Hanicka had been married to a Christian for more than a year. But of course the Germans didn't believe him and wanted to see the marriage licence. Well, that wasn't a problem, Mr. Stein had that all right. But one of the Germans was a suspicious sort, and he went to the parish church, and when he saw that the record was entered over another one that had been erased, there was trouble."

"They locked Father Venhoda up!" said Vixi.

"Yes, they did. The poor man was sent to a concentration camp. But God did not abandon him, and in His mercy He arranged for Father Venhoda to meet Archbishop Beran in the camp. Of course the Most Reverend Father Beran wasn't archbishop at the time, that came after the war. Both of them survived. But Father Venhoda had to have an operation immediately afterwards. Just imagine!" And the priest turned his pale, trusting eyes upon me. "If I were to tell this story to a foreigner, to someone who didn't live here under the Germans, I don't suppose he'd believe me, and I wouldn't blame him. He was already an elderly man, I mean Father Venhoda, about sixty, and some Gestapo or SS man or whatever kicked him so hard he broke one of his ribs! Think of it! There were no doctors in the camp and the rib punctured his lung, so when, thanks be to God, he came back after the war, he had to go straight to the hospital for an operation. I understand they had to remove half of one lung! Just imagine!"

He looked at us as though he had just told us something extraordinary, something exceptional, and not one of those ordinary stories that were a dime a dozen. I reached for the last piece of cake.

"Father Venhoda never really recovered from the operation," said the priest. "He served holy mass for a time after that, but the altarboys had to help him whenever he knelt. Then the poor fellow couldn't hold the chalice any more. And once — it makes a body want to cry, just thinking about it — he dropped the Host. The poor man, the poor man," said the priest, shaking his head, and a sentimental tear flowed down the creases of his face. The romantic sunset beyond the rocks tinged the tear with pink, and the priest wiped it away with his hand. "He was so upset at dropping the Host that he prayed far into the night, kneeling on his prayer-stool until he fainted. And he never got up again. His neighbours wrote to the archbishop — we all knew they'd been in prison together — and the archbishop came and administered the last rites. He had such a wonderful death, such a wonderful death! He would often pray to Saint Joseph — by the way, Miss Koziskova, did you know that Saint Joseph is the patron saint of happy deaths? A happy death is the greatest gift God can give a Christian. I mean, that death should not catch us unprepared, you understand?"

Vixi nodded. "And what happened to Hanicka?" she asked.

Father Doufal wrung his hands, a sign that her fate had been terribly sad.

"It's an awful thing! Not only she and the Steins, but the Soukups too, father and son! They all died in the camps, and only the Lord knows how!"

He fell silent. Several more tears slipped down his cheeks along the pathways of age. I found myself suddenly angry, and thought, "The sentimental old fool!" The cake was now eaten and I felt a twinge of conscience — "You're a real pig, sir! I had no idea!" Vixi would tell me afterwards. It was almost dark in the room. The sun set behind the spires of the rock formations, Father Doufal turned on the lights, and at once that beautiful unreality vanished. It's stupid, I said to myself. So I ate his whole cake. So what? It's all just living kitsch anyway.

3.

Perhaps it had been kitsch. The small statue with the doll-like face, too. And yet. . . . But that old story was only a melodrama now, not a tragedy.

The little priest with his ribcage kicked in, the Jewish girl with a name straight out of a nineteenth-century Czech novel, the pious country lad, the God-fearing farmer, all perishing romantically in a textbook concentration camp. It's not reality any more, I said to myself, it's just a horrifying fairy-tale. I set the pale blue statue of Saint Joseph back on its wooden penis. The SS men had turned into metaphors, the Gestapo were evil old witches, but those who came later, in another country — our country — had not entered the mythology at all. They weren't even that interesting any more, because it was all a rerun anyway.

4.

I turned away from the window and looked at the back of Father Godfrey. He was wearing a black poplin shirt with a stylized clerical collar and was looking uneasily out the window at the main campus of Connington College. Outside, long-haired rebels were yelling, "Pigs out! Pigs out!" and I had a paradoxical aural hallucination: I heard them shouting, "*Sieg heil! Sieg heil!*"

"At the root of all evil is Vietnam," Professor Almswith was saying from his chair by a small coffee table. He was an expert in modern poetry. "It's high time we pulled out. It's a filthy war."

The thin, neurasthenic Father Timothy said, "Of course. But — but aren't you afraid — don't you ever think about what might happen when we leave?"

"Nothing too awful," laughed Almswith, displaying an expensive set of dentures. "The fat cats all have Swiss bank accounts. Experience tells us they'll be looked after. And the Communists won't hurt the poor people."

I looked at the priest, anxious to see what his reply would be. "Certainly, experience . . . ," he nodded. "But — have you ever been there, professor?"

"Where?"

"To Asia?"

"We're not living in the age of Marco Polo," replied Almswith. "One doesn't have to have been everywhere."

"I worked there for a while," the thin priest said, almost in a whisper. "I went over as a missionary, but for health reasons. . . . You know, in the villages — and they mostly live in villages — people who aren't really rich at all are considered wealthy. Some people on welfare here might be better off materially, you know — but in Asia, people with next to nothing might, for instance, hold some public office . . . or perhaps they're — active believers . . . and — "

He stopped and Professor Almswith said, "I know what you're trying to say, Father. But do you know how many people are dying every single day in this war?"

Father Timothy hung his head.

"Revolution is a cruel thing," Almswith went on. "We all know that. Even *they* know it," and he nodded his head towards the window and took a sip of the Manhattan he'd ordered before supper. "But they say, correctly, that waiting costs more, even in terms of human lives, than revolution."

Although I didn't want to — and I mentally kicked myself for doing it — I said, "Who figured *that* out?"

Almswith, the thin priest, and Fry all looked at me. Fry was an expert in the Christian-Marxist dialogue.

"No one," said Almswith. "But it's not too hard to work it out. All the modern revolutions put together have certainly not cost as many lives as two thousand years of exploitation and war."

Talk is silver, silence is golden, I repeated to myself quickly, to suppress my terrible desire to speak, to ask questions. Whenever I did suppress it — which was most of the time — it was the right thing to do. On those few occasions — but even then I'd always got out with my skin intact. I'd been lucky. But God knows who's right — I'm not a philosopher. Sometimes, for a heightened effect, I give my operettas philosophical titles. But if we've waited two thousand years already. . . . We've managed to come so far; are we capable only of technological miracles? But I couldn't put it into words. It was too complicated.

"Yes. Revolution is a wonderful thing. For a while," I blurted.

But the expert in modern poetry didn't recognize the Hemingway quote. He smiled condescendingly. "Naturally, you're prejudiced. I can understand that. I'd probably be prejudiced too if I were in your shoes. My advantage is that the excesses of revolution have never done me any harm. I can be purely rational about it."

I wilted before his perfection, with nothing more to say.

Father Godfrey, a fat black cloud by the window, was still staring mutely at the mob of students, hippies, and black men in frizzy Afros that had been gathering on the campus since morning. That very morning, Father Godfrey had celebrated twenty-five years in the priesthood, in the air-conditioned Connington cathedral where, precisely according to post-Vatican II liturgy, a new communion table stood in front of the older altarboys, and rosy-cheeked, athletic choirboys had sung, "*Vivat pastor bonus, vivat in aeternum!*" Father Godfrey had celebrated mass, broadcast (entirely in English) over the sound system. But the sermon was awkward, and what it revealed was not Christian humility but the nagging feeling that his quarter-century in the priesthood had been pretty much a write-off. "*Pastor bonus!*" he said bitterly as we were walking back from the church together, past a colourful clutch of fancily dressed young blacks. "Who listens to me? Whom have I *really* helped?" Now he stood by the window, immensely overweight—again that sign of piety—and tortured by the loss of meaning.

I stood up and went over to the round black figure. The campus newspaper lay on the windowsill, with large headlines and a prominent article by someone who had just had to post bail and was complaining that the Connington prison was no different from Dachau. Outside the window the students, looking like beggars in ragged clothing, marched in a circle and waved placards with slogans so uninventive that I immediately forgot them. The sun beat down on them from a blue sky and suddenly they were little altarboys bearing monstrances, walking in procession through the medieval countryside from the sandstone spires. . . . A hallucination. I was angry with the dead priest; he'd infected me with a plague of doubts that were eating away inside me, transforming themselves into a bad conscience. Had I entirely lost the art of declaring my support for whatever form of power happened to be sitting in the saddle, in the most present of present times? Never fear, I would learn again. And I would never ever get involved in anything again, here or there, because I couldn't change anything anyway. It was their affair. And anyway, what could I do, I, the author of silly operettas? It was just that, from the depths of absolute forgetting, the foolish Father Doufal had suddenly invaded my life again. All because of Juzl's stupid detective story.

I heard Father Godfrey's hoarse voice say, "They're here!"

Policemen appeared across the campus green.

"Pigs're coming, pigs're coming!" a female voice shrieked right below the window. "Peace now! Peace now!"

Sieg heil! Sieg heil! I stood on tiptoe and saw her. It was Marie Pecakova again. Fat, shapeless, braless, in the briefest of miniskirts, she was shrieking as though someone were slicing her flesh with a knife. Men in plexiglass masks were advancing across the grass and this poor, heavily overweight girl was suddenly sitting in the staff room in Hronov, and it was Milada Maresova and she was saying, "It's a harsh measure, comrades, I'm aware of that, but Bolsheviks have always been able to display harshness. . . ." I felt as though I were going crazy. God, were they *everywhere*?

The police went to work. Truncheons thumped, tear-gas bombs exploded, and a boy ran across the campus holding his head. Blood was seeping between his fingers.

Professor Almswith clenched his fist. He was wearing a small, antique cameo ring. "What do you say now?" he asked me, half-closing his arrogant, professorial eyes. "Don't you think they have truth on their side?"

The temptation was too sweet. It was a timeless situation and too many lines had already been invented to suit it.

"What is truth?" I said.

Almswith merely made a face; here was one quotation he did recognize. He turned away and drummed his fingers on the glass. The boy with the bleeding head was still running and yelling and beside him, trying to keep up, ran a CBS cameraman, filming him with a hand-held camera. He stumbled and then stopped, realizing he couldn't keep up, and then, scarcely losing a beat, whipped his camera around professionally and trained it on one of the plastic-visored men from Mars, who was crudely laying into a black woman.

"Yes, this is just what you see in a police state!" said Almswith at the window, loud enough for everyone to hear.

This is just what you see. . . . I stared out at the campus, where another Martian was about to wallop the cameraman with his truncheon; he noticed just in time that it was a representative of the mass media and, pulling his swing short, struck himself in the knee instead. He went down, but an instant later he was on his feet again, furiously massaging his leg while the cameraman eagerly recorded his scoop. Just what you see. . . . I remembered those quiet, orderly streets, not a soul anywhere, just the proclamations: *For expressing approval of the murder of the Deputy Reichsprotektor, SS-Obergruppenführer, and Chief of Police, Reinhard Heydrich, the following people were shot, with their families* . . . , and streets full of flags and banners and pom-poms, and I realized that the language of Shakespeare doesn't even have a word for it. . . . I saw those cellars straight out of "The Pit and the Pendulum", where heads were pummelled into putty . . . and no one sees what goes on but everyone knows, because everyone is like the three proverbial monkeys. . . . "This is what happens! And we have it right here! Here and now!" I heard Almswith saying.

Leaving a trail of ugly dark spots on the white cement, the boy reached the sanctuary of the Le Corbusier library, and I turned back to the group around the coffee table.

Professor Fry was listening to Father Timothy.

" . . . perhaps," he was saying, "perhaps for undeveloped countries. But in advanced countries . . . as soon as you satisfy material needs, other needs suddenly become more pressing, and I'm not thinking of culture so much as the need for freedom. . . ."

Why don't you drop it? I thought. Do you think we can change each other's minds?

"You're thinking in outmoded concepts," said Professor Fry. "Freedom, like all intellectual notions, is evolving. It accumulates new, non-traditional meanings. It's only with the liberation of man from material dependency, from existential pressure, that a genuine, far deeper and more internal — "

I made a face — I couldn't help it. I'd heard this before, from the folksy, far less erudite Comrade Prochazka, the school principal, who had put it in terms not much simpler at the ideological crash course where Irena Znenahlikova passed her gonorrhea on to me. He told us how, in our informer-infested land, the mystical butterfly of a new freedom would emerge from the cocoon of revolution. Rehashed freedom, Gellen had grinned back then. Rehashed, my friend. Deeper, more internal — that was all discovered by Epictetus, my friend, and I don't suppose I have to remind you what they called Epictetus? The slave philosopher, my friend. The slave philosopher.

Outside the window, the fat girl danced beneath a banner calling for FREEDOM NOW! and screamed directly into the plastic-covered faces of the police, like someone who had taken leave of her senses:

"Piggypiggypiggy, c'mon piggypiggypiggy!"

It was all a matter of comprehending necessity, Gellen had said. In ancient Rome they called it law and order. And this freedom, he'd grinned, is called. . . .

"Piggypiggypiggy, c'mon piggypiggypiggy!"

But does anyone really need so much of this freedom, I asked, and I looked again at Marie Pecakova, who was performing a clumsy veronica in front of the Martian bull.

"PIGGY!"

The plastic-visored cop gave the fat girl a clout over the head with his truncheon. Father Godfrey hissed in an intake of pain, as though he were the one hit, and from the corner of my eye I saw the clenched fist with the cameo ring rising, clearly symbolically, towards the panelled ceiling of the common room. The porcine squealing became a howl and the woman, bleeding, collapsed on the cement terrace and thrashed her thick legs at the searing sun.

5.

As I expected, Suzi kept her promise one hundred per cent. In fact, she'd transformed herself into the Platonic ideal of whorishness. She strutted into the foyer of the Kaiserhof Hotel plastered with makeup; she was wearing a metallic blue mini and her neckline plunged almost to her waist, revealed the tantalizing fact that she wore no bra and didn't need one. With blithe self-defacement she had covered her own beautiful dark blonde hair with a synthetic platinum wig. I almost thought she'd overdone it. But I relaxed when I saw the expression on Anton Pavlovich's face: Suzi clearly took his breath away. I lurked behind a palm and watched him stop dead in the middle of the coconut matting, while Arashidov expanded his wrestler's chest and stepped forward so briskly that his wide trouserlegs flapped as if caught in a breeze. Suzi wriggled her hips, Arashidov offered her his arm, and the revolving door spun them both outside and directly into the Morrises' Hillman.

I jumped in as well.

A minor complication arose. Suzi hadn't come to Vienna for her health; she had a job at the Schwarzweissklub, and she asked Morris to take her there. The problem was that I hadn't bothered to explain to Arashidov who his platinum whore really was, since it had never occurred to me that Suzi would make such a deep impression on the apparently asexual writer. So when she asked Morris to take her to the club, Arashidov assumed she was simply planning to take her money and run, as agreed.

"Wait a moment, miss!" he said, and in his clumsy English he made an effort to persuade her to come drinking with us at a cheap bar where they served *Heuriger* — fresh young white wine.

Suzi — Stanislavsky would have been proud of her — entered fully into her role. Donning her most cynical, *demi-mondaine* look, she said out of the corner of her mouth, "*Veefeel?*"

Arashidov, not knowing German, looked questioningly at me.

"She wants to know how much you'll give her."

The man from the land of hardboiled socialism had no idea what the going rate for Viennese prostitutes was. Swayed, perhaps, by the cheap magnificence of Suzi's dress, he was obviously guessing on the high side.

"Daniel Josefovich," he whispered excitedly, "can you help me? They gave us a ridiculous per diem and I've already drunk it up. How much do you think?"

"All I can lend you is a hundred schillings. It's probably not enough."

Morris pulled up in front of the Schwarzweissklub. The entrance was brilliantly lit, brighter than a noonday sun. A shiny black porter in silver livery stood there, surrounded by winking artificial stars.

"*Hundert Schillink?*" suggested Arashidov.

"*Pff! Mein Amerikaner gibt mir hundert Dollar!*"

She gave her bare shoulders an exquisite shrug of scorn, opened the car door, and slid out. Her wig held high, she strode proudly past the saluting doorman and into the bar.

Arashidov followed her wriggling hips with a look of misery on his face, while dancing stars reflected merrily in the material of her dress. He shook his head sadly. "*Amerikanets!*" he said, with envious sarcasm, and suddenly he was overcome by a terrible fit of Russian rage. He shook his fists towards the checkerboard doorway of the club so vehemently that the doorman backed away in alarm.

"*Svoloch imperialisticheskaya!*" yelled Arashidov. "Dollars, that's all you want, dollars! But just you wait!"

The notion of playing second fiddle to the imaginary American client of an imaginary Viennese whore had goaded him into a fit of political chauvinism.

Along with the *Heuriger,* the Tirolerhof served enormous plates shaped like cornucopias and filled with different kinds of cheese. Arashidov stuffed his mouth with several varieties at once, felt thirsty, and in the wink of an eye downed a quarter-litre of the new wine. By now he'd forgotten about Suzi and was proceeding to soft-soap Morris; he'd got a novella of Morris's accepted for publication in the Soviet Union and had then gone on to translate it magnificently. The novella told the story of a young delinquent in a Borstal. Morris had written it in the first-person singular, in slang and mostly through dialogue, and in writing it he'd shown an intimate knowledge of the subject and the social milieu. His most recent book was a travelogue about his trip around the Soviet Union, but when he asked Arashidov (while pouring him more *Heuriger*) about translating that into Russian, Arashidov muttered something evasive. They were considering it, he said, but they wouldn't be giving the job to him.

"Why not?" asked Morris.

I knew that Arashidov was lying; the truth was that he simply didn't want to spoil his reputation at home by translating a work in which Morris's knowledge of his subject and milieu was far inferior to that in his novella. Then it came out that among the things Morris's Soviet guides had not told him was the story of how Arashidov had done over the novella for translation. Arashidov immediately, and with great verve, set about to correct this omission.

The novel, he said, had charmed him. "Michael Williamovich, it is a masterpiece!" he said. But the brilliance of the text had not blinded him to some of the pitfalls inherent in the job. So before he did anything else, he created a Plan.

"A plan?" said Morris, astonished.

Arashidov spread out a paper serviette among the scraps of cheese on the table and then, with one of the twenty-five felt-tipped pens he'd bought that day (for his friends and their mistresses), he sketched out a replica of the Plan:

THE PLUSES

The novel is:

a) A shocking portrait of the inhumanity of capitalism, etc.
b) Shows the rottenness and decay of capitalism, etc.
c) The delinquents are the fruit of exploitation, etc.

It is written in the 1st person sing: told in the hero's own words, and even though no one has told him about the revol. solution to soc. problems, etc. it is a shocking denunciation of:

1) capitalism
2) American imperialism (the Korean War, where the hero refuses to be sent)
3) nuclear war (Make Love, Not War)
4) religion (blasphemous swearing, stealing from poor boxes in churches, etc.)

PROBLEMS AND THEIR SOLUTION

1. Written in argot. Sol: Write an afterword mentioning the old English tradition of crit. realism (Dickens, Sam Weller, Tressell: Ragged Trousered Philanthropists). Also mention the tradition of British folk humour (anthology: The Songs of British Miners, pub. Foreign Literature in Translation, Moscow, 1962). Also mention Shakespeare: the dialogue of the rude mechanicals in Mid. Nights Dr. etc. In the translation: translate into standard literary Russian, indicate argot by hints & suggestion, etc.

2. Scenes depicting drug abuse. Sol: shorten the scenes, perhaps leave them out altogether.

3. Erotic scenes. Sol: rewrite, shorten descriptions, drop strong language and the entire copulation scene.

4. Scenes of homosexual love. Sol: cut them out, replace with short linking text.

5. The character of the prostitute. Sol: expand on the motif as to why she became a prost. (small pay, an exploited store clerk, etc.)

6. References to Soviet concent. camps, to Stalin, etc. Sol: Tear page out of copy to be sent to publisher's reader; retype (without refs) with explanation that the cat tore it up.

7. Novel merely shows soc. probs. but gives no proper, i.e., revolutionary, solution etc. Sol: Mention in afterword: The Soviet reader is politically aware, and can fill in blanks himself. Admit this is a weakness, but understandable: writer still young, hasn't been to U.S.S.R. yet. Stress: has been invited and promised to come when he finishes new novel and film.

GENERAL REMARKS

Offer the book for reader's report to:

1. Someone from Novy Mir;
2. Josip Ilich, via Anna Grigoryevna;
3. Yevtush., Voznes., Kuzhnets;
4. Leonid Nikolayevich (*Nota bene!* Can't read English: — keep it a secret in the pub. house and warn him not to blow it!)

BACKUP: Ask the following to write an Afterword (when translation complete: don't let them see original!)

1. Michail Antonovich (maybe through Anna Grigoryevna);
2. Kyril Vasilich.

NOTE: Indicate to Nikolai Petrovich that through confidential sources we know the author is secret member of the Com. Party of Gt. Br. (get Anna Grigoryevna to confirm).

Anna Grigoryevna, Arashidov explained as soon as he had sketched out the reproduction of his plan, was a ballerina in the Bolshoi Theatre who had the traditional Russian love of literature, and was surrounded on all sides by that other traditional Russian reality, old-fashioned rose-sending admirers. One of the most persistent was Josip Ilich, the notorious critical whore who was mentioned in the list of potential readers. Anna's role was to soften him up and encourage him to write a positive report, because only his support would give weight to a recommendation by the liberals from *Novy Mir* and by delinquent writers like Yevtushenko, Voznesensky, and Kuzhnetsov. As well, Anna was to try to persuade the drink-sodden winner of many Soviet and foreign literary prizes, Michail Antonovich, to write the afterword (Arashidov himself would provide, on request, a draft of the afterword which Michail Antonovich would merely need to sign) and this would silence critics in the Cultural Bureau. Difficult as this mission was, there was real hope that Anna Grigoryevna would succeed; several years before, when Michail Antonovich had spoken to the students at the Academy of Ballet, Anna Grigoryevna had been among those who asked for his autograph. She was the only one the master had chatted briefly to, and later he had invited her to his dacha, where he had tried to seduce her. Anna Grigoryevna was to complete this conspiratorial hat-trick by flirting with Nikolai Petrovich, editor-in-chief of the Foreign Literature Publishing House, and saying that she had met Morris at a reception in London and that he had confessed to her, swearing her to strictest secrecy, that he was a crypto-Communist.

Morris looked shocked and the pretty Molly put her hand over her mouth. Arashidov, however, did not notice their discomfort, and went on to explain that he had managed to steal a bound copy of Morris's novel from the British embassy library — where, as a delegate of the Union of Soviet Writers, he'd been attending a party to celebrate Queen Elizabeth II's birthday — and had written a dedication in it — "To Ann Grigoryevna, the Russian Fairy" — and then forged the writer's signature, so the girl would have something to show Nikolai Petrovich.

Arashidov went on to explain the case of Leonid Nikolayevich, the last of the readers, who was to write a report on the novel although he knew no English at all. "The old man is wonderfully generous," he said lovingly. "He never spoils your fun and he has never once refused to lend his support to a good thing. I wrote a draft of his report too, and then, this good old man, he rewrote it to give it his style. Every schoolchild in our country knows how he writes; it's very difficult to imitate."

"I don't believe I've heard of him," sighed Morris.

"He's our greatest living fabulist," said Arashidov. "He's eighty-eight and still writing. He wrote his report — it's a pity I didn't bring it with me, Michael Williamovich — in the form of a fable about a pike, that's your novel, and some carp, our Russian writers, who don't strive for truthfulness and artistic mastery but would rather lie about in the swamp of their honoraria. The report helped me a lot."

"And who's Michael Antonovich?" asked Molly Morris hoarsely.

"A member of the Academy," said Arashidov. And then he swore with fervour: "That *durak* Michail Antonovich! He wouldn't write it in the end, the swine! Anna practically crawled into bed with him, but he's so afraid of sullying his reputation in the Praesidium that when he read your novel, Michael Williamovich, he threw her out. What a bent spine the bugger has! Scared shitless! A motherfucker! A traitor to Mother Russia! And for him I made a special version of the translation, just for him! In my version, the hero comes under the influence of a Communist and takes part in a peace march! May a plague shrivel his vitals!" The memory of all that pointless work got Arashidov even more worked up. "So in the end, Kyril Vasilich had to write it. But he's an asshole too; he did such a lousy job that it made matters worse, and for a while the whole project hung by a thread."

The confused English novelist could only mumble something in reply, while Arashidov sampled the emmentaler, then the goat's milk cheese, and finally some edam, washing them all down with long draughts of *Heuriger.* Then he started describing, with great gusto, how with Anna Grigoryevna's help he had wheedled a report out of Josip Ilich that was full of unqualified praise; how, apart from the cowardly failure of Michail Antonovich, no one else had let him down; how the only scene he had had to cut entirely was the homosexual one and then, out of respect for Morris, he had limited the new linking text to two sentences; and how, on the other hand, he had defended the drug scene almost in its entirety (he had cut only one paragraph explaining how to cultivate marijuana at home) and in the end hadn't even had to expand on the theme of the exploitation of prostitutes. In the sex scenes he had cut the expressions that referred to sex organs but otherwise had left — and carefully translated — all descriptions of the act of love itself, and in general had larded his translation, which was into literary Russian, with such an enormous number of lexicographical and syntactical allusions to the argot of Moscow juvenile delinquents that the enraged Academician Pestilenko, to whom the editors gave a copy in the later stages of the Morris Affair, labelled Arashidov the greatest corrupter of the Russian language since Byliny. Arashidov then provided a translator's note that deftly stretched a safety net of quotations around the whole dangerous work, and finally Kyril Vasilich, in his afterword, confirmed the precision of Morris's insights into juvenile delinquents, their ideology, and how gangs are formed, and stressed that all this corresponded to his own observations from his work among the young people of Moscow. And thus, having been read by several editors (including the editor-in-chief), armed with annotations and afterwords, corrected, cut, interpreted, and in all possible aspects edited, explained, recommended, guaranteed, and underwritten by the signatures of the editor-in-chief of the publishing house and his underlings, the work was finally delivered by the responsible editor to the secretariat of the publishing house, where the secretary was to rubber-stamp it and deliver it to the production department.

But the office secretary, Irina Petrovna — a fiftyish member of the Moscow Committee of the Union of Soviet Women — opened the manuscript at random, and her eyes encountered the word "*lifchiky*". Her suspicions aroused, she leafed through it some more and saw the word "tits". She leafed further and found the word "ass" used in a context that had nothing to do with zoology. That was enough for her. Flushing red, she took the manuscript not to the production department but to Leontiye Andrejevich, chairman of the Party organization in the publishing house, who also happened to be the business manager. The economist unearthed a number of other naturalisms, read the afterword by the director of the reform school, and found a serious ideological error that had escaped even Nikolai Petrovich's watchful eye: to claim that the insights of an English bourgeois writer (by virtue of his being a subject of her Britannic Majesty, Morris's origins had suddenly been improved by one social class), however progressive he might be, into the life of English juvenile delinquents were in any way equivalent to the *Soviet* experience with hooligans was an insult to the Soviet Union. A Party meeting was quickly convened and Arashidov was summoned before it. The meeting dragged on into the night, then split into several other meetings at ever higher levels, until at last, in consultation with the Minister of Culture (who was a woman), so many experts had been asked to write new reports that Anna Grigoryevna wasn't able to visit them all. As a result, some of them did what was expected of them. On top of that, the minister got in touch with the Soviet ambassador in London, who talked the matter over with a secretary from the Communist Party of Great Britain, and it came to light that Morris had lied to Anna Grigoryevna about his secret membership in the Party. On the other hand, the Central Committee of the Party in Britain praised Morris so highly, as being a non-Marxist but of impeccable proletarian background and a true voice of the working class, that the minister, after making discreet inquiries in the Central Committee about the probable course of Soviet foreign policy in the near future, approved publication of the novel, on condition that it not be available to the public but merely to some five hundred important pedagogical specialists in youth reform institutions. And that — after a final reworking of the translation, not by Arashidov but by Comrade Jelizareva, a functionary in the Pedagogical Institute — is what happened. Fortunately, however, most reform-school pedagogues had children, mostly of delinquent tendencies, who stole the copies from their parents' bookshelves. And so not long afterwards, from Moscow to Vladivostok, an enormous number of typescripts of the book were in circulation, made in the *samizdat* fashion — that is, the price of borrowing the book was typing out several copies and passing them on. Some copies included scenes excised from the official version, and the language was restored to its original level of corruption, based on a version that Arashidov himself had prepared especially for *samizdat*.

It was only now that Morris understood why Arashidov, despite several reminders, hadn't been able to send him a single Soviet review of his book. And I had the impression that Morris was also beginning to understand why Arashidov was so reluctant to talk about translating his recent travel book.

We were finishing our tenth litre of *Heuriger* when a café orchestra with a fat zither player took its place on the podium. The tearful music aroused feelings of guilt in Morris; he realized that we had only talked about him and his work, although Morris's translator was also the author of original fiction which, unlike Morris's, had been honoured with an important literary prize. Unfortunately Morris was at a disadvantage here because he didn't know any of Arashidov's works. Still, he feigned interest and asked what he was writing just then.

The question caught Arashidov off guard. He gazed intently at the Englishman and then, in the grip of a conditioned reflex, looked around cautiously. Finally he leaned across the table and brought his head close to Morris's. His tipsy voice sounded conspiratorial as he switched from broken English to his mother tongue, and my head soon began to ache from the job of translating for him. But the *Heuriger* gave me strength and fluency.

"Michael Williamovich, do you know my book *The Legend of the Man on the Tractor*?" he asked darkly, knowing full well that Morris had no way of knowing it. It had never been published outside the socialist camp, although ten years previously it had earned him his last literary prize, from the Ministry of Agriculture and Chemical Fertilizers. I, however, did know the book; I had helped its Czech translator versify the incredibly stupid song lyrics the author had larded his narrative with. It was one of those mass-produced, stereotypical stories about a rebellious Moscow youth who, against his will and on orders from the Komsomol, goes to Siberia to help carve farmland out of the virgin steppes. There, in a generally traditional manner, he is reborn as a good Soviet citizen. Despite its orthodoxy, the book — or, more precisely, a scene in which the hero's girlfriend goes skinny-dipping in a pond on the steppes and is discovered and practically raped by the not yet completely reborn hero — provoked what passes for public discussion in the Soviet Union. "You've never heard of it, of course," belched Arashidov, and Morris shook his head. "You haven't missed a thing. It's a piece of shit." I translated, and Arashidov, who knew the expression from his reading of contemporary American fiction, nodded approvingly. "But my next novel, *The Legend of the Man with the Vodka*, Michael Williamovich, is going to be the truth about that shit."

Arashidov looked around again, brought his head close to Molly's sweet-smelling hair, and then, in a basso whisper appropriate to a recitation of Pushkin, hissed, "We are deep, deep in the Siberian steppes. Near Merekve Lake they are making a collective farm out of nothing. A typical Soviet labour brigade is there, full of thieves and con-men and hookers and pimps, all on the lam from Moscow because things were too hot for them there, and citizens who want to improve their political profiles, and hooligans who want to get into university, and a lot of people who've been released from the camps but still have a term of exile to serve. Oh, and two simple-minded jerks who've come out of sheer stupidity. It's a hot summer. Clouds of mosquitoes swarm in from the swamps every evening. The latrines are rank. There's nothing to eat but potato soup, and herring on Sunday, washed down with goat's milk, plus whatever you can trap on the steppes. It's beyond the range of television; the only radio station is from Nepal and the KGB jam it. You live in wooden barracks, twenty to a room, boredom in the evening, hard labour all day. Half the tractors aren't running, there are no spare parts, there's only one doctor in the whole camp, and he believes dysentery is caused by evil spirits so he cures it by fumigation.

"Up to this point," said Arashidov, "it's a pretty standard exposé, full of the kind of objective difficulties the Soviet people have always known how to struggle against — always, of course, with the help of Marxleninist doctrines. But what helps *my* heroes," and he stressed the possessive adjective with considerable pride, "is boozing and fucking."

In the mouth of the Stalin Prize winner, these two words sounded almost terrifying. Molly Morris darkened, although her husband used words like that in his books as a matter of course.

"Suddenly," said Arashidov, "just when the August heatwave is hitting its peak, the workers discover a terrible thing: they're running out of vodka!"

"Oh, no!"

"*Da, da,*" Arashidov nodded. "So they get together, think things over, and draw lots, and who should the lot fall on but the Jew, Jakub Izakevich, a fence for stolen goods, a pimp, and a secret believer. His instructions are to travel to the nearest city for a new supply of vodka. But the nearest city is Leninogorod, eight thousand versts away!"

"How many miles is that?" asked Morris.

Arashidov waved his hand. "You drive and you drive and you drive and you drive and you drive and you drive and you drive," he said in a singsong voice, "you drive for days and days and weeks and weeks and months, and you're still not there. Siberia is vast! Siberia is endless!" He stretched his arms apart and knocked a wine bottle, fortunately empty, off the table. The waitress understood this to mean that he was ordering another.

"And that is why Jakub Izakevich, although it is only August, hitches up his sleigh. He knows that when he returns from Leninogorod with the vodka, the wide steppes will be covered with snow." Arashidov nodded and told us how Jakub Izakevich drove and drove and drove and drove and drove and drove and drove, and I was beginning to think he'd become a record with a stuck needle when he paused, took a drink, and choked. Morris's wife pounded him on the back and that got him moving again. "Finally," he continued, "sometime around the anniversary of the great October Revolution, Jakub Izakevich arrives in Leninogorod, makes his purchase, loads the bottles into his sleigh, and starts the journey back. But as soon as he leaves Leninogorod it starts to snow, and before long Jakub Izakevich and his sleigh are slogging through a heavy blizzard. Late that same evening he finds himself in a God-forsaken village, where he asks for lodgings for the night. They bed him down in a stable, but next morning, when he's about to pay for the bread and cheese they've given him, he discovers a terrible thing. He has no money left! He has accidentally spent his food money on the vodka. Now what?" Arashidov stared wide-eyed at the new cornucopia of food Morris had discreetly ordered at the mention of cheese, filled his mouth, and, when he'd swallowed some of it, went on to tell how the muzhiks flatly refused payment in "comradely credit". "The only thing Jakub Izakevich can think of is to offer them vodka. The muzhiks look at each other and then, without a word of discussion, they nod. They even give Jakub Izakevich a little extra to take with him: smoked shoulder of bear. And then he drives and he drives and he drives and he drives and he drives and he drives and he drives — "

Arashidov had become a stuck record again, so I said, to bring him back to the story, "Until that evening, when he comes to another village?"

"*Da, da,* Daniel Josefovich," he said gravely. "And as soon as he arrives, he offers them vodka instead of money. They give him a room in the local Soviet. Next morning he drives and he drives and he drives and he drives and he drives — "

"Until he comes to a third village?" I interrupted.

"No!" cried Arashidov. "He discovers a strange thing." He stopped the story while he washed his mouth out with *Heuriger,* and we were silent.

"What's that?" asked the Englishwoman finally, in a small voice.

"The supply of vodka does not diminish," he said triumphantly.

"But — how?" she asked, still mystified.

"Just that. It simply doesn't diminish. He gives it away, he barters it, he drinks it himself, but it makes no difference. There are still just as many bottles as before. It's like when Christ fed the multitudes with those three small fishes."

"You're not going to put it that way, I hope," I said.

The fat zitherist began to sing a song about Lili Marlene, accompanying himself with tinny, melodic washes of sound. Arashidov once more lowered his voice.

"The farther Jakub Izakevich travels from Leninogorod across the snowbound steppes, the more muzhiks there are, all eager to trade bread and cheese for vodka. Then it occurs to him that he could sell the vodka. First he sells it for a ruble, then he adds a kopek, then ten, then another half-ruble, and still the muzhiks buy vodka as though they can't get enough of it. The money begins to pile up and still — "

"The vodka doesn't diminish!" cried Molly. She was getting into the spirit of the thing.

"*Da,* Molly Brianovna, the vodka does not diminish. And then Jakub Izakevich is possessed by the spirit of Mammon." Arashidov rolled his eyes terribly and swallowed a piece of cheese. "He says to himself, 'Should I return to the collective farm, where a man is eaten alive by mosquitoes and the latrines are so foul that not even the pungent aroma of Aire de Moscow can disguise it? Who needs that? No, I shall turn to the east. *Ex oriente lux.* I shall go to the far side of the world, selling from my inexhaustible supply of vodka, and I shall get rich, and in Vladivostok I will get myself a mistress!'"

And so Jakub Izakevich and his undiminishing supply of vodka set off into the steppes, into that vast white sea with only the black skeleton of a frozen tree drifting in it here and there, and dark little islands of forgotten villages. He sold and he sold, and the vodka remained undiminished.

"But very soon," said Arashidov, "a rumour sweeps through the wide steppes: the legend of the man with the vodka. And muzhiks come on skis from distant villages, they trek over the endless hills on snowshoes, the wealthier ones hitch up their troikas, and Party secretaries drive up in automobiles. And from mouth to mouth, the length and breadth of Mother Russia, flies the name of Jakub Izakevich, the man who brings us vodka, our joy, our mother, our savior! Until at last the story reaches the ears of the militia."

He stopped, and opened a new bottle of wine. Morris's wife covered her mouth with a small hand in anticipation of the horror to come. "And the militia mount up and set off on horseback into the steppes to hunt down the man with the vodka." Tears were now streaming down Arashidov's cheeks; in the ancient tradition of his land, he was publicly moved by his own story. "But news that the militia is after the man with the vodka travels faster," he said, with satisfaction. "The warning flies from mouth to mouth, Jakub Izakevich begins to zigzag across the steppes, and the muzhiks, driven by the fear that the militia will kill their benefactor, swarm out of the villages in greater and greater numbers to buy vodka while there is still time. And Jakub Izakevich, hunted by the militia on one side and by thirsty muzhiks on the other, zigzags across the steppes, and he zigzags and zigzags and zigzags and zigzags and zigzags — "

"Oh for God's sake, stop it!" cried Molly Morris. "What happens next?"

And Arashidov slipped into another groove and described how Jakub Izakevich took refuge in stables, abandoned herdsmen's huts, and local Party secretariats, still selling and selling, and I opened my mouth to stop the record but Arashidov did it himself, with the brief refrain, "And still the supply of vodka does not dwindle. No matter how much he sells, there is still a mountain of bottles under the canvas cover of his sleigh, and in each bottle is vodka, as pure and clear as crystal. And since the militia can't catch Jakub Izakevich on their horses, the Father Czar in Moscow sends — "

"Wait a minute!" I said. "Wait just a minute, Maxim Gavrilovich!"

Arashidov looked at me foolishly for a moment, shook his head, and went on:

"All right. The chairman of the Supreme Soviet in Moscow sends them a big snowmobile. But that doesn't help either, because they can't catch the man with the vodka, not even with a snowmobile. And do you know why?"

He looked questioningly at Mike Morris, and then at the pale Molly.

"The snowmobile is too slow?" suggested the pragmatic Brit.

Arashidov raised a finger and waggled it at Morris. "No. Because the People hide Jakub Izakevich!"

He took a drink. I knew the story would soon come to a sad end, for Russian literature knows no happy endings.

"They hide him as they once hid Vladimir Ilich," sobbed Arashidov. "But even so, there is one man, Kuzma Judasevich from the village of Golgotka, who betrays him. The miserable bastard is after a state decoration!" Forgetting that he was now in Austria, Arashidov spat on the floor. "It's evening. Jakub Izakevich and his faithful horse have just entered a narrow valley where the people of Golgotka have sent him to hide for the night. But as soon as he enters the valley he sees the big snowmobile, and beside it Kuzma Judasevich, pointing him out to a lieutenant of the militia. Jakub Izakevich stops his little horse and tries to turn around, but he can't. The valley is too narrow.

"And now the lieutenant gives the order, rat-tat-tat-tat-tat, and the militia fire at Jakub Izakevich, gunning the poor man down. Waves of gunfire echo across the wide steppes, and the muzhiks of Golgotka come running up to find Jakub Izakevich lying in a pool of his own blood. They fall on their knees before the lieutenant and cry, *'Batyuska Leytyenant!* You've killed Jakub Izakevich. But don't destroy the vodka!' But the lieutenant is young and he too wants a medal. And he gives the order and rat-tat-tat-tat-tat, the vodka is gone! Gone!" Arashidov groaned. "They have destroyed every last bottle. The bottles fall shattered into the snow, the slivers of glass glittering and the vodka, pure and clear as crystal, soaking through the snow and into the earth!"

There was silence at the table, underlined by the wailing of the orchestra. Arashidov pulled a much-used handkerchief from his pocket and blew his nose so loudly that the zitherist sent him a withering look. Struggling to hold back his tears, he finished his story:

"Next spring, when the snows melt and the steppes are turning green, water begins to bubble out of the earth at that very spot. And the water is pink! All the muzhiks cross themselves in wonder. But that is nothing to the wonder they feel when they taste the water. Because it's not water, it's vodka! Pink vodka, like the kind with paprika in it. This is the blood of Jakub Izakevich, the martyr. And the story of the miracle is carried by word of mouth the length and breadth of Russia, and muzhiks come from far and wide; and from the cities, members and functionaries of the Party come secretly and collect the pink vodka in wooden buckets, and still the vodka keeps flowing and flowing and flowing and fl— " and Arashidov suddenly hiccoughed violently, grabbed the edge of the table, and stiffened. The *Heuriger* was starting to get to him.

"You forgot to add," I said, "that Kuzma Judasevich repents and casts his medal into the sanctuary of the Regional Party Committee headquarters and departs and goes away and hangs himself."

But Arashidov struggled to his feet and rushed out.

He came back some time later, dejected and deeply unhappy. He sat down, took a pinch of emmentaler from the tray, then put it down on the table beside him. Morris tried to express his sympathy, but Arashidov was inconsolable. "You don't know shit about our lives, Michael Williamovich! *Nichevo!* It's far worse, far worse than you can imagine." Again he opened his eyes wide; his complexion was green. I thought the *Heuriger* was still working, but Arashidov was a hardened drinker; through the byways of immoderation, he was coming back around to literature.

"Tell me, Michael Williamovich: who was the greatest writer of all time?"

He fixed his burning eyes on Morris. The Englishman was embarrassed and thought hard. I could see that he wanted to please the Russian soul of his unhappy translator.

"Tolstoy?" he suggested, questioningly.

"Pfui! Tallstoy!" grimaced Arashidov, mimicking the Englishman's pronunciation. Morris drew back in shame and for a while tried to measure Arashidov's mood. Like everyone slightly interested in literature, he had heard something to the effect that the author of *Crime and Punishment* was a *persona* practically *non grata* in the homeland of socialism. So, repressing his political sympathies, he said quietly, "Dostoevsky?"

Arashidov merely waved his hand dismissively.

"Shakespeare?" suggested Morris, even more timidly. By now he'd guessed that Arashidov was probably an Anglophile. As it turned out, he was right; he was only wrong in his choice of author. Arashidov put a frightful expression on his face, bugged out his eyes, then pulled himself up and leaned far over the table towards the stupefied British couple. In a voice full of triumph and pious enthusiasm, he roared:

"The greatest writer in the world is George Orwell, of course!"

"You can't mean it!" said the pretty Molly.

"Oh yes I can!" said Arashidov, with the authority of an Old Testament patriarch. "And even George Orwell knew bugger-all!"

6.

The party at the Czechoslovak embassy was slowly breaking up. As I was putting my empty glass down on the corner of a sideboard, Mr. Schultz walked by me.

"Comrade Sulc!" I said.

My interest didn't please him, but he stopped.

"I've been thinking more about it," I told him.

"About what?"

"About the so-called miracle in the Chapel of the Virgin Mary under Mare's Head."

"Oh, that." It was clear that the pleasure was still exclusively mine.

"Yes. I remember one of the articles written by that editor. There was a man called Pecen, or something like that, who was there at the time — at least, that's what the article said."

Sulc was wearing a well-tailored suit. His long arms hung motionless by his side and he said nothing.

"Or maybe it wasn't Pecen. But I think that's what it was. I know it was a rather odd name."

After what seemed to be some quick, hard thinking, he said, "There used to be a Pecen working for Security in those days. I think there was, anyway. But he wasn't there with us."

I looked into his evasive eyes. Why was I getting mixed up in this? Why? Perhaps I'd been infected by the general audacity that was going around.

"Wait a minute. Now that you mention it, I do remember," said Sulc. "Pecen was named in that anonymous letter. The one they printed.

But comrade — as you and I both know, anonymous letters belong in the waste basket."

And having been instructed once again by this former (and probably present) employee of the Secret Police on a principle of moral behaviour, I said no more about the matter.

7.

Until I got back to Prague. There I ran into Juzl in Charles Square. He was hurrying out from under the shadowy portal of St. Ignatius, a feverish light in his eyes and his cheeks ablaze. Almost too cordially, he shook my right hand; he had a habit of squeezing your hand with all his strength while gripping your shoulder with his other hand. Perhaps this was something he'd picked up at the seminary.

We sat down on a bench in front of the church. Juzl was wearing a bright silver cross in his lapel, a novelty that the newly revived Catholic retail outlet, Charita, had just put on the market. He told me it was for Catholics who were not ashamed of their faith. I thought briefly of Julia, furiously crossing herself in the Church of the Virgin Mary of the Snows after one of Father Urbanec's prehistoric sermons. Now she was a sweet payroll clerk with seven children, all named after Czech saints: Ludmila, Anezka, Vaclav, Vojtech, Jan, Prokop, and Vaclava. No doubt she was enrolling them all in non-mandatory religious courses; that fall, for the first time in years, religious instruction was to be allowed in the schools. But from that pleasant memory, I turned back to Juzl.

"I read your article, Mr. Juzl," I said, "but it didn't satisfy me. Tell me more."

"I couldn't talk about everything," he said. "You're well aware, of course, that certain things can be used against the Church. And I wouldn't want that to happen, particularly in connection with Father Doufal. But I discovered a terribly important circumstance." He moved closer to me. "This Pecen left the Church because a priest seduced his sister and she had a child out of wedlock. Pecen was sixteen at the time — a sensitive boy, obviously. So you can imagine — " He put his hand on my shoulder again. I could feel it burning through my thin summer shirt, almost as though he had a fever. Perhaps he did. "As you know, stories like that have always been among the most effective arguments against the Church, demagogic though they may be. That's why I didn't want to mention it in print."

He removed his burning hand from my cold shoulder. I thought how much alike they were, bad priests and bad functionaries. Unpleasant facts were suppressed so they wouldn't harm one institution or the other. But Juzl, like all believers, didn't see the parallel. All that mattered for him was the difference: one served God, the other served the devil. And he had no doubts about which was which.

"Up to that point, Pecen had been a very religious kid," he continued. "He'd even been an altarboy, led a Catholic Scout troop. But in technical school he came under the influence of a Communist teacher, and when that business with his sister happened, the teacher naturally turned it to best advantage. Pecen went to the vicarage and, without his mother's knowledge, announced that he was leaving the Church. Then he joined the Youth Union, then the Party — Pecen came from a very poor family — "

"An interesting example of the genesis of fanaticism. He goes from being disillusioned with one kind of moral authority to — "

"That's not quite how it was," Juzl interrupted. "He was never a fanatic, at least not according to his mother. He was a quiet person. He did join the Party but he was never an activist, and he never harmed — "

"And then he joined the Secret Police — "

"The old woman never knew that until this year. That's another reason she wrote to me. She still can't believe it. Pecen was trained as a radio technician and he told her he was working at the Tesla plant in Prague. And then — he died in prison! She can't understand that that's exactly how a lot of secret policemen meet their end!"

"But why in prison?" I asked.

He turned his whole body towards me. The sun caught the small cross in his lapel and momentarily blinded me.

"The old woman claims he finally returned to God. In those days it didn't take much to get yourself arrested — sometimes a public declaration of faith was enough. They never told Mrs. Pecenova or his sister why they arrested him. But that wasn't so unusual then either, and the women never even thought of finding out more. Even now they're reluctant to try. They're both simple, pious women and they're terrified of Communists — God knows, with good reason. They were only told that he died in custody."

"Did they beat him to death?"

"I don't know."

"What else do people die of in prison?" I was thinking of Gerta, who had survived a bout of hepatitis in Auschwitz. "The organism builds up all kinds of resistance in prison."

Juzl shrugged his shoulders. "Ultimately, what matters is not Pecen's death — or even Father Doufal's — but what happened in the chapel."

"I know," I said. "That's what you said in your article."

Juzl went off to his office. It was a sweltering August day and I thought I might step into the church to escape the heat. As I expected, the interior was pleasantly cool, a sensation I remembered from my years as an altar-boy, although this church was baroque rather than Gothic, and the sun fell through its clear glass windows and landed with full force on the altar. The interior had recently been restored and gilded. Paid for with government money — one of the strange paradoxes of a regime that with one hand did good deeds and with the other committed bloody sins. But of course, the repairs had been done for the benefit of tourists from the West.

I glanced up at the dome; it was decorated with white scrolls, bosses, and rosettes, like a cake done up with butter icing. A host of little plaster angels seemed to be frolicking joyously in the icing, their arms stretched up towards the eye of God at the peak of the dome. *This is a materialistic regime,* I heard a familiar voice say, *yet it supports the birth of myths.* I looked around: there were only a few old women sitting in the pews. *It guarantees people work as does no other system in the world.* Where had I heard that voice before? *It provides free medical care for its citizens yet subjects them to permanent nervous stress and an arbitrary system of justice. It renovates medieval cathedrals yet empties them of priests.* Throughout the countryside the red onion-domes of small baroque churches peep over the rye fields; and in lush green valleys, miniature wayside chapels shine like virginal brides. I frowned. And on the pathways through the fields, young priests die racing their motorcycles from church to church as they try to administer five or seven masses each Sunday at five or seven different villages — our country's bizarre version of dirt-bike racing. Who said that? Who? . . . Then I remembered. Of course — it was the black-haired son of Laura, that sweet daughter of the bourgeoisie. Coming from a bullhorn, under the statue of the uncanonized saint. He was the one. I frowned. It's a progressive regime and it fights against obscurantism. And in this fight they accidentally stepped on the toes of one naive obscurantist. It can happen to the best of philosophies.

I looked around the church again. Not only had it been freshly renovated, but it had a conscientious spiritual custodian. Under the main choir hung large billboards which the priest had decorated with pretty calligraphic notices. He must have taken a lot of trouble with them; he had used inks of various colours and embellished them with scenes from votive pictures.

I stopped in front of one billboard given over to the cult of Mary. A careful hand had put up fifteen gaudy pictures arranged in three rows — pictures of a kind that had been banned for years and weren't available anywhere. But these had survived the times of adversity, carefully concealed in some prayerbook. They looked brand-new; even the frames of paper lace were flawless, like the lace on virginal underwear. For each one, the careful hand had written a history of the location, the statue, and the miracles that had taken place.

I stared at them as though beholding a bouquet of cornflowers on the brow of Tutankhamen's mummy. Crudely coloured Madonnas in bishop's mitres floated above pictures of small chapels that might well still be standing in some far-off place. The Mother of God of Three-Peak Mountain, the Virgin Mary of Pine Hill, the Blessed Virgin of Clay Peak, the Mother of Our Lord of Zerotin, the Virgin Mary of the Seven Stones. The names of these weather-worn sanctuaries — sanctuaries so inconspicuous that they had escaped the state's attention and had all but disintegrated — evoked a harmony of wood, wind blowing across mountaintops, the yeasty smell of processions of pilgrims long since gone to their graves. Cone-shaped Madonnas with tinier cones, holy infants, in their arms. Jet-black Virgin Marys looking like African bishops caught in the crowns of linden trees. Madonnas of supernatural origin: *In the year of Our Lord 1712, shepherds found this statue in a wild rose bush;* Madonnas from far-away places: *This statue was brought to Rose Mountain by Count Kolowrat from the Dutch city of Eindhoven where, from time immemorial, she had stood in the capitulum of the cathedral;* home-grown Madonnas: *and from the beam from the arch of the burnt-out church, a countryman from Zerotin, Benes Zalman, carved a statue of the Blessed Virgin.* They were oddly imperious, these little wooden queens: *the shepherds carried the statue to the decanal church, where it was placed in a side altar. At night, however, a wild rose branch grew out of the altar and the statue was found facing the place where the shepherds had found her. So they built the chapel in that place.* Frequently the whimsical miracle-worker herself asked for shelter: *The Mother of God appeared in a dream to Countess Zahorska and said to her: "Three miles to the east, on Clay Peak, I wish to have my chapel!"* They also performed feats of magic: *At night, however, the statue vanished from the church, and the next day people from a neighbouring village found her in a hollow tree. They carried her back to the church, but she disappeared again; again they found her in the same tree. When this happened a third time, they realized that the Mother of God had taken a liking to this place.*

Shafts of sunlight striped the golden altar, just as those golden bars of light had fallen across the reliquary of the poor priest so long ago. Motes of dust swirled in the rays. The Madonna was on display in a silver case, and she was dressed like an opulent mannequin, like an urban empress, in silken lace. She was still worshipped; old women in black were kneeling before her, and there was even a young man in a checkered shirt among them. Perhaps the Office for Ecclesiastical Affairs had granted her the privilege of representing, to the present-day world and its pilgrims from the lands of convertible currency, all those other Mothers of God rotting away in damp chapels in the woods, their paint slowly cracking in the wind that howled through those wild ravines among the rocks, helpless to help themselves despite all the miracles they had performed in the past. Incomprehensible pilgrims in backwater retreats, rural shepherdesses with only the animals for company, capriciously curing the poor, who might have been better off in another world. Beautiful statues representing tall tales, little folkloric queens from the colourful dark ages. Unforgotten virgins sprinkled with the aroma of pine, white brides. . . . *As late as the mid-nineteenth century, pilgrimages were held to the Mother of God on Three-Peak Mountain. Later the custom died out and the chapel fell into disrepair. In A.D. 1928 the statue was transferred to the decanal Church of the Lord in Klokoty, where it is situated on a side altar and is worshipped by believers to this day. . . .*

A strange bitterness came over me. I looked at the rows of Madonnas with their haloes picked out in gold, hovering in the clouds in defiance of gravity, and I whispered to myself the wistful epithets ascribed to them in the yearning poetry of illiterate peasants. Blessed Mary of the Swollen Oak, intercede for us. Mother of God by the Swallows' Nest, hear our prayer. Mother of Our Lord from the Valley of Lindens, have mercy on us.

A crowd of people with Leicas around their necks gathered beneath the choir while a guide explained to them, in loud English with the accent of an RAF pilot, something about Brokoff and the Dientzenhofers. . . . No, my dear little saints. No, your time has passed. The only people left today who believe in your miracles, or persuade themselves that they do, are frustrated deserters from the seminary life like Mr. Juzl. Your chapels have fallen into disrepair and the weather has stripped away your colours. You are old now, and too tired to give blind girls back their sight. And you too are old — dumb, wooden, and dead — oh Mother of God under Mare's Head. Only your spouse could muster an incomprehensible, half-hearted, embarrassing gesture. Not at the bidding of the heavenly Father, though, but at the hand of a dead secret policeman.

8.

Over a stretch of green grass laid like a carpet across a gently undulating landscape rolled a formation of golfmobiles driven by men in shiny orange and red shirts. I was lying in the shade of a pine tree with Mr. Pohorsky, whose job it was to shave the grass of the Connington golf course for two dollars less a dime per hour.

Before coming to the U.S.A., Mr. Pohorsky had been a labourer for four years. For twelve years before that he had worked in the uranium mines in Jachymov and Pribram, not of his own free will, and before that he had taught natural science and physical education for three years. Before that, equally against his will, he had broken rocks near the German village of Buchenwald, not far from the home-town of Goethe and Schiller, and for three years before that he had been a natural science teacher, and before that he had studied for four years at a teachers' training college, the son of a low-level postal official. Now he was lying in the shade of the pine tree, delighting in America — in the healthy outdoor work, in the fresh air, and in how polite and considerate the men in the golfmobiles were.

He had good reason to be content.

"They almost didn't let me in," he said, blissfully recalling difficulties overcome. "For a year I rotted in a gymnasium in Vienna — it was the only dormitory they could find for all us refugees — and my prospects looked pretty grim, I can tell you."

"You? A former political prisoner?"

"That was the problem. You know how it is — I'd chalked up seventeen years of prison and it wasn't that easy to explain to those jerks from U.S. Immigration that you can end up in prison and still be innocent. Damn their hides! Anyway," he sighed, "I was a bit of a jerk myself. I admitted I'd once been in the Party."

"This is news to me, Mr. Pohorsky."

"No news at all." He spat at an approaching squirrel, slipped off his tennis shoes, and wiggled his toes luxuriously. "I entered the Party as a young jerk in 1941, under the Nazis. And right after the Communist takeover in '48 I left the Party as an old jerk, under the Bolshies."

"Why, for God's sake?"

"Because, like I already told you, I was a jerk. Two days after Klem announced that the Happy Days of the People's Democracy were here, they chucked the head of Sokol in our town into prison. Burival his name was, a butcher. A great guy — we were in Buchenwald together. He'd get parcels of food from home but he gave everything away, mostly to me. So he came back a bundle of skin and bones and I was as plump as a baby pig."

"I can't believe that, Mr. Pohorsky."

"All right, a skinny pig, then," admitted the greens trimmer. "The fact is, Burival was a fine fellow. He'd always say, 'Mirek my lad, go ahead and fill your face. I filled mine for fifty years. You're younger, you need it more.' He was fifty when they picked him up for being head of Sokol. They didn't mind the athletic part, but neither lot was going to put up with all that patriotism."

"Wait a minute—when who picked him up? Didn't you say you were in Buchenwald together?"

"Both the Bolshies *and* the Nazis, of course! For the same damn thing. What kind of a question is that?" said Mr. Pohorsky, annoyed. "That was why it pissed me off. The Bolshies said he was bourgeois and Sokol was a bourgeois organization. So I told them, 'Fair enough. If Pepik Burival's in the clink, then Miroslav Pohorsky's not in the Party. And I threw my card in their face."

"That was a stupid thing to do," I said.

"It sure was," admitted Mr. Pohorsky, and then he told me how, after endless inconclusive interviews at the American embassy in Vienna, and with immense self-denial (he felt like an informer, although he was careful to name only people who were demonstrable swine), he inquired politely why his ancient membership in the Communist Party was being held against him, when so many far more recent Party members had sailed right through. And so the immigration officer explained to him the philosophical basis of their hesitation.

"'When did you join the Party, Mr. Pohorsky?' he asks me. He was a real prick, a slimy cocksucker who looked like he did his hair with axle-grease. So I told him May 1941. And he says, 'Under the Nazi occupation?' 'That's the one,' I told him. 'But these other gentlemen,' he says, 'the ones you were wondering why we let them immigrate to the United States, do you know when they joined the Party?' 'I haven't the faintest idea,' I said, 'because they were in Prague with their noses in the trough. While I had *my* nose up against a seam of high-grade uranium ore in Pribram. How the hell do you expect me to know?' 'It was after the Communist take-over,' grins the bastard, 'in March 1948. And that's the basic difference.' 'You're damned right it is,' I says. 'They're a bunch of radishes!' I had to explain that one to him, and about a month later, when he finally understood, he says, 'Right, Mr. Pohorsky, that's exactly right. You joined the Party when it was a *life-threatening*—those were his words—a *life-threatening* thing to do. But *they* joined it when it was life-threatening *not* to join.' 'Exactly,' I said, and it took me several months and I still didn't understand it. Would you?"

He looked at me with his blue eyes. I laughed. "Well, as a matter of fact, there's a certain logic to it."

"Sure. You're an intellectual," sighed Mr. Pohorsky. "I still didn't get it. 'Mr. Pohorsky,' says old axle-grease, 'you must have been a *real* Communist if you joined when you could have been shot for it. But I think we're right to assume that those other gentlemen were never real Communists. Either they joined the Party because they were scared, or they were forced into it, or they did it to get ahead. But you — what did you do?' 'I don't follow you.' 'I mean right after February 1948?' And as the light began to dawn even in my dim head, he shovelled it to me raw: 'While those other men were joining the Party, you actually *left* it. Now, how can you tell us you're not only a *convinced* Communist, but an *iron-clad* one, since you left the Party because of an injustice to your friend Mr. Pushival? In other words, your motives were *idealistic.* How can you guarantee you won't get mixed up in some similar activity in the U.S.A., out of similar motives?' And he gave me this ugly smartass grin, and I was so dumbfounded all I could say was, 'Oh, I see,' and I went back to that stinking gym. It was a clear case."

In the end it was a member of the John Birch Society (which Mr. Pohorsky thought was a charity) who saved him from another year in the gym. The man had done a rather freely edited interview with Mr. Pohorsky for the Hearst newspapers. He described him as a penitent renegade who, having personally experienced the perversity of Communism, had converted to Christianity (this much was true); now the Communist conspiracy of liberals in the White House was preventing him from entering the country. The article eventually helped Mr. Pohorsky get his immigration papers, but it also brought him to the attention of Prague, and on the strength of that one article the Secret Police promoted him to the status of long-time secret agent, first for the Gestapo and later for the CIA, and they began to confiscate his letters to his wife and daughter in Myto. So that the two women wouldn't get suspicious — and also to punish Pohorsky the traitor, indirectly — the cops told them Mr. Pohorsky had been beaten up by Arab students at a revanchist meeting in Munich, where he had delivered a passionate speech against Czechoslovakian aid to President Nasser. They said that the Arabs had broken both his legs and that while he was in hospital the doctors had discovered that he was suffering from lung cancer, a consequence of his long years in the uranium mines, and that he was now on his deathbed. Therefore, they delicately informed Mrs. Pohorska and her daughter, they were not to expect any further letters.

Mrs. Pohorska had long years of experience and normally she wouldn't have believed what the cops said. Under the circumstances, though, their story about the lung cancer seemed probable enough. But Miss Pohorska told the story of her father's critical condition to a friend of hers who was with the air division of the Army Volunteer Club, and not long afterwards the pilot hijacked an air taxi to Vienna and met Mr. Pohorsky, who was clearly enjoying good health. Thus the allegedly dying man learned of the alleged revanchist meeting in Munich, and as soon as he arrived in the U.S.A. he began to look not just for work, but for someone who was going back to Czechoslovakia who would smuggle a message to his family. After two months of living on bread and tea he got a job cutting grass in Connington, and now I agreed to be his secret courier.

The colours on the golf course burned with a special brilliance in the mild New England sun. Against the emerald green of the grass the men on their golfmobiles looked like psychedelic posters. Mr. Pohorsky asked me if I would mind helping him get a kink out of his back, and after I'd done so he took a sip of tea from his thermos flask and explained, "This is what keeps me going. There are anti-carcinogenic substances in tea, and it's only because I belt back a couple of litres a day — and it's strong stuff," he said, swirling the inky liquid in the plastic cup, "that I've managed to survive. You know, man, I worked for half a year right in the uranium mill. They usually stuck the belly-achers and the priests on that detail because most of them snuffed it. When the guys started throwing up they'd whip them off to the so-called infirmary, and there they'd just fall apart. What a fucking bunch of bastards."

"What's a uranium mill?"

"That's where they grind down the ore. It's kind of like a stone-crusher. There's always this fine dust in the air, like fog. Uranium dust. The guys working in the mill were twelve times more radioactive than the guys working underground." In the somnolent New England sun it almost seemed as if Mr. Pohorsky were making it all up. "And you know, it was in that mill that I began to believe," he added.

"Believe what?"

"In God. Maybe it was because there were so many priests there. And I also started believing that sooner or later there'd have to be a general reconciliation — us, the Commie bastards, the whole country."

"Do you still believe that?"

"Sure," said Mr. Pohorsky. "At first I thought like most of the boys did. Did you know Mila Vanicek?"

"How could I? I wasn't there."

"They called him Full-Nelson Vanicek. He was a former champion in amateur Graeco-Roman wrestling. He came from Myto too. Apprentice butcher; as it happens, he worked for Pepa Burival."

"Why did they lock him up?"

"Come on — for the same thing we got locked up for. Being a jerk. And being a jerk, he'd always say, 'What's the best way to deal with a Communist? Knock his teeth out, break his arms and legs, pull out his fingernails one by one, and then throw him on the manure pile and let the pigs finish him off.' I subscribed to that too, at first." Mr. Pohorsky took another sip of his miraculous tea.

"Things like that shouldn't be said out loud. Not even in prison."

"Damn right. In the end this one guard, Frank the Terrible — that was just the nickname we gave him, his real name was Novak — anyway, when Vanicek kept shooting off his mouth like that, Frank the Terrible poked both his eyes out. And when he saw what he'd done, that he was in real shit, he finished him off with his pistol so he wouldn't get any heat from the warden. Said it happened while Vanicek was trying to escape."

Mr. Pohorsky finished his cup of tea and threw the dregs at the persistent squirrels.

"Yes indeed — violence begets violence," he said. "If we can't find a non-violent way out of this, it'll all go right down the toilet."

I was distracted by the nearby buzzing of a small gas motor, and I raised my eyes from the fleeing squirrels. A pair of fluorescently attired golfers was sailing by. In one of the carts I recognized the silver-haired professor of atomic physics, William Burleigh; in the other was Dr. Hrzan, a visiting professor from the Czechoslovak Academy of Sciences. Mr. Pohorsky told me that originally he'd asked Dr. Hrzan to take the message to his wife, but that recently Hrzan had decided not to go back. Annoyed by his decision, Mr. Pohorsky showed me a clipping from *Time* magazine — a letter from Hrzan in which the internationally known scientist, after twenty years in the Communist Party (he'd joined in February 1948), served notice to the Central Committee that as a protest against the Soviet occupation of his country he was returning his Party card. His decision to defect had obviously been helped along by the fact that Connington had just offered him tenure, but *Time* made no mention of that.

Mr. Pohorsky screwed the top back on the thermos and wiped his mouth with the back of his hand.

"There's nothing like tea! Tea refreshes, wakes you up, preserves your health," he said. He was in a fine mood.

"You should patent your discovery. Americans are obsessed with cancer, because they haven't got much else to be afraid of."

"That's a good one," he chuckled.

"I'm serious. Or at least sell it to some tea company as advertising copy. They'd pay you — I don't know — maybe a thousand bucks. I'll write the text for you, if you like. And you can give me a cut."

"That's a *really* good one," laughed Mr. Pohorsky. "But I'm serious. Tea contains anti-carcinogenic substances. It's a proven fact."

"So much the better. Don't they have a law here about telling the truth in advertising, or something? As a matter of fact," I said, looking at Mr. Pohorsky, who had once more stretched out luxuriously on the grass, "what worries me is that the tea companies won't believe you."

"Why shouldn't they? I'm living proof, aren't I? There are anti-carcinogenic substances in — "

"That's not what I meant. They'll believe that part, people believe any nonsense here. I was thinking of — "

A little white ball arced through the clear air, and Dr. Hrzan vanished behind a yellow cloud of fine dust as he swung awkwardly in the sand-trap. A humid breeze mingled the scent of pine trees with the smell of pipe tobacco from the veranda of the beige and pea-green clubhouse. Mr. Pohorsky was nodding off beside me on the grass, brushing away an insistent butterfly with his hand. His fingernails were cracked and broken.

"Mr. Pohorsky," I said, lying on my back under a fleet of white rococo clouds sailing across the Rhode Island sky, "you're a kind of living chronicle of political prisonerdom. You wouldn't happen to know anything about the case of that miracle-working priest from the Virgin Mary under Mare's Head, would you?"

"Of course I would," Mr. Pohorsky snorted. "They beat him to death."

"You don't know any more than that?"

"About the beating he got? No."

"Not just about the beating. About the whole affair of the false miracle."

"Sure I do. In the first place, it wasn't a false miracle at all. It was the real McCoy."

"Come on, Mr. Pohorsky. I know you're a believing Catholic, but you're a man of science too."

He sat up and looked at me intently. "Look, does the name Kopula mean anything to you?"

"You mean the poet?" I had the absurd feeling that the world had just shrunk, as if by divine intervention.

"And does 'A Litany to Joseph's Wife' mean anything to you?"

"It does. I once heard it recited."

"I spent two years in Bytyz with Honza Kopula. And I know what inspired him to write that poem."

"Mister Pockorsky! Mister Pockorsky!" we heard a female voice cry behind us.

"Yes?" roared Mr. Pohorsky.

A woman in a white dress stood on a knoll. She looked about fifty, which meant she must be at least sixty.

"My husband's rolled his golfmobile, right at the seventh hole," she called. "Would you be kind enough to come and help turn it over?"

"I'm on my way," roared Mr. Pohorsky, putting on his tennis

shoes. Then he jumped to his feet and, very nimbly for his fifty years, ran off across the bright green grass.

9.

I first learned something about Josef Pecen's past on the Vindobona Express on my way back to Prague from the conference on the *roman nouveau.* The previous day's Czech newspapers were on sale in the station in Vienna, and in one of them I found another instalment in Juzl's series:

> As our readers may remember, we had been unable to learn much about a Mr. Pecen, one of those who took part in the installation of the remote-control device. Since then, we've been contacted by Mrs. Evzenie Pecenova, the mother of Josef Pecen, who lives in Prague with her married daughter. According to Mrs. Pecenova, her son died sometime in the summer of 1949 in the Pankrac prison in Prague. This raises interesting new questions: why was Josef Pecen arrested? And how did he die?

The article was unusually brief and inconclusive. If that was all Juzl had turned up, then he was just reinventing the wheel. Disappointed, I picked up a copy of *Wien am Abend* from the seat; my eye was immediately caught by a headline in one-inch type:

> SOVIET DELEGATE TO NEW NOVEL CONFERENCE IN SCANDAL

I was alarmed. The first thing that occurred to me was that Arashidov had got plastered again last night, without me there to protect him from the hookers of Vienna. But fortunately the scandal concerned not the Lenin Prize winner but his chaperone. Anton Pavlovich Chekhov, the newspaper said, had been taken to District One police headquarters and charged with assault after an incident involving Czech singer Sue Kajetanova. Chekhov had punched her in the stomach in the Sacher Café on Kohlmarkt, causing her to lose consciousness. At a trial the next morning, he told the court that he'd acted in self-defence because she'd slapped his face. Oh, Zuzana! I sighed blissfully. Apart from the fact that this was not the best argument to present to a gallant Viennese court, it appeared that Anton Pavlovich had uttered lewd remarks to Suzi and made an immoral suggestion although she swore to the judge that she had never seen him before. Anton Pavlovich was given an unusually high fine for creating a public nuisance, and took refuge in the Soviet embassy. Suzi then announced that she would sue him for damages because of her minor injuries. A short while later the Czechoslovak ambassador visited her in her hotel and then, in an exclusive interview with a reporter from *Wien am Abend*, she stated that she was prepared to refrain from suing. "The affair has a certain piquancy," the reporter wrote, "given the present political tensions between Czechoslovakia and the Soviet Union."

Unlike Juzl's boring piece, the article in the Austrian paper cheered me up. Suzi was obviously well known in Vienna; her export LP, *Rock Riffs*, had sold fifty thousand copies, the reporter said. I was glad to hear it.

I put the *Wien am Abend* aside and looked at the passing countryside. A white church tower gleamed beyond a field of rye; a little farther on there was another one. I had the feeling someone was looking at me through these white eyes, someone who could see deeper into my soul than I wanted. For a brief moment, I was touched by the terror of eternity.

8

■

A Mystical Picture

I.

"I'll tell you what you are!" said an excited Comrade Ponykl. "You're a miserable goddamn priest-lover! And you're only writing these goddamn articles about this tragic case for your own sneaky reasons! That's all the rage right now, isn't it? You think the Party's just a gang of fatheads who never did anything but screw up!"

We were sitting in Juzl's office — I as silent as a mouse, because I hadn't been able to escape when Ponykl burst through the door unannounced. The pistol-packing Party worker of Hronov was nineteen years older now. His skin was more wrinkled, his features were sharper, and his manner, once so full of an ebullient, self-assured aggressiveness, was now that of a pugilist trying to battle back from the corner of the ring. He spoke with a rancour I hadn't noticed those many years ago; back then, he'd been more of a jovial beer-barrel philosopher, a man of the people. But back then I'd only really seen him with the Grand Master, when he was proposing a simultaneous chess match for collective-farm chairmen. Now he was sitting face to face with the class enemy and shouting his head off. Perhaps this was how he'd browbeaten Bozena's father and the other kulaks.

"Doufal was a con-man, goddamn it! He swindled people! He set the whole thing up for a bunch of superstitious old women — and now you're using it to — to disorient our young people!"

"What do you mean '*our* young people'?" Juzl interrupted acidly.

Ponykl was enraged. "I know you. You'd like nothing better than to alienate them from us. First it was jazz, then it was rock and roll, and now it's religious superstition, right? But we won't let you get away with it."

"Who is this 'we' you keep talking about?" Juzl persisted. "The leadership of your party admits that its whole Church policy was handled badly, and it's trying to make amends. I'm merely trying to help them out. So who do you mean by 'we'?"

The old man looked ready to burst. He managed to control himself, but his face was red, and I knew he was getting ready to counterpunch. And counterpunch he did, in a line straight out of a socialist realist novel.

"We Communists, *Mister* Juzl! But just you wait: you haven't heard the end of this yet!"

"Relax," said Juzl, "and answer me one question, if you can: why are you so convinced that Father Doufal was guilty, and that the anonymous letter-writer is lying about that remote-control mechanism?"

"Because I knew the man, that's why. He was a crook and a narrow-minded fanatic!"

"A crook who allowed himself to be tortured to death for his faith?"

The old man flared up as though someone had stuck him with a needle. "Don't start all that again! He died of stomach ulcers. You lot think you can blame everything on Beria's gorillas."

"According to eyewitnesses, Father Doufal had all the fingernails on his left hand torn out."

"Look, some scatterbrained broad . . . it was nineteen years ago! She probably made the whole thing up just to get herself in the papers. And that goes for the old bag too, the one with the flowers. How come all of a sudden everybody's got total recall? None of that stuff proves anything, none of it!"

"It proves more than anything *you* ever came up with in your trials back then, which you dismiss as merely 'impairing socialist justice'," said Juzl very quietly.

"They were all crooks! Slansky, Clementis, Horakova, the whole damned gang of them!" shouted the old gunslinger. "And that 'martyr' of yours was no better! Maybe a lesser crook than Slansky, but a bastard anyway. All right, so maybe we couldn't *prove* everything we had against them, but they were conniving sons of bitches and they deserved to hang! All those traitors and exploiters!"

"I don't know who you think Father Doufal was exploiting."

"He was swindling the people because he wanted to bring back the exploiters!"

The old man pounded the table with his fist and turned so red I became worried. And Juzl obviously didn't want an old Party veteran to have a stroke in his office, because he said, almost consolingly, "Maybe we should get back to the matter in hand. You wrote me that you can prove Father Doufal was guilty. How?"

"I saw him, didn't I!"

"Father Doufal?"

"Sure. In that movie. I saw him pull the string, and then the statue moved."

"When did you see this movie?"

"Right at the time. They put on a special show for us at the local movie house."

"You mean, for us Communists?"

Ponykl flashed Juzl a dirty look. "Right, us Communists. And they also invited all those old bags, the ones who spread the rumour about a miracle. They could see with their own eyes how that sonofabitch priest bamboozled them. Of course, it didn't change their minds a bit; what else is new? They went on whispering, saying it *was* a miracle, it *was* a miracle." The old man was trying awkwardly to mimic those by now deceased old women. "But tell me this, okay? If it was a miracle — and there's no such thing, right? — and if, like you said, he'd have died rather than take anything back — then how come he let them show him pulling the string?"

"Did you recognize him for sure? In the movie, I mean," Juzl pressed him.

"You're damn right I did. How could you take Doufal for somebody else? A huge fellow, big as a mountain, with a mug like a dried-out doughnut. Tell me," and to my great alarm he suddenly turned to me, "could you take Doufal for anyone else?"

"I never knew him," I said quickly.

Ponykl peered at me suspiciously. "You sure?"

I nodded.

"Anyway, it doesn't matter." And he turned back to Juzl. "If it wasn't the real Doufal in that movie, my name ain't Ponykl. I can still see him, like it was today. It was Doufal, all right! And he pulled the string and the figure nodded, just like in a puppet show!"

No sooner had he slammed the door behind him than Juzl asked, as I knew he would, "Do you two know each other?"

"I was in Hronov a couple of times in a panel discussion," I lied. "Some amateur group put on one of my operettas and this guy was a local functionary or something."

Juzl's curiosity was satisfied. I was relieved.

"What a horrible person," Juzl sighed. "But in this case I don't suppose he's lying. He's smart enough to realize that there might still be a copy of the film around, and if it turned up. . . . But you said — "

"Yes. I saw it too. They ran it as part of a newsreel sometime in the summer after it happened. The fellow in it — at least, as far as I can remember — was more like a beanpole than a mountain. Black hair, glasses with thick black frames — "

"I don't understand," said Juzl.

I laughed. "You don't read detective novels. Let me give you some help. In every decent piece of detective fiction, you ask yourself three questions: who? how? and why? In this case, we've had the answer to 'who' right from the start. The film was made by the Secret Police. And now we have the answer to 'how'."

I looked at Juzl and he looked back at me. He didn't understand. People as straight and direct as him, as full of faith, have no insight into the criminal mind. Chesterton must have been an exception.

"They simply made two versions," I said. "In one version, Father Doufal played himself; in the other, they hired an actor. Now we only have to answer the last question: why?"

"Why the two versions, you mean?"

"Of course."

"I — I haven't a clue."

He looked at me as though he expected me to help him out once more. A while before, when it began to be possible again, I'd written three or four detective novels. I'd never really considered my operettas serious writing, but I secretly believed that my detective novels were more honest literature than most of the books that passed for serious literature then. I always revealed the truth (about the criminal, at least) mercilessly and completely: I never kept back anything.

"They must have had some reason." The mystery bothered Juzl. "Maybe, as you said after your talk with Sulc in Vienna, they had to reshoot it because some of the original film was damaged. Could that be it?"

"Maybe. By the time they developed the film, poor Father Doufal may have been, shall we say, unusable." Then I thought of something. "Wait — Sulc didn't actually claim the film was spoiled. On the contrary, he made a point of saying he didn't know for sure."

I thought for a while, and suddenly both versions, Sulc's and Ponykl's, made sense.

"Of course! Ponykl's line is basically the same as Sulc's: why did Father Doufal allow himself to be filmed if he was innocent? And if he let himself be filmed why would he then go and die for his faith? But unlike Ponykl, Sulc made damned good and sure not to make any outright claims. *Maybe* the film was damaged . . . *maybe* it had to be reshot . . . they transferred him to another case . . . and so on." I felt the excitement of detection mounting within me. "It's obvious!"

"What's obvious?"

"Sulc *knew* two versions existed. He invented that stuff about poorly exposed stock just in case we managed to dig out the incriminating copy somewhere. Ponykl doesn't *know* there's another version."

Juzl nodded eagerly.

"And what's more," I said, "I'll bet Sulc also knows *why* there were two versions. But how do we get it out of him?"

Suddenly Juzl made up his mind. "I'm going to Vienna!"

"Sulc won't tell you anything. He never says more than he has to."

Juzl's decisiveness just as rapidly evaporated. "You're right. And the Ministry of the Interior is sabotaging me too. They claim no copy of the film was ever preserved. Not even in their archives."

"They may not be lying. Some things just don't get preserved. But maybe some witnesses are still around. Write an article about it."

This excited him again. "You mean, asking anyone who remembers that film to speak up?"

"Asking anyone who was at the screening in Hronov to speak up," I said. "The one Comrade Ponykl was at."

2.

I handled my compulsory attendance at the conference on Makarenkovian pedagogy in the usual way: I told Vixi to wait for me at the edge of the woods near the pond, then I went back to town and signed in at the Municipal Theatre. I exchanged a few words with three comrades of legendary vigilance, and when the program got under way I went to the washroom and crawled out the window. In less than an hour, I was sitting beside Vixi again.

"Sir, do you think it's possible?" she asked urgently, still unnerved. "Could it really and truly have happened?"

"It's nonsense," I said, and I lay down on my back. My darling was sitting there in a dirty white T-shirt and her once-white tennis shoes; from a distance she must have looked like a white spot in the summer landscape. At the far end of the vista before us, where the countryside rose gently to the mountains, another white spot stood beneath wild pinnacles of rock.

Vixi stared into the distance and said, "What if it's not nonsense?"

"Don't worry, it is. You were asleep too, and you dreamed it."

"I did not. I didn't get loaded the way you did last night. The doll moved. I mean Saint Joseph," she corrected herself, and after a moment she crossed herself as well.

That made me laugh.

"I wouldn't laugh too much if I were you. After all, it happened because of us."

"What makes you think that?"

"You're a queer Catholic. First I spend two months trying to seduce you and all you can say is you mustn't do it. Then we do sin, and when we get a clear sign you pooh-pooh it."

"So what did he do, shake his fist at you?"

"I don't know what else you'd call it. His arm was stretched out and he leaned forward, like this," and Vixi held up her arm and tilted her beautiful body forward, just the way a statue sitting on a rocking chair would move. "I thought I'd have kittens!"

"I hope not. But if you do, it won't be from being scared."

"Don't blaspheme, sir. It was because of me, because I sinned. A lot."

"So did I."

"But I sinned more."

She looked at me uneasily, then decided to admit to something I'd noticed anyway, even with my hangover.

"I pressed up against that hiker who was sitting next to me. I wanted to make him horny. During holy mass! I don't know what got into me. It's a terrible sin!"

"It certainly is. I'm surprised you didn't turn to stone, like Lot's wife."

"She turned into a pillar of salt," she corrected me. "What *is* that, anyway?"

"A column made of salt," I told her.

"I know that, but what does it *mean*?"

"It's one of the mysteries of faith."

She looked at me suspiciously, then said, "You're a real scoffer, sir! You don't believe in anything at all. So why wouldn't you — you know — get involved with me? I want the truth!"

"I've already told you: I was afraid of sinning. Now my conscience has a heavy load until my next confession, and it's your fault."

This took her aback. "That's true," she said after a moment. "My God, I'm such a bitch. All that time I couldn't think of anything but how to get you into bed."

"You didn't just think about it — you tried with all your might."

"I guess I did," she said, embracing her legs with her arms, as she so often did, and resting her chin on her knees. "But I only did it because I love you."

"You can't expect that argument to stand up before God."

"It won't stand up with Father Doufal, either. We better not do it any more until we're married."

"Or we can just go to confession every time we do it," I said, suggesting a solution that was common among engaged Catholic couples.

She measured me with her eyes. "Sir, you really *are* a scoffer!"

"You mean that after all that, you're suddenly turning pious on me?"

"Yes, I am. Because of that miracle. And you don't even believe it happened. You're like Saint Thomas — he didn't see it, so he didn't believe it."

"And he was still a saint," I pointed out.

"Because he believed in the end."

"When he saw for himself."

"But you know what Jesus told him? Blessed are those who have not seen and yet — "

"You didn't believe either until you saw," I reminded her.

"But at least I believed then. You're a doubting Thomas."

"No I'm not," I said. "I believe."

"In what?"

In what? If only I knew, Vixi. I stretched out my arm and described a half-circle over the summer countryside. "I believe something exists that's responsible for all this." The pinnacles of the rock city were veiled in a delicate haze, a cloud of vapours drawn off the meadows by the sun. "I believe that this something has the same esthetic taste as we do. And that some things should be done, and others shouldn't."

"If that's all you believe, you're not much of a Catholic."

"But I am. Quite a bit of one, in fact."

"It seems like a pretty small bit to me."

We were silent.

A gentle breeze drifted across the countryside, announcing the arrival of evening. The green meadows and yellow fields formed an abstract pattern — strips of grass, strips of gold — and running among them, in graceful curves and undulations, stretched a dirt road. The breeze brought with it echoes of the sobbing voices of the morning:

"In-ter-cede for us!"

A small cloud of dust rose above the crest of an undulation in the landscape and in the midst of it, nodding back and forth, was a red and white banner on a long staff. Behind it was another one, and something gold sparkled, all in the cloud of dust; then slowly a black procession appeared over the crest, with coloured banners above it, and in the middle of the procession, at the very centre of the cloud, was a green priest with a golden sun in his arms. His voice, diminished by the distance, echoed across the blazing waves of rye:

"Saint Joseph, who never knew the Blessed Virgin, and yet became the guardian and protector of her Child. . . ."

And the wailing of the old women: "In-ter-cede for us!"

They came nearer. The priest's voice now chanted somewhat louder, "Saint Joseph, who fled into Egypt with Mother and Child, fleeing from the mercenaries of King Herod. . . ."

"In-ter-cede for us!"

"Saint Joseph, who taught Christ our Lord to be a carpenter. . . ."

"In-ter-cede for us!"

Vixi stiffened, as taut as a string, and crossed herself. The procession was coming nearer. On the banner carried in front by a tiny altarboy, I could now make out an image of the Mother of God. The imposing figure of Father Doufal was also getting larger. He was carrying an antique monstrance made of thin strips of gold radiating like rays of light from a dark centre where the Host rested, looking like the eye of God on the priest's reliquary. He was surrounded by old men and women, a tiny, shrunken host of people. In front of them was an altarboy with the censer, another with a little bell, and the small boy with the banner. They walked slowly, approaching as though they were walking into the eye of a camera, and the priest's head in its black biretta towered over the white Sunday kerchiefs worn by the black-clad women. This must have been how the monk Albert approached five hundred years before with a band of his faithful followers, under one banner, drawing near to the valley of Hronov . . . walking through the wild poppies . . . in the same cloud of dust . . . *for one generation passeth away, and another generation cometh, but the earth abideth for ever. . . .*

I shook myself out of my momentary madness and made a wry face. With a vision like that, I wouldn't make it very far in my career as a pedagogue. By now the procession was so close that I could see the expressions on the old women's faces. They seemed more trancelike than usual, and their singsong wailing was more intense. Down the wrinkles on their faces flowed tiny runnels of pure rural perspiration. Father Doufal's face also glistened with sweat, and he seemed in a strange state of bliss. "Saint Joseph!" thundered his voice, "who quiet and of humble heart loved the Blessed Virgin above all else. . . ." "In-ter-cede for us!" sang the old women, like a jazz quartet. There was not a trace in the Father's voice of the shyness and modesty I had heard when he'd shown us the results of his wood-carving. This was the voice of a Crusader in a horsehair tunic, leading his children through the Saracen desert. "Saint Joseph . . . ," he sang.

I no longer heard the words. The procession walked right by us, but no one noticed either me or Vixi. They passed like a mirage. Even the stalwart priest who had taught Vixi the catechism, who had sat here with me, not long before, talking of the birds and the stars, now stared with sightless eyes at the blue sky; perhaps he was watching the larks swooping and dipping high in the air above the banner. I couldn't take my eyes off his face. It seemed to have been carved by a woodcarver more skilful than he, but working in the same style, with similar tastes. . . .

Vixi jumped up.

"Come on! Let's go with them!"

"Don't be crazy! We can't!"

"We have to!"

"I'm not going to get myself thrown out of the school just because you thought you saw something."

She stood there indecisively and then, unhappily, she almost implored me, "You won't go with them?"

"Out of the question! And you won't either."

"Yes I will," she said. "I have to, since you're such a scoffer. Then at least you'll go to purgatory instead of hell."

She turned away and her bright, well-brushed hair flashed before my eyes like the flag of some hopeful lost cause, the red ribbon ablaze. Vixi ran down the slope and joined the very end of the procession.

I tagged along in the distance far behind them, gritting my teeth. Incense mingled with the resinous aroma of the woods into a single, intoxicating cocktail; the tinkling bell blended with the scolding of the birds the little procession had disturbed. As the group slipped slowly through shadows alive with bees and butterflies, I wandered along a deep path between two banks of clay, where the green moss was flecked with gold wherever a shaft of sunlight managed to penetrate the treetops. Occasionally I glimpsed red from a banner, a ribbon, or a flowery kerchief. All the way, the antiphony of the priest's voice and the old women's wailing continued.

When we began to get close to the town, I circled around ahead of the procession, ran to the Municipal Theatre, climbed back in through the bathroom window, and entered the auditorium (making sure the three vigilant comrades saw me) just as Ivana was delivering her concluding address on the theme: "No One Is Beyond Reform: Dialectical Education on the Road to Socialism".

It was getting dark by the time I extricated myself from a circle of garrulous and boring comrades. I turned down Ivana's invitation to go to the café with the district inspector, and very circumspectly went up to the church. Vixi was sitting on a bench outside, under the green trees. I nodded for her to follow me and then walked quickly into the lilac bower.

"They're saying their rosaries in there," she said. "The procession went straight to the church and now they're praying."

"So you've got over it, then?"

She shook her head. "Can you explain it, sir?"

"What is there to explain?"

"The statue of Saint Joseph actually moved!"

"So what?"

"He was warning me."

"Oh my!" I said.

We sat on an old bench in front of the chapel. Hronov was sinking into night, and an evening mist rising from the lilac bower made the church's glowing yellow windows seem framed by a diffuse corona, like little clouds, with the candles inside making copper-coloured points of light in the glass.

I put my arm around Vixi's shoulders.

"Vixi?"

"Hmmm."

"I love you, you know that."

I ran my lips over her silken cheek.

"I'm glad."

"Come to my place. The widow will be asleep by now."

"I can't."

"Come on."

"No, I won't come."

"Oh, God!"

"You're taking the Lord's name in vain," said Vixi, "and you're exciting sinful lust. I'm going home."

She stood up.

I got to my feet as well, cursing myself for having so thoughtlessly set this creature on the road to salvation.

"Vixi," I said, "I swear on my soul I'm Catholic. But these things shouldn't be taken too literally. Come with me. I'm crazy about you, and God will forgive us."

"No He won't," she said. "If you know it's a sin, He won't forgive you."

As I stood there looking at her, I felt I was in the presence of a real miracle. Could I, through lies and the clap, have brought the heathen Vixi to true faith? The ways of the Lord are indeed strange. *Quia absurdum, turpe, indignum.* I took her by the hand, but she pulled it away.

"Let me go, sir! We really have to let this thing cool down!"

Unexpectedly, she gave me a soft, wet kiss on the mouth, and then ran into the shadows of the lilac bower. I saw her running away, that improbable Hronov Mary Magdalene, that will-o'-the-wisp of youth, with a twinkling cloud of stupid fireflies around her.

One of them lit on my arm — an unpretty, leggy-looking beetle with a beautifully incandescent bum. I flicked it into the darkness; its little light came on and it flew away unsteadily among the lilac bushes, now no longer in bloom, after the others, after Vixi. I lay down in the grass, and stayed there, cursing and suffering, far into the night. I thought a little about faith and rejection too, although not much. I believed in rejection, but not in faith. The worst of it was that there was nothing you could know with certainty.

I fell asleep. Towards morning, the cold and the dampness woke me up. I stood up and went on a short jog around the woods, partly to get warm and partly because I was young, frustrated, and well rested. Then I decided to go straight to the school and make myself a cup of coffee in the staff room. I ran back through the lilac bower, past the widow Ledvinova's little house. I could see her in her century-old dressing gown through the open kitchen window, making breakfast for her two sons, the pastors, who would be getting up soon so as not to be late for their shift. As I ran past the church, I noticed that the front door was open.

That was strange, so early in the morning. I stopped. The morning mass began at six, and it was barely four-thirty. I looked around. The first workers hadn't yet appeared on their way to work; there was no danger that anyone would see me go into the house of darkness.

Cautiously, I entered the church. Candles were still burning quietly on the altar, but by now they were short stubs with not much life left in them. The sound of someone contentedly snoring carried through the silence. The robust priest was lying on the steps leading to the altar, fast asleep.

3·

Juzl handed me the letter over the Cinzano on the café table. I glanced at the signature: "Respectfully yours, Albina Knizakova."

"Your regular correspondent?"

"I think this is the answer to your 'Why?'"

I read.

Dear Sir, I'll tell you why the communist swine made another movie with someone else, not Venerable Father Doufal, because in that first movie they showed us it really was Father Doufal and he pulled the string like they said in the papers but it was the Virgin Mary what moved, not Saint Joseph, but at holy mass it was the other way round and they never took the trouble to ask nobody what happened because they think they eat wisdom for breakfast and know it all so they fixed up the Virgin Mary but it was Saint Joseph that moved, the patron saint of Father Doufal on the intercession of the Most Blessed Virgin Mary. And you ask why Father Doufal let them use him in the movie, well it was because he wanted to give us a sign that they were lying through their teeth and nothing was fixed up before because it was Saint Joseph that moved and not the Virgin Mary and he knew we would understand and anyway Saint Joseph moved as a sign of Father Doufal's death and martyrdom, because his name was also Josef and we said right away the movie was a fake and they were just trying to fool people because the communists don't know the difference between the Mother of God and the Guardian of our Lord and those miserable creatures, they found out what we was saying and arrested seven of us and poor old Pavlicek died when they were questioning him of a heart attack and I testified as the Lord told me to and I told them about those flower pots and the swine arrested me for it and I spent five years in prison but praise be to God I came back with my health and all of this is God's truth, sir, and Aloisa Rivnacova from Cermna can back me up if she's still alive, she was only 62 when it happened but the rest were older and will now be resting in the arms of God, like our saintly martyr, the Venerable Father Doufal, Respectfully yours—

"Well, there it is," I said, putting the letter down.

Juzl nodded. "They got it wrong. It was the hand of God at work."

"Maybe." I shrugged. "In any case, the comrades didn't listen to the voice of the people; they just went ahead and mechanized the statue of Mary for the filming, according to their original plan."

Juzl's eyes were no longer looking at me, but somewhere beyond me, where I had never been able to look, or at least had never been able to see anything.

"Yes. But then how come Saint Joseph moved?"

Yes, how come, for God's sake? I sat there over my Cinzano, like Lot's wife.

9

■

The Final Solution

I.

Mr. Kohn — diminutive and plump, with rosy cheeks and curly hair — raised a glass to his mouth and moistened his pink lips with gin. His eyes were empty of hope as he scanned the evening crowd in the Connington bar and said, with sadness in his voice, "I'm an American now, I pay my taxes and I've managed to accumulate a decent bit of net worth, but I'll tell you frankly, I'm not at home here. Thirty years in the United States, doctor, but I still have the Liben gasometer and the Prague skyline in my mind's eye, and I swear to God I can still see the little shop that belonged to my late father, with the bell that always tinkled when you opened the door. That was home to me. This — " and he swept a plump arm in a circle that was meant to include Connington and New England, "this is what I call Babylon."

"But still, Mr. Kohn, I take it you don't regret leaving?"

"Regret? I'll tell you what I regret, doctor. I regret having *had* to leave. And that's the difference, do you see? It's one thing to *want* to leave; it's another thing entirely to *have* to."

2.

A telephone rang, but I didn't know where it was. Gradually I realized that it was *my* telephone, that it was night, but that I was still in the middle of a bad dream — though I didn't know what it was about, I only knew I was relieved to discover that it was a dream and not reality. The room was dark, but my eyes slowly grew used to it. A yellow streetlamp shone outside my window. And the telephone was ringing. When that happens at night, it's always terrifying. My watch glowed three-fifteen. I reached for the receiver.

"Smiricky."

"The experiment was a failure," said someone's voice.

"Who is this?"

"Paternoster."

I was relieved. The author of utopian novels was a notorious drinker. A call from him in the middle of the night was nothing special.

"Art thou in heaven?" I asked. "And how did you get there? Johnnie Walker or Chateauneuf-du-Pape?"

"I'm not in heaven, my friend. I'm up shit creek. And so are you."

"Not me. I'm sleeping. If you want to talk yourself out of a drunk, call up Sarka. Good night!"

I hung up.

The room was quiet. In the distance I could hear the growling of an airplane. The Prague airport was about five kilometres west of where I lived; when the wind was from the west the pilots would turn for their final approach right above my house, and it made a terrible noise. I'd got used to it, though, and usually slept right through the ruckus.

I lay in bed, my ear half cocked for the familiar sounds of night traffic on the main street through Brevnov. There seemed to be more noise than usual for that time of night and, if anything, it was getting louder. I opened my eyes again. The yellow streetlamp shone through a halo of late-summer mist.

The telephone exploded again. I reached for it.

"The experiment was a failure."

"Go to hell!" I said with feeling, all the while listening to the rumbling in the air overhead. To my half-awakened brain it sounded like more than just some nighttime Boeing that, perhaps because of the fog, was circling the airport waiting for clearance to land. Then the unawakened half of my brain suddenly became fully conscious. The author of utopian novels had no more explaining to do. What I'd experienced before his call was not a dream; it was two nightmares becoming one — the nighttime and daytime dreams merging into a single nightmare of reality. I repeated into the receiver — and against my will, an unexpected hatred crept into my voice — "Go to hell, Paternoster!"

"I'm already there. So are you. The Brothers have come."

"Those airplanes? Is that them?"

"And that ain't all. There's a tank spearhead moving in from Melnik. They should be outside your place pretty soon. Take a look out the window."

"I'd have heard them. Tanks rattle like a truckload of scrap metal."

"Of course, I forgot — an old tank commander." Suddenly Paternoster seemed alarmed by something. "Holy shit!"

"What's the matter?"

"Foglar's got that tank manuscript of yours, right? Before Dubcek that would have been enough to get you high treason!"

Now I was alarmed, even more than Paternoster. Against the voice of common sense, I had taken my novel *In the Red Panzerkorps* out of its fifteen-year hiding place with my aunt in Popovice and brought it in to the suddenly liberalized Writers' Union Publishing House. Vohnout had just been thrown out and replaced by Foglar, who had earlier been thrown out by Vohnout. In the historical situation now emerging, signalled by the rumbling of aircraft overhead, my venomous satire on the people's army was as dangerous as it had been once before, long ago, when it fell into the wrong hands. I began trembling in my bed like a bowl of gelatine, but I replied heroically, "What of it?"

"My friend," said Paternoster, "if I am up shit creek, then you are, at the very least, in the large intestine. If I were you, I'd get my ass down to the office and take that manuscript back to Popovice as fast as I could. I'll bet you Vohnout is on the first tank in here, and that's the last you'll ever see of the manuscript. Until it's on the table in front of the state prosecutor — "

"Go to — "

Then I heard it outside my window. I remembered the sound well; those first few days in the army, it was terrifying. Then you got used to it. But in the course of eighteen years I'd got unused to it again, and my heart fell into my pyjama bottoms.

"They're here," I said to the telephone.

"The tanks?"

"Right."

"I tried calling Hejl. No one answered. You know, man, I have a feeling the boys from the KGB are already at work."

By now I was trembling violently. "Don't be crazy!"

"I hope I am," said the author of utopian novels. "Well, so long, and Abyssinia in Siberia."

He hung up.

I shot out of bed and, on legs that seemed about to give way underneath me — just as I'd described the sensation several times in my detective novels — I wobbled to the window.

The noise outside sounded like a truck carrying a load of old garbage cans, and the scene might have come straight from one of Paternoster's novels. Out of the early morning mist, one after another, emerged a line of squat monsters, messengers of truth. Sitting on top of them in a cluster of automatic rifles, looking warily at the windows as they went by, were adolescents from the land of the bright future.

I realized that my old sarcasm, at least, had not abandoned me, and my knees began to take orders from my head once more.

3.

Mr. Kohn nodded philosophically.

"Do you think I wanted to leave? Of course not. I was still hanging around Prague as late as May of '39. I couldn't make up my mind. There were awful rumours being whispered about — they'd put us all into camps, they treated people like animals, we'd all die — but you didn't know anything for sure. That was the worst of it: nothing was certain, neither the good rumours nor the bad. But going to a foreign country — well, I was forty-five at the time, I could only speak Czech and a touch of German, I had a small factory and no capital abroad, and you couldn't take anything out any more — I tell you, doctor, it was a tough decision to make. When you're pushing fifty and nothing is certain, and horrible things are happening no matter which way you turn. That's the worst of it. When there's nothing, nothing at all that's certain."

I nodded. I understood Mr. Kohn very well. I was forty-five too, and I had no capital anywhere. But all that was behind him now; he had nothing worse than death to look forward to. And it would clearly be a luxurious death in a well-equipped hospital. I looked at his grief-filled eyes and the pink cheeks of this well-preserved old man of seventy-five and I suddenly found myself envying him. It was the envy of Ecclesiastes.

4.

I rushed through the early morning streets on foot. I'd given up the idea of taking my Felicie out of the garage; the stream of tanks seemed endless and they were creating iron traffic-jams at the intersections. There had been several boys in front of my house throwing bottles and rocks at the soldiers.

It was scarcely four in the morning, but a mob of people was already storming into the streets: dishevelled women in nightgowns, weeping;

unshaven men shouting vulgar but appropriate insults; young men in colourful shirts holding up clenched fists, not in the fashionable greeting of those days, but in a gesture essentially older and more of the people. Alongside the shuddering tanks ran a crowd of high-school girls shouting out in tearful class-room Russian:

"*Pachemu? Pachemu vy priyekhali suda?*"

I moved quickly and silently through the streets towards my overwhelming goal. The tanks were just like the ones in my imprudent novel, except that nervous adolescent boys cradling deadly weapons in their arms were staring down from them at an alien world — staring at the girls trotting along beside them, at the unexpectedly defenceless crowds that poured into the streets to meet them (their *politruks* had promised them organized gangs of Zionists armed with the latest American war technology), at the strange, un-Russian, medieval city. The *politruks*, in newly issued knee-length *rubashky*, were standing on the tanks near the cannon, frowning at nothing in particular. Occasionally a private would look around at the golden epaulettes as if seeking instruction, but the officers maintained their sphinx-like hauteur. Once this city had been looted by Swedish mercenaries, and later it had been crushed by the naked will of an army of German National Socialists. Now I felt that a low, earth-crawling darkness guided by electronic computers was rolling over the land.

At the corner by the Church of St. Antonin the street angled sharply to the right and each tank had to stop, execute a clumsy manoeuvre, and lurch towards the embankment. I walked past one tank with its left track churning up paving stones and streetcar tracks. On its mudguard perched a *politruk*. He was small but had pumped himself up to full height; he wore a padded vest and brandished a revolver, and a nose like Maxim Gorky's protruded from his potato-like face. On his cap shone a bright ruby star, that symbol of anything and everything under the sun. An irritated certainty of the sanctity of his every act lingered in the bushy eyebrows beneath the star, but I could see that he was beginning to wonder if they hadn't ended up in the wrong country by mistake. Another troop of young girls in miniskirts had gathered around the tank and they were shouting, in heavily accented Russian:

"*Pachemu? Pachemu? Kontrarevolutsiyi u nas nyet!*"

I noticed that the ordinary soldiers clustered around the *politruk* on the tank were gaping at the bare thighs as though hypnotized. They might never have seen so much of a girl's leg exposed so publicly before.

"*Pachemu? Pachemu?*" shouted the girls, and real tears flowed from their eyes.

The *politruk* scanned them with an evil eye used to surveying the steppes. In the mix of emotions that flitted across the potato-like face, sanctimony had triumphed for the moment; he had undoubtedly been warned that the miniskirt was a symptom of the restoration of capitalism.

"*Pachemu? Pachemu?*" wailed the band of girls in their grade-five Russian. Suddenly — above the shouts, the clanking of the armoured vehicles, and the roar of motors — a shrieking woman's voice rose like a siren. She too spoke Russian, but this was the beautiful language of Lermontov, with all the accents in the right places:

"*Idite domoy, ruskiye fashisty!*"

The *politruk* automatically raised his pistol, ready to shoot. A young man with a bazooka sitting near his feet wept, shedding tears like the girls in the miniskirts. The officer wrinkled his eyebrows and looked for the source of the piercing voice. High above the crowd towered the grey head of Bozena Pokorna, the six-foot-five translator of classical Russian literature. Not long before, at the bloodthirsty meeting at the Writers' Club, it had been she who, ignoring the Prague Spring and all its manifestations, had uttered another memorable slogan about staying away from politics. Now she was standing there in pink curlers and a shabby peignoir, betraying principles gained by bitter experience:

"*Ruskiye fashisty, idite domoy!*"

The *politruk* easily picked her out from the crowd of young girls. They stared at each other for a moment, the officer and the translator, both with a similar hatred. Then the officer waved his pistol and from the depths of his inflated chest he roared like a bear:

"*Smert fashizmu! Smert kontrarevolutsiyi!*"

The crowd seemed to swell and roar. Several young men put their fingers in their mouths and whistled, and a wave of jeering, mocking shouts rose from the people. A street-boy drew a swastika in chalk on the glacis plate of the first tank, right under the boots of the sobbing bazookaist. And over all the hubbub, again, came the piercing voice of Bozena Pokorna:

"*Smert sovyetskomu fashizmu! Smert sovyetskoj kontrarevoluctsiyi! Idite domoy!*"

The girls in the miniskirts, momentarily silenced by this exchange of opinions in perfect Russian between the officer and the translator, came to their senses and immediately took up the slogan:

"*Idite domoy, ruskiye fashisty! Idite domoy, ruskiye fashisty!*"

A slickly dressed mod armed with a transistor radio shouted, in English:

"Russians, go home!"

It was beautiful, and hopeless. I hurried around the corner. I did not want to be there if the terrified adolescents on the tanks decided to resolve this battle of words with their automatic rifles.

5.

"And all you ever heard was, what will they do with us? Will they clap us in a ghetto but let us go on living, or take us away somewhere and kill us? Yes, doctor, that was the question that filled our minds from morning till night, and then from night till morning. Thoughts work away at you, whether you want them to or not. It's awful. A living nightmare, doctor. You walk through the streets surrounded by people who aren't in any danger, and you're right there beside them, faced with exile or death. And nobody gives a good goddamn, and why should they? What do they care for you? You're the one who's in it up to your neck, not them."

Mr. Kohn was silent for a while. Several black men and their women, all wearing Afros, were pushing up to the bar around us.

"I know what you're talking about, Mr. Kohn," said Mr. Pohorsky. "It's like when they were taking me past Wenceslas Square in the paddy-wagon and I saw the name of a movie on a marquee: *Tomorrow There'll Be Dancing Everywhere.* And they were carting me off to the uranium mines in Jachymov."

6.

I couldn't get to the publishing house on Prikopy Street. The tanks were jammed up at Prasna Brana, and a lively debating circle had formed around the immobilized steel chariots. I turned into Senovazne Namesti. In front of the former stock exchange a man in civilian clothing was being slapped around. He was an obese, grey-haired fellow with an arrogant-looking mouth and he was shouting, "Please, let me be. Is big mistake!"

"Is big mistake, sure buddy, ees wery beeeg mistake," said someone beside me.

"Who is he?"

"A member of the Soviet gestapo. They taught him to speak Czech in Moscow, but they didn't do a very good job of it."

Another blow fell and the alleged agent began shouting at the top of his lungs. His Czech was indeed transparently foreign and the fellow decided to come clean.

"*Ja ne sovyetskiy! Ja tolko ruskiy! Byelogvardeyskiy emigrant!*"

The circle of people around him was taken aback. They were politically sophisticated enough to distinguish between Russian nationality and Soviet imperialism. A man in a checkered shirt, his arm poised to land another blow, scowled. "So you're an old Prague Russian, eh?"

"*Da! Da!* From nineteen hundred twenty!"

The man in the shirt took a moment to weigh the heavy Russian accent and then shot back, "Who commanded the Russian troops that liberated Prague in 1945?"

"Marshal Konyev!"

The man in the shirt landed a powerful blow that knocked the alleged White Guardist to the sidewalk.

"Take that, you old Prague Russky!" said the man in the shirt. "I guess you've never heard the name Vlasov, right?"

"*Da, da,*" the fellow mumbled. "Vlasov. General Vlasov — " but the man in the shirt kicked him so hard he landed back on his feet.

"Back to your own kind, cocksucker," he said in disgust, and kicked him in the rear again. The agent set off at a brisk run. Several more blows landed, but he was soon out of reach.

A young man in overalls said, "We should have slit his throat. He'll turn us all in."

"Him? He was scared shitless. He won't remember us."

"Then he'll name people he does know and blame it on them. That's what they did in the fifties, isn't it? At least that's what you said."

The man in the shirt said nothing.

I turned and hurried on.

7.

"Well," said Mr. Kohn, "then you know what I'm talking about, Mr. Pohorsky. That feeling — it's a terrible thing. When you're not free any more and you're not dead yet. To make a long story short, I hung around in that state of mind until May '39 — and then suddenly it was too late. The lid came down. They weren't letting Jews out any more. And the moment they slammed the door, anything in the world seemed better than sitting inside that cage. Anything. Even begging for a living on a street-corner, or slogging it out from dawn to dusk in the Ruritanian outback; even dying in some hospital for the poor, but in a bed, at least, doctor! Anything was better than that inhuman fear you get when you're trapped like an animal. The terror, wondering what they'll do with you. Because I'll tell you, doctor, man is not a piece of livestock, and the worst thing that can happen to him is to die like one. And those poor bastards — but you know this, of course, gentlemen — they all died like animals."

I knew it, of course. Through the bobbing Afros I could see in my mind a picture taken, God knows why, by an SS man who ended up with a bullet in his head. An Allied soldier pulled the photo out of the dead man's pocket and sold it for a tidy sum to an illustrated magazine. Naked old women, fat naked middle-aged women, some running through the rubble beside a kind of rubbish heap, some just sitting on the ground in attitudes of resignation, shamefully naked before the eye of the camera, their loose stomachs hanging down over the triangular patch of human fur, their breasts pendulous, naked not from the mercenary impulses that drive gate-fold bunnies but stripped by command, terribly naked, still holding tightly — responding to an impulse that no longer made sense — to their naked children. White, untanned women's bodies, puffy with age and idleness. In human clothes they would all have been kind or haughty or dignified Jewish mommas with extravagant hairdos and earrings in their old ears. Yes, there is nothing worse for a person than dying like a piece of livestock.

"And if it hadn't been for Bondy I'd never have got out of that cage, gentlemen. I'd have been turned into a bar of soap like the poor buggers who stayed behind."

8.

I pushed my way through the people gathered in front of the museum. One of the armoured vehicles had gone out of control and crushed a telephone booth. I forced a passage through the thick crowd in the deafening roar of the iron cavalcade and I remembered another telephone call a few years before, also terrifying. That time it had been Ludmila calling — the woman I called Lida or Lizetka.

"*Servus,*" she said. It was eleven o'clock at night. I recognized her voice; she was the only one who ever greeted me in the old Austro-Hungarian style.

"Hi, Lizetka."

"I want you to come over to my place."

"Now? Why?"

"Time was, you never asked why."

Her call annoyed me. As a sex-starved noncom I had been irresistibly hypnotized by her green eyes in a railway compartment on the way from Kobylec to Prague. Her husband was in an infantry regiment in Kobylec and she made me an erotic martyr, her own private toy, for as long as I was in the tank corps. She was practised in the act of seductive inaccessibility, and kept me hanging until one day, when my stint was over and my first operetta was playing, she gave in — though I suspect I owed it more to her weakness for writers in general than to any special feelings she had for me. It was a perfect case of forbidden fruit, and after two weeks of extramarital fornication I cooled off. Her pride was hurt and she burned. But not with love, of course.

"It's almost midnight, for crying out loud."

"Time was, you'd come running at three in the morning, darling."

That was true; there was no point arguing with her on that account. I decided to resort to cynicism.

"Time was."

"Do I take it you don't love me any more?"

I knew it was not love that moved her now, but wounded pride. Unfortunately her pride was distinctly hypertrophic.

"Don't you love me any more, Daniel?" she pressed.

"Sure I do. But it's a little late now."

"It's never too late for love."

"It is for mine."

She was silent for a moment. I imagined her reclining on her couch, overcome with anger.

"Let me tell you something, darling: it is not as late as you think. So pull yourself together and get over here, pronto."

"Look, Lizetka, go stuff yourself!"

"It's in your own interest, darling," she said. A certain malice in her tone made me uneasy.

"What did you say?"

"I said you'd better come quickly, if you know what's good for you."

I was overwhelmed by the feeling, common under socialism, that I was about to land in trouble.

"Look, Lizetka," I said, feeling quite unsure of myself, "I'm not really interested."

"You will be," she assured me. "I have an interesting novel here. It's called *In the Red Panzerkorps*. Do you understand, Dannypoo?"

Ten minutes later I was sitting in a taxi heading for Radlice, my heart beating in my throat — not in anticipation of a night of love, but because in the novel in question — my novel — the multiple infidelities of Ludmila Neumannova-Hertlova were described in rather venomous terms, including some blow-by-blow descriptions of her love-making skills. My God, how could she have got her hands on the manuscript?

I soon found out. Lizeta, dressed in nothing but a transparent negligée, said in tones calculated to arouse terror, "Look here, darling, I don't so much mind that you lend this tripe of yours to your buddies without even checking to see whether they happen to be my buddies as well." That fingered Paternoster, although a mere two weeks before, when I'd given him the manuscript to read (on the promise that he'd keep it to himself), he had certainly not been her buddy. "Nor do I really mind that you describe me as a Zizkov hooker," she said, truthfully, because basically she enjoyed her reputation as a whore. "I don't even mind that you describe me as a completely *asinine* whore, or that you say I have an ass like a *horse*," she went on, moving from truth to lies and from there directly to deliberate hypocrisy. "What really insults me is your *cynicism*. I'm not a stupid Communist, you know, but enough, my dear, is enough. I can take a lot, but I still have my socialist convictions. And in all tolerance, Dannykins, and even given my sense of fun, this book insults me as a socialist!"

I looked at her, panicky and perspiring. The association of socialism with this woman, who was ruled by a lust beyond that of any other woman who had ever dominated me, was utterly surrealistic—like a roast leg of goose in the middle of a monstrance.

"And besides that," she said, "I do believe you've revealed a few military secrets."

"Surely not!" I exclaimed, paralysed.

"Oh yes," she said. "But we can let more competent authorities be the judge of that."

She looked at me. I was speechless, so she continued. "I've been thinking of taking it straight to the Ministry. Of the Interior."

She stared at me with her evil, haunting eyes. Under the thin nightgown, her nipples were erect. My heart began to beat in wild terror again, because in these matters I was in absolutely no doubt. Lizeta was entirely capable of carrying out her threat.

For a long time that night she played with me, like a very cruel cat playing with a terrified mouse, until at last she allowed me to pull the nightgown from her and perform an act of compulsory love—from behind, perhaps to demonstrate that her ass was not at all like a horse's, but was a trim, virginal little bum. But it was still like a horse's ass. In that, and in everything else, my description of her had been precise.

9.

"Bondy? Who was he, a relative from America?" asked Mr. Pohorsky.

"No sir. A friend. A born idler. I met him around the end of May, on the embankment, and Bondy was all ironed and squeaky clean, as always; he was even wearing a carnation in his lapel. By that time, just so you'll get the picture, gentlemen, Jews were slinking about through the back streets. But here was Bondy as though nothing had happened. No cage, not a sign of distress. He sees I'm all worried and he says, 'What's the matter?' and I tell him what a schlemiel I am and how I'm stuck there.

I could have been out of here, I say, and in South America or somewhere, poor maybe, but safe. And all Bondy says is, 'Kohn, since you're an old friend of mine, come with me!' And we went. You'll never guess where."

"Where, Mr. Kohn?"

By the bar, just as in the old blues songs, one of the black dudes began quarrelling with a beautiful chocolate-skinned girl, and gave her a shove. Her Afro wig toppled off among the drinks, revealing a charming curly head covered with miniature braids. An ancient blues wail emerged from an enormous mouth.

"To the *Staatskommando der Wehrmacht*, gentlemen!" said Mr. Kohn. "There were guards at the gate, but Bondy just flashes them a pass and they let him in. Let him in? They practically salute him. And you know what I look like, doctor. Well, it's nothing compared to Bondy. It couldn't have been an oversight."

And Mr. Kohn pointed ruefully at his enormous schnozz.

10.

Then she lay beside me the way she liked to, on her belly, with her magnificent ass glowing white in the moonlight. A lace curtain caressed us in the breeze of the open window.

"Lizous?" I said.

"Hm?"

"Where's the manuscript?"

"I thought you'd want to know."

"Where is it?"

"In the safe. Over there."

She pointed with her foot to a small safe on the bookshelf; it was where she locked up letters from her lovers, to keep them from the jealous but lamentably weak Dr. Robert Neumann. In the moonlight her leg was unabashedly naked. But it didn't arouse me. My freedom was at stake.

"Give it to me."

"I'll have to think about it, darling."

"Are you going to try to blackmail me?"

She raised herself up on her elbow. In the white moonlight, her breasts formed two beautiful white slopes separated by a narrow path. "Is this kind of blackmail so unpleasant?"

"No, but I'll enjoy it more when you give me back the manuscript."

I realized that I was in a classic situation and that I was behaving with classic helplessness.

"I'm afraid not, my love. I know you," she said. "You're as perfidious as all the rest of them put together. Your little novel stays in the safe."

I had an idea, and got up. There were cigarettes on the writing desk, but her handbag was there as well.

"What are you doing?" I heard her say behind me; then there was a thump as she jumped out of bed. I was scrabbling inside her handbag, and she moved right in beside me.

"Give that back!"

She tried to snatch the handbag away. I grabbed her around the waist and we tussled until I managed to throw her back on the bed; she had muscles under that soft surface. As we rolled around on top of each other she stuck the handbag underneath her and held it there with both hands. I sat astride her and grabbed her by the neck.

"Are you going to murder me?" she hissed mockingly.

I was sitting on her belly with her excited breasts clamped between my thighs; suddenly it excited me too.

"I'll kill you," I said, but with her whore's instinct, she could tell my resolution was weakening.

"Not like that. They'd catch you right away."

I let go of her neck. At once she began to taunt me. "Do a good job of it, darling. Make it first-degree murder. It'll be great."

The moon ignited her green eyes. I tried grabbing for the handbag, but she arched her back with all her might and I lost my balance and fell down with her. She jumped off the bed and her bum flashed white in the moonlight again as she ran out of the room. I couldn't follow her because her parents were asleep in the room across the hall. They were serious Catholics, and to the many other mysteries of that faith they added one of their own: an inexplicable tolerance for their daughter's fornications; still, I didn't want to push her that far. Angrily, I flopped down and lay there on the bed, aroused, full of hate, alarmed and exhausted. Then she returned. The moonlight lent a lovely opal sheen to her skin. I lay on my back with my hands behind my head. She hopped onto the bed and mounted me like a horse, placing her hands on my shoulders and swinging her full breasts, with their dark, erect nipples, just above my face. Her basilisk eyes sparkled and she said, "And now you're mine, Daniel, in case you had any doubts. You'll come when I ring your bell, and if you don't, the Secret Police will be the next to ring it."

The idea excited her so much that she began to work her wonderful ass back and forth in my lap.

11.

"And another soldier opened a great high door for us, all covered with gold and decorations," Mr. Kohn went on, "and then we were inside and in front of us, behind a table big enough for at least twenty people, sat a general with a monocle in his eye. As soon as he sees Bondy, he says, '*Servus, Bondy! Was kann ich für dich tun?*' You may not believe it, gentlemen—I know I didn't—but he offered to help just like that. A Nazi general. And you know who it was?"

"No."

"General Blaskowitz. If the name means anything to you."

It did. Blaskowitz had engraved his name into the emotional history of my generation as a signature on the very first of many sinister posters written in Czech by one of the general's Sudeten German advisers, which ended with the delightfully anti-sentimental warning, "Anyone who oppose the Army of the Reich will be shooted." Yes, we knew who General Blaskowitz was.

12.

In front of the Melantrich building in Wenceslas Square I caught sight of Juzl. He was as pale as a corpse, but the little silver cross still shone proudly in his lapel. A crush of steel was flowing up the centre of the square, and I had to shout to make myself understood.

"What are you going to do, Mr. Juzl?"

"We're going to print an extraordinary edition. A proclamation against the invasion."

"I mean you personally?"

He looked around in confusion, but didn't reply.

"You should disappear. If you can, that is. Do you know if they've occupied the western border yet?"

"Apparently not. The crossings to Austria and Germany are still open. But . . . I'm not leaving."

"You should."

Juzl looked intently at the river of rattling iron and said, almost absently, "You go. I have to stay here."

He took me by the arm. The red-white-and-blue flags that were fluttering in the windows everywhere now lit his pale cheeks with historical flashes; he looked a little like a harlequin. He spoke as if in a trance.

"I just got back from Hronov last night. I have in my hands definitive proof that what took place in that chapel cannot be explained by natural means."

His pale eyes stared intently at me, though God knows what they saw. Over his shoulder I could see the Soviet power moving slowly across my field of vision — a power that always reduced the art of war to numerical superiority. There were just too many of them. And Juzl stood there unshaven and pale, and full of his truth — his irrelevant nonsense — while behind him the ugly caterpillars crawled across the square.

"All the more reason for clearing out."

He shook his head. "I can't."

"Don't be crazy!"

A heavily crewed tank behind him moved to avoid a munitions truck. An iron stegosaurus . . . and before me was this incomprehensible Don Quixote . . . his Dulcinea in a small, moss-covered chapel . . . and he said to me, "I see a sign in this. If *he* showed that he could die for what he believed in, what right have I to run away?"

"I don't know what he showed," I said. "They simply beat him to death. He couldn't escape. You can."

"He could have confessed, like others did. He could have survived. But he chose to die."

"And what about everything you've discovered? If you stay here, no one will ever know about it."

The stegosaurus angrily ripped up a piece of curbstone and the roots of a decorative tree and then, with a screech of metal on metal, sideswiped the munitions truck.

"If I were to leave, anything I wrote would only be words. But I saw it with my own eyes. And someone else saw it with me. Two people, in fact. In the West," he said, looking around the square, "I couldn't prove it anyway. They wouldn't believe me. And God very seldom manifests His truth to the multitudes."

I lost my temper. "I know God is cruel, dammit. I know He's a miserable elitist. But in the West, at least you'd be able to — "

Something cracked, and the enormous, overheated body of the tank rumbled towards us. We jumped out of the way, each in a different direction. The tank came to rest on the sidewalk; on it was a clutch of young soldiers who looked as terrified as I felt. One of them was sitting on the mudguard, his hobnail boots pointing directly at the chest of a weeping teenager in a miniskirt. It was like an outrageous symbol. I looked for Juzl and just then heard a shot. I whirled around and saw an old Praga car loaded with freshly printed newspapers pulling out of Melantrich Passage. As it backfired again, I turned back to the soldier on the tank. His eyes nervously scanned the windows on Wenceslas Square, his automatic rifle at the ready; behind him, a cluster of barrels bristled at the crowd. The echo slapped against the façade of the National Museum at the top of the square and the Praga exploded yet again. A flock of pigeons clattered into the air from one of the cornices. The soldier whipped his gun up and fired a long volley in the general direction of the pigeons. The barrels bristling behind his clean-shaven head turned to follow the chatter of his gun and the whole crew let loose a cannonade of gunfire. As I dropped to the ground, I caught a glimpse of the tank's turret spinning around to face the National Museum, and then a graceful arc of tracer bullets spattered against the neo-Renaissance façade. A glittering waterfall of glass showered down as the gun worked overtime.

Panic broke out on the sidewalk. People crawled into the passageways. A fat lady heaving herself out of harm's way like an enormous dung beetle suddenly collapsed beside me and lay on her stomach, groaning and flailing her arms and legs helplessly in the air. Carefully I crept behind a lamp post. On the prow of the tank the riflemen were kneeling in battle-positions, and the *politruk*, who looked just like the one at St. Antonin's, shouted to direct their fire, essentially at the pigeons.

During a lull in the gunfire, I heard something rustling above me in the crown of a tree. I raised my head. A white pigeon tumbled down through the branches onto the paving stones, its wings drenched in blood. It twitched once or twice and then died. As so often in my life, everything seemed to be an embarrassing symbol.

13.

"And Bondy says, in German, 'Nothing. Just a trifle. My old friend Kohn here needs an *Ausreisepass.*' 'Just for himself, or for his family too?' says General Blaskowitz. Bondy looks at me, and I still can't believe I'm not dreaming. But I take courage and say, 'I'd also like one for my wife Heda, if you don't mind, for my daughter Hana and my son Jakub, and my mother Berta Rehorova. And for my brother Arnost, if it's possible. He's still single.' And all the time I'm thinking General Blaskowitz is just making fun of me the way people like him always made fun of Jews, but he says, 'A mere detail,' and calls for his secretary. To make a long story short, gentlemen, in half an hour I was high-tailing it straight home like a jackrabbit, with passports for my whole family!"

"That's unbelievable, Mr. Kohn! How do you explain it?"

"Don't ask me, Mr. Pohorsky. I didn't ask Bondy either. It was a miracle."

"A miracle?"

"What else could it have been?"

14.

When I finally reached the publishing house, I could see at once that it was all over. In the entranceway stood another mass product of those fertile Soviet wombs, cradling an automatic rifle and standing with his legs apart, his feet in hobnail army boots. Behind him, leaning against a sign that said WRITERS' CLUB, an officer with a cigarette dangling from his lips watched the action in the street with a mixture of curiosity and well-schooled hatred.

I looked up at the balcony outside the meeting hall. It seemed a long time since Kocour had exposed Vohnout's strange evolution and Marie Burdychova had confessed her problematic sin. Now three Soviet officers were standing up there, and one of them was studying a suspicious-looking statue on the cornice of the National Theatre through a pair of binoculars. Others — political officers led, no doubt, by Vohnout — were probably searching Dasa Blumenfeldova's shelves for counter-revolutionary literature. Thanks to her inappropriate eagerness, she earned a mention in the notorious Soviet *White Book on the Counter-revolution in Czechoslovakia.* I felt myself breaking out in a cold sweat. My first serious (and now counter-revolutionary) novel, written fifteen years ago, was on Blumenfeldova's shelf, right at the top, along with illustrations by Brabenec, the homosexual painter. He'd done them during breaks on a major work, a large canvas called *Alice in Penisland,* and he'd made all the officers look like misshapen potatoes.

The nightmare that awaited me now would be far worse than the one Lizeta had put me through, although her perversity was almost Roman and her sexual greed was practically insatiable. I'd given Paternoster a real tongue-lashing, and he'd tried naively to pry the manuscript out of her. She just laughed at him, of course, but because he burned for her he hung around for another half year, without making any progress towards either goal. The situation was so desperate that occasionally, in moments of temporary insanity, I seriously considered murdering her. On one occasion I resorted to the less drastic relief of getting plastered at the Pinkas Tavern — and that's how I was finally saved.

There, in the packed pub, I met my former tank driver, Andelin Strevlicek. We hadn't seen each other in almost two years. He was also out drinking, but he was drinking for joy. His sixth child had just been born, his first son. After he'd told me, with atavistic pride, about the height and weight of his male heir, we wandered into the forest of nostalgia — and I got an idea.

Andelin Strevlicek was also a victim of female treachery, and his case had made him a legend throughout the Seventh Tank Battalion; officers from other units would find various excuses to come and see this living rarity with their own eyes. He was an exceptional tank driver and mandolin player. Evening after evening, throughout his first year of service, his mandolin sang out his pent-up longings. Then, as a member of a variety-show group that played at harvest-home concerts in the neighbouring villages, he started going out with a girl in Lopotin, and his evening serenades came to an end. It soon came out that he'd got the girl in the family way. But because Strevlicek was an existentialist by nature, he looked on the bright side. Armed with a doctor's certificate stating that the girl really was pregnant, he was given an otherwise unattainable three-day leave to get married. Clean-shaven, decked out in his dress uniform, and glowing with pleasure at his unexpected holiday, he walked past us to the gate. We were just cleaning the tank after a week of exercises in muddy terrain, and we envied him.

But when he came back he was crestfallen. "Gentlemen," he said, "she didn't tell me she already had two kids, both of them girls."

"She was married before?" I asked — a little maliciously, since the status of the two unannounced children was pretty obvious.

"No," said Andelin, "she had both of them on the wrong side of the blanket. One's a gypsy," he added gloomily. "But otherwise she's a good girl," he said, and began to cheer up. "Anyway, who cares? I'm a locksmith, I can support a wife and kid. And if I can support one brat, I can support three."

"Of course. You're a locksmith," I said, and with the royalty I'd got for a song about a model soldier who teaches illiterate gypsies how to read the army newspaper, I bought a bottle of cheap fruit wine, and we got drunk to celebrate his instant fatherhood.

His luck stayed with him. Six months later he got a telegram that said: SAFE ARRIVAL EVERYONE HEALTHY, and soon after that he got another three-day leave to see his first proper offspring (and have it christened, though he didn't tell the commander that). I was intrigued by the telegram's wording; why did it say "everyone" when only two lives were involved? But Andelin's in-laws were simple folk, no doubt ignorant of the finer points of grammar, and when I saw the excited Andelin trying to turn his dress boots into black mirrors I put the question out of my mind.

He came back three days later, as crestfallen as he'd been after the wedding.

"What's the matter, Andelin? Is this kid a gypsy too?"

"You don't know the half of it, man. There's three of them."

"What? Three little gypsies?"

"They're not little gypsies. They're mine. They got the same snout as me," he said, pointing to his typically Czech snub nose. "But gentlemen, they're triplets. And every one of them cracked below," he said dolefully. We stood there between the bunks and no one laughed. The tragedy of a man who'd begun his stint in the army as a bachelor, and in barely six months was going back to civvy street the father of five daughters (one of whom was a gypsy), was too devastating. This time the whole unit pooled its resources and we went drinking in the Jolly Tankman in the only village that wasn't out of bounds.

And luck smiled on Andelin once more. There was an accordion duo playing dance music in the pub and Andelin, when his usual method of consoling himself ("I'm a locksmith, and if I can support three brats I can support five,") didn't work, requested the song that goes, "I'll drink, and drink, till I've drunk it all away"; then he grabbed one of the five occasional prostitutes hanging round the bar and dragged her onto the floor, where he intended to dance a solo with her. The accordion duo started playing, Andelin sang the first verse in a heart-rendingly defiant voice, and after the words "I still have to drink you away, my gallant lass," he brought his foot, in his hobnail boot, crashing down on the floor — and collapsed. He tried to stand up, roared in pain, fell over again, looked at us with astonished eyes, and declared, "Fuck me, I've buggered my leg!"

In the military hospital, it turned out he was right. The injury was diagnosed as a lateral fracture of the shin, and it allowed Andelin, a true child of fortune, to spend the rest of his army stint in a hospital room normally reserved for officers, where he was installed as one of the main attractions of the base. Not surprisingly, he soon began to look on the bright side of things again.

Now, in the Pinkas Tavern, Andelin heard me out with his usual cheerful good humour. "For you, old buddy, anything," he said. "All you have to do is case the joint, make sure the coast is clear." I gathered he was rapidly getting into his role as a gentleman burglar. "This safe," he declared, "is going to be a pushover."

We got drunk on beer.

Afterwards I began to take steps to carry out the plan. It wasn't hard to get a key to the Hertl family house. Lizetka's parents always left an extra set of house keys hanging on a nail in the hall, and I replaced them with a collection of keys that had piled up in my drawer over the years. Andelin had copies made and the next day I put the original set of keys back. Then I waited until Lizetka's husband was working the Saturday and Sunday shift on his paper and invited her to spend Saturday with me in a famous *Absteig* called Zamecek just outside Prague, where wealthy and important actors, painters, and Party members went to dally with lovers and mistresses. I knew Lizetka was a snob and wouldn't refuse my invitation, and indeed she didn't. I didn't have to worry about her parents; for twenty years, they'd gone to the movies every Saturday night.

Andelin did a masterly piece of work. Early Sunday morning, an enraged Lizetka called me, and it was without a doubt the most pleasant conversation I'd ever had with her.

"Smiricky," I said, picking up the phone.

"Daniel, you're a pig! I hate you!"

"Likewise," I said.

"You're a tasteless, shameless, idiotic animal!" she shrieked. "Where did you steal the key to my safe? How dare you go through my things like that?"

She filled me with respect for Andelin's craftsmanship. My Robin Hood had obviously cracked the safe so skilfully that he'd left no signs of forced entry.

"In the first place, if you'll allow me to say so, Ludmila," I said, drunk with my new feeling of freedom, "we're not talking about your things, we're talking about *my* things. And how I stole the key I'm certainly not going to tell you."

"You're disgusting!"

"Likewise. And by the way, in case you didn't notice, I was sitting beside you all yesterday evening, along with all those celebrities."

There was a moment of silence while she tried to sort that one out. "No one else was interested in that manuscript. It must have been you. And nothing else was taken, either."

"Well, my dear Liduska, you may have contacts with the Secret Police, but I've got contacts with a slightly different underworld."

"I don't care how you worked it, you're a goddamned burglar!"

"There are some decent people among burglars."

"And you think you're a writer, and a serious writer at that! You shit! You shit! You *shit*!"

"Tut-tut, Lida, that's an ugly word, coming from a lady. And I never said I was a serious writer. That little novel you stole from me is nothing but a light, inconsequential bit of fun about the army — except that, as you so rightly guessed, it's politically somewhat risky."

"Who's talking about the stupid crap you write? I'm talking about that childish joke you couldn't resist, you goddamned intellectual! You disgusting jerk! And I'll turn you in, for burglary and theft!"

She was in a rage because she was smart enough to know she was helpless. But her reference to the childish joke interested me.

"So you didn't like my little joke?"

"I'm going to wipe my backside with it, you idiot!" she screamed, and she slammed the phone down.

So the joke was something material.

Suddenly I became alarmed. I remembered that one of the things I'd described in my novel, in great detail, was the story of Andelin's marriage.

15.

"Had Bondy and Blaskowitz been buddies at the front during World War One?" asked Mr. Pohorsky.

"Bondy? Don't be ridiculous. Bondy faked an IQ of minus five when that war was on. No, it was a miracle. Except," Mr. Kohn sighed, "except that I often ask myself: why me? Why me, of all people? What did I do that was so virtuous I deserved to be spared?"

Yes, I thought. What has any of us done, good or evil? The ways of the Lord are indeed inscrutable.

"Spared," Mr. Kohn nodded his curly head, "at the price of turning me into an exile without a country. And without a mother. Did you know my mother didn't leave with us? She said she was too old to go gallivanting about on the ocean. She was sixty-three. Of course, she'd married an Aryan after Father died, and that saved her. Just imagine — she survived it all. The war, Stalin, everything. She's still alive today. Ninety-two years old! And she hasn't seen me since '39. When I think of how much I loved her — and then last year I understood for the first time. I was spared so I could be punished."

"Punished for what, Mr. Kohn?" I asked.

"For being shit-scared, doctor. For being unforgivably shit-scared. And for selfishness. When you think about all they had to go through before they were killed — "

Mr. Kohn pulled out a monogrammed handkerchief and blew his nose. It sounded like the trumpeting of a sad, helpless elephant.

"Ever since the war ended, gentlemen, I've wanted to go back. The problem was that my American business was just getting off the ground and I couldn't afford to leave. So I kept putting it off and putting it off, until '48. By that time, as they say, I was *ein gemachter Mann*, and along came the Communist putsch and that little factory of mine, the one my stepfather, the Aryan, was running, got nationalized. Tell me now, could I, an American capitalist, go back home in those circumstances? No, I couldn't. And what was more, my mother sent me a message with one of the escapees — the new ones, I mean, the ones running from the Communists — not to come home yet, that times were uncertain and she heard they were getting ready to come down on the Jews again. So I said to myself I'd wait a while longer."

Mr. Kohn played another mournful fanfare on his tragic schnozz.

"But always, gentlemen, I was thinking about going back home. Daydreams, of course, but you know how it is. And you know what always snapped me out of them?"

"What, Mr. Kohn?"

"The cage. That feeling — that the lid would come down again. That I'd get there and suddenly the door would close behind me. And that's a terrible, inhuman feeling, gentlemen, because cages are not for people. That feeling that I'd be in a cage, just like in '39, but with no Bondy to come to the rescue this time, and no General Blaskowitz either."

Mr. Kohn took a careful sip of gin, which was against his doctor's orders. Some kind of truce had taken place at the bar; the pretty black woman, her wig on her head once more although slightly askew, was winding herself around her somewhat mollified partner.

"And did I have a nose, gentlemen!" said Mr. Kohn. "It started all over again. They closed the borders, just the way the Nazis did, and no one could get out. People escaped through the forests, over Sumava; they were shot at, innocent people were sent to the camps again — and this was hardly four years after the war. They died like cattle again. There weren't as many of them, but there were quite a few. Murder is always a terrible thing, whether there's one or a hundred of them."

"There were more than that, Mr. Kohn," said Mr. Pohorsky. "About three hundred went to the gallows alone. I'm not counting the rest — I mean the ones who were shot escaping or died in hospital. Just those that got hanged. Some of them more than once."

Mr. Kohn was horrified. "More than once, Mr. Pohorsky?"

"Yes sir, more than once," said Mr. Pohorsky, and out of ironclad habit he looked around, focused suspiciously on a long-haired young man who had just come into the bar with a red star sewn onto his college jacket just above the Phi Beta Kappa symbol, then brought his head close to Mr. Kohn's. "Like Franta Vohanek. He was in a cell with me and some agent testified that he was connected with the CIA, so they gave him the rope, but before they strung him up they wanted him to name his accomplices. So they showed him a list and said they wouldn't hang him if he'd just point to who was in it with him. But Franta hung tough. So they led him into the yard, put him under the gallows with his hands tied, the hangman was feeling his neck — and just then Judge Ryba, a bloody swine who crawled up the Nazis' assholes during the war, shouts, 'Stop!' so they untie Franta, take him back to his cell and then to interrogation, and they tell him again: just show us the names on the list and you won't hang, you'll serve a light sentence and be back home at the first amnesty. And Franta didn't even know anyone on the list. He might have said what the hell. He could have pointed to any name he felt like, since he didn't know anyone. But he was tough. In a couple of days he was under the gallows again, his hands tied, with the hangman feeling his neck — "

"That's awful!" said Mr. Kohn, reaching for the forbidden gin with a trembling hand.

"Anyway, to make a long story short," said Mr. Pohorsky, "they played that game with him for half a year, Mr. Kohn. Franta lost track of the number of times they did it, and he got so used to it that he said if they didn't truss him up a couple of times a week and shove him under the gallows for a little excitement, he almost missed it, because the boredom in prison is enough to kill you sometimes. Anyway, one fine day they trussed him up and took him out under the gallows, the hangman reached out for his neck, Judge Ryba said nothing, and *crunch!* Franta was swinging there like a chrysalis on a thread."

They had to bring Mr. Kohn another gin.

16.

I went to our next meeting in the Pinkas Tavern gripped by a terror worse than the first time. If Andelin had read the manuscript, I could expect anything. He was such a simple man that it would never occur to him to blackmail me. At best I could expect my jaw to be broken by a locksmith's fist; at worst — without a lot of hemming and hawing, and perhaps inspired by his wife — he would do what Lida had only threatened.

When I saw him behind a foam-capped mug at a tightly packed table, my heart stopped; there was no manuscript in sight. But I was an alienated intellectual, and I was psychologically misjudging this man of the people, this father of six. He welcomed me with noisy enthusiasm. As it turned out, he'd devoured my work in a single afternoon and had recognized himself in Corporal Albin Chrobacek. But instead of being upset that I'd written the truth about him, as Lizetka had been and as all my higher-placed acquaintances would have been, he was delighted and proud.

"You did a great job, buddy!" he said, raising his beer mug and clinking it against mine in a toast. I couldn't believe my own luck. "That part about me busting my shank was a riot. But you forgot some details," he added, and then proceeded to demonstrate that he had a far better memory than I, causing me to speculate that he might have made the better writer had his ambition not been entirely satisfied by the consumption of fifteen to twenty half-litres of beer a day. He chided me for forgetting to describe the visit of the *politruk* Hospodin, the idiot hardliner who tried to prove that Strevlicek had hurt himself deliberately to avoid manoeuvres. "But old Captain Matka gave him such a chewing out that Hospodin didn't know his ass from his elbow, not that he ever did anyway. And then Matka started visiting me in the hospital and we got bombed on cheap muscatel and he told me, I kid you not, that his first two brats weren't his either."

Then the exhilarated locksmith began to unwind a whole spool of reminiscences from the army. During a brief pause, when the waiter was exchanging our empty mugs for full ones, I asked him anxiously if he had the manuscript with him.

He laid a heavy hand on my shoulder. "If it's okay with you, I gave it to my sister to copy out."

"Your sister? To copy out?" I was horrified.

"Don't worry, she can type with all ten fingers. She took a course. She'll be done in a week."

"Andelin! What if someone else gets hold of it?"

"I said not to worry, old buddy," he said, with some irritation. "Do you think I don't know my way around here? Two of my brothers are in the slammer for trying to cross the border. And the sister's boyfriend — her fiancé, actually — is in Leopoldov. The dumb jerk — he was telling a joke and didn't bother to look who else was listening. But she can keep her mouth shut. And I only want it for myself, as a souvenir. You'll have to sign it for me."

A week later he really did show up with two manuscripts, and in one of them I wrote: *For Andelin, one of the heroes of this saga.* He was immensely pleased with it, although I had to explain what a saga was. Then he told me that Lizetka's safe had been child's play and that all it took was an ordinary jiggler. He had to explain what a jiggler was.

"By the way, did you leave anything in the safe, Andelin?"

"Did I leave anything in the safe? Of course not," he said. But skilful safe-cracker though he was, he was a lousy liar; he flushed perceptibly.

"Come off it, Andelin, there must have been something. Lida told me she'd wipe her ass with it."

"She said that? She must be a real wh — "

"Okay, she said backside. Now what was it?"

"All right, old pal." Andelin was almost choking with laughter. "I didn't want to tell you in case you got pissed off at me. Do you know that English novel *The Feathered Serpent* by Edgar Vallats?"

I began to suspect what was coming. I nodded.

"I just left a piece of paper there that I tore out of a notepad on the table. I didn't leave anything of my own there, in case you're wondering. And I drew a kind of hand on the paper and then wrote *You can't escape revenge — The Black Hand* in great big letters, printed it, so they couldn't identify me by my handwriting. And then I stuck it in the safe. A pretty neat joke, don't you think?"

I had a good long laugh. You have no idea *how* neat, Andelin.

For a while after that I was nervous, not because I thought Andelin might squeal — he was obviously too honest for that — but because of his love of convivial drinking and his sister's probable love of gossip. But nothing happened. They knew how to keep their mouths shut. And Lizetka stopped calling. About a year later, she covered her losses when the son of a high Party official committed suicide over her.

But now the peril of this still unpublished manuscript was looming over me again, sitting somewhere just behind my neck. I had no doubt that Vohnout knew how to keep his silence about some things. But in my case, he had no reason to keep his mouth shut.

It was afternoon. By now, Soviet war technology must have arrived at the Austrian and German borders. I packed two suitcases and put them in the Felicie, but only so that later I'd have nothing to reproach myself with. Subconsciously I was waiting for the classic ring of the doorbell. On my way home I'd listened to various transistor radios carrying the first broadcasts from the underground stations, and the first manifestos broadcast by heroes — or suicides, since they announced their full names — condemning the arrival of the fraternal armies. The world-famous playwright spoke drily and logically from his hiding-place; he was followed by the histrionic Vrchcolab and finally by Bukavec, who spoke in a trembling voice. Then a female announcer, who sounded oddly familiar, warned people to beware of an ambulance with the licence number AC 3215. She said it was being driven by KGB officers disguised as hospital attendants who were arresting people on a list. Perhaps I was on some list as well.

I had scarcely closed the second suitcase when I heard the classic ring. For a second I thought I might faint, but the ringing repeated at regular intervals and I realized it was only the telephone. I picked up the receiver.

"Danny? This is Sylva."

I felt a sudden rush of relief.

"Look, Danny, I don't know what to do. Milan's in Paris, and I tried to call him but they tell me they can't get a connection."

That's what I call bad luck, I thought. Sylva had come back from Paris just the day before, with both her children.

"I'm just packing my bags, Sylva. If you want, we could all go to Paris."

"Great idea. Thanks," said Sylva, as though I'd offered to take her to the Slapy Dam a few miles up the Vltava.

Half an hour later I was bundling Sylva, her two small children, Martina and Martin, and their three enormous suitcases into my Felicie. One of the suitcases simply wouldn't fit.

"Couldn't we leave it here?"

"Oh no, please, I don't want to do that," she begged. As always, she looked stunning. For the long and possibly dangerous journey she had put on the briefest of miniskirts, made of snakeskin, which she'd just brought back from Paris. The extra suitcase, which was more like a trunk, probably held similar rarities. As I looked at this marvellous example of Czech womanhood, I suddenly felt very patriotic. I decided that I would take all her skirts, mini or maxi, to Paris, even at the risk of my life.

I lowered the Felicie's convertible roof and placed the gigantic trunk on its end in the back seat.

The tiny blonde Martina was delighted. "Are we going without a woof?"

"We are."

"Gweat!"

"Gweat!" echoed Martin. "We'll all catch colds."

"That's enough, kid! In you get!" said Sylva.

She lifted Martina and put her in the back seat beside the suitcase. When she leaned down for Martina's little brother, the micro-mini revealed a magnificent set of thighs, and instead of the usual stirring in my glands I felt the swelling of an impersonal pride. Sylva sat Martin beside Martina and my pride increased: both little kids looked irresistibly pretty sitting there beside the towering suitcase, like a painting by a salon artist. The job of transporting this Central European beauty through a cordon of oriental steel so intrigued me that I was gripped by a wild chauvinism and completely forgot my own fear.

We drove out of the quiet residential district onto the main artery through Dejvice. Tanks were parked along the sidewalks, and around each one was a circle of people brushing up on their Russian. Ideological discussions were in full swing and the soldiers were losing their voices. I saw one of the many, almost identical *politruks* pull a copy of *Pravda* out of his kitbag to make his point, and begin to quote from it in the dramatic fashion of official army readers. Laughter broke out in the circle around the tank, and someone handed a leaflet printed in Cyrillic to an adolescent who was looking out of the driver's hatch. The big-eared head immediately vanished into the dark interior of the war machine, along with the leaflet. Meanwhile the reader's voice broke as he attempted to shout over the laughter, but he went doggedly on. The leaflet distributor held out a whole bundle of his wares towards the dark hatch; a large hand emerged and grasped at them eagerly, then snatched them back inside.

We turned and drove alongside a fence made of rough boards around a building site. It was covered with large signs. SVOLOCH IDITE DOMOY shone in the noonday sun in burning white letters almost as tall as a person, and along it a six-foot-five figure was walking from letter to letter. It was Bozena Pokorna — no longer in curlers, and wearing a flowery dress instead of a dressing-gown. She had a bucket of white paint in her left hand, a brush in her right, and she was scrupulously adding the proper diacriticals, which the sign-writers had left off.

I'd known Milan since youth. My youth, that is — his childhood. Now I was zipping along the empty highway to Plzen at ninety kilometres an hour, his beautiful wife — a former pedicurist Milan had discovered for his first film — beside me, and behind us, in the back seat, two artistic consequences of the director's discovery. They looked like Milan back in the days when he used to stand by the beer taps in the Port Arthur tavern in Kostelec, where his Uncle Ulc had sent him for beer, gazing with rapt admiration at our powerhouse. We were swinging "Sweet Georgia Brown", the Port Arthur was trembling from the assault of our five-sax line (we were before our time in this), and little Milan forgot himself and took public sips from his uncle's beer until old Barta leaned over the bar and gave him a clout on the head. And then life, unbelievable life, took over and made me a third-rate sax player and, a quarter of a century later, a successful librettist, and the awestruck Milan was dealt the role of a world-famous movie director; he was now in Paris getting ready to direct his first non-Czech film.

All at once I saw tanks on the road ahead of us and I had to slow down. They were going at a snail's pace, veiled in swirls of dust. I turned to Sylva and met her magnificent copper-coloured eyes. For all my patriotic resolve, our situation was precarious.

"Should I try to pass them?"

"If we don't, it'll take us a century to get to the border."

I stepped on the gas and soon we were right under the rear of the last armoured monster. Eight legs in hobnail boots were dangling off the end, hanging over steel plates. I pulled out and slowly moved forward through clouds of dust. The awestruck eyes above the boots were fixed on Sylva's proud face. She looked a little like Queen Nefertiti and she knew it. Scornfully she stuck her lower lip out, and held the expression until we had slipped past the prow of the tank and turned back into the middle of the road. Another assembly-line *politruk*, sitting by the cannon, cast his eyes over Sylva's thighs. We pulled up behind the new tank, submerged in dust and a deafening roar. Both the little Czech children stared in silent amazement at the hot iron creatures.

Little Milan had been living with his Uncle Ulc involuntarily, a victim of the times. He came from Metuje, where his father taught school. A local informer had notified the Gestapo about the activities of a certain Mr. Kadera, who belonged to an underground Communist resistance group, and Mr. Kadera was nabbed. While they were beating him in the kidneys, demanding that he name his contact, Mr. Kadera got what he thought was a good idea: he named Milan's father. Of course, Mr. Forhont wasn't a Communist contact man at all; he was a supporter of President Masaryk and apart from that he was entirely apolitical. But Mr. Kadera's mind was dulled by the beating, and he reasoned that since Mr. Forhont was innocent and therefore knew nothing, he could give nothing away. He thought the Germans would just ask Mr. Forhont a few questions and let him go.

Mr. Forhont really did know nothing, but unlike Mr. Kadera, who was trained in conspiracy, he was incapable of making anything up; he simply went on stubbornly protesting his arrest, which he referred to as a mistake. Unfortunately, one particularly well aimed boot of *die geheime Staatspolizei* happened to crush Mr. Forhont's temple, and he died before providing any information. So they pulled in Milan's mother and treated her in a similar way, only somewhat more cruelly because, as it turned out, she was a Jew of the second degree according to the Nuremberg Laws. According to those same laws the ten-year-old Milan was a third-degree Aryan and therefore got off with his life, and so Mr. Ulc, the owner of a grocery store in Kostelec, came for him and started sending him out to the Port Arthur for beer.

17.

"And so, as they say, the years went by," Mr. Kohn continued. "Back home things started improving a little and around 1956 Momma wrote to say they'd promised to give her a passport. You can't imagine how excited I was! I hadn't seen her for seventeen years. But then, *boom!* Hungary. And Momma didn't get her passport. By this time she was eighty years old, so I said to myself, maybe you'd better go and see her yourself. I was an American citizen, naturally. But as soon as I began to think seriously about going, gentlemen, I started getting cold feet all over again. The rational part of my mind said, 'What's there to be afraid of, you old fool?' But my fear didn't listen. You know, if there are reasons for being afraid in the first place, your rational mind can never give you a hundred-percent guarantee. So then I went to see a shrink, but he was no help at all. I kept having the same dream: I cross the border, have a sudden fit of panic, and try to back up—but the barrier's already dropped behind me and I'm back inside the cage. It's the emigrant's dream, gentlemen, and if you haven't had it yet, you will have."

"I have, Mr. Kohn," Mr. Pohorsky assured him. "Exactly the same one."

"And it wouldn't take much—maybe just a kick. I have a weak heart, my liver's not up to scratch either. It wouldn't take much and I'd drop dead like a dog on the pavement—"

"That's what you think now, Mr. Kohn," said Mr. Pohorsky, trying to cheer him up. "But you can always stand a lot more than you think. I even survived the uranium mill. And you know why? It was only thanks to—"

And Mr. Pohorsky acquainted Mr. Kohn with his tea therapy.

18.

"Where are they going, Mummy?" said little Martina's voice in the back seat.

"I don't know, Martina."

"Why are they making such a wacket?"

"Because they don't know any better."

I glanced in the rearview mirror. Martina began shrieking at the soldiers sitting on the mudguard just a few feet away.

"Don't make such a *wacket*! Don't make such a *wacket*!"

"Don't make such a *wacket*!" added her brother, loyally; he was a half-hour younger than she was. He added something that sounded like "doody buggers".

"Mawtin!" said his sister reproachfully.

The adolescents turned their blank faces from the beautiful mother to the beautiful little girl. As we pulled away from them one of them raised his hand from his automatic rifle and waved uncertainly, and a smile lit the wide face under the ruby-coloured star.

"*Chto ty na nas krichish, dyevochka?*"

I stepped on the gas. To my ears, it sounded as though the soldier was just trying to reach out to a fellow human being. The little girl scowled.

"Mummy, what's he saying? Can't he talk wight?"

"He's speaking Russian, Martina, you understand?"

"Why is he speaking Wussian?"

"Because he's an evil, stupid Russian," said Sylva, and she made a contemptuous face at the soldier. The gunman blushed, the hand that had made the friendly gesture sagged, and the child shrieked, "You evil, stupid Wussian!"

19.

In the café where the enormous ear had been rocking back and forth on the chair, trying to get close to us, Gerta had said, "A concentration camp is the best cure for anything that ails you. In Auschwitz I got over a case of hepatitis with no medical attention, and to this day I have a liver like a teetotaller. Even mental illnesses seemed to vanish. Anita Petrmichlova, the daughter of the alderman Petrmichl, she got mixed up with the Abwehr and then she wouldn't put out for some dodo from the SS. She was half-Nazi, for crying out loud, and you should have seen how the concentration camp cured her of that! After the war she joined the Party."

"Fine, Gerta," I said, "but some people the camps didn't cure. You said yourself— "

"Oh, you're thinking of my Robert? You bet it cured him. Once, before they arrested him, he told me, 'If I were ever convinced that what they say about Comrade Stalin is true, then all my work would have been a mistake.' Robert didn't die uncured, he— "

"But you were telling me about that other fellow, the one who— "

"Ota? Sure, you find madmen everywhere. When they hanged him he shouted, 'Long live the Communist Party of Czechoslovakia!' right under the gallows. Darkness at bloody noon all over again. And the ones they finally let go, most of them were falling all over each other to swear their oaths and get their Party cards back— "

"You too, Gerta?"

"Are you crazy? Anyway, most of them only did it because they were afraid. And they knew what they were afraid of, too."

"I don't know, Gerta," I said then. "Are you sure it was just cowardice? Hus was a Catholic till the bitter end— "

20.

"Mummy, when will we get to Daddy's?"

"It won't be long now, Martin. Are you hungry?"

"Yes."

Sylva reached into the handbag beside her on the seat. We were trapped again and going scarcely twenty-five kilometres an hour. I wanted to take a shortcut to avoid having to dodge in and out through this endless column of war machines, so I turned off onto a side road. It was not marked with the usual sign. The underground radio stations had appealed to people to take down street signs and signposts, and name-plates from doors in apartment buildings, and people had responded well. In many places they had improved on the original idea; the sign at the turn-off said PUTIM, but I wasn't misled. I knew this road, and—like everyone in my generation—I also knew Good Soldier Svejk, whose wanderings had taken him to that town. The sign was like a family joke. All the same, the deliberately misleading road sign turned out to be a problem. About fifteen minutes later we ran into another armoured division that knew neither the road nor the book, and apparently had to get to Putim to fulfil some strategic plan or other. And so we were in a jam. By taking considerable risks I managed to pass several of the iron coffins, but then the road grew narrow and the squat tanks took up the whole roadway. Our Felicie was stuck between two of them, and we had to adjust our speed to theirs.

21.

"Believe it or not," said Mr. Kohn, "I've never been afraid of death; I was only afraid of dying like an animal. It's a kind of modern fear. I bet decent, law-abiding people in the past never knew it— "

"Aren't you exaggerating a bit, Mr. Kohn?" I said. "Why would they do anything to you? You're an American citizen. And you're not a political person, are you?"

"I suppose you're right. It's an irrational fear, I know that. But who can say? And it's pointless to talk about it." He sighed. "To make a long story short, sometime in '64 they finally gave Momma a passport. But she was eighty-eight by that time and all the excitement made her ill and the doctor wouldn't let her travel. I don't know—I began to see a sign in all this, the hand of God or something, and that made it harder for me to conquer my fear. I was sure they'd dig up something to use against me and I'd end up dying like those poor people. Like an animal."

"Let me tell you something," said Mr. Pohorsky. "*They* were the animals. In Rovnost there was this guy called Valchar who had a little specialty. He crucified people. For fun, naturally — he took them down again after. And his buddies didn't actually nail them to the cross, they just tied their hands and feet and gave them a spongeful of vinegar to drink, like they did to Jesus. But one day one of the crucified men — he used to be a lawyer, a fatso, Dvorak was his name — he had a bad heart and he gave up the ghost."

22.

As we moved along slowly in a cloud of dust, a suspicion took root in my mind that gradually became a certainty. The tank squadron that had been dragging us along what was supposedly the way to Putim had irrevocably lost its way and was now chugging aimlessly through the southwestern Bohemian countryside. An officer in a tank helmet was standing in the turret of the lead tank, flirting first with a map and then with the countryside, and occasionally roaring something into his throat mike. The charming landscape flowed by, the lengthening shadows of the apple trees fell across the tanks, and the navigator, wedged into his turret, turned the map upside down and spoke into the mike again.

Suddenly the tank in front of us braked to a halt. I almost ran the Felicie into its rear end. Then all the tanks, obviously acting on orders, turned off their motors and everything fell silent. It was ominous. In the back seat, Martina said in a clear voice, "Mummy, I'm firsty."

"I'm firsty too!" said Martin.

"We're trapped," I said. "The brothers haven't a clue where they are."

Excited voices were arguing on the lead tank. I noticed that an old woman with a goat was watching the unusual intruders from the edge of the woods.

Sylva handed Martina a bottle of Kofola.

"They fell for that sign to Putim," I said.

"Shit!" said Sylva.

The commander in the tank helmet jumped down from the lead tank and ran over to the old woman grazing her goat on the hillside. The old woman tried to retreat into the woods but the goat, its mouth working on a tuft of juicy grass, refused to follow her. The soldier jumped forward in one mighty leap and caught the old woman by the shoulders. His voice, affable enough for a soldier, carried clearly through the evening air.

"*Babushka — kuda Pilzen?*"

Another voice, closer to us, said, "*Day nam popit, dyevochka!*"

Behind us, Martina began to yell, "Mummy! Mummy! He's taking it away fwum me!"

Sylva whirled around angrily and in the rearview mirror I saw a dust-covered soldier beside the Felicie, quickly pulling his hand back from the Kofola bottle like a boy caught stealing cookies.

"What do you think you're doing?" Sylva pounced.

"*Nichevo.*" The soldier smiled awkwardly. "*Ja chochu napitsya.*"

"Drink your own drinks. Or tighten your belts, you hicks." Sylva thrust out her lower lip magnificently. "Martina — don't cry just because of some Russian."

"She's not cwying because of the Wussian," said Martin. "She spilled the Kofowa all over her dwess."

Sylva lost her temper. "Damn it! Look what you've done! A new dress, covered with Kofola!"

"*Eto Coca-Cola?*" said the soldier, pointing at the bottle with great interest.

"*Shto sluchilos?*" came a bass voice behind us. I turned around. One of the assembly-line *politruks* was standing on the edge of the road, frowning suspiciously at my elegant red car.

23.

"And when that stuff with Dubcek started up," said Mr. Kohn, "well, you can understand; for a long time I didn't want to believe it. They're all Communists. But then news started coming through. Former political prisoners had their own club. They were going to allow other political parties. Rehabilitations. And people started going for visits and coming back all enthusiastic. And finally even Lewith got his courage up — remember Venus chocolates? He was very big back home before the war. They confiscated his factory right in 1945 because he had about eight hundred people working for him. When he went back, he was as shit-scared as I was. I asked him if he'd drop in on my mother. So when he comes back he says, 'Kohn! You've got to go there. Either a miracle is taking place, or we're all *meshugga.* I'd say we're all *meshugga*, so do yourself a favour and go while there's still time. And your mother says you should come too, says she won't be around for ever — look, why beat around the bush — she's ninety-two, she's running out of steam and I'd be lying if I told you different. So go quickly. You can't imagine it — it's beautiful. Hradcany! Mala Strana! They've opened a lot of the old palace gardens to the public. It's beautiful, I tell you, a real fairy-tale. So shake a leg, Kohn, see for yourself, before it goes down the toilet. I give it until Christmas, maximum.'''

24.

"*Davay pasport!*" commanded the officer.

I looked at Sylva. "It seems we're in the shit."

"Tell them to stuff it!" said Sylva.

"*Davay pasport!*" said the officer again. "*Vy inostrantsi?*"

"*Da,*" said Sylva.

The officer was surprised and stepped back. He was joined by another officer and they both looked at our licence plate.

"That wasn't the wisest thing to say, Sylva," I said. "They probably know their licence plates. They'll see we're not foreigners."

We looked at the officers. One of them pulled out a booklet, leafed through it, then peered at our plate again. As I had feared, the first one said, in very unpleasant tones:

"*Vy Chekhoslovaki!*"

"*Da,*" said Sylva, stupidly.

The officer was still scowling at us when he noticed Sylva's enormous suitcase in the back seat. He pointed at it and asked threateningly:

"*Shto u vas v chemodanakh?*"

"None of your business!" said Sylva. This threat to her personal property suddenly improved her linguistic abilities. Fortunately the officer, fascinated by his own suspicion, didn't notice.

"*My priyekhali razbit kontrarevolutsiyu!*" he said haughtily to the bristling young woman. "*V etom chemodane mozhet byt oruzhiye.*"

"Why is he carrying on about 'rouge'?"

"*Oruzhiye* means something else," I said quietly.

"What?"

I said nothing. I didn't think Sylva was taking a recoilless cannon to Paris in her enormous suitcase, but I still felt a chill of fear.

The officer stepped up to the rear of the Felicie and looked around superciliously. Then he nodded to two soldiers on the tanks and pointed to Sylva's suitcase.

25.

Trofim and Sasha looked superciliously at the façade of the Rudolfinum concert hall in Prague, while Irina kept looking at Paternoster.

"Have you seen the Palace of Music in Moscow?" Trofim asked. "It's far bigger than this."

The Rudolfinum was about the seventh building that Paternoster and I had shown these three students from the Industrial School for Costume Jewellery in Omsk. Paternoster's brother was the principal of a similar institution in Prague but was too busy to take them around, so he had asked us. As with the six previous buildings, the Russian guests found this structure inferior to the architectonic wonders of their homeland.

"But it's a pretty building all the same," said Irina to Paternoster. She praised it — as she had praised the six others — to appeal to Paternoster. To me her motives were clear. Like so many educated Russian girls in the early sixties, she longed to marry someone outside the Soviet Union. I had been cool to her from the beginning, so she was focusing her efforts on the author of utopian novels instead. Paternoster was incapable of being cool in any situation or under any circumstances.

I knew this kind of would-be bride only too well. I remembered the tragic case of Tonda Lenecek, a semi-illiterate stagehand who travelled to Moscow with the National Theatre and brought back an associate professor of gynecology. Two years later, in a fit of recurrent and well-founded jealousy, he strangled her and was sentenced to twenty-five years in prison. I also remembered, with some bitterness, the collapse of the mildly critical literary monthly *Maj*, indirectly brought about by another Soviet bride who yearned to marry anyone as long as he was a foreigner.

The Central Committee had been itching to axe *Maj* ever since its editor-in-chief, a poet by the name of Homola, had written a review describing Comrade Vohnout's poems as "socialist kitsch". The outraged Vohnout easily found run-of-the-mill ideological errors in many other articles in the periodical, and because Central Committee members were pathologically sensitive to any criticism of anything, they slowly got ready to lower the boom. At this point, however, like a bolt of lightning, the news spread through the Party apparatus that Homola, that weasel, had just become engaged in Moscow to Jekaterina Adzhulina, the daughter of the minister in charge of Siberia. Comrade Kaiser, head of the Party's Cultural Department, quickly called off the Central Committee's attack and the radicals on the editorial board of *Maj*, secure behind this nuptial rampart, moved to the offensive by publishing an essay on socialist realism written by the Trotskyist Tenke, who had been executed, just to be on the safe side, right after the Victory of the People in 1948.

Unfortunately, none of the radicals could foresee that Jekaterina Adzhulina's pathological lust for marriage would have the effect of cooling Homola's desire. But that was precisely what it did. Homola started drinking, and two months before the wedding date (they had a proper engagement in the best bourgeois tradition) he went to the Café Bikini with an old childhood friend — a friend who was married already, but unhappily so. Soon both men were seized by the illogical but not uncommon desire to seek out female company as a relief from their disenchantment with their own women. They didn't have to look far; at the very next table were two young things from Brdy who had come to spend Saturday in Prague.

The young things stayed over until Sunday.

Time went by, and the wedding was almost at hand. Then one day a tall, full-bearded man who looked like Krakonos, the wild spirit of the mountains, strode into the editorial offices of *Maj* and demanded to see the editor-in-chief. He didn't look like a writer, but he carried a stout cane of knotted wood that commanded respect. So they let him in to see Homola.

About a week later we were having an editorial meeting. Someone had just proposed that, beginning with the next issue of *Maj*, we start printing work by Zamyatin. His proposal was supported by Hejl, the world-class playwright, who had elbowed his way onto the editorial board as leader of a young radical group. Homola was chairing the meeting, but he seemed absent in spirit and was certainly a little drunk. He showed no signs of realizing how dangerous this discussion of the extremely dangerous Zamyatin was. Just as Paternoster and I were about to suggest a tactical delay to fend off a catastrophe that not even the daughter of a gulag overlord would be able to prevent, the door flew open with an abruptness that only happens in movie comedies, and there she stood, Jekaterina Viktorovna Adzhulina herself. She wore a shining white suit shot through with silver thread (the suit was imported from Paris); a diabolical aureola of raven-black hair surrounded her ivory face, and her black eyes blazed. She was magnificent, imposing, and obviously irate. She ran an eye full of evil intent over our group and then, in five Cossack-like steps, marched up to the chairman. Homola was struggling to his feet in terror but a button on his fly caught the handle of the drawer, and before he could stand up Jekaterina landed a murderous roundhouse right on the side of his head. Then she whirled around, took five more steps, and strode out of the editorial office, slamming the door behind her so hard that a portrait of Ernest Hemingway tumbled off the wall. Reeling from this blow of Tartar intensity, the editor-in-chief fell over backwards in his chair, taking the drawer with him and covering himself with poetry manuscripts, two English detective novels, and a box of condoms, purchased too late.

Later we learned that Jekaterina had flown in from Moscow on the morning TU457 and taken a taxi from the airport to the editorial offices, where she had told the driver to wait for her. After delivering her blow she had taken the cab back to the airport, got back on the same TU457, and gone straight back to Moscow, where later that same evening she managed, with the help of a Congolese journalist, to be unfaithful to her unfaithful fiancé.

Of course, word of the incident got back to Comrade Vohnout, who passed it on to Comrade Kaiser, who immediately called a council of war in the Central Committee.

A few days later the whole editorial board gathered again, in a very subdued mood, in the Church of St. Wenceslas. The man with the beard was there too, this time minus the walking stick; he wore a black suit and in the light of the candles on the altar he glowed with satisfaction. Before the altar knelt Homola with one of the two young things from the Café Bikini, who was, quite unjustifiably, wearing a wreath of virginal myrtle on her head. The rest of us still found the whole situation incredible.

But Comrade Kaiser believed it, and a couple of days after the wedding he gave orders for the cannonade to begin. Hired hacks fired off appropriate salvos of negative reviews, and before long — by a decision of the Central Committee in response to a wave of indignation among the literary public — the literary review *Maj* was unceremoniously axed.

But Jekaterina Viktorovna, the unrelenting Soviet bride, was so deeply affected by her Czech lover that she soon ditched her Congolese journalist. Several years later, when the literary radicals had regrouped and taken over the editorial board of a magazine called *The Golden Fleece*, she collared its editor-in-chief, Malecek, at another Moscow conference. This time the wedding was carried out Bolshevik style, with no bourgeois shilly-shallying, and Comrade Kaiser, who had just been training his rockets on *The Golden Fleece*, had to change targets. Out of spite he nipped in the bud an attempt by young Catholic authors to take over a literary journal called *Head.* Let it be said to Jekaterina Viktorovna's credit that although Malecek beat her, she fell genuinely in love with Czech literature, and played an important role in temporarily protecting *The Golden Fleece* after the tanks arrived, when Malecek became a deputy minister for a brief time; then she followed him to the Congo, where he'd been appointed ambassador just to get him safely out of the way.

26.

"So fear and *Heimweh* were shooting it out inside me," said Mr. Kohn. "I was homesick for Momma. Who ever had the good luck to be seventy-five and have his mother still alive, and the bad luck not to see her in thirty years? So I made up my mind. Heda and I filled out applications for Czechoslovak visas—and the moment I hand them in, those army manoeuvres start up inside Czechoslovakia. So I put it off again. Then the armies leave and we pack our bags, but there's another crisis, a big summit at Cierna, but then Brezhnev and Dubcek come out hugging each other and Lewith says, 'It'll hold together, like I said, at least until the plums ripen. This is your last chance, Kohn. In six months there'll be no more of these whiskery kisses, just knives in the back again.' So I took a deep breath and off we went." Mr. Kohn swallowed a liver pill and told me about embarking on the SS *United States*, as he had never flown in his life and didn't intend to start now.

27.

Because those Soviet *jeunes femmes fatales* were still fresh in my mind, I remained forbiddingly cold to Irina. The more reckless Paternoster couldn't control his lust; he may even have slept with her. But he avoided having to marry her. That privilege was reserved for an economics student called Janecek who got so crazy about Irina two years later that he tried to ask for Soviet citizenship—he thought that would make her happy. But Irina acted fast. Playing the woman who would make any sacrifice to be with her man, she made Janecek go back to Prague (with her), then go on vacation to East Germany (with her) and visit Berlin, then escape (with her) to West Berlin, and move (with her) from there to Frankfurt, because she didn't feel safe in Berlin. In Frankfurt she lassoed a West German lawyer and divorced Janecek. The lawyer moved (with her) to Canada, where she ran off with someone called Leonardi who, thanks to his Mafia connections, owned a cotton plantation in South Carolina and a chain of motels.

But all that came later. Back then, in front of the Rudolfinum, she was only seventeen. The 1960s were just beginning and Irina walked with a sexy little wiggle along the banks of the Vltava, in a beribboned dress, and made gazelle eyes at the smouldering Paternoster.

"But the stonework is wonderful," she had said, when Trofim declared that the Kremlin was far more colourful than the Gothic cathedral of St. Vitus. And when Sasha remarked that the lookout tower on Petrin Hill wasn't as high as the spires of the Vasily Cathedral, Irina observed that "It makes your head spin so marvellously!" And when Paternoster dragged us off to the new Jewish cemetery to see the grave of Franz Kafka (stunned by the vision of Irina's shapely legs, he forgot that these people we were showing around were costume jewellery apprentices), and Trofim dismissed it as a garish display of bourgeois taste or the lack thereof, Irina retorted that, even so, the cemetery was "wonderfully romantic!" Unable to watch Paternoster melting away so pathetically before my eyes, I remarked that it was the Nazi occupation that had turned the cemetery into this romantic ruin. Irina's doelike eyes became basilisk-like and she turned a withering gaze on me, while Trofim lectured us on how the Americans had destroyed Dresden while the Soviet people were busy defeating the Germans.

28.

The Kohns' Cadillac went along in the hold of the SS *United States*, and his black chauffeur travelled tourist class. They docked at Le Havre, reclaimed the Cadillac, and were at the German border by nightfall. The trip across West Germany took them two days. As they drew near the Czechoslovak border, Mr. Kohn's invincible fear turned to panic.

"I was ready to tell John to turn around, that we were going back, Momma or no Momma. By the time we reached the barrier I was absolutely terrified. A guy in a green uniform steps out of the customs office. He had that star on his hat and his uniform looked so kind of slept in, so rumpled, so *Eastern*, that I said to myself: My God, if this guy ever got his paws on me — "

Meanwhile the long-haired fellow in the jacket with the fraternity pins had managed to sell some of his newspapers to the black patrons, so he looked around and then made for us. Mr. Kohn stopped talking. He seemed transfixed.

"Guerrilla newspaper, gentlemen?" said the long-haired young man, sounding just like a newsboy touting the evening tabloid. He spread his wares out in front of us. A traditional portrait of Lenin, imperfectly reproduced from an imperfect reproduction, stared at us from page one. "Only twenty-five cents!"

As though hypnotized, Mr. Kohn pulled out a half-dollar with a portrait of John Fitzgerald on it and exchanged it for two copies of the paper. Suddenly the young man reminded me of the Jarda Bukavec I had known back in Hronov.

29.

"Hey, stop that, all right?" Sylva called out, and she turned to me.

"Look, tell them to stop it."

"Do you have a warrant to search private citizens?" I asked. Given the situation — with my small Felicie sandwiched between several tons of fighting steel — it was an idiotic thing to say. I'd also forgotten that I couldn't speak Russian.

"*Shto?*"

"Do you have — a warrant — "

"*Pozvoleniye?*" The *politruk* puffed up his chest and in an almost ceremonial voice said, "*My priyechali rozbit kontrarevolutsiyu!*"

He looked over the rolling countryside bathed in the light of an attractive sunset. Then he silently nodded to the two soldiers. One of them grabbed the suitcase and another raised a pick to smash it open. Sylva rushed at them with a shout.

"*Stoy!*" roared the officer.

"Stop it!" Sylva shrieked. "It's not yours!" She fought like a cat until the officer pulled out what must have been a twelve-millimetre revolver, and pointed its huge muzzle at her back. "Aren't you going just a little too far?" said Sylva, and pouted disdainfully. "How about putting that thing away? If you're not careful, it might go off!"

"*Ruky vverkh!*" said the officer.

"What's he talking about?" Sylva asked me.

"He wants you to put your hands up."

"Why, for crying out loud?" Offended, she turned back to him. "Look, how about putting that thing away? It's making me nervous."

But the officer did not lower his pistol. Once more he gave the nod to his underlings and, uncertainly, they slipped the point of the pick under the lid.

"For God's sake, will you lay off? It's a new suitcase!" she cried. She tried to join battle once more, but this time the officer leaped dramatically between her and the luggage and stuck the barrel of his gun into her stomach.

"Sylva, I think you'd better let them go ahead," I said.

"Then tell them to let me unlock the damn thing, at least. It's a brand new suitcase, cost me almost a hundred in Tuzex, and now they want to — "

I explained her suggestion to the officer. Reluctantly he removed his pistol from her navel and Sylva, her lower lip in an attitude of maximum disdain, unlocked the baggage and dramatically flung back the lid.

"Feast your eyes, bumpkins!" she said, presenting us with the view of a rich assortment of fine women's lingerie, some in shades of pastel, others sinful black, red, or striped, and all of it transparent. The Red Army stared at the collection in amazement. Then the officer slowly drew himself up to full height and regarded us with suspicion.

"*U vas eto dlya blata?*"

"What doesn't he like now?" asked Sylva.

"He suspects you of selling this stuff on the black market."

"Tell him to keep his stupid ideas to himself, all right?"

"This all belongs to her," I translated.

"*Shto vy vryotye* — " the *politruk* began, and then, just as suddenly, he stopped. I could feel his suppressed rage. He ran his eyes over the Felicie, over the neatly dressed children, and over the countryside again. He uttered a strange sigh, then reached into the suitcase and pulled something out. It looked like a brassiere, only the entire upper half was missing. With a look of distaste the officer stretched the thing out in both hands, stared at it, shook his head, and emitted the sound of someone who has once again been persuaded of a great truth.

"Jesus, don't let him hold that thing up here in front of all these hillbillies," said Sylva. "All I need is for them to try and rape me!"

"That's Mummy's bwa!" cried Martina happily.

I glanced towards the tanks. A big-eared private was staring at what the *politruk* was holding up in the pink light of the setting sun. A head in a padded leather helmet emerged from the driver's hatch, the eyes agog at the outlandish garment. In that moment I longed to be a painter. Not an abstract expressionist, but a realist like Akademician Gerasimov, in order to capture, in his idealized photographic style, that strange scene: the pink light, the glowing countryside, the sophisticated war machinery, and against that background the racy scrap of underwear and, transfixed by it, the childish blue eyes of a people who can be made to do anything at all.

But I was no painter; the best I could do was sketch a stylized cat to amuse Martina. The moment passed, the scene vanished for ever. The officer shook his head again and laid the bra back among the rest of the shameless items crammed into the suitcase. At a gesture from him the soldiers closed the suitcase (not without some effort) and jumped back onto the tank, while the officer clambered back up to his post by the cannon. The motors roared, a cloud of orange dust rose, and those squat monsters moved forward along the road that, according to the signs, would take them to Putim.

Later, in Paris, Sylva told me that they'd palmed a box of birth-control pills from the suitcase. We both tried to imagine what would happen when the tank crew ate two dozen anti-baby pills. Probably nothing at all. They always have had strong stomachs.

30.

"I know it was paranoia," said Mr. Kohn. "Why should they be after me, Kohn from Providence, Rhode Island, when I didn't even complain when they confiscated my factory back in '48? But what can you do? If it hadn't been for Heda, I'd probably have told John to turn around and go back. But Heda took my hand and gave it a squeeze and we slowly passed under the barrier. And nothing happened — they didn't even bother searching us. We drove through a woods, and suddenly the woods stopped. It was evening, we were driving down into a valley with the sun at our backs, and what do I see but a Boy Scout troop marching along the road ahead of us. Scouts! Just like — what is it? — thirty years ago, gentlemen! Little runts with knobby knees, green shirts, and knapsacks, led by a scoutmaster in short pants, who was also the only one wearing one of those wide-brimmed hats that Mounties wear. As soon as I saw them, my fears began to melt away. I mean, if Scouts could go on the march there again. . . . Anyway, the shadows began to lengthen and the land, gentlemen, gave off this wonderful smell, and everything was, I don't know, sort of — small — like in a fairy-tale. Those tiny villages with worn down, dilapidated houses, but you could hear cows mooing everywhere, and smell hay and barns . . . and there were posters saying 'Long Live Dubcek!', and the roads were narrow and full of potholes. . . . Gentlemen, after those German highways and motels and Texaco stations, I suddenly felt I was not only back home again, but thirty years back in time as well! Quail running across the fields, little girls in kerchiefs riding bicycles down the road, signs in Czech everywhere — and those village names! I tell you, gentlemen, I read them out loud and it was like saying a prayer: Jestrebi, Svina Lada, Pohorska Lhota, Okruhovice, Provodov. Then it got dark. John turned on the headlights and those white-washed road markers started flashing by and I remembered how I used to go driving with Momma and Dad along roads like this, with those white stone markers on the shoulders. Dad had an old Praga . . . and my fear had gone, the *Heimweh*, everything, and I could hardly wait to see Momma again. By that time we were almost in Prague, and I said to myself, no! We'll enter Prague by daylight. I can't go dropping in on Momma at midnight! Besides, I want my first glimpse of Prague to be in full sunlight. I want to be well rested. I remembered everything. I knew without even looking at the signs that the road led past the Hotel Hubertus. We used to drive there for Sunday lunch; at that time it was a full day's outing in our Praga. So I said to John, 'John! Take this side road here!' And John turned off onto a small road and pretty soon we were deep in the woods, and the pine-cones smelled heavenly. . . ."

31.

A few days later Trofim called Paternoster and suggested we have a farewell party at which — in his words — we would have some drinks and conversation.

There was conversation, but more drinking. The party took place in a flat belonging to Paternoster's brother, the principal of the costume jewellery school, and the principal's seventeen-year-old daughter, Vera, took part as well. The Soviet troika showed up with six bottles of Stolichnaya vodka and a package of paprika. They dissolved the paprika in the vodka to create a Bloody Natasha, and we soon forgot our ideological differences. In fact, the combination of vodka and hot pepper turned Paternoster into a sex maniac; he almost stripped Irina naked before our eyes. His brother had to straighten him out and drag him off to the shower stall in the kitchen.

While Paternoster was cooling off, Irina was telling Vera about the second of her great expectations from this trip to Prague: she had saved some pocket money by not eating and wanted to buy one of the transparent Italian raincoats known as "condomcoats", but she didn't know where to find one.

"Sometimes they have them in the House of Fashion," said Vera, who was rather bored because her father had forbidden her to drink. "What kind do you want? Pink, white, or pale blue?"

"Oh, any colour."

"I've got two of them. One's white and the other's kind of honey-coloured."

"Two?" said Irina, astonished.

"Would you like to see them?"

Vera, who was wearing jeans (which Trofim had frowned at), opened a modest little wardrobe in the corner to reveal about ten hangers holding colourful dresses. On the inside of the door was a large mirror.

"Oh!" sighed Irina.

Vera took out a hanger that held two raincoats. She removed the first one, a honey-coloured coat, and handed it to the girl from Omsk. "Want to try it on?"

A look of enchantment appeared on Irina's pretty face. Worshipfully, she slipped into the raincoat and ran her hand over the transparent plastic as though it were mink.

"*Och, kakoye krasivoye!*"

And she turned around in front of the mirror.

"Want to try the other one?"

As if slipping from one dream to another, Irina slipped out of the honey-coloured one and into the white one. Fortunately Trofim didn't understand the Czech nickname for the coat, so he didn't intervene. He too seemed enchanted (and somewhat alcoholized) as he watched Irina revolve before the mirror, wrapped in PVC and moaning in an anguish of longing.

"The honey one looks better on you," said Vera. "I'll give it to you if you want, as a souvenir, okay? Honey doesn't suit me anyway."

I noticed that the honey-coloured raincoat had a tear in the hem, while the white one was like new. But Irina failed to spot this. She flung herself around Vera's neck. "*Och, Vyerochka!*"

We watched this scene silently and drank our Bloody Natashas. The diabolical drink had obviously dulled Trofim and Sasha's patriotism because the gift — a rather demeaning one — didn't upset them; they didn't even say anything about the superior qualities of Soviet condomcoats.

Irina's attention was caught by something else in the wardrobe. "*Vyerochka, mozhno posmotret?*" Without waiting for Vera's nod, she took out a pretty blue linen dress with white buttons.

"Oh! How beautiful!"

"That's just a washable dress," said Vera. But Irina was pulling out yet another one: a garment of wine-coloured velvet with a tight body and flared skirt. The girl from Omsk gasped. When she saw a corduroy suit in a poisonous green colour, she whimpered as though she were at the climax of some not entirely moral delight.

"*Vyerochka* — this is really all yours?"

Vera replied grudgingly, so that her father, who was bringing the still-dripping Paternoster back into the room, would hear her, "I don't have *that* many things."

Another rummage through the wardrobe produced a brocade sack dress which had enjoyed a brief revival along with the Charleston; it was golden yellow with a brilliant violet zig-zag pattern. Irina was trembling by now.

"Want to try it on?" asked Vera good-naturedly.

"*Ach, Vyerochka,* may I?"

Then something happened that I couldn't believe at first. Irina bent over, grasped the hem of her puritanically long skirt, and without the slightest hesitation or uncertainty pulled the dark blue dress over her head and stood there before us in a pink slip. The slip had been washed many times and mended in several spots with green thread. Beneath it were round shapes which Trofim might with some justice have described as superior to any bosoms he had seen in Prague.

But alcohol has always been an enemy of progress, and the Bloody

Natashas had Trofim well on the road to cosmopolitanism; he merely smiled lecherously. Steam began rising off the still-damp Paternoster, while Sasha swallowed hungrily. Then Irina pulled the gold and violet sack dress over her head.

Once again I was struck by the profundity of the old saying. These clothes made the apprentice girl from Omsk into a Paris *vedette.* Feverishly she rotated back and forth in front of the mirror, admiring her unbelievable self. Vera put on a record with the song "Teach Me the Charleston, Granny", but no one had to teach Irina anything. After a five-second mini-lesson, she and Vyerochka put on a pretty performance for us.

This was too much for Paternoster and he retreated back into the kitchen. Trofim, doubled over, staggered to the toilet. The record ended and Irina, quick as lightning, pulled the sack dress over her curly head and wriggled into the wardrobe in her slip. On the next record, which had recently been withdrawn from the stores, Suzi's voice declared with satisfaction that "Armstrong Ain't No Russian". Irina emerged from the wardrobe in a white prom dress covered with rainbow sequins and performed a belly dance before the mirror, turning her back to us. Emboldened by the drink, Sasha flung an empty bottle into the corner and tried to do a version of a Cossack dance, but he fell down on the carpet and lay there listening to Suzi's syncopated wailing. Trofim came back from the bathroom, relieved, and began to drown out Suzi's voice with a song in the Omsk dialect. Judging by the enthusiasm with which the recumbent Sasha joined in, I concluded that the song wasn't out of the Komsomol songbook. At last a freshly showered Paternoster came back, grabbed Irina, and danced some rock-and-roll figures with her while she changed, on the run, into a trouser suit of devilish black material. I asked Vyerochka for a dance and the party turned into a disciplined (Vera's father came back into the room and stayed) but still Bacchanalian event, enlivened by the occasional striptease by Miss Irina Byelovyezhnikova.

Irina's ecstasy over the clothes moved Vera to a generosity unheard of in a poor Czech girl. When we finally left, long after midnight — carrying Trofim between us — she gave Irina not only the condomcoat but the washable blue dress with the buttons and a good-as-new bra. She wanted to give her a pair of older jeans as well, but even though Trofim was unconscious and Sasha was stubbornly plying us with Radio Jerevan jokes, Irina refused. A girl who appeared in Omsk in pants might well have been lynched by the local Party committee.

32.

"It was ten in the evening when we pulled up in front of the Hotel Hubertus. And it was eleven-thirty when we finally lay down in our wide, sweet-smelling beds, with the woods murmuring outside the window, and the stars visible over the treetops. By this time I was calm and relaxed, and I'd started making plans. We'd buy a villa somewhere around here — Lewith said they were for sale everywhere — and Momma and I would move in and everything would be all right at last. I'd come back home. I fell asleep and dreamed that the little bell over the door of my father's shop was tinkling and Momma was there behind the counter, smiling, and she looked just the same as she had thirty years ago when I'd last seen her. Oh, my!" sighed Mr. Kohn.

33.

Wedged in between the tanks, we jounced along through the whirling orange dust, with the roar of the vehicles in our ears. When we had almost reached the main highway to Domazlice, I tuned the radio to an underground station. A familiar young woman's voice was just saying, " . . . the National Artist Marie Burdychova will speak." I turned the volume up.

"Is she the one who wrote *Hanka the Brickmaker*?" Sylva asked.

"Yeah," I said, "she wrote it. A long time ago."

"It's a very nice book," said Sylva. "When I was a girl I must have read it at least five times. I knew bits of it almost by heart — "

I waved my hand to silence her and from the car radio, punctuated by the crackle of atmospheric static, came a familiar, croaking old voice: "In this tragic hour, I wish to address the people to whom I have looked all my life with love and respect as our models: to the representatives of the Communist Party of the Soviet Union. And I say to them: I curse you! You have betrayed a cause for which so many people laid down their — " The signal faded and her words were lost. I tried to find the station again but couldn't.

When we reached the main highway, I stepped on the gas and extricated myself from the convoy, which ground to an uncertain halt. I saw the commanding officer studying the map again. His *politruk* was pointing towards the setting sun, perhaps to explain which way was west. It was twilight and from the eastern horizon a noticeably symbolic black cloud was climbing into the night sky. On the other side, a Technicolor sunset suffused the sky with brilliant oranges and golds. The officer made his decision and the noisy convoy rattled into motion and headed towards the black cloud, while we drove into the sunset. We were moving fast now and the road was suddenly empty, quiet and cool. Before we knew it we were driving through a dark woods. Martina and Martin had long ago been silenced by sleep in the back seat. Sylva said, "Please, you have to stop right now or I'm going to have an accident."

I drove to the shoulder and Sylva reached for the door-handle.

"You could have told me that long ago," I said.

"That's a good one. And what about them? They'd have had to stop their whole armoured division, or whatever you call it."

I pulled on the hand brake and Sylva sprinted into the ferns. I did the same on the other side of the road. With blessed relief I pissed on the dark plants, and before my inner vision another realistic canvas appeared, one I would paint if I were Gerasimov: a regiment of the occupying army blocked on a narrow Czech country road by a red Felicie, waiting until Sylva Forhontova finished peeing.

I walked back to the car and leaned against it. The trees were whispering, it was a beautiful summer night, and out of the woods rolled the aroma of eternity, untouched by political turmoil in a tiny country in Central Europe. The highway split the forest to reveal a parallel strip of starry sky above — a beautiful August sky that glowed like a black velvet tablecloth strewn with glass diamonds. I lay beside Vixi on a narrow bed in the small attic room of her grandfather's cottage, and through the tiny open window the night showered us with special effects: stars not hidden by smog, the aroma of apple trees in the orchard and dried fruit in the attic, the pungent odour of old wood around our wooden bed, the smell of the enormous red-and-white-striped comforter filled with goose feathers, the sweet smell of thyme from the linen closet, the mossy emanation of the thatched roof and the strange, disarming, and incomprehensibly delicious tang of manure, in which the stench of the cowshed was imperceptibly transformed into the aroma of bread and the musky odour of that young body, of Vixi, the sorceress of Hronov . . . the smells of a summer night in a country cottage in the Eagle Mountains.

34·

Vixi's unknown past and the home I'd never seen surprised me. For me, Vixi was inseparable from that yellow T-shirt, the tennis shoes, the blue ribbon in her hair, and the rococo girls' dormitory where the crucifixes had been replaced by colour prints of Stalin, Gottwald, and his bigshot in-laws. Now here was this cottage with a pine-wood barn behind it, a short distance from a thatch-roofed village and a white bell-tower, high on the side of a hill near a wood — a cottage made of thick wooden beams with tiny windows and, in the sitting room, portraits of Saint Florian, Saint Vaclav, and Saint John of Nepomuk painted on glass (an inheritance from the great-grandfather; Vixi's grandfather was an atheist), as well as an extensive kitchen oven and unpainted furniture. It was here, incredibly, that Vixi had lived from the day the old man had taken her from her dead mother in the maternity ward until the day she had moved to the dormitory in Hronov; she had had to walk over the hill to Machov, seven kilometres away, to attend primary school and then the municipal school. And it was here that she returned each weekend while I played billiards in the *fin-de-siècle* games room of the Municipal Hotel with Comrade Ponykl, or drank whisky with Gellen in his elegant dacha. The old man had no electricity; the cottage was too far from the village and it would have been expensive to run a line out to it. We sat in the light of a kerosene lamp, eating potatoes and cottage cheese from a large wooden bowl and washing it down with sour milk: the old man, Vixi, her cousin Antonin, his young wife, Ruzena, and I. On the sideboard, wrapped in white linen, was an enormous loaf of rye bread, baked in the oven that gaped blackly at me behind the old man's back.

"None of it's true," said the old man. "They're all talkin' through their throats! Martin Stoklasa? Josef Zima? Think either one of 'em would ever in their lives think of murderin' anyone?"

"They was framed 'cause they didn't want to join the co-op, that's why," said Antonin. "That horse's ass Ponykl been sniffin' round here all the time last little while, tryin' to persuade us all to join up. But there ain't gonna be no co-op in Maslova Lhota, and that's that."

He pounded the table with his huge fist. The table had no cloth on it, and the wood had been scrubbed until it was white and the grain stood out, beautifully polished.

"Why did they pick them to frame if nobody wants to join?" I asked.

"Oh, there's some that'd join right away, sir. Malina for one, or Berousek," said the old man. "All of them that first off haven't a pot to piss in and second off can't stand the smell of work. It's fellows like that are eager to join a co-op, you can bet on it."

"All they want is to take what we got, that's the point," said Antonin angrily. "Take away what our fathers and grandfathers took out of the earth with their bare hands!" He was brushing up against the territory of legend, but then he pulled back to concrete detail. "And why'd they frame Stoklasa and Zima and Benisko, Mr. Smiricky? Because they're the best farmers in Lhota, that's why. Kulaks? I'll give them kulaks! If everyone went about their work like Josef Zima, things'd be a lot different around here, I'll tell you. You'd have to see him. Forty-seven and he looks sixty-five, all from hard work."

"And what about the mercury?" I asked, referring to the fashionable way for CIA agents to do away with collectivized cows in socialist drama; the method appealed to prosecutors who were lacking in imagination, and it was now beginning to show up in police reports. "That's not true either?"

"True?" snorted the old man. "I never in my born days heard nothin' about no mercury. Rat poison I might believe, but mercury?" He pointed a callused finger at me. "And if there was anything like that went on, then Honza Nohejl done it on his own. It'd be just like him, the schemin' little bastard. Never had nothin' except two left hands, and the better-off farmers around here have been supportin' him for years because they couldn't stand to see him go under. A hundred-year-old woman could do more in the fields than him."

"I'll tell you how I think it was, Mr. Smiricky," said Antonin. "In Tresnova Lhota they threw Honza out of their co-op 'cause he was lazy. He wants to get even so he crawls into their cow barn with a butcher's knife, but that son-of-a-bitch Ponykl nails him, and at the police station they slap him around a bit and pretty soon Honza's dancin' to their tune. Always did anyway. And now he's goin' to sing whatever they want him to. So he says Martin Stoklasa was plannin' to kill the chairman of the district national committee or whatever they want. That's how it was." Antonin took a deep drink of sour milk. "But I'll tell you one thing: Ponykl ain't gettin' back into Maselna Lhota except over my dead body! And there ain't gonna be no co-op here!"

"Father Doufal says a co-op doesn't always have to be a bad thing," said Vixi. "If people get together and help each other, the way Christians should — "

"The good father should keep to his pulpit and leave politics to them as understands it," thundered the old man, forgetting that this was the Party line at the moment. "Help each other? I'll tell you what a co-op is, my dear. The hard workers work for the lazy bums."

Vixi never said another word. Later we lay on the hillside in the thick, ancient grass, Cygnus bright in the sky.

"Vixi, did Father Doufal really defend the co-ops?"

"Well — he just said that some things the Bolsheviks do, Christians should have done long ago."

"Son-of-a-gun! So he is a progressive priest. I'd never have thought that."

"He's not a progressive," said Vixi. "He said even the devil can do good deeds when he's after souls that belong to God."

"I beg your pardon. So he's not a progressive priest. Progressive priests see the Communist Party as a direct continuation of the Thessalonian community."

"Of what?"

"Nothing. It was a kind of early Christian co-op."

"He doesn't see anything like that in the Party. He says the Communists don't follow God's commandments and that will finally bring them to ruin."

We were lying on our backs and a cool breeze caressed our bodies. A cow mooed down in the village. The pale starlight made Vixi's nose look white. She remembered something.

"Hey, sir, did you read about this Milan Straka guy?"

"Milos Straka," I corrected her. Milada Maresova had recently mentioned the case of the progressive informer in the staff room.

"Anyway, the model pioneer. When I went to my last catechism lesson, Father Doufal was sitting at his desk reading some mag or other and shaking his head, and when he saw me he said, 'Miss Koziskova, I'm just reading something my mind doesn't want to believe. About someone called Milos Straka, Miss Koziskova.' Vixi was a real mimic and she did a wonderful imitation of the priest's voice, with its tone of constant wonder. 'He's a young lad — it says here he's ten years old — and here's what's hard to believe, Miss Koziskova: he informed on his *own father* for listening to Western broadcasts on the radio.' 'There's more than one like him around,' I said, and he said, 'Well, perhaps. Bad children are always with us. But that's not the point. Now they're holding this child up as a *model* for other children to follow! In the newspapers, Miss Koziskova! They say he's a Czech Bertik Morozov. You don't happen to know who Bertik Morozov is, do you, Miss Koziskova?' Do you know who Bertik Morozov is, sir?"

"Pavlik Morozov," I said. "He's a kind of Soviet Goody Two-Shoes. Turned his own father in for plotting to kill some Bolshevik commissar or something. So the kulaks did him in — the boy, that is."

Vixi thought a while. "Did his father really try to kill that commissar?"

"That's what they say. I guess even Father Doufal would have to approve of turning your father in under those circumstances, wouldn't you say?"

"Probably. But Straka was only listening to the Voice of America."

"We're applying the experience of the great Soviet Union to our own limited Czech circumstances," I said.

"All the same — who knows the real story with Bertik Morozov?"

"Pavlik."

"All right, Pavlik. Maybe he was mad at his father for beating him, so he made it up."

"For God's sake, Vixi, don't go blabbing around ideas like that!" I was horrified by Vixi's psychological insights, which tended in a very different direction from the criminal theories of the time. "Pavlik Morozov has a place in the Kremlin martyrology."

"In the what?"

"He's on a list of Communist saints tortured to death. It's like the Roman martyrology — that's a list of Catholic saints who were tortured to death for their faith. Like Saint John of Nepomuk, for instance."

Vixi's mind pounced on a theme that interested her more than the mythology of the Communist Party.

"Hey, d'you know what Kamila Doruzkova said? She read somewhere that King Wenceslas the Fourth had Saint John of Nepomuk killed because he slept with his wife. All that stuff about him not wanting to betray the secrets of the confessional was just an excuse. He had him drowned in the Vltava."

"Maybe it was different. Maybe Saint John simply didn't want to tell King Wenceslas who was shagging his queen and the king got royally annoyed and accused him of shagging her himself."

Vixi was silent, and a wrinkle appeared over her white nose. She was thinking again.

"You know what's really awful, sir?" she said. "Some things you'll just never know for sure. Everyone says something different, but what's the *truth*?"

"You mean about who was shagging the queen?"

"That too, but I mean in general."

"You mean, did Pavlik Morozov's dad really plan to murder the commissar? Or did Pavlik merely work out the revolutionary possibilities of the time and try to use them to his own advantage?"

The black wrinkle almost overshadowed Vixi's white nose.

"I just don't believe it, sir, because the Communists say it's true and all they ever do is lie. But supposing it was true? Who'd believe them?"

We lay there silently, staring into the starry sky. It was pleasant to philosophize in the sweet-smelling air. How did Vixi put it? The same way Pontius Pilate did: "What is truth?"

"One thing is certain, and therefore important," I said. "Little Milos Straka turned in his own father for listening to the radio — no one's life was at stake. And the Communist Party of Czechoslovakia is holding him up as a model for other children."

"Wait, that's — " Vixi held her hand to the stars and began counting on her fingers. "The first one: You shall believe in one God. The second one: Don't take the name of the Lord — "

"It's against the Fourth Commandment," I said. "Honour thy father" — and a sudden wind rushed out of the valley — "and thy mother — "

" — that thy days may be long, I know," Vixi interrupted, "and that thou shalt prosper on this earth. Why 'on this earth', sir? Don't they care in heaven whether you honour your father and your mother?"

"I don't know," I said. "I don't know how they look on these things in heaven."

35.

"I was asleep for about a minute," said Mr. Kohn, "and suddenly there's somebody shaking me. I wake up — half wake up — and I see it's the chambermaid. 'Mr. Kohn,' she says, and I look and I see she's crying. 'Mr. Kohn, get up! The Russians are here!' And do you know, gentlemen, how I felt when I got over the first shock? Have you any idea how I felt?"

I shook my head. So did Mr. Pohorsky.

"That the lid had come down. The lid had finally come down. And I was trapped inside. And this time, no Bondy and no General Blaskowitz!"

36.

My thoughts were interrupted by a crackling sound. Sylva emerged from a cluster of dry ferns.

"Danny! Just a little way over there, there's another road, and I can hear someone speaking English!"

"Come on!"

"Hey, maybe they're diversionists. Let's go have a look."

It seemed absurd to think the Americans would send soldiers across the border to get mixed up in a local crisis.

"You wait here, with the kids," I said, reminding her that she was a mother, and I crept off into the ferns.

Soon they began to thin out and I could see a white district road that for some reason ran parallel to the main highway. In the starlight I could see the sparkling outline of a big American limousine. Voices were coming from inside.

"We won't get out of here! We won't! I know we won't!" It was a hysterical voice, and another one, calmer and deeper, was trying to soothe it:

"Take it easy, boss. We can just wait here till morning."

"They'll find us and kill us!"

"Hey now, boss, none of that talk."

There was a moment or so of silence, then: "How could you get lost? Don't you have a map?"

"There were no damn road signs anywhere, I told you that, boss."

"Oh God, oh my God, I'm done for!"

Another voice joined in, this time a female one:

"Shut up, Izzy. You're in no danger at all! Be quiet and try to get some sleep!"

The people were too rattled to be diversionists. I jumped over the ditch beside the road and walked up to the limousine.

"Good evening," I said in English. "Can I help you?"

A black man wearing a chauffeur's cap stuck his head out the window. "Evening, sir. We've just run out of gas."

"You wouldn't happen to be Czech, would you?" came a voice from inside the limousine, speaking Czech.

"Yes, I am. At your service," I said.

"My name is Kohn," said the voice. "From Providence, Rhode Island."

37·

"Did you talk to him?"

Barta, smooth and elegant as usual in a white shirt and a hand-knit tie, was sitting behind the heavy desk directly under a portrait of President Svoboda and the First Secretary — the new one. The bright façades of the Washington street glared harshly through the window.

I was my old self again. I confessed. "There was no way to avoid it. And besides, I'm interested in what he has to say. I'm planning to write something about emigrants. A play, perhaps."

Barta was toying with a silver snuff-box. He wore a massive, lavishly decorated wedding ring on the sun-tanned ring finger on his left hand. I looked at the photograph of a young woman, his new wife, and a child on his desk. The child was too small for me to make out what sex it was.

He nodded. "If you need anything before you leave for Prague, give me a call. I'll arrange it for you if I can. I've only been here a month, so I'm still just getting my bearings."

When I first came here on my Ford Foundation grant, another comrade had been sitting in this office, saying nasty things about the Soviet Union. Now my old acquaintance was in his place.

"What did Hrzan actually say his reason for emigrating was?"

"You mean in private? He said he's got more opportunities in Connington than in Prague. I don't know whether he meant scientific or financial opportunities. They gave him tenure in less than a year, with a full professor's salary."

Barta's eyes met mine. "In plain Czech, he betrayed his country for a mess of pottage."

I couldn't recall right away where in the Bible that image came from. I didn't even know what pottage was. But it certainly wasn't from the writings of Marx. I looked at Barta's thick, heavily engraved ring.

"A sack of gold would be more like it," I said. "And of course he repeated the familiar thesis — that the 1950s had come back, with all the consequences."

I looked Barta in the eye again.

He smiled. "That's exactly what people like Hrzan want to believe. But the Party learns from its mistakes. There's no going back, either to what came before Dubcek, or to what he brought with him."

Saying nothing about what Dubcek's era had meant to him personally, he went on. "Dubcek was inevitable. Too many unresolved problems had accumulated and Novotny put them off instead of dealing with them. So he's responsible too, in a way, for what came with Dubcek."

He was preaching now, and his old theoretical, academic certitude returned. I was fascinated by his hands. They were flashy, bureaucratic hands, with that ring.

"In any case, one guarantee that the 1950s won't come back," I heard him say, "is the fact that Comrade Husak is now at the head of the Party. Don't forget that during the period of the Cult of Personality, he was in prison."

How can I describe his look? Fishlike? Expressionless, certainly. Perhaps the look of a tiny chip in a large mechanical brain that was trying to reprogram itself. Reprogram? Or was it simply adapting its old ways to new circumstances? That was the question. Or was there a difference? And that ring finger . . . with its heavily engraved ring. . . .

The office was air-conditioned, but I felt hot all the same. I wanted to get away.

"So you can arrange to extend my travel documents?" I said, interrupting his lecture on political philosophy.

"Yes. You've got a serious reason for it and — well, quite simply, comrade, I know you," he said, whatever that meant. He picked up my passport and put on his thick-rimmed glasses.

I knew him too — Comrade Barta — even though I wasn't trained for it. Better than he knew me.

That wasn't the only surprise that awaited me in the Czechoslovak embassy in Washington. In the vestibule I was prepared to meet a well-known stereotype, the man-of-the-people comrade in an American off-the-rack outfit, but I had no idea it would be Ponykl.

He recognized me at once.

"What you up to here, teacher? I mean, Comrade Writer?" He greeted me with genuine pleasure at first, but then immediately became suspicious. "You here legally?"

"Of course. I'm writing something about political emigrants."

"For Prague?"

"For Prague."

"You know, I seem to recall you signed that manifesto, didn't you?" He looked at me with wavering distrust.

"I fell for it, Comrade Ponykl. I had no idea what was really behind it. And don't forget, there was, well, pressure in the air — "

"Right. Psychological terror," said Ponykl. "They didn't try that stuff on me, though. I'm tough. But I understand. You're an intellectual, and there ain't much you can do about that. Sometimes it takes you people a while to get it."

As he stood there looking me over, a new wave of suspicion crossed his cramped, ageing face.

"Before I forget — did you have anything to do with that Juzl fellow?"

"Nothing at all. Somehow he managed to find out I was teaching in Hronov at the time — when that business happened there. He tried to get something out of me, but I didn't know very much. In my opinion," I said, just to make sure — and suddenly it occurred to me that in his plaid jacket Ponykl looked just like the petty mobsters in those Humphrey Bogart movies I'd seen in Connington, put on by the student revolutionaries — "in my opinion, there was something phony going on there."

"Right enough, comrade. He was a clever bird, that holy man from Under Mare's Head. But we mopped the floor with Juzl. The sonofabitch! He tried to use an unfortunate accident to spread his reactionary ideas."

"Is he doing time?"

"Not yet," said Ponykl. "For the time being, he's doing manual labour. That won't hurt him none." He leaned closer to me. "We'll lock him up later, when things are a touch more normalized."

He flashed me a grin, held it for a while, then put on an official face again and straightened his shoulders. "So you're writing what, comrade? About emigrants? Just do a good job of it and write about what a bunch of losers they are — runaways!"

"You know I will, Comrade Ponykl."

"I remember the time you made that speech about Comrade Lenin — you put it real well," he said, with a dreamy expression — that is, as far as his petty mobster's face would allow it. And then, to my horror, he began to quote from some overblown bombast unfamiliar to me: "'Perhaps even tomorrow a great conflagration will sweep the world, the great conflagration of world revolution that will destroy all the filth of the world in us and around us and will set a bloody exclamation mark to mark the beginning of mankind's true history.'"

He looked at me.

"You got it just right. I got a copy of your speech from Comrade Hrozna, the principal, and I've still got it stashed away somewhere."

Oh my God! The overblown bombast was suddenly coming home to roost. I was the one who had originally produced this stuff, back when Hronov was celebrating its five-hundredth anniversary, and I'd rehashed it several times without making many changes — first for Lieutenant Hezky, commander of my platoon, then later for a meeting of the Revolutionary Trades Union in that big publishing house, then for an occasion — I could no longer remember which one — in a theatre. My God, was I one of the ideological fathers of this muzhik standing before me now?

"That's why I was disappointed when I saw your name on that manifesto, comrade. But now I see you've found yourself. The Party never — "

And he began to reproduce the usual truisms, dear to my ears as they are to the ears of all sinners longing for absolution, for a return to the security of familiar libations and truths. But Vixi had said, "What is truth?"

I shuddered. Ponykl had said his piece and was staring at me with his dead eyes peering out from the lizard-like folds of his ageing skin.

"And what about you, Comrade Ponykl?" I said with comradely good humour. "What are you doing here? You're the last person I'd expect to find in Washington."

"The Party needs solid cadres for sticky places like this," said the petty mobster. "You'd never believe how many revisionists of all sorts there was in the diplomatic service. I mean like our former ambassador — he was another goddamned right-winger! They've recalled him. He was one of our working-class cadres, too. Spent twenty years in our embassies abroad. And then he lets us down."

He gazed at the Tiffany window by the main entrance and folded his hands behind his back. There was a bulge in the side of his sports jacket, but perhaps he'd simply chosen the wrong size.

"I tell you, I've thought a lot about it in the last little while," he assured me.

"About what?"

"About how comrades like you — well, not exactly like you, you're not in the Party and you only wobbled a bit there — but I'm talking about some Communists. And how they let us down. Hell, they betrayed us! Educated comrades! We sent them to academies and universities, so how come they let us down? But me, I've only got grade eight, right? And I didn't let them down."

He turned away from the Tiffany window and rested his eyes on me. They looked at me unwaveringly, directly, like the eyes of an animal that suspects nothing.

"I guess it depends on the individual," I said.

"The individual's got bugger all to do with it," he said. "They all let us down! National artists too! Writers, professors, even some of our generals. You'd have to go through the lot with a fine-tooth comb before you found someone who'd admit he was wrong. Not to speak of someone who never fell for that reform crap in the first place. No sir! All them highly educated comrades, they were all part of the counter-revolution. And you know why that is?"

I didn't know, but I was eager to find out. Why was it that the truth of comrades Barta and Ponykl was attractive only to comrades Barta and Ponykl? It was a serious problem and I longed to discover the answer. Maybe it would tell me about the question Vixi had posed so long ago.

"I don't know," I said.

"I racked my brains for a long time," said the gunslinger, nodding his small head. "But in the end I went at it Marx-Leninist style. All those comrades let us down," he explained, and he actually raised a finger, "because they don't have the class instinct I do. I have it, and I always had. So with me they can't get nowhere with those goddamned intellectual notions and the like."

He shook his old, wrinkled head, now protruding from a white collar and a flashy American sportscoat.

"Anyway, what is it you want here?"

"I'm supposed to pick up an extension of my travel permit."

"Take a seat, then. Comrade Cultural Attaché's got someone in there right now."

So I sat down on an upholstered chair in the vestibule, under one of the many renderings of Prague Castle by Setelik, and I watched while the scourge of God from Hronov directed the trickle of visitors to their various destinations. And the years began to unravel backwards, that strange and wonderful skein of years and people and reversals, until they came to rest at a point where Zdenka Prochazkova, the rangy phys-ed teacher, was ridiculing me:

"If I may say so, Mowgli, that speech of yours has certainly put you in Ivana's good books!"

"Didn't you like it?"

"Who cares what I think? Ivana's opinion's the main thing. You do know how to say the right things to please her!"

"I meant what I said seriously. On the whole, I mean."

"Did you seriously mean it seriously?"

"On the whole."

I was walking Zdenka up the hill to her house. Her husband was now the Inspector of Schools for Bohemia and came back from Prague only once a week, if that, and on special occasions. She was walking beside me in a shapeless skirt and a pale blue summer sweater, her sweat-dampened hair unkempt. She looked at me with wry skepticism.

"What I mean is—look, Zdenka. It wasn't Lenin's fault that all kinds of bad eggs joined the Party."

"You talk as though you were in the Party yourself."

"Nuts. I'm only trying to be fair. You've got men like Grimm, who turn every political change to their own advantage, and then you've got people like your husband. I just want to be fair, that's all."

"Oh, yes indeed, Mowgli. You're so fair you're sometimes just dumb."

That made me angry. I really had meant what I said. Her husband had spoken to me prudently at the political indoctrination course and he hadn't used a single cliché that got my back up. I hadn't yet realized that this was a special gift, an ability, and not a sign of purity at all.

Not long after I'd made that speech about Lenin at the town's five-hundredth anniversary, and then accompanied her home and provoked her into calling me a fool, Zdenka came up to me in the staff room and said, "Look at this. Can you make any sense of it?"

She handed me a letter written on the letterhead of the Ministry of Education:

> Dear Comrade,
> I'm happy to announce that the Foreign Placement Committee of the Ministry has unanimously decided to appoint you the Physical Education teacher in the experimental Czechoslovak

school in Cicero, Illinois, U.S.A. The comrades value very highly your work both in physical education and in politics, and your contribution to the development of the Czechoslovak Union of Youth in Hronov.

The rest of the letter contained technical information which I didn't read. I grinned at Zdenka and said, "Congratulations! This is quite something!"

"It is indeed. Something strange."

"Why strange?"

"Because I didn't ask to be sent there at all. As far as I know, it was Milada Maresova who was supposed to go to Cicero."

"But not to teach physical education."

She looked sharply at me. "Wait a minute — are they sending two teachers from Hronov?"

She looked around and then, like a burglar, approached the box where the janitor put the staff mail and quickly rifled through it. In a moment she was holding three envelopes in her hand. She examined them, held up one for me to see from a distance, then put all of them back and came back to where I was standing.

"She's got one from the ministry too. Jesus, Mowgli, I can't go to America with her!" She picked up her letter thoughtfully. "Anyway, I'm not going."

"Why not, for God's sake?"

"Because, little brother, there's something about this that stinks. I didn't ask for this, and as far as my political work goes, that's a joke. It's true my girls won the regional basketball tournament, but someone just stuck the Youth Union label on it, and if that's a contribution to the development of the Youth Union then I'm a — "

"Your subjective opinions don't matter, it's the objective results that count," I said, and into the staff room walked Milada. Both of us quickly pretended to be absorbed in marking papers. Milada went to the box, picked up her letters, scanned the return addresses, and eagerly opened the one from the Ministry of Education. As she read it her face flushed with blood. Angrily she tore the letter into pieces, crumpled them and flung them into the waste basket, slammed a pile of notebooks on the table, and ran out into the corridor.

Zdenka rushed to the waste-paper basket.

In my office, we carefully put the crumpled scraps back together:

Dear Comrade,

The Foreign Placement Committee of the Ministry of Education has reconsidered your appointment as teacher in the Czechoslovak School in Cicero, Illinois, in the U.S.A. Given the fact that in the meantime several openings have occurred elsewhere that require someone of the highest pedagogical and political qualifications, the Committee has decided to alter its original decision and, because of your exceptionally high qualifications, to appoint you to fill a particularly demanding position. At the suggestion of Comrade Prochazka, the Inspector of Schools for Bohemia, you have therefore been appointed principal of the Czech school in the spa town of Kudowa in the district of Kladsko in Poland. As you are no doubt aware, a Czech minority has lived in this district since the time of the Prussian wars, when it was lost by Maria Theresa. During the Nazi occupation the majority, under great pressure, claimed German nationality. It was only after the liberation of Kladsko by the Red Army and its annexation by the People's Republic of Poland that the Kladsko Czechs resumed their Czech nationality. Of course we should not deny that most of them did so to avoid being transported away as Germans. Children of compulsory school age who have grown up in such conditions for the most part do not know any Czech or, if they do, then very badly. Most of them have little understanding of the stormy political developments in this area. It will therefore be incumbent upon the political abilities of the principal to insure that these Germanized Czech children become not only good Czechs, but also highly conscientious and politically mature citizens of socialist Poland. I am convinced that you. . . .

This was followed by another encomium on Milada's political maturity and correctness, then some technical instructions and the signature of the minister.

"Well, she got what she wanted," I said.

Zdenka frowned at the letter.

"Why would my old man do a thing like that?"

"He probably saw through her," I said. "I've always had a higher opinion of him than you have. This proves I was right."

"Mowgli, please don't forget that I've lived with him for seventeen years!"

"Sometimes strangers understand those closest to us better than we do ourselves," I said, reciting an old saw. But sometimes old saws are completely wrong. This one was.

At first, all of this seemed to me like a deliberate punishment meted out by an intelligent school inspector. The Kudowa spa was about two hours' slow walk from Hronov, on the other side of the border between Czechoslovakia and Poland. At one time it had been possible to cross the border with normal ID, but with the intensifying of the class struggle both fraternal states had suspended this practice. Now Kudowa was in a foreign country and you needed a valid passport as well as travel documents to go there. The bearer of such instruments was allowed to cross the border once every six months.

Starting the next day Zdenka took two days off, and three days later, once again in my office, she said, "This whole thing is turning out to be very embarrassing."

"Why?"

"I was in Prague yesterday, at the ministry."

"And? Are you going?"

"I turned it down."

"My God! You're trampling on your own good luck."

She laughed sourly. "Look here, Mowgli, I'll tell you how it is if you keep it to yourself. My old man arranged for me to go to Cicero, just the way he arranged for Milada to go to Kudowa."

"I still don't. . . ."

"To disabuse you of some of your illusions: he set Milada up because once upon a time he tried to get her into bed. But she considered adultery with a member of the Party immoral, so now he's paying her back."

I must have looked uncomprehending, because she added, "I'm surprised you would find something like that hard to understand, Mowgli."

"What I find hard to understand is how anyone could lust after Milada," I said, so I wouldn't appear entirely stupid.

"You see? I've always said you were a human cub among the — "

I looked offended so she went on. "Of course he wasn't lusting after her — but she was making eyes at him and Olda thought a fling with her could advance his political career. What he didn't realize was that through him she was worshipping the Party, and maybe even Lenin. If he weren't so overweight, Olda would look a lot like Lenin."

"The old devil! But why did he arrange for you to go to Cicero?"

"I'll give you three guesses," sighed the rangy phys-ed teacher.

This time I got the right answer the first time. Dr. Crippen and bunglers like him had, for the same reason, bricked their wives up in cellars. Prochazka the modern-thinking Leninist had merely tried to place the Atlantic Ocean between himself and his wife.

But I hadn't known all this when I was walking Zdenka home two days after my own Leninist speech, when she said, "You're so fair you're sometimes just dumb."

It annoyed me and I retorted, almost like one of the comrades, "Have you got anything against Lenin?"

"No, no I haven't," she'd replied. "I don't care very much, that's all."

We were walking through the orchard. The apple trees had just blossomed; a breeze was swaying the tops of the trees and a perfumed rain descended upon the phys-ed teacher. She was veiled in a white cloud of swirling petals.

"You know what I think Lenin was, Mowgli?"

"No. I think he was a genius and an idealist."

"I think, Mowgli," said the phys-ed teacher, "that he was the devil."

Alarmed, I looked around.

Behind us a fat lady was crawling up the slope. But I guessed she was out of earshot.

38.

Mr. Pergl put the reel on the projector and threaded the film through the gates.

"You'll see for yourself, Mr. Juzl," he said. "I screened it as soon as I read your last article."

He switched the projector on and through the windows of the booth we watched the nineteen-year-old drama that, according to the Ministry of the Interior, had not been preserved even in their archives. Fortunately it had been preserved in a secret collection of curious film documents gathered by the projectionist at the Hvezda cinema, Mr. Pergl.

The drama that he projected was not typical of his collection, which was composed mainly of brief nude scenes cut out of X-rated pictures. I had already seen this film once, but I couldn't remember it; it had been nineteen years ago and at the time I'd been distracted by Vixi, who'd been holding my hand in the dark. Looking at it now was like seeing it for the first time.

It began with a full shot of the chapel under Mare's Head and then cut to a close-up of the altar and both statues. In the projection booth of the Hvezda cinema I suddenly felt surrounded by the atmosphere of that long-ago morning, feeling sad after the sensual delights of the night before, hearing the wailing voices of the old women — but instead of those voices the auditorium below me was filled with amplified narration peppered with ideology. Then the camera panned to the pulpit where the priest stood ready.

I stiffened. The priest's face was unclear, but I had vivid memories of the techtonics of those ancient features. One thing was certain: this Savonarola in glasses was not Father Doufal. This was not the sturdy priest with hands like spades. Whoever it was, I had the feeling I'd seen him before. But during the past twenty years I had seen too many crude faces close up, and this one was shot from too far away. The narrator explained the mechanism as the relevant details flashed on the screen: the hook in the back of the statue and the steel wire that led from it over a series of pulleys to the pulpit. Then this began to blend with another image and another voice, but no longer thanks to the director's artistic design. The story of the little blind girl, the light-giving rain, the cows, the donkey . . . a hole drilled through the wooden railing and into the pulpit, a handle on the end of a steel wire . . . a cricket singing in the grass . . . then a cut to a close-up of the statue, nodding as if it were trying to bow. . . .

"D'you see that? It was Saint Joseph that moved!" Juzl's voice mingled with the voice of the narrator and the voice of the dead priest. "Exactly the way Mrs. Knizakova described it. In the first version it was the Virgin Mary. This is the second version, the one they showed in all the cinemas."

Another cut, this time a close-up of a hand. A booming voice announced ideological excommunication. *Our Father* . . . and a pan to Saint Joseph bowing obediently. I felt as though I'd suddenly woken up.

"They threw out the first version," said Juzl.

"Could you run it again?" I asked Mr. Pergl.

He complied.

The white chapel, the Virgin Mary, Saint Joseph. "They didn't throw out the *whole* first version," I said. "They kept some shots." The bespectacled Savonarola in the pulpit.

"You don't mean these shots?" said Juzl. "That isn't Father Doufal."

"Watch this now," I said. The camera travelled up the steel wire . . . *Holy martyr* . . . from the hook on the statue, over the first pulley, the second, the third . . . *intercede with God for us* . . . to the hole in the pulpit . . . the wire handle. . . .

"Now!" I said.

The hand pulling the wire . . . *who slapped the face* . . . a wide, farmer's hand . . . *of the blasphemous man.* . . . The last joint on the ring finger was missing.

Juzl breathed out suddenly. "That's him! That's his hand!"

"Yes," I said. "It's the hand of a living saint."

It was phantasmic, terrifying . . . and magnificent. After nineteen years, through the miracle of film . . . a carpenter's unpriestly hand, scarred by a worker's wound. . . .

"Of course, by that time he was dead. When they spliced this copy together."

A hand. A wire. And the puppet bowed down. The hand again, the wire, the thundering voice from the amplifier cursing it all, damning it all, casting it all into the fire. . . .

Suddenly I realized it was not the hand, that strange, modern relic, that terrified me most. But what it was, I did not yet know.

10

■

A Trip around the World

I.

From the studio, Briza announced that we could start. I sat down at the microphone opposite Lester, and Suzi sat down on my right. Jana Hloubava went into the control room.

I could see her on the other side of the glass. The artificial light exaggerated the circles under her eyes. I realized I'd never seen her look cheerful, as though her appearance and the spirit of the times were somehow in harmony. I remembered her at the airport, scurrying after General Yepishev. But then, at least, she'd been a fresh young girl in a miniskirt. She still wore the miniskirt but her complexion had yellowed, she seemed wilted, and a strand of silver shone in her black hair. She lit a cigarette. Briza turned on the red light.

Lester and I began to read the commentary.

Our program was orthodox and sentimental, not for the teenage generation. We played only swing. The needs of the rock and roll fans were taken care of by a young married couple, who'd just been told that their half-hour program had been suspended.

"When we were sixteen, they sold Brunswick records here. Every true swing fan called them 'Brunshviky'," Lester said. I followed the script as he read, waiting until he reached the marked passage that I was to read. Some good old-fashioned talk about saxophone heroes allowed me to forget briefly the sword of Damocles hanging over our heads, and the question everyone was asking: not whether it would fall, but when.

The pressure inside my head, which had persisted ever since I'd driven the Felicie — alone — back across the border in an easterly direction, had relented a little. "It was the custom in those days," Lester went on, "to include only the name of the band on these records, not the singer, because the band was what sold records. One of the most famous swing bands of all time was led by the hunchback Negro drummer Chick Webb." Lester had an even, monotonous voice, and a moustache that he wriggled ironically from side to side. It was an old habit of his. Sometimes his flat voice and the moustache with its expressionist waggle seemed like symbols of a movement we all belonged to, a movement that had no agricultural implements in its logo.

A quarter of a century before, in the great hall of Lucerna, a younger Lester, already sporting his moustache, had introduced the swing band that the beer-sipping little Milan Forhont had listened to in the Port Arthur tavern in Kostelec. In this band I had tried poorly but with great enthusiasm to imitate Coleman Hawkins, while Lester, working within the guidelines laid down by the *Reichskulturkammer* or some such authority, announced drily, "The joyful rhythm of the following composition, 'Our Bull Got Spooked', by Jiri Patocka, reflects the joy of living joyfully — in other joyful words, *Kraft durch Freude.*" Then he would wriggle his moustache and here and there someone in the audience would laugh — everyone understood what was going on — and we would start playing "Tiger Rag". Lester's moustache quickly became a secret sign.

He came to the marked part and I took over. "Sometime in 1939, we heard a female singer perform with this band. At the time, she impressed us with her perfect swing style." Lester had also put out an illegal magazine called *Swingtime* in which he published valuable information about the rising star Glenn Miller and his Modernaires. When the war was over he shone as the editor of the legal monthly magazine *Jazz*, but not for long — periods of full legality never lasted very long in Lester's life. After the Victory of the People he submerged himself, with his impassive face and his eloquent moustache, in the anonymity of a musical agency, where he returned to the roots. He began to write articles about American folk music for the orthodox periodical *Musical Horizons.* Among the radicals, who had withdrawn even further from public life into what they themselves called inner emigration, where they did nothing for the public at all, Lester's reputation was that of a frightened conformist — a reputation he later confirmed by not signing a single manifesto during the Prague Spring. "Her name was Ella Fitzgeraldova," I said, "and for Chick Webb she sang the swing number 'I've Got a Guy'."

"Right after the invasion, we were broadcasting from the army studio in

Vinohrady," said Jana Hloubava. "They found that, so we started shuttling between Karlin and Michle. People were fantastic. When word came that the Russians were onto us in Vinohrady, I was helped over the fence by a guy from the People's Militia. Everyone was fantastic. But the whole thing collapsed in the end anyway. Either they had their own spies on the inside, or people talked too much — "

"Or some realized, after the fact, that they'd been a little too daring," said Lester.

"Possibly," said Jana Hloubava. "Or they recognized my voice — "

I recalled that dusty road and the small radio in the tiny Felicie caught between two enormous tanks. That voice — of course.

"But they'll let you go on working here in Light Music, won't they?" asked Suzi.

"For the time being. Except that today I got called in by Knourek, the new boss, you know?"

We nodded.

"He was all upset and he said I should watch what I said, because in the last variety show I made some dangerous allusions in my continuity and I should bear in mind that it was only thanks to him that I hadn't been arrested yet. 'But they'll lock you up in the end anyway,' he told me. 'They have a Soviet adviser working in the Ministry of the Interior now, and they'll have a little chat with you all in the end' — that's what he said."

The pressure inside my head pushed violently against my temples.

"For this reason I would recommend," the poet Vrchcolab had intoned, and I, still in uniform, had listened intently to him, along with Lester, who was sitting beside me in civilian clothes as the musical adviser, "that all cultural officers be sent urgent instructions recommending the following: *a)* that they make sure no concert orchestras use mutes, which deform the optimistic tone of the brass instruments, turning it into a painful wailing sound; and *b)* that they use every means at their disposal to dissuade orchestra leaders from using saxophones of *any* kind, because of their hybrid, cosmopolitan, and decadent timbre. They may substitute the violoncello." Lester nodded his agreement to each point in Vrchcolab's edict, and when the poet had finished talking he stood up and, as was expected of him, gave his expert opinion. In highly technical terms he explained what gave the saxophone its special timbre, that the hybrid sound was not caused merely by the reactionary politics of Adolph Sax but by the reed mouthpiece in combination with a conical metal tube. Lester also explained the source of the progressive sweetness of the violoncello, but unfortunately he waded too deeply into specialized terminology relating to hand positions and fingering, so that the commission got the impression that because of the exceptional technical difficulties involved, the violoncello could only be properly played by a virtuoso. Then Lester returned to the conical construction of the saxophone, comparing it to the clarinet, which has a cylindrical bore. The assembled commission heard all about overblowing in twelfths and octaves, complete with musical examples which Lester very nimbly sketched out on the blackboard. Since most of those present could not read music, the commission concluded its hearing by drawing up a circular for orchestra leaders recommending that *a)* in every case where there was a local virtuoso capable of playing a violoncello, the orchestra should engage his services instead of those of a saxophonist; and that *b)* in amateur orchestras saxophones should be used rather than clarinets because overblowing in twelfths, as the clarinet is played, was an older and therefore less progressive technique. . . .

"And now listen to Webb's singer in 'I've Got a Guy'," I said into the microphone, and nodded at Lester. In the sound booth Briza brought the music up under the continuity, and we listened in silence as Chick Webb's saxophones bounced up to Ella's solo like light-footed kittens.

"And on top of everything else, my tooth aches," said Jana Hloubava.

"Want a pill?" asked Suzi. Jana nodded and Suzi pawed through her handbag. "One or two?"

"Three. I've been hitting the pills pretty hard recently."

She swallowed them and washed them down with coffee.

"By the way, Suzi," she said, "Knourek also said that that kiss of yours isn't going to pay off in the end."

"He can go to hell!" said Suzi, making a face. "I'm going to kiss whoever I damn well feel like. And it's not going to be him!"

Using long-winded sociological and musicological analyses that he'd prepared for the Cultural Department of the Central Committee of the Party, Lester had been able to persuade Comrade Kaiser that the musical re-education of young people urgently required a new magazine to take the place of the former *Jazz*, which had been banned. Overwhelmed by Lester's arguments, Comrade Kaiser finally asked what the name of this magazine would be, but when Lester suggested *Rhythm* or *Syncopation* the head of the Cultural Department shook his head and said it would be called *Melody*, because the Party was *against* rhythm, since rhythm excited the passions and was therefore anti-rational and, by extension, anti-Marxist. Lester agreed, and in the first number of *Melody* he published an article entitled "How They Poison Young People's Minds in the U.S.A."

— a sociological and musicological study of Elvis Presley which included the scores of two of his hits and a huge photograph of Elvis, accompanied by a quotation from Comrade Kaiser about the dangers of succumbing to base passions. Thus Comrade Kaiser, who until that point had been known to only a few people in the Prague intelligentsia, became a household name, and Presley's two songs could soon be heard, sung by groups of young people with guitars, in municipal parks from one end of the country to the other. But because Lester hadn't dared publish the English lyrics, there were soon about five different domestic versions — at least one of which was politically objectionable because its lyrics employed an acronym for the local police.

The First Secretary, who had not yet been dethroned, had organized a party — perhaps to advertise how different he was from his gloomy predecessors — for pop stars. He arrived in the same silver-threaded suit that he'd worn when he sat on the terrace of the Hrzansky Palace and listened attentively to the world-class playwright. Suzi, who was always emotionally excitable and spontaneous, kissed him for the photographers. Since the First Secretary's government was now inevitably heading towards final dissolution, Comrade Knourek's prediction was not without substance.

For the time being, Suzi didn't seem worried; she smoked and drank coffee as usual. But the girl with the circles under her eyes was worse off, for her voice couldn't be confused with anyone else's and her sin was more than just a photogenic kiss. When I'd been in Paris delivering Sylva, back when the invasion was still newsworthy, *Paris-Match* had published another photo. It had shown the announcer of one of the underground radio stations in Czechoslovakia, with her face shadowed and invisible, since *Paris-Match* played by the rules of conspiracy. All you could see of her, shining out of the shadows, were those unmistakable legs in the mini. I longed to take a picture of the face now, for *Paris-Match*, but I don't suppose they'd have bought it — it was three months later, life had stumbled on, and other, more newsworthy news was filling the front pages. The announcer had fallen down the public memory hole and the advisers could get her ready for the frying pan at their leisure. Or not. It was entirely up to them.

Ella sang and we listened, enthralled — as we always were, every time — by her message, and on the other side of the sound-booth glass Jana Hloubava, the tired little angel, nodded her melancholy face to the slow rhythm. And the years swung forward and backward across a long quarter of a century, and Lester and his moustache suddenly swelled up and took on the gigantic proportions of the now-defunct monument to the dead marshal. But I realized that Lester's work had been destroyed too, that what Vrchcolab hadn't been able to accomplish with his radical philosophizing about saxophones he had accomplished with his radical appeals for the democratic elimination of all that was Communist from the Communist Party. The pressure in my temples grew, and it was very unpleasant.

"Do you want to hear a protest song?" said Briza after the broadcast.

We nodded eagerly, and he got up and went into the booth. We were silent. Both girls veiled themselves in clouds of nicotine smoke. Lester sat between them and the clouds came together above his head in a bluish-white halo.

A piano tinkled from the speakers. Then two voices, singing in harmony:

> Pee-pee Pytchorin Street
> That's where my baby lives,
> In Pee-pee Pytchorin Street,
> In Moscow, that's where she lives.

We listened to the young Ella until she'd finished the vocal and Webb's sax man slid into a magnificent, sobbing solo. Then Lester raised his eyes to look at Suzi. Everything had been dialectically turned upside down. They hadn't been destroyed — neither by Vrchcolab, nor by General Yepishev. Lester would simply go on sitting through boring meetings ("he signed nothing, was not involved in the counter-revolution") and nodding in agreement when the old Kaisers and the new Vrchcolabs had their say. Again he would obfuscate their opinions through clarification, and smuggle sweet saxophone poison into their programming for young people and for the occupational army — or I fervently hoped he would. The unobjectionable name of his magazine hadn't changed since that first critique of Elvis Presley, but the contents had altered radically. Now the only people in its pages who wore their hair short were Negroes of Armstrong's generation.

It was and was not a protest song. It was swung by two young, mocking voices, and they were saying something you couldn't quite put your finger on, something uncensorable. Suzi sighed, the smoke slid tenderly over the yellowish face of Jana Hloubava, Lester wriggled his moustache horizontally in an inaudible semantic joke.

> I think it's really neat
> That Pee-pee Pytchorin Street

sang the two unknown lads, now with an energetic tempo, and the semantic joke was underlined by the pulsating rhythm of a military march. Helpless similes chased each other through my head. Similes for the ways of the mere spirit, arched over by a thundering power.

> Pee-pee Pytchorin Street

they sang with tender passion,

> That's where my baby lives
> In Pee-pee Pytchorin Street. . . .

I knew they couldn't destroy Lester unless they killed him.

Chick Webb finished with a honeyed chord and Lester, in a voice devoid of all intonation, said, "We have here in the studio our number-one singer, Zuzana Kajetanova, and we're going to ask her a question: Zuzana, could you identify the singer who has just sung that song for us?" Suzi squirmed nervously in her chair — whenever she had to speak instead of sing in public, she was a bit nervous — and said, "Well, I certainly think it very well might be — of course, Ella Fitzgerald." "Wonderful, Zuzana," Lester said, delighted, again in a completely neutral voice. "How did you recognize her? That was Ella when she was eighteen, after all." "Well, she's got that kind of voice, you know? She can really cut loose, and her voice is relaxed and, you know, free. . . ."

I thought of an obvious comparison from ancient history, Rome defeated by Greece. It may take us a century but the spirit of "Pee-pee Pytchorin Street" will triumph over the trumpeting of the big tubas in the end. But the century flows on and we're a little lost. Me, Lester, Suzi, and most of all Jana Hloubava, because she caught General Yepishev out in a public lie. We're all a little lost. Even if historical experience teaches us that the distant future is ours, what good will it do to us? Who was ever consoled by history?

> That's where my baby and me meet,
> Down in Pee-pee Pytchorin Street

the two supernatural voices sang energetically, and the song went on and on, in its stupefying carousel of lines:

> Pee-pee Pytchorin Street
> That's where my baby lives,
> In Pee-pee Pytchorin Street,
> In Moscow, that's where she lives.

Then it was lost in a fading echo.

"What a knockout," I said, the way Vixi had, once upon a distant time.

2.

It was when the finals were approaching. "What a knockout," she said. "What are you going to do about it?"

The final exams were not only approaching, they were right around the corner. All the girls in the graduating class — including Bozena Stoklasova, who had incurred public disgrace by denouncing her father as a criminal in exchange for the privilege of being admitted to the finals — had stopped dating the boys at the school of stonemasonry and, with the rashness native to their sex, were attempting to stuff their brains with an enormous mish-mash of misunderstood fragments from many branches of knowledge.

And I was in the soup.

"Sir — what are you going to do about it?" Vixi repeated.

"I'd love to know myself."

Putting aside the letter Ivana had given me that morning from the Ministry of Education, I looked at a tatty mimeographed sheet bearing the heading:

SOCIAL SCIENCE
Introduction
Social Welfare under Feudalism

When I had joined the staff in Hronov, my colleague Miss Rivnacova had turned the subject of Social Science over to me with obvious relief. Along with it I had inherited this dog-eared scrap of paper. I had tried in vain to determine, first from my predecessor, then from Ivana, next from the district inspector, and finally in a written inquiry to Prague, what — apart from the text on the mimeographed sheet — was supposed to be the proper subject matter of this new science. The ministry had introduced it in what had previously been called the Family School only that year, both to emphasize the socialist nature of the institute, and in the interests of making the curriculum scientific. It was an expression of the same tendency that had transformed Cooking, a subject taught by Evzenie Vikusova, into the Theory of Nutrition, also taught by Vikusova.

But I was in deep trouble. My subject appeared in none of the old curricula, under any other name, and because it was deemed one of the main instruments of "scientification" the ministry had set aside four hours a week for its instruction in the fourth year. To my query, they replied that the course outline and the textbooks would be provided "in due course".

They were not. Ever.

In the end I abandoned my quest to discover the substance of this important science and instead, for those four hours a week, taught the girls an old novel called *The Pimp* which, because of its highly social theme and the Party membership of its author, Egon Ervin Kisch, could perhaps have been construed to represent an aspect, at least, of social science. And now, three weeks before the ultimate test of our students' mental maturity, Prague had decided that final examinations would be conducted in the subject.

I sat with Vixi in my office pondering a letter in which the very same ministry that had never delivered the course outline and textbook demanded that I work out "sixty to seventy examination questions" and send "two copies to the Social Science Section of the Matriculation Department of the Ministry of Education for approval."

"A fine mess," said Vixi.

The hot June sun was streaming into the office, and I told her, rather sharply, to keep her smart remarks to herself and try to think of a way out of this instead. We both reread the succinct mimeographed introduction to the mysterious science in the hope that some kind of enlightenment might ensue.

> Under the feudal system, social welfare in the modern sense of the word was practically non-existent. Though it is true that the feudal lord was responsible for caring for those of his serfs whom age or sickness prevented from working, this "care" was limited to the occasional bestowing of miserable alms, or else it remained entirely on paper, because there was no practical way to ensure that anything was done.
>
> The only institutions even remotely resembling modern social welfare were the hospitals for the poor, run largely by the Church and particularly by several charitable monastic orders. This, of course, was merely a cloak beneath which the Church, the greatest exploiter of the Middle Ages, concealed the evil it committed at the expense of the working social classes, the serfs and the rural and urban poor.
>
> These hospitals had very primitive facilities; there was practically no hygiene, the sick were made to lie by the dozen in unventilated halls, and often the only care provided by the

uneducated and superstitious monks was the so-called "sacrament" of supreme unc—

(The next instalment of the textbook will follow within a week.)

And here the text, of which the Ministry of Education had delivered fifty copies, ended for ever.

"What can I do with this?" I sighed with a faint heart.

Vixi put on one of her implausible, eager-to-be-of-help expressions and, with a bright orange fingernail, began to count the lines.

"Twenty," she said. "And they want sixty questions from you. That means—twenty goes into sixty three times—for every three lines, one question. That's not so bad."

"Vixi," I said, "where were you when the Good Lord passed out the brains? You must have got that talent for chess by accident."

"You can forget about *that* talent," replied Vixi. "The Grand Master has mated me."

"That was fast. When he was here in Hronov it looked like a draw."

"Anyway, it was sheer luck I lasted as long as I did," said Vixi, and then came back to the mysteries of immediate concern to us. "Look, what's so awful about one question every three lines?"

"It's the other way around," I pointed out. "We have to make up *three* questions for every *one* line."

"Jeepers creepers! 'Under the feudal system, social welfare in the modern sense of the word was practically non-existent.' Three questions from that? Jiminy Cricket!"

"Well, how about this? Question number one: Did social welfare exist under the feudal system?" I looked inquisitively at Vixi and saw that she had already grasped the principle involved.

"Question number two," she said. "What kind of social welfare existed under the feudal system?"

My mind went blank. "How would you put the third question?" I asked.

The familiar perpendicular lines formed above Vixi's nose. After a moment she said brightly, "Theoretically, some form of social welfare existed under the feudal order. What was it like in reality?"

"That might do. But it needs a little more variety."

In five minutes we had the first three questions ready:

1) Did social welfare exist under the feudal order?
2) In what way did feudal society care for its welfare cases?
3) In theory there was a primitive system of social welfare in the Middle Ages. What in reality was the case?

I sent Vixi out for booze and we got down to work. With the aid of a bottle of house liquor from a nearby pub, the work soon became a game, and by midnight we had come up with sixty-seven completely different questions. One of the side effects of the alcohol was that we never tried to answer any of them.

The ministry approved the questions and we mimeographed them in Hronov and handed them out to the girls. With Ivana's permission, the windows of the dormitory shone into the darkness till midnight, two hours after the girls' normal bedtime; some of the lower-form students took advantage of the crisis to slip the sculptors from the school of stone-masonry past the backs of their matriculating schoolmates.

One evening, as Vixi and I were walking back from the pond, I peered through the window of Evzenie Vikusova's house and saw a group of her pale students intently discussing something with her, although there were no final exams in the Theory of Nutrition.

"It's obvious," whispered Vixi, standing beside me and looking through the tangled lilac bushes into the privacy of Evzenie's home. "They want to glut the examination board and they're working out a way to do it."

"Glut?"

"Like getting them drunk, only with food."

So that was it: a secret strategy based on the Theory of Nutrition. I began to look forward to the finals.

Just before the exams were scheduled to begin, Ivana called a meeting of the graduating class and pleaded with them all to wear their Youth Union shirts to the exams, both for the sake of the school's good name and in the interests of decent results. "It's not in the regulations, comrades," she said, "but it will make a favourable impression on the comrade chairman of the committee, and it will demonstrate the hundred per cent membership rate we have in the school."

We had the hundred per cent membership, all right, but only a maximum effort mustered the necessary number of Youth Union shirts. Finally, on Ivana's orders, students in the lower forms lent their shirts to the graduating class.

And so, on Monday morning, we took our places in the staff room — dressed in our Sunday best, I full of intimations of disaster. On the preceding day the lower-form girls, also on Ivana's orders, had provided the room with what were referred to as "decorations", so that it now appeared ready to host some kind of Marxist masquerade ball. On the same day Ivana had been to the hairdresser's (it was Sunday, but the hairdresser had a daughter in the graduating class) and now, instead of looking like a bulldog, as she usually did, she resembled an enormous poodle. The diminutive chairman of the examining committee was all but lost in her shadow. The chairman, a former teacher in a school for retarded children, had advanced to become the principal of a nursing school in Prague by becoming progressive at just the right moment. I sat at the very end of the table, beside Milada Maresova, who had also come wearing her Youth Union shirt.

The first student, Adamova, was summoned. She was as pale as Pierrot. She drew a piece of paper with her first question on it, fumbled, dropped it on the floor, recovered it, read it, then relaxed. Her exam turned out to be a decided success. She conversed in Russian about the life of Comrade Stalin; she analysed a poem by Michal Sedlon called "The Pig Feeder" and said that it held a dignified place in the great revolutionary visions of the Czech revolutionary poets of the nineteenth century, Svatopluk Cech and Jan Neruda. In Marxism her question was "What does the dialectic method consist in?" and she rattled off the appropriate passage from the textbook, including two typographical errors. Ivana seemed to swell with pride at such a clear example of intelligence, and Adamova reached for the final question. It was in social science.

With evident relief, she read it aloud to the committee: "Describe the nature of health care in medieval hospitals."

Then she took a deep breath and began. "Under the feudal system, social welfare in the modern sense of the word was practically non-existent. Though it is true that the feudal lord was responsible for caring for those of his serfs whom age or sickness prevented from working, this 'care' was limited to the occasional bestowing of miserable alms, or else it remained entirely on paper, because there was no practical way to ensure that anything was done. The only institutions even remotely resembling modern social welfare were the hospitals for the poor, run largely by the Church and particularly by several charitable monastic orders. This, of course, was merely a cloak beneath which the Church, the greatest exploiter of the Middle Ages, concealed the evil it committed at the expense of the working social classes, the serfs and the rural and urban poor. These hospitals had very primitive facilities; there was practically no hygiene — "

"I think that will be enough," said the chairman, interrupting her close to a rather critical moment. "What do you think, comrades?"

Following Ivana's lead, we all nodded in satisfaction, and the perspiring Adamova was sent out to allow us time to discuss her performance briefly. We did so, Adamova was summoned back and told that she had passed with honours, and she was released, flushing with delight.

When she had disappeared into the hallway, a brass gong sounded. Such an un-Marxist sound startled me. The door into the corridor, which had just closed behind Adamova, opened again, and into the staff room came a curious but fascinating mirage: Doruzkova, Chebenova, Zdarska, Pelantova, Sinkulova, Chocholousova, and Kotykova, objectively the seven most beautiful girls in fourth year, each in a blue Youth Union Shirt somewhat taut around the breasts (for the younger students from whom the shirts had been borrowed were less amply endowed). Upon those breasts, across a uniform that represented the correct world-view, each had pinned a feudalistic lace apron, the kind worn by chambermaids on stage. Each carried a silver tray laden with refreshments, and they entered in single file.

The plan Vixi had told me of was about to be executed.

The girls approached the table and then, as if they were about to put on a display of gymnastics, the odd numbers turned left and the even right, leaving the most beautiful of them all, Jarmilka Kotykova, standing directly in front of the former pedagogue of the mentally retarded. When each of the girls had taken up her position and turned to face her respective member of the committee (I had drawn Sinkulova, a baroque angel), they dropped an exemplary curtsy and set their trays on the table. Such a well-trained unit would have pleased the generalissimo, let alone the chairman of our committee, whom Ivana was quite openly watching. She was not disappointed.

"Oh! Oh!" he exclaimed.

The girls reversed their manoeuvres and filed out of the staff room, displaying enormous white bows of embroidered muslin that bobbed up and down on their very tight skirts.

I roused myself from my enchantment and looked at my tray. Beside a gigantic beaker of vermouth there was something with a powerful aroma served on a seashell. The chairman was already tasting his and exclaiming, "Oh! Oh!"

The exams had begun very promisingly.

They continued in the same vein. Barabasova was next in the sweat-box, and she was equally well prepared: she did well in Russian conversation (the life of Comrade Lenin), analysed a Czech poem (Jan Vrchcolab's "Vladimir Ilich's Night in Hronov"), and expounded on Marxism (the three sources, the three components). In social science her question was "Discuss the social function of the Catholic Church in the Middle Ages."

"Under the feudal system," she began, "social welfare in the modern sense of the word was practically non-existent. Though it is true that the feudal lord was responsible for caring for those of his serfs whom age or sickness prevented from working, this 'care' was limited to the occasional bestowing of miserable alms, or else it remained entirely on paper, because there was no practical way to ensure that anything was done. The only institutions even remotely resembling modern social welfare were the hospitals for the poor, run largely by the Church and particularly by several charitable monastic orders. This, of course, was merely a cloak beneath which the Church, the greatest exploiter of the Middle Ages, concealed the — "

"Wonderful, comrade," the chairman interrupted her. "I think that will be enough. What do you say, comrades?"

We quickly agreed, although Milada Maresova gave me a peculiar look. When the chairman told Barabasova that she had passed with honours, Milada opened her mouth to ask me something, but then changed her mind.

Cabova, who was next, got the question "Was there any way of guaranteeing social welfare under feudalism?"

"Under the feudal system," she replied, "social welfare in the modern sense of the word was practically non-existent. Though it is true that the feudal lord was responsible for caring for those of his serfs whom age or sickness prevented . . ." and the chairman stopped her after the line: "The only institutions even remotely resembling modern social welfare — "

Cermakova's question was: "How were the hospitals in medieval society financed?"

"Under the feudal system," she answered, "social welfare in the modern sense of the word was practically non-existent." The chairman cut her recital short as well; he too began to give me strange looks.

When Cihakova spoke on the theme "Duties of a social nature imposed upon the feudal lords by the social system" and began her reply with the words: "Under the feudal system, social welfare in the modern sense of the word was practically non-existent," the chairman listened to her for a long time, and didn't give her an A until after "often the only care provided by the uneducated and superstitious monks" —just when I was beginning to fear she might end with the words "The next instalment of the textbook will follow within a week."

But Cihakova left with her honours mark, and just as the chairman turned to me and was about to say something, in came the Seven with lunch, like a veritable *deus ex machina.* It was a princely affair: roast beef with a beautiful pyramid of dumplings drowned in a cream sauce that Vikusova had anointed with port. This was preceded by a cream soup with raisin-sized mini-dumplings, and followed by a sweet pastry buried under a mountain of whipped cream. When we had finished that we were confronted by a huge chocolate cake stuffed with a buttery filling and set in a base of pudding and custard. Either the chairman was a very hungry man or he was fond of eating (in the end it turned out that he was a notorious glutton), for he stuffed himself into such a state of drowsiness that when Cincibusova, given a question on hygiene in medieval hospitals, replied, "Under the feudal system, social welfare in the modern sense of the word was practically non-existent," and continued almost to the end of the mimeographed page, I had to utter the obligatory "I think that will be enough" myself, because the chairman displayed scarcely any signs of life and merely nodded agreement in a reflex action. On the other hand, the perilous state of fourth-year social science was not lost on Ivana. Whenever she looked at me uneasily, I pretended to be blowing my nose. As for Milada Maresova, by this time she was frowning. The next candidate, Drahokoupilova, drew the terse topic "Personnel in feudal hospitals" and replied in full right up to the phrase "beneath which the Church, the greatest exploiter of the Middle Ages," at which point Milada leaned over to me and said, "Comrade, this is outright sabotage of a very important subject."

The program for that day was eventually concluded by Ejemova's dissertation on the subject "The function of the monastic orders in the medieval system of social welfare". She began, "Under the feudal system, social welfare in the modern sense of the word was practically non-existent," and the chairman, who had been paralysed by an enormous supper — ragout, turkey with caviar stuffing, a three-layered Pischinger cake with rum-filled candy — said to me, "Comrade, I get the impression that in your subject the students are reproducing what they learned in a rather mechanical way, instead of developing the ideas themselves in their own words."

That evening, Ivana had me on the carpet.

"Good Lord, comrade, what on earth have you been teaching them?"

"I don't know. They all got different questions."

"Then why did they all parrot exactly the same answer? 'Under the feudal system social welfare in the modern sense of the word was practically non-existent. Though it is true that the feudal lord was responsible — ' and so on and so forth?" It was clear that Ivana had absorbed the entire essence of this new science as thoroughly as my students had, merely by listening. "Don't you see, comrade? It will bring us all into terrible disrepute. Tomorrow, if they all start off 'Under the feudal system — '"

Unfortunately I was pretty sure they would, and I came clean. I told Ivana all about the ill-conceived principle of making three questions out of one line.

"Why didn't you come to me about it sooner?" she wailed.

"I didn't want to bother you. Anyway, what could you have done about it?"

"I don't know. Something."

In the end she decided that I should call a meeting that night in the dormitory, and order the girls to at least stammer and hesitate when they replied.

The meeting was convened in the former dormitory chapel. Evzenie Vikusova, who from the outset had been seconded as head of diversionary tactics, also took part. After what had happened the first day, her strategic role was that much more crucial.

"We'll serve more wine," she decided, as soon as the meeting began.

"And we'll give the chairman a bigger glass," suggested the captain of the food-carriers, Kotykova.

"And Maresova too," said Chocholousova, and then, startled by her inadvertent lapse, corrected herself at once: "I mean *Comrade* Maresova."

"She doesn't drink. Unless — " and Vikusova thought for a moment, "unless we slip a little something into her lemonade. But the question is, what?"

"Sleeping pills?" suggested someone in the nervous crowd.

"Who'll test us in Russian if Maresova nods off, smarty?"

"Ivana!" cried Maleckova, one of the proletarian girls, from the back of the room.

"Girls! You mean 'The Principal'," Vikusova admonished them, out of sheer habit.

"But Comrade Principal speaks Russian like a Chinaman," said Maleckova.

"Just forget the whole idea," the cooking teacher decided. "Maresova will have to remain awake."

"I only hope she limits her attention to Russian," I interjected.

"Fat chance," said Maleckova.

Then Evzenie quickly outlined her original plan. "Perhaps we could do it this way. You girls can stand behind your respective members of the committee, and whenever their glasses are empty you can fill them up."

The assembly murmured with hope.

"That won't work," I said, dashing that hope. "Only the person being tested at the time is allowed in the room."

A hum of disappointment. Then Adamova asked to speak; class solidarity, rooted in the quite classless base of common terror, was still intact, so those who had already passed the exams had come to the meeting as well.

"Couldn't us girls who've finished stand and serve the wine? I think we'd all agree to that, wouldn't we, girls?"

The new graduates all nodded eagerly.

"It's worth a try," I said, "but I'm not sure the principal will approve."

"And we'll change the menu, too," said Vikusova. "We'd planned to serve roast chicken on bacon, but we'll cook something heavier. Capon à la Czernin, with mayonnaise sauce and truffle — "

"And for dessert those buns with nougat filling, the ones you wanted to save till Wednesday," piped up Bozena Stoklasova.

The girls were right in their element. From a pedestal where a statue of the Blessed Agnes of Bohemia had once stood, a government-issue bust of Stalin (made of papier-mâché and painted bronze) gazed down upon them. Beneath his whiskers was the familiar sinister grin, as though he were pleased by the materialistic approach taken by these Youth Union girls. Nevertheless, I decided to force them to consider an intellectual plan of action as well.

"It's my fault for not foreseeing the problem," I admitted, and I felt the girls accepting me into their jittery midst. "But we'll have to try and make the best of it. Maybe you can vary the way you begin your answers."

They stared at me like a clutch of terrified rabbits: thirty-five otherwise experienced young ladies for whom social science, quite rightly, meant nothing whatsoever.

"But how can we do that when we don't know anything except what's on that piece of paper?" cried Erazimova desperately. She was first in line the next morning. "How can we vary — "

"Look here," I said. "Social science is almost like Marxism. Let's take a concrete question," and I looked at my list. "For example, 'The limits of social welfare provided by the feudal lord to his serfs.' Whatever you do, for God's sake don't start: 'Under the feudal system social welfare in the modern sense of the word' and so on. And don't grind it out like a hurdy-gurdy. Say something like 'In order to define the limits of social welfare provided to the serfs by the feudal lord — ' and speak nice and slowly, and hesitate every once in a while — 'we must first clarify certain fundamental terms. For example, "feudal lord".' That's a term you know from Marxism, after all, so you can say the feudal system consisted of several different classes, and then you can compare it with the system of slavery, for instance, and then say something about the bourgeois revolution — you've learned that already too. I heard you rhyming it all off today at the crack of a whip."

The girls, in their perspiration-stained Union shirts, nodded enthusiastically. The second girl on the list next morning, Formanova, said, "That ought to work. Or we can go from the feudal lords to the gelds — the guilds? — anyway, about how the free cities give rise to the middle classes among the tradesmen and that kind of thing, can't we?"

I agreed. Vikusova, instinctively faithful to the principle of materialism, added, "And one more thing. Tomorrow morning, before we begin, we'll serve them glasses of vodka and Mr. Smiricky here, or perhaps the principal, can propose a toast. It would be best to propose it to Comrade Marshalissimo."

"Comrade Generalissimo," whispered Zemankova, the class climber, who was second-last in the alphabet and therefore condemned to a particularly long and painful wait.

"To Comrade Generalissimo. And when they've done that they can toast President Gottwald, and then — anyway, the principal will think of someone else. A glass of hard stuff on an empty stomach goes to the head quickly. And Jarmila," she said to the leader of the group — which called itself the Sextet, I discovered later, even though there were seven of them — "don't forget to pour the chairman a double."

Next morning, at a meeting before the chairman arrived, the proposal to create the post of wine-glass filler-uppers was vetoed by Milada Maresova. "The matriculation examinations are a celebration — " she said.

"That's just the point," Zdenka Prochazkova interrupted.

" — of reason," Milada went on, "and education. On the whole, it's appropriate that we serve refreshments, as a visible proof of the affluence socialism has brought us all." (In fact the food has been donated to us, quite outside the rationing system, by the director of the National Meat Enterprise — a former butcher by the name of Chocholous, father of one of the Sextet.) "But alcohol in large amounts is a throwback to the bourgeois era." Milada preached with such fervour that Ivana didn't have the courage to put the matter to a vote. But she was still warrior enough not to admit complete defeat, and she insisted on the morning toast. Her ideological justification for a glass of hard stuff on an empty stomach — that it was analogous to a libation to the gods of antiquity — was somewhat dubious, but because she substituted Comrade Stalin and the present leadership of the Party for those gods, her decision was unassailable.

A few minutes later, when the chairman arrived, Ivana stood up, raised her glass (they had poured the chairman a large gobletful of vodka), and spoke on the theme of J. V. Stalin with such passionate conviction that we had the distinct impression that Father Czech, the legendary national patriarch, had discovered the Vltava basin in the fifth century A.D. only thanks to the marshal's teachings.

Erazimova came forward, rattled off a flawless definition of exploitation, conversed in Russian about the Great Patriotic War, analysed with ease the poem "One Hundred and Ten Per Cent Joy" by S. K. Neumann, Jr., and in social science drew the following question: "Examine the real meaning of the charitable activity of the medieval Church." She swallowed and, clearly battling a conditioned reflex, began rather hesitantly. "First we shall have — ah — have to clarify our terms. For instance — ah — the Middle Ages. Mmmm — the Middle Ages — ah — ended when America was discovered by the Genoan — ah — the Genoan merchant Christopher Columbus." She swallowed again, then continued. "America — ah — is a state," and she hesitated again, conscientiously, "where even today, ah, there still exists — hmmm — exploitation." She looked helplessly at the committee, and her pleading eyes fell on me. I had to help, but I could think of nothing to say.

"Correct, comrade. You said 'exploitation'," and I thought furiously, then said, "Could you — ah — develop that idea somewhat?"

Inspiration gleamed in Erazimova's eyes. "When we speak of exploitation," she cried, and she began to recite like a gramophone record, "we do not mean it from the moral but from the economic point of view. Exploitation consists in the capitalist's appropriating a portion of the surplus value created by the workers," she recited, and I was helplessly aware that she was repeating word for word the memorized text she had already parroted less than half an hour before, in her reply to the question on Marxism.

Unfortunately the chairman noticed this too. The early-morning drop of the hard stuff had evidently sharpened his faculties, and he interrupted her in a rather unpleasant tone of voice. "Yes, we know that. You've said that already. But the question is about the real meaning of the charitable activity of the medieval Church. Keep to the point."

Vikusova, who on her own initiative was sitting at the far end of the table, stood up, causing an interruption. The chairman looked around at her, rather annoyed, but she merely flashed her gold dentures at him and vanished from the room.

Once again I met my student's desperate eyes. "Come on now, Erazimova," I said feebly. "Just relax, now. The question is clear enough. Was the — ah — shall we say, the assistance to the sick the real point of the health services provided by the exploitative feudal Church?"

Erazimova shook her head, swallowed, and wiped her forehead with the palm of her hand. Large, dark circles began to appear under the arms of her blue shirt.

"No, it wasn't," she whispered, and then swallowed again. "It wasn't because — "

Silence.

"Well?" said the chairman.

Erazimova looked at him and turned into a rabbit staring at a python. "Because," she swallowed, "under . . . under the feudal system . . . social welfare in the modern sense of the word . . . was practically non-existent. Though it is true," she swallowed again, then went on with growing confidence, "that the feudal lord was responsible for looking after those of his serfs whom age or sickness prevented from working — " The chairman slowly began to raise his hand; Erazimova noticed this and began to accelerate. " — this quote unquote care was limited to the occasional bestowing of miserable alms or else it remained," and the chairman's hand had reached its zenith and had begun to shake in the familiar sign that meant "*Hold it!*" — "on paperbecausetherewas," the frantic Erazimova poured out the text in a high-pitched voice, "nopracticalwaytoENSURETHAT — " and the gong went off, the door flew open, and the Sextet entered with a great flourish, their outfits enhanced this time by starched white capes. Through the doorway I could see Vikusova straightening the bow that hung down over the bottom of the sexual angel Kotykova, but by this time Doruzkova, at the head of the line, was gently nudging aside the stupefied Erazimova and making a right turn. A teapot materialized in front of each of us, along with a hypertrophied cake made of some marzipan-like substance of yellowish hue and crowned with a marzipan star. Unfortunately it had six points but, mercifully, Milada Maresova failed to notice.

"Comrade Chairman," said Ivana with a cheerful smile, while with a hand she thought was hidden from his view she shooed Erazimova out of the room, "today our students have prepared a little surprise for you. Comrade Maleckova's father has just come back from a construction job in the Mongolian People's Republic and he's brought some genuine jasmine tea with him."

"Oh! Oh!" exclaimed the chairman, lifting the lid of the teapot and inhaling deeply. "Oh! Oh!"

We drank the tea, which smelled of a perfume shop, and in the conversation that followed, Erazimova's performance was classified as rating an A-minus.

Perhaps the chairman was allergic to jasmine tea. Up to this point he had been taciturn and had intervened in the machinery of matriculation only sparingly. After drinking the tea, however, he came to life in a very odd way. Formanova's turn was next, and although she was a Jew and the oft-promoted pedagogue of retarded children had recently published an article in the *Teacher's Gazette* attacking Zionism as an instrument of American reaction, she aroused the most lively interest in those formerly rather dull eyes. No sooner had she begun to recite her answer to the question in Marxism with what was now the expected proficiency (I was astonished at how diligent these girls were) — "Historical materialism teaches us that the decisive motive force in society is not ideas but contradictions" — than the chairman became expansive. "Marvellous! Wonderful!" He turned to Ivana. "It's been ages since I've seen such well-prepared students, comrade! Historical materialism teaches us! Isn't that delightful! Such political awareness in girls so young! I'm astonished!"

My first thought — and Ivana's too, for she was blushing — was that the chairman was being sarcastic about the obvious, mindless rote learning on display. But the teacher's euphoric frenzy went on for about five minutes before he finally calmed down and invited Milada to test Formanova in Russian. They talked about Gorky, and the chairman was possessed by a fresh fit of enthusiasm. For another five minutes, or perhaps it was ten, he exclaimed on Gorky in loud, clichéed superlatives, and during the test in Czech Formanova was scarcely able to utter the words "*Anna the Proletarian* is a novel by Ivan Olbracht that cap — " before the chairman began to recount a long, confused story about the trials and tribulations of a shoemaker in the Bata concern. "What was the fate of the serfs whom sickness or old age prevented from working?" Formanova, exactly according to plan, led off, "First we have to clarify certain concepts. For instance, 'fate' — I mean 'serf'," and the chairman clapped and behaved like the judge in *The Club of Queer Trades*. "Magnificent! Wonderful! First we have to clarify certain concepts! Under the feudal system social welfare in the modern sense of the word was practically non-existent. Though it is true that the feudal lord was responsible for caring for. . . ."

"There's nothing to worry about," Gellen assured me. "The only thing is that you get a bit of a hangover afterwards. It is addictive, but a week is too short a time to get the habit. As a, shall we say a euphoric, it works pretty reliably. Did he carry on a lot?"

"By the end he was doing almost all the talking. The girls just sat there quietly, and we simply handed out the marks."

"Jarmila told me," laughed Gellen, and from his cabinet he pulled out a bottle of whisky. "Shall we have a little of our own euphoric?"

Whisky was one of the reasons why I'd taken to keeping Dr. Gellen company during his night shifts. I also felt at home in his company.

"I have to thank you. If it hadn't been for the euphoric, I'd have been in deep shit."

"Thank Jarmilka. It was her idea."

"I didn't know she knew anything about drugs."

"She doesn't. She just wanted 'some pill that would make him forget who he was' — those were her very words. So I picked out the best I could for her."

He handed me a whisky and we touched glasses.

"Death to the Communist Party of Czechoslovakia!" said Dr. Gellen, imitating the hollow enthusiasm with which exhortations for long life were usually pronounced. "Death to the Great Stalin!"

I said nothing. There were too many wires in the walls. Instead of responding to his toast, I asked, "How long have you known Jarmilka?"

Gellen grinned wryly at me. "I performed an appendectomy on her last fall. I tell you, my friend, slicing into that snow-white belly seemed like sacrilege."

I wanted to dwell on the theme of Jarmila's snow-white belly, but the nurse rang; there was someone in emergency. I accompanied Dr. Gellen down to the first floor. A slim, pretty young woman in white stockings and a permanent wave got up from the benches against the wall. Beside her on the floor was a basket from which hung the familiar limp head and neck of a well-fed and expertly slaughtered goose. The neck of a bottle was also visible.

"Good evening, Doctor Gellen. I just came to show you — "

"Ah, it's you!" Gellen exclaimed delightedly, and the young woman turned scarlet. "So, let's have a look at you." He took her by the chin and turned her head from side to side.

"You can hardly see it at all," she murmured happily into his hand. "I brought you a goose, and a drop of slivovice." Gellen was still holding her chin and mumbling with satisfaction. "Lojza's so relieved, Dr. Gellen, and I expect you're glad too that it healed so good."

"Like the nose of a newborn babe," said Dr. Gellen, letting go of her chin. "Next time your husband is splitting wood, tell him to keep his eyes on the job."

The young woman blushed again. "If it weren't for you, doctor, my life would have been ruined."

I looked at her nose. Around its tender little tip there was the scarcely visible pink thread of a scar. It rather suited her, a subtle distinguishing mark on the simple, attractive rural face. Your life won't be ruined, my dear, I thought, but the good doctor may complicate it a little. And I felt slightly envious that my friend didn't even have to leave the hospital for, as he put it, his pussy. I walked out into the warm June night, suspecting nothing of what awaited me the following day.

It began promisingly, suffused with the blissful sensation that my students and I were saved. To be on the safe side they had plied the chairman with the euphoric tea at breakfast, and now he stood on the station platform assuring Ivana over and over again that these final exams had been the most wonderful in his life. He also promised to arrange to chair the examination board at our school the next year. I didn't care, because by that time I would be in uniform.

The train connecting Hronov with the nearest district towns was only half an hour late, but it nearly left without the chairman. He was so wrapped up in what he was saying that Ivana had to lift him up onto the step and hold him on the platform, to keep him from falling out of the car. We stood there in a row and waved, false smiles on our faces and profound joy in our hearts. When the train went around the bend at the semaphore, the chairman leaned far out over the railing and sent Ivana a long kiss. Then he vanished.

We looked at each other and Ivana said, "Well — that takes care of the finals!"

Just then someone behind us said aloofly, "Honour to work, comrades!"

I froze, then turned around. There on the platform stood Jarda Bukavec with two other men, one older and the other younger. The older man had immoderately wide trousers and wore a menacing, shapeless hat on his head. His face was pinched and cold-looking.

"Grand Master Sergei Alexeyevich Petrofim, chess champion of the Soviet Union," said Bukavec, by way of introducing the sinister-looking man. "And this," he said, indicating the younger man, "is Comrade Lukac, the Deputy Minister of Education."

And so we held one more extraordinary meeting at the conclusion of that agitated school year. The deputy minister, Lukac, as cold as an Arctic char, sat beside Ivana, and in the place of honour opposite the principal sat Petrofim, his dark blue wide-brimmed hat on the table in front of him as a mark of rank and distinction.

"Perhaps we ought to, indeed we should, take into account," Ivana began in her maudlin voice, getting ready to deliver her usual Marxist-Makarenkovist arguments, "the fact that Comrade Koziskova is still young and unreasonable, and that she's an excellent — or at least pretty good — student. If the collective were to influence her in a positive — "

Petrofim raised his hand like a metropolitan of the Orthodox Church and mumbled a long and angry speech. No one could understand what he was saying except the deputy minister, who had obviously been well trained.

"The Comrade Grand Master points out — quite correctly — that if it only concerned him, he would simply dismiss the whole matter. But in this case, through his person, the entire Soviet Union has been crudely and profoundly insulted."

"On one hand, the Comrade Grand Master is of course right," Ivana began her rebuttal. "But on the other hand — "

The deputy minister, however, was unmoved by the arguments of Makarenko. "Look here, comrade — this whole matter is a clear case of arrogance crying out for punishment. Worse yet — if I'm not mistaken, it has all the earmarks of a carefully planned act of provocation. What is the comrade's family background?"

"She's an orphan!" Ivana replied quickly. "Her mother died in childbirth and no one knows who her father is. You know, comrade," and Ivana lowered her voice and paused deliberately before uttering the most favourable aspect of Vixi's political profile, "she's an illegitimate child. She lives with her grandfather; he's a small farmer with a holding of five and two-tenths hectares."

"And one of the bitterest opponents of collectivization in all of Maselna Lhota," said Milada Maresova harshly.

"You see? It's just as I thought," said Lukac, his voice hardening. "She comes from a reactionary environment! It's obvious that she was trying to provoke an incident by deliberately insulting the Soviet Union in the person of the Comrade Grand Master. She can't be allowed to continue her studies. Call her in at once!"

To gain time, Ivana now resorted to a lie: she said they would have to bring the girl in from Maselna Lhota, since she'd already left to spend the weekend with her grandfather. That wasn't true, and I knew that Ivana knew it wasn't. I also knew that for the two hours before the tribunal met again, Ivana would be in the girls' dormitory rehearsing Vixi in her role as penitent.

Before she left, Ivana also tactically divided the enemy. She entrusted Milada with the job of giving the special guests a tour of Hronov, and she ordered me to pacify Bukavec.

I dragged Bukavec off to the Municipal Restaurant. I soon realized, though, that, unlike Petrofim, Bukavec was not especially upset.

"The whole thing's really pretty funny," he said. "But you've got to understand Sergei's way of looking at it. I'd never beaten him — just squeezed a draw out of him a couple of times. Until now. And since he can't take it out on me, he wants to take a bite out of the kid. He can't stand losing. Most Russians can't."

"Shouldn't you be sticking up for Vixi? I mean, if it weren't for her, you'd never have beaten him."

"Out of the question, man. Petrofim often goes around for drinks with Comrade Stalin. It's not a good idea to get on his wrong side. Confidentially," and he took a typical look over his shoulder and then, just as typically, leaned close to me over the table, "Borisov could have been champion for sure, but he's a Jew and Comrade Stalin will never invite *him* for drinks. You know how it is — sometimes it's better to make a bum move on the board than in real life, right?" He sat back in his chair. He seemed to have matured politically since our last encounter under the moon. Then, in a normal voice, he said, "But I tell you, man, the whole thing's a riot!"

One day, Bukavec explained, Petrofim — who was actually a cousin of Bukavec's wife — had shown up unannounced at his house in Dejvice, saying he'd come to Prague on a whim. He'd heard how beautiful the city was — that is, he'd been to Prague four times, but always just for a tournament, and this time, he said, he wanted to see the city as an ordinary tourist. So Bukavec spent three days taking him around to see the beauties of the capital. But his in-law seemed abstracted, inattentive, and altogether too incurious for a simple tourist. Petrofim couldn't even work up any plausible enthusiasm for the Bethlehem Chapel, reconstructed — mainly to attract tourists — on a spot where it was thought the great Jan Hus might once have preached.

Bukavec began to suspect that there was a woman behind Petrofim's trip to Prague, and so on the fourth day he invited him to The Golden Well, an outdoor restaurant on the castle hill overlooking Prague, where they could enjoy the beauties of the ancient city over a bottle of wine. As they were drinking, Petrofim asked with studied casualness, "Jaroslav Karlovich, have you ever heard of a town called Hronov?" "I have," replied Jaroslav Karlovich, with a jolt of alarm. "It's in north-west Bohemia, near the Polish border. Why?" "I was just wondering. I hear they have a wonderful old town hall." Petrofim abruptly changed the subject: "What's that strange spire over there?" and "That green roof, is it baroque?" and then, again casually, he asked what the train connections were like. "To where?" "To Hronov." "I don't know." Bukavec's suspicion that the Grand Master had a mistress in Prague yielded to a suspicion that was, to his taste, even more tantalizing. "I've only gone there by car." "So you know Hronov, Jaroslav Karlovich?" "Pretty well. I played a simultaneous match there not too long ago."

Petrofim asked about two towers and the building that housed the Ministry of Pensions, and then said, "How was it? Interesting?" "How was what?" "The simultaneous match — do they have any talented local players?" The tantalizing suspicion became a certainty, and Jaroslav Karlovich looked his distant in-law straight in the eye. "As a matter of fact, they do. There's a child prodigy in Hronov. Actually, she's not a child, strictly speaking; she's seventeen. But she came within a hair of beating me, Sergei Alexeyevich." "In the simultaneous match?" asked Sergei Alexeyevich innocently. Bukavec tried to fix the Soviet Grand Master's eyes with his, but Petrofim kept looking away. "No," said Jaroslav Karlovich, "she was too nervous. I played a match with her by mail. Her name is Vlasta Koziskova."

And that was how the international Moscow-Hronov-Prague chess triangle collapsed. I'd known all along that Vixi was full of surprises.

Ivana put Vixi in a nylon blouse and presented her to the deputy minister in the manner of someone introducing Mary Magdalene. The grand masters did not attend the tribunal; only Lukac and the teaching staff were present. Except for Milada Maresova; she was so enthralled by the chance to spend some time with a distinguished Soviet guest that she was willing to forgo the opportunity to watch the destruction of one of the class enemy. She took both chess masters to a roadhouse in "Rock City", the rock formations outside Hronov.

The deputy minister proved quite capable of handling things on his own. He was public prosecutor and judge wrapped up in one, and presented his case in a speech magnificently prefabricated from the most highly approved phrases of the time. The son of a small factory-owner and therefore a working man, he had moreover demonstrated his loyalty by following little Pavlik Morozov's example. In his introductory remarks he dissected Vixi's crime in all its abysmal abhorrence; then he went on to outline the still more abhorrent punishments that dangle over almost everyone's head in a socialist society; and he ended by praising the great mercy of the Party and the working people, who allow every citizen, though he deserve only death, the chance of salvation.

"You will go to work for two or three years on one of the great labours of socialist construction, comrade," he said, pronouncing the sentence, "and if, through honest work, you demonstrate a change in attitude, the Party will allow you to complete your studies."

He was finished. The silence that now reigned was filled with inexpressible thoughts.

At last Ivana spoke up. "Well, Vlasta darling, have you anything to say?"

Vixi had wept bitterly and sincerely (though not in repentance) while listening to the statesman's speech. Now she raised a red nose to the deputy minister and sobbed, "Comrade Deputy, I beg of you! I promise I'll never do it again!"

This formulation, also prefabricated and classic, merely moved the deputy minister to another cliché, this time from the realm of folk wisdom: "It's no use locking the stable door after the horse has bolted, comrade. You should have thought of that sooner."

"Comrade," said Ivana, moving cautiously onto the counterattack, "Comrade Koziskova has only one year left before she graduates. I think that if she made a pledge — " But the factory-owner's son held out his hand like Caesar in the Colosseum.

"The horse has already bolted," he repeated. "If this were just some local act of delinquency, or something that concerned our own people's democratic republic, well then, of course, we could simply dismiss it and that would be that. But this concerns the Soviet Union! The land of the Great October Revolution, comrades! Please bear that in mind!"

He swept the staff room with a threatening glance, as if daring anyone to dissent. For some reason, high-ranking comrades all did this whenever they talked about the cradle of Communism.

"I agree with you completely, comrade," Ivana began again, bouncing like a ping-pong ball off the apparently all-consuming vision of Vixi's crime. "Of course — " But suddenly, and quite unexpectedly, Zdena Prochazkova broke in, and her voice betrayed feelings smouldering within her which, were they to erupt, would probably cause the deputy minister to flee from the staff room under a hail of fire.

"I still don't understand, comrade! Would you please explain exactly how Koziskova insulted the Soviet Union? Just because Bukavec checkmated Petrofim?"

"Zdena — please, don't bring that up now," groaned Ivana.

"How? Could you please explain that to me, comrade?"

The deputy minister glowered at her and Ivana clasped her hand to her heart.

"I believe I've explained it already."

"Then I'm probably stupid, but I didn't understand."

"I'll explain it to you later, Zdenicka!" said Ivana, growing desperate.

"I want to hear it now! And I want to hear it from the comrade deputy minister!"

Lukac sighed. "It's all so obvious, comrade. Koziskova committed fraud with the intent of ridiculing the Grand Master of the Soviet Union. And a Grand Master of the Soviet Union represents the Soviet Union."

"In chess," said Zdena. "An ordinary, stupid game, and moreover it's a leftover from feudalism," she said — the line I would quote much later, without indicating my source, in my operetta *A Game with Emilka.*

The deputy minister was horrified. "You are talking about a game, comrade," he shouted, "that Lenin himself enjoyed playing."

"Koziskova wasn't playing with Lenin!"

"Zdenicka, please, I know this matter has got us all upset!" pleaded Ivana. "But we have to keep a cool head — "

Vixi began to howl.

"And anyway," said Zdena, unmoved by the general fear and confusion in the air, "it was Comrade Bukavec who defeated Petrofim. So if anyone insulted the Soviet Union, it was Bukavec."

"That's where you're wrong, comrade!" roared the factory-owner's son. "The Soviet Union was not insulted because someone defeated Comrade Petrofim in chess, but because that victory was attained by fraudulent means, with the clear intention of ridiculing Comrade Grand Master Petrofim!"

"That's not true!" wailed Vixi. "I didn't try to ridicule anyone. I only thought it would be a — a good joke!" and she burst out crying again.

"A joke? A fine joke! This little joke of yours, comrade, involved the Soviet Union. And that's where the fun stops!" said the deputy minister. Then he realized that this might be taken the wrong way, and added, "The Soviet Union is sacred to all progressive people the world over."

"You're absolutely right, comrade! But — " Ivana was trying again to put matters right, but Zdena Prochazkova interrupted, "Does that mean no one is allowed to defeat the Soviet Union? Even in chess?"

"Of course they can!" shrieked Ivana. "But on the other hand — "

But the factory-owner's son outshouted them all. "*If* — " he roared, so loudly that even the howling Vixi fell silent, "*if* Comrade Bukavec were to defeat the Comrade Grand Master Petrofim in a proper, public match — even though something like that is *extremely* unlikely — *then* the Soviet comrades, I am sure, would swallow their pride and accept it in a sporting spirit! But this match, comrades, was a *hoax*, the intention of which was to *ridic* — "

"Why are you calling it a hoax?" shrieked Zdena. She did not have the deputy minister's capacity to harangue, but her voice suddenly had an edge to it that I'd never noticed before. "They played according to the rules, didn't they? The only difference was that Bukavec wasn't afraid because he didn't know he was playing Petrofim. And when fear was no longer a factor, the better man won."

"You can't construe it that way, Zdenicka!" Ivana's hand was now firmly clutched to her heart.

"Why not? Let me ask you this: would there be any hue and cry if Petrofim had beaten Bukavec, and not the other way around?"

For a moment that silenced everyone. With a single blow below the belt, Zdena seemed to have kayoed the advocate of correct opinions. But he wasn't going to let himself be counted out — not yet.

"Naturally there wouldn't be, because then it would be our own domestic affair and — "

"Why domestic? Petrofim is a Russkie, isn't he?"

"Comrade!"

"I mean a Russian."

"In — in that case," stammered the deputy minister, "there would be no — ah — attempt at intentional ridicule of the Soviet Union in the person of — "

"Nonsense!" said the phys-ed teacher resolutely, and then, with iron logic, she added, "How can you know that? The most you could say in that case would be that the attempt failed."

But her logic alarmed me, and sure enough, the factory-owner's son, steeled more than others in the class struggle because he had to work harder than those of more lowly birth to defend the position he had won, immediately jumped on the potentially false syllogism. "There, you see? You see, comrade? You're admitting that there was such an intention here. And unfortunately, it succeeded!"

"Now just a minute! You'd have to prove that such an intention was there."

But the deputy minister knew his Vishinsky. "The girl has confessed as much! She herself called it a joke!"

"But I didn't mean it that waaaaaay!" wailed Vixi.

"A joke about the Soviet Union? Comrade? About the country that liberated us in a bloody, four-year war against Fascism in which untold millions of her best sons fell — "

"They didn't fight that war on account of us!" Zdena yelled. I felt another stab of alarm, stronger this time. My friend was flushed and utterly beside herself. She had gone too far this time. An awful silence fell over the room. Even the principal's usual ability to bounce back seemed to have failed her.

The deputy minister said, almost in a whisper, "How did you mean that, comrade?"

"Exactly the way I said it. The Russians didn't go to war because of us. They only entered the war when Hitler invaded them. Before that, they had a pact with him. They didn't start fighting Fascism until it began to burn them directly, if you want to know the truth!"

Zdena's excitement had reached a hysterical pitch. It occurred to me that Comrade Prochazka might no longer have to conspire to have his wife transferred across the Atlantic to be rid of her. The stunned silence persisted and became sepulchral. Ivana was gasping for breath, and the hand which she still held pressed to the region of her heart was, I suspected, no longer there for purely theatrical reasons.

Zdena suddenly heard the silence, like a cold wind from the grave, but I don't suppose she cared any more. "We're always carrying on about liberation," she said, calmly now but with great disdain. "The big powers always get into each other's hair, dragging anyone they feel like along with them whether they want it or not, and then they expect us to thank them for it afterwards. And they call it liberation. Well, you can take that liberation and stuff it."

"Co-comrade!" stammered the deputy minister. He was perspiring now and ran a finger around the inside of his collar. "You're speaking — you're speaking about the Soviet Union! And loyalty to the Soviet Union is the hallmark of every citizen in the People's Democratic — "

"But comrade, Comrade Prochazkova *loves* the Soviet Union!" Ivana, by some miraculous effort of will, had mobilized the remnants of her strength. "I can vouch for that myself! She trained our students to do Russian folk dances! For the anniversary of the Great October Revolution! It's a pity you couldn't see how magnificent it was, comrade."

She looked around imploringly for help. Evzenie Vikusova alertly picked up her signal and said bravely, "That's true, Comrade Deputy Minister. And Koziskova here danced a solo," and she flashed a toothy golden smile, but with little effect. "She was wonderful. You'd have loved her!"

She meant well, but her mention of Vixi reminded the deputy minister of the original, if now not the most serious, crime that he'd uncovered at the Social School. He gritted his teeth so tightly that the veins stood out on his temples, then said coldly, "Well, I don't really think there's anything else I can say. After what I've heard here today, I see no other possibility than to report this whole matter to the Comrade Minister himself."

He stood up, pressed his ministerial briefcase to his chest, and by mistake walked through the door leading into the principal's office.

Ivana saw her chance at once, and pushed him back inside with her stomach just as he recognized his error and was turning around.

On their afternoon outing into Rock City, Milada Maresova showed the chess masters the chapel where the Secret Police had discovered another deliberate hoax not long before. Petrofim and Bukavec had their picture taken with the miraculous statue and Milada later gave us a copy as a souvenir; the grand masters were standing on either side of the statue with their hands clasped as if in prayer, like actors in some amateur farce.

I managed to have a few private words with Bukavec during supper, when we both went to the toilet together. I asked him whether he couldn't get Petrofim to change his mind. He refused even to try. He was afraid of his mustachioed god, and could therefore resist any temptation to annoy his prophet.

"Anyway, man, it's completely out of the question now. The deputy minister said one of your teachers insulted the Red Army soldiers who fell in battle, and I mean, seriously, that's going a little too far."

I was annoyed; I hadn't expected an old schoolmate to talk like a politician, especially in a pissoir. It must have been obvious to him by now why I was so interested in Vixi's fate.

Ivana and Maresova took the deputy minister and the grand masters to the station. Through Vikusova, Ivana had asked Zdena and Vixi to wait for her that evening in her office, so I said goodbye to them both in front of the school and walked slowly through the town, past the church, and through the lilac bower to the little chapel.

The new priest was tacking something to the glassed-in parish notice board. From an upper window in the rectory a striking woman in curlers was leaning out; she was the cook the new priest had brought with him. I looked back at the notice board and saw CATHOLIC CLERGY PEACE INITIATIVE shining out in big red letters. I realized that not only would Vixi not finish Social School, she would not even finish her instructions in the catechism.

Later I learned that for some time after the arrival of the peace-loving priest, the most stubborn of the old women of Hronov were taken every Sunday in a haywagon by the pious old farmer Sochora to the nearby spa of Belous. There, by a spring of mineral water that had miraculously cured the Princess von Schaumberg and Lippe of infertility, Holy Communion was served by the eighty-five-year-old retired Dean Rambousek. Eventually, however, Sochora was arrested for conspiring against the republic, Dean Rambousek was retired to a concentration camp for priests, and the pious old ladies were scattered to the winds.

Once more I sat on the bench outside the little white chapel, waiting for my two friends to show up, and in my mind I said farewell to Hronov. That day I had received an unexpected letter from the district army command, inviting me to appear without delay for induction into military service. This was several months earlier than normal; as the letter explained, there was an extraordinary summer draft this year. My first reaction to this sudden loss of freedom was rage — I even considered demanding a deferral — but the wave of anger soon subsided. Freedom was just an illusion anyway.

Hronov, that sweet-smelling garden of light and trees, twinkled below me as if in response to the luminous messages of the stars above. The phosphorescent town below me was teeming with young people, such people as are often driven mad by the injustices of the world — but only for a brief time. And I was young too, and I thought little of the future. I was quick to catch fire and quick to cool off. I was beginning to forget the priest who had so recently vanished without a trace. Were it not for the progressive cleric who was uglifying his church with that quisling manifesto, I might not have wasted a single thought on that carver of statues.

I wondered what the new pastor would do with those half-finished figures. Would he complete Saint John to please the nursing sisters in the hospital? He didn't look like a wood-carver. Much later, I learned from my former students that he filled the churches of his large parish with ugly plaster saints mass-produced by a branch of the collective farm in Svinna Lhota. Eventually he was arrested and sent to jail; it turned out he'd been selling the ancient statues from the old churches to an Italian Communist businessman, and replacing them with the conveyor-belt saints.

For a long time, and with no great difficulty, I would even forget the girl who was now walking through the lilac bower below me, arm in arm with the phys-ed teacher. First there would be Janinka, the wife of my commanding officer in the Third Tank Battalion, then a singer, Venus Paroubkova, then Ludmila Neumannova-Hertlova, called Lizetka, then. . . . As for the phys-ed teacher, I forgot about her almost as soon as she was out of sight.

"How can I face my grandad?" wailed the forgettable girl sitting on the bench between me and the phys-ed teacher. "He'll give me an awful thrashing."

She burst out crying, and the sound of her sobbing carried across the town through the quiet night under the stars with their promise of bliss, and she was crying over more than the thrashing she anticipated. But the world, the old whore, did not hear her.

"What happened in Ivana's office?" I asked Zdena over Vixi's head.

"We're all going our separate ways, Mowgli. You to the army, Vlasta to a work brigade, and I — "

"You — ?"

"Ivana kept at him until he promised not to report it to the minister. About me running off at the mouth about the Soviet Union, I mean. But she had to promise to discuss my case at the district level."

"What will they do to you?"

"You know Ivana — she'll pull something out of a hat. At worst I'll have to teach in a one-room school somewhere in the border regions."

"Poor Prochazkova!" I sighed. "You turn your nose up at Cicero, Illinois, and you end up teaching children their ABCs in some God-forsaken hole in the mountains."

In the philosophic tradition of people in all tyrannies, Zdena replied, "It's better than making mailbags. But now Ivana and I have got to work something out for Vlasta. We can't let her go to Ostrava and be raped by some goddamned Commie foreman."

Vixi began sobbing with renewed vigour.

In the end things didn't turn out too badly for Vixi. Her grandad did give her a thrashing, as expected, but the good Dr. Gellen wrote her a medical certificate saying she was allergic to industrial ash, and then found her a place as a nursing assistant in the district town of Zeleny Hradec. Also as expected, Zdena's big-shot husband used her fall as an excuse for a politically justified divorce and then married a comrade from Prague who was twenty years his junior. Zdena taught for about two years in the Eagle Mountains and then one day, while skiing, she broke both her legs, and because the Rescue Service found her too late they had to amputate them. I myself survived a load of trouble in the army when, to endear myself to Venus Paroubkova, I wrote an insulting swing arrangement of "The Marshal Budenny Song" for the Third Tank Battalion orchestra, which outdid Benny Goodman on that occasion but was afterwards disbanded. I survived other scandals as well, and once I was out of the army I began a successful career writing operettas. After several more defeats, Bukavec finally checkmated Petrofim at an international tournament in Moscow, shortly after the generalissimo died; it was the height of his chess career. And on August 21, 1968, Ivana locked herself in her office at the Social School and hanged herself with a piece of clothesline.

11

■

A Confusion of Tongues

I.

Vohnout had not seized my treasonous novel, nor had he rumbled up to the publishing house atop the first tank. For reasons that no one understood, he had kept well out of sight. As soon as it was clear that the Red Army had no specific instructions for dealing with the conquered publishing house, Foglar once more occupied the editor-in-chief's office, and now Paternoster and I were sitting there with him while Foglar, over a bottle of slivovice, attempted to reassure us.

"No, boys. Kocour finished Vohnout's career once and for all. Vohnout's got himself a job in wholesale book distributing and he wants to stay well clear of things from now on."

As the house tactician Foglar had been notorious for his misjudgements, which were founded on an embarrassingly indestructible optimism. The invasion hadn't changed him a bit.

"Still, I'll take my manuscript back," I said. "You say you can't publish it now anyway."

"That's right. You take the piss out of the army a bit too much, and they're a little sensitive about that just now, especially since they didn't fire a shot this time."

Within the publishing house, the only immediate consequence of the occupation by Soviet armed might was the disappearance of all the felt-tipped pens, and a sudden depletion of letter paper (the Red Army soldiers used it in the toilet for hygienic purposes, and then discarded the sheets into large cartons they had brought into the cubicles from the storeroom). As well, the illustrations to my novel — the potato-faced officers rendered by Brabanec, the author of *Alice in Penisland* — vanished, although all the other illustrations survived untouched. The author of science fiction, who couldn't have been more unlike Foglar the optimist, concluded that the KGB now had the drawings and intended to use them as documentary evidence of the treacherous counter-revolution in Czechoslovakia.

Foglar disagreed. "No, boys," he said, lowering his voice as if to deliver a prophecy, "nothing will happen." I thought the hidden microphones would pick his words up anyway, and decided that from now on I wouldn't say anything, not even something apparently irreproachable. "They're not as strong or united as they seem. It's only a matter of time before a Soviet Dubcek appears."

"Are you talking centuries or millennia?" remarked Paternoster, and Foglar — like all optimists, utterly lacking in irony — said gravely, "I give them four or five years, maximum. Look at this!"

He opened a drawer in his desk, devoutly pulled out a piece of lined paper, and spread it out in front of us. It contained something written in heavy-handed Cyrillic script:

> Forgive us, dear comrades! It is not our fault. But we have to obey orders, or el. . . .

"You know where I found this? Here on my desk, under the glass. Under a snapshot of my wife!"

"Aha," I said. Unlike Foglar, I attached no vital significance to this attempt to communicate across the deadly barriers of military discipline.

"Someone interrupted him before he could finish, do you see?" said the editor-in-chief, pointing to the uncompleted word. "Isn't it touching? It was probably some big-eared soldier with his head shaved, but they haven't completely gummed up his brain. Do you realize the risk he ran, writing that? If they'd caught him, they'd have— Don't you think it says a lot?"

"Absolutely," said Paternoster. "Fools like him have always existed in Russia. About one fool to every ten million muzhiks. But don't forget, they've got Siberia to straighten them out."

"You fellows are incurable pessimists!" said Foglar, waving his hand dismissively. "The fact is that they've got the message: the whole nation's behind Dubcek. They'll be satisfied if they can persuade us to stay in the Warsaw Pact; aside from that they'll leave us alone, you'll see. Basically, we've got it made!"

2.

The feeling that I was the only sensible person in a world populated by fools and people of habitual intemperance had haunted me throughout the Prague Spring, and now, after my return from France, it intensified. The habitual intemperance, once a turn of phrase, had become a reality. The days flew by, from the snow-white morning depressions, full of intimations of Siberia, through the exhausting struggle of unjustified hope against easily justified despair that took place during the endless, aimless daytimes — in theatre dressing rooms, in editorial offices, and in clubs. Everyone was drinking; hope rose with the level of alcohol in the blood, until it began to seem almost justified, for alcohol is the best substitute for argument. The talented novelist Nabal — despite having landed a one-room flat in Prague just before the invasion, after much intrigue — returned to the Krkonose Mountains and took up residence in a small, lonely cottage. Kocour went to Zurich to attend a conference on the aesthetics of Max Bense and, while he was there, asked for political asylum. He returned to Czechoslovakia after receiving a sharp reprimand from the leader of his surrealistic group, Alfred Cepelka, a psychiatrist and soprano saxophonist with an obscure Dixieland band, who threatened to expel him because surrealists do not abandon Apollinaire's Prague — not even when it becomes a sinking ship. Vrchcolab, Bukavec, and several others flew between Munich, Paris, Geneva, and Prague, trying to stir up Western public opinion against Soviet militarism, and found themselves under attack by German opponents of American militarism. Perhaps they were trying to figure out, as they travelled, what the KGB intended to do with people who had said, written, or signed something before the invasion.

Apart from a fairly innocent application to join the Club of Non-Party Writers, Paternoster had been fortunate enough not to sign anything. His new, mildly reformist novel was only half written (and he had begun to rewrite it before even starting the second half), and he had told me, in the luxurious apartment that Milan Forhont's American producer had rented for him in Neuilly, "Either I go back now, with the risk that entails, or I emigrate. Which is like the difference between having internal and external haemorrhoids. Or else I stay out of the country for a while and then go back in a year or so when things are clearer, eat humble pie in public, and spin a few yarns about the horrors of capitalism. But I don't think my readers would appreciate that, so I'm going back now."

He had given no realistic thought to the possibility of making a living in the West as a writer, and he was too lazy to consider going back to his original profession, internal medicine. In any case, he'd been writing utopian novels for years now, and had completely forgotten his basic anatomy.

"I'm going back too," I had said, without thinking the matter through logically.

We'd gorged ourselves for the last time on the oysters which Sylva, in her ignorance, served by the gross, and I'd followed Paternoster's Fiat east.

In Prague I came down with a bad case of alcohol poisoning and then, through a Western journalist of my acquaintance, applied for a Ford Foundation grant.

The Ford Foundation grant was slow to arrive, Foglar's optimistic predictions became less and less plausible, drunken parties now began before lunch, and then one day in January, in Wenceslas Square, a young student named Jan Palach set himself on fire.

An outraged Sarka handed us the newspaper with trembling hands.

"Have you seen this? The absolute swine!"

We were walking up the stairs of the philosophy faculty to the main lecture hall. The walls of the stairwell were covered with slogans that, though they demanded the impossible, were still unrealistic. RUSSIAN OCCUPIERS, GO HOME! and WE DEMAND A U.N.-MONITORED PLEBISCITE ON THE PRESENCE OF SOVIET ARMIES OF AGGRESSION! and JAN PALACH GAVE HIS LIFE FOR YOU! DON'T BETRAY HIM!

"I can't believe such low-down, shit-licking quislings could even exist!" wailed the tipsy Sarka, thrusting a copy of *Zpravy* into our hands. This was the new, post-invasion organ of the loyal Marxist-Leninists and was financed by the Soviet police, written and printed in Dresden by employees of the Ministry of the Interior who had fled to the G.D.R., and brought to Prague in Soviet military vehicles that, according to agreements signed by the Czechoslovak politicians who had been taken by force to Moscow, were not subject to the normal customs inspection at the border. "They're animals! Can you believe it?" said Sarka, almost in tears.

Unlike most of the other articles in the paper, the one headlined TRAGIC VICTIM OF THE COUNTER-REVOLUTION was signed: Zikmund Herodas. Many such improbable bylines could be found in the paper, and they were generally pseudonyms of the more timid quislings. But I still remembered the leaflet that Jana Hloubava had shown me in the Cloisters Wine Room, and I knew that this particular *nomen omen* belonged to one of the more daring quislings. This time the author made no mention of the deposed President Novotny, whom the earlier pamphlet had praised for consistently denying the obvious murder of a handful of Jews, but he did offer a novel explanation for the young martyr of Wenceslas Square. "Several Western agents persuaded this inexperienced and disoriented student to take part in their demagogic plan," he wrote, without quoting a source for such damning knowledge. Then he went on to say that "these agents gave the gullible university student a liquid which, they said, burned with a so-called cold flame. The naive lad thought that this would make an impressive political provocation, and he agreed to play the role of a 'living torch', which would burn, of course, with a harmless flame. The criminal agents, however, cruelly betrayed the lad and, instead of the harmless liquid, gave him — ordinary gasoline! Thus, in one blow, they rid themselves of a witness to their foul conspiracies and at the same time provided sensational grist for the counter-revolutionary mill."

"Not a bad idea," said Paternoster approvingly. "The only problem is that it probably doesn't make a heck of a lot of difference whether you burn to death in a normal flame, or in one that's only a couple of hundred degrees centigrade."

"Is that a fact?" cried Sarka. "Is a cold flame really that hot?"

The former physician nodded. "I can't remember the exact temperature, but I wouldn't advise anyone to stick his hand in it."

Sarka caught his sleeve. "You have to tell the students that. We'll read the article to them, and then you can tell them what you just told me."

The prospect horrified Paternoster. We were walking past an empty plinth from which a statue of Lenin had just been removed (Masaryk had stood there before Lenin, Adolf Hitler before him, and for twenty years before Hitler it had been Masaryk again, who had been there since the original statue of Franz Josef II was removed) and replaced by a black wreath bearing the initials J.P. (the wreath would remain for another three months before being replaced by a bust of Lenin). Paternoster looked around and mumbled something about having to go to the men's room first, and disappeared. Later he claimed the crowd had been so thick that he hadn't been able to get back into the lecture hall.

The hall was indeed packed and, again, there were symbols everywhere. We sat down behind the lectern and the crowd gazed at us through myriad eyes — the same crowd that not so long ago had listened to the bullhorn addressing them from the pedestal of the statue of Jan Hus in the Old Town Square. Again those nubile young girls in their miniskirts were here, and the young men in Che Guevara beards, but wearing the Czechoslovak tri-colour on their sweaters instead of a red star. Today they no longer needed the theoretical arguments that Laura's son had supplied. The allied superpower, sulkily demanding love, had provided them with the argument of personal experience.

I was here as a victim of moral terror, as the Leninist with the Leica who had once concealed himself behind the pillar might have put it. (I didn't see Barta here today.) The moral terrorists had come to my flat: two girls in cheap, thin mourning dresses and two bearded young men with black bands around their arms. They asked me to speak, and under the circumstances I didn't have the heart to explain my private view of the Prague Spring. Outside my window lay the ashen, steely-grey skies of another January; the tower of the Church of St. Marketa, established in the ninth century on the ruins of a pagan temple, stood there in the bare winter landscape like a finger raised in warning. The four mourners looked at me with the clear, doelike eyes of youth, which no victorious revolution has yet been able to fuck up, and both girls had tears in their eyes. When they left, an incredible pile of cigarette butts remained in the ashtray. But no matter how long they sat there, I couldn't bring myself to tell them that I was not, heaven forbid, a revolutionary like the others they wanted to hear from, that I never had been, that I had always believed in chipping away at things because it was a strategy that, over time, would drive Goliath himself to a nervous breakdown. Nor did I want to say that they had fallen for the sweet talk of the spoiled brats of revolution who had set the terrible machinery of the proletarian dictatorship in motion twenty years before, with no risk to themselves and as a great lark, and then, for a long time after that, had danced their circle dances on that same terrible machinery. And then when they began to grow old and to see through it all, they became nostalgic for the euphoria of revolution, and because they had never had to pay the price of their own enthusiasm they had begun beating Goliath with their tiny little fists. But David is victorious only in the old Jewish fairy-tale, and now Goliath would crush them, these embarrassing playboys of Marxism-Leninism.

The afternoon felt unreal, like a nightmare. Hejl, the world-class playwright, spoke as though he were talking to students in Berkeley, California, and not in a lecture room at Charles University with its bugging devices all neatly connected to the KGB listening post in the Party hotel. "If we try to salvage what we can of the January reforms," he said—referring to the present Party line of First Secretary Dubcek, whose days were already clearly numbered—"then without realizing it we are merely supporting the gradual transition from the present state of things, when the country still has a leadership, powerless though it may be, that the majority of the nation supports, to a state in which the individuals in this leadership will be replaced, one by one, until one fine day we wake up with a totally collaborationist regime—and one that, unlike today's government, *will* have power, although it will hold that power only at the discretion of the occupier, and be limited by his will. And such a government will very quickly and very completely destroy everything we hope to salvage. If we continue to obey the so-called prudent appeals for calm issued by today's leadership, we are only lending substance to the illusion that the occupier is trying to create around the world, which is that we are dealing with the situation ourselves, that the occupier is not interfering. The outrage that world public opinion expressed over the occupation will gradually subside, and in the end the occupier will have a free hand, through its puppet government, to do whatever it wants."

The playwright paused to drink some foul-looking water from a carafe, and then went on to deliver a wildly optimistic appraisal of the old whore he called the World.

"We ourselves must stand up and resist. We must hold a general strike, we must force the occupiers to cast aside the fiction of non-intervention and resort to open military dictatorship by the Red Army. In this way we will expose to the whole world the naked truth about this so-called fraternal assistance and arouse the conscience of the world from the slumber into which it will otherwise irrevocably fall."

He sat down to a storm of applause. My embarrassingly concrete imagination gave a rather unpretty shape to the abstract notion of an "open military dictatorship". I saw again those familiar and specifically European cattle cars, on wide-gauge tracks this time, carrying these moist-eyed young girls and their Guevaras to those snowy regions that Arashidov had wanted to write into unorthodox legend but never did. I shuddered, then told myself I was being paranoid. They were no longer what they'd been when we were twenty. Maybe the odd one here and there might be, but there shouldn't be any more cattle cars. Still, the past always shows the potential of the future; there was nothing to rule out that possibility. We were dependent on the whims of people who thought that—

For the middle-ranking officer, perhaps a *politruk*, had asked, "How could you let things slide so far, comrade?" Then he'd reached into the bookshelf, knowing exactly what he was looking for, taken out a slender volume, and placed it on the desk in front of Foglar. "And you call yourselves a socialist publishing house!"

"But that's a collection of poems by Stanislav Kostka Neumann," protested an astonished Foglar. "Neumann, comrades, was a Communist even beyond the grave! He didn't even waver during— " He'd been about to say "the Moscow Trials" but he stopped himself in time.

The *politruk* nodded sadly. "So much the worse, so much the worse! Progressive poetry—with *this* on the cover?"

He rested his index finger on a delicate pen-and-ink drawing of a young nude by the lusty old national artist Hrusovsky, an immensely tender fellow. Foglar felt (he told us afterwards that he didn't know why) like crying. He tried to explain to the officer that before Neumann had grown older and become impassioned by politics he'd been more interested in the sexual revolution, and that the collection of verse adorned with the delicate nude was an early work from that period, often considered by critics to be the poet's best.

"That's exactly what I mean, Frantisek Premyslovich!" said the *politruk*, wagging his head reproachfully. "This is what you publish of the poet's work! An early, immature book, and one which is very likely politically erroneous. You give no thought whatsoever to how you are distorting the image of this progressive artist among young people!" He sat down, shaking his head, then tossed back a glass of vodka and looked squeamishly at the immoral drawing on the cover. "You are editors, after all. How could you let something like this get through?"

We were dependent on the whims of people like that. Now Bukavec was speaking. It was a confession — much like the one I'd listened to on the terrace of the Hrzansky Palace, except that it was fuller, and in public this time. I listened to this ancient fellow student of mine freely admitting that he had informed on three employees of the Revolutionary Trades Union Movement for praising Hemingway and having once been Boy Scouts. He had turned them in, he said, because he'd been blinded by the devil, and had believed that he would be helping to liquidate the enemies of the working people. Two of those he betrayed were sent to concentration camps but fortunately survived; the third was sent to work in the mines, where he died in an unfortunate accident. Bukavec begged the assembly to spit on him, but none of the Che Guevaras or Joan of Arcs did so. Bukavec then began to enumerate his more commonplace sins, and by now it was too late to tell him to leave me out of it; for the second time he apologized to me for the article that had once inadvertently provided my play with such good publicity. At this point someone entered through the rear doors and I could hear loud whispering, from which I understood that a call had come from the radio station saying that Russian tanks had occupied the airport again. I felt the vampiric atmosphere of that foggy afternoon weighing on me. I looked around. Yes, nodded a red-headed Guevara, a colleague who was standing in line for an Austrian visa had just called to say that an Austrian official had told him the same thing. One of the students was dispatched to the airport by motorcycle to scout out the situation.

Bukavec had finished his confession and was now moving onto the attack. "The world is ruled by two imperialist superpowers, the U.S.A. and the U.S.S.R.!" he warned. "Don't be misled, my friends, by fine-sounding speeches from Moscow about socialism. I know their socialism. It's a police state! And because they've never gone through the bourgeois-democratic phase of development, they are incomparably more hypocritical and therefore more dangerous than America." He was shouting now, and the veins stood out on the temples of his moon-shaped face. But no policemen in plexiglass helmets burst through the door. The older and therefore more experienced police state knew that such methods led nowhere; instead, they surrounded the university, the city, the entire country, with the vampiric atmosphere of terror. The large eyes of the crowd took in the Grand Master's message, the Gospel according to Bukavec—just as, less than a year before, they had eagerly devoured the Gospel according to Vladimir Fischer—while their colleague was on his way to the airport by motorcycle, for the Troglodytes might already have decided on the course of action that the world-class playwright wanted to force them to take. Bukavec revealed further familiar truths, there was more whispering among the students, then the red-headed Guevara told the crowd in hushed tones that his colleague had called from the airport to say that there were no tanks there, it had been a mistake, they had only intervened in Boleslav because some people in a protest march had stoned a barracks where the occupying forces were billeted. Bukavec then began an appeal to that old whore, the World, but Boleslav was not enough to rouse the conscience of a planet full of Biafras, Vietnams, and Siberias. Now a young girl in a crumpled dress of black stood in front of the microphone: Jan Palach's girlfriend. She spoke about her final conversation with Palach as he lay in the oxygen tent, covered in ointment. He had no regrets, he said, but wanted no one to follow his example. The girl began to cry and could not go on. The large eyes of the crowd were covered by a film that glistened in the white light of the January afternoon. A lad in a black sweater jumped to his feet to announce a resolution addressed to the students of the World, and it was put to a vote. I recognized him. So he was here after all, he'd been here the whole time—the evangelist who had spoken beneath the statue of the martyred priest, the not entirely Aryan son of the beautiful Laura Widemanova. He read his resolution in a perfectly beautiful voice crying out in the wilderness. He radiated the conviction that a student who turned himself into a mass of fried flesh in protest against a might cleverly camouflaged as right would interest the girls and Guevaras in foreign campuses. "Colleagues the world over!" was how the appeal began, the appeal they flung into the face of the old whore called the World.

Towards evening I was sitting in Paternoster's bachelor flat in a villa in the residential quarter of Baba. "You know what Vrchcolab's daughter Renata told me, man?" he asked. "She said they're holding a vigil in the dormitories, reading Palach's last will and testament and singing the national anthems in between. Sarka's there too and says she's going to stay with them. Can you beat that? Intelligent people, and all it takes to screw their minds up is one hysterical psychopath. They'll end up forcing the Russians to put in a military dictatorship, just the way Hejl wants them to. I tell you, our common sense has gone right down the tubes."

I looked through the french windows into the winter night. On the lot next door was a building under construction, made of mottled white marble. The graceful arc of a white staircase rose into the air, ending with a step that led into space. Glazed brick walls rose to the sky; they were not roofed in. A handful of stars twinkled overhead.

"Hejl!" sighed Paternoster. "He's under the impression that he's playing an important political role in an important historical period. But from the clinical point of view, he's a psychopath with a martyr complex."

"He'll soon get satisfaction if he carries on like this," I said. "Who's building that house? Not Suzi? I heard she bought a piece of property somewhere out here."

"No one's building it any more. At least, not for the time being. The prime minister started it — that was before the reforms broke out. He borrowed two hundred thousand from the president for it, and when they both got the axe the construction just stopped."

He came over to the window and both of us looked out at the unfinished marble staircase. It reminded me of Xanadu. Oh God, I sighed to myself, the whole world is full of strident symbols. Human torches. Statues of martyrs. Potential martyrs. Debauched patricians. Sons of martyrs. Mothers of sons of martyrs. Wives of martyrs.

Wives of martyrs, mistresses of cynics . . . something was forcing its way to the surface of my awareness, but for the time being my mind was clouded with anxiety and whatever it was couldn't get through. Ancient martyrs like that fifteenth-century priest. Fresh martyrs like the boy who poured gasoline on himself. Recent martyrs like the parish priest with the horrifying manicure — mistresses of cynics, wives of martyrs — why was there always a woman mixed up in it?

"I expect a new Prague Spring will be putting out shoots any day now," said the author of science fiction. "It'll be slightly different from last year's model, but pretty soon the masons will be swarming around next door. By fall they'll have the roof on."

3.

"In a relatively short time after the revolution, even the former members of the exploiting classes will comprehend that the revolution means a better life and greater justice for them as well," droned the chairman of the meeting in a lifeless voice. His left hand was resting on a book in a red cover and he stood there in a three-piece suit beneath a garish poster representing a group of Chinese frolicking around a huge head of Mao Tse Tung. The speaker's chestnut hair was conservatively slicked down and his twenty-two-year-old face was clean-shaven. He differed from a bank clerk in only one detail: there was something large and ostentatious in his lapel. Later, from up close, I saw that it was another Mao Tse Tung, a smaller one made from a kind of plastic. In the playful rays of the Connington sun, it was rather colourful.

For the first time since my arrival in Connington, I found myself among young people who dressed as I did. The common-room floor was not sprawling with the usual mixture of Guevaras in tasselled leather jackets, girls in short shirts that, in a confusion of terminology, they referred to as dresses, and disciples of an oriental deity with saffron sheets over their jeans and tiny braids of hair hanging from shaven skulls. Here everyone was sitting politely on chairs. There was even a Milada Maresova making careful notes at a small table beside the chairman, an expression of zeal on a face which combined cruel benevolence with charitable obstinacy.

Beside me sat an unremarkable youth with pimples on his nose, and beyond him a man in a red and white checked shirt like a lumberjack's; I gathered from the discussion that he represented the working class. Over the next few days I caught a glimpse of him several times, lounging around the livelier street corners on Telegraph Avenue, sitting over beer in the hippie bars, and leafing through paperbacks in the second-hand bookstores. Someone later told me that he was Larry Dale, a working-class poet. In the shop where they sold the most progressive avant-garde literature I even found a mimeographed book by Larry Dale, nestled between an anthology called *Cunt Poems* (with a muff of real hair glued to the cover) and another thin volume daubed with its creator's own blood (which, when dried, looked like spots of desiccated diarrhoea). Dale's book was simply called *Songs of a Worker.* I read about half the poems on the spot; they were the thoughts of Mao Tse Tung retold in the author's own words and mixed with echoes of verse I had once read in *Masses & Mainstream.* The poet had stripped the mixture of all remnants of rhyme, rhythm, and poetry and chopped it up into lines of roughly the same length. He was asking eighty-five cents for the book, but in the same shop the same amount of money would get you two mysteries by Dashiell Hammett—who had been a Communist too, after all. I chose Hammett over the workers' poet.

Between the poet and the pimply youth was the only other person at this progressive gathering (besides myself) who was there by mistake: a dozing hippie with a greasy mane of hair and a shirt flaunting savage flowers spattered with dried grease from an excessively juicy hot-dog. He arrived after the meeting had begun, slumped into a chair, and fell at once into a sleep that appeared to have been artificially induced. He revived, however, as soon as the chairman began advocating bloody revolution as the most appropriate road to the completely gentle society. By the time he had finished his description of this rose-scented apocalypse, the hippie had regained full control of his faculties.

"Thus even former members of the exploiting classes will, in a relatively short time, understand their proper place and join in the task of building the new society." The chairman smiled with exaggerated warmth and invited us to ask questions. The hippie, by now fully aroused, immediately put up his hand.

"And what," he said, with a hiccup, "will happen to those who don't want to join the revolution? Who don't understand?"

A trace of condescension seeped through the boundless amiability of the chairman's smile. "Well," he said, "an absolute majority *will* comprehend and join the revolution, in a relatively short time."

"Yes, but what about the minority, the ones who don't?"

"Well," said the chairman, "they would be such insignificant exceptions to the rule that we don't really need to worry about them. Of course, those who stubbornly cling to their exploitative positions and resist the revolution with weapon in hand," and his smile mellowed, "will be liquidated."

"Come off it, man," said the hippie. "I'm not talking about anybody clinging to their fucking exploitative positions, and I'm not talking about armed resistance, either. I just mean people who don't understand, right? Like, they don't want to join. Guys like you and me, you know, who aren't exploiting anybody and don't want to fight against anything. They just want to live and let live, you know? They just don't understand, that's all."

"Why shouldn't they understand?" asked the chairman in surprise.

"Oh, shit! They just don't. How should I know why?" He punctuated the urgency of his question with a sudden wave of his arm, then slouched over to one side of his chair. He appeared to find that position quite natural.

"But they *will* understand," the chairman reassured him, "when they read these two books."

He lifted them up: *The Thoughts of Chairman Mao* and *Mao Tse Tung on the Cultural Revolution.* "Then they will understand that the bourgeois social scientists, so called, have artificially obscured the essence of a problem that is simple and clear. All those mountains of studies in bourgeois sociology and psychology have a single aim: to confuse the working class, to keep it from realizing that in reality nothing is complex and, on the contrary, everything is very simple: exploitation, the class struggle, armed revolution, after which, in a relatively short time, the — "

"Armed revolution, eh?" said the hippie, interrupting the speaker's refrain.

"Yes," replied the chairman. "Chairman Mao says that guns and bullets are the instruments of revolution."

The hippie raised a protesting finger to the sky and waggled it back and forth in the air. "Oh no, man. Bullets won't work in America."

"Well, what do you suggest, then?"

"Love!" cried the hippie. "We all gotta wake up the love that's inside us and then injustice will . . . like . . . disappear. . . ."

His voice trailed off and he fell asleep again. The chairman exchanged glances with the girls in the audience and they all sneered patronizingly at the idea of love.

I asked to speak and the chairman nodded. "You say bourgeois social scientists have artificially complicated problems that are really quite simple. Do you think things will continue to be simple after the revolution?"

"They'll be even simpler," said the chairman. His voice was less amiable now. I could tell he didn't trust me, though I was dressed the same way he was. "Instead of antagonistic conflicts between the people and their exploiters, there will be non-antagonistic conflicts among the people that won't have to be resolved by violence."

"And what makes you think those conflicts will be simpler?"

The three females present turned to look at me. In their eyes I could see not the pity they had accorded the hippie, but something approaching distaste.

"All the sources and instruments of progressive science will be available to the people," declared the chairman. "There is no problem that the people, in its great wisdom, cannot solve."

I carried the argument no further. I have long been allergic to that hermaphrodite animal to which Leninists have attributed the same conflicting characteristics as the ancient Jews once did to Jehovah. I did not want to be gratuitously malicious, and besides, it occurred to me that this zealous youth in the three-piece suit might report to some zealous comrade in the Progressive Labor party, and he to someone else, until eventually a rumour about a provocative reactionary from Prague reached the ear of some Czechoslovakian secret agent posing as a political refugee in Connington. Ultimately the tale might end up in my file in Prague's cream-tiled Ministry of the Interior, somewhat complicating my hitherto simple life in a society that had already been through not only a simple revolution, but a very simply liquidated counter-revolution.

So I merely nodded. It must have seemed that I was agreeing with the non-existence of problems that the people, in its infinite wisdom, would be unable to solve, because, in a manner that was nothing short of kindly, the chairman smiled once more.

"Any more questions?" he asked.

"Yes," said the representative of the working class hoarsely. "What about art after the revolution?"

The benevolence on the chairman's face gave way to pure pleasure. He picked up the little red book, leafed through it, finally found what he was looking for, and looked blissfully at the workers' poet.

"Mao Tse Tung says the only creator of revolutionary art is the people, and the people in turn are the only consumers of revolutionary art. Art belongs to the people."

The girls, the workers' poet, and the unremarkable young man all nodded. Unlike them, I had heard that definition of art many times before — although it had been variously attributed to authorities such as Stalin; the Soviet Minister of Culture, Mrs. Furtseva; someone called Comrade Tesnohlava, a district officer in charge of culture whose words had once been quoted in the Hronov *Sudlice*; and Comrade Kaiser, among others — so it didn't strike me as being so fresh and original.

"Notice the pregnancy, the precision, the classical simplicity of the idea," the chairman continued. "No bourgeois aesthetics would be capable of anything like it."

The audience murmured its appreciation while the hippie once more roused himself to full consciousness.

"What kind of art will it be?" he wanted to know. "I mean, like, what will it be about?"

"It will be revolutionary art," said the chairman, "and it will express the interests and the feelings of the people."

"How?"

"In a revolutionary way," smiled the chairman. "Realistically."

"Fuck it, man!" said the hippie. "I mean, like how? What are they going to write about?"

"About everything the people are interested in, everything that will make the people more noble and lead them to an even deeper understanding of the revolution."

This must have been too complicated for the hippie, for he shook his head, though perhaps it was only to wake himself up. Suddenly I felt as though I were watching a painfully amateur theatrical production in some jerkwater town of a drama that had played the outside world long before. My head swarmed with recollections of Lester, of my novel *In the Red Panzerkorps*, of Comrade Kaiser, the ersatz musicologist. But still I didn't speak, inhibited by my fear of omnipresent secret agents. Besides, the hippie had just thought of something else.

"Are the Beatles revolutionary?"

The chairman became very animated, perhaps because here was a concrete item he could critically demolish. Those ancient Party hacks I used to listen to would also become more concrete when tearing apart bourgeois art, even though it made them no more precise.

"No. The Beatles are profoundly reactionary," he said enthusiastically. "The content of their songs is banal and bourgeois — mostly about love — and their music is based on a suggestive rhythm that stimulates the passions. Thus they distract the attention of our youth away from the only serious problem confronting this society — how to wage class war. And so the Beatles are profoundly reactionary."

Something familiar in the timbre of his voice reminded me of Comrade Kaiser and I was carried relentlessly back through time from Connington College to a period about fifteen years before when, just as the hippie was now shaking his head, Lester had been nodding his. Only then it had had to do with Glenn Miller.

"So, like, what will songs be like after the revolution?" asked the hippie.

The chairman began his answer almost before the hippie had finished his question. "Not long ago I heard a good example of the kind of song I mean. It's called 'Joe Hill' and it's about a working-class revolutionary who was executed by the American fascist police. It ends with a beautiful message: 'Don't mourn my death — organize!' That's the kind of thing people should be singing, not 'Yellow Submarine'. And people *will* sing songs like that after the victorious revolution. Because they capture all the — " and he began to ramble effortlessly on about the spiritual life of his hermaphroditic "people" and my private time machine carried me away from Connington to Lucerna, the large concert hall in the middle of Prague where Lester and I had been masters of ceremony for a concert given by Bert Singer, the progressive American folk singer; the young people packing the hall had applauded thunderously to the plonking of Bert's banjo and his song about Jenny, whom the people's artist wished goodbye.

The concert was moving swiftly and surely to a triumphant climax. Lester and I took turns at the microphone, conveying to the audience the approximate contents of Singer's songs or, when we felt it was more prudent not to translate them, regaling them with tall tales of the American Wild West that we'd taken from Botkin's *Treasury*. The crowd's reaction inspired the songster. During the intermission he said, "Magnificent audience! I'd never have believed that such contact was possible with people who don't even understand me."

But it was only after the intermission, when he sang "My Darling Clementine", that the crowd of seventeen-year-olds reached boiling point. The song had recently been popularized by Suzi Kajetanova, but instead of singing a faithful translation she had used a Dadaist text written by a Czech songwriter and intellectual. After a five-minute round of applause and two encores, Singer was no longer satisfied with mere audience contact; he longed to be understood.

"Could you please translate the next song before I sing it?" he asked. "Word for word?" And he handed us a page torn from a mimeographed magazine. The song was called "Working Class, Unite!" The contents were extremely anti-American, anti-capitalist, and pro-Communist, and the versification was somehow all too familiar. Lester's moustache twitched. "If I were you, Bert, I wouldn't translate it." "Why not?" Lester's moustache twitched again, in the opposite direction this time, and he said truthfully, though without getting to the heart of the problem, "It just can't be done on the spot like that. Nowadays poetic lyrics are the thing here. If I translate this off the top of my head, it's going to sound pretty stilted." Bert dismissed the idea with a wave of his hand. "That doesn't matter. The important thing about this song is not *how* it's said, but *what* it says," he declared, little suspecting that he was repeating a famous aesthetic maxim of Comrade Kaiser. He insisted that Lester step up to the microphone.

In that popular, expressionless voice of his, Lester began to translate: "Unite, working class, unite and march forward. On the horizon the sun of socialism is shining brightly." The hall fell strangely silent; Bert attributed this to the audience's heightened interest. "In unity is strength; we shall get rid of the bourgeoisie," Lester droned on, his moustache dancing. "Under the Red Star of justice, the people will win, will win, will win." His voice faded away.

Beaming, Bert commenced plonking his banjo into the sepulchral silence, then burst energetically into song. "Working class, unite and march forward — "

The temperature in the hall dropped lower and lower, until the chill came through to the singer. Towards the end of the song he made two mistakes. When he'd finished, a few dozen of the most polite in the audience offered up a smattering of applause. It was such a shock to Bert that he made seven mistakes in the next song, and after the show (the audience left without even giving him an encore) we spent a long time trying to persuade him that he hadn't been singing to three thousand young reactionaries (Goodness, no! After close to twenty years of socialism?) but merely to three thousand young men and women for whom a certain configuration of themes was extremely unpopular, because the mass media never let up on them and otherwise gave space and time to their favourite pop stars only when they felt the need to castigate them.

We had obviously managed to enlighten Bert somewhat, for in the recording studio he scrapped his plan to record "Working Class, Unite!" (a song he had never recorded in the capitalist U.S.A.) and instead did "Jenny Goodbye" and "My Darling Clementine". The resulting single became a bestseller.

Meanwhile, back at Connington College, the discussion had moved on.

"These books contain it all," said the chairman, pointing to a pile of pamphlets. "A revolutionary must read a great deal and educate himself. Above all, he must read the works of Chairman Mao," and he raised three volumes, "then the writings of Comrade Lenin," raising two, "Comrade Stalin," raising one, "and of course the works of Marx and Engels," and he raised *The Communist Manifesto*. "Only an educated person, a comrade well versed in books that tell the truth, can be a staunch Marxist-Leninist and a disciple of the thoughts of Mao Tse Tung."

I was overcome by a devilish urge to shock. Moreover, it seemed to me that even a Czechoslovak secret agent could hardly see this as a particularly sensitive theme now.

"You named Stalin as well," I ventured. "But as I understand it, Stalin committed a number of serious crimes, and — "

"Comrade Stalin," the chairman interrupted me, and suddenly he was no longer gentle, "made certain *errors*. Only Soviet revisionists talk of crimes. In socialist countries they tell the truth about Comrade Stalin: he was one of the geniuses of the revolution."

"But Russia is a socialist country, is it not?"

"At the present time it is ruled by revisionists. That makes it an imperialist, not a socialist country."

"What about Czechoslovakia?"

In the wake of the recent invasion, the chairman was well informed about Czechoslovakia; he was able to instruct me without a moment's hesitation.

"Czechoslovakia *was* a socialist country," he said, "but not any more. The revisionist Dubcek clique turned the socialist character of the country back towards capitalism."

"Then why did the Russians occupy it?"

"That was a typically imperialist intervention by powerful revisionists against weaker ones. Czechoslovakia was essentially a colonial country *vis-à-vis* revisionist Soviet imperialism, and the Czechoslovak people rose up against — "

"When was that?"

"Just over a year ago."

"But that was when the revisionist Dubcek clique came to power."

The chairman smiled again, but it was a condescending smile. "The revisionist Dubcek clique merely attempted to redirect the rightful wrath of the Czechoslovak people against the Soviet imperialists and at the same time to exploit this wrath to restore capitalism. Meanwhile, however, the people's interests that were most in conflict with the imperialist interests of the Soviet revisionists had to be defended by the Dubcek clique in order not to set the people against itself."

I was astonished. It was so simple that even those present understood; they all indicated this by nodding knowledgeably.

"But the Czechoslovak people," the chairman assured me, "have already seen through the lies of the Soviet imperialists and the intrigues of the revisionist Dubcek clique. Supported by the people of the People's Republic of China, the People's Albania, and the revolutionary struggle of the people throughout the world, they will cast off the yoke of Soviet imperialism."

"That's great," I said. I was overcome by my feeling of futility and said, rather faintly, "But — listen, I could be wrong, but didn't Czechoslovakia become a colonial country, as you put it, under Stalin? Have you ever read Solzhenitsyn?"

"Who?"

"Sol-zhen-NIT-sin," I said, attempting to pronounce it as I thought Americans might.

"Who?"

I tried again, distorting the pronunciation a different way.

"What was the name?" asked the chairman irascibly.

"I'll spell it for you." And letter by letter, I spelled for him the name of that premature prophet from the depths of the Russian tradition. "He's a Soviet writer," I said. "He writes about conditions in Soviet prisons and concentration camps in the Stalinist era."

"I don't read revisionist writers," the chairman shot back. "We already have enough specialists in blackening socialism right here in the United States."

"But this particular writer is being persecuted by the imperialist revisionist Soviet clique," I said. "They don't allow his books to be published in Russia."

"So where do you know them from?"

Where? I realized I had stumbled into a blind alley. And indeed I had.

"They were published in America," I conceded. "I've read them in an English translation."

"Then it's obvious," said the chairman, garlanding himself with a victorious smile. "This writer is simply consciously or unconsciously an agent of American imperialism and therefore he has come into conflict with the interests of the Soviet imperialist revisionist clique. So they persecute him. The Soviet imperialist revisionist clique," he intoned, causing me to wonder for a moment whether English had the same kind of tongue-twisting pronunciation exercises for children as there were in Czech, for he repeated those long words without a single slip of the tongue, "on the one hand openly joins forces with the American imperialists, but on the other hand tries to defeat them in the imperialist struggle to carve up the world."

He looked around at his flock, who nodded at him, then declared proudly, "I don't read authors like that. I read books from which I learn the truth," and he placed his hand reverently on the tiny red pile in front of him.

"It's been estimated," I said quickly, "that from thirty to forty million people died in Stalin's concentration camps. Is that in your books?"

A chair cracked. I turned; the man in the red and white checked shirt had risen out of his seat and was starting angrily towards me. I saw now that he was enormous, with a huge chest, and in the neck of his shirt, which was unbuttoned despite the chilly weather, was a glint of fiery red hair.

"Stop that bourgeois muck," he growled, advancing a step forward.

"The information comes from reliable sources — "

"Are you going to stop that reactionary shit?" the chairman snapped at me. For the first time that afternoon, he seemed to have lost his composure.

"But if you want to know the tru — "

"Did you hear what I said?" snarled the workers' poet. He was right beside me now. "I told you to can that bourgeois muck."

"Look — "

He didn't. He took my collar in one of his bearlike paws, turned me around, and gripped the seat of my trousers with the other. I had a flash recollection of my Jewish uncle, Mr. Mintz, who had once been physically ejected from the Café Paris in Prague by members of the Sudeten German National Socialist Party for taking exception, out loud, to their HeilHitlering. Uncle Mintz had thrashed his legs in the air as they carried him. I tried not to thrash mine, but it's almost impossible to avoid when someone is carrying you by your collar and the seat of your pants. Milada Maresova very helpfully opened the door and I felt the terrible and easily manipulable (if you know how to go about it) might of the working class bearing me across the foyer of Connington College. It seemed I could not escape these symbols made flesh, even in America. Milada Maresova ran on ahead to open the main door, and I flew down the steps onto the sidewalk of Huron Street, landing right at the feet of a Chinese girl in a miniskirt.

She was so startled that the bundle of textbooks she was carrying tumbled to the sidewalk and scattered. *Aristotle: Logic*, I read on the spine on one, as I helped her gather them up, and I cursed inwardly. They cropped up everywhere and in everything; it seemed almost deliberate.

Then the drowsing hippie landed on the sidewalk beside me. The revolution had cast him out as well.

4.

The day before I left for Connington, Foglar called.

"They've found them!"

"What?"

"Those illustrations. They were under some old galleys. And there's something interesting on them. Come and have a look."

I didn't want to. Prague was preparing for the funeral of a young man who may have been a psychopath, but who did what he did, after all, in a psychopathological time. Rural policemen, brought in for the funeral from all parts of Bohemia, stood in groups on street corners, carrying automatic rifles. A huge black flag hung outside the Faculty of Arts. But I'd had enough; it seemed to me that the young man's insane act had merely slowed the inevitable descent of the sword of Damocles and I wanted out. I was in no mood to visit the publishing house, but in the end I went.

With an air of mystery, Foglar took from his drawer the original endpapers, which the painter had filled with a whole Hermitage of officers' heads, and placed them dramatically on the desk in front of me. The officers stared out from the glossy paper, their meddlesome stupidity accentuated by oversized epaulettes covered with the appropriate constellations of stars. Something was written under each head, but it was not in the painter's hand. It was in crudely printed Cyrillic script, like the experiment in communication that Foglar had found on his desk. *Eto izvyestnyy durak, polkovnik Yevgeniy Denisovich Prokhorenko* — I sounded out, syllable by syllable, the words written under a misshapen head with two large warts. And under a tubercular, potato-like head with slanting eyes: *Eto golova proklyatoy svinyi Leytyenanta Gleba Grigoriyevicha Byelokhvostova.*

"What did I tell you?" said the editor-in-chief, glowing. Even under the black flags his optimism did not forsake him. "There's no Russian like a Russian."

I looked sharply into his eyes. But he was not a spiteful man. He obviously had no idea that he was quoting a former president. After the fall of the Nazis, and before he murdered his best friend, Slansky, Gottwald had said exactly the same thing of the Germans.

The Air India Boeing lifted off from the airport the next day, leaving beneath it a black carpet of winter cloud and, beneath that, the city with the funeral procession winding through it. In the procession marched the Che Guevaras, their pale girlfriends, weeping women, and men who clenched their fists, though not because they were revolutionaries. The procession radiated an ominous, dark pathos that reduced everything to a single thought whose simplicity would have suited even the most radical disciple of Leninist doctrine.

An hour later the Boeing landed at Orly, where the sun was shining and jovial customs officers were joking with a dark-eyed Indian woman who had tried to conceal a bottle of Indian liquor in her luggage. We changed planes and took off into the friendly sunshine, and in another forty minutes we descended into London. In the airport a group of uniformed schoolgirls were skipping across the hall towards the Alitalia gate, probably headed for Capri and their half-term vacation. Later, high above the waves of the Atlantic, I got drunk on gin and, with my hearing sharpened by the alcohol, eavesdropped on an argument between a British-American couple over a musical comedy where, as far as I could make out, the actors appeared stark naked on stage. The husband disapproved, and his wife was carrying on about what sounded to me like the social revolution. In my dazed state I wondered what this had to do with stage nudity. It was some time before I realized that she was talking about the *sexual* revolution.

The next day, the head of the Slavic Department at Connington College held a commemorative ceremony for Jan Palach, but only a handful of people came: a few emigrants from the Baltic republics, two Spaniards (out of solidarity), an official representative of the Student Council, and a senator from Wyoming, probably because he'd gone to school with the head of the Slavic Department and happened to be there on a visit. The senator gave a speech, and though he didn't say much about the suicide, it wasn't his fault — he knew practically nothing about it. On the other hand, he was eloquently indignant about the poor turnout. "Where are the students?" he asked, with a rhetorical flourish. "I look around me and I don't see them. Why are they not sitting here on these chairs? Why are they not appealing to the conscience of the world, and crying out, '*Ecce homo*'? What did they have to do that was important enough to prevent them from showing up?" he thundered in well-schooled tones. "Do they believe that the drama unfolding in Prague has nothing to do with them? Have they forgotten the words of Thomas Paine: 'Where there is no freedom, there is my home?'" I could see that the official student representative didn't understand the paraphrase of Paine's words; the context was missing, and he wasn't sure he knew the name.

After the assembly, the head of the department explained that the commemorative service had clashed with an interesting squash match, as well as a meeting of the Women's Liberation Front where a famous feminist from Harvard was supposed to appear. Her fame was based on her refusal to wear a brassiere, so most of the men were at that meeting as well. Humphries, the Connington administrator for the Ford Foundation, told me, "The senator shouldn't have been so demagogic. I thought it rather undermined the dignity of the occasion."

Next day the senator spoke at nearby Sandfield University, where he talked about democratic forms of protest. But the students wouldn't fall for his argument. At a prearranged signal they rose to their feet and, chanting the strange slogan "Ho, Ho, Ho Chi Minh", went out to smash the windows of the university library. They pulled down the Stars and Stripes which was flying from a flagpole in front of the library, and poured beer over it.

That evening, the Harvard feminist and a long-haired professor joined us in the Faculty Club. A year and a half before, the professor had been sentenced to five years in prison for assaulting a police officer and inciting to riot. His original sentence, I learned, had been four years, but during his trial he had exposed himself several times, and the judge, who was a prudish man, had added a year for contempt of court. Now the professor was talking about his concern for growing police terrorism. He explained that just because he was still on probation he had had to post a ten-thousand-dollar bond to get a visa to fly to Cuba to take part in a congress on the tactics of urban guerrilla warfare. Fortunately several revolutionary organizations had undertaken a fund-raising drive for him (he had recently been appointed to a chair in the History of Revolution), and he was now set to fly to Cuba the next day. I got drunk on gin and tonic and had to retire to vomit into the toilet.

When I came back, the feminist leader was talking about how she disagreed with the Soviet type of proletarian dictatorship. She wouldn't want to live under such a system, she said, but she would submit to any dictatorship run by Che Guevara, and she would certainly prefer that to the dictatorship of Richard Nixon. Everyone expressed agreement and Humphries, who couldn't keep his eyes off those liberated breasts, turned the conversation to the latest sensation on Broadway, which was interesting because, for the first time in the history of theatre, masturbation to the point of ejaculation was being portrayed on stage. Professor Rosenfeld, a literary scholar, compared the play in question to the latest novel by a famous Jewish writer, and informed the gathering that the author of the masturbatory play was now writing a new comedy featuring defecation — which, unlike masturbation, posed some technical problems. Then the feminist confessed that recently she had been plagued by nightmare visions of the President of the United States. She was terrified that under politicians like Tricky Dick, as she called him, America might lose those last slender remnants of civil liberties and personal security remaining to it.

Originally I had intended to try to turn the conversation to the suicide in Prague, but I began to doubt that they would be interested. They were surrounded by so many horrors that the voluntary death of a single individual must pale by comparison.

The very next day I got drunk again. I'd been invited to a party by Dr. Jiri Hrzan, who had been in Connington since the spring of 1968 as a research scientist and had not long ago been given a tenure-stream appointment. He and his wife, he told me over the phone, had just put a down payment on a house, and they were giving a house-warming party for several Czech friends. They'd had a party for Americans the day before, so there'd be no foreigners at this one, and we'd all be able to chew the fat over things of interest only to us Czechs. Kucera — a professor of political science and a former dean of the Faculty of Economics in Prague — would be there, Hrzan said, and Dr. Srkavy, an Egyptologist in Prague and now in Connington, and finally Mr. Juricka. The latter was actually a seasoned American, Hrzan laughed, and he'd really turned the tables on the regime. He'd spent six years in the New York office of the International Monetary Fund as the Czechoslovak representative. Not long ago his contract, which had already been extended twice, had run out, and in light of the purges going on there, Prague had recalled him. But Juricka knew his way around, Hrzan said. He'd asked for an audience with the executive secretary of the IMF, who had a streak of sentimentality and a Ukrainian grandfather, and the secretary had personally extended Juricka's contract for another two years. Prague had to swallow it.

Hrzan and I were sitting on the new chesterfield, the IMF official was rocking in a colonial-style rocking chair, and we were all sipping the whisky that Mrs. Hrzanova brought round on a tray. She had plenty of sex appeal and was wearing a rather skimpy, fashionably shiny dress with what was called the Wet Look. "They can't touch me," the IMF official was saying. "My passport is valid until 1973. They wrote me a nasty letter, of course, telling me to come home at once, but I didn't even reply. I want nothing to do with that gang of thugs."

Everyone nodded. I didn't feel entirely at ease among these people, because they were all, wives included, Party members, and I was still suffering from a deeply rooted reflex that forbade me to speak ill of the Party in the company of its members. Now that I was abroad, the reflex remained but its essence had changed. I had the impression, probably based on my own reactions as a lapsed Catholic, that speaking ill of the Party would somehow hurt their feelings. So for the most part I simply drank.

"The sewers burst open and now everything is just pure filth," said the Egyptologist. "But that's the natural result of all compromise. Mark my words, it won't be long before everyone in Prague is collaborating."

"The big mistake," said the political scientist, "was that President Svoboda didn't shoot himself in Moscow the way he threatened to."

The Monetary Fund official waved his hand dismissively. "The big mistake was that the president didn't mobilize the army. They should have fought! It would have cost some lives, but it would have stiffened the national backbone. The Party's been bending it into submission for twenty years, and as soon as it straightens up a bit they bend it again."

"But don't forget, our people know how to get along in a situation like that," said the Egyptologist.

"That's what's so awful about it!" shouted the Monetary Fund official. "I know exactly what you're talking about. All that artful dodging, those clever scams, the sham loyalty, helping each other in shady deals. But that's what undermines the national character the most! And it's been going on, if you count the Nazi occupation, for thirty years now!"

The political scientist said, "Dubcek should have been far more radical right from the beginning, and to hell with what Moscow thinks. He should have called that Party Congress in the spring, instead of waiting till it was too late."

I took a gulp of whisky and was reminded of Dr. Gellen; he too had drunk Chivas Regal. Some of it went down the wrong way and I began to choke. This turned their attention to me.

"Perhaps we should ask our colleague here what he thinks," said Dr. Hrzan. "He's the only one of us who has the advantage of never having been in the club. How do you see things, Mr. Smiricky? Shouldn't we have pushed the reforms forward with more energy when we had the chance?"

By this time I was well into my cups, and besides, alcohol in the windpipe is a very distracting thing. It took me a few moments to realize that by "club" he meant the Communist Party.

"I don't know," I said, shrugging my shoulders and wiping my jacket with a paper napkin that had an American flag on it. "My slogan has always been 'Svejk, not Caesar', but — "

"That's exactly why we are where we are!" shouted the official. "Behaving like Svejk is a fine thing, but just look at what it's done to people. They're no longer capable of action."

Usually my guiding principle is that everyone has a right to his own opinions and that it makes no sense to enter into polemics. Yet the whisky, the quiet town of Connington, and the fact that the only cops around were American made me feel braver.

"Look here," I said, turning to him, and I felt my courage — or whatever it was — begin to fail me. "I don't want to make any personal accusations here. But about that failure to act, wasn't it your own — I mean your former par — what I mean is, there hasn't been much choice since '48. It was either behave like Svejk, or take the consequences. . . ."

"He's right," Dr. Hrzan laughed heartily. "He never collaborated the way we did."

"Never collaborated?" said the official, looking around at the company. He was obviously of a choleric nature, because he turned red and looked outraged. "I don't know who collaborated here!" he said, and his eyes came to rest on me. "I believed in it. And if you define collaboration, it's clear that. . . ." I stopped listening to him because I realized he was getting ready to accuse me. *Per definitionem*, and I could almost hear Gellen saying it, collaboration is cooperating with the enemy. O holy syllogism! He believed, therefore they were not the enemy, therefore he was not. . . . I never believed. But was Ivana my enemy? What should I have done? Put a bomb in her office and blown up the Health and Social Workers' School? Should I have sent Foglar a bottle of slivovice spiked with deadly poison, just to prove that I was capable of acting? Back then, when Vixi was languid among the lilac trees, this man had believed. He had certainly participated enthusiastically in political activities. After all, there was that comfy little job with the International Monetary fund in New York. . . .

Suddenly I felt a rush of abnormally normal anger. "Back then, we imagined it would be completely different!" I heard him say.

"What?" I shot back. "Hasn't the dictatorship of the proletariat turned out exactly as planned?"

Dr. Hrzan laughed heartily again. "He's right — there's no getting out of it. We collaborated, even when we'd known for a long time who we were working for. Some of us kept it up right into the sixties."

He looked around meaningfully, but I had no idea what the factions were inside the Connington Party organization.

"We fought!" called the Monetary Fund official. "And I don't know — "

"I think we should drop the subject and have another drink," said the Egyptologist. "What's the point of recriminations? What's done is done. All of us have come to terms with that already."

Dr. Hrzan's wife — looking as though she'd been dunked in water, the secondary indicators of her sex standing out under her dress — poured the Chivas Regal and said, "Please don't look at these glasses. You wouldn't believe how hard it is to find something even a little bit tasteful in America. Most of the shops are full of kitsch."

And so she shunted the conversation onto another and more amusing track, and as we all became inebriated, she began rubbing her damp indicators against me. Dr. Hrzan didn't look like a man with the potency of a Dr. Gellen and he wasn't holding his alcohol as well either. But such things no longer interested me.

5.

I left Connington and did not come back until just before my return to Prague. The generous Ford Foundation grant allowed me to weave my way across the beautiful United States from the Atlantic to the Pacific, on the trail of literature and thus of my own youth, when I was an avid consumer of American novels and movies. To the town of Hannibal on the banks of the Mississippi, then by Greyhound Bus through the sagebrush and the burning Nevada desert to Virginia City, to a romantic summer night under a wide sky among the ruins of Jack London's giant house in Moon Valley, then a sharp turn to the south to Beverly Hills and Santa Monica, Tarzana, Culver City . . . a finger placed sentimentally in a wound in the pavement in front of Grauman's Chinese theatre on Sunset Boulevard, following the stiletto heel of a girl called Judy who died that summer. . . . Everything in my life was a symbol. In feverish excitement I sped along the desperate highways of Utah and Nevada, across the Dragon Mountains, those huge symbolic skeletons in the dead arm of a river . . . into Mormon cities where I hung suspended in the waters of the Great Salt Lake, battling against biologically inexplicable flies . . . into Las Vegas, where I lay under the moon in the warm waters of a swimming pool on the roof of a white hotel, the fountain of neon cascading below me from the façades of gigantic houses of shame. I was in the grip of nostalgia as the Greyhound flew across the country, slicing through the green fields of Iowa until I found them — the little immigrant town of Spillville, the church of Saint Wenceslas, baroque names on the stained-glass windows and a statue of Saint Joseph on a side altar, a forgotten story among forgotten stories, meaningless, entirely lost in the blood and gore of the world. And another feverish fit — across the country to the South this time, to the town of Oxford, and Faulkner was dead by then too, and from there south-east to South Carolina, Georgia, where I saw dilapidated shacks from the bus, and barefoot brown piccaninnies stuffing themselves with popcorn, a grey-haired old man with an arthritic knee showing through a hole in his trousers, dragging himself slowly along a dusty road with a sack on his back . . . and I didn't know where he was going, or what was in the sack. And the Greyhound carried me on past wooden shacks, a pot-bellied man in a stained shirt sitting in front of each one with a can of beer close to hand, filthy children, dogs and chickens in the dusty roads, a strange, apathetic poverty, and I didn't know yet if it was real apathy or to what degree it was real poverty, poverty of the body, poverty of the soul, but I wandered through dilapidated towns where air-conditioners purred quietly in the twilight of rotting wood, and in a dream I saw the gallimaufry of my life, my I-know-that-I-know-nothing. Then through Menlo Park by car with a clever Czech co-ed and the American groom she had ensnared, along Seventeen Mile Drive, green lawns wet with a fine, refreshing mist from the Pacific Ocean, while the clever Czech girl talked about an undercover cop in Prague who'd fallen in love with her (for even undercover cops have love lives) and, like an altruistic minnesinger from a medieval romance, had got her a passport, knowing she would not be coming back. Then back to the South, which pulled me to itself like a bad conscience. One night, in a Holiday Inn near Atlanta, I found an old *Frankfurter Allgemeine* in my room, probably left behind by a German businessman or tourist. It contained a message from Central Europe: EIN SELTSAMER SELBSTMORD, the headline said, and I read, with the Georgia stars outside my window:

> *Prague.* Jaroslav Bukavec, a 45-year-old Czech Grand Master in chess, was found in critical condition in his cell after being held in custody for two months in Prague's Ruzyne Prison. He was dead on arrival at Pankrac prison hospital. He had a fractured skull, a broken neck, two broken ribs, and a severe brain concussion. According to a brief report given by the prison authorities to Mr. Bukavec's widow, he committed suicide by beating his head against the wall of his prison cell. Mr. Bukavec, who was arrested two months ago for "damaging the interests of socialism", was one of the strongest supporters of the former reformist Czechoslovak Communist Party boss, Alexander Dubcek.

I sat there in the hot night under the Georgia stars, the purring air-conditioner damping the sound of cars speeding down the freeway in the distance, and I tried to weigh things in my mind but couldn't, tried to weigh those nightmares, things observed but unspoken, and I drank half a bottle of Johnnie Walker, and while that strange picture gallery ran through my head I tried to weigh my life, his life, many lives and books and tricks and stories, and I felt myself drifting off to sleep, but before I did I reached for the Gideon Bible and, following an old superstition, opened it at random and blindly stabbed my finger at the page. . . . *And when he had thus spoken, one of the officers which stood by struck Jesus with the palm of his hand, saying, Answerest thou the high priest so? Jesus answered him, If I have spoken evil, bear witness of the evil: but if well, why smitest thou me?*

I fell back on the soft bed of the Holiday Inn and quickly lost consciousness. Everything, everything, was an embarrassing symbol.

6.

"You never seen it? Never? And you say you was all over the States?" said Ponykl, astonished. "You shouldn't have missed it, comrade. It's the only thing here that's any good, if you ask me. They used to have it back home too, when I was a kid."

He got up from behind his little table, which reminded me of the Ministry of the Interior in Prague, and the eyes in that desiccated face were ablaze. In his plaid off-the-rack jacket he seemed to light up, and he talked with great excitement.

"They usually have it on TV, so take a gander at it sometime when you get the chance. Channel eleven, mostly. But it's better to go see it live. You'd piss yourself laughing! Sure, I know it's all a set-up, but they run it like a circus and it's fantastic! Last time," and he choked momentarily with the rush of happy memories, "last time they had this huge, fat guy, must of weighed close to four hundred pounds, Haystack Humphries or something like that. He climbs into the ring in them blue jeans with the bib and braces, like farmers here wear. And you should of seen it! He was fighting someone called Schmidt, a bald-headed Kraut, a real devil of a guy. And they didn't waste no time getting down to it: pow, bam, they were slugging each other in the stomach and in the teeth, didn't matter, and talk about strangle-holds! I tell you, if they'd of done it for real they'd of been dead, the both of them. Finally Haystack Humphries pins Schmidt down with his stomach. The Kraut pretends he can't get out from under him, the jerk. Like I say, it's arranged before they start. But it's a real hoot and I bet you've never seen nothing like it."

The flame in those sunken Hronov eyes, eyes that had already seen so much, seemed to turn golden, and his voice became almost tender. Even Ponykl, it seemed, had sentimental memories.

"I tell you, comrade, I always feel a hell of a lot younger when I watch that stuff. I can still remember when the rasslers used to come to Hronov. Hajek's Arena used to be the best. He had Randolfi in his stable, the European champ, but my favourite was Varga, a middleweight. He had this special hold, they called it an American Necktie, turned everyone blue. It's true it was a setup there too. Pepa Horak, the guy who worked on the self-acting twiners at Mautner's cotton mill, he'd always volunteer, told me once he got ten crowns for every match, with five extra if he got scraped up and bled. Most of the time it was all arranged, but not always. Young Leps used to volunteer a lot too, the son of old Leps, who had the biggest butcher store in Hronov. He never let them buy him off 'cause he never needed the money. He was built like a young bull and he didn't give a damn for no one. Once he tossed Randolfi out of the ring and they had to revive him. By that time Randolfi was getting on in years, but young Leps didn't give a shit. He was a real arrogant bastard, a damned bourgeois brat. But don't worry, I gave him what he had coming to him during the currency reform. He tried to change more money than he had a right to, through one of his old employees. Anyway, he cooled off in the slammer and when he came back on an amnesty he was so skinny his own mother never even recognized him. But where was I?" He sank back into the distant past again, running a hand with prominent veins through his thinning brushcut. "Anyways, later they hired a farmhand from Kostelni Lhota and him and Pepa Horak and someone called Matatko, I think, all of them got paid under the table so they'd like be volunteered before young Leps could get in, that was the idea. Oh, those were the days!"

He lit a cigarette. I noticed that it was a Partyzan, the cheapest brand of cigarettes available back home; you had to hold them level or the tobacco — or whatever it was — would run out. They probably sent them to Washington in the diplomatic pouch. His sportscoat might be American, but he remained faithful to his socialist vices.

"At first young Leps complained," he said, his wrinkles softening in a blissful smile of nostalgia. "But they told him to go to hell, and he was so desperate for a fight he volunteered for a boxing match without knowing the first thing about boxing. Hajek had a boxer in his stable too, a guy named Lenecek, a tough cookie even if he wasn't that big. So they start pounding each other and before long young Leps's face is all bloodied up. He hadn't a clue how to keep his guard up so he took it in the honker and the eyebrows — one of his eyes looked like a rotten egg — but like I said, he was a real bull for a fight and he held in and then, man, he got mad, and when Lenecek slipped on an apple core somebody threw into the ring, young Leps winds up and without even looking what he's doing he gives him a roundhouse right in the solar plexus and Lenecek's kayoed. They gave him a hundred and fifty crowns for beating him, and young Leps actually took it! He didn't even need the money — they had more than a million at home, three million by the time the currency reform hit them! The bourgeois swine! I guess he figured the money was honestly got, but what Pepa Horak took, they was bribes, right? Anyway, comrade, those was beautiful times. Randolfi, Varga, they'd come every spring and set the ring up close to the old town walls, because by that time it was warm, and I remember once Varga pulled Pepa Horak's arm out of joint and he went to his house afterwards and apologized. They lived in a shack out in the wagon colony . . . I tell you, they was beautiful times. . . .

The door of the cultural attaché's office opened and a long-haired young man walked out, all red in the face.

"Goodbye," he barked at Ponykl, and from the gate, through which the golden sun was streaming in from the Washington boulevards, he shouted, "That's the last time I'm ever coming here!"

"We got no use for hooligans like you anyhow, you bum," roared the tiny mobster, and then he turned to me. "You can go in now, comrade. The comrade cultural attaché is free."

I walked through the mahogany door. Behind a heavy desk, right beneath a portrait of President Svoboda and the new First Secretary, sat Barta. He was leaning on the desk, which bore a photograph of his new young wife and small child. He wore a heavily decorated wedding ring, and glasses with thick black frames, a kind I'd never seen him wear before.

The shock of sudden, unexpected recognition knocked the wind out of me for a moment. But I recovered my composure.

"May I come in, comrade attaché?"

He took off his glasses and looked at me with naked eyes—expressionless eyes in an expressionless face beneath a slick haircut. He recognized me.

"Welcome, comrade!"

The cultural attaché.

The last time I had seen him had been in a film. But then he hadn't been wearing a well-made business suit, or a hand-knit tie. And he hadn't taken his glasses off.

12

■

The Virgin Mary under Mare's Head Revisited

I.

Laura laughed. "So, take your choice. Either the electromagnet was transferred from the Virgin Mary to Saint Joseph by persons unknown — or else it was a miracle. Who the persons unknown could be, God only knows. The examination of the chapel, the inspection of the statues, and the installation itself — all that was done with maximum secrecy, if you know what that means."

"Not as well as you do," I said.

I had asked Slavek Machal to introduce me to her as soon as I got back from America. I knew she'd been ill — terminally ill, they said — for some time, and with Juzl removed from Prague by forces that were dead set on purifying the ideological atmosphere of the capital city, I felt — absurdly, perhaps — that the solution of the mystery lurking about the Virgin Mary under Mare's Head now depended on me. After all, I was a near eyewitness to the sensational happening in the little chapel above the poisonous meadows around Hronov. And Laura, as I now realized, was the last insider of that murky affair still living in Prague. How much longer she would continue to live was an open question.

Laura took my dig in the spirit in which I'd offered it. "Thank you. In any case, I fully expected that reporter — what was his name, Juzl? — to come looking for me. It might have occurred to him — since it occurred to you — " and she smiled, her shiny pink lips as charming as the debutantes at an American Institute annual dance, "that Barta was my husband and that no secrecy is ever maximum enough to come between husband and wife. Why didn't he look me up?"

"Because he never connected Barta with the miracle. Nothing pointed to it. I didn't realize it myself until I met him in Washington."

"Oh, I see."

She still had the beautiful, haughty mouth of the affluent young. But otherwise Laura was no longer as pretty as she'd been at the time of the Cuban crisis. Not even all that fancy English tea she used to drink back when Slavek was rushing to jerk off in her bathroom had been enough to save her from the cruel scourge of the Lord. The light, a greenish reflection off the dome of St. Nicholas Cathedral, highlighted a delicate pattern of wrinkles on a face horribly aged by illness.

"To make a long story short," she said, "you know roughly what happened. And what does it matter now, anyway? When they showed that first version of the movie in Hronov and word went around about the mistake, Barta took it out on the priest."

"And the priest died."

Laura's shoulders stiffened and she stubbed out her cigarette. The stack of butts in the ashtray reminded me of the neat pyramid that had once piled up in front of Jana Hloubava, though for different reasons.

"He said he lost his temper. I don't know. He was never a rash person. But it could happen to anyone — sometimes something gets you so upset that you lose control."

I thought of the murders committed in fits of passion that I'd studied in the *Criminological Gazette* when I was trying to break into Czech literature through the back door of crime fiction. And I remembered the priest's fingernails, carefully taken care of, one by one. But I said nothing.

"There were a lot of unresolved mysteries around the whole affair," she went on. "The biggest one, though, had to do with taking out the electromagnet. As you know, Pecen ran out of the chapel right after the miracle; he complained to Sulc afterwards that he'd felt sick. As I recall, he said he'd even panicked inside the chapel. Sulc said it was because Pecen had been an altarboy when he was a kid. It was a genuine case of recidivism — he'd been a very religious little boy."

"So I gather. But then he turned Communist after some priest apparently got his sister in the family way. A radical change of faith often goes back to an experience like — "

"I know all about Pecen's prehistory," Laura interrupted me, as though she didn't want to hear about it. "The last thing Pecen wanted was to go back into the chapel at night to remove the electromagnet, but they finally persuaded him to do it. Sulc went straight for the Virgin

Mary, but Pecen lifted Saint Joseph up first. There was nothing underneath it. They found the device where they'd originally put it: under the Virgin Mary. Pecen suddenly got squeamish again and ran out. Later he went on sick leave. Anyway, Barta got the idea that the priest had fiddled with the statues."

"But how could he have done that? When? And why?"

"Barta's hypothesis went like this: the priest, God knows how, got wind of the plot and kept his eye on the chapel. Or one of the old women kept her eye on it for him — maybe she hid in the bushes or somewhere. Pecen installed the device about midnight Saturday. The priest waited until Pecen cleared out, then simply shifted the electromagnet from the Virgin Mary to the other statue — and please, don't ask me why! That's what Barta was trying to get out of him. Some time after the miracle the priest put the electromagnet back in its original place, so that when our people came to remove it, it was where it should have been. Under the Mother of Your Saviour — if he is your saviour, Dr. Smiricky?"

I ignored the sarcasm. When I was attempting to enter Czech literature through that back door, I also studied Western models of detective fiction. Everything in those sources was cool, analytical, logical. Criminals confronted with Nero Wolfe's summary explanations were also cool, logical, absorbed in the Montenegrin's deductive prowess, almost as if they were reading a detective novel themselves. Now it was my turn to grin. "Your first explanation is extremely improbable, your second one impossible. After the miracle, Father Doufal left the chapel with his flock and they walked to Hronov in procession. He prayed all night in the Hronov church. And your people took everything apart before midnight."

"How do you know that?"

I told her how I knew.

"But then who did it?"

I shrugged my shoulders.

"According to Barta's hypothesis," said Laura, lighting another cigarette, "the priest figured out a way to beat security at their own game, using their own weapons. If he'd merely shifted the electromagnet from the Virgin Mary to Saint Joseph, it would only have been a miracle for the believers in the chapel, just as security planned it in the first place. But by putting the device back where it had been he made the whole thing seem, even to the police, like a — well, perhaps he thought it would look like a miracle, or at least something inexplicable. And later, after they arrested him, they took him behind the altar and he saw that the pulleys and steel wire were still installed on the wrong statue — the one that was supposed to move but didn't — and he got another idea. That was why he was so willing to let himself be filmed — he understood that for the people who'd actually been in the chapel, a film showing the wrong statue moving would be incontrovertible proof that a real miracle had taken place."

"Is all that Barta's deduction?"

"No. The priest admitted to them why he'd co-operated with the filming," said Laura, letting the smoke out of her mouth. Thin wisps caressed the cosmetic tectonics of her face, the greyish blue mingling with the bright green reflection from the dome of the baroque cathedral. Laura hadn't changed in that regard, either. She wasn't satisfied with a flat in some cheap highrise development on the outskirts of Prague. This was a six-sided room in the tower of an old town house, with Lenin looking out of place among the Copenhagen plates and a collection of china shepherdesses.

"But that was the only thing he confessed to," she added.

"When I talked to Sulc in Vienna, he claimed that Father Doufal also confessed to setting up the pulleys and the wire."

"Sulc was lying. The priest never confessed to anything else. And then — after he was gone — Barta began to wonder if maybe Pecen had got mixed up, if he'd put the magnet under Saint Joseph by mistake, forgotten about it, and then panicked when Saint Joseph moved because he was afraid they'd give him a rough time for screwing up. In any case, they got themselves into a nice ideological muddle. A miracle involving Saint Joseph in a chapel dedicated to the Virgin Mary! In those days that was a serious mistake."

"I know," I said. "But how could a former altarboy have confused Saint Joseph with the Virgin Mary? And how could Pecen have managed to put everything back under the Virgin Mary before they returned to dismantle it Sunday night?"

Laura stared at me through the smoke, and the wrinkles in the corners of her eyes deepened in an ironic smile.

"In other words, we're right back where we started. It was either persons unknown, or a miracle. Which of course I don't believe."

Certainly not, Laura, I said to myself. Your faith is of a different kind. You had it back when you drove Slavek mad, and later, when you screamed that you'd strangle poor Fischer with your own hands. Everyone loses control sometimes, you say . . . is that faith still with you, Laura?

"In other words, Barta didn't bother trying to figure out who put things back the way they were," I said. "And when the priest croaked, he took it out on Pecen, right?"

Laura nodded.

2.

Mr. Pohorsky repaired the hole, and a seventy-year-old who looked fifty pushed the ball into it with her club and then drove her golf cart to the sandtrap. Another ball came flying through the air onto the green, nearly beaning Mr. Pohorsky. Shortly afterwards, a golf cart laboured over the rise bearing Professor Burleigh and Dr. Hrzan. Mr. Pohorsky wiped his dirty hands on his trousers, walked back to the pine tree, and with immense satisfaction lay back on a bed of pine-needles.

"Well now, about this poet fellow, Honza Kopula," he said. "When we were in Bytyz together, he told me he'd been in the slammer with Pecen, in Pankrac, when they were grilling them. That was before they did Pecen in because he got reconverted to the faith."

The ultramarine sky radiated a holiday warmth and all was beautiful in God's world, just as the old song said. "He ended up believing there really was a miracle in Hronov," Mr. Pohorsky said. "He set his contraption up under the Virgin Mary, he was sure of that. But he had some kind of premonition, at least that's what he told Kopula. From the minute he got his orders to join the unit that was supposed to fix the miracle, he felt leery of the whole operation. But he went along with it because he said he had this bone to pick with the Lord. Then Saint Joseph moves. And when he finally puts together every last scrap of courage and goes back to dismantle it, he finds everything right where he put it in the first place, under the Virgin Mary. That was what brought him back into the faith." Mr. Pohorsky laughed. "After that, they tried to get him to confess that he'd been an agent of the Vatican all along, and that he'd only left the Church as a cover and he'd put that thing under Saint Joseph on purpose. But he wouldn't confess. Then someone was clumsy enough to tap him on the head with a steel-toed boot, and that was the end of Mr. Pecen."

Mr. Pohorsky turned on his side luxuriously and looked at me. "That's why Kopula wrote that 'Litany to Joseph's Wife'. It was Saint Joseph's miracle, but Kopula was a sucker for women so he dragged the Virgin Mary into it too. The idea was that Saint Joseph moved at her behest. Oh God, I tell you . . . Kopula. The poor bugger. He suffered like a dog in the camps. He couldn't jerk off like the rest of us because it was a mortal sin and he was scared, so he used to have wet dreams instead. Jesus, the others gave him a hard time! There was a guy called Votruba, slept on the bunk underneath him. In for rape and murder. He got twenty-five years, like Kopula, and he had women on the brain. He'd teased the hell out of Kopula, always taking digs at him, like the thief on Christ's left hand. He claimed the name Kopula came from 'copulate' and that said it all, so what the hell was he trying to prove with all his religious bullshit. Kopula would argue back and say his name came from the Czech word *kupole*, a church dome, but the other was what stuck, naturally."

"What was Kopula in for, anyway?" I asked. Dr. Hrzan had stepped out of his golf cart and was taking a few warmup swings. Then he put the club back in his bag, removed another one, and took a few practice swings. "As a Vatican spy?" I asked. "Or because he made secret copies of a photograph of the archbishop and passed them on to former Boy Scouts?"

"That was part of it," Mr. Pohorsky nodded. "But the main thing they had against him was that at a public meeting of non-believers he called Jan Hus a heretic. They gave him twenty-five years to think it over. He'd have got less for espionage or for pictures of the archbishop because he didn't actually do those things, but he did say that about Hus. They had witnesses. It seems he got into a bloody argument with someone called Magister Saun at the meeting. Anyway, as I say, they gave him twenty-five. They locked Saun up with him too, but just for five; he got off lightly because he was an atheist," said Mr. Pohorsky.

3.

"It's a pretty awful story, isn't it?" I said.

Laura said nothing. It was evening now, and the room was dark. The gas lamps went on outside the window and the light fell across the writing table where that small bronze bust of Lenin stood.

"There are worse stories in the world," she said finally.

"You mean like Jack the Ripper?"

She shook her head. "No. I mean famine, depression, colonial wars. This was all worked out perfectly rationally, and it would have served a useful purpose. We had to show the Church in a bad light, because after February 1948 the Church was the last real bastion of reaction. Especially among simple people — the very people who, in the logic of things, should have been on our side. And Barta had no way of knowing that the priest had stomach ulcers."

Again I wanted to ask but didn't. That too fell within the framework of the perfectly rational. The end justified even the priest's final manicure.

The first few drops of rain fell on the metal shade over the streetlamp, reminding me of the room where my sad mistress, Rebecca Silbernaglova, had lived before she emigrated to Israel. Before she was killed. There had been a streetlamp like that outside her window too. We would lie on the couch, a cake-shop Sunday outside, and Rebecca would tell me stories of her life in the Theresienstadt ghetto. But Laura's story had nothing to do with Rebecca. Or perhaps it did. They were both stories of those means, and the ends that justify them.

4.

The ballast of anxiety that had fallen away in the Air India Boeing that carried me, a year before, against the direction of the earth's rotation, descended upon me again when I sailed back a year later in the same barque. This time the anxiety was blunted by philosophical skepticism gained in a land that drowned its ancient ideals in effluence and then slowly transformed them into seductive and halting slogans. And I could see that face before me all the time, suddenly brought into focus by the glasses, and I couldn't shake the thought of the editor, Mr. Juzl, whom I'd last seen on the square as the Marxist-Leninist tanks opened fire at a flock of pigeons.

Back in Prague, Juzl was nowhere to be found. He'd been thrown out of the newspaper. I was summoned to the Ministry of the Interior, where, despite being treated with ostentatious politeness, I spent an unpleasant day. With a clear conscience I wrote a confidential account of my journey to the U.S.A. in which I betrayed both Dr. Hrzan and the official from the International Monetary Fund. The police made no mention of my having signed the Dubcekist manifesto; they merely confiscated my passport. It was a situation equal to Mr. Kohn's worst dreams. I started drinking again, and feverishly wrote a 1920s musical to avoid, for various reasons, writing about the present — until I was reminded of it by a certain proclamation issued by the Prague Municipal Theatres, one of many similar proclamations in which citizens, committees, and commissions retracted earlier proclamations which they had been seduced into signing by the Right and the Zionists during that counter-revolutionary year.

From the Marxist point of view, a valuable discovery had been made: after twenty years of re-education by a revolutionary government, and changes in the base and the superstructure of society, a nation had allowed itself to be seduced in the course of a few months by a counter-revolution involving approximately ninety-five per cent of the population — in other words, a counter-revolution with far greater mass support than any of the revolutions in history. This confirmed the correctness of Lenin's implicit thesis that people are fools and it makes no sense to waste one's time over them; that one must instead organize an enlightened minority that will lead all the rest into paradise. And practice had taught yet another lesson: this minority may be infinitesimally small as long as there is a strong foreign army to back it up.

The proclamation of the Municipal Theatres caught my attention not only because it was, in itself, an absurdist text of a high order, but because it included the name of my unforgettable friend, and Laura's lifelong admirer, Slavek Machal. A long-ago afternoon on the ramparts of the royal castle, the beautiful Laura, and those still more ancient times before Lenin became a factor in her life — everything came back to me from the depths of time and the repressive will, and the proclamation itself sounded to me like a voice echoing from those ancient times, now revived:

> The artistic council of the Municipal Theatres of Prague has examined the reaction of audiences during certain performances, and has decided to remove from the repertoire the following plays: Molière's *Ode to the King*; Albee's *A Delicate Balance*; and Machal's *Monkeyshines.* The company had a positive ideological purpose in presenting these plays, and that this was understood was confirmed in many reviews, including reviews in the Party press. But the company cannot remain indifferent to the unwanted and often provocative reaction of audiences, who often vulgarize a spurious relevance to the present day which they think they see in the action, thus undermining the artistic intention of the works. The company desires, through its artistic endeavours, to express its full support for the high ideals voiced not long ago in a speech by Comrade Indra of the Central Committee of the Communist Party of Czechoslovakia in the V. I. Lenin Works in Pilsen.

I knew the speech referred to because I'd read it in the paper. The Central Committee member had spoken about the urgent need to kick all hardened counter-revolutionaries out of the mass organizations, and also about the fears rampant among part of the population that the bloody terror of the fifties would now come back. To such people he offered assurance in the form of a historically unfounded assertion — that "Communists are not butchers."

Directly beneath the speech was a review of a movie by a progressive Greek director who had recently achieved some renown for a film about the Greek junta. His new film was based on a book about the Slansky show trials, the victims of which Mr. Vohnout (once more editor-in-chief) had once wished a dog's death. "The film," wrote the reviewer of the

Party paper, "is deliberately calculated to arouse anti-Communist sentiments in the audience. For example, it exploits the reactionary slogan 'Lenin, wake up! They've gone mad!' which unfortunately appeared on the streets of Prague when the counter-revolution was being put down thanks to the timely intervention of the Warsaw Pact forces. If Lenin really had awakened, gentlemen, he would have given you a good swift kick!"

This folksy expression enlivened what was otherwise just another boiler-plate text. I had no doubt about the correctness of the writer's judgement as far as Lenin was concerned, except perhaps that Lenin would not have administered the kick himself. Lenin was a tender, sensitive soul. He had others to do his dirty work for him.

Right under that review was an article by Zikmund Herodas about the problems of the Cult of Personality:

> In the twenty years of socialist construction, only one church was built in the entire republic. During the eight months that the counter-revolution prevailed, construction permits were issued for twenty new churches in Slovakia alone. And it is interesting that while the construction of new factories and schools had constantly been hampered by a lack of material, everything necessary for building these churches was suddenly, as if by a "miracle", available. It is also interesting that, although there has been a shortage of masons for years, the construction of these churches is still proceeding at an unprecedented pace. Citizens who have otherwise never expressed much interest in voluntary labour when it was needed are now donating hundreds of thousands of man-hours in their free time to the construction of these useless buildings (which include five new manses). In the community of Cataj they are even helping the twelve (!) remaining Jews put up a new synagogue. The Party, however, cannot look passively on at this gross waste of work and material, and must begin kicking live flesh.

Again that expressive word. In spite of myself, I had to admire the consistency with which Herodas took pokes at the Zionists. He certainly could not be accused of lacking principle.

Slavek and I met at the villa of the old poet Jaroslav Seifert. After the invasion Seifert had suffered a fourth heart attack, and was now confined to his easy chair. Slavek, though not bound to such Christian duties, paid him regular visits to keep him company. The old man wrote melodious lyrics and was the only poet of his generation who still had a large following among young people. In his own youth he had had a strong sex drive — always an advantage for a poet — and he had combined this with a genius for language. For fifty years now he'd been writing verse of increasing freshness and wry self-mockery on the subject of the charms of young women and the delights of drink. Within the framework of these Omar Khayyamesque themes, the proportion of poems on women to those on wine would occasionally shift. During the Prague Spring, women had dominated his song; now they had almost disappeared, and when we visited him the poet was working on a pessimistic divan on dandelion wine.

And an old sin was gnawing away at his conscience.

Almost as soon as we stepped into his bedroom, which doubled as a study, he turned his watery eyes on us and cried, "Mr. Machal! How shall we ever render an account of ourselves? Tell me, how can we ever justify having been Communists?"

I was astonished. I had no idea the Master had once been a disciple of Marx's teaching, and I didn't think his massive audience of young readers knew it either. Even much of the older generation must have forgotten, since in living memory the Master had sung the praises of nothing more progressive than breasts, thighs, and cups of wine.

But Slavek had been expelled from the Party just a month before, and the Master's cry of anguish caused him some embarrassment.

"You were never a Communist, Master," I said soothingly. "Not really."

"Oh, but I was, Mr. Smiricky, I was," said the tender lyricist. "Of course, I knew bugger-all about what I was doing. Jiri Wolker and I used to drink wine together. He was a polite young man from a good family and we used to carry on about Lenin. We knew bugger-all about him too, of course, but it sounded so lovely: ' . . . and on the living and the dead — he smiles — Lenin. . . .'"

"You wrote that?"

"Yes, Mr. Smiricky, I did," admitted the Master. "I wrote it. And Lenin didn't even know how to smile. He could only grimace. Under his whiskers." The Master pulled the corners of his watery eyes up with his fingers and did a credible imitation of the grimacing revolutionary. "But back then that escaped our notice. You know how it was. There were poor people everywhere, asthmatic washerwomen all red from the hot water, old women who should have been sitting on doorstoops and looking after their grandchildren, but they couldn't. There was terrible poverty then, gentlemen. But how could anyone know that the outcome would be such shit!" And the Master gestured with disgust at a copy of the Communist Party daily. It was spattered with spilt wine.

For the first time, Slavek spoke. "I've thought a lot about it, Master. The problem goes back to Lenin. It wasn't just Stalin who spoiled everything."

"It's in *Marx*, Mr. Machal! It's all there in Marx!" lamented the poet. "And we read him like the Bible! Jiri Wolker knew *The Communist Manifesto* by heart. He'd always recite it when we were somewhat tipsy, along with Apollinaire's *Zone*, which he knew by heart too. We were all good lads, gentlemen, with our head full of good deeds. We shot our mouths off about revolutionary violence, but in our heart of hearts we believed that nothing would happen to anyone, that we would simply get rid of injustice, nothing more. That was our revolution, gentlemen! It would help everyone and harm no one."

"Not us," said Slavek. "We knew we'd have to lock up the reactionaries for a while. But the prisons would be something like reform schools, rehab centres — "

"Was that really how you and Laura saw it?" I interrupted.

Slavek was taken aback by my question, but he nodded. "Yes, it was. At one point Laura even wanted to study penology. She had this notion that she'd go into a women's prison and they'd re-educate the wives of factory owners — "

"And instead of that, gentlemen, what we got was ketchup!" groaned the Master. Hearing Laura's languid name had made him sit up for a moment. "Did you read about that? Do you remember? They crushed those poor buggers' balls. Making ketchup, they called it."

Slavek turned red. "Yes, I read it. That was when I started to see how things really were." He frowned silently for a moment, then declared, "In some situations revolutionary violence is necessary and therefore permissible. But sadism — never!"

The Master turned his teary eyes on Slavek. "And how would you achieve that, Mr. Machal? Would you go and be a prison guard yourself? Do you really think your Laura would become an instructor in those re-education facilities? For violence you have to have hired thugs. Those who talk about it would never harm a fly — to carry it out you need thugs, gentlemen, people who will do anything without batting an eye."

"That's just it," said Slavek sadly. "I've thought a lot about whether you can have revolutionary terror without sadism. And I guess you can't. And I can't accept sadism, for any end."

I felt sorry for these two curious Communists, one a fellow-traveller fifty years ago, the other barely a month out of the Party. But Barta was still a member of the Party, and he always would be. And what did that say about the Party? I made a face.

"Well," I said, "Lenin would answer that you can't make an omelette without — "

"Are people eggs to be broken?" lamented the Master. "And is the Party God, that it should have absolute power over people's lives? Did the Communists create mankind?"

"No, but they want to save it."

"Save it?" the Master snapped. He remained silent for a while, then shook his head. "Mr. Smiricky, I don't see any crosses anywhere with Party secretaries crucified on them. Their backsides have just got a little bigger, that's all, to fit the back seats of their chauffeured limousines."

He was so upset that he began to have palpitations of the heart, and we thought it better to leave him in peace.

It was as we walked back down to the city, following the route we'd once taken around the castle, that I asked Slavek to introduce me to Laura. I told him about my discovery at the embassy in Washington, and about the conclusions I'd drawn after looking at all the accessible links in the chain. Slavek was dismayed but he promised to arrange a meeting with her. And talking to her wouldn't be dangerous, he said. Laura had changed too — like the rest of us.

We stopped at a railing overlooking Prague. No changes were visible here. The city was still beautiful. But it occurred to me that most of its present beauty derived from the baroque period, the dark age of Czech history.

5·

"Why did your first husband have to die?" I asked Laura, without regard for her feelings.

She laughed. "Human reason is susceptible to illness too. The intention was correct: a warning to real traitors. But then everything turned bad. Yes, you're right. It all became pathological. But the Party is cured now."

"Cured?" I hesitated slightly, but we were all in the same predicament now. Perhaps it really wasn't dangerous to talk like this with Laura. "What about those writers in Russia? You know their names, even though their books aren't published here. Don't you think they have *some* truth on their side?"

"It's a petty truth. For them — and probably for you, too — their petty truth hides a great truth that not even an age of pathology can destroy. That millions of muzhiks, who would otherwise be living like animals to this day, have free medical care. That no one is dying of hunger. That no one knows the despair of unemployment."

"Are there no other kinds of despair?" I asked. "The despair of unfreedom?"

Laura laughed again. "Freedom is a luxury. It will be available to all when Communism comes. After the world revolution. People must be educated for freedom. They must grow into it. Ripen."

"Re-educate them?" I smiled wryly. "Not change the social conditions they live in?"

6.

Perhaps I was being hysterical, but I laughed so hard I couldn't stop.

"What's so funny?" said Vixi, annoyed. "So they're inviting us to an old-fashioned pig feast. What's the matter, haven't you ever heard of that before?"

"I was just remembering — " and I doubled up with laughter again. "Vixi! It's been twenty-one years! Those final exams, remember? That was a feast!"

"It wasn't as funny then as it is now."

"Nothing's as funny when it's actually happening," I said. "But after a time it becomes funny. Otik Silber actually published a novel this year — a funny novel — about Auschwitz. That's the basis of our historical optimism, Vixi. One day, we'll all be laughing. Did anyone in Maselna Lhota even notice that there was an invasion?"

"I expect they did, Dr. Smiricky!" she said venomously. "While you were rolling about with black floozies in California last year, there were no pig feasts in Maselna Lhota. For the first time in about fifteen years."

Again, I couldn't help laughing. I took Vixi around the waist. She was definitely not plump — just a bit fuller than she had been back then.

"You're still better than all the black floozies in the world, Vixi."

"Hey, let go of me. I'm not interested in picking up any nigger's disease, okay?"

"Vixi! That's racist!"

"No sir, that's sexual hygiene! Did you go to the prophylactic clinic for a check-up when you got back?"

"No, I didn't," I admitted. "I saw one too many movies in the U.S.A. and it turned me off diddling completely. Except once in Nevada, when I went to a whorehouse, purely out of curiosity. But when the girl found out I was from the East Bloc she started up a conversation about

Solzhenitsyn. She was practically the only American woman I met who even knew Solzhenitsyn existed. We got so involved in our discussion that nothing else happened."

"Of course not. You were always pretty good at stringing a line," said my loved one. "Like all those Catholic excuses you used to dream up for not starting anything with me. That was pretty funny too."

"That wasn't funny at the time, either — at least, not to me."

Green and gold spots from the sunlight and the leaves fluttering in the breeze moved languidly across Vixi's face, across her pert little nose and her green eyes. We were walking through Stromovka Park and Vixi, a flicker of contempt on her face, turned to look at a slim, pretty girl in tight-fitting pants who was walking with her arm around the waist of a man of uncertain, though certainly not white, race. I knew, however, that her contempt had nothing to do with the man's colour; though she'd tried to hide it from me, my backstage spies had once reported that she'd taken up with someone from the chorus of an American company touring *Porgy and Bess.* No — Vixi felt contempt because the girl was so young, so slim, so pretty. Then, perhaps remembering her Porgy, she cast an uncertain sidelong glance at me and passed on to me something of what she'd learned in the venerealogical clinic where she was employed.

"Venereal diseases have been spreading like wildfire here, ever since they allowed people to travel abroad. Before that we had only a couple of cases of syph a year, and they were usually gypsies. Now they've had to open a whole new department."

"They'll be closing it again soon," I said. "We'll be healthy once again, protected from the dreaded spirochetes by the familiar curtain." I laughed. "Let's go to the pig feast."

And we went. I, Vixi, her two children, the younger of which was mine as well, and Vixi's gloomy husband, Vojtech. Not long before, he and his wife had joined the Third Order of St. Francis, which legally non-existent order demanded vows of purity. So Vixi became a nun, but she soon overcame the fears aroused by my recent visit to the Nevada whorehouse. She was a fine nun, Vixi. There was always something special about her.

I was somewhat anxious about this trip. So far, Vojtech had no idea that Vixi had once been my student, whereas I was afraid the cousin in Maselna Lhota would remember. To allay my fears, Vixi wrote the cousin a letter explaining that if it came out she'd have a divorce on her hands and two kids to worry about. The practical-minded cousin would understand that. The grandfather was pushing ninety; we could safely assume he'd be senile.

I stuffed them all into my Felicie and set off in a direction almost opposite to the way I'd driven two years before, with Sylva and her twins. Vixi's children were quite a pair too. Fifteen-year-old Anezka had brought her guitar with her, and though she knew only three chords, she sang a surprisingly large repertoire of songs all the way. I'd never have believed you could spew so much anti-Communism into the world through three simple chords. Little Vojtisek, who was ten, joined in occasionally with his choirboy voice, but in the rearview mirror I saw that on the pretext of fraternal banter — and right under the nose of the sleeping man who was named on his birth certificate as his father — he was adroitly managing to brush up against his sister's budding breasts. He takes after his father, I thought cynically, and after considering it for a moment I decided that Anezka did too. At least, she was pretending not to notice her brother's games, and all the more zealously singing songs like "Ivan, Go Home". For twenty years the Party had tried fruitlessly to create an authentic modern Czech folklore; the invasion had accomplished it in a matter of months.

As we drove through the flat, central Bohemian countryside, bluish mountains slowly appeared in faint outline on the horizon. Then the landscape began to roll and the shadows lengthened as the Felicie slipped along the yellow road. We drove through Hronov without stopping and climbed the narrow road into the womb of the mountains, to Maselna Lhota. The town huddled in a fold in the hills, covered with shadows and echoing with the lowing of cattle in the co-operative cowsheds. I took a deep breath of the unchanging aroma of the countryside and drove through the blue shadow out into the sunlight, reddening now as evening approached, and up to the brow of the hill where the cottage of Vixi's grandfather stood.

7.

Laura's black eyes shone at me out of the dark, glowing faintly in the reflection from the streetlamp. "You know, I still don't know who you are."

"I'm nothing," I said. "I'm just a silly question mark. Forget about me. And go on talking!"

Laura lit up again. It must have been her thousandth cigarette. Her moist pink mouth glistened in the flame of the match, and as she half-closed her eyes they glittered with a black light, of coal, of hell.

"We define freedom as the possibility of acting within a consciously perceived framework of necessity. Necessity in history means structures that exist independently of human consciousness. But there are people active in society who are gifted with a heightened awareness and will-power, and these people set certain goals. It is through such people that the laws of society operate."

"Then what is democracy?" I asked. "You're grossly underestimating people. Everything is decided by an elite! And what makes your elite so elite anyway?" I was losing my temper, but Laura remained calm.

"Their loyalty to the Party," she said. "Based on a profound understanding — "

I interrupted. "'*Unsere Ehre heisst Treue*'?"

"What?"

"Nothing, Laura." I shook my head. "It's just a slogan some soldiers used to wear on their belt buckles. That's all."

8.

I left Vixi and the rest of them to talk over family matters in peace and walked down to the village, now immersed in a blue twilight over which the setting sun had stretched a bright canopy of orange cloud.

As I walked past a cottage that was overgrown with moss and had a high television antenna emerging from the roof, a middle-aged woman stepped out the door and greeted me.

"Good evening, sir! This is quite a surprise!"

A face full of sun-baked wrinkles beamed at me from under a kerchief, but there was nothing in the face, or in the flowered skirt or tow-cloth blouse, to suggest who this was. "Just a moment," I said. "Do I know you?"

"I recognized you right away. You haven't changed at all," the woman laughed. "I'm Bozena Stoklasova. Beniskova now. You probably don't remember me — "

Face to face with this sun-browned country woman, I was struck dumb by the cruelty of time. But how could I not remember? Fortunately, time leaves the beauty of memories untouched.

"How could I not remember, Miss — I mean Mrs. Beniskova!"

She invited me inside and poured me a glass of buttermilk — they didn't deliver beer to the co-op store until tomorrow, she said. Her three children retreated at their mother's command, along with four colourful kittens and a tame crow, and their astonished eyes stared out at me from the top of the broad, tiled kitchen stove. Bozena's husband had gone to the district town and wouldn't be back until later that night. And so we reminisced . . . and into the reddish light that came into the room through the tiny window (I asked her not to turn the lights on) those beautiful names fell like emblems of a time now lost, and a life long since dead: Kamila Doruzkova, Jana Chocholousova, Eva Formanova, Jarmila Kotykova. . . . They'd got married, most of them, had about fifty children among them, got divorced. Jarca Adamova had been killed on a motorcycle, Jirina Sinkulova was a somebody in the Party, and Andulka Maleckova, the proletarian of the class, had died of improperly diagnosed hepatitis. . . . I remembered Bozenka's father, the kulak who had been convicted, and later cleared, of conspiracy to murder.

"Daddy died," said Bozenka. "He came down with the rheumatic fever in prison and when he got back they put him to work on the state farm in Blazejova, in a calving station. It didn't do his health much good, but — "

"They put him in a what?"

"Well, he didn't want to come back to Lhota since they'd done him so much harm here. And they'd taken away our farm. So he went to work as a night watchman in the calving station. But all those nights — Somebody has to stay with pregnant cows overnight, see, so they can help if it's needed, or so if things get bad they can call in a vet. Father worked nights there. But during the day he couldn't bring himself to sit around doing nothing, so he mostly helped with the calving and sewed harnesses. That was a hobby of his — he could make fine harnesses. But his heart was weak from the rheumatic fever, the doctor said, and he took a heart attack. And he hadn't even turned sixty-two. My father-in-law, I mean Mr. Benisko, if you remember him, he was in prison with him too."

I nodded. Benisko the kulak. The kulak with slightly less acreage, who was therefore sentenced by the strict but fair laws of class justice to a somewhat shorter term in prison.

"He survived my father. He died this year; he'd just turned seventy. At least he lived to enjoy his grandchildren. But he was in for ten years. Karel, my husband, they wouldn't give him a job in the co-op because of his father. They wanted to take him on because Karel's good with machines, so the chairman went to see Ponykl — you remember him?"

"Of course I do."

"Anyway, the chairman told Ponykl that Karel was hardworking even though he was the son of a kulak. But Ponykl wouldn't let him in. So Karel went to work in the quarry — that was all right as far as they were concerned — and they didn't take him on at the co-op till 1960. He was never happy in the quarry, even though he made good money. Karel's a farmer right down to his boots."

Bozenka looked out the window. Outside, in the pink evening light, a gaggle of white geese rippled by, driven by a girl in a red kerchief.

"And, Mr. Smiricky, do you know what happened to the principal, Mrs. Hrozna?"

"I do." I didn't want to talk about it; it occurred to me that Bozenka might not have such fond memories of her as I did. But Bozenka began herself, and *in medias res*.

"Did you read the article they wrote about her back in '68, in the *Sudlice*?"

"I did, Bozenka."

She got up and walked over to an old-fashioned hand-painted commode, and opened it. Through the aromas of the oven, of wood, bread, and eiderdown comforters, came the smell of apples. From underneath the linen she took a bundle of letters and newspaper clippings carefully tied with pale blue ribbons. She was another collector.

"I've got it all here," she said. "This is what they wrote about her," and she read: "'Most citizens of Hronov still have vivid memories of how the principal of the Hronov Health and Social Workers' School, Ivana Hrozna, using a combination of terror and threats, compelled B. Stoklasova, the daughter of Martin Stoklasa, to write a shameful denunciation. . . .' They mean this," said Bozenka, pulling a yellowed clipping from the bundle. "But you know, Mr. Smiricky, she was only trying to help me. It was because of her that they let me finish school at all."

"I know," I said. And what good had it done Bozenka in the end? What had all those superhuman efforts of Ivana, Hronov's own Mother Courage, ultimately led to? To suicide. I grimaced. To that end of all ends.

"I couldn't just leave it at that, could I? So I wrote a letter to the *Sudlice*. I'll read it to you — if you're interested, that is."

"I am interested, very," I said.

Bozenka leaned towards the window to catch the dying pink light, and read:

> Dear Sir,
>
> In the last issue of your esteemed newspaper you published an article that contains a reference to Mrs. Ivana Hrozna, principal of the Social School in Hronov. It says that she compelled me, through terror and threats, to make the declaration that you printed in your paper on June 19, 1949. However this is not true. Mrs. Hrozna did not force me to do anything; on the contrary, she tried her best to allow me to write my final examinations, despite the fact that my father, M. Stoklasa, was sentenced to prison as a kulak and a traitor. She succeeded in

this, and I owe it to Mrs. Hrozna that I graduated from the school. I would kindly request, therefore, that you correct the impression left in the article referred to above. Mrs. Hrozna, the principal, harmed no one. All the girls in her school will attest to this, including K. Doruzkova, now Nejezchlebova, who in that same issue of your paper published a declaration in the name of the Czechoslovak Union of Youth for our class.

Respectfully yours,
B. Beniskova, née Stoklasova

"Did they publish it?" I asked.

"No. I went to the newspaper offices once when I was in Hronov, but the man who was editor told me it wasn't the right time to start airing such complicated matters in public, because the important thing now was to drive the conservatives out of public life. And he said Mrs. Hrozna was one of the most conservative of the lot. He said he'd publish it when the time was right. But then the Russians came, and the very same day Mrs. Hrozna — well, you know what she did."

We sat in silence for a while, thinking about Ivana. I remembered how she'd manoeuvred the deputy minister back into her office, trapping him there. How she'd cried over Vixi's loss in the simultaneous chess match. How she'd stood up to Milada Maresova and misused quotations from the holy scriptures of Marxism-Leninism for — what? For what?

"And you didn't try to have it published afterwards?"

"I can't now," said Bozenka. "Now the *Sudlice* is full of letters accusing people of all kinds of things. It's awful, Mr. Smiricky. Mainly Mr. Grimm's doing, if you mind him?"

I nodded.

"He's the editor now. He publishes the things people said under Dubcek, and then they go after them and some of them even lose their jobs. If it's a decent job, that is. If I published the letter now, it would look like I'd joined the collaborators, and I can't do that. Especially not after what they did to my poor father, God rest his soul. And that editor, the one I talked to in '68, he published some kind of self-criticism, that's what they called it, but they sent him to work in a dairy anyways. And if I told them now what he told me then, they'd probably throw him out of that job too."

Bozenka looked out the window again. "It's about time to milk the cows."

"It's time I went too, Bozenka."

"People would think I was an informer," said Bozenka. "And anyways, it wouldn't help Mrs. Hrozna now, would it?"

9.

"The theme of this meeting where Kopula got himself in trouble was 'Master Jan Hus: Precursor of Armed Revolution'," said Mr. Pohorsky, while I squinted against the Connington sun, watching Dr. Hrzan as he tried in vain to whack the ball out of the sandtrap. "Professor Nejedly himself — our notorious first socialist Minister of Education — was the keynote speaker. He couldn't find enough good things to say about Hus, what a progressive man he was, how violently he was opposed to the Church, and how the Catholics, compared to him, were inhuman bastards. Honza Kopula couldn't stand it, so he tells Nejedly that the Church hasn't oppressed a non-Catholic for at least two hundred years, whereas the Church itself is now being oppressed by the Communists. Hus was a Catholic priest, he says, and it wasn't the Church he was opposed to, but bad priests. Unfortunately he went too far and became a pigheaded heretic, and he got what he deserved. At that point Saun jumps up and lights into Professor Nejedly too. He says Comrade Kopula here is right to point out that Hus was a Catholic priest — he was a pious little busybody who believed in God, the same as all the rest, and as the comrade rightly pointed out, he got what he deserved. And he, Magister Saun, couldn't understand how the Communist Party could praise an idolator like Hus, who'd been willing to go to the stake for his God! In other cases, and rightly so, they've made short work of people who've done nothing more than deceive others through superstition. Professor Nejedly got pissed off, so did Honza Kopula, and both of them lit into Saun, so Saun got pissed off too, and that's when the actionable statements began to fly. The Communist Party was betraying the revolution when it praised a priest — Saun said that. And Hus was not only a heretic, he was the Antichrist hiding under the guise of piety — Kopula said that. Saun's remarks were far more incriminating than Kopula's, but because he was an atheist they didn't come down as hard on him. But they really hit Kopula. Wherever he went he kept having bad luck with atheists. In the slammer he ran up against another one, Valchar, one of the screws — I think I mentioned him before. He found out Kopula was praying and stuck him in the uranium mill. Birds of a feather, he said, because most of the guys in the mill were priests. That's where Honza picked up his cancer. I told him to drink more tea but he wouldn't because of the caffeine and other poisons in it. Oh, by the way, did you mean what you said about that ad?"

"Absolutely," I said, trying desperately to recall what ad Mr. Pohorsky was talking about. Then I remembered. Surely to God he hadn't taken it seriously? "This Valchar," I said. "I can't remember.

Who did you say he was?"

"He was a monster, man, I tell you. I get goose-pimples just thinking about him," said Mr. Pohorsky.

"Violent?"

"You can say that again," said Mr. Pohorsky, waving his hand. "Remember the lawyer who croaked on the cross? That was Valchar who did him in. But all the same, I can tell you — " and Mr. Pohorsky became philosophical. "Well, once I was belly-aching about the grub and Valchar comes up to me, grabs me by the lapels, and looks at me with these burning eyes of his — he was part gypsy — and he says, you know what he says to me?"

"No, but I can guess."

"You won't even come near," said Mr. Pohorsky. An orange Mohawk Airlines jet was moving through the ultramarine sky. In the distance Dr. Hrzan hit the ball straight into the sandtrap and then got into his golfmobile. A squirrel jumped out of a pine tree and crept up to Mr. Pohorsky, sniffing his trousers as Mr. Pohorsky lay on his back talking with his eyes closed. The squirrel hopped past his trousers and approached his head.

"Valchar says, 'Pohorsky, you're a sonofabitching capitalist. You want to bring back capitalism, right?' And he shook me like a sack of potatoes. He was strong. 'But we ain't letting capitalism come back, Pohorsky! You understand what I'm saying, Pohorsky? I went hungry. My father was unemployed and started drinking. Mother and the rest of us starved. Capitalism will not be restored, Pohorsky. It can't be. If I have to tear you apart like a snake, it won't come back!'"

The squirrel tickled Mr. Pohorsky's whiskers and he opened his eyes.

"Bugger off!" he said to the animal, and it fled and scampered up the pine tree. "I almost felt sorry for the poor bastard," said the greenskeeper. "When you get right down to it, he couldn't help what he was."

10.

"Laura," I said, "do you think ideology is stronger than the police?"

Laura laughed. There was a scarcely perceptible tone of contempt in her laughter. "Man is inclined to evil, right? Well, we're convinced it's the other way around. In primitive societies, man had a powerful sense of the collective, of mutual help. In that way he was good. It was class society that turned him into an evil animal. Communism will eventually replicate the relationships in those original societies. It will awaken all those old, original virtues in man."

"Nobility? Sensitivity? Love?" I said. "Or hatred, hypocrisy, cruelty, selfishness?"

All the humour went out of Laura's eyes, even sarcastic humour. "For the time being," she said, "we're still living in a divided world. But people, decent, noble people, are emotionally susceptible to notions of their own decency. It's hard to be rational about it. The invasion, of course, was a terrible emotional blow. But at the very least, the social avant-garde has to remain faithful to its own rationality."

"There's more to man than rationality," I said. "And you said yourself that even reason has its own illnesses."

II.

Alka-Seltzer, that miraculous cure for the excesses of the night life, put me back on my feet. It was ten in the morning. I had no idea when the evening with Hrzan's little Party cell had ended. I sat on the edge of my bed in the guest room of Telluride House and watched as an unseen postman slid a letter under the door. It bore an Italian stamp and a two-month-old postmark. Who could be writing me from Italy? It was Bukavec.

> Dear Danny,
> I'm writing this from Lago di Como, where I'm playing at a spring tournament. I heard you left Prague in a hurry and I'm wondering if you didn't let your pessimism get the better of you. Keep your chin up, my dear friend! Things only seem black — the advent of better times is closer than we think. For example, there are three Soviet grand masters here at the tournament with me. At first they only parrotted what they'd read about the invasion in the Soviet press, but in a couple of days I was able to persuade them that it was an international crime. And I have their assurances that once they return to Moscow they will explain the truth to people wherever they go. I know, you'll say it means nothing, it's a drop in the ocean. But make no mistake — grand masters have a greater authority among ordinary people than writers, not to mention politicians. When Petrosian says something, it has more impact among ordinary people than if the First Secretary said it. And the government can't touch them — if anything could arouse the Soviet people from their political lethargy, it would be the repression of famous chess players by the police. The situation in the

U.S.S.R. is by no means as hopeless as it seems.

When the tournament here is finished, I'm going back to Prague. I did so many rotten things there—I even hurt you, and the girl who invented that delightful twist on chess by mail. Imagine a kid like her playing two grand masters off against each other! I should really thank her; she enabled me to beat Petrofim, which I'd never have had the courage to do if I'd known who I was playing. What was her name? I'd like to look her up and ask her to forgive me.

I've come to realize that for years I've been serving the devil. The Communist Party is nothing but his latest incarnation. Now I have to make amends, at least in part. I've been reading the Bible a lot. What a magnificent, truthful book it is! What shall it profit a man if he gain the whole world . . . ? I, old friend, must save my own soul.

Yours for ever,
Jarda Bukavec

The telephone rang. The cheery voice of Dr. Hrzan. "How do you feel after last night, my friend? What are you up to?"

"I'm reading the diary of a madman," I said. "In this land of television, I find myself longing for classical literature."

12.

Gellen leaned towards the fire dying in the fireplace and added several logs. He took a few pages from a pile of newspapers, crumpled them, then noticed something and stopped.

"Here's a document for you, my friend!" he said. "'A Letter from the Central Committee to all Party Organizations'."

I was standing by the window. The white chapel of the Virgin Mary under Mare's Head shone like a star in the cold spring night. Behind my back, I heard Gellen's voice: "I have to give them one thing—Party documents are fine examples of the dialectic method in action. Listen to this." And he read, "'It was we Communists who were never afraid of criticism.' What do you make of that?"

What did I make of that? I closed my eyes and the chapel disappeared. I turned. "It's true, they were never afraid of it. But there's no dialectics in that. If anyone ran off at the mouth they had his balls cut off."

"And you don't call that dialectics?"

I thought for a while, then grinned at my friend.

"I suppose it is."

"Right. Let's read on: 'It was we Communists, our Party, who found the strength within ourselves to reveal and make amends for the tragic shortcomings, errors, and mistakes that took place during the era of the Cult of Personality.'"

He looked at me with a question in his eyes.

"Ostentatious use of the majestic plural," I suggested. "It would be interesting to try to locate the individuals who spurred that group into finding the strength within itself in the first place."

"Who? Listen: 'The Action Program from the spring of 1968 bore clear evidence of pressure from right-wing opportunists. Thanks to types like Ota Sik, Josef Spacek, Josef Smrkovsky, Frantisek Kriegl, Vaclav Slavik, Eduard Goldstucker, and others of their ilk'—I love that phrase," said Gellen. "Comrade Grimm back in Hronov was very fond of it. Tell me, do you remember Comrade Grimm and others of his ilk?"

"I do. Read on."

"Where was I: ' . . . and others of their ilk, many passages of a right-wing opportunist and revisionist nature were written into the Action Program.' To give ourselves an idea of what the comrades have in mind, we need only look at a speech made by Comrade Indra at a meeting of the Politburo last week." He turned around, reached into his bookshelf among the crime novels, and pulled out a green folder. "I keep my valuable documents in a special place," he said, and pulled out a clipping that was obviously from *Rude Pravo*. "'It's also high time,'" he read, "'that we stopped overdoing those "rehabilitations". Not everyone who was prosecuted in the fifties under the terms of socialist justice was innocent—' and notice, my friend, all the things that can be labelled 'socialist'. Do you remember a certain series of bathtubs?"

I nodded.

"'And please note that this statement takes us to a qualitatively higher stage in the development of the Party's courage. The Party, which once found the strength within itself to reveal its tragic errors and mistakes, is now finding the strength to reveal that the necessary revolutionary measures taken in the fifties, later revealed as mistakes and errors, were so declared as a consequence of those very mistakes and errors. And because two negatives make a positive, the necessary revolutionary measures taken in the fifties were necessary, and therefore, by definition, not erroneous and mistaken.' Am I not being magnificently dialectic?"

"You are," I assured him. "And it will be the Party and only the Party which will always find enough strength within itself to reveal future errors and mistakes. If anyone else finds the strength to reveal any errors and mistakes made by the Party, the Party will grind him into tiny pieces."

The logs were blazing furiously in the fireplace and Gellen, his face aglow in the light of the flickering flames, was again transformed into a provocative devil. Provocative. . . . Everything fit together, just as in a detective novel. On the basis of assumptions that were possible, if somewhat implausible. And if the impossible is eliminated, then what remains is true. . . . I stopped myself. Yes, but only in detective fiction of the classical school . . . in Edgar Allan's work. . . .

But what had Gellen done the night after, when the Father stayed at his prayers so long that he fell asleep on the steps leading to the altar? Outside the window, the stars were shining.

Vixi and Gellen's bedmate had carried me back to Hepner's cottage after midnight. Gellen had been drunk then too. Sulc and Pecen had come to dismantle the device the next day, after dark — let's say around ten o'clock. Father Doufal had left the chapel at the head of his procession about three that afternoon.

I turned back from the window. Gellen was still reading the Party document.

"No, no," he said, "I'm not emigrating anywhere. Of all the professions we have here, spectators are, historically speaking, the most important."

13.

"Listen, Mr. Pohorsky," I said, "that business about breaking necks and pulling out fingernails and throwing the Commies on the manure pile — "

"That bastard Indra!" said Mr. Pohorsky. "Read this!" He undid his shabby windbreaker and took a thick wallet out of an inside pocket. Instead of folding money, however, it was full of newspaper clippings. On the lawn, which he had trimmed himself only yesterday, he set an article in front of me that, according to a note written in ink in its margin, had come from the *Literarni Listy* of August 1968:

> On July 27, during a speech in Ostrava, A. Indra, a member of the Central Committee of the Communist Party, said, "There is evidence of a growing danger from the right, and various right-wing 'clubs' have been formed to provoke our working people. This was illustrated by a recent meeting of K231 in Usti nad Labem. A member of the executive of this so-called club of citizens unlawfully imprisoned in the 1950s, a certain Pohorsky, said publicly that 'the best way to argue with a Communist is to punch his teeth in, break his neck, pull out

his fingernails one by one, and then throw him on the manure pile and let the pigs finish him off!' "

I put the clipping down. "Oh well, it's obvious now where I — "

"Just go on reading it to the end," said Mr. Pohorsky, pushing the clipping back into my hand. "It was written by — " and he looked at the clipping, trying to find the name of the author, " — by a Mr. Vrchcolab. Never heard of him. Maybe you know who he is. But he did a great job! Go on, read it!"

I took the document and found the place where I'd left off. What followed was not a quote, but a text by a poet I knew quite well.

> Mr. Indra, whose conservative sympathies are well known, didn't bother to quote any more from the speech of this "certain" Mr. Pohorsky. Why not? The answer is clear if we read Mr. Pohorsky's speech to the end. Unfortunately for Mr. Indra, participants in the meeting at Usti nad Labem tape-recorded the entire meeting and provided our paper with a transcript. Right after the words "let the pigs finish him off", Mr. Pohorsky said this: "At the time, I too subscribed to what my friend Vanicek said. Later I realized, however, that cruelty begets cruelty, revenge begets revenge, and that if all of us want to extricate ourselves from the situation into which the years of Stalinism cast us, we — former political prisoners — must shake hands not only with Communists, but also with our former guards and torturers. Only in a state of general reconciliation, the kind that Comenius spoke about so long ago, is there hope for the Czechoslovak experiment.

I looked at the politician lying on his back in the Connington grass. "Never mind Vrchcolab. You said it very nicely yourself, Mr. Pohorsky."

"It was nothing," said the grass-barber, dismissing the comment with his hand. "They weren't my words, anyway. Honza Kopula kept babbling about it all the time he was in the uranium mill. All I did was bring it up to date a little, that's all."

14.

"The Party is going back to Lenin," said Laura.

An issue of *Tvorba* lay on her table. "Can I read you something?" I said.

She scowled, but nodded.

I opened the magazine and looked through its ideological supplement for a while. It didn't take long to find what I was looking for. The sentences I wanted to read to her were branded in my memory like a fiery sign.

> He was as uncompromising as he was human. . . . He demanded, in the interests of putting down an uprising in Nizhni Novgorod . . . that hundreds of prostitutes be shot or driven out of town. . . . In June 1918 he wrote Zinoviev: "Today we in the Central Committee have learned that in Petrograd the workers wished to respond to the murder of Volodrasky with mass terror and that you . . . prevented them from doing so. I protest categorically against this! We are compromising ourselves. We have been threatening mass terror and now, when the time comes to act, we instead impede the entirely justified revolutionary initiative of the masses."

Laura interrupted me. "Wasn't that the rational thing to say? Didn't such things save the revolution?"

I shrugged my shoulders. "Maybe. But that *was* a revolution. There was shooting and people were murdered, on both sides." I looked straight into her eyes. "Can you really say that's how it was here, around and after 1948?"

She said nothing.

"I know what can be said about that time," I said, putting *Tvorba* aside. "The *only* thing that can be said about it is that it was the disease of reason. And people died of that disease. A priest, for example — from the Virgin Mary under Mare's Head Hill."

Laura lowered her eyes and pulled out another cigarette. "I told you Barta did that when he was angry and upset. And he didn't know the priest had ulcers."

"I wasn't just thinking of that priest," I said, and again I deliberately refrained from mentioning Father Doufal's manicure. Laura, it seemed to me, was biting her lip. Her eyes slipped down to the small bust of Lenin glowing in the dusk. Once, in Moscow, they planned to build a Palace of the Soviets a hundred metres taller than the Empire State Building. The last two thirds of the structure was to be a statue of Vladimir Ilich Lenin covered with sheets of bronze. The idea was that when the sun had set and the streets of Moscow were engulfed in the gathering darkness, Lenin's head would still be aglow, casting reflected sunlight down into the gloom.

I looked at the burning bust and at Laura's tired face.

"Yes. Applying those principles is a problem, and Lenin was a genius. Stalin — "

"You know what Stalin did, Laura?" I interrupted her. "A minor thing, something that relates to the problem of application. Lenin banished democracy from the life of society, because society is crawling with the class enemy and democracy can be misused. But Stalin understood that because of Lenin's measure, the class enemy was able to penetrate the Party. Democracy existed only within the Party, and therefore it was only within the Party that it could be misused. What he did next was entirely logical. He applied Lenin's doctrine of terror to internal Party conditions. Completely logical. But can there be democracy where there is terror?" I asked. "And terror, naturally, doesn't mean just blood. I don't know what the soul bleeds, when it bleeds."

15.

"But the thing is, Mr. Smiricky, we wanted to go too," insisted Mrs. Pohorska. "They were giving passports to everyone then but, believe it or not, Mr. Smiricky, they never gave them to us. I kept going back, until finally sometime in the spring of '69 they told me we'd never get a passport because they said Father was engaged in hostile activity abroad."

Mrs. Pohorska pulled a newspaper out of a voluminous net shopping bag. "They put this kind of thing in the papers about him quite a bit," and she began to read slowly and with some difficulty, holding the newspaper from her at arm's length. "'People like Pohorsky and others of his ilk, who after the arrival of the fraternal armies fled across our borders and now live in the U.S.A., where they are richly rewarded for their treason — '" She stopped and looked at me. "Is it true that Father is living so well?"

"He spends his whole day on the golf course," I said.

"Does he really?"

Mrs. Pohorska was astonished. I explained to her what Mr. Pohorsky was doing all day long on the golf course and she spat symbolically. "I knew it was all lies! And I told him, Mr. Smiricky, back in '63, when they let him go, I said, Father, that's enough politics. You've had to pay for it before and you will again. But he wouldn't listen, Mr. Smiricky. He was a driven man."

We were talking in a room belonging to Mrs. Pohorska's cousin, whom I had contacted according to Mr. Pohorsky's conspiratorial plan, and who had in turn contacted Mrs. Pohorska. "They'd nab you if you went to see her yourself," he'd told me. "They're opening her letters, I've found that out for sure." So I made the contact, Mrs. Pohorska turned up at her cousin's in lightning-quick time, and I passed on the address of a obliging Yankee from Connington where Mrs. Pohorska could write to her husband, as well as the news that Mr. Pohorsky had not been kidnapped by Arabs, that he was not lying in hospital but was alive and well, prosperous, and working at the university.

Mrs. Pohorska took out a red handkerchief and wiped away her tears. Her eyes were tired and reddish from constant crying and she had long since forgotten how to speak normally. Whenever she opened her mouth, her voice came out in a kind of wail.

She blew her nose and then pulled from her bag a page that must have been torn out of some Western magazine, because the paper was glossy.

"Father hasn't let up, not even over there, Mr. Smiricky! And he's ruining our lives here. Just take a look at what he's up too."

She showed me a full-page ad with a photograph of Mr. Pohorsky on it. He was standing there as large as life, a steaming cup of tea in his hands and a television smile on his face. A graphic artist had retouched the gaps between his teeth so that they shone in solid white splendour. TEA HELPED ME SURVIVE! ran the caption under his picture, in brilliant orange lettering, and beneath that, in smaller type, was the story of how, thanks to tea, he had survived the uranium mill, with the additional claim that Chiswick Tea contained the highest percentage of the antitoxin thein. Mr. Pohorsky was a man of great fantasy.

"When did he send that to you?"

"He didn't — I told you, they confiscate all his letters. The cops brought it to me. They said they wanted me to see how Father was flinging mud at the republic. But Mr. Smiricky, everything he says here is true! He did work in the uranium mines. The only thing is, the tea he drank was different, not this — " and she squinted at the ad, " — Khiz — vix." She blew her nose again and then told me that Anicka, her daughter — a bank clerk — had been thrown out of work a month before on orders from above and now had to work on a state farm as a labourer. Mrs. Pohorsky herself had scrubbed floors for twenty years in a canteen for miners, so they couldn't really do anything worse to her.

"And was any of this worth it, Mr. Smiricky?" she wailed. "I mean Father getting so involved in supporting Dubcek? Just between us, Dubcek was a Commie like the rest of them. And he fooled around too, I can tell you. Just look at this!"

She took another *corpus delicti* from her well-stocked cache. It was amazing how many people had turned into collectors of curiosities; I was reminded of Gellen's green folder. But Gellen was gathering *acta theoretica.* Mrs. Pohorska's interest was fixed on the concrete.

It was an ordinary postcard, but it had a picture on it that I would not have expected to find in the hands of this old lady. It showed a naked woman and, standing behind her, an obviously naked man. The man was embracing the woman around the neck with one hand, and fondling her breast with the other. The girl was completely visible, *en face*, with curly black hair in her lap. The man was hidden behind the girl, with only a hairy leg and one hip visible, and his head cocked sideways and peeking out from behind the girl's naturally dark-blonde hair.

I didn't recognize the bodies, but the heads belonged to Suzi Kajetanova and our former First Secretary.

"There, you see, Mr. Smiricky?" said Mrs. Pohorska. "And his mouth was full of fine talk about the nation! And all the while he was carrying on like that! With a hussy like her! And him a father of three!"

I looked at Suzi's dear face and at the face of the man who had been groping after truth on the terrace of the Hrzansky Palace, after that ever-elusive perpetrator in the mystery stories of our lives. Then I tried to explain to Mrs. Pohorska that Comrade Kaiser and his Department of Culture had — somewhat amateurishly — turned into collage-makers. They had failed to destroy Suzi's popularity by circulating the rumour that she had peed on working people's heads from the balcony of the Hotel Hvezda. Nor had they succeeded in limiting the First Secretary's popularity by accusing him of being an agent of the CIA. Now, I thought, they would be more successful. People usually deny their saints the right to indulge in something that is human and indulged in by everyone else.

16.

"Laura!" I implored, almost like Mrs. Pohorsky. "I know your son. He's utterly different from you. I heard him speak twice. Today he's as young as you were then, when you were all converted to the faith."

"When we recognized the scientific truth," Laura corrected me.

"Do you think your son has no more than his faith?"

Laura turned her head into the shadow and remained like that for a while. But she was not wiping away tears, nothing like that. Soon she looked back into my eyes again and her ashen face was firm; gaunt, but firm. She had the pink lips of Miss Widemanova.

"I feel terribly sorry about all this, I really do. It kills me, you know? I'm his mother and I have — "

"Maternal feelings?" I suggested. I knew I was being cruel, but my sarcasm seemed to snap her out of it.

"Apart from that, I'm still in possession of my reason," she said, "and therefore I know that when Vladinek gets up there with his bullhorn, he is, unfortunately, a demagogue. Like everything else in the world, the Party is imperfect. But it still provides the nearest thing in the world to a perfect, scientifically run society. We're making this revolution with people, not with angels. But our system forces even the crooks to do good — in the general sense, though not necessarily in the narrow circle of their personal influence — that is, if they want to hang on to their sinecures. People live better here."

The essence of science, Laura, is precise definition. Who are the people? And who are they not? It was the kind of question a demagogue like Vladinek might ask, but I asked it only to myself.

17.

"Mummy, what's for supper?" asked Vixi's Vojtisek.

"You'll see," she said.

And we did see. Ruzena and her oldest son, Pepik, brought a pot from the stove and the Koziseks' kitchen filled with the aroma of abundance. The kitchen hadn't changed much in twenty-one years: a large room in a wooden country cottage with a low ceiling and small windows, and the same holy pictures hanging just below the ceiling — Saint Florian, Saint Wenceslas, Saint John of Nepomuk — and the plain, unvarnished wooden table permeated with the smell of cottage cheese and vegetable soup. The only changes were the electric light, replacing the kerosene lamp that had once hung from the beams, and, in the corner, an enormous Hungarian television set.

We gathered around the table. Vixi's diminutive grandfather, who was celebrating his ninetieth birthday, sat at the head of it. Ruzena, buxom and pink, took the lid off the pot. A column of delicious steam rolled out, and she dished up enormous mounds of boiled pig — the head, the tail, and the hocks — into the stoneware plates in front of us. We took grated horse-radish from a dish, and slices of bread from a basket (the bread was store-bought, that was another change; the grandfather's oven was now cold). We must have looked like a poster I remembered from my teaching days in the lilac town, depicting an idyllic vision of socialism as a perennial feast. Even Ruzena the plump housewife seemed to have stepped straight out of the poster; she was wearing the same Sunday-best blouse of white cotton with folk embroidery on it, and she portioned out the chunks of boiled pig with a smile of unclouded bliss.

"There ain't nothin' like boiled pig's head," cackled the old man, taking his first mouthful. Already his moustache was dripping with grease.

"But it needs horse-radish," said the cousin, Antonin. "Unless anyone wants mustard; we got that too."

But no one did. We were already tucking into our boiled pig. The delicious meat aroused my latent gluttony. It was evening, in a cottage in the mountains, the family sitting around the supper-table eating boiled pork. A kind of atavistic Gargantuanism awoke inside me. I gobbled down a boiled ear and Ruzena, smiling, served me a piece of hock, the succulent skin still bearing stiff bristles. I swallowed the hock, chasing it with large amounts of horse-radish.

"They'll be another pig ready by Christmas," said Antonin. "Six, seven hundred pound. By then they'll be two hundred, two hundred and fifty bottles of fruit wine ready too, plus at least fifty bottles of slivovice. Plus a ton or so of spuds — "

"Are you going to have another feast when you kill that pig?" asked Vixi's fifteen-year-old daughter, Anezka.

"You're dang right we are," said the cousin. "And you all have to come. We'll really fill our faces!"

The delicious fatty juices flowed into my stomach. Outside the window, the lower branches of a burgeoning apple tree nodded languidly in the breeze. There is a feeling of great security in the aroma of pork. I hadn't experienced anything like it for two years, perhaps more. The skin tasted better to me than all the sirloin steaks in all the Holiday Inns of the world.

"People are finally gettin' on the right track," Antonin said. "They've figured out it's better to just get on with the work and not worry about nothin' else. And not go traipsin' off the devil knows where, way the other side of the ocean. Take Jirka Zima — when the Russkies came, he took off. And what's he doin' now? Workin' in a factory somewheres in Canada. Least he was. Now they've chucked him out of work. Says they got unemployment over there."

"Should of stood home, sat on his ass where he belongs," cackled the old man. "All this gaddin' about. Home is home, damn it!"

"Jirka Zima?" I said, and then stopped. But it was too late.

"You remember him, Mr. Smiricky," said Antonin. "They locked his dad up with old Stoklasa and Benisek, sayin' they was poisonin' animals. You taught Bozena Stoklasova — "

"I read about it in the papers," I interrupted hastily. "They said they'd rehabilitated them all."

"Course, what am I thinking, you never taught here," backtracked the cousin, winking awkwardly at Vixi; he'd just about spilled the beans. But Vojtech Novotny was too absorbed in the boiled pig, or perhaps in his own thoughts, to notice.

"Their Jirka — Jirka Zima, that is — had to work on the state farm in Jaromer. At the beginnin' it was no piece of cake, I can tell you, but then he married the accountant's daughter and they gave him the livestock to look after, and he started doin' pretty well. He bought a car, their boy got into high school, he built a house — "

"What'd he run away for, then?"

"He pissed his pants. When Dubcek was in, Jirka shot his mouth off a lot. Got some kind of agricultural union going — "

"He shouldn't have done that," I said.

"Damn right!" croaked the old man. "What the hell business was it of his to go around settin' up unions? And anyways it was just another Communist swindle like all the rest of them things. He should of stood put and been happy with what he got. Them Communists hassled his poor father till he died in jail, so why didn't Jirka just keep his damn fool mouth shut?"

Vojtech Novotny suddenly sat up. "I disagree," he said, with sudden interest. "They tortured his father to death. It was quite natural that he wanted to clear his name."

"What do you mean, clear his name?" the old man snorted. "Everyone knew Zima was innocent. Do you think people are stupid? It was those sons of bitches Ponykl and Nohejl who dragged him into it. Of course, they let Nohejl go again, the dumb clucks — they put him away for perjury under Dubcek, but now he's out walkin' around again. They say he works in Zeleny Brod in the National Committee. Don't imagine he'll get much work done there, though. He always was a lazy bastard, never liked the smell of work. That's why he got mixed up with the Secret Police in the first place. Stinkin' layabout!"

"That's exactly it, Grandad," said Novotny, trying to redirect the flow of the old man's hatred in the right direction. "That's the kind of people Jirka Zima was coming out against in '68 when — "

"That's just what I'm sayin'!" said the old man, cutting him off. "Was there any call for him to be comin' out against anyone? What was he doin' gettin' mixed up in them Communist swindles anyway, the jackass?"

"Grandpa's right," said Ruzena. "Why should we bother about them? Let them argue themselves silly in Prague. We'll just carry on here in our co-op as best we can!"

We were silent for a while, revelling in the wonderful flavour of boiled pig. The old man smacked his lips energetically and mumbled something under his whiskers.

"So the co-op is doing well?" I asked.

"Thank God, yes," said Antonin. "Last year wasn't too good, with the invasion and all. We didn't get much per unit. But this year everything's back on track, and I reckon that, countin' the goods we take home, we'll be getting two, two and a half a month."

"And what about the life of the spirit here?" asked Vojtech Novotny in a tone of dissatisfaction.

"You mean with mass and all?" said the cousin awkwardly. "Well, we — I mean our family — we was never great churchgoers, you know that. Grandad left the church back in 1918. But they do celebrate mass here. There's a young priest comes in from Hronov on a motorcycle every two weeks. The one they had before got locked up, must be two or three years back. He got mixed up in some scheme for sellin' statues or somethin' like that. Lazy as a bedbug, that one was. There was never any masses in Maselna Lhota while he was around. But the new one, he's younger and he's leanin' into it pretty good. Roars around on his bike like the devil. Only thing is, people don't turn out for him much. Just a few old women, the odd teenage girl — the priest is young and good-lookin', see — "

Vixi's husband shook his head sadly. "It's just the opposite in the city. Religious life hasn't been this intense for a long time. And a lot of young people are going to church. I was wondering," and he looked at the grease-slicked old man, who was obviously full but was still stuffing himself, "do you happen to remember a priest called Father Doufal?"

"The one the Commies murdered?" asked the old man indifferently. "How could I forget?"

"Did people here talk about him? Did they follow that series of articles in *The People's Democracy*?"

"Oh, I wouldn't say so, no," said Antonin. "We knew what was goin' on back in '49 — we knew the Commies set him up, just like they did Stoklasa and Zima and Josef Benisko. Poor bugger. But there was lots like him."

"But it actually was a miracle," the poet insisted.

"So they say," admitted the cousin. "Have some more pig meat, lad. You're not eatin'. Here, take a piece of this trotter. Look at all the lovely fat on it!"

We submerged ourselves again in the delights of pork fat and gravy. Saint Florian, Saint Wenceslas, the patron saint of Bohemia, and Saint John of Nepomuk, the holy martyr to secrecy, looked down upon us impassively from their perch on the beam. Chickens were clucking outside the window. I felt wonderful. A delicious laziness came over me and I wanted nothing more. If this could have gone on and on, with cooked pork and horse-radish tomorrow, the day after, and so on, I would have wanted for nothing more, nothing at all. It was probably better, as Cousin Antonin said, to get on the right track and then stick to it. Any right track. Boiled pig, horse-radish, the bliss around the kitchen stove, peace and brotherhood among nations. And to top it off, let the radio play some music — if need be, even symphonic music.

Suddenly the poet felt sick. He wasn't used to so much fatty food all at once. For twenty years he'd eaten in the hospital canteen, and although in time he'd been promoted from a washer of corpses to an orderly, he still didn't make the kind of money that would allow him to eat well. So now the aroma of camomile tea blended with the smell of boiled pork. They put him to bed in a tiny bedroom with a striped eiderdown, and stars beyond the window, and Vixi was free. We went for a stroll on the hillside to help walk off the food, as the cousin put it, before we went to bed, and to remind ourselves, twenty years later, of the magic of a village night in the mountains.

The magic was delightful and refreshing. The village lay like a swarm of fireflies in the valley, and there were clear skies above the jagged silhouette of the mountains.

"Time is a terrible thing," I said. "Time is a traitor. I'm forty-five. And you must be — what? — thirty-eight, Vixi?"

"You mean you can't remember?"

"I think I'd rather forget. When we were here last — it was just before that big anniversary in Hronov, remember?"

"And before the big screw-up in the chess match," she said. "Look, prof, did you know Bukavec came to see me?"

"When?"

"When you were in America. He came to apologize. He wanted me to forgive him."

"Which you did, I hope."

"He really begged me. But I played stubborn," said Vixi. "Now I feel like kicking myself. I hear they fractured his skull in Pankrac prison."

"They say it was suicide."

"Sure it was! But even if it had been, they'd still have him on their conscience. If it wasn't for them, he'd have gone on playing chess and never given suicide a thought. Assuming he ever did. But you know what I regret most?"

"What?"

"I told him he ruined my life when he blew the whistle on me."

"Didn't he?"

"Of course not," said Vixi. "So I'd have graduated from school, and instead of being a nurse's aide I'd have started as a tea-lady with a high-school diploma. Then some playboy would have knocked me up because I was dumb and boy-crazy. It would be practically impossible to ruin a life like mine."

We were silent. A meteor streaked down the sky, like a bright tear falling.

"What do you want for yourself, Vixi?"

"Me? Nothing any more. The usual things. I want the kids to grow up. I want Vojtisek to be a doctor and Anezka to be smart enough to land herself a doctor."

"You landed two," I said.

"They landed me, is more like it. You know what I mean?"

She was right. Another tear of white-hot iron dropped from the sky.

"What do you want for yourself, sir?"

Me? I was intoxicated by the magic of the village night and, like everything else, it became a symbol. That night, no doubt, it meant something different than it had twenty years before. Though God knows. I hear some verses in my head. . . . *Surrounded by a mystery . . . like blind men, we do grope through darkness . . . only Jesus is the light. . . .* Who had sung that? The Moravian Brethren at the widow Ledvinova's? Or some other bearded men? Or was it all just a. . . . *One generation passeth away, and another one cometh: but the earth abideth for ever. . . .* I heard those distant, wailing voices, many of them almost certainly dead by now . . . the kind faces glowed . . . singing along with an out-of-tune lute and a wheezing, asthmatic harmonium, a violin, a trembling flute, and what do I want for myself? Not much. Almost nothing.

"I want to die, Vixi," I said.

"That's not true," said Vixi. "You just made that up now."

A new meteor dropped its tear among the stars of Orion. But I wanted nothing. It was cold by now, and Vixi wasn't wearing a sweater. Soon we returned to the warm cottage.

18.

Suzi rushed round the corner of the corridor, all out of breath. She ran with her knees tight together, her hair was stringy, and traces of two days' worth of makeup were still on her face.

"Hi! Am I late?"

"Ten minutes later than usual," said the bandleader, Vaclav Bor.

We went back into the studio. In daylight and in her street clothes,

Suzi looked like a brazen, slovenly servant girl from a 1920s working-class dance hall. Her complexion, without makeup, was ashen brown, and when she forgot to hold her face at a professional angle she looked either scrawny or, from another angle, slightly puffy. A dirty shoulder strap peered out of the low-cut neckline of her crumpled dress, and she had three ladders of different lengths on her left stocking; her shoes had not seen polish since the day she bought them, and there was a large, pinkish splotch on her breast, probably from some red wine that hadn't quite made it to her mouth. Whenever I saw her like that, with her tongue hanging out, going straight from the bus where she'd spent the night — strengthened not by sleep but by dextroamphetamines — and rushing to the raw morning recording studios, to the cold morning theatres for rehearsal, to an early morning recording session at the radio building, and asking, "Am I late?", she reminded me of an American film, originally called *Stage Door* but for the sentimental Czech market translated as *A Butterfly in the Spotlight.* During the day she was a caterpillar, but each evening she swept out into the footlights as a beautiful, scintillating butterfly.

She was nervous. She tried to ingratiate herself with the production assistant handling the recording console; she'd even brought her a present, a special foreign recipe for goulash. She gave me a peck on the cheek — a gesture she usually omitted. When the bandleader, who had a cold, was suddenly overcome by a fit of coughing, she offered him some sticky lozenges and promised to knit him a Norwegian sweater on their next road trip. And then, when they stuck the score in her hands, she suddenly remembered she hadn't been to the bathroom yet and rushed out of the room.

"What's the matter with her?" I asked Bor. "Is she all dexed up this morning?"

Bor shook his head. "No, it's not that. She signed a loyalty oath for the minister. Her name was on a list they published in *Rude Pravo* and now she thinks she's marked for life."

"Well, not everybody signed it," I ventured.

"Most people weren't even asked. They want signatures mainly from aces like her. And besides, they've got something on her: she once kissed Sasha Dubcek."

"You signed it too, didn't you?" I asked cautiously.

With his characteristic frankness, Bor replied, "Like shit I signed it! All I signed was an attendance slip at the door. Next day we were all in *Rude and Depraved*, not as 'those present' but as signatures of some fucking statement of loyalty to the Party or whatever it was. I called them up right away, but of course they didn't print a retraction. So I started telling everyone I met that I hadn't signed a goddamned thing and that I wasn't loyal to the Party at all. Hardly anyone believed me, so I said to hell with it. And now we're doing a tour of the Soviet Union, too."

Bor's band was sitting in the sound studio on the other side of the soundproof glass, laughing at something.

"This will be the first time in two years, won't it?"

"Yeah. We came back from the last one two days before the invasion."

"What was it like?"

"A real hoot, man, you know how it is?" Bor delicately unwrapped Suzi's lozenge and went to wash it under the tap. Then he popped it into his mouth. "A hoot," he repeated. "We did a string of concerts in Azerbaijan, Baluchistan, I can't even remember all the names. The only time you ever see a Russkie there is in the Party secretariat, and we never went there. But fifty thousand people show up at the concert, most of them young, and in one place there was this enormous herd of horses around the stadium, more horses than we probably have in the whole goddamned country. And they had these buggies with a kind of archlike rig for the horses, just like you see in those old paintings."

"Troikas?" I asked. "In Baluchistan?"

"Yeah. Or maybe it was somewhere else, I get these places mixed up. You know how it is on the road. But it was hot, man, like the tropics. And we had this concert one Sunday afternoon — you should have seen Suzi sweat! All morning we were pouring this local piss into ourselves, camel beer or something, and Suzi got so plastered she almost tossed her cookies over some guy wearing a suitcaseful of medals at some reception that evening, and to make matters worse he was Russian, a Party secretary. For a week afterwards we all smelled like camels."

"Even Suzi?"

"She was the worst of all. You know how she can knock them back with the best of us. But you can't imagine a better audience, man. We get up there on stage and everywhere, as far as you can see on all sides, there's these flat faces with squashed noses and shaved heads. Soldiers. In Ordzho or Kydze or wherever there was this huge military base, a missile base, so they say. And there they all were, staring at us like we'd come from Mars, but as soon as we started playing they applauded so loud after every number that the horses stampeded and they had to round them up with helicopters."

"You're exaggerating," I said.

"Like shit," said Bor. "The encores were half as long as the concert."

"What did you play for them? Russian folk songs?"

"What we always play — pop in the first half, straight jazz in the second. Suzi sang twelve choruses of scat, almost tied her vocal cords in a knot. No, man, we didn't play any goddamned Russian folk songs," said Bor, "except for 'Policko, Pole', and we swung that. When they were sending us off next day there was some local tamburizza band there imitating it for us, and they almost swung it, man. They got good ears. But we heard later that some Party secretary banned them, because when a Bulgarian delegation came to visit they played the Soviet anthem with some blue notes smuggled in."

"You're putting me on."

"I swear to God it's true," said Bor, who was probably lying. "At least, that's what Volodya Lifshitz told us later, in Vladivostok. That Party secretary — "

"The one Suzi barfed on?"

"Almost barfed on," Bor corrected me. "He got into shit with Moscow because of the anthem — some local careerist in Ordzhokydze blew the whistle on him. So the secretary raked the band over the coals and now they're playing *kalinky* again. But Volodya says they have tapes sent to them secretly from Moscow and they're transcribing Ornette Coleman for the balalaika."

"Now I know you're kidding," I said.

Suzi came back from the toilet. They stuck a sheet of music, written specially for the coming tour, into her hands. She'd never seen the song before, but there was nothing unusual about that. She sat down in a corner with the music for a couple of minutes, then got up, declared she was ready to wing it, and went into the studio. I put on a set of headphones.

The song was a waltz, but naturally the band didn't play it in straight three-quarter time. The title of the song — "A Party, after Leo Tolstoy" — was somewhat unconventional and clearly directed at the Soviet official who would have to approve it. The lyrics purported to be inspired by *War and Peace.* Suzi, more by instinct than by reason (with which she was not particularly well endowed), understood the pretence, and her magnificent voice wove ornaments suggesting worlds of forbidden allegory around the innocent waltz:

The marshals come, the marshals go,
Inviting ladies to the dance. . . .

Through my mind flashed a memory of Lester — under a swastika in the Lucerna hall — introducing "The St. Louis Blues" as "The Song of Resetova Lhota" — that same old tactic, now refined by a quarter of a century of saintly dissimulation and *reservatio mentalis.* But now, as always,

I was drawn into the paradise of that voice, the only paradise we had left here. It had to be a gift from God, because that was the only hypothesis that could explain it. Her voice played with the marshals, drawing them in quadrangle time over the triangle of the waltz, and I could see them in my mind as large spheres, the top half covered with medals, the bottom half red and polished like black mirrors:

The marshals come, the marshals go. . . .

General Yepishev strode towards the airport building but the waltz held him back, the brass instruments underlining his terrifying burlesque of a parade-ground step, four-four over three-quarter time, while Suzi's voice, like drops of poison, slipped over the waves of the "Blue Danube". Everything was, as always, something else instead—

Inviting ladies to the dance. . . .

The generals, I hoped, would not understand; but the shorn-headed young recruits from the peanut gallery might—the lads who wanted to make off with Martina's soft drink; who yearned to communicate but were interrupted; who, in legends spread by touring foreign bands like Vaclav Bor's, transcribed Gerry Mulligan for the mandolin . . . and the saxophones soared into a wailing swing riff while Suzi sang a piercing soprano scat. The chief engineer leaned over to the production assistant, and as I took off my headphones I heard him say, "Goddamn it, Jitka, she's cooking today."

The girl handling the tape machines nodded blissfully.

When they'd finished recording the final take, Suzi ran up to me. "Danny, will you come to the canteen with me for a coffee?"

I was astonished. It was always I who had to invite her, and she almost never had time. "Of course, Suzi. I'm yours for as long as you want."

She smiled nervously and, against all expectations, took my arm.

19.

The graceful curve of the marble staircase ended in a vacant marble frame. In that frame stood a beige lady in sunglasses, watching a gang of workers dragging a large door up the marble stairs. The embossed copper plates on the door glistened.

I was leafing through the manuscript of Paternoster's new work.

"Give it back to me," said Paternoster. "I have to rewrite the whole thing, from start to finish. Everyone will recognize Hejl and Pinkava, and they're national heroes now, so it's going to be about as easy to write the truth about them as it is about that so-called hero Julius Fucik. Give it here."

I gave him back the manuscript and he locked it in a deep drawer.

"They really are heroes," I said. "To behave the way they're behaving when they know very well what the Russians are capable of— "

"It's a martyr complex," said Paternoster. He waved a paper he'd picked up from his desk and handed it to me. "I'm telling you, every abnormal behaviour pattern has a psychopathological cause. And when the KGB and Russian tanks take over your country, the only thing normal is keeping your mouth shut and your opinions to yourself. You should read this," he said, tapping the piece of paper. "This is more to the point than any of my utopias."

'Hmm," I said. The beige lady gracefully waved a hand in a glacé glove; one of the workers took off his hat and wiped his forehead with a handkerchief. I looked at the paper. It was a questionnaire and it concerned me. It had a wonderful title—INFORMATION ON RETURNEES—and in the corner, in red, the word CONFIDENTIAL! The questions were such that, if Paternoster answered them truthfully, they'd hand me over to the Ministry of the Interior for drawing and quartering. One of them went: "What did the returnee write to you about in his letters from abroad? (If you have the letters, attach them to this form!)" And that was the least dangerous of the questions.

"How are you going to answer that one?" I asked him.

"I'll say you wrote about broads. That's the only thing that sounds credible in your case. Though I get the impression you lost interest there, am I right?"

He got up, went over to the liquor cabinet, where he kept his tobacco, and refilled his pipe. "But I tell you," he said without turning around, "some people are going to be annoyed you came back."

"You mean because they won't be able to declare me a traitor?"

"Well, there's that too. But I was thinking of people like Nabal. Not long ago he said that the more people stay abroad, the bigger print runs the rest of us will have."

"The rat!" I said. "And here I praised him everywhere I went. But he's wrong. The Party will put an end to such reformist greed."

Paternoster puffed on his pipe and I was intoxicated with the sweet smell of imported tobacco.

"Why the hell did you come back, anyway?" he asked. "Couldn't you go on writing your operettas over there?"

I shrugged.

"Don't tell me you were homesick for the mother country!"

I shrugged again. No — I hadn't been homesick. It was more a feeling that I'd lost interest in life. The lid had come down. The cage door was shut. Not the same cage door Mr. Kohn had been so afraid of. People were still travelling abroad — not everyone, but some — and there were no monster trials. It was a less material, a less definitive cage. A cage lined with dry straw and provided with a bowl of milk.

"I came back for the broads," I said. "They're not as demanding here, yet. Over there, they're all sex maniacs. And for the two of us, my friend, the age of potency is slowly coming to an end."

"Speak for yourself," said Paternoster, "but just between you and me — " He waved his hand dismissively. "But what the hell. The real fuckup is that they've invited us — that is, me, Nabal, and old Kopretina — to join a five-member writers' commission to sit down with the Ministry of Culture. They want us to bury the old Writers' Union. It's not a nice prospect."

"Did you accept?"

"What could we do? The minister told us in no uncertain terms that while they appreciate the fact that we didn't get mixed up in anything during the counter-revolution, if we don't get mixed up in this latest scheme of theirs now they won't appreciate it one bit."

"So all your caution wasn't worth a damn in the end."

"If you're in a river of shit, it makes a big difference whether you're down at the bottom, or up on the surface paddling your canoe. And I tell you, my friend, that shit we're in now is going to be around for a long time. Besides, maybe we can help in some way."

It was the classic excuse of all such canoeists in all such rivers, and I made no comment.

"Just wait, though," he added. "They'll think up something for you too. You should have stayed in America."

We were silent. I looked out the window. The toiling workers were using all their strength to fit the door into the marble portal. The lady in the beige suit was standing to one side, directing the operation with her pink gloves.

I could smell the fragrant smoke behind me. Paternoster had come over and was looking out the window too.

"She's Mrs. Ex-Prime-Minister," he said. "Now Mrs. Member-of-the-Praesidium."

"So the once-abandoned Xanadu is moving rapidly towards a successful conclusion."

The men finally set the bronze door on its hinges and the beige lady tried it out.

20.

The lighting in the radio station canteen was fluorescent and it made Suzi's gaunt face almost unrecognizable. It was past lunchtime and we were sitting there over two sloppy cups of Turkish coffee. Suzi was in her worst caterpillarish phase.

She came right to the point. "Danny, do you think I'm a whore?"

She stared at me, her eyes dilated by whatever drug she was on.

"Suzi! I've always wished you would be — but every time, you prove to me that you're not."

"You know what I mean."

I smiled at her. "Yes, I know. And no, I don't think you are — not at all."

"But other people do. Look at this." And she placed a letter in a torn envelope on the table in front of me.

I took the letter out of the envelope and read:

> Kajetanova, you whore!
> We loved you, but now you can go to hell. You signed your life over to the occupiers and their servants, and as far as we're concerned you're finished. Go ahead and sing for the Kremlin murderers who enslaved our country. Get drunk on their vodka while the cops back home arrest us and lock us up. On the anniversary of the invasion they picked up Hynek, Olda, and Pavlina from our gang, stripped them naked and beat them, then threw them out of school. And what were you doing, Kajetanova, you whore? Necking with Husak? Just like you fucked Dubcek, except you didn't deserve him. We hope you fuck your way all the way up to Brezhnev, you whore, because as far as we're concerned, you're dead.
>
> Your former fans,
> Petr and Honza

It was worse than I could have imagined. Suzi stared at me with panic-stricken eyes. "Don't pay attention to things like this, Suzi," I said. I tried to sound encouraging but I couldn't keep a false note out of my voice — and Suzi had perfect pitch. "We all know you didn't do anything bad."

"Danny, please believe me! I didn't want to sign it, but they told me they wouldn't let me sing if I didn't!" she said miserably, and she didn't have to say any more.

"I know, Suzi. You couldn't let them silence you. And most people know how it is. These kids," and I pointed at the letter, "are young and foolish. They don't know any history. They were obviously never taught about the early Christians."

Suzi's eyes, made wider and more attractive by the drug, questioned me. "I don't understand," she sighed at last.

"There were two kinds of early Christians," I said. "The public Christians and the secret Christians. The public ones let themselves be thrown to the wild animals. The secret ones made sacrifices to the Roman gods during the day, and at night they took communion in the catacombs. The Church recognizes both kinds: the ones who were eaten became saints, but it was the others who survived and eventually spread the teachings of Christ all over the world."

Suzi thought hard, and a faint hope kindled in her eyes. "I honestly didn't want to sign it, Danny. But they went after me in a really filthy way."

"I can imagine they did."

"Maybe you can't. Did you — did you see that picture?"

I nodded.

"Danny," she said imploringly, "believe me! You know me! I swear to you, I never had anything to do with Dubcek. I only kissed him that once, that was all!"

"You don't have to explain it, Suzi. I know a photo-montage when I see one. And they did a pretty lousy job of it."

"Didn't they? Vaclav Bor saw that right away, too. The director showed him the picture so he'd stop working with me, but he didn't want to let him keep it. He said he was only pointing it out to him, as a friend. And Bor told me. I was so outraged I got a lawyer and told him to sue."

She was so derailed by the gall of the Party Cultural Bureau that she forgot herself and grasped my hand. I could see the tenor saxophonist Hreben, the most notorious gossip in the band, looking at us from the counter where he was picking up a belated lunch, and I remembered that Suzi's present husband was more jealous than any of her previous ones. But I didn't care.

"The trouble is, my lawyer's in the soup because he was handling political rehabilitations in '68. And the public prosecutor wouldn't accept my suit because he said the perpetrator — the one who did those photos — was unknown and you can't sue an unknown perpetrator. Oh well — I guess you probably can't."

"Perhaps he could be tracked down, Suzi," I said, trying to keep her spirits up. "The director showed the photograph to Bor. That means he's circulating libellous material."

"They accepted a suit against him, but the judge remanded the case."

"Till when?"

"He didn't give a date. That probably means till forever," Suzi said, resigned. "Because in the meantime they published the photograph abroad — someone sent me the magazine from Munich. And the lawyer said it made things worse, not better."

She raised the cup of coffee with a trembling hand and looked at me over the rim. It was covered with dried coffee grounds.

"I don't have the magazine with me. I lent it to Mr. Lester. I'll call him and ask him to bring it to the Lucerna bar tonight — that is, if you're coming . . . ?"

"Of course I'm coming, Suzi."

She smiled gratefully at me. "And they dragged something else out against me too. They said I was there when Hreben said the Communists were a criminal organization. They had a tape-recorder hidden in the dressing room. They played it back to us and said either we sign and go to Russia on a state tour, or we never appear in public again. And they said it was us who sent the pictures to the West German magazine ourselves to make the regime look bad, and that qualifies as slandering the republic, and with that and the tape they have enough on us to put us in jail."

"Oh, Suzi!"

Before me that sweet, gaunt face which seemed to understand nothing . . . and how could it? . . . how could sweet Suzi understand that higher wisdom which concerns itself with children evacuated to survive and a nation destined to be destroyed . . . which comes from the region of means justified by all manner of ends . . . how could my butterfly girl understand the mind of the justifying bishop of all this?. . . Oh, Laura!

"Then they said there was another aggravating circumstance in my case, because that time in Vienna they said I dishonoured that Russian writer — what was his name?"

"Anton Pavlovich Chekhov?"

"That's him, the swine! Not the other one — he seemed pretty decent."

21.

"Laura!" I implored. "Laura, supposing we admit that evil is necessary to establish good, that still doesn't stop us from calling it evil — "

"Certainly. And the necessity is a question of degree."

"And," I asked, "who determines the degree? The Party?"

"The Party," said Laura.

A weariness came over me. The long march around the vicious circle of her fidelity had worn me out.

"What is the Party?" I asked, like Pilate. And I washed my hands of the acts for which I bore no responsibility. The evil acts and the good. What else could Pilate do, if the grace of God wasn't upon him?

"Laura," I sighed. "Remember what your party was saying twenty years ago? About everyone eventually understanding? In twenty years, almost no one has."

"That's the consequence of the mistakes the Party has made over the past twenty years," said Laura. "People were taken advantage of by — "

She didn't finish the sentence.

"By whom?" I pressed her. "Traitors? Foreign agents?"

She looked at Lenin's bust. "Look, you're an intelligent man," she said, pushing Lenin a little farther away from her. Now the tiny head glowed in the light of the streetlamp, somewhat, I imagined, as it would have glowed over Moscow had the gigantic project ever been realized. "There may have even been the odd agent here or there. I doubt it, but I don't know. But the absolute majority can be divided into two categories. In some cases, the categories overlap."

I waited to see what she would say.

"Madmen, and people with ambitions. Or, if you wish — idealists, and those who needed to hear themselves talk."

"And who are now occupying the posts that the madmen and the ambitious tried to occupy?" I asked.

"The idealists."

"Madmen, in other words — ?"

"No," she said. "There are two world-views and two kinds of idealism. Didn't you ever go to political schooling? You must have been asleep." She grinned. "Our world-view uses objective social forces for the benefit of the masses. Regardless of what the subjective motivations are."

Her remark chilled me. Someone once told me something similar. Where was it? In the shadow of that monument to the heretic who was burned at the stake? Yes — and it was one of her husbands. And he was commenting on the views of her son.

22.

Suzi fell silent, then swallowed a pill from a familiar white tube and washed it down with coffee from the disgustingly unclean cup.

"But, Danny, I still shouldn't have done it. I should have let them put me in prison instead!"

Tears welled up in her panic-stricken eyes. Now it was my turn to take her hand. "What good would that have done, Suzi? A temporary sensation for the scandal sheets on the other side of the hill."

"It would have been more than that. But I swear I'd have let them lock me up if I'd been sure they'd let me sing again after I got out. But you know how it is. They've put me through so much already."

She pulled out a handkerchief that rivalled the government-issue coffee-cup in front of her for grubbiness. They had put her through a lot. I remembered the trial . . . how many dollars had been involved? . . . Twenty-seven, or was it thirty-seven? And then that business about urinating from the balcony. . . .

Her tears made their way down through yesterday's makeup. Suzi lifted her awful handkerchief and blew. "Danny, I feel wretched. I'm terrified they'll boo me off the stage tonight." I looked at her. She finally burst into sobs, smearing her face with tears mixed with makeup and bits of old chewing-gum that had stuck to her handkerchief. She wept inconsolably, while I marvelled at how full of infinite variety are the variations on class warfare provided for by Marxism-Leninism. It occurred to me that if Comrade Kaiser were endowed with the power of telepathy, he would at that moment have declared me a cynic for whom nothing is sacred, not even the doctrine for which revolutionaries bled and died. But I know they bled and died for that doctrine. That's precisely why I'm a cynic, Comrade Chairman of the Bureau for Culture. . . .

"They won't boo you off the stage, Sue," I said. "You'll crack off a few Beatles numbers and they'll carry you out on their shoulders. You'll see. I'm telling you, people love you, Suzi."

She took my hand again. "I know you're fond of me, Danny. But audiences are — they can be awfully fickle, you know?"

"Not this audience."

"You think so?"

I pressed her hand until the tender little bones in it cracked. Then she thought of a colossal but rather moving stupidity. "I'm — I've always kind of — held you at arm's length, Danny — "

"Not at all, Suzi. Listen, I respect you for it."

"Seriously?"

"Seriously. It's one of the things I like about you. You're kind of old-fashioned. I don't mean in music," I added quickly. "I mean you're faithful to your husbands." She didn't notice the plural. "Hey, I'll tell you what — I'll bring you some real French cognac tonight. And you'll sing like a nightingale." For the first time since we'd entered the canteen, she smiled. Then I thought of a way to cheer her up even more. "And listen, that other Russian from Vienna, the one you said seemed decent — remember him?"

"The one I played the hooker for?"

"That's right. Arashidov. He was a great guy, wasn't he? He got drunk that time with Morris and said insulting things about the Soviet Union until four in the morning. Anyway, you know what he did?"

Suzi shook her head.

"When the brothers committed their act of fraternal love, I found his signature on one document."

"Was he one of the ones who demonstrated in Red Square?" asked Suzi breathlessly.

"No. He was one of the ones who signed a Declaration of the Union of Soviet Writers greeting the heroic people of Czechoslovakia who were rescued from the horrors of the counter-revolution by the brotherly act of the armies of the Warsaw Pact," I said. "So there you are."

23.

The rain outside the window slackened off, and the metal shade over the streetlamp sounded like a toy drum. It reminded me of Rebecca again, but she was dead. I used to go to visit her on rainy Sunday afternoons like this, and we would lie on a squeaky couch and comfort ourselves with the illusion that the world couldn't harm us. But it could. Life is a whodunnit and the perpetrator is truth. It's a bad whodunnit. The perpetrator always gets away.

Laura was sitting in deep shadow while the wind swung the streetlamp outside the window back and forth. She laughed. "This conversation of ours . . . it reminds me of arguments some of us used to have—how long ago? Twenty-five years! God! A quarter of a century! We used to argue like this at university, sometimes all night long. We never agreed about anything."

"Yes," I said. "It was beautiful. As long as they were just student bull-sessions."

24.

Vixi hurried back from her catechism class all excited. I saw her white tennis shoes flashing in the dusk of the lilac bower and her silken hair shimmering in the light of the full-bellied moon. Then she dropped exhausted beside me on the bench.

"Sir! You won't believe this! Father Doufal wanted to get married!"

"Well, if that doesn't take the cake!"

"It sure does!"

"And I always thought that as far as the opposite sex was concerned, the most he ever thought about was the Virgin Mary. He's a fine one. Listen, did he ever make a pass at you during catechism class?"

"Sir! You always see the dirty side of things."

"Look who's talking! And since when do you call things like that dirty?"

"Ever since I've been going to catechism," she shot back. "And he didn't want to get married when he was already a priest. It was when he was still single. I mean, before he became a priest. When he was still a farmer."

She snuggled in comfortably beside me and I pressed my face against her silken hair and looked through it at the moon. It almost blinded me. It hung in the sky like a polished bowl, and seemed closer than usual.

"His parents died when he was only eighteen," Vixi went on. "He was their only son, so the army didn't take him — in those days they didn't take only sons. But farming was hard. He had to work like a horse to keep the farm going. He had nine hectares. It doesn't seem like a lot, but if a man's got to work it alone — "

"So that's why that old debbil woman got to him, is it? With nine hectares, finding a bride couldn't have been much of a problem."

"Don't make fun of him, sir! As a matter of fact, it *was* a problem." She wriggled around and her hair tickled my nose. "I don't think Father Doufal was much of a one for it."

The idea of the grey-haired priest tortured by the urgings of his glands seemed laughable to me. So as not to make Vixi angry, I tilted my head back and looked at the sky through half-closed eyes. The moon was awfully close. It hung over us like a slowly descending silver Host, shining so intensely that it almost seemed to warm me with the cold flame of youth. I closed my eyes. I could hear Vixi telling her story as if from a distance, from a great distance . . . from a Gothic cathedral where Grandma and I used to go for litany . . . from a time that existed only in old people, that no longer existed in the world. . . . "Father Doufal was a shy man," said that distant, long-ago voice of my Hronov girlfriend . . . . "He never went dancing, he was always polite to the matchmaker but he didn't like anyone the man suggested. So he worked the farm for fifteen years — until he was thirty-three, the same age as Christ at the end of his life, he told me." "Perhaps it didn't mean anything, Miss Koziskova. But perhaps . . . ," and the voice fell silent. The afternoon sun poured through the window of the vicarage, the heat lifted the dust off the old furniture, and the priest sat in a dusty aureola, searching through his memories with pale eyes. "I was introduced to Karolinka," he said, and Vixi thought a new note had entered the priest's voice, not a profane note — he was still pious — but more lively, perhaps. He was no longer speaking of theory vitalized by prayer. . . . "She was a — well, today you'd call her a serving girl. At the Zabehlickys', who had a big farm. And you know, Miss Koziskova, I was taken with her, as they say, at first sight." "He said, 'I was taken with her,'" said Vixi, "not 'I fell in love with her.' He was *taken* with her. He speaks awfully old-fashioned. . . ." And she told me how, after two months, they came to an agreement and went to the parish house to have the banns published, because the Holy Church didn't recommend a long engagement, and in the case of a small farmer there was no reason for it. The banns were read out three times from the pulpit. Then it was only a week till the wedding. "I was at the tailor's, Miss Koziskova. I had to have a proper suit made for the wedding because I had nothing black to wear. By this time the suit my father, God rest his soul, had handed down to me was too small — I'd last worn it at his funeral, and I'd filled out a little since then, you know. And so, Miss Koziskova, I was standing in Master Vavruska's workshop, and the master was fitting me for the suit, sticking pins in it, you know, when Auntie Hadrouskova came flying into the yard and I could hear her shouting before she came through the door, 'Mr. Vavruska, is Pepik Doufal there with you?'" "Doesn't that sound strange, sir?" marvelled Vixi. "Pepik Doufal; that's what she called Father Doufal. Anyway, the master tailor called out through the window that he was and what did she want, and the aunt rushed in, hesitated, and then said, 'Pepik, don't be alarmed, but. . . .'" "And of course I was alarmed, Miss Koziskova; it was as if something had suddenly stopped inside me, and my aunt said, 'Pepicek — Karolinka was run over by a car.' 'Is she — ' I said, and my aunt said, 'She is, Pepicek. She's with the Lord.' And so, Miss Koziskova, I didn't get married." The priest nodded his farmer's head, " . . . and sir, he had tears in his eyes," said Vixi. "One tear ran down his nose and he had to wipe it away. He must have been very fond of her. . . ." "Master Vavruska clasped his hands, Miss Koziskova," he told Vixi, "and then he grasped my shoulder and said, 'Pepik, I'm terribly sorry. And the suit . . . if you haven't got the money for it, I can give it to — ' but I shook my head and I said, 'I'll need it for the funeral, Mr. Vavruska.' And so, Miss Koziskova, instead of a wedding, I provided for Karolinka's funeral," he said, wiping his nose, where tiny red veins had mapped out the years of his life. "And I still hadn't turned thirty-four. Then one day that fall I was ploughing out in the fields and I'd had this strange feeling all morning. I hadn't even had breakfast, I just wasn't hungry. Ever since Karolinka died I'd kind of lost interest in things, lost my appetite, but you know, Miss Koziskova, a farm needs to be kept up, the animals need feeding and the fields need working. So I was ploughing that day, it was almost noon, a warm, dry day." "And sir, Father Doufal suddenly began talking different than he usually talked," said Vixi. "More like a farmer, you know?" " . . . I'm turning over a furrow right near the road and suddenly, in the distance, I hear a roar, an automobile engine, and I stop ploughing and wipe my forehead and along the road, it was more of a cart-track really, Miss Koziskova, all dust, anyway along comes a beautiful automobile, black with chrome trim, all shiny as if they'd just polished it up, and it's slowing as it comes towards me. I look inside and it's the bishop, Miss Koziskova, so I quick cross myself and the bishop smiles and blesses me, and the automobile drives on and leaves me there in a little cloud of dust." The priest fell silent, then blew his nose long and loudly into a red handkerchief. "Like you," I said to Vixi. "Sure, like me," said Vixi. And then he said, "And Miss Koziskova, it suddenly felt as though a hand was placed on my shoulders forcing me to kneel . . . and I knelt down and I looked at the dust rising slowly towards heaven, and the sky was azure blue — it was a clear fall day, not a cloud anywhere — and in that dust, that little swirling cloud of dust, Miss Koziskova, suddenly there he was, right in front of me — Saint Joseph! He was suspended in the air, with a halo around him that shone out of the dust . . . Saint Joseph, Miss Koziskova!" "How did you know it was him?" Vixi asked. "He was holding a white lily," said the priest. "That's Saint Joseph's flower. It symbolizes purity, Miss Koziskova. And I held my hand out to him and suddenly I heard, just as I'm hearing you, Miss Koziskova, I heard Saint Joseph say: 'Josef,' he says, 'Josef, be as I am!' I heard him as clear as I hear you, Miss Koziskova, and I knew exactly what he wanted me to do." The priest fell silent again, and put his enormous handkerchief back in his pocket. "What did he want you to do?" Vixi asked. "It was a call, Miss Koziskova. We call it a late vocation. After all, I was thirty-three. And when he said, 'Be as I am!' Saint Joseph was telling me he was the husband of the Virgin Mary but he never knew her as a wife. Just like me with Karolinka. I didn't hesitate, but sold the farm and went to study for the priesthood." "But he hadn't even been to high school," I objected. "Well, he went to the Jesuits and told them about his vision," said Vixi. "First he went through the Episcopal Secondary School, then they accepted him at the seminary, then he became a priest. . . . Oh sir, isn't it a beautiful story?" In the cold glow of the moonlight, she turned her face to me; it was lit from below by the purple reflection of the lilac blooms. It was not, however, one of her standard, improbable expressions. "Isn't it beautiful, really?"

"It is," I said. "A little too beautiful to be true."

"But it is true!" she said indignantly. "Father Doufal wouldn't lie!"

"I'm not saying he's lying," I said. "He was a devout farmer, his bride-to-be had just died, he was working hard on an empty stomach, it was hot — "

Vixi's face fell. "You're impossible, sir," she said. "You try to spoil everything."

"I don't like doing it," I said. "And maybe I'm wrong."

"Maybe you just are!" said Vixi with renewed hope.

25.

"It will be just as beautiful again when these ideas are fully realized," Laura assured me.

"Every idea brought to fruition is awful, don't you remember?" I said, quoting a line from a play by her devoted admirer Slavek Machal.

She laughed.

"Life is an aphorism, right? But aphorisms work because the wit in them overshadows reality. They are half-truths."

Yes, you're right, Laura, I said to her, but only in my mind. Concentration camps are a half-truth, full employment is a half-truth. The life of the body is a half-truth; the death of the soul a half-truth. But what, Laura, is the whole truth?

There was nothing I could do but try to resolve this *nescio* in an old, tried-and-true fashion. I put on a wry face. Life is a whodunnit, the perpetrator is truth, and no one ever runs the perpetrator to ground, so the whodunnit is a bad one. That's an aphorism too.

Is it also a half-truth?

A gale was blowing up outside, rocking the streetlamp and lashing its pale light across Laura's face. She was old, wrinkled, ill. I should have been afraid of her. But she was Slavek's platonic love. And I knew that despite what she said, she was not taking advantage of this new boom in Leninism. Perhaps that was her defence — to withdraw, before death, into the security of student bull sessions . . . those beautiful theories. . . .

She worked in a library. An ordinary office job. She didn't do anything for the Party any more. But there were others who did.

26.

The clock showed ten. I turned on the radio — I needed to listen to some music, something. "And now, our regular political commentary on current issues and events," said the announcer, "by Rudolf Kucera." Tepid female intonation, rather attractive no matter what she was saying. Then a male voice came on.

"Last night the National Assembly unanimously withdrew the eighteen resolutions it passed between May and August of 1968. Some of our foolish and incorrigible critics will see in this proof that our National Assembly has lost its freedom to make decisions. They will claim that dark and unspecified forces have compelled our elected representatives to submit to the will of so-called conservatives and collaborators. Well now, my dear right-wingers, our people know very well that just the opposite is true. In 1968 the National Assembly took a full four months — yes, four months — to pass those eighteen resolutions. That will give you some idea of what kind of pressure was brought to bear on our representatives by proponents of — I do not hesitate to use the expression — white terror, before the right-wing elements were able to mislead and force a majority of them to comply with their wishes and pass those reactionary resolutions. I repeat: a majority. For kindly notice, dear listeners, that not a one — I repeat, not a single one — of those eighteen resolutions was passed unanimously! In each case there was opposition, sometimes less, sometimes greater. The fact that all of those same eighteen resolutions have now been unanimously rejected by the National Assembly in one day, in a single day, is *not*, dear listeners, proof of the assembly's lack of freedom, but on the contrary, of its *freedom.* Yes, its freedom. Our freedom! Communist freedom. Today our comrades in the National Assembly are no longer subjected to the constant witch-hunts that raged when press, radio, and television were dominated by right-wing extremists; today they are no longer exposed to the tender mercies of the white terror, and thus they may *freely* and *unanimously* vote according to their innermost convictions. Our comrades in the National Assembly, after — "

I switched off the radio. The image of this group of elected representatives, who had so often voted any way that was required of them, suddenly retreating in confusion before the white terror of Jana Hloubava was so comic that I burst out laughing.

"What's so funny about that?" Vixi asked.

"I'm just following an old blues recipe."

"Don't talk so damned educated, sir!" she said.

"*When you see me smilin',*" I said in English. "You know a bit of English, don't you, Vixi? *I'm smilin' to keep from —* "

27.

Perhaps — and things began to fall into place like the pieces of a jigsaw puzzle — perhaps, almost certainly, Laura had done a lot for the Party in the past.

"Why didn't you throw me out? You knew I wanted to talk to you about that — about the miracle, didn't you?"

She was silent for a while, then said, "It doesn't matter any more. I guess that's why. You can't put anything in the papers about it now, and I — "

She lit her thousandth-and-first cigarette and began to talk. Her voice, probably because of all those cigarettes, was rather hoarse.

"You quoted Slavek's aphorism to me," she said. "Every idea brought to fruition . . . and so on. The simple fact is, some people get used to it and some people don't."

She inhaled hungrily and half the cigarette disappeared. Outside, the wind and the raindrops were playing a wild drum solo on the spectral *Blechtrommel* of Rebecca's streetlamp.

"Get used to what, Laura?"

"Don't ask such silly questions," she said. "It had to be that way, I'm convinced of it. It's just that I never managed to get used to those — concrete details — "

Ah Laura, I said to her in my mind, you beautiful mistress to Party discipline. Laura the proselyte. Why, for God's sake, must everything be made up of details? If I could have had Father Doufal's faith, I might have said that the minor details were the work of the devil. The work of God is vast, general, redolent of the sandalwood of the future . . . a six-hundred-pound pig. . . .

"Have you heard the story of King Lavra and the willow tree?" she laughed. "King Lavra's barber was forbidden to tell anyone that the king had donkey's ears, so the barber used to whisper his secret into an old, hollow willow tree in the woods."

Thank you, Laura. I don't think I deserved that. It's just that I was always lukewarm, not like you —

"And anyway, I haven't told you anything you didn't already know. Or couldn't piece together from what you knew. You're not a bad detective," and she paused and inhaled the rest of her cigarette, then carefully set the tiny butt aside on the yellowed pyramid. It rolled down the burnt-out side of the pile and came to rest under the bronze Lenin, an ugly, charred little corpse. "You should have been the one to join the security forces," she said, "not — "

She didn't finish the sentence.

"Not — not you, Laura?"

"Not me," she said.

"Laura," I said, taking it slowly, and I felt terribly depressed.

Words that belonged in a detective novel rolled like foreign bodies through the texture of her twilight, through the beautiful, sad music of the streetlamp — tennis rackets, youth that has a sixth sense for the evils of a world fucked up by its daddies, youth, responsible for everything and nothing . . . crude words from a whodunnit in the context of a great poem . . . but such is the world . . . *c'est la vie* . . . this is how our world evolved. . . . "Laura," I said, "Juzl knows almost everything about Sulc and Pecen. But there were three people who installed those devices in the chapel. There was a woman with them, someone called Koernerova. Juzl wasn't able to dig out anything about her — not a thing. Have you any idea why?"

The streetlamp, Rebecca's sun, lashed her face again with its pale light. Laura was old now and she would die soon after this, like Rebecca before her and, before her . . . but it was Laura, love in a blue shirt, Laura, who swore by reason because they brought her up to wear perfume and play golf and she was too full of life, too far away from lazy afternoons asleep on the well-trimmed grass . . . she would certainly have noticed Mr. Pohorsky there, because for her, unlike Comrade Hrzan, caddies and groundsmen were people too, but that awful dialectic . . . *it is transformed into its opposite* . . . the negation of a negation. . . . She swore by reason because she passionately believed in it. Because she was a woman, and not even the feminist leader from Connington could liberate her from the slavery that was in her, in that supple and gentle organization of tissue and chemistry, which we men do not possess, and from which comes life and therefore death as well. . . . Laura, so much a slave that a prison guard had to shout at her, to remind her. . . . Consciousness is a function of the brain . . . the brain is the seat of logic. . . . *We are governed by certain undefinable forces to which ideas only serve as guides*. . . .

I closed my eyes. I remembered the time she had come into Slavek's office, stunning legs visible beneath a pretty spring dress, to speak to Barta. Then she had divorced the murderer Barta, although both of them still swore passionately by their all-powerful reason. Laura, who believed that she did not simply believe, but knew. . . .

And I believed that I now knew who had written Juzl that anonymous letter, and why, and why the writer had invented a false name for the female officer.

28.

I did bring a bottle of French cognac to the dressing room, and Suzi tossed back two shots in a row and, after a short pause, a third. The Lucerna hall was quickly filling up. Through a crack in the curtain I saw the usual Che Guevaras and their silken-haired girls. Suzi was terrified. Even her husband of the moment, a bass player in her back-up band, wasn't casting murderous glances at anyone who tried to cheer her up, as he usually did; he actually told me that the cognac was a good idea. But Suzi, now once again transformed into a butterfly, was struggling to keep from fainting.

Lester beckoned to me from his dressing-room door. I went in and he handed me a magazine. "Sue called and asked me to bring you this."

"Her nerves are shot."

"In that case," said Lester—wiggling his moustache to the left, indicating a smile—"I'll try to neutralize things right off the top."

The magazine was one of those sensationalist German tabloids and it wasn't even on glossy paper. I opened it. The article was headlined FROM THE PHOTOLABS OF PRAGUE and it was illustrated with a pair of photographs. The first one I already knew: Suzi, the First Secretary behind her in the throes of passion, the sinfully black muff of hair in Suzi's lap contrasting sharply with her naturally blonde head of hair. The headline read, THE FIRST SECRETARY AND THE FIRST LADY OF PRAGUE ROCK. . . . The second photograph showed the same two naked bodies up to the neck, but the heads were different; they were people I'd never seen before. Below the photograph the headline continued: . . . IMITATE DANISH PORN MODELS KÄSTRIN AND JUPP.

"Couldn't they find some local whore to pose for them?" I asked.

"I guess they were afraid she'd talk."

"Something should be done with this."

"It's already been photocopied. It's going to be circulated," said Lester.

The stage manager stuck his head in the door, and Lester got up. Through the open door I saw Suzi standing ready behind the closed curtain. Her knees were trembling visibly.

I sat down in a chair and closed my eyes. I felt nervous too, almost frightened. In the vision of memory, separated from the present by my eyelids, a scene from the Connington College campus appeared—the preposterous senator from Wyoming who had dared to defend democracy, and the outraged whistling, the stamping, the shouts of the long-haired crowd who wanted not democracy but the dictatorship of the beautiful Che. An absurdly inappropriate scene. It had nothing at all to do with the private suffering of a single lightweight muse. Lester's monotonous voice came over the loudspeaker in the dressing room, with all its far from monotonous timbres.

"Good evening, my very dear friends, and welcome to our last concert before we leave for the Soviet Union." Someone in the hall gave a piercing whistle, someone else joined in, and as the whistling and shouting grew Lester had to pause. When the noise died down he continued in exactly the same intonation, without the slightest animation. "All of us can still remember vividly the arrival of the fraternal armies almost two years ago. For the first time since that memorable day, which none of us will ever forget," he continued like a music box, "our singers will be going to the land where tomorrow means the same as yesterday here," and he twitched his moustache and the uncensorable change in the classic line by Julius Fucik was understood perfectly by the public, "so that we can show our Russian teachers how we sing here, and what we sing. . . . In the joyful rhythm of the following composition," said Lester's voice, as level as the ocean horizon, "the joy of the joyful life is reflected, for, as we all know, *Kraft durch* . . . ," and I had to shake my head, because it was a hallucination, *déjà vu,* black magic probably caused by an identity of the place and the incantation, revived, like the spirit Marbuel, a quarter of a century later. . . . I drove the spirit out and Lester was saying, " . . . and now, for our first singer of the evening, I want you to welcome the lovely Suzi Kajetanova, with a new song by Alois Posledni and Karel Mikes—'Please Leave Me'. . . ."

The moment of truth had arrived. I covered my eyes, which were already closed, with the palms of my hands. I imagined Suzi briskly walking through the curtains with a glowing, professional smile on her face, as she'd done a thousand times before, a caterpillar transformed into a butterfly of the night, going to meet the decibels crashing onto the stage. Everything became mixed up in my mind. This time it was not identity of place, but of time and the subject, and the spirit Marbuel or the spirit Amodiel who was eagerly coming to life. Suzi was not standing in front of the boys and girls in the Lucerna; as she opened her mouth the Connington crowd, in fringed leather jackets, fell silent, and she sang . . . *When love is over, you should go* . . . . It would be hard to imagine a more banal song . . . a more brilliant song . . . and cries went up from the Connington students, perhaps of disapproval, and the silence was gradually permeated by chanting and Suzi sang, "*Ach, I didn't know your true self!* . . . and the long-haired revolutionaries yelled louder, until their chanting became a roar in which Suzi's voice was soon, very soon, lost. . . . *You forced your love upon me! Go away, now I know who you are* and they were whistling now, and apple cores, eggs, and tomatoes pelted down on Suzi, for they had never known food shortages in Connington. *Leave me! I don't want to be with you any more—just go AWAY!*—in her piercing high C, and everything was drowned in a terrifying, insane jungle roar of stamping and whistling—

— I opened my eyes. Suzi was staggering through the curtain, perspiring, flushed, shaken, with that jungle racket in the background. She popped something into her mouth and held out a blind hand, someone handed her a glass of cognac, she tossed it back, turned around, and went back out to face the growing cheers — and I drove out Marbuel and realized with enormous relief that I was not in that unhappy, enslaved land where the Connington golf greens were tended by Pohorsky the traitor, but in Prague, in a land safe now from a similar fate, and that all that noise on the other side of the curtain was coming not from the Connington greenhorns but from the ancient boys and girls of Prague, that generation whose ugly caterpillar would one day perhaps be transformed —

29.

Two kilometres outside Maselna Lhota, I drove down the narrow road that wound its way through the fields and among the small hills and led to the highway. Then I drove flat out into Hronov. That morning the sky was overcast with a grey mist, and around ten the clouds banked up into reddish formations that looked like apocalyptic horsemen. I dropped Vixi and her family off at the Hronov station, waiting until they waved to me from the window of the noon express, and then drove off towards the horizon, where a lone granite peak loomed like the back of an irritated stegosaurus. The Dragon's Hole.

Once, somewhere, I had driven through another fairy-tale countryside like this. Storks had been flying through the air — enchanted princes — and the postmaster's romantic château had stood out against the horizon. Now the granite cliff was a dragon's lair, and the ruler of heaven used his gigantic brush to rearrange the clouds into a terrifying study in grey and black. The grass on both sides of the road was a poisonous green. The rock wore a coat of scrubby pine and its flat stone face looked west. The dragon stood at the foot of the cliff and roared.

I stopped the car some distance away and looked at my watch. It was five to two; the dragon would be falling silent any minute now. It was tall and extended, made of iron and wood and covered with granite dust, and somewhere its hidden jaws were noisily chewing up stone. Beneath the cliff, a crane on caterpillar treads loaded huge boulders onto an iron cart, and beside it stood two men, also covered with dust. The crane swung erect, then turned away, and the two men leaned into the iron cart and pushed it along a sagging set of tracks towards the dragon. I could see their feet, in lace-up boots, digging into the crushed stone ballast as they pushed with all their strength to keep the cart moving. The only people here were these two, the crane operator, and probably someone in the bowels of the dragon. It was a lonely place, a strange kind of purgatory. What was keeping them here at a job that combined the solitude of the plough with the inferno of an early nineteenth-century factory? I knew what kept at least one of them here.

The crane operator jumped down to the ground and ambled towards the dragon. The two men with the cart slowly pushed their load to an opening in the board wall, into which an endless iron conveyor belt rattled. They tipped the cart up, the boulders in it clattered onto the metal conveyor, and the dragon began to swallow them. The crane operator joined the other two. He lit a cigarette, then held out his match for one of the men to light his. A few fat raindrops fell on the Felicie's windshield.

I raised my face to the composition in black and grey; murky rainclouds were scudding along beneath it. The men standing at the foot of the dragon took shelter under a wooden roof and rain drummed on the roof of the Felicie. The hands on my watch gradually approached two. At last the dragon abruptly fell silent. A small door in the wooden wall opened and a fourth man came out. All four of them walked over the crushed stone to the path.

They approached the Felicie through the rain, their collars turned up. Their flat cloth hats, crude jackets, trousers with patched knees, and boots of stiff leather were all covered with dust that was slowly dissolving in the downpour. Two of them were carrying old-fashioned lunch buckets. They walked silently, quickly, indifferent to the rain.

I waited in the Felicie. As they walked past each of them gave me a brief glance, then kept on walking. It was the fourth one. I would probably not have recognized him, but he was the only one who stopped and smiled. He looked like a man from one of Corot's paintings. A three-day stubble and the dust had covered his face with a perfect mask.

The road rose through the fairy-tale countryside into the mountains. The windshield wipers made fresh fan-shaped openings in the dusty windshield and the road wound forward through the spruce and the pines. Beside me on the seat sat the dusty stone-cutter Juzl.

He had wanted to be close to the chapel, he said. When they fired him from the newspaper he went to the district of Zeleny Brod, where it turned out that the director of Municipal Services, under whose aegis the Dragon's Hole quarry operated, was a secret Catholic. It was the will of God, said Juzl. Comrade Grimm, the faithful Marxist from Hronov, whom Prague had now appointed to the local National Committee, opposed the presence of a counter-revolutionary journalist in his quarry, but the director was desperate for another hand; in the wake of the invasion, three of his employees had left the country. Besides, there was little danger that the journalist would put the wrong ideas into the heads of his co-workers. In the belly of the dragon was Vavrin, the former owner of a stuccoing firm, and the last man in the district who knew this dying craft. Kubicek the cart handler had once owned a small hotel. The only one who might have felt threatened by Juzl's presence was the crane operator, Janda — he was a real worker, a labourer's son, but he was also a long-haired hooligan who played bass guitar in one of the eight rock and roll bands in Hronov, and he'd been in bad odour politically ever since the invasion, when Comrade Grimm had noticed him chalking swastikas on the sides of Soviet tanks. (Fortunately for the cause of peace and progress, a reporter from *Pravda* had used photographs of Janda's swastikas to provide final proof of the Hronov counter-revolutionaries' true sympathies.)

In the end Comrade Grimm recognized that the Dragon's Hole was an appropriate place to punish political offenders, and Juzl's future was secure, probably for some time to come. "Others are far worse off than I am," he said in his usual voice, full of wonder and piety.

A flat clearing appeared among the trees, with a long wooden building in the middle. A platoon of soldiers in Russian army gear was marching across a concrete air strip towards some engines of war parked under canvas camouflage covers. Long, thin, eager probosces protruded from the covers. We drove by, leaving the scene behind us.

But the stone-cutter had noticed them. "The local girls won't go out with them," he said. "So not long ago they brought some female prisoners from Russia. One of them ran away and hid in the rock city — "

"Up where your chapel is?"

Juzl nodded. In the rock city, where half a millennium ago a small band of the faithful had hidden. But the clergy had caught them anyway, and had burned them at the stake.

"They sent out a search party and found her," said Juzl. "But rather than give herself up, she jumped off the rocks and killed herself."

We were driving through a dark wood that was growing darker by the minute. Emerald-green flashes of moss shone in the dark passages between the trees and big burdock leaves glistened as though wax had been poured over them.

"In the West they call these *Czech stories*," I said. "Pretty soon it's going to be a synonym for tall tales. It's generally thought that Czechs make them up. For understandable reasons, of course — they do try to be fair to us."

"In the West," said Juzl bitterly.

Raindrops ran down the windshield. A ray of sunlight penetrated the treetops and fell on the road in front of us. We drove into a meadow and the sudden transition from darkness to light almost blinded me. The rain began to thin out. The sun shone from behind the clouds, illuminating a village nestled in the woods and dominated by a building that looked like a sanatorium.

Juzl pointed to a cottage surrounded by firewood stacked almost to the eaves. "That's the one," he said. "It belongs to the Rerichas. We met in the chapel. Mr. Rericha did some painting there. When I found work in the quarry he said, why don't you move in with me?" We were almost at the cottage. "Mr. Rericha's a widower. He lives here with his old mother."

Someone was chopping wood behind the cottage. A white mongrel rushed out of its doghouse and flung itself joyfully on Juzl. The axe-blows stopped and a thickset man appeared around the corner. My first reaction was alarm — for a moment I thought I was looking at the dead priest. The heavy farmer's body, the face creased with the tectonics of time, short, greying hair in a brush-cut. The man laughed awkwardly with his eyes, which looked pale in the sun. But it was not the priest. His name was Matous Rericha.

In the dark parlour, with her back to the stove, an old woman sat on a low stool. She might have been a hundred. She tried to get up but Rericha said, "Please, sit down, Momma," so the old woman offered me her hand, all bone and vein, and looked for a long moment into my face. I didn't know if she could really see me or not. One of her eyes was motionless and probably blind, but there was a faint spark of life left in the other. "God bless you," she whispered, "and welcome." She had no idea who I was, and she obviously didn't care.

We sat down at a table by a window as tiny as the one in Vixi's grandfather's cottage. It was the same kind of mountain cottage, except that cousin Antonin's place was full of children and dominated by a buxom housewife. Here there were two men, one on the threshold of old age, the other at the end of his youth, and a century-old woman. Still, the place was neatly kept, and warm. A cosy haven against the dangers of the world. Which, as life had taught me, is an illusion.

Juzl placed the familiar folder on the table in front of me. I had seen it last in the Slavia Café. The articles in that unfinished series, which two years before had caused a modest stir, mainly among Catholic readers, had survived the recent changes. But the last article existed only as a galley proof.

"Do you still remember what Father Urbanec told us when we paid him that visit?" said Juzl, and then, without waiting, answered the question himself. "That the anonymous letter with the sketch of the electromagnetic device was sent to me by the Secret Police? That was after witnesses had established that the other device, with all those pulleys and wires, couldn't have been in the chapel before the miracle took place. Here's the letter."

He put the sketch in front of me. I remembered it well.

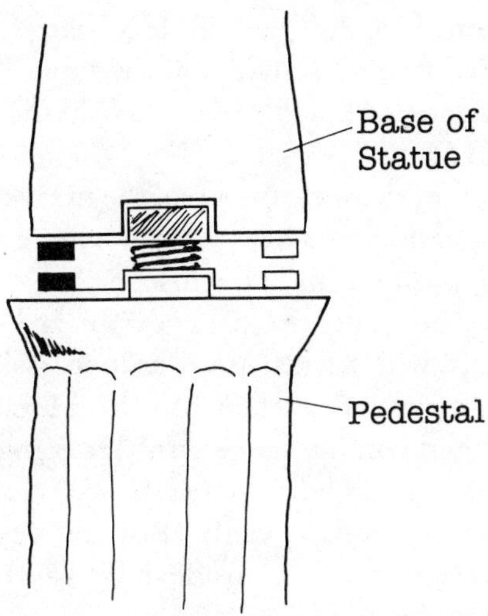

He placed a finger on the drawing. I noticed calluses on his hands that hadn't been there before. With one or two exceptions, I rarely notice things like that.

"That thing should have been installed in the statue of the Virgin Mary," said Juzl, "but then some unknown person shifted it, they say, to the statue of Saint Joseph. But," he said, and his voice was trembling, probably from excitement, "I went to the chapel and I discovered that it would have been completely impossible to transfer it from one statue to the other."

We looked each other in the eye.

"In other words — ?" I said.

"In other words there was no electromagnetic device in the first place. Father Urbanec was right. The police invented it *ex post facto*, when the impossibility of the pulley system was proven."

I still didn't understand, but I felt strange, and oddly trusting. I would have been satisfied with his word and his faith. But he provided me with proof.

"Just like the first time, the Lord led them into confusion. They obviously made that sketch according to their old documentation, without bothering to check the statues on the spot. And because they invented the pulley mechanism for the statue of the Virgin Mary, for the first version of the film, they had no preliminary sketches of Saint Joseph. They made the second version of the film in a hurry, without installing anything new — someone simply hid behind the pedestal and moved Saint Joseph by hand. That's why they never discovered that it would have been impossible to shift the mechanism from one statue to the other without making complicated alterations.

"This is Saint Joseph," he said. His head was so close to mine that I could feel him breathing excitedly on the table. "The base of the statue has a round wooden peg that fits into a hole in the top of the pedestal. And this is the Virgin Mary."

He laid another drawing on top of the first sketch. "You see? She has a hole on her underside, and her pedestal has a protuberance that fits into it. It's just the opposite from Saint Joseph."

He stared at me intently, his eyes ablaze — perhaps from his mad obsession, perhaps with a truth that was inaccessible to me. I stared at his work, executed in piety, I saw his proof, and I felt a chill down my spine. All my life I'd been coming across embarrassing symbols, but this. . . . Was it possible that Juzl hadn't noticed?

"That's all very well," I said. "But you've missed something. You simply turn the electromagnet upside down, and then you can transfer it from one statue to the other."

Juzl never took his eyes off me, but the shock and disappointment I expected didn't appear. He merely shook his head.

"No you can't. Take a good look — my drawings are proportionally exact. There's a difference of a centimetre and a half between the diameter of the peg on the Virgin Mary's pedestal and the diameter of the peg on Saint Joseph. The hole on the Virgin Mary is narrower!"

Was it really possible that the stone-cutter hadn't noticed this most embarrassing of all symbols, this immoral little joke that you could hardly suspect a baroque wood-carver of having deliberately made? Or was it only my rude imagination, the blasphemy of a non-believer in our modern age? What did it mean?

My Catholic friend stared at me, or rather through me, at something I couldn't see. According to legend, Mary Magdalene was. . . . *Quia turpe, quia indignum* . . . it had followed me too, from my first encounter with the water nymph, the naiad who led me to the miracle. . . . Nothing human is to me . . . to the pure at heart, everything is . . . man, created in the image. . . .

What did it mean, if anything?

"God struck them with blindness," I heard the voice of Matous Rericha say.

God? Blindness?

"Do you have that anonymous letter here?" I almost barked at Juzl. He leafed through his folder.

> Your conjecture is a nice one, and very brave. I'd be a happy man if I could believe it, if only because certain people would be highly upset if it were true. Unfortunately, however, I must disappoint you. Saint Joseph was moved not by the power of God the Father, nor the Son, nor the Holy Ghost, and certainly not by the Virgin of Virgins, but by the power of the Secret Police —

Of course. I was right. I knew that style all too well. The sarcasm of a man who, as sometimes happens, had absolute power over women. Not even Laura was exempt. The intonation of a person whose world-view consists in ridiculing present and past gods, because he is already living in the next century.

I looked up from the old letter. But what role, I wondered, could he possibly have played in all this? The father of the daughter of the mother of my son? When technically it was impossible?

Matous Rericha and Juzl stared at me intently with the eyes of faith, as if they were expecting that I would confirm their logic: yes, everything fits, it must have been a miracle. But I, who never believed anything because no faith had been given to me, did not believe. Even though my reason cried out: *Yes!*

Someone put a hand on my shoulder, a hand of bone and vein, and said in a wheezing voice, "You were there too! When Saint Joseph gave the sign!"

I felt a terrible wave of shock go through me, from head to toe. The old lady was crouched over me and her one good eye was glaring into mine.

"Momma! Please!" said Mr. Rericha.

The old lady said no more. She turned away and disappointedly shuffled back to her stool.

"I feel wonderful here," said Juzl. "Everything that happened the year before last somehow showed me the way. Did you know I wanted to be a priest?"

I nodded.

"Now it's too late. The seminaries have enrolment restrictions again, and they wouldn't be allowed to admit me anyway. Here I can be useful." He looked out the window, then went on. "I don't know if you can imagine what it's like to be free of ambition. It's a wonderful feeling. I used to be ambitious, did you know that? Back when I began writing those articles. My motives for writing them weren't entirely pure. I flattered myself that I was being a big investigative journalist, exposing something — but now God has taken all that ambition away from me. It's a great act of grace. I have a deep certainty, and I want nothing more — "

Outside, the day was clearing. After the rain, the mountain countryside looked fresh and washed. Evening was approaching.

"But no one will know about the miracle now," I said. "No one will print your findings."

"God doesn't need to be constantly convincing everyone. Not the way they do. He offered proof to a handful of the faithful. God — " The stone-cutter stopped. In the distance I could hear a faint tinkling, almost like one of those tiny bells in a puppet theatre. I shook my head, but I wasn't imagining it. It was real. What was reality, though? A handful of the faithful — like those around the priest who went to the stake — and now, around this priest . . . an absurd continuity. . . .

"He'd have saved Sodom if he'd found ten just men. Perhaps it's true today, too, that the fate of the world rests on such a handful — "

A cruel God. And what about the rest?

"It's time we were going," said Mr. Rericha.

"Where?" I asked.

"To the home. Every Friday we have an evening rosary worship service, and when the priest from Hronov is free we usually have holy mass too. Will you come with us?"

"Of course."

"I always take Mother in the wagon," said Mr. Rericha. "Our mare died last year — "

"I'll drive you," I said quickly.

It was scarcely two hundred metres away, but we drove. Near the entrance to the sanatorium, a motorcycle was leaning against the wall. A black helmet swung from one of the handlebars.

"The Reverend Father is here, Momma!" said Mr. Rericha joyously.

As I parked the Felicie beside the motorcycle, a nun in a wide white cowl came running out. I opened the door, and the nun and Mr. Rericha helped the old lady out of the car. It was difficult. Old Mrs. Rerichova wasn't heavy, but she was stiff and could scarcely bend down to get through the door. Finally I offered my hand and the old lady grasped it. Once again, she gave me a piercing look with her almost blind eye.

"You *were* there!"

The nun looked questioningly at me, and behind the old woman's back Mr. Rericha made a sign to indicate that his mother was no longer in full command of her faculties.

We led her down a long corridor to the door of the chapel. The sanatorium had an odd staircase — it was narrow, with a wooden groove running up either side, close to the level of the steps.

"The home used to be in Prague," Mr. Rericha whispered to me. "The Vincentinum Home, you may remember it. For people born with incurable handicaps. After February they took it over for some offices or something and they moved the patients out here, and I'd say they're better off for it. The air's cleaner here." He pointed to the wooden grooves. "The nuns had to make some changes here themselves. Most of the poor souls can't walk and the stairs are all but useless. I helped them a little with the harder work."

Suddenly I thought of something. "Are the nuns here from Prague too?"

"Some are. But most of them are from down in Hronov. They used to work in the hospital there, but as soon as one of them directives came out that only civilian nurses could work in hospitals — "

We went into the chapel. Clearly it had once been a gymnasium. Part of a Swedish ladder was still fixed on the back wall — but what would cripples need a gymnasium for? By the front wall there was a strange altar. It was a triptych like the old Gothic altars, but it shone with almost psychedelic colours. In the centre panel a pink Christ with a puppet-like face was suspended in space, his blue eyes searching all corners of the former gymnasium. On each of the wings were saints in a similar pink and pale blue, against the background of a green landscape that looked as though it might have been inspired by a chocolate box. Saint Peter and Saint Paul were there, each holding the instruments of his torture, eyes like poppyseeds staring out from permanent-waved beards. The hand of Mr. Rericha had left traces of his colourful faith on the entire highland district. Who knows, I thought; maybe in some future time these bright, shriekingly colourful saints will be on display in museums. An absurd continuity.

Mr. Rericha helped the old lady into a pew and disappeared through a door beside the altar. Juzl went over to a harmonium by the wall and I sat down in another pew. The pews — there were only four of them, ancient, worm-eaten, carved ages ago by a hand that worked by eye — had obviously been brought here from some abandoned chapel. In the first pew sat three ageing nuns, in the second one, two old men and three old women. I sat in the third one, with a girl with a black rosary and a pretty face.

But surrounding the pews were wheelchairs, and the sight of what was in them made me feel ill. Perhaps they were human, but they looked more like a fantasy by Hieronymus Bosch. I understood why they had been removed from Prague, the city of programmatic optimism. Before me, like oversized, misshapen vegetable marrows, were three hydrocephalic heads with shrunken faces, like the primitive war trophies of headhunters. Twisted skeletons with arms put askew by rickets . . . legless trunks, male and female, creatures that were no more than shadows lying on cots, shades of Oranienburg. And right beside me, a white skeleton with transparent skin stretched over the bones — a creature, perhaps a man, perhaps a woman, stretching out a single, swollen, fingerless hand . . . and from the head leered a set of bared teeth, for the creature had no face.

I couldn't bear to look at them, and turned away. Among the beds and wheelchairs stood several younger nuns, in their fifties perhaps, who were wiping the creatures with damp rags. I felt my stomach rising.

But something compelled me to look again at the creature beside me with a skull instead of a face. And it was not just a perverse compulsion to see alien horrors, a distant appreciation of the suffering of others. For among the constructions designed to support those heads full of water, among those monstrous figures in the wheelchairs, I had noticed something. A sturdy, brave nun was bending over that white skeleton, wiping the skull, with its tiny, blinking eyes, with a white washcloth. And I recognized her. It was the same brave nun who had once so adroitly examined my unpleasant disease and spoken, almost with joy, about the archbishop's imprisonment. Sister . . . Udelina? Perhaps. Udelina. For all those twenty-one years, while I — she had been bending over this spectral human being, soothing the living skull. She had the same sixty-year-old, kind, unnaturally — unnaturally? — good-natured face, the same speckled, dextrous, certain hands. She was one of those ten. . . . O Lord, I called out in spirit, though I did not believe in Him or in His miracle, Lord, what does all this mean?

The bell tinkled. Juzl began pumping the pedals and placed his fingers on the keyboard, and the grand voice of the harmonium soared through the gymnasium. Mr. Rericha entered through a door beside the altar, his vestment somewhat close-fitting on his thickset body, and he carried a large missal in his hands. For a brief second I again had the impression that kind Father Doufal was walking towards the altar in his oft-washed shirt — but then the priest walked out after Mr. Rericha. He was young, handsome, and rosy-cheeked, with chestnut hair — a healthy young man from the mountains — and with his blue eyes and pink cheeks he could have been Mr. Rericha's model for Christ, Joseph, and Mary.

Again I was overwhelmed by that sensation of unreality, the feeling that everything was symbolic of something else, that I was in a world that was constantly coming to an end and yet did not end, that I in fact belonged here, somewhere in a thatched cottage, that here was my original home, in the humility of this surrender — but as always, the feeling lasted only a brief moment. Then I was once more sitting in the gymnasium, the doll-maker's phantasmagoric work before me, and around me was a living horror, not from Hieronymus Bosch, but from a building in Prague where they made room — for what? For another, possibly more monstrous . . . ? "Jesus, King of Heaven and Earth, Angel choirs before thee bow!" wailed the nuns, joined by Juzl's bar-room tenor and the bleating of two or three of the creatures in wheelchairs. Then, in a clear, powerful voice, the young priest said, "*Introibo ad altare Dei!*" as if there had never been a Vatican council, and the doll-maker replied in thundering Latin, made strange by his Krkonose accent: "*Ad Deum, qui laetificat iuventutem meam!*" For here, the rituals of the Church survived intact. I remembered the tortured priest and I wanted to weep. I'm getting old and sentimental, I told myself, but it wasn't age that made me feel that way. It was the fact that I didn't understand it, that I didn't believe in it, that I didn't believe in anything. Because I wanted to believe but couldn't, and therefore wanted at least to understand. *Quia absurdum. Quia turpe. Quia indignum.* And I suddenly thought of Vixi, full of life once, back then, and Ivana, the old fool, and Zdena Prochazkova, also languishing in a wheelchair somewhere, and Milada Maresova, and Bozenka and her kulak father, while the handsome priest at the altar was doing everything just the way it was done when I was a boy, back when Father Meloun would raise high the Host with great effort and under his vestments I would see his black trousers and the white laces he used to tie down the cuffs of his long cotton underwear. I had left this place, and I felt I should return but there was nowhere to come home to. I thought of Mr. Pohorsky and Dr. Hrzan, of the First Secretary and of the river tenderly enfolded within its green banks, of the gifted novelist and how delighted he'd been by all the departures, of the awful fat girl who howled when the man from Mars hit her over the head with his truncheon, of the running boy who left a trail of blood behind him, and I thought of Bukavec, of Irina in her pink slip, of Arashidov, who could not have approved but signed anyway, of Suzi and Lester, of his religion of jazz, of Sylva and Martin and Martina, of the locksmith Strevlicek, who saved my bacon, of his gypsy baby, of Mr. Kohn, who was so afraid of being caged, of Sarka Pechlatova and the author of utopian fiction, of the beige lady and her white marble staircase that led to heaven, though I never mounted it and never will, of Julia Nedochodilova and the strange nunnery of Father

Urbanec, of the thousands of altars in the world and how many were actually graced by the presence of a loving Jesus Christ — and suddenly I awoke from my reverie and was back in the gymnasium, but the harmonium wasn't playing any more and I could hear the squeaking of wheels, and see the wheelchairs with their white, living monsters and the white swans floating through the air beside them. Mr. Rericha was supporting the one-eyed old lady and her eye was on my eye and she wheezed at me, "You *were* there! And you fell asleep then, too!"

But I wasn't asleep now. I was completely conscious, myself once more — Daniel Smiricky, a misguided counter-revolutionary of minor importance, re-educatable, the author of librettos for musical comedies, of detective novels and comedy films, fearing God less than he feared the world, a skeptic. I said, "Granny, I've already told you, you're confusing me with someone else."

30.

I lifted Saint Joseph up to put him back on his pedestal, but with his glossy coat of fresh paint he slipped from my hands and fell to the floor. Tenderly I knelt down to the miracle-worker who had survived, in the solitude of this chapel under Mare's Head Hill, for more than two hundred years, and I saw that his end had finally come. The impact had split him lengthwise, opening him up like a book. When I looked into the statue I felt the touch of God's hand once more, and I knew that, against His own interests, He was giving me a sign. The phallic protrusion on the bottom of the statue was not an integral part of the saint, but was in fact a plug glued into a cavity bored in the base. . . .

31.

The red log was burning down in the fireplace and Gellen was silent, listening, smiling his habitual ironic smile. I was talking like a fictional detective. On a string of deduction I strung pearls of fact; some of them were separated by twenty-one years, but together they created a chain at the end of which I held the perpetrator. And the co-perpetrator of murder *ante factum*, since because of his little joke a country priest and a pious undercover cop had been beaten to death.

Gellen merely grinned at my accusation.

"My friend, I didn't invent the system where telling a joke can send a man to the gallows, and therefore I in no way bear any responsibility for the bloody mischief it creates. Besides that, my dear Poirot, there are serious flaws in your deductions. There isn't a court in the world, not even a Czechoslovakian court, that would find me guilty on the basis of your proofs."

"Tell me what those flaws are."

"Have you forgotten about that little party where the two of us got so plastered that your girl had to carry you back to Hepner's cottage and mine had to lug me off to bed? That was about two in the morning. At eight o'clock the old woman went to the chapel to water the flowers, and by nine the shepherd and his flock were already there."

"Perhaps you were only pretending to be drunk."

"My friend, do you recall that line of bottles on the mantel?" Gellen pointed to the fireplace, where a log was twisting in its final, incandescent agony. "It was still there in the morning, except that by morning all the bottles were empty. If you recall, my girl had colitis and wasn't drinking. Yours was sipping her lemonade like a sweet young thing from finishing school. And if you'd downed all those bottles yourself you wouldn't be sitting here today — taken in that amount, alcohol is a lethal poison."

"And Sunday afternoon?"

"On Sunday afternoon, when my girl and I were leaving the cottage, we could still hear the believers carrying on in the chapel. They were wailing and screeching and falling all over themselves. That was about three o'clock. The girl had to be in Prague by five because of her husband. If you don't believe me, you can ask her; she heard the noise in the chapel herself. I remember she made fun of it on the way back. Oh, wait a minute, you can't ask her," he backtracked, looking embarrassed. "She took off after the invasion. But maybe we could get her address. She's somewhere in Australia — or was it South Africa? — with her husband."

I laughed. "You got to Prague at five, turned around, and you could have been back by seven-thirty or eight o'clock."

He turned the bottle of Chivas Regal upside down, but only a few drops fell into his glass. "Theoretically possible, Max Carrados, but a little improbable, don't you think?"

I pulled a wry grin, the way he liked to. "All supernatural or preternatural agencies are ruled out. Father Ronald Arbuthnott Knox said that," I said. "And once the impossible is ruled out, what remains must be true. Regardless of how improbable it may be. Those two principles still apply."

"In literature, my friend — in cheap, second-rate pulp literature. Not in real life," said Gellen.

"So how do you explain it?"

"Quite simply," he said, and my old friend grinned, more glibly than I. "It was a miracle."

I lay in the wide bed in the upstairs bedroom of Gellen's cottage, where he — perhaps — had spent that drunken night. Through a triangular window in the angle of the roof I looked at the stars. But I wasn't thinking of that night — I was thinking of a far earlier time, when I was sixteen or seventeen, when I lay on the bed in my own room looking through the window at mysterious Betelgeuse, mechanically saying the Lord's Prayer while thinking about life, the life which still lay before me and was yet to come. Thinking about that badly written whodunnit in which the perpetrator is truth but can never be run down. Sometimes, perhaps, a solution beckons enticingly, but it always turns out to be far-fetched and improbable. Beautiful as it may seem, it only works in literature.

All I wanted to do was sleep. Outside the window, the stars — those embarrassing symbols of vanity — burned clear and bright.

ABOUT THE AUTHOR

Josef Skvorecky is Professor of English at Erindale College, University of Toronto. He emigrated to Canada after the Soviet invasion of Czechoslovakia in 1968, and he and his wife, the novelist Zdena Salivarova, continued to keep Czech literature alive through their Czech-language publishing house, 68 Publishers. Skvorecky was the 1980 winner of the Neustadt International Prize for Literature. His novels include *The Cowards*, *Miss Silver's Past*, *The Bass Saxophone*, *The Engineer of Human Souls* — winner of the 1984 Governor General's Award — and *Dvorak in Love.* In 1990 the Skvoreckys were awarded the Order of the White Lion, Czechoslovakia's highest recognition, for their services to Czech literature.

ABOUT THE TRANSLATOR

Paul Wilson lived in Czechoslovakia for ten years, working as a translator and English teacher, and playing with an underground rock band, The Plastic People of the Universe. He was expelled in 1977. In addition to other novels and short stories by Josef Skvorecky (including *The Swell Season*, *The Engineer of Human Souls*, and *Dvorak in Love*), he has translated works by many Czech authors, such as Bohumil Hrabal, Pavel Kohout, and Vaclav Havel. He now lives in Toronto, where he is Associate Editor of *The Idler* magazine.

A NOTE ON THE TYPE

This book was set in a version of a type face called Baskerville. The face itself is a facsimile reproduction of types cast from moulds made for John Baskerville (1706-1775) from his designs. Baskerville's original face was one of the forerunners of the type style known to printers as "modern face" — a "modern" of the period A.D. 1800.

Composed by Cybergraphics Co., Inc., Toronto
Printed and bound by Arcata Graphics,
Fairfield, Pennsylvania